The Visioneers is a new kind of novel.
It invites you to participate in a
transformative learning experience that
generates awe in human possibilities.

It will uplift and empower you
to continue your travel on journeys
destined to create a future of quality for the
Earth, its citizens, and all its living systems.

It will touch your heart
with age-old truths,
even as it challenges you
to understand new paradigms
that set our lives in a global future.

It will open doors for those
in business, education, and
human resource development,
who seek to build
enterprises, communities, and learning places
ready to meet the challenges of
a 21st century renaissance.

The Visioneers also stands alone as entertainment.
It is a powerful story of romance, mystery and suspense,
with a memorable cast of characters, who once encountered
will become part of your life.

For those with a positive future vision,
it is a treasure experience to be cherished.

The Spirit of Yes from page 216
Yes opens the doors to the possible

Yes

Yes is an affirmation
    built on a thousand noes.

No to
    death, pain,
    sickness,
    sadness,
    and bad compromise.

No to
    lethargy,
    fuzzy thinking,
    mediocrity,
    and boredom.

Yes begins
    with intention
    to take little yes steps.

Yes to
    vigour,
    to strength
    and striving,
    to hard work
    and homework,
    to study
    and learning,
    and thinking,
    to writing,
    and being.

Yes to
    embarking on journeys,
    to questing and questions.

Yes to
    dancing
    and singing,
    to poetry,
    music,
    and laughter.

Yes to
feeling
    and friendship,
    to well-being,
    to good food,
    and good drinking,
    to beach walks,
    to popcorn and movies,
    to fireside chats
    and pillow talking.

Yes to
    fun places,
    to wilderness spaces,
    to mountains and climbing,
    to playing and dreaming,
    to planning and deep seeing.

And when the chorus of yeses
    rings out in celebration,
    fueling the heart with wild courage,

It's easy
    to take giant leaps
    to say:
        YES
    to growing,
    to being,
    to soaring,
    to living,
    to loving,
    to me
    to you
    to us.

So
    I can,
    I will,
    and I do!

—Lea Star

Who are the Visioneers?

Answers from the book . . .

"(The Visioneers) are citizen-activists, who seek to give power to ordinary people by awakening inside their minds the visions that are there, for themselves, their families, their communities, and the world." (page 268)

"We are a group of twenty ordinary people from many countries who have come together on an enterprise to change the future of the world." (page 78)

"It's a grand dream. But it's also a possible future. Our task as Visioneers is to show how to move the possible to real." (page 89)

"Now you and your Visioneers, and many millions of like-minded souls across the planet, are moving to take history away from the brink, toward the horizon." (page 161)

"The path of the Visioneers calls for all good men and women to step forward, to step forward in such numbers that no power on Earth can stop them, in their intent to build a future that is good and true and decent." (page 173)

" . . . the Visioneers are acting . . . They're out in the world. They're grabbing attention. They're pulling up the blinds. They're throwing open the windows. Today we're a curiosity. Tomorrow we'll be a force so strong that all the El Condors of the world will tremble in their eyries for fear of it." (page 188)

"(The Visioneers) are wakening the dulled imaginations of a tidal force of human potential to create a different outcome. They are stirring up the listless energy of a population at drift to identify a shared vision of what life can be like on this planet in the 21st century, instead of what it is likely to be like if conditions don't change." (page 308)

"The spirit of the Visioneers . . . is demonstrating over and over again, in every country, among the rich and poor alike, that people acting together to enhance life can and do make a difference." (page 391)

" . . . the Visioneers . . . are running with nothing more than human spirit and hope and belief in a better world that they can build with their minds." (page 421)

" . . . you've learned that to speak about impossible things, you must first move your position to higher ground. From there, they no longer seem impossible. That's what the Visioneers are doing, moving people to higher ground in their minds." (page 475)

Quotes continued on page 526

"Congratulations on a spiritually moving and uplifting script."

—Dorothy Blandford: Entrepreneur

"It is a powerful book, absorbing to read, vivid and emotional at times, and stimulating throughout. I was especially moved by the wonderful attitude of everyone working together for a mutual cause; something I have not experienced since the War."

—Peter Marchant: Senior Citizen

"The book was an inspiration!!! It gives new meaning to the words rejuvenation and revitalization . . . This book ignites a spirit of human power . . . The children are the future. It is good to see that you have incorporated children of the world as being influential and dynamic sources of energy."

—Judy Magrill: Graduate Student

"The Visioneers will inspire people of all ages to gather under its banner and spread its message of the limitlessness of the human mind."

—Jane Fredeman, Ph.D.: Simon Fraser University

"In this time when young adults are finding it difficult to get excited about the future, this book is a blessing in disguise. *Carpe diem*: Seize the day."

—Sarah Berghofer: University Freshman

About the Author

Des Berghofer is a man with a passionate concern for the future of the planet and its citizens. *The Visioneers* floods with his strong belief that people who understand the larger picture will care for their earthly home. He developed this value growing up in a farming family in Queensland, Australia. It was here that he first learned to love the Earth.

Fondness for knowledge and discovery led him to the University of Queensland where he earned his first degree and became a teacher. This profession took him across the world, first to Great Britain, then to Canada, where he learned to look at the future as a discipline of study. He was awarded a Ph.D. in Educational Administration by the University of Alberta, and went on to become Assistant Deputy Minister of Advanced Education in the Government of Alberta. During ten years in this position, his thinking developed extensively about the pivotal role that education is playing in developing the future of the planet. This was strengthened by extensive national and international experience through the Council of Ministers of Education, Canada, and on many delegations to the Commonwealth, China, and Unesco.

Moving from government to the private sector in 1988, he co-founded Creative Learning International in Vancouver, where he continues to work with his partner, Dr. Geraldine Schwartz, on developing skills of creativity, leadership, and visioning with clients from business, government, education, and the community.

From this wide-ranging life experience has grown a strong conviction for Des Berghofer that creative learning must become a primary force to produce a positive outcome for the future. It is from this thoughtful and seasoned perspective that the story of *The Visioneers* is written.

the VISIONEERS

A Courage Story about Belief in the Future

Desmond E. Berghofer

Creative Learning International Press
Vancouver, Canada

The Visioneers is a work of fiction. The characters are fictitious. Where historical figures appear, their portrayal is as characters of fiction. When people occupying real offices are mentioned, the characters depicted in those roles are imaginary and do not represent current or past incumbents of those offices.

The poem *Yes* (page ii) and Esther's response at the wedding (page 394) are taken from the private collection of poetry by Lea Star with permission of the poet.

All references to Scripture are from *The Holy Bible,* King James Version. The Prayer for Peace on page 176 is from the *Siddur Sim Shalom* published by the United Synagogues of America.

Copyright © 1992 by Desmond E. Berghofer

All rights reserved. No part of this book may be reproduced, transmitted or utilized in any form or by any means, electronic, photographic or mechanical including photocopying, recording, or by any information storage and retrieval system without permission in writing from the Publisher, except for brief quotations embodied in literary articles and reviews. Inquiries should be made with the Publisher at the address below.

First printing September, 1992

Canadian Cataloguing in Publication Data

Berghofer, Desmond E. (Desmond Edward), 1938-
  The visioneers

  ISBN 0-9696173-0-5

  I. Title.
PS8553.E73V5 1992 C813'.54 C92-091484-5
PR9199.3.B47V5 1992

Published by Creative Learning International Press, 503-1505 West 2nd Avenue, Vancouver, British Columbia, Canada, V6H 3Y4

Cover Design Geraldine Schwartz, Ph.D.
Logo Anne Rees

Printed on recycled paper
Printed in Canada by Friesen Printers

To Gerri
whose love and support make all things possible

To my mother
who has been steady and strong for me all my life

And for Sarah, Katie, and Charlotte
who with all young Visioneers everywhere
deserve a better future than the one we are currently
delivering to them

Acknowledgments

No book is ever written from the solitary mind of the author. Each of us is formed in part by other minds who touch us along the way. Many of these we meet in the books, articles, films, television programs, radio broadcasts, and various presentations that absorb our interest from time to time. Still others speak to us in conversations of meaning; yet all too frequently we forget how our thinking was shaped by an encounter of this kind. To all such unnamed sources of inspiration and guidance I freely acknowledge my indebtedness in shaping the broad themes of this book.

Over the course of the past twenty years the direction of my thinking has moved steadily towards a mounting concern that human beings are not managing their planetary heritage well. It would be easy to become pessimistic in the face of the evidence, but I am fortunate to have been influenced by mentors who encourage the opposite perspective. Chief among them is Willis Harman, whose own contribution towards creating a more positive future is substantial. His kind and supportive review of a bulky manuscript is gratefully acknowledged.

I deeply appreciate, too, that several others took the time out of busy schedules to be my first readers and provide helpful comments to make the book better. It is particularly gratifying to know that the story and ideas have touched the hearts and caught the interest of those who like Marilyn King, Mona Brookes, Norma Milanovich, and Nathan Segal are making their own substantial contributions to prospects for a more hopeful future. Similarly, I am most grateful for the encouragement and guidance I received from Dorothy Blandford, Jane Fredeman, Margaret Legg, and Peter Marchant.

Among the younger generation, for whom the future has most significance, my daughter, Sarah Berghofer, has been both a supportive reader and a steady source of inspiration and advice. In like spirit Judy Magrill has encouraged me to believe that the book will speak meaningfully to young adults now formulating their contributions to life as citizens of the 21st century. I thank Judy and her husband, Barry, for being supportive early readers.

Several other busy people who agreed to read the manuscript are gratefully acknowledged: Milton Fruchtman, Jerzy Wojcieckowski, Wayne Kines, Arthur Erickson, Agnes Fessler, Shelley Lederman, George Pratt, Trevor Turnbull, and Frank Klassen.

Appreciation is due also to those who provided generous assistance on the technical aspects of putting a book together. Byron Johnson of Friesen Printers and Patty Osborne from the Vancouver Desktop Publishing Centre were particularly considerate. Shona Ralston made a monumental effort in typing most of the text under severe time pressures, and still found energy to be an enthusiastic reader. Abby Jeffs' cheerful contribution in typing the first part of the manuscript is also acknowledged.

Finally, there are really no words to express the debt of gratitude owing to my wife, Geraldine Schwartz, whose supportive and great-spirited partnership of this work was present from beginning idea to final product. Her unflagging enthusiasm for making a contribution of service to humanity places her in the foremost ranks of the Visioneers.

Contents

Foreword

Readers of the heart begin here.

Dear Fellow Reader:

The book you are about to enter is not an ordinary reading experience. It is a journey which leads to a new country, a "promised land" in which, transformed and empowered, you will become a planetary citizen of a new and future time.

In order to travel to this place, some preparation is required. Each of us brings to every new experience a set of paradigms, concepts and beliefs that determine our perception of reality. These are the ultimate limits which act as blinders to the wider world of truth. To achieve the potential this book has to change you forever in a life-enhancing way, you must be prepared to suspend the set of judgments that hold your blinders in place. You must be prepared to *hold fire and think deeply.*

This journey includes the truths of ancient times passed down both in our genes and through the wisdom of our ancestors. It contains new and future truths about our state-of-the-art understanding of human consciousness as the energy that fuels our world's engine. It encompasses the truth of the heart that we feel authentic, and the truth of the spirit that transcends religious dogma, to embrace the mind of humankind. It uplifts us to see the hope of what can be as we become children of a common God, brothers and sisters of the soul.

This book is written in the tradition of great literature since the first storytellers of our kind entranced their fellows with tales of imagination, of mystery, of suspense, of romance; and it is written in the new tradition of the visual cinema of the mind's eye, where frame after frame of exquisite beauty unfolds in a flow, exposing us to our deepest humanity.

It is the story of the triumph of good over evil, taking into account real world events, people and places. Carefully researched, it comes from the mind of a new renaissance author, knowledgable about the world, who clearly understands the current scientific findings about consciousness and energy. It provides an easy learning of all those things that will stretch our belief system into a more flexible and expandable shape, a shape amenable to a quality life in a future to which we all must go.

Finally, it is a personal call to action to the reader to become a Visioneer, an engineer, a pioneer of a better future, a future that begins with oneself and moves to the realm of a relationship of meaning with others. Once this book has touched your heart, you will want to give a copy to those you love and care about. This book is a gift of love and of life.

—*Geraldine Schwartz*

To The Reader

You are about to plunge into an unusual creative engagement. In the pages that follow you will find yourself, from beginning to end, at the centre of everything that happens. Though rich with characters who show no hesitation in running away with the action, this story never allows you to sit back as dispassionate observer. No. You're in the thick of it from start to finish.

Just as all of us are caught up every day in the future we continuously create for ourselves, so you, as reader, are the chief participant in the action and energy of this drama. Indeed, when the subject is the future of life on the planet, how could it be otherwise? Each of us, simply by being here, is an active participant in determining the outcome. So it is in this story, where struggle, adventure, fellowship, and love take flight with high hope for what the magnificent human mind is capable of achieving when engaged to the full.

The events in which you're invited to participate take place after 1992. You can choose the date. The technological sophistication of human life and the pressures for action will increase the later you leave it; so you can be the judge. However, one thing is clear. The longer it takes for something similar to this story to happen, the more grave will be the outcome for the planet.

So, you're welcome here. Come along. Take your place at the centre of the action, and join the characters waiting for you in the pages ahead. For the most part, they will become your friends. Travel with them as a co-conspirator in an adventure that ultimately speaks to life well beyond the story told here.

You're the chief among the Visioneers. Look to the future. Catch the wave. Enjoy.

—*Desmond Berghofer*
Vancouver
July, 1992

Cast of Characters

YOU, THE READER
There from the beginning, moving the action

YOUR MENTORS
Winston Churchill
Charles Dickens
John Kennedy
Anne of Green Gables

THE VISIONEERS

The Original Team	*First Recruits*
President M'buta Mutsandu	Teenagers in Vancouver
Bill Bates	Lord Nigel Feversham
Indira Murti	Lady Pamela Feversham
Daniel Thomas	Prince Rupert of Wittenstein
Mark Venture	Vladimir Rostov
Esther Fisher	Anna Borodino
General Francois Soulière	Boris Dubrovsky
Theresa Romano	Zhao She Yuhan
Sally Hearst	Baba Satyananda
Nicholai Andropov	The African Contingent
Boris Gunther.	Julia McCarthy
Junichi Yakasawa	Arthur Rhinegold
Luis Valdez	Diane Koplitz
George Cardinal	George Walker
Carmen Santander	Senator Wilfred Brown
Jeremy Hiscox	Jenny Lovicks
Irene Henshaw	
Karl Ibsen	
Mohammed Hussein	
Lin Yuen	

OTHER MAJOR PLAYERS
> Pamela Barrett
> David Roth
> Mina Roth
> Kamal Rashid
> Colonel Aaron Greenberg
> Cardinal Claudio Vachiano
> Peter Hemphill
> The World Leaders
> President Miriam Suchinda
> Rivka Fisher
> Tevi Fisher
> Judith Kaplanski
> Deborah Segal
> Bob Venture
> Alice Venture
> Rabbi Ruvain Ben Sabbath
> Reverend Gordon Ringthorpe
> Anton Salman
> Haim Shamir

THE EVIL CONNECTION
> The Army Captain
> Elmiro Perez
> El Condor: Carlos Palmira
> Elvira Ramos
> Larry Porter
> Patrick Harrigan
> Michael Sullivan
> Alberto Gonzalez

PART ONE

Gathering
Strength

CHAPTER ONE

Heroes
and
Heroines

Hello. I know it's not customary for the author of a novel to step right up in the first chapter to meet the reader. However, the relationship we are to have throughout the following chapters of this story is not the usual association of author and reader. You see, I need your imagination to carry the action forward. In fact, you and I are co-creators of what happens here.

Let me explain how this works. This a story about inventing the future. We begin, you and I, with a common concern on this score. We understand that the world and the planet are in great difficulty. The way ahead is by no means clear. All of us on the Earth as intelligent human beings face an enormous challenge of inventing a sustainable future. Confronted with that reality, you are invited here to use your imagination to help create a story of hope for the world. It's an adventure story. It's a love story. It's a quest led by high ideals of courage, trust, and belief in the nobility of the human spirit to ultimately make the right choices.

You are asked to use your imagination to build the story as a creative visualization. This means that you're a full participant in everything that happens. There are many heroes and heroines filling the following pages, but foremost among them is yourself. You're also going to find that you become very attached to some of these characters. After all, they are receiving their life through your imagination, so how could you not care about them, especially when they get into difficulty. For there are villains in this story, too. They will emerge as vividly as the heroes and the heroines,

3

and you'll be caught up in the action of how to steer the story through to an outcome of bright and shining prospects.

My role in all of this is to be the guiding hand behind the scenes, encouraging you continually to go at it full heart. To help with that I ask you to keep a number of metaphors and images in mind. The first is to see the future as an ocean of turbulent waves when a big surf is running. Let's begin there now, in a real ocean where the waves are cresting three or four metres high and rushing in to crash relentlessly on the beach.

Imagine above the ocean a blue sky with puffy white clouds drifting lazily. Imagine the long rolling waves and the sun-drenched sand stretching away on both sides into the summer haze. You're waist deep in the surging water, with a powerful undertow sucking at your feet. Now in the breakers, you strike out to get through them to the heaving blue swell beyond.

Once through, you float in momentary calm, riding effortlessly on the backs of the long rollers, your eyes scanning for the big one. Suddenly it's there, towering above you, a mountain of water poised ready to crash. Too late, you've misjudged it. Your feet are sucked out and the full pounding thunder of the wave is all around you. A useless cork, you're flung, twisted, turned and crushed. In an instant you're on the bottom, face grinding in the sand, then turning over and over, gasping, choking, until you're flung up onto the beach, staggering, looking for your feet. Then you're sucked back, crushed again, and finally spat up onto the safe sand, dazed, breathless and scared.

You stretch out soaking up sun, regaining strength, getting ready to try again. On your feet, more cautious now, you move out into the breakers, watching skittishly for another dumper.

Look out! Here it comes again, bigger than the last one, brutish monster, snarling down at you through white-flecked teeth. Not this time, you say, I'm ready for you. You suck in air, fill your lungs, and dive deep into the bowels of the beast.

The pounding force is gone. You feel the surging energy passing above. You dive deeper, towards the bottom, where it's calmer still. You've outwitted the fiend. It's murky here in half light, with the salt stinging your eyes. Your breath is beginning to go, You climb up to where the surface should be.

For a few seconds in open sunlight, your lungs suck in air. Your eyes are wide open searching for signs of what to do. White foam beats all around. Where are you? Good grief, you're in the line of breakers! Too late, here it comes again, the whole ocean falling on top of you! Dragged, pounded, ground, upended, you're disgorged back up onto the beach, gasping and foolish.

There has to be a better way. You soak up the strength and energy from the sun. On your feet again, you move back into the water, really cautious now, your neck stiff and sore from the last pounding. Into the breakers you go, striking out hard, to get through them, really through them, out beyond the crashing turbulence, into deeper water. Put fear aside, you're out here to play with the giants of the universe. One lifts you up in a great swelling surge of energy. You feel the power and match yourself to it, swimming up to the crest. Content, the wave sweeps on, passing you to his brother. Down the trough and up the other side you go. You've got the feel of it now. It's quieter here, there's time to feel the sun on your shoulders. The beach and the surf seem far away.

But there's little time to look back to the beach. Your eyes scan the heaving blue humps ahead, watching for the tell-tale beginning of a crest, positioning yourself, manoeuvring, getting ready.

Here she comes! What a beauty! Just arching up into the sky as if she wants to leap right out of the ocean. Go for it! Go now! Strike out, pull yourself up onto it. A few powerful thrusts and you've got it. Yes! Here you go! Oh, what a beauty! Head up, in the sunshine, eyes open, you see the beach rushing towards you. All around, the boiling, surging, thrusting energy of the wave lifts you, propels you. Now, it's broken, and still you ride it, as it flattens out, coming in, in, in, right in. The sand is under your feet, and you're running, laughing, exultant, right up onto the beach. Arms up, you salute the sun, the sea, and the sky, co-creators of the surge of life.

A Glimpse of the Future

So there you have it. In your imagination you've created the experience of struggling with the waves, finally to emerge triumphant, knowing how to ride them into the beach. And that's how to use the ocean and its waves as a metaphor for the future.

There are three ways to go. The first is to be dumped through misjudging the coming force. The second is to dive for cover, to get out of the way of the juggernaut, only to find this a temporary respite, for behind it lies the same crushing power as before. The third is the exhilarating experience of riding on the crest of the wave, using its full energy to lift you up and carry you forward, head in the sunshine, eyes open, searching for opportunity.

So that's how we're going to look at the future, as a turbulent ocean full of waves of opportunity. The experience just now in your imagination with real waves tells you that it's hard enough when you try to ride them on your own. How do you get all of the people in the world to do it together? That's the real challenge of the future. You understand that our common concern for sustainability derives from the fact that we now have five and a half billion people on the planet whose combined activity is stirring up this ocean of turbulence. How do we learn together to ride the waves of our own making and avoid being dumped by them?

Now a new thought comes to mind. What if all of us out here in this ocean of turbulence turned our eyes on the future and tried to shape it? What if we put up some clear visions of what the future could be like if we all pulled together? Then we could bend every effort of mind to ensure that it turns out that way. What a difference that would make! We'd all be riding on a wave we helped to shape. How much better that would be than the crashing turmoil and conflict we now have of people and nations acting blindly from their own small view of the world.

We need to become Visioneers. Yes, that's it—a new word for a new age. Pioneers of the future. We'll go visioneering, all of us, shaping and riding the waves of the future. We'll do it in our minds first. There we can create the visions of the possible, teasing them out, building them up until they become so real that they're the life force carrying us forward. We'll ride every wave in to moments of celebration, right up onto the beach, our feet finding the sand in an exultant dance of accomplishment. Allowing time to soak up the sunny pleasure of it all, we can then go back out and set ourselves to do it again in a pattern of continuous achievement.

Visioneering! What an idea! What a possibility for the world! What a triumph of mind—to be able to explore the future and make it happen! What better time to begin than now!

Sweeping the Earthscape

So now we have the idea for our story. It will tell of how you as both reader and participant create characters and travel with them on an adventure to show how, in the real world, we might invent the future. The place to begin is with the Earth itself, so you move now in your imagination to sweep across the Earthscape.

Imagine the same blue sky as before with puffy white clouds drifting lazily. Below, you see the baked red earth of an African landscape speeding by, vast motionless and empty. Your breath catches at the hard, bright energy of the open savannah ringed by the dome of an incredibly blue sky. You're gathered up and swept into the scene where you move along as weightless spirit, a silent invisible observer of the unfolding panorama.

From the red earth you travel across green plain, mountain, and jungle to the immensity of a heaving blue ocean. Breaking the surface, the humps of whales catch your glance. For a moment you're amongst them, out of the vista into the action, riding with them in the seascape. Then on you go again, tracing the shoreline of another continent, vast unending kilometres of empty Australian beach, stretching away beyond sight, baking open in blazing sunlight.

With breathtaking speed you travel on, and find yourself now resting for a moment in the empty silence of giant ice caves at the edge of Antarctica. From here your cinematic course sweeps up the coast of South America. It touches at the islands of Galapagos among strange eternal creatures of a forgotten world. Then on you go again above the vast expanse of the Amazon jungle, steaming in tropical heat, where the mighty river threads its passage through the powerful, life-supporting lungs of the fragile planet.

Ironically, it's here that you first encounter evidence of human interaction with the Earthscape. Stark gouges are hacked out of the jungle, and as you sweep low over the smarting landscape, you see the struggling efforts of small, impoverished holdings, where men and women seek unprofitable ventures of crop and cattle where before the jungle held its footing for all recorded time.

Suddenly you become aware of a deep and spreading pain. This is not the physical suffering of a distressed body, but rather the spreading agony of a natural system drifting out of balance. All of the wonders you've just visited seem now in jeopardy, and the searing pain you feel is the great gasping of a planetary system responding to sharp and mounting intrusion.

This is the signal for you to travel northwards to the great industrial machine of North America. Here you arrive on the doorstep of megalopolis where people are swallowed and disgorged from buildings in perpetual motion, while the air crackles with the electrical energy of powerlines, radiowaves, and television signals. Everything seems to be held together by electronics in which the digital passage of immeasurable bits of information links the world in a continuous, twenty-four hour day of unrelenting activity.

Across the Atlantic Ocean you sweep eastwards into Europe where old and new crowd on top of each other, as industrial heartlands belch clouds of noxious fumes and smoke into open sky. Below, parliaments and assemblies grind along in endless discourse as doctrine and ideology struggle to find something that will work to put human affairs in order.

Your cinematic flight now takes you east again across the great land mass of Asia into the world's most populous territory of China and India. Here ancient civilizations struggle with the future, while at the eastern edge the economic miracle of Japan surges along at meteoric speed.

From here you move south west into the heart of Islam where, though geographically small, an enormous ideological-religious conflict with Judaism keeps the whole world on edge. Where there could be symbols of a golden age of progress, a Jerusalem for all seasons, there's little more than violent acts of terrorism and reprisal that fuel the basest instincts of the human species.

Away to the south lies the tragedy of Africa, the vast forgotten continent, where grinding poverty, corruption, and the misery of famine hold too many of its millions in continual fear, anger, and hopelessness.

You could go on, but this is enough to give you the sense of the challenge that lies ahead. You've seen the vast and delicate fabric of the natural world and the chaotic activity of its most intelligent species. Both are locked together, inextricably interwoven in the dance of destiny.

Let the Action Begin

Now we come back to the task at hand: to build a vision of the future to which we would all like to travel. The adventure is about to begin. Your imagination is primed for the task. We are well met, you and I, for this journey together.

Let's go full heart to meet the heroes and heroines of the story. They will become our friends, as, indeed, I would like to think you and I can also be. Our quest together is a noble one. Let's begin.

CHAPTER TWO

The Mentors Assemble

Y OU'RE IN A SPECIAL PLACE tucked high up on a ridge among tower-ing mountains. It's a five-sided log house built out of half metre thick, fire-killed spruce. Each log is carefully shaped to fit the curve of the other, caulked and bonded against the piercing bite of the wind and driven snow. On three walls huge picture windows open out to the breathtaking vista of rocky range, hanging glaciers, towering spruce and pine, alpine meadows and an aquamarine lake almost filling the valley floor three hundred metres below.

Against one wall a friendly, open field-stone fireplace crackles merrily, dancing flames licking blackened stonework. Along the other wall, stretches a bookcase containing all the books you've ever read, together with important magazines, newspapers, reports, and journals. Built into the centre of the bookcase a large television screen looks out with powerful stereophonic speakers on either side.

This is your thinking place. Sheepskin rugs are scattered on the pol-ished, hewn wooden floor. Five solid comfortable leather chairs stand positioned for warmth and view around the fireplace.

You're sitting alone in one of the chairs. You remember with a grimace the confusion and turmoil of the waves. You know that the ocean is still out there and you're in it, but you have time now to be inside your mind to think. Here in this beautiful place created out of your imagination, you have the space and time for it. And you've come to think about the future. What was the word? Visioneering? Yes, that's it. You're going out in your mind to explore the future and shape it to your liking—to shape it so well that you feel yourself moving comfortably into it. You sense that this is right for you , because you've been here before.

That's a nice thought. It would be good if it were so easy. What about all those other people trying to find their place in the future? Perhaps your ideas won't fit with theirs. Then how does it work? You can't be in the future by yourself. You can only be there with other people. How can we put something together that will work well for all of us? If visioneering is to succeed, there has to be a meeting of minds. What evidence is there of that in the world? Not much. All of history right down to yesterday is full of people arguing and fighting for competing futures. How can we expect that to change? Only by embracing faculties of mind little used in the past, but ready to be developed when we choose to do so.

The Lion Returns

"Now that's an interesting proposition, indeed!" A loud stentorian voice booms in your head.

Startled, you look around. You're no longer alone in your thinking room. Seated in a chair by the fireplace, looking directly across at you is a squat, unmistakable figure: heavy-set features with famous bull-dog visage and penetrating gaze staring right into you. You've been joined by Winston Churchill.

"We could have used some better faculties of mind earlier this century. Too late now, of course, to change that, but I like your idea of trying it for the future. One way and another, we made a mess of things—all in the name of trying to come back from the brink, where one crazed lunatic after another was intent on taking us."

"Thank you for coming," you say. "I'm honoured to have one of the world's pre-eminent statesmen in my thinking room."

"Yes, well, that's all right. Now we have to get on with it, don't we. I had my turn. We had a tough time of it. We turned back one of the most abominable scourges in the history of civilization, but we left a lot of poison lying about to fester new sores. You can never win at that game. We suffered crushing defeats, one after the other, but we triumphed in the end. That mad dog, Hitler, almost had his way, but we stopped him. That was as much as we could do. Now the world has a whole new set of dangers to imperil it. I like your idea of visioneering to get people thinking sensibly and listening to each other. It'll be the dickens of a job to pull off, though."

The Immortal Creative Genius

"Did someone mention my name?" A new voice is in your head. You look and a second figure has appeared, sitting opposite Churchill. He's well-dressed in a dark nineteenth-century suit with high, stiff shirt collar and cravat. His hair is long and slightly unkempt, and his face, lively and energetic, displays a wisp of beard. His voice has the rich colour of the seasoned actor.

"I say, this is a beautiful spot you have here. Rather different from London and the English countryside. Good company, too. I'm so glad you brought me along."

You understand immediately that you now have Charles Dickens with you, and with him his myriad of characters: David Copperfield, Ebenezer Scrooge, Joseph Marley, Mr. Pickwick, and all the rest, not here in person, but present behind the darting, lively eyes of their creator.

"That was a fine entrance you made, Charles." Churchill is nodding approvingly at the newcomer.

"Well, I always had a flair for the theatrical, and when your name is in the language, you should make the most of it, especially when it's used by one of our great statesmen. I'm so pleased to see you, Winston."

"I see you two know each other," you hear yourself saying, a little lamely.

"Of course," replies Churchill. "Everything we've done is out there to be known. But that's not the point, now. We're here to put the future on a better track. It's an interesting prospect. I'd like to have another shot at that. What do you think, Charles?"

"Yes, indeed." Dickens gets up and begins to pace the room enthusiastically. "You know, I showed how to do that with Scrooge in *A Christmas Carol*. I'm rather pleased with the way the world keeps bringing that back every Christmas. It would be a lot better if they learned something from it, though. I'm certainly keen to lend a hand on this visioneering project. We just might make a difference now that the stakes are so high."

As you sit and listen to this exchange, you suddenly have a great sense of hope. The constant pounding and beating of the waves is never far from your mind, with all those people and ideas and products churning around inside them. But here in this quiet space in your mind you've been joined by two great spirits who played boldly on the world's stage of their time. Through you, perhaps their wisdom can help to chart the future of a new age.

A Shining Presence

But wait, there's a new presence in the room. "Whenever anyone mentions high stakes, I'm there every time."

The slightly nasal Bostonian accent is instantly recognizable.

"It's good to see you, Winston. And you, Charles, what a pleasure! And look at this place! If this isn't God's country, I don't know what is. Where are we anyway? It's got to be Canada. Look at those mountains and glaciers. It is Canada, isn't it?"

He had come into the room like a hurricane. Striding with springing step he had grasped Churchill by the hand and pumped it, slapped Dickens on the back, and is now holding out his hand to you, eyes twinkling, the familiar lopsided grin filling his face.

"Yes, it's in the Canadian Rockies, Mr. President," you say, your heart rising noticeably as you greet John Kennedy. "I'm so glad you've joined us."

"I wouldn't want to miss it. It's a great idea you've got—visioneering. Yeah, I really like that. It's got a ring to it. And all that business out there with the waves. Absolutely brilliant. You looked pretty foolish getting dumped, though. I certainly know what that feels like."

"You saw all that?" you ask. You hadn't realized who might have been watching your performance with the waves.

"Absolutely. That's why I'm here. Anyone with that kind of spirit and guts to get out there and battle with those monsters deserves to be helped. You know, this visioneering idea is not that different from what we did in the sixties with the Apollo project. We said we'd put a man on the moon by the end of the decade, and we did it. We burned that idea into the minds of everyone who could contribute and then we let them go at it. The result was a miracle. We did it then. People can do it again now. Visioneering! Yes, that's a wonderful idea for a new century. What do you think, Winston?"

Churchill is on his feet now, his back to the others, feet apart in characteristic defiant stance, staring out at the vista below.

"Yes, I said as much before you got here." His voice booms out slowly. "We need to shore up spirit and courage. Just give people with real blood in their veins and a stubborn pride in their chests, some encouragement, and they'll go out and find a way." He turns back to face the room. "But you've got to get them moving. Put some fire in their bellies and they'll kick the stuffing out of any petty despot that comes along."

Kennedy is laughing. "Yeah, I remember, Winston, what you said to those Brits of yours during the war." He puts on a Bostonian-Churchillian accent. "We'll fight them on the beaches. We'll fight them on the streets. We'll fight them in the hills. We will never surrender. I always wondered what you'd do if you ran out of countryside."

"We did," Churchill smiles. "That's why I saw to it that America came in to help."

"Gentlemen," you interrupt, "I'm extremely honoured to have you here in my thinking room. I'm not sure where you've come from, but I assume I brought you here with my imagination to help me with what I would like to do to invent a better future. Your wisdom and experience from your own times will, I'm sure, be very profitable. How should we begin our discussion?"

A Precious Jewel

"Excuse me, but I don't see how you older people should go on talking like this without including someone young enough to see herself doing marvellous, exciting things in the future. After all, that's what the future is all about—dreaming your dreams and making them happen. And who's better at that than we young folk, who perhaps don't know enough about how to be cynical and pessimistic."

All eyes have turned to meet a new arrival. Actually there are two new figures. In the foreground, moving into the centre of the room is a bright-eyed young girl of sixteen or seventeen with an outstanding crop of red hair hanging loose and flowing around her shoulders. Dressed in a high-necked puffy white blouse and a long swishing green skirt, she brings a dazzle of colour and energy to the room. In the background, an older woman wearing a trim black suit smiles somewhat wistfully at her bolder companion.

"Hello," says the young girl, extending her hand and dropping little curtsies to the distinguished men in the room. "My name is Anne with an 'e'. I'm really Anne Shirley, but everyone knows me as Anne of Green Gables from Prince Edward Island. I also call myself Anne of a Thousand Dreams. I'm all of the Anne's and Alice's and Jane's that you read about in books. We dream our dreams to make the world a better place. I think that might be just what you need to help you see things differently. This is the lady who created me. You see, I never was a real person like you gentlemen, so I thought I should bring my creator with me."

The older woman steps forward and speaks in a rich, full voice: "My name is Lucy Maud Montgomery. I was listening to your discussion and thought that Anne should be here. Now, if you will excuse me, I shall be on my way."

Charles Dickens raises a hand in protest. "I say, don't do that. It was very clever of you to put one of your people on the centre stage, so to speak. I wish I had thought of that. Please stay."

"You have so many characters, Mr. Dickens," says Miss Montgomery. "Anne is my special prize. I will leave her with you. Thank you for your kindness. I must go. Goodbye, Anne. I know you will speak well for both of us." With that she is gone.

"Well, then, gentlemen," says Anne, "you were about to have a pro-

found discussion. Please don't let me interrupt. I'll just be quiet and listen."
She sits in one of the vacant chairs, folding her hands in her lap, looking
attentive and alert.

A Profound Discussion

Churchill strikes a parliamentary pose, thumbs hooked inside his vest, and
begins.

"First of all, we have to establish one clear fact. The future is not simply
going to happen. It will be a result of everything people do, and it will roll
over them like a great wall of water sweeping up out of the ocean of times
past. That wave is gathering force now. It's building up from the staggering
accomplishments of the world's scientific laboratories and research establishments and being converted into instruments and procedures that give
humanity incredible power over nature. But at the heart of the wave are the
thoughts and passions of human minds, goaded on by the idea that power
and dominion are the universal goods. These two forces have come together now, scientific knowledge and a passion for domination, and they're
battering relentlessly against the natural systems. The issue for the future
is how to change the direction of such thoughts. I speak here for both
genders, for I understand well the impact of women's thoughts, and I
welcome their growing prominence on the world's stage. But so far, there's
no clear evidence that the accumulated thinking of men and women is
taking a different direction from the past, while the course of events is
sweeping relentlessly towards an apocalyptic end."

"You mean, I think, Mr. Churchill," says Anne, "that people must think
more like a mother nurturing her children than like an Alexander conquering the world."

"That is exactly what I mean, Anne."

"How to do that," President Kennedy is speaking now, "when you've
got your finger poised to push the button of a multi-megaton bomb, or your
foot on the accelerator of a 300-horsepower convertible streaking down the
highway—you know, that's the issue. We understand intellectually what
needs to be done, but somewhere in the gut is this passion to out-perform
everyone else, and when you've got the technology and the money, the
passion is to do it, no matter what."

"But the 'no matter what' is beginning to matter a lot," Anne has spoken
again.

"Anne, dear," replies Kennedy, "you've put it exactly right. The 'no
matter what' is staring everyone who pays attention right in the eyeballs.
We're talking here about a poker game in which we've put practically every
chip on the table, and we're betting we know more than that other guy

we're playing against. The trouble is the other player is God and He's not going to be easy to beat."

"But why does it have to be a contest at all?" Anne is on her feet now, pacing. "I'm sorry, gentlemen. I said I would sit and listen, but I'm just so upset by what you, Mr. Churchill and Mr. Kennedy, have just said. I mean, I'm not upset at you. You're expressing the issues so grandly and accurately, but it's almost as if there's no alternative to disaster and chaos, that there's really no future at all. Well, I'm sorry, I just don't believe that. No, I'm not at all sorry I don't believe that. I believe you can have vision and purpose and a sense of grand things you want to do with your life without the need for it to place the whole world in jeopardy. I mean, what's the sense in that? There's no sense in that, and I just don't think people are going to let it happen, especially the young, who've still got most of their dreams left to dream. No, I just don't believe it. What about you, Mr. Dickens? You've got such a wonderful imagination. Can you imagine a world without a future?"

"If I could, I don't think any of my characters would forgive me for it," replies Dickens. "While many of them didn't have very attractive personal futures, they always had hope. Even Sidney Carton on his way to meet the guillotine could see the advantages of his course of action, and Scrooge, of course, when he was shocked into facing bleak future prospects made a marvellous transformation.

"Now that's what appeals to me so much about visioneering. It's capital in every aspect. Can you not see people of every stripe warming up to it? Why, it'll be a veritable feast of adventure for them. Just imagine being given the chance to create your own future—and to really do it. There you are in the boardroom and the chairman gets up, popping the buttons on his corpulent vest, and says, 'Ladies and gentlemen, today we shall begin to create the future'. And all the executives will smile and nod, not wishing to disabuse the old man of his notion, but conspiratorially knowing that he's not altogether of sound mind.

"But he will continue to beam at them. Let's call him Humpington, shall we? So there's old Humpington, red-cheeked and bright-eyed, sweeping aside the boring agenda book he has in front of him, with all of its ridiculous 'whereases' and 'possible options' and mealy-mouthed corporate mumblings. And he says, 'Come, come now, let's get to it! Smithers, you're a bright fellow, tell me what you'll be dong here five years from now.'

"Now Smithers is the lean, sad-faced controller, who has never taken two steps without checking that he's putting his feet exactly in someone else's footprints. Well, with old Humpington beaming his ridiculous question at him, Smithers' collar shrinks, and his face turns a shade of purple as he grabs for his water glass, bumping his spectacles askew, and waving his left hand for support from his fellow business partners at the table.

"And, of course, Miss Greenfield from Marketing comes to his aid saying, 'Why only yesterday Tom and I were talking about that.' Tom is Smithers, you know. Everyone uses first names except old Humpington, who pleases himself about that, just as he does about mostly everything else. But Jenny Greenfield is speaking and she says, 'I told Tom that what we should do is put together a huge chart that we could hang on the wall over there that would have all of our potential customers and products and markets spread out in colour, and then we could map out our direction with a huge red arrow that everyone could colour in every day. And Tom said that it was a great idea and he would certainly approve my requisition for coloured pens and put it under special projects with a little asterisk beside it to show that it was an original thought.'

"Well, of course, Humpington is delighted and he comes around the table and gives Jenny an effusive hug, and very soon everyone is into the spirit of it, talking about prognostics, and scenarios, and strategies. Why, within five minutes, there were thirty-seven creative ideas being explored, and there wasn't a man or woman there, even including Smithers, who couldn't do it. And that's the way Humpington and Associates began their practice of visioneering and now every day it's a race to get to the office to put the next piece of the project together."

Dickens has presented all this in grand oratorical fashion and now stands beaming at everyone, looking for all the world like his imaginary Humpington, Chairman of the Board and leader of the visioneering team.

Anne claps her hands and does a little dance in the middle of the room.

"Oh, yes," she chortles, "that's the way to think about it! I know you made all that up, Mr. Dickens, but it really could be like that. I can just see it. Everyone from company presidents to government leaders to teachers in school to families around the dinner table—everyone imagining the future they would like to see and working away at it to make it happen. That way, they could be sure about the future, because if everyone imagines something good and reasonable, then I'm sure it will happen. Don't you agree, Mr. Kennedy and Mr. Churchill?"

"Well, of course," John Kennedy is quick to respond, "though it becomes a little more difficult when you've got hard heads on different sides of an issue coming up with conflicting ideas of what the future should be like. But the way to start is to get people doing it, then we can refine the process as we go along."

He turns to Dickens.

"I must say I'm impressed with you Charles. All that stuff about prognostics and scenarios and strategies. It's very mainstream and not exactly in vogue for a nineteenth-century novelist."

"Well, we do try to stay current. Seeing that we're all here in our host's imagination, I believe we should try to address the issues with the concepts of the day."

"Quite right," Churchill is speaking again, "and now I believe we should get on with it by laying out a tactical plan. That's what our host expects of us, is it not?"

All eyes turn to you. You've assembled this group in your thinking room. They're obviously ready to participate fully in the assignment and their performance will be as stimulating and successful as your imagination allows them to be. They're not here as themselves, but as composites of what your imagination can put together. Drawing on what you can visualize as their response to the challenge of an age not of their making, you'll gain insights for action. You're not sure what will emerge. You know only that the issue is important. You recall vividly the challenge of the waves and that it demands from you and everyone else on the planet a response that's truly exceptional and unprecedented. The future is at stake. Anne's impassioned plea for sense to prevail rings in your mind. You see the wave of the future cresting around you and all your contemporaries. You're calling for every vestige of creative energy to lift yourself and the others onto that wave, to ride it confidently and enthusiastically into a future that's rich and positive, and worthy of the incredible power of the human mind to fashion and sustain.

A Plan of Action

Your assembled team is on hand and ready to assist.

"You're quite right, Mr. Churchill," you say.

"Winston," he interrupts.

"You're quite right, Winston," you continue. "We need a plan of action. Charles and Anne have already shown the way. We need practical examples for the world to see the process at work."

"Very well, here's what we should do." Churchill has taken the floor again. "First, we need to drive right to the heart of the matter by getting our governments and their bureaucracies into anticipatory stride. By nature, they're entrenched conservatives standing too much on ceremony and too little on leadership. That was all right in its day, but that time's past. They have to learn, and learn quickly, to lead with the neck. If someone tries to wring it, or lop off the head, so be it. You've got a better chance to dodge a falling axe than to get out of a crowded chicken coop.

"Second, business. Like democracy, capitalism is a grossly inadequate economic system to work under, except that there's no better one in the world. Now that the iron curtain has been hauled back up in Europe, we can see the consequences when men and women aren't given the opportunity for initiative and enterprise. These will be the catchwords of the future. Let's stake out the ground for them now.

"Third, education. This should be the energy source, but it's become the exhaust. We need to fire up the minds of the young with visions of the possible and not dull them with the banalities of erudition. Every boy and girl should be a Visioneer of the future possible. They have the potential in their minds. We must help them grasp it with their hands.

"Fourth, the community. This is where people live. If it's not alive with passion for the decent and beautiful, then it can be a nest-bed of snakes and vipers striking with venom and violence.

"These are the four arenas in which we must perform and demonstrate the power of visioneering. I see it as a bold and enlivening enterprise and propose that we begin without delay."

"You make some excellent points, Winston," John Kennedy is speaking. "Now, what we need to do is put spirit to the action. Everywhere in the world a great apprehension has crept into the minds of men and women. As knowledge and technology expand, people stand timid in the face of it. What they've forgotten is that human consciousness comes first, before invention. The world is on the edge of a new adventure. The 20th century has been one of the most savage in human history. Now we're on the threshold of a new millennium of promise unknown to any previous generation. The seeds of greatness have been sown in the muck and grime of battle on too many fronts, in the barbarous atrocities of too many dark days, in the blind ignorance of what our energies of progress were doing to the planet. But the seeds have been sown nonetheless, and a harvest of riches is at hand for those who can now be good stewards of the land.

"The time to move is now. Everywhere our project can be the symbol of hope, courage and determination. With eyes firmly fixed on a positive future vision, people can, weave the fabric of the destiny they desire. That's the message of our project. We're about to begin the journey. Let's show the world what it can mean to be in our company of Visioneers."

"Bravo, Mr. Kennedy! Bravo, Mr. Churchill!" Anne is on her feet hugging each of the speakers. "Oh, I'm so excited now! That's exactly the spirit and plan we need. Oh, where do we begin?"

"Why, at the risk of sounding banal in the presence of such impressive oratory," Charles Dickens is speaking now, "I suggest we begin at the beginning. Our host assembled us for this session. We seem to be agreed on a course of action. Our spirits are up for it. Now we're on call for Scene I of our exciting drama."

His words bring a close to this session in your thinking room. Suddenly you're alone. The atmosphere is electric with the energy of your mentors. You close your eyes to rest before the action begins.

CHAPTER THREE

Enter
the
Visioneers

ALONE IN YOUR THINKING ROOM you search in your mind for symbols to guide you in your quest. Your mentors were very quick off the mark. The outline of a plan of action is already in place. Before you meet with them again you want to take a moment to create some images to anchor your thinking.

You already have the metaphor of the wave, rolling, cresting, and breaking in the ocean of turbulence. You return there now in your imagination and look up from the foam-flecked swell where you see the great blue dome of the sky. Yes, that's it. What better symbol for unity on the planet than this? From horizon to horizon it envelops the world, a quiet cocoon of shelter to the living planet. Somehow there must be a way to turn every eye skywards, and let human minds see the endless possibilities that come from living in peace and harmony under its protective dome.

Now you look again and with a flash of insight you see the way to do it. Before you is another image. It's a silver bridge arching up into the incredibly blue sweep of the sky. You lift yourself up, out of the water, onto the bridge where a moving sidewalk takes you along. What if all the people on the planet could do this? Travelling together on the silver bridge across the friendly sky would be a powerful image for building a future of peace and cooperation.

You turn and look down into the ocean where now you see millions of people of all ages, nationalities, and colours. And you see that every eye is turned towards you. You open your arms and beckon them to join you on the silver bridge. You see the strain in every face: black, brown, white; men, women, children. Everyone is straining to break free to join you. But no one comes. Something holds them back. Something binds them to the tumult and the torment of their present. They don't have the power yet to lift themselves with vision onto the silver bridge. But they're only a breath away, and you know you must stay to help them. You cannot ride the silver bridge alone.

You have your images now. You're ready to proceed. Back in your thinking room, your mind is filled with the shining brilliance of the silver bridge arching up into the blue sweep of the sky.

Creating the Team

"That's an excellent image. Now, you must get your spirits up. There's much to do, and we're ready for it."

The voice is friendly and reassuring. You feel a firm hand on your shoulder. Charles Dickens is at your side. He gives you a nod of his head and one enormous wink.

Instantly, your other three mentors are in the room.

Winston Churchill stands solidly by the fireplace, his jaw firm and eyes penetrating. "We must begin without delay. We are at the turning point." His voice is grave. "This past century, which began with such promise for peace and prosperity, can only be judged as a disaster of unmitigated proportions. We must put the genie of national greed back in the bottle or face the consequences of total chaos. It's past time to take a different tack. We must begin today, this minute, to assemble the pieces for a new project for humanity."

"Oh, yes!" Anne's voice is anxious with anticipation. "Let's make it something so wonderful that it will light up the minds of everyone everywhere with new possibilities for just being the best that we can be. But not doing it to win or triumph or to beat someone else. We need everyone to be the best they can be. That's the way we all can benefit. We need to care for each other—each one helping the other to climb up onto the silver bridge. Oh, I can see it! I really can see it—and I know we can make it happen."

"Yes, Anne, we can make it happen," President Kennedy is pacing up and down the room. "Winston's idea of a central human project is brilliant. It will be the model for a new order. You can't expect people to move unless you can show them something worth moving to. We need to gather the key people for a general planning session right away."

He turns to you.

"You're the important player here, you know. What an opportunity— to engineer a new human project to be a lighthouse for the future. You took the first step with your concept of visioneering. The second was to get us together here in your thinking room. Are you ready for the next?"

"Why, yes." You're somewhat surprised at your own forthright response. The infectious spirit of your guests is spurring you on. "I can get people together right here. I'll create a visioneering centre next door. It will be the design space for the architects of the future. Who should be included?"

"Well, it's pretty clear to me we need a cross-section of the kind of people who can make a difference," the President is continuing. "It should be easy enough to arrange. They're all in your imagination anyway. We just need to stimulate your thinking to get the best mix. You certainly need to begin with a good political leader, not from a super power, that's too high profile. A good third-world leader would be the best bet. Along with him, a capable administrator and some others who can make things happen: engineer, industrialist, developer, architect, folk like that."

"Don't leave out a military man," Churchill adds. "You'll need a good strategist. And a good newspaper man: someone to blow hard, but to do it intelligently. You'll need an historian, too, to put some perspective into things."

"Now, Winston," John Kennedy chortles, "Why don't you just name yourself and be done with it?"

"Yes, well I did think of that," the old man replies, "but I'm in the high command on this project. We need these other people at the operations level."

"Then let's make sure we include those who can be sensitive to the yearnings of the human soul." This suggestion comes from Charles Dickens. "We need a poet, a teacher, a man of the cloth, a performer, and an artist."

"Don't forget some young people," Anne speaks out, "a boy and a girl, and we should have a mother, too. There's no one who appreciates the future more than those caught up in the creation and nurturing of life."

"Then I suggest we also include a farmer and a scientist from the life sciences." This is your own suggestion. "And I certainly think we should have someone from an aboriginal culture who feels deeply for the natural rhythms of the land."

There's a pause now as everyone reflects on the suggestions that have been made. Charles Dickens brings the process to a close.

"Hurrah for our team of Visioneers! Can't you just see them, assembling, getting ready for the work. There's old Mutsandu, President of Yarawi in Africa with his black smiling face, and young Miss Henshaw peeping over her glasses just fresh out of her schoolroom in Edinburgh. General Soulière with his full chest of military ribbons from Paris extolls the virtues of military discipline to Mark Venture, head of Venture Engineering in Brisbane, Australia. Karl Ibsen, the Norwegian architect, is discussing gothic architecture with Jeremy Hiscox, reader in history at Cambridge, England. Then there's Sally Hearst, high school student from Auckland, New Zealand, meeting her pen pal Nicholai Andropov from Moscow for the first time. The Welsh poet, Daniel Thomas, has a rapt audience for his oratory: Boris Gunther, dairy farmer from the Rhine Valley; Junichi Yakasawa, President of Yakasawa Incorporated, Tokyo; Carmen Santander, dark-eyed Spanish singer and dancer; William Bates, publisher of New World Press, Los Angeles; and George Cardinal, Chief of the Red Earth Band in northern Alberta, Canada.

"Add to this Theresa Romano, mother of two sons and three daughters from Naples; Esther Fisher, Israeli artist from Tel Aviv; Lin Yuen, senior secretary in the Peoples Republic of China; Mohammed Hussein from Jordan and head of a project planning commission at the United Nations headquarters in New York; Indira Murti, biologist from New Delhi; and Father Luis Valdez from Santiago."

"Now here we have a full assembly of Earth people which, for a Victorian novelist from London, shows a grand stretch of the imagination. Would that I could have included them in my circle along with my David Copperfields and Martin Chuzzelwits and Sam Pickwicks. It was a different time, and as fertile as I found my garden then, the human landscape of the 21st century is so much richer that my spirit soars with the sense of what we can do together on this project. My friends, it's a grand endeavour. God bless us in its pursuit and its accomplishment!"

They're all pressing close with excitement. Anne throws her arms around you and hugs you tightly, then embraces all the others. The men are shaking hands all around. Your heart swells with the sense of what you're about to undertake. You close your eyes a moment. The room spins. You sink into your chair resting. You're alone now, gathering energy to begin.

Arrival by Silver Bridge

Imagine a blue sky, with puffy white clouds drifting lazily, and in it your silver bridge arching across the blue space. Suddenly the sky changes colour to the soft pinks of daybreak, then to deep purple of grapes and royal robes, and you're moving on the silver bridge, across the sky, watching it change colour now to emerald green and lilac, a whole kaleidoscope of different hues and patterns, enveloping you, washing over you, calming your spirits, quieting your mind.

It's warm and sunny, the sky is blue again, and you step off the silver bridge onto the grassy slope beside your mountain retreat. Adjoining the building is a new structure of log and blue mountain stone, stretching expansively across the slope, tucked among tall, ancient spruce and pine trees, looking out across the vista of open grassy hillside, mountain ranges, and the deep valley with its amethyst blue lake sparkling in the sunlight in the valley below.

You turn and look up into the sky where the silver bridge stretches away until it fades from view. As you watch, something changes. Slowly materializing out of the blue haze, some darker outline of figures on the bridge move towards you, gliding effortlessly, on the moving sidewalk, growing larger as they come.

The lead figure is almost at the end of the bridge now where it touches the grassy slope between two tall pillars of shining silver. He steps off. You recognize him instantly from Charles Dickens' description: tall, black, smiling, with friendly round face, and silver hair. He is wearing cool, white African robes, flowing easily over his ample frame. This is President Mutsandu from Yarawi.

And behind him, one after the other they come, stepping off the bridge, gathering on the hillside, greeting each other, smiling, shaking hands, embracing, their voices and laughter drifting up to you. You see them clearly, men in casual summer shirts and slacks, women in bright colours, many nationalities, about twenty in all, younger faces and older, various shades of white, suntanned, black and brown, all smiling, looking fresh, relaxed, and expectant for adventure. This is your company of Visioneers, arrived from across the Earth, assembled, eager and ready to begin, waiting for you to join them to design the new project for the human family.

You move down the hillside towards them. All eyes turn to you, friendly and enthusiastic.

"Friends," you begin, "welcome. You've come to be here together to undertake a great work. It can't be clear to any one of us what we must do, but together we have the knowledge and the power of imagination to build a vision in the minds and hearts of people everywhere. It will be a vision of what we can as a human family make of this world. It will be a future of meaning and fulfillment, a powerful, continuing life force for the happiness and well-being of all."

"Bravo, my friend!" It's Mutsandu who speaks, and his voice is rich with the golden warmth of his homeland. "You bring a good message. We're glad to be here, and are eager to begin. Let's go now to the place of assembly to share our ideas and tell what's in our hearts."

First Meeting in the Visioneering Room

In an instant, the scene has changed and the new arrivals are assembled in a large round room of the visioneering complex. It's full of light from the bank of windows around the perimeter, and from the huge glass dome above that opens the interior to the sky. The Visioneers have all found places around a continuous circular desk of richly polished wood, light grained and pleasant to touch. The desk is one of several arranged in concentric circles, open at the front and rising in tiers above floor level, where there is an open space about fifteen metres across. In this space, in full view of all participants, a huge world globe slowly turns, glowing iridescent, showing continents, oceans, islands, in full earth tones of brown and green and gold and blue. There are no boundaries or names, only the continuous natural features of the living Earth. As you look more closely, you realize that the globe is not solid. Rather, it's a three-dimensional image, a hologram, projected into the centre of the room, visible to everyone as if solid, but existing only as an image. The remainder of the floor is clear, carpeted in light blue and white, a mirror image of the sky visible through the dome above. The Visioneers sit in comfortable, high-backed, white leather chairs, that turn to allow them quiet conversation with their neighbours, while at the same time providing a full three hundred and sixty degree view of everything around.

This is the Visioneering Room, heart of the complex you've created to fashion a rich and meaningful future for the world.

Mutsandu speaks: "Friends, we have come from our homes to this place to do a great work for the world. Each of us sees from our experience a small piece of the whole, but we know in our hearts that we face a grave danger. It's the danger of ignorance and indifference, of being too small in our minds to know how to act when great deeds are called for. The Earth lies open and exposed to the products of our minds. We see it turning there," and he gestures to the giant globe in the middle of the room, "in its rich dress of brown and green and blue. We see it above in the blue vault of the sky. We see it out there through these windows in the mighty sweep of this great landscape. We see it all, and yet we seem to know so little.

"Or, if we know it, we do so little to show it in our actions. My country is small, the people are poor, we scratch out our living the best way we can." As he speaks, the globe dissolves, and into the centre of the room come the sights and sounds of an African village. Everything is in three dimensions, real life people and animals, and flies, and fruits and vegetables, and dust, and sunbaked earth, and clumsy, squat buildings built of red clay and thatch. Everything pulses with the activity of men, women and children, going about life in the dusty streets.

"We sell the timber from our forests," Mutsandu continues, "and the copper from our mines for what we can get for them from the industrial world. In return, we obtain some medical facilities and drugs for the people, and some schools and educational supplies for our children, and some new technology for our agriculture and our water supplies. Life goes on, but we don't know where it's going on to. Just one day after the other, which was, perhaps, all right once, but isn't anymore, because the rest of the world is going somewhere, and we want to know where it's going, and if it's good, we want to go there, too. If it's bad, we want to be able to say, we don't want to go. But now we're lost. All over the world there are poor people who are lost, and they're all searching and grasping for whatever they can, and in time, the Earth cannot bear the pressure of it."

"Come on, M'buta, you can't have it both ways." It's Bill Bates who has spoken. He's a large, well-built man in his late fifties; brown hair thinning on top; square, solid face; blue, penetrating eyes. "Look, I come from Los Angeles, and a greater contrast with what you're talking about, you couldn't imagine." As he speaks, the African village dissolves, and is replaced by the roaring rush of cars on the Santa Monica freeway. There are no people in sight, only vehicles, and tall square-cornered, glass-encased buildings, as far as the eye can see, which isn't very far, for a thick, blue-brown haze envelops the cityscape, shrouding the hills to the north and east and blanketing the beaches and the Pacific Ocean to the west.

"Just look down there and you can see what we've got." Bates waves at the scene, raising his voice to speak above the roar of the traffic. "But inside each of those cocoons of cars and buildings there are people, millions of people, and they're all doing their thing, going full-tilt to make a go of it. And some of them are doing very well financially, and they use it, every chance they can, to get the hell out of there, and go somewhere else, where the air's cleaner, and the sky's a little bluer. They go on safari to your country and they leave their dollars behind, and your people are a little better for it. And the Americans think it's wonderful, so long as they can get a good hotel room and some coffee and a steak. They wish they could stay there forever. Then they high-tail it back to L.A. to get back into the rush of what, for them, is the real world. Does that make any sense? I don't know. Maybe it does, maybe it doesn't. But everyone is busy at doing it, and they don't seem to have much time to think about doing it any other way."

"And there lies the tragedy of the human gap," Indira Murti is speaking softly as the turbulent Los Angeles scene disappears and the globe returns. "We have created a world of great activity, but very little reflection." She smiles, almost shyly, a tiny figure in a magnificent, coral pink sari. She's young, no more than thirty-five at most, but her deep brown eyes and relaxed features bring a sense of wisdom to her years.

"In the race for techniques and profit," she continues, "people have forgotten that their conscious human minds are part of a universal consciousness, which includes the Earth, our mother. By seeing themselves separate from the Earth, people are using their living energy to run in conflict with the universal life force. It's very destructive, both to the individual and to the Earth. We need to learn again that all reality is energy. In the beginning, it was energy, and in time, it coalesced into matter, but the energy remained locked inside. And when human consciousness came into the world, it came as energy, able to touch the inner parts of reality and set itself in harmony with that energy. But human consciousness also has the power of analytical enquiry, to probe as it were from the outside, to discover bit by bit the complexity of the whole, but never, never in this way to be able to touch, let alone understand, the universal energy that runs through everything."

As she speaks, the globe dissolves and is replaced by soft waves of blue light, rippling across the empty space in the centre of the room, reaching out to envelop each of the Visioneers as they listen to her voice speaking softly, almost musically. She continues.

"Through our science, we have discovered the power of mechanical advantage, and we have learnt the chemistry of the elements, but we have not found, we do not know, the binding energy of the cosmos of which we are a part. To discover that, we must go deep inside our minds, which are part of that energy, and we must take our instruction for what to do from that deep inner wisdom. And from that wisdom, we can build our systems of economics, and our patterns of relationships, not relying only on the reasoning, intellectual attributes of our mind, but using those faculties to support what we have learnt intuitively from the deeper recesses of our being."

"Well said, Indira. That's very powerful." Mark Venture has entered the conversation, his Australian accent pleasant and friendly. He is tall, well built, good looking, with suntanned face, and twinkling blue eyes. As he speaks, he places his large strong hands in front of him, slowly locking and unlocking his fingers.

"What you're saying is that we've bought into a way of thinking and acting that's no longer good for us. Is that right?"

Many heads around the table nod.

"But built into our brains—or is it in our minds—anyway, somewhere in our mental faculties, we can get inspiration to see things differently. Not to accept, for example, that the only way to make newsprint is to cut down our forests, or the only way to grow food is to pour fertilizer into the soil."

"It's deeper than that," Daniel Thomas' dark eyes are alight with excitement, his long black hair brushing the shoulders of his blue denim shirt as he speaks. "It's in seeing the inner vision that we have the power. The mind—and I should tell you it is the mind and not the brain. The brain is an incredible piece of living tissue with billions of neurons and neuro-transmitters and the like. But it's only tissue. The mind is energy, free flowing, boundless energy, whizzing around the universe, knowing no boundaries of time or space, and because of that, it can see visions of what otherwise seems impossible, and know truths for the future that for today seem untrue."

"Yeah, well, wait a bit, I was coming to that," Mark Venture interrupts. "You see, I'm an engineer, and I know a bit about how you build things. And you certainly can't build them if you can't first see them in your mind's eye, so to speak. Sometimes you can't even build them then. I remember the stories of the engineers who were working on the Sydney Harbour Opera House with those great arching sails going up into the sky like bags full of wind. They could see them all right, but do you think they could build them? Those sails defied all of Newton's laws and a few more to boot; but in the end, the engineers did it because all the time they could see them, and they knew there had to be a way to do it."

"Exactly, Mark, every artist knows that the vision is the first part in creation." It's Esther Fisher from Israel who has joined the discussion. She is small, but her presence glows with strong energy as she leans forward in her high-backed leather chair. The same spirit shines in the rearing white unicorn with golden horn which decorates her soft pink sweater. Her curly auburn hair frames the delicate features of her face, which, without makeup, glows fresh with healthy beauty.

"I work in oils on large canvas, and before I begin, I must feel the energy of what I want to paint, filling the whole space around me. It's as if I'm a part of it and it's a part of me. And then, slowly out of the energy field, emerges with great clarity the image of what I want to create. It's there in every detail. I can see it, every part of it, every brush stroke, each splash of colour, separate, and merging with the other colours to create something greater than all of the other, a synergy of all the parts, a composite, coming right out of the mind onto the canvas.

"Can we here, together, create a similar vision for the world? The future is in our minds. Can we begin here in this room to see it? Can we clear our minds of all the bitterness, the old truths that don't serve us well, the evil that intrudes like a dark cancer growing to choke out the life when it's first destroyed? I think we can do that. I know we can do it. And if we can do it here, then we can find a way to take it out to the world. And that would be a wonderful thing to do. Don't you think so?"

Her voice, her question, hangs quietly in the air, as every mind considers and searches for response.

Mark Venture's glance meets hers, and something passes between them, almost imperceptible, just a fleeting contact, but a connection nonetheless. When he speaks, the words are for the room, but the intent is for Esther.

"Yes, that would be a great thing to do. And I can already see the start of it. It begins with leadership. We're running headlong into a world where danger comes not from an external source but from what's happening inside—inside our organizations, inside our communities, inside our own minds. This is the most insidious kind of danger. It's like a cancer. It's there growing, but you don't know it, until suddenly it explodes, and it's running all over your body. To deal with danger like that you have to have the kind of leadership that allows people to discover who they are, to celebrate their strengths, to recognize what needs to change, and then to press on to continually strive to do better."

"There's no blueprint for where we have to go. In Australia, we'd say we're somewhere out back of Burke with the truck broken down, no help for hundreds of miles over sun-scorched plains, and only enough food and water to last a day or two on fly's rations. To get out of a situation like that, you've got to have a lot of intestinal fortitude—guts, if you like. But more than that, you've got to have a vision of where you're going, so that it's seared in your mind . And it's got to be a place that's better than where you are now. Otherwise, you'll never make it. And you've got to be able to get everyone else on the truck to see it too, so they'll have the hope to continue on.

"And there's got to be rules, but they're internal rules, because no one can be standing over you to see you do the right thing. You've got to believe that people are better than a mob of sheep, milling around, too stupid to know what to do for their own good.   .

"You know, Esther, your friend Moses was a good example of the kind of leader we need today. In fact, that Exodus story is a pretty good metaphor for what we've got to do now. That pack of Israelites was an unlikely group to make it across the desert and the Red Sea into the promised land, what with their chickens and their kids and their few bits of household belong-ings. The whole mob of them moved out because they had a vision and a hope of somewhere better to be.

"And there was Moses prodding them along. He was no great shakes as a speaker, but he had the fire of God in his eyes. He was quick to tell them that first they had to believe in themselves and the idea that they could be better if they gave up what they had and went in search of something more.

"Well, of course, the difference between that situation and this is that we're not on any kind of exodus. There's nowhere to exit to. We need to put our brains to work to see where we're going to be in a few short years if we don't do something different from what we're doing now. We need to get a vision of what something better can be. And we need to commit every bit of our energy to making that vision happen.

"We're all leaders and followers at the same time. We have to be good at both and be able to tell when we need to be one or the other. And I suppose that's the definition of a Visioneer, someone who's able to engineer a preferred future by being a good leader and a good follower. That's who we are, ladies and gentlemen. Welcome to the band of Visioneers!"

He pauses and smiles shyly.

"Sorry about the speech," he says. "I'm not used to running on like that, but Esther got me going."

The whole room breaks up into gusts of laughter and shouts of "Well said, Mark", and General Soulière from Paris, who is sitting beside him, stands up and twirls Mark's chair around in salute amid more shouts of praise and applause.

On his other side, Theresa Romano, short, well-rounded mother of five from Naples, lifts him from his chair and hugs him into the folds of her ample body.

"Oh, you're so right, " her voice is deep and rich with the passion of the Mediterranean. "We are the Visioneers. But it's not just for us, the vision. It's for the world, and most of all, for the children. I have five of them at home in Napoli, my little ones. I have their photographs." She fusses around inside a huge black leather handbag looking for the photographs.

But there's no need. In an instant, the children are in the room, centre stage, running through the narrow, cobble-stoned streets of Naples, two boys and three girls, aged five to fifteen, the little one, Maria, black-haired, dressed in pink, running hard with little legs, hand in hand with brother Stefano, the eldest, almost tugging her off her feet, as they run, shouting and laughing. And out of the doorways of other houses pour more children, dodging under the clothes hanging on sagging lines across the street, running, just running hard, faces alive with youth, their voices shouting, filling the room, until the whole of the centre space is filled with children, from every land, eyes glowing, eager, passionate, full of fun and laughter. They've left the streets of Naples and are thronging into an open field, filled with sunshine and green grass. Stefano appears again, now with little Maria on his shoulders. He's waving a large blue flag, held high on a long pole, sky blue, with a large white circle in the centre of it, representing the world, and in the circle, a huge white V for Visioneers. Little Maria carries her own small flag, waving it furiously, and suddenly all of the children have flags, and it's a dancing sea of blue with the bold white V waving high and free as the children weave and dance around the field, then thread out into a long line, with Stefano and Maria in the lead, and head off down a winding, tree-lined road, singing. Their words float up and fill the room, where the Visioneers are sitting transfixed by the spectacle, until the children are gone and all that remains are their voices and the song, and the words repeating over and over again:

"We are the ones, going to the fore.
Big ones, little ones—all of us are here.
Small world, big world, reaching out to all.
Up, up and upmost—the mighty Visioneers!"

Theresa Romano is almost overcome with excitement. Her large round face is wet with tears. She bobs up and down and weaves from side to side. Suddenly, she spots the two young people who are part of the visioneering team, curly blonde-haired Sally Hearst from Auckland, New Zealand, and long-faced, sad-eyed Nicholai Andropov from Moscow. They're sitting together on the opposite side of the room from Theresa. As the sound of the children's song fades, she runs in a kind of ample, rolling motion, like a tug boat on a light swell, around behind the chairs of the other Visioneers, and comes between them, one arm around each, hugging them to her.

"Oh my dears, " she sobs. "I'm so glad you're here. My little Stefano and Maria, there, aren't they wonderful, and all of the others, little Visioneers, all of them. And here you are, part of us. You can go back out and be leaders to the children of the world. And I'll go out and tell all of the mothers that they needn't be afraid for their children. They must tell them to dream their dreams, and to not be afraid, but to work and play together in hope and love. Because that's the true way of the world, not the bitter, ugly, fighting that we've known, as if we have to battle with everyone else for a small piece of something to call our own, when all the time there's plenty there for everyone, because that's the way the world is. God has seen to it, and we must learn the truth and teach it to our children, so that they can find more hope and joy in living every day."

As she finishes speaking, the children's *Song of the Visioneers* comes up again, and the voices fill the room:

"We are the ones, going to the fore.
Big ones, little ones—all of us are here.
Small world, big world, reaching out to all.
Up, up, and upmost—the mighty Visioneers!"

Sally Hearst's eyes are shining. She's just sixteen.

"I don't know what to say," she exclaims, half laughing and half crying at the same time. She rubs at her eyes. "This is so wonderful. I mean, wow! Nicholai, how can you sit there so quiet? There's all of this stuff happening here. I don't really know what's going on, but it feels good and right. Back home in Auckland, everyone just pretty well takes things for granted. We kids are mostly interested in our own things. Quite self-centred, really.

"But now I can see how much more there is to do. It's like, wow! the whole world has opened up, and I'm right here in the middle of it and looking out and seeing everything. And all of you people, all of you who've spoken, it's so wonderful what you're saying. There's so much we can do to set things right in the world. All we have to do is to see things right.

"Like you say, Theresa, if you see plenty, there is plenty. And that's your answer, too, Mr. Mutsandu, there's plenty of everything in the world for your people. We all just have to see it that way. And that's what you meant, too, didn't you, Indira? The wisdom to see what we need to see, to know what we need to know is inside us, like a life force, and if we get in touch with that then we're boundless and free and can go whizzing around the universe, like Daniel says.

"Oh, I've learnt so much already. What do we do next? When do we start? Come on, Nick, don't just sit there. Tell us what you think."

She pushes him good-naturedly on the shoulder, smiling encouragement. He turns his wide sad eyes on the room. He's only eighteen, but could be twice that age.

"I think it's very hard," he says, "to get people to reach out beyond themselves to others. In my country, we've been very good at performing— in the Olympics, in the ballet, in hockey, in the circus. The select few, brought together and trained, become the best in the world at what they do.

"But the rest of us have been very unhappy. We knew things weren't working well, but we had to tell the lie and say that everything was fine, and if we didn't, there were those watching us to catch us out, and some of them were our best friends. Most of that is changing now, because the lie was just too big, and finally everything fell apart. Now we're trying to rebuild it, but when we do, will we do it any better? I don't know."

"Well, of course you will, you silly goose," Sally chides him. "That's why you're here, to see how things can be and go and do them."

He smiles at her, shrugs a little. "Yes, I see, I will try. I'm a good listener, and I do want to believe you."

That seems to be the signal for everyone to get into the discussion. Conversation opens up all around the room. In the centre, the great round globe reappears, turning slowly, providing a continuing reminder of the reason they are together.

The guttural tones of Boris Gunther from Germany are raised in animated discussion with Junichi Yakasawa, the Japanese industrialist. Boris is a farmer and he weeps for the growing toxicity of his soil, the unwanted spin-off from the industrial machine. Junichi understands and speaks of his efforts to turn enterprise toward human fulfillment rather than consumption.

Across the room, Luis Valdez speaks softly with George Cardinal. The small-framed Roman Catholic priest from Santiago is a sharp contrast with the big-boned Cree Indian chief from northern Alberta in Canada. Valdez has seen the despair of the peasant farmers in his parish in Chile. Cardinal knows from the inside the bitter grief of native people, who want to hold the Earth, but are caught in the vortex of industrial development that gathers them up and sweeps them aside before they can taste more than a morsel of the promised meal. Together, the two men strike a common bond, destined to take them soon into the dangers of the conflict that erupts when the passion of men's souls are stirred to act against an all-pervading evil.

In another group, the mood is different. The warm Latin energy of Carmen Santander from Spain strikes a chord with the dry English wit of Jeremy Hiscox, history professor at Cambridge. Irene Henshaw forgets her Scottish reserve and bursts into gales of laughter at the prospect of Jeremy seeking to engage again in the conquest of the Spanish armada. The joke is quite lost on Karl Ibsen from Norway, but in pleasant good humour he offers to design a villa they might share to blend the baked heat of a plaza del toros with the soft fragrance of an English country garden.

One remaining pair have withdrawn a little from the group and stand together at the bank of windows, looking out across the grassy hillside to the saw-tooth Rocky Mountain range in the distance.

"There's one thing we must never forget," Mohammed Hussein speaks softly, almost reverently, "we each come from two great civilizations whose greatness can endure forever."

Lin Yuen, a senior secretary in the People's Republic of China, nods slowly. "Yes," he says, "where the foundations are strong, the structure can withstand much agitation."

These are prophetic words for all of the Visioneers in the room. Little do they know at this time the extent to which each of them will soon be tested and how deeply they will have to search in and beyond their traditions to find the way ahead. The conversation continues as the sun drops slowly behind the mountains and long shadows creep across the landscape.

◆ ◆ ◆

You have met your band of Visioneers and they have learned a little of each other. Brought together in the mindscape of your imagination, they've come upon the stage where now they'll start to play out the drama of a time between times. You don't know where this will take either you, or them. You sense only that this must happen, and that you'll see it through to the duration when your part in it will be done. For now, you can enjoy the company of your friends and accept your role as mentor and student of the experience.

CHAPTER FOUR

The
Project
Is Set

W hen you arrive in your thinking room, the others are already there ahead of you. Churchill stands legs apart, in the middle of the room, chewing on an unlit cigar, facing the door, waiting for you to come in. Kennedy is at the window, dressed in casual slacks and blue sweater, hands in pockets, staring out at the landscape. Dickens, seated in a chair by the crackling fire, leafs through a magazine. Anne has a sketchpad and is surreptitiously sketching the bull-dog stance of Churchill, a mischievous smile playing on her lips. As you enter, they all turn expectantly to face you. Churchill takes the cigar from his mouth and stabs the air.

Empires of the Mind

"Venture is a good man," he almost growls. " You need to put him in charge of operations. Soulière hasn't said anything. He seems weak to me. You need to beef him up a lot. Bates is a disappointment, too. For a newspaper man, he doesn't have much of an opinion. You'll have to get him out of that Los Angeles smog so he can see what's going on in the world. Mutsandu has good potential, but he's too naive to be effective yet. Get him out of Africa into Washington, Tokyo and London, so he can find out what power is all about. The women show promise, particularly that spunky little Fisher person from Israel. She'll be solid when the going gets tough. And that Indira Murti is smart. You have to get her to a position of influence. She sees the truth of what I said years ago, that the next empires will be the empires of the mind."

"Oh, come on, Winston, we don't want any talk of empires here," President Kennedy intervenes. "That's ancient history. Planetary steward-ship is the only way into the future. We didn't understand that in my time. When I launched the Apollo project, I wanted to get American confidence back by making a superhuman effort. That was all. And we achieved the goal. We put man into space.

"But the outcome was different from what we expected. Through the eyes of the astronauts, we looked back to Earth from space and realized our responsibility for this planet. And it's a heavy responsibility. It's the num-ber one issue. Everywhere the old territorial boundaries are coming down. The Berlin Wall was a symbol of that. When it went up, it marked the beginning of an era of balkanization worldwide. When it came down, it marked the beginning of a new world future. That's where things are now.

"The world's heading for what I would call a WE future: Wholistic Entrepreneurial, where the number one issue for people will be to invent a global economy that promotes the well-being of the planet as a whole and everyone on it. No more empires—American, British or Russian, but a real Commonwealth of Nations."

"Bravo! Mr. Kennedy! That's it exactly," exclaims Anne. "That's what the visioneering project is all about. It's an effort by a band of ordinary people to write a new kind of future history—away from competition and conflict towards cooperation and sharing. You're right, Mr. Kennedy, it has to be a WE future. That's the only kind that will work."

"I say, this is getting exciting," Charles Dickens has joined in. "Plane-tary stewards, WE future, future history, empires of the mind. And here we have this unlikely band of Visioneers showing the way. It's a great story. I wish I had written it. Does anyone know what's going to happen next?"

"Yes," growls Churchill, "the rest of you are going to keep quiet long enough for me to make my point." He glances at them a little, then smiles, roguishly.

"I don't mind admitting that I'm an old Empire man. But I can go beyond that and be a planetary steward with the best of you. And that's my point about the mind. If we're going to shift the foundation of the way things are done on the planet, people have to shift the way they think. You can't be the steward of a planet until you can see clearly in your mind what planetary life is about. And I can tell you, it's a whole lot more than tribes running around in jungles, which is where we started, feeding off the land and killing each other when they trespassed on the other's territory. That's where we began and we haven't progressed beyond that right up to the bloody, barbarous 20th century. We just became more proficient and blood-thirsty in the slaughtering, pretending all the time to cloak it in the fine dress of civilization, but slavering like hungry hounds to bite off another piece from a shrinking, rotting corpse."

Anne emits a little gasp at the vehemence of the Churchillian rhetoric and drops her paint brush.

"I'm sorry, Anne, if my images strike you as lurid, but we're never going to do what needs to be done if we don't see things for what they are. Out there is a snarling, gnashing, grinding, tearing plethora of teeth, and if we're going to put this band of Visioneers into the thick of it, we had better be sure they're up to it.

"That's what I meant about the mind. The battlefront is now at the level of mind. The ultimate force is mindpower. We know it can be nourishing and profound, but it can be rotten and cankerous, vile, hideous, and wicked almost beyond the point that decent people can imagine.

"This has been the century of Nazi gas chambers and human ovens; chemical weapons spraying death over unsuspecting civilians; bombs raining out of the sky dropped by disciplined technicians in tiny cockpits onto hundreds of thousands of unprotected people and all the products of their heritage; and the ultimate incendiary Armageddon of the atomic bomb, blackening the entire landscape with the charred remains of whatever was there and poisoning the environment into a long devastated nuclear winter.

"All of this is as recent as yesterday. The elements of it are in last night's news. And tomorrow is already here, lying waiting, open and exposed to whatever wickedness or wisdom the human mind chooses to release upon it.

"That's why I insist we put this visioneering project onto a war footing. I have a plan for doing that, which, with your permission, I'll lay out for you."

Churchill pauses and looks around the room. "Okay, Winston," Kennedy replies, "since when did you need anyone's permission to say what's on your mind? You've grabbed each of us by the throat. You've got our attention. Now, let's hear the plan."

Changing the Mindscape

Churchill takes up a position by the fireplace. Kennedy and Anne find chairs and sit down. Churchill motions you to come forward and you take the large comfortable chair in the centre of the room where you sat when you first met the group.

"The goal is to change the mindscape," he says. "The mind is everywhere at once. It's the foundation of history. If we want the future history to be decent, it has to be seen that way first in the minds of the men and women who'll determine what happens. The hardware we have for thinking about that is pretty well set. Our brains have been in place for several million years, born and reborn every generation, abused and nourished by circumstance and intent, but nonetheless set.

"And it seems from both ancient and recent understandings and experience that this human mind of ours has an infinite capacity. But we choose most of the time to chain it down, to lock it up in small dark rooms where little light can penetrate. What our project is about, is unlocking some of those chains, and throwing open some windows to let light into those prisons.

"The only way humanity can move forward is to see every human mind as a centre of creative energy. They must drop the categories that a more primitive mindware put in place. Remove the barriers that divide: black-white, east-west, liberal-conservative, protestant-catholic, Jew-Arab, capitalist-socialist, management-labour. There's no place in the future for those paralyzing, conflictual categories. While we hold to them, it's not a WE future, but a THEM and US future, and some of US now have such power to wield against THEM that we can and we will bring everything crashing down around us.

"So that's why I said we have to put our effort onto a war footing. It's not a contradiction. I'm not talking about another war between THEM and US. I'm talking about a state of mind that says there's peril all around, and we have to move quickly to secure some strategic advantage before we're overwhelmed.

"This can be the world's most triumphant celebration of human creativity. Up to now we've been outstandingly successful as a species in creating objects from our imaginations. Now we have to create a new world order. And the process is the same. We must begin in the mindscape, with the vision of what that new world order will be. We have to imagine it before we can do it.

"And it's not enough for us to imagine it here in this room. Nor is it enough for the Visioneers to imagine it in their assembly. Nor for select individuals in different countries of the world to imagine it. That's where it will start, but it won't be possible until there's a groundswell of educated imaginations in every part of the world, in every field of endeavour, in every colour of skin, in every stripe of religion, ethnicity, and cultural upbringing—all of them accepting as a great enterprise of worth, the building of a shared vision of the future.

"It will begin in the mind. It can begin nowhere else. Our enterprise, our project, is to take the steps now to change the global mindscape. We have a band of Visioneers to do it with. And we must guide them to secure the utmost strategic advantage to achieve our goal."

Churchill pauses again. Every eye is fixed on him intently. Charles Dickens is leaning forward, completely engrossed.

"Yes, yes," he murmurs, "the mind is the place to start. It's the most powerful force on Earth. Go on, my good man, tell us what you see for our Visioneers. How do they change the mind of the world?"

"Your phrase is right, Mr. Dickens," Churchill rejoins, "the mind of the world! We begin by understanding that the world can and does have a mind. It's a manifestation of the collective consciousness of all the minds existing on the planet. The great project of the 21st century will be the gathering of these minds into a single, resolute purpose for the betterment of the Earth and everyone on it. The nation state that we have designed is an imperfect concept. At best it's a stepping stone to the place where we now must go: planetary stewardship. And we can't get there unless we turn five and a half billion minds from a multitude of cultural ignorances into a unified mindframe. They must see that human fellowship in union with the life systems of the planet is the only possible way for a decent future life.

"Creating that mindscape is the momentous task of our band of Visioneers. They must seek out the pressure points and touch them to move the power levers of politics and wealth and military might with a new and more powerful force: enlightened vision of human destiny. That's the object of our efforts, my friends. That's the mission of our Visioneers."

Again he pauses. Anne is almost beside herself with expectation.

"Go on, Mr. Churchill, go on," her voice is breathless with excitement. "What's your plan? How do you see it unfolding? How can we help?"

A Congress of the Global Mind

Churchill strides across the room to the bookcase and lifts down a large, heavy, brass-bound globe of the world and sets it spinning on a coffee table in front of the fireplace. John Kennedy and Charles Dickens are both watching and listening attentively, each appreciating the high order performance of a master statesmen.

"That," says Churchill, gesturing to the spinning globe, "is in peril. We must save it." He puts his hand firmly on the globe and stops the spin. "We begin by sending our emissaries to strategic pressure points throughout to stir minds to act. Here, here, here, and, here." He stabs his finger into various parts of the world. " The exact locations don't concern us now. I'll outline them in due course. That's step one. Step two calls for a grand assembly of world leaders. And mind, I'm not talking here of the posturing apology for power-broking that goes on in the United Nations in New York. That's a patchwork affair, already an anachronism of a past mindframe of warring combatants grabbing for territory and control. It's done some good work in its time, but now we must go beyond it. I'm talking here of a Congress of the Global Mind, where the central task is creative, not defensive. We must build with the full energy of creative human minds, the best in the world, the vision of a new world order, leap-frogging over the calamitous inadequacy of past and current thinking.

"The change will come, not because people choose to do so, but because they are being swept there by the force of mind at work in the world. The energy centres will be our Visioneers, led there by the power let loose by this one grand enterprise for which we few have been assembled.

"And after that comes the unfolding. A millennium of effort to achieve the vision. To do what could not be done in all the millennia preceding because minds were fragmented and at war, and could grasp only at small pieces, limited by their vision. But now the vision will be bold, written large on the great skyscapes of the universe for every eye to see, and the human mind will reach the ascendancy of which it's capable when limitations are set aside.

"That's the way I see our enterprise unfolding. If you're in agreement with the generality, I'm ready to move to the specifics."

The Incarnation of Evil

Sensing the need for others to take the floor, Churchill moves to the empty chair and sits. Anne, enraptured, reaches across and squeezes his hand, whispering, "Thank you", just loud enough for all to hear. Kennedy is smiling and nodding appreciatively. However, it's Dickens who seizes the moment to speak.

"Splendid!" he almost shouts enthusiastically. "You've set the vision with magnificent eloquence. Now we shall run with it. But first, I must introduce a caution, not to in any way dilute the rich body of the wine you've poured for us. By no means. But, rather, to enhance its bouquet and aroma by setting it in the context of what I have come to understand about the human character."

He stands up and adopts a theatrical pose by the fireplace. One hand is in the pocket of his brown, country-coloured slacks, while the other fumbles absently with the gold watch chain hanging across the lavender vest under his high-buttoned tweed jacket. His sharp features are alive with the energy of his thoughts.

"You've spoken, Mr. Churchill," he continues, "with great passion about the nobility of the human species. I agree. All my work was dedicated to the release of that virtue in the human condition. But as we all know, and no one better than you, sir, there's a darker side. It becomes manifest in individuals whose very presence seems foreordained to bring disaster and misfortune by attacking the very heart of noble enterprise.

"I'm speaking, my dear friends, about the incarnation of evil."

His body stiffens. His eyes are hooded. His hands gesture furtively in front of him, clawing at the air as if it were a thick and heavy substance.

"When our Visioneers go forward, they will encounter such evil, and we should not anticipate that they'll have an easy time in dealing with it.

"There'll be the brutish lout, thick of skin and mean of mind, whose only thought is for himself. With huge strength in great hams of hands, he'll not be averse to crushing the life out of a weaker party, if rage and expectation incline him to it. These are the thugs of life, born of our species, but somehow infected with a carbuncular disorder in their blood that poisons all their outlook.

"And on the female side, though it pains me greatly to say so, for no one more than I admires the beauty and the virtue of the female soul with all of its capacity for unconditional love and generosity. But, as I say, on that side, too, there is the treachery of evil, boiling over with passion for vindictiveness; and erstwhile beauty, shifts before the very gaze into hard lines of unremitting hostility and vengeance. Such women are a blight to any enterprise, for they strike with venomous ferocity and can inflict telling and sometimes mortal wounds on the unsuspecting.

"But worst of all is the high priest of incarnate evil, intelligent and lithe of mind, but totally absorbed with illusions of grandeur, himself portrayed in his mind as conquering hero, sweeping all obstacles aside as irritants to his deluded dreams of conquest. He has no time to wait for the promulgation of his wickedness. It has festered inside his being for an incubation period, then erupts with a swiftness and violence that amazes and confuses all those who might otherwise have stood firm against it. No quarter is given to an enemy. Life has no value if it does not support his aggression. Instant executions, mass exterminations, diabolical perversion and torture. Nothing is too extreme for the wickedness that drives him on with maniacal determination for conquest.

"The world knows all these archetypes, and the various paler shades of their distemper. They are there irresolute, unforgiving and unrepentant. They are the treacherous minority, mutations of the mainstream of the life force that otherwise empowers and ennobles the universe. As we move now with this grand venture, we must be wary and prepared for their emergence, lest they strike a telling blow at the heart of our enterprise."

The room has grown still and the air hangs thick with the implications of what has just been said. Dickens, a trifle uncomfortable as the purveyor of the message, shrugs a little and sits again without a further word in his chair by the fireplace.

A Fountain of Love

"But what about love, Mr. Dickens?" It's Anne's turn to intervene. Dickens raises his eyebrows and gestures to her to continue.

"I know what you say is true, and I know you've said it only for us to be prepared. But we can't just let it lie like that. I mean, Mr. Churchill has set our vision on the grand expanding horizon of human achievement. That's a far greater force than the ugly picture you described.

"I believe that at the heart of the human spirit is an unquenchable fountain of love. It's the one sure and enduring life force. Even those despicable mutations you've just described have the capacity to love. No tyrant or cold-blooded murderer has ever lived who wasn't touched at one time by love.

"It's there for us, for all the world, if we just look for it. I believe that there's a great river of love coursing through all life on Earth. As we reach now for the higher levels of human consciousness that Mr. Churchill described, then we'll learn to drink more deeply of this stream of love.

"When the road is hard, and the going seems almost impossible, our Visioneers will remember that. It'll shine in their eyes and glow in their acts and the whole world will be moved by it.

"I just know that's the way it will be."

A Time of Passage

"And the world is more blessed than any of us can imagine by the Annes in it." John Kennedy has come over to her and extends his hands, smiling. She reaches up to him. He takes both her hands and lifts her to her feet, and embraces her long and affectionately, his boyish face buried in her hair. When they part, he continues to hold her hand.

"Stand with me a moment, Anne, while I say one or two things." They turn to the others, standing hand in hand by the fireplace as he speaks.

"Winston, you've described where we must go, and I agree. Charles, you've cautioned us of the villains we'll find along the way, and I know them well. Anne, precious Anne, you've reminded us of love.

"All that I can add is the vision of what I see. I see a time of great turmoil coming for the world. It's a time of passage. In America, we had great waves of immigrants come to our country. They gave up almost everything they had to take a chance on a new beginning. They were coming to a land about which they knew very little, and what they did know was probably false expectation.

"But they all held one common passion in their hearts—hope for a better future. In their time of passage from the known to the unknown, they were borne on by their hope for a better outcome than they otherwise would have. Those who were ultimately successful in their new adopted land were the ones who could enliven hope with vision, who could see themselves successful in whatever they did. As they gained more knowledge of their new surroundings, they quickly sharpened and adjusted their vision to take advantage of the opportunities that abounded.

"So it is now with the world. It's a time of passage from the outmoded mindframe to the new that Winston has so eloquently described. My vision is a 21st century filled for the first time in the history of civilization with a common purpose for the betterment of all life. It will be a planetary culture, interconnected with information systems designed to tell people how well they're doing in the movement toward the vision, what adjustments need to be made, what temporary sacrifices are required.

"It'll be a world filled with love of learning, for no one can be a planetary citizen without striving for the whole of life to know and appreciate all the wonder of such a world. Minds will be enlarged with education systems that seek to remove all limits, to encourage, to reward the achievement not only of the individual best, but also the collective effort.

"It will be a time when my own words first uttered in the heyday of my presidency can take on new and enlarged meaning. People will ask not what the world can do for them, but what they can do for the world. Everywhere the boundaries will be pushed back, and the inequities bridged by ordinary men and women acting with intent.

"Above all, Anne, it will be a world of love, because people will take away the barriers of distrust and division and difference, and once they're gone, the full flow of affection can pour forth unhindered.

"It's time now to hand the baton to our team of Visioneers, to wish them God speed and the safe assurance of our continuing attention to their best efforts."

The Crushing Burden

His words settle into the stillness of the room. All of their words hang in the air, like a heavy mist with the sun shining through it, splitting into a kaleidoscope of rainbow colours: Churchill's ringing oratory to convene a Congress of the Global Mind, Dickens' searing depiction of the evil that infects the human psyche, Anne's passionate belief in the power of love, and Kennedy's grand vision of a new world order of cooperation and caring. All of it hangs in the air, pulsing, shifting, shining, and waiting. Waiting. Waiting for what? Waiting for you. Waiting for you to take the next step. Because all of this is in your mind. These characters from history and fiction who are so comfortable and close to you now, exist only in your mind. Their words, their visions, their passions, all are in your mind. And they're building to a crescendo of challenge. And you're staring down a long tunnel of shimmering light, where everything is possibility and nothing is certainty and everywhere is complexity.

Suddenly, the weight of it all has settled on your spirit as a huge, smothering burden of responsibility. And you want to get out from under it. What do they expect of you, these mentors? Why are they here in your mind? Why are you here? And where are you? Where is this place, your thinking room? What is happening to you? What are you expected to do next?

The boiling passion of confusion erupts and you turn with hostility and anger on your mentors. Your words cut with knife-edge savagery into their rainbow mist of future possibility.

"You seem to forget, all of you," you say, "that none of this is real. None of you are real. All of it is imagination—my imagination. What do you expect of me? I'm a single, simple, one person, flesh and blood with an existence—though I'm beginning to doubt it—outside the meandering mindfest of future possibilities. What do I know of the ways of the world, the pressure points of high places, the strategies of change? It's too much. You're expecting too much of me. I can't see, I don't know. What you're asking is too much. You're proceeding as if I'm not here. But I am the only one who *is* here. And it's suddenly all too much, and I don't think I can do it."

Your words out, Churchill pounces on them with a vengeance. He springs from his chair, standing in front of you, nostrils flaring with anger.

"What do you mean, you're not up to it? When you set your foot to a path, you don't turn back just because the going gets tough. There's no way back for you, for any of us. There's only forward. You began the venture. You assembled us. You came up with the idea of visioneering. Now we must get on with it, because to go any other way is futile. The choice is out of your hands now. It's been made. The only issue is how best to move forward. And we're here to see to that. You've got the Visioneers at hand. You've heard the general outline of where we are to go. Now you must play your part in taking us there."

The old man's anger is full blown, but not overbearing or intimidating. His passion is with the venture. His frustration is with any delay to the enterprise. His eyes burn into your mind as much with need as with intensity.

President Kennedy has come up beside him. His wide blue eyes stare into your heart.

"Life is a continuous choice of doing what you sense to be right," he says, "or backing off to take what seems an easier path. But in reality, there is no choice. If you take the second way, you've lost the field. There's no choice when it comes to great enterprise. There's only courage. Courage to take the first step; courage to see it through, no matter what; courage to stand alone, if necessary; courage to face a hundred thousand hostile eyes and say, 'This way we go because any other is unacceptable.' You have that courage, my friend, otherwise you wouldn't have begun, and we wouldn't have joined you. We understand the load you carry, but only you can carry it. Take a moment now to find your courage, and you'll see it's not so bad."

His face is calm and reassuring. Churchill's glowering visage has softened a little and now is set firm and resolute. Anne and Dickens join them. They don't speak. Anne's sweet girlish features are apprehensive and appealing. Charles Dickens' gaze is good-humoured, and he nods his head up and down, a tiny smile playing on his lips, which widens in expectation of your response.

At that moment, the cloud of doubt is lifted. You see before you four great minds and spirits, assembled at your bidding to join you in visioneering. This can only be to nourish a project of great worth. Your heart is lightened. You step forward, smiling, grasping their hands, one after the other, and over again, the mood lightening, laughing now, backslapping, embraces all around, even Churchill, hugging you like a jovial pooh bear in decidedly good spirits.

"My friends," you're saying, "thank you for being here. I'm sorry for my outburst. I'm quite recovered now and ready to proceed. Indeed, I'm more than ready. You're right, all of you, there is no choice but to go on. There's so much to do. The world can't continue the way it is, and all of us must do whatever we can to move the change to where it must go—into a 21st century of collaboration and effort to resolve differences and bring more justice and equity. It can happen only if these ideals are in the hearts and minds of ordinary people. I'm determined now to do my part. My band of Visioneers is ready to do theirs. With your guidance and support, our achievements will be spectacular.

"Mr. Prime Minister, I believe you have some specific instructions before I bring my team together."

A Bold, Audacious Plan

Churchill is positively beaming now. He strides back to the globe. Everyone gathers around.

"Yes, well here's the drift of it," he says. "I don't need to go into all of the details. Mark Venture will work them out with you. He's a good man, the right kind of leader for this project. Here are the essentials.

"There's a summit conference of world leaders set for six months from now in April at the United Nations in New York. Most of them will be there. They'll meet to discuss and argue about all the usual things: trade, embargos, arms reduction, pollution control. None of it will amount to any great improvement because they'll all come to the meeting from the same position: How do I get as much as possible for myself? While that kind of arguing is going on in New York, millions of lives elsewhere are destroyed through poverty, war, lack of hope, and all the rest of the sorry blight we know so well, exaggerated now by the cataclysmic coughing and wheezing of a dying environment.

"The task of the Visioneers between now and then is to make sorties into every corner of the globe to get a groundswell of action going to put pressure on the leaders to make some real changes. Of course, this won't make much difference because all those people are carrying around the wrong mindframe in their heads, and they won't act differently until they think differently.

"That's when we play our trump card."

He pauses and looks around the group for effect.

"Okay, Winston," laughs Kennedy, "you've got our attention. What's your big play?"

"We kidnap the leaders," Churchill says triumphantly.

There is a stunned silence.

"By Jove! That's got some spirit to it," Charles Dickens exclaims. "Can't you just see the headlines in the New York Times? SUMMIT LEADERS DISAPPEAR. Or in the tabloids: PRESTO—NOW YOU SEE 'EM, NOW YOU DON'T. And the story lines goes on. 'At precisely 2:10 p.m. today, Eastern Daylight Time, after a copious lunch of roast beef and good red wine, the leaders of the most powerful nations on Earth vanished into thin air. Aides and officials sat dumbfounded looking at the empty chairs, while a security guard at the door was heard to remark: Hey, don't blame me. I'm here to keep the lunatics out, not the big cheeses in. A thorough search was made under the tables in the clothes closets, and in the men's and ladies' washrooms, revealing absolutely no trace of the missing statespersons. It's as if they vanished into the hot air of their own debate.'"

"Yes, I see it right away." President Kennedy is rubbing his hands, roguishly. "You lift the power brokers out of their seats of influence and plunk them down here in the Visioneering Room without any of their trappings of office and it becomes quite a different debate. In the meantime, though, you've got a vacuum back on their home front, and that could be dangerous, Winston."

"Of course," Churchill growls, "that's why the Visioneers have to do their work well beforehand. Immediately the opportunity opens up, they move in with their new manifesto for planetary stewardship. They send this new message crackling instantaneously across all the communication networks of the world, in every language, and look to the fall-out as people respond."

"It's certainly a risk—change through manipulated chaos," Kennedy muses.

"Far better than death through enforced constipation," Churchill rejoins.

"Precisely," Charles Dickens intervenes. "It's pure genius with a stiff spine and I salute you for it, Winston. What do you say, Anne? As the tactical novice among us, you no doubt have a fresh perspective."

"It's a dream," she replies, "and that's where the best part of life begins. But we must go beyond the dream to act. Mr. Churchill is showing the way for that. I can hardly wait to see what happens."

"It's settled, then." Churchill moves to bring the session to a close. "Mark Venture is to be summoned now to put the next piece in place. We wish him and his band of Visioneers good speed on their epic adventure to create a future to match the higher aspirations of the human mind."

With that, they're gone. Left alone, you slowly begin to realize what an astonishing prospect lies ahead. Up to now, everything has been imagination. Figures from history and literature conjured up in your mind along with a fictional band of Visioneers. Now Churchill has introduced a new element. You are to thrust your characters into the real world and bring the present live leaders of the nations into your imaginary setting. The meeting he referred to is in New York in six months' time. You're well aware of it. The media have been exploiting it for several weeks. It's to be an extraordinary session of heads of governments at the United Nations, convened by special invitation of the Secretary-General. The purpose of the meeting is to develop fresh insights for the world of the 21st century. Well, Churchill certainly proposes to give them fresh insights. Something not on the agenda: a quick trip by silver bridge to the Visioneering Room, while the Visioneers redirect world affairs. What an absurd, bold, exciting, brilliant idea!

Smiling, you relax back into your chair gathering energy for the task that lies ahead.

PART TWO

The
Venture
is
Launched

CHAPTER FIVE

First Steps

Let me make sure I've got this straight. Winston Churchill wants me to lead the Visioneers in an assault on the world's governments." Mark Venture is staring hard at you, his handsome sun-tanned face creased in a querulous expression of disbelief.

"Well, not exactly an assault," you reply. "More like an intervention."

You're seated with Mark on the patio outside the Visioneering Room in the brisk mountain air of a clear autumn morning. Two steaming cups of coffee sit on the table between you. He's been listening intently as you outline the discussion with your advisors.

"Yeah, well you can call it what you like. It certainly sounds like an ambitious scheme. But I've always been an admirer of Churchill, and if you say he's on the team, then I'm impressed—and Kennedy, too. That's a powerful combination. But a large part of their greatness, you know, was their nerve to deliver an aggressive knock-out punch. Where do you suppose this new interest in a collaborative future of planetary stewardship comes from?"

"I expect they see more broadly, now," you reply. "In power, they had to respond to the pressures of the day. Now they see from a cosmic perspective. However, their earthly charisma is still very much in evidence. It's a combination that can do more to change the world than they could accomplish while in office. They're looking to you to lead the effort in their stead. Are you ready for that, Mark?"

"It seems to be the Moses syndrome all over again. It's strange, I just mentioned that to Esther in our meeting the other day, now here I am being handed the assignment. I don't know if I'm ready for it. How could anyone know that? But I'll do it, if that's what you mean."

"It's exactly what I mean."

"Good, well, let's get to it. If we're going to pull this off, you'll need to be pretty swift with that imagination of yours. We'll need to move our people in and out of tricky situations very fast. Some of it will be dangerous, too. We won't know how it's going to come out, and if it goes badly for us from time to time, we have to be ready for that. Do you understand?"

His expression is serious now. He's already in role, looking ahead, sensing the problems. You know exactly what he means. You can have no favourites or preconceived notions of outcomes. Events must unfold as they will, in response to his leadership and the actions of the Visioneers. The play is out of your hands now. You're the vehicle. Mark Venture and his Visioneers are the players.

"Yes, I know what I must do," you say.

He nods, stands up, and goes into the Visioneering Room to begin the play.

In the Andes

Six heavily armed soldiers wind their way on horseback single-file up the narrow mountain road high in the central Andes of northern Chile. Father Luis Valdez wipes the perspiration out of his eyes, and adjusts the focus of his binoculars. He grunts in dismay as the image sharpens, revealing the sallow faces under floppy felt hats and green jungle shirts criss-crossed with bullet belts bulging with cartridges. Each soldier has a submachine gun slung across his back and the butt end of a high-powered rifle protrudes from a long leather scabbard next to the saddle pummel. They ride easily, reins held loosely, relaxing to the labouring sway of the horses as they pick their way up the slope among rocks and holes on the rough mountain trail. Saddle bags and pouches bulge, probably with more ammunition, and each rider carries a tightly bound bed roll across his horse's rump.

"Here, take a look." Valdez passes the binoculars to George Cardinal lying on his stomach beside him. Cardinal screws up his eyes, stares for a minute, then lays the binoculars aside.

"It's our welcoming committee," he says. "We'd better get ready for them."

Marathon Miracle in Vancouver

From the upper level in B.C. Place Stadium in Vancouver, Sally Hearst and Nicholai Andropov sit looking down on the spectacle below. It's an incredible sight. The huge domed arena is filled with the colour and sound of Marathon Miracle, a forty-hour rock festival of performers from across Canada and the United States. The stadium seats are packed with 25,000 stamping, chanting, spectator-participants: average age 17; enthusiasm level 95%; exhaustion point, close to maximum.

It's 7 p.m., Sunday evening. The festival began thirty-nine hours ago at 8 p.m. on Friday. Since then, more than 500 performers have stormed, caressed, attacked, beguiled, abused, and otherwise entertained the audience from the 200 square-metre stage out in the playing area. A dazzling plethora of multicoloured lights have stabbed and probed convulsively on performers and audience alike, cutting them up, casting them out, contorting, contrasting, confusing and conveying them all into a heat-soaked conflagration of unremitting motion.

But above, beyond, and outdazzling all of the dazzle has been the sound. Fifteen amplifiers, each one powerful enough to fill the stadium on its own, have whipped and cracked the hard rock frenzy from stage to audience to domed roof and back again, crashing down at decibel levels too high to think about, then suddenly softening into melody as sweet as summer rain, before the next crescendo.

The audience, restless and eager, have embraced the sound and spectacle entirely, some of them continuously since the start, others coming and going, all of them giving mind, body and spirit to the total experience. And now they're moving with tired, but undimmed anticipation toward the finale.

Sally grabs Nick's arm and points to a spotlight, still unnoticed by most, tracking a solitary figure across the stadium floor.

"Come on Nick, there's Theresa. It's time for us to move."

A Unesco Connection

Paris. The severe uninspiring architecture of Unesco headquarters appears suddenly out of the morning mist. The taxi weaves the remaining 100 metres through the traffic and swings into the crowded driveway among other taxis and large black embassy limousines with their countries' pennants standing up bravely on the front fenders. Behind, more than 150 flags of member countries hang limp and lifeless atop their poles in the misty morning air.

Francois Suullère, Boris Gunther, and Junichi Yakasawa get out of the taxi, show their identification badges at security, and proceed inside. The stream of delegates is continuous, but not heavy yet, as it's still only 9 a.m., and the assembly doesn't come to order until 10 o'clock.

The three Visioneers move inconspicuously through the delegates. All three are dressed in blue business suits, even General Soulière, who has chosen to abandon his uniform for increased anonymity before they make their move.

Outside the entrance to the main assembly hall, they pause for a moment to have a whispered conversation, then split up, each going to his appointed task.

Rendezvous in Scotland

Evening shadows lengthen in the short October twilight as a lone piper plays his sad lament on a small stone bridge, a few kilometres from Balmoral Castle in central Scotland. The mournful melody, rich in cadence and spirit, rises and falls, sweeps and dips, spreading out across the dusky landscape, enveloping all who hear it in the strange and lovely tones of this northern land. Eventually, the piper moves away unseen into the darkness, and with him goes the melody, fading, returning, and fading again until it has melted into the evening air. The sound of the running stream replaces it as the pulsing theme of the soft and gentle evening.

Waiting by the roadside, the two Visioneers sit in silence caught in the spell of the magical pipes and the lonely landscape. Irene Henshaw's eyes are filled with tears, her heart touched that she can share this moment in her native country with her new friend, Jeremy Hiscox. Both of them sit quite still, letting the magic of the evening settle on their spirits, and waiting for the start of their mission.

Suddenly, 200 metres away, flickering through the trees, two sets of car headlights appear, coming slowly along the narrow country road. Irene and Jeremy exchange glances and quickly move to their positions, waiting for the vehicles to arrive.

Rowing into Russia

The splash and creak of the oars are just audible over the light wind ruffling the surface of the lake. Daniel Thomas pulls energetically at his task. His long black hair blows loosely in the wind and his face is turned to catch whatever warmth it can from the weak Russian sunlight of late October. Bill Bates, sitting in the stern of the boat, hunches down into his black leather jacket, as his eyes search the distant shoreline for the cabin.

"Aha," he exclaims, "I can see it now, over there, on that spit of land, jutting out into the water." He fumbles for his binoculars to look more closely. "Yep, that's it all right. Looks like it's been there for a hundred years. No sign of anyone about, though."

"Just give them time," rejoins Daniel in his lilting Welsh voice. "You can be sure they're looking for us just as keenly as we're looking for them. Would you be a good fellow now and give my knee there, the one on the right, you know, a bit of a rub. It's cramping up on me."

Bates leans forward to comply. "Say, do you want me to take over the rowing? I'm a bit out of practice, but I could get us there."

"No, if it's all the same to you, I'd like to stick to our arrangement. I'll do the rowing, and you do the carrying. That computer and transmitter there are going to be a dead weight once we land. How far is it to go now?"

"A bit over 400 metres. You're doing just fine on the oars. We'll enter you in the next Olympics. Does Wales have a team?"

"We did, but the poor devil got worn out, you know, from competing in every event. We buried him last month." Daniel bursts into gales of laughter at his own joke, and breaks out singing into a sea shanty.

Suddenly, Bates grips his companion's knee and raises a hand for caution. "Hsst," he says, "I see something now." He looks through the binoculars again. "Yes, three of them, they've spotted us. They're coming down to the beach."

"Is our man one of them?" asks Daniel, "a big golden-haired fellow with a red beard."

"Yeah, there's no mistaking him. There's a woman, too. A big buxom gal. Looks like she could sling a bag of potatoes over each shoulder."

"She's yours. I'll stick to the one with the red beard."

Daniel pulls the rocking boat a little harder through the waves.

Bates mutters good-humouredly: "I always knew you poets were a strange lot."

He lays the binoculars aside and settles back on the hard seat, watching the three figures on the beach grow larger as Daniel pulls them in.

Out of the Forbidden City

Mohammed Hussein draws a deep breath to take in the sense of where he is. He stands in the flood path of Chinese history. Before him lies the huge, hard, open space of Tiananmen Square; behind, the walls and palaces of the mysterious Forbidden City. Surging between the two, the constant flow of early morning Beijing traffic, bicycles and buses bears a human current of activity back and forth to work, to study, and to find other ways of passing time on yet another working day in modern China.

He looks at his watch: 10 a.m., still fifteen minutes before he expects to meet Lin Yuen. They haven't seen each other since the first meeting in the Visioneering Room. He remembers well their conversation about the great traditions of China and Islam. Now he's here in the Chinese capital, to feel for himself the enormous crush of this reality, gaining a sense of what it means for the future of the world.

He turns and enters the gates of the Forbidden City. For the next fifteen minutes he wanders aimlessly and unnoticed through the gathering crush of Chinese people and foreign visitors. He strolls through tranquil gardens, ascends and descends countless sets of time-worn steps, brushes by grotesquely beautiful statues symbolizing power and defiance, glimpses the remains of treasures of untold worth. All of it crowds into the space of these few minutes before he must set his hand to help fashion a new piece of history. Surrounding him here is the beauty and the savagery of thousands of generations of power, corruption, achievement and treachery. Awaiting him beyond these walls is an unknown challenge, to raise new standards for a future history.

Somewhere in the back of his mind he remembers fragments of a poem by Mao Tse-tung: ". . . Six hundred million people, strong in unity, firm in principle can shore up the falling heavens . . . "

He's back at the gate. He sees Lin Yuen hurrying towards him across Tiananmen Square. Mao Tse-tung lies in his tomb a few hundred metres away. The treachery which spilled out student blood on the stones of Tiananmen Square is still fresh in memory. History is unravelling. He grasps Lin Yuen's hand and together they hurry in eager conversation across the Square towards the Great Hall of the People.

Searching in India

The ancient Leyland diesel bus lurches to a stop in a cloud of dust just outside the village of Katsuri in southern India. Indira Murti and Carmen Santander descend onto a sunbaked rocky path leading off across listless countryside toward a line of low, green hills a few kilometres away. Behind them, the bus-driver flashes a face full of teeth as he calls good naturedly: "Now, you have a good day ladies and pay no mind to any of the roguish fellows you might meet on the road. They're harmless country boys more scared of their shadows than bold in their tricks."

Carmen turns and flashes him her brilliant Latin smile. Indira, if she hears, pays no attention, for she has already shouldered her backpack and is setting off along the dusty path. They make a striking contrast with the languid landscape. Carmen is spectacular in her low-cut, white peasant blouse and green-red-orange-yellow striped full skirt swaying on her ample hips as she hurries to catch up to Indira. Her companion is crisp and trim in light green shirt and slacks. Both wear broad-brimmed straw beach hats to protect against the baking sun.

"Well, here we are," laughs Carmen. "So this is your country. It's not very different from Spain. Where are all the people? I thought India was full of people."

"They're here," Indira replies. "We'll meet plenty soon enough. At this time, they've got more sense than us to be out in the noontime heat."

"Ah, yes, Siesta. We should rest, too. What's our hurry?"

"Just up ahead the road crosses a stream. We can rest there."

In fifteen minutes, they reach the place. A tree-shaded stream crosses the path in ankle-deep gently running water. Carmen lets out a little yelp of delight, kicks off her sandals and splashes into the water, lifting and swishing her skirt in girlish glee. Indira, more restrained, removes her shoes and socks and joins her friend in the stream. Laughing, they hold hands as they step gingerly from rock to rock. Suddenly, Carmen squeezes Indira's fingers as she gasps: "Look there, who do you think they are?"

An old white-bearded man and two young boys have come out of the trees to stare at the young women.

"Hello," smiles Indira. "We're on our way to Ventagiri. Is it far?"

The boys look to the old man, their grandfather, to reply. "Not far," he says. "Why do you go there?"

"We have business with Baba Satyananda. Do you know of his work?"

At this, one of the boys leaps into the air and begins to hop in circles, first on one leg, then on the other, and completes the performance with an accomplished mid-air somersault. His brother, all the while, is shouting and dancing and egging him on.

"Six months ago," the old man says, "little Rami here, the acrobat, was a cripple—before we met Baba."

"And Grandfather was almost blind," shouts Rami's brother. "Now he sees like a hawk and takes us every day on new adventures."

Indira and Carmen exchange glances.

"You would say, then, that Baba is a remarkable person?" asks Indira.

"He's a man of miracles," replies the grandfather. "Do you have something to ask of him for yourselves?"

"Not for ourselves," Indira's voice is quiet but eager. "For the world."

"Ah, for the world. That is good. I don't know much of the world beyond Katsuri, but what I hear is not pleasant. Baba is a very kind man. He can help the world. He'll be pleased you've come."

With that, the old man takes the two boys by the hand and waves good-bye to the visitors. They head off upstream and are soon lost to view among the trees. Indira and Carmen smile at each other and without speaking, hurry back to gather up their shoes and continue quickly on their journey to find Baba Satyananda, Man of Miracles.

Into Africa

"Mutsandu, you're a crazy devil, but I love you. Look out for the tree! Aggh, he misses the tree and hits the rock! My poor Swedish mother would turn in her grave if she knew her son's brilliant career was to be cut short by a mad African in a Land Rover."

A tiny cloud of dust spreads out from the speeding wheels of the bright green vehicle as it cuts a crazy zig-zag path across the African savannah. It's a tiny pin-prick of motion in a vast landscape. Grass, trees, sky—all blend into one endless vista of shimmering heat haze. Wild and open, the grassy plain stretches out to the tangled range of scrub-covered mountains a hundred kilometres ahead.

At the wheel of the Land Rover, President Mutsandu allows himself a short burst of wild abandon. He remembers earlier, less stress-filled days when he crossed this plain, not in a presidential vehicle, but in the long, loping stride of an Olympic-class runner. With the top open, Karl Ibsen is jumping up and down on the passenger seat, grasping the edge of the windshield as Mutsandu leaves the dirt road and weaves and bounces the truck across open country.

Ahead, a herd of grazing zebra raise their heads at the sound of the approaching vehicle. They begin to run. Spotting them, Mutsandu twists the wheel, almost dislodging Ibsen, and sets off in hot pursuit.

"Aiyee! You mechanized maniac. Look at those black and white horses run! Come on, M'buta, they're getting away! Aiyee! Look out! There's a ditch up ahead! You're going to hit it! Stop, man, stop! Aggh! Too late. I can't watch."

At the last moment, Mutsandu has come to the same conclusion about the ditch as his frenetic companion.

"Hang on, good friend!" he shouts. "We don't want to lose you."

He stands on the brakes and twists the steering wheel to the left at the same time, bringing the Land Rover around in a capsizing skid. Karl Ibsen's weight is just enough to stop them from turning over, but combined forces of gravity and momentum are too much for his grasp. As the vehicle lurches to a stop, Ibsen somersaults over the windshield and lands sitting bolt upright on the front of the hood above the hot radiator. In an instant, he leaps into the air again, grasping the seat of his pants and races thirty metres away from the now stationary truck and its wildly guffawing driver.

Still unable to control his mirth Mutsandu gets out of the vehicle and comes over to his erstwhile passenger. He puts his arm around the dancing Ibsen, who now also bursts out laughing.

"See, my friend, we're alive," says Mutsandu, "and have chalked up another memorable moment for our biographers to write about."

"If that's what Presidents do to enter the history books, I'd rather stay a humble architect."

" Would that it were all so easy," Mutsandu's mirth is subsiding now. "Ah, my friend, you can't know how much I love this wild open country. I'm sorry if I frightened you, but I can share nothing more valuable with you than the love for my country."

"You know," Ibsen replies, "I think I actually believe you. But where are we, anyway?"

"Over there, you see, that range of mountains. That's the western border of Yarawi. My cottage is just a short way into the hills. We'll be there before dark. My wife and family will be looking out for us. Tonight, we'll have a grand meal together and tomorrow, we begin our work."

Australian Home

"There it is, Esther, down there, among that clump of fruit trees. Can you see it? Come on, don't hang back."

"You go ahead, Mark. This is a moment you should have to yourself. I'll be right behind."

Mark Venture and Esther Fisher have driven over 150 kilometres from Brisbane to find this place. Though he continues to live in Australia, Mark hasn't been back to his childhood home in over twenty-five years. Now, more than ever, he has felt the need to do so, and to share it with Esther, his new close friend among the Visioneers. They left the car two kilometres away on the sandy road at Westbrook Crossing where the creek is running fast, a metre deep, across the ford. They came over by foot on the railway bridge and cut across through the iron-bark forest, following the cattle tracks until they came to the homestead fence where the old house stands, a hundred metres further on.

Mark hurries down the hill to the old, picket fence, rotting away now, but still flecked with traces of white paint. He pushes open the rusty iron gate and comes down the path to the front of the house.

Everything is smaller than he remembers it as an eight-year-old, climbing in the old peperina tree and playing on the front lawn with his Kelpie dog, Blue. The wide spread of the verandah circles the entire house. It sags now in places from age, and the weather boards badly need a coat of paint, but otherwise, the house seems sound enough. He bounds up the steps and in an instant is rushing through the rooms, all empty, but otherwise, just as he remembers them.

His own room, at the back, is tucked in beside the water tank where it looks out onto the orchard. The sun used to hit here first on cold winter mornings, and he would want to stay in bed, but his mother would soon dig him out with the smell of sausages sizzling for breakfast, replacing the lure of the warm bed.

The kitchen is the one room unchanged from the old days. Mark's brother, who now owns the property, still uses the kitchen when the men are down this way for shearing or mustering. The old wood stove and kitchen table remain in place along with the built-in cupboards with their sliding glass doors. In the space above them, between the ceiling, was his secret place where they never could find him in hide-and-seek.

"Hello." Esther has come in. "It's lovely, Mark. Please tell me about it."

For several hours, they browse through the house and the old sheds and barns surrounding. They make tea on the old wood stove and he tells her the childhood stories of the place. It's growing late when they leave and head off back through the bush the way they came. On the high ground, by the railway tracks, above the place where they left the car, they sit in a clump of large scattered rocks and look over the darkening tableland. Mark falls silent and Esther comes close, touching his arm.

"What is it, Mark? Are you thinking about the others?"

"Yes," he replies. "I feel responsible for them, you know. They're all out there, and none of us knows how it's going to turn out. It's no longer a game. No more silver bridges in the mountains and a comfortable Visioneering Room. We've got a wild plan underway and for most of it, we can't be sure how it'll turn out.

"But I knew I had to come back here to touch this place again. It's my life and soul, you know. There's some strange power in this land for me. I've thought about it for years, but it wasn't until I took on the leadership of our project that I felt I had to come back— to get myself set for what's to come. And I wanted you here with me. It means a lot that you came."

"I want to be here, too, with you. It's so strange and different for me, but somehow I feel at home here."

They sit silent for a while. It's quite dark now. There's no moon, but the stars have come out full blaze through the sharp night air following the recent rains.

"Just look at that sky," Mark says quietly. "To be part of that, Esther, is such a privilege. Every place where the Visioneers are, night or day, they're under that sky—and everyone else, too—every living, breathing soul, under that great dome of space. If we could only grasp the significance of that and put all of the other stuff we call life into that perspective, we'd be in tune with ourselves. Do you think we can find the wisdom for that, Esther?"

"If enough of us can, we can show the way, and when others follow, it can be spectacular! 'Six hundred million people, strong in unity, firm in principle, can shore up the falling heavens.' "

"Who said that?"

"Mao Tse-tung, leading the Chinese revolution. 'And I, behold, I establish my covenant with you, and with your seed after you . . . neither shall there anymore be a flood to destroy the Earth.' That's God speaking to Noah. I think he meant a covenant for the preservation of all life for all time.

That's why we'll be successful in our venture and you, Mark, properly named for it, will lead us there. God is with you and all of us in this enterprise."

They fall silent for a moment. Then Esther speaks again.

"You know you have to send me to Jerusalem, don't you, Mark. I'm ready to go now."

Her words are like a knife in his side.

"It's too dangerous, what must be done there. I've been trying to find another way."

"I know, but it's my country. I must go."

"I'll join you. As soon as I get things settled here."

"That'll be good, and I know you'll be with me at all times before that."

She takes his hand, and together they make their way down from the rocks under the star-filled sky to their car waiting below.

Taking Stock

The images on the screen fade and you take in a deep breath, preparing for the next piece. You have been watching each part of the unfolding drama on the large television screen in your thinking room. It feels very real now. Activity is underway. The Visioneers are out. The enterprise is launched. You feel the excitement building as you engage with the participants in this audacious scheme to change the world. You reflect for a moment on the scope of it.

Most enterprises, even the boldest have boundaries: creating a business empire, investing in the market, assembling development projects, launching military attacks. Even the wildest of these pale in comparison to the scheme you and the Visioneers have under way. It has suddenly become very heady stuff, and you can feel yourself rising to the excitement.

"Humph! We've got things started. Now to put the screws to it."

He startles you. You weren't expecting company. But then it's his plan, so it's not surprising to see him here following it.

"Hello, Winston," you say, whirling in your chair to greet the now familiar dominating presence in your thinking room. "What do you think? Are we doing it right?"

Churchill gestures expansively for effect.

"We've got this whole round globe of human pig-headedness," he growls. "First, we've got to spread our arms to get hold of the actors, then we'll squeeze them tight, until their eyes start to pop out of their sockets. That's when they'll see things differently. Yes, we've made a good beginning. There are some weak spots, yet, but Mark Venture is getting his team in place. The issue now is to move quickly and keep the pressure on. Once the thoroughbred is out of the stable door, you have to get set for the ride.

We've got a good hold on the reins. Now we have to grip the beast with our knees and give him some room to run."

As usual, Churchill's graphic images startle your imagination. However, before you can reply, the television set springs into life and Mark Venture's face fills the screen.

"Hello," he calls, "what's gong on there? We've got to get moving."

"Yes, so I've just been told," you reply.

"Oh? Who by?"

"Winston Churchill."

"Oh? Is he there with you? I don't see him."

"You're not supposed to. At least not yet. However, I can tell you that he's pleased you've got the horse out of the stable. Now all you have to do is ride him."

"It wouldn't be so bad if there was only one horse," Mark smiles ruefully. "Right now, I've got a whole mob of them, galloping off in all directions at once. That's what I wanted to talk to you about. Are you ready for the next piece?"

"Certainly, what would you like?" You smile to yourself at the ease with which you are falling into the role of joint conspirator with Mark Venture.

"Okay, well we've got South America and Africa covered. There are plenty of people in Europe to do what needs to be done there. I'll keep an eye on Australia myself. By the way, what do you think of my boyhood home?"

"It looks just fine. You came from there, so that's a good recommendation."

"Yeah, well, thanks for the compliment. I'm also going to move Junichi Yakasawa out of Paris to Japan, so get ready for that. Bill Bates will have to get back from Russia to the United States. There's a lot to be done there. I think Theresa and the two kids are going to have a lot of fun with those teenagers in Vancouver. If anything is going to change the world, that should do it. We've got things underway in China, and Indira and Carmen are going to turn up something interesting in India. That leaves the Middle East, and Esther's going there."

You see a cloud flicker across his face.

"Mark?"

"Yes?"

"Don't worry. She'll be all right."

"Yes, well, it's a tough place to be on your own, but I'm planning to go there myself as soon as I can.

"So there's the picture. Any last thoughts before we go?"

"Yes."

"What?"

"' . . . The game's afoot:

"Follow your spirit; and upon this charge cry—God for Mark Venture! The world! and the Visioneers!' "

You're quite pleased with your quote. Mark spots it right away.

"Shakespeare," he says. "*Henry V*, breaching the gates at Harfleur. Slightly corrupted in the quote to suit our present situation."

"Exactly," you reply.

"Well, 'Once more unto the breach, good friend, once more.' I'll be in touch again soon."

He is gone.

A gravelly voice says in your ear: "Horatius at the bridge faced fearful odds—but how could man die better? With his brave companions he won the day. So shall we."

Winston Churchill, ever the old soldier, has had the last word. You're alone again. The fire leaps in the hearth. Outside, the sun touches the mountain tops. The new day has begun.

CHAPTER SIX

The
Circle
Widens

FATHER LUIS VALDEZ AND GEORGE CARDINAL are hastily putting the finishing touches to the installation. Old Santa Maria, the Mission of the Holy Virgin, is well located for the work to be done. Perched on a table top 1500 metres above sea level in northern Chile, it looks out north, south, and east to the sky-scraping peaks of the higher mountain ranges. Four hundred kilometres to the west, the Pacific Ocean crowds in on the rugged coastline.

They've used an old stone house at the back of the church for the equipment. From here, they plan to shoot a signal to a communication satellite from which they hope it will be picked up by a number of networks across the continent, if not live, then for rebroadcast later. The task now is to get started. They'll begin this evening. Between now and then they must deal with the soldiers they saw on the mountain trail a few hours ago. They can be expected to arrive any time now.

"I'll go and prepare to meet our visitors," says Valdez. "You must stay here out of sight. I can pass for what I am, a parish priest. You'll attract too much attention. Hopefully, they won't be so curious as to search the mission thoroughly. If they do come out here, then we must do what we must do to protect the enterprise."

Cardinal nods solemnly.

Outside, it's a bright October morning. The smell of spring is in the air. Everywhere around the mission the trees and shrubs swell with green new life, and along the ditches beside the road leading down to the village, a carpet of red, white and gold wildflowers bid a merry welcome to travellers.

At the moment, there's no one on the road. Father Luis has donned his black cassock and busies himself weeding an overgrown garden bed in the front yard of the mission by the crumbling stone fence. Presently, he sees the three figures on horseback coming up the last 200 metres of dirt road from the village.

He pays no attention at first, as if three heavily armed soldiers riding by the mission were a normal occurrence. However, when they rein in at the gate and sit there silently on their horses, observing him, he straightens up, wincing a little with back pain, and waves them a greeting. The horses stamp and snort, steaming from their exertion, shaking their heads and jingling their bridle buckles.

"Hello, good morning," Father Luis smiles, speaking in the Spanish dialect of the region. "It's a beautiful day to be out."

There's no response from the soldiers. They continue to sit silently observing him. Up close, the details of ammunition belts and firearms are the same as he had observed through the binoculars, but the close proximity of concentrated, lethal firepower brings a chill to the warm spring morning. Valdez walks down to the gate, intending to discourage them from coming onto the mission grounds.

"I'm Father Luis Valdez. Can I help you with something?"

He notices that the central figure of the trio is wearing the designation of captain on his shoulder epaulettes. The man's face is hard, a stubble of unshaven beard adding grimness to his expression.

"A priest is no help to anyone," the man's voice is pitched hard and sharp. "What are you doing here?"

"Well, right now, I'm trying to bring some order to these flower beds, but otherwise, I'm in charge of the mission."

"The mission is closed. It has been for twelve months. I personally shut it down and escorted the priest out. I ask you again, what are you doing here?"

"Well, the mission has reopened. I've come with personal instructions from the bishop. I'm sure you'll find everything is in order."

"I don't care about your instructions, priest. I don't want you or your mission in my territory. I should have burned it down. This time I will. Who is here with you?"

"No one. This is a small place. The church can't afford an assistant."

"I heard different, priest. I heard there were two of you: the other one a foreigner."

"I had help moving in from the diocese, but I'm alone here to run the mission."

The captain nods to the other two soldiers.

"Look around," he says curtly.

They half smile, half leer at Father Luis, and touch their heels to their horses' flanks. They brush past him at the gate, so close that one of the stirrups bumps his arm. The smell of horse sweat and leather is thick about them. The butts of their highpowered rifles pass by at eye level.

One of the soldiers rides up to the front door, dismounts and goes inside the church. The other deliberately rides his horse over the flower bed where Father Luis had been working and disappears around the side of the church in the direction of the stone house where George Cardinal is keeping out of sight. The captain pulls a small radio transmitter out of his saddlebag and the air crackles with static as he calls and listens for a reply. Luis Valdez walks away a little, giving the man space to display his peevish temper. Apparently satisfied, the captain shuts off the radio and returns it to the saddlebag.

"You know why I don't like priests, priest. You come in here with your words of brotherly love and better health and education for the poor people down there in the village and out on the farms. You cause unrest. You create a disturbance. I don't like that. I want to keep things just the way they are. That's my job: keeping order, and the best way to do that is to make sure nothing changes. I don't want any trouble-making priests getting under my skin. You understand me, priest."

"I hear what you're saying," replies Valdez, "but I come only in the name of God and love and peace. Such a mission can bring no harm, only good."

"Take your God, your love, and your peace," the soldier retorts, his eyes flashing with hatred that Valdez has seen a thousand times before, "and wrap them up with your virgin and your Christ, and get out of here, priest. I want you gone, do you hear me? I'll see to it personally that you go."

Just then, the soldier who had gone inside the church, comes out, mounts his horse and rides back to them at the gate. He is carrying a small, wooden crucifix, which he had taken from the altar in the Chapel of the Ascension.

"Nothing but the usual stuff," he grunts. "I brought you a souvenir."

He hands the crucifix to the captain, who takes it and smashes it hard against the gate post. He throws the broken pieces at Valdez's feet.

"This is what I will do to you and your God if you don't clear out of here, priest." His voice is quintessential malevolence.

"Miguel!" he shouts. "What's keeping you?"

The second soldier reappears on the other side of the church. He has ridden all the way around. As he comes back, he forces his reluctant horse over another flower bed, crushing the plants and kicking aside the rock border. He leers at Father Luis.

"Nothing different from last time," he reports. "The priest lives in the old pig sty out back. There's no one else around."

"All right, priest," says the captain. "I have other vermin to exterminate more irritating than you. But I'll be back, and it will be best for you to not be here when I do."

He jerks his horse's head around and kicks sharp spurs into its flanks. The horse leaps with the stab of pain, and the three of them take off in a shower of small stones and dust, heading back down towards the village.

Valdez watches them go until they're out of sight, then hurries back to the house where George Cardinal is waiting.

"How much did you see?" Valdez asks.

"Not much. One of them rode by the house, but he didn't try to come in. He seemed to be more interested in prancing around on his horse than in carrying out a search. What happened?"

"Nothing yet, but that captain means trouble. He got some orders on his radio to back off. I expect he's acting without authority. But we can probably expect interference from him in the future."

"All the more reason to get started here. They're expecting our contact on the network at 8 p.m. sharp our time. That leaves us just a few hours to check out the equipment. Let's get to it."

George Cardinal goes through a closet door into a small space on the side of the house, inconspicuously added as a transmission room. Luis Valdez pauses a moment to glance at the small pieces of broken crucifix which he has carried back from his encounter at the gate. Sadly, he sees in them a measure of the hard and broken reality of this vast and violent continent. He tucks them in his pocket and turns his mind to the future.

Sensational Performance

Theresa Romano has reached the huge sprawling stage in the middle of the domed stadium in Vancouver. The strident, punishing sound of Men at War has lifted the audience to fever pitch. This grim-faced group finishes their piece with an electronic explosion of sound and laser light, cutting and stabbing into the frenzied spectators, culminating in a mushroom cloud of dry ice and red-orange, billowing light on stage. The sound ceases abruptly. The wild-eyed, sweat-soaked performers scurry off stage. Men at War have launched their Armageddon. Silence settles as the symbolism touches the audience. Then, out through the angry billowing cloud onto front stage, steps the corpulent, motherly figure of Theresa Romano.

Six searing spotlights pick her out. She is dressed simply in a plain white evening gown, a single silver pendant flashing at her throat. The audience remains hushed, curious to find out who this woman in white is who has stepped out of the wreathing cloud of death and destruction left by Men at War.

Theresa is making a bold gamble. As a young woman she had trained as an opera singer, and though she never reached the stature of international performer, she remains a talented artist. She is gambling that she can bring the power of her training and presence to grab and hold the attention of this rock-crazed audience of young people. Unaccompanied, in a clear voice like a bell ringing on a distant church steeple, she begins to sing. The melody and words come from deep within the human spirit. It's the ageless song, *Amazing Grace*, and its captivating melody casts its spell on even the most frantic of the young people in the stadium.

As she finishes, the silence among the audience is profound. She opens her arms wide and calls out to them:

"Now, my children, sing it with me, with new words for the new age."

She speaks the first line, then motions them to join her as she sings it through. Hesitantly, they begin.

"Amazing Grace, how sweet the sound."

Then the second line:

"That calls to us to hear."

And the third line, more confidently, swelling:

"We once were lost, but now we're found."

And the fourth line, full voice:

"The time to come is near."

The final four lines sweep up and fill the stadium as 25,000 eager teenage voices reach for the stars.

"Amazing Grace, our hearts inspire
Show us the way to see.
Our dreams, our hopes, our great desire:
To grow, to live, to be!"

And then again, she takes them through it, and somewhere from behind, a band picks up the melody and the whole stadium overflows with sound as the eager young voices sing for their future, led by this unknown woman, dressed all in white, who has appeared suddenly in their midst, stepping out of the symbolic cloud of death and destruction.

The song ends. Theresa smiles and bows. A crescendo of applause and shouts of approval break out and continue, wave after wave, the audience on its feet, stamping and cheering. Theresa, standing in full spotlight, continues to smile and bow and wave, acknowledging the applause. She is joined on stage on either side by Sally Hearst and Nicholai Andropov.

Theresa motions for silence. Slowly, the cheering subsides as the audience, curious, wants to see what will happen next.

"Thank you, thank you," Theresa calls. " You're so kind. I love you all, my children. My name is Theresa. I am here with my friends, Sally and Nick, to ask you to join us in the greatest adventure of all time. We want you to join us as Visioneers to change the world."

As she speaks, a great arc of lights overhead flash on spelling out in letters a metre high, VISIONEERS. Backstage, the event organizers have formed in a hasty huddle. The promoter, red-faced, perspiring, is demanding explanations.

"What's going on here? Who's that woman out there? Who let her onto the stage?"

"I dunno, sir," replies the M.C. "She kind of just appeared outa the smoke. Before I knew what was goin' on, she had everyone singin'. It's a hell of an act, though. If I tried to stop it now, the whole place would come down."

"What's this Visioneer stuff? And who put those lights up?" The promoter turns his fury on the stage manager.

"I dunno," he replies, "they just kind of materialized."

"Lights materializing! This woman appearing out of smoke! What kind of a fool do you take me for? I want you to go out there now and get her off the stage."

The leader of Men at War has been listening.

"I wouldn't try that, fellas, if I was you. This lady, whoever she is, has a message—and those kids out there are payin' attention. I suggest you guys shut up and listen, too. You've got a smash hit on you hands. Don't blow it."

Indeed, the audience is now paying rapt attention to Theresa.

"There are just a few of us now," she is saying. "But soon, with your help we can be millions across the world. We have a vision. It's very simple. We see people everywhere, and especially young people like yourselves, banding together, working on great projects, each one led by a vision of what you really want to do. Projects that are good, that bring joy and happiness.

"Just imagine. Will you imagine with me? I want you to dare to see how this might be. In every city, town, village, out in the country, everywhere you go, in every land, all races and nationalities and colours—young people, like yourselves, just doing good helpful projects for people, to make things as good as they can be, then making them better. What a difference that would be! Very soon, we wouldn't have to worry nearly as much about the bad things out there because the good things you're doing would start to take over. It's so simple. And it can begin with you young people. I'll call you my bambinos. I have my five bambinos at my home in Napoli in Italy—little Maria, and Gina, and Isabella, and Lorenzo, and Stefano, the eldest. I want them all to grow up in a world that's free and healthy, where the air is clean, and the food is good, and there's enough for everyone and they have a nice bed to sleep in and can go to school where they can learn how to dream big dreams and how to make them real. And they can all learn to share and listen and work out differences by doing good things together. What a different world that will be! Can you imagine that with me? Because that's where we must start, by seeing it in our minds, by being Visioneers, by being the people in the world who stood up one day and said, we want things to be better. Then instead of thinking of all the reasons why they couldn't be better, we thought of all the ways they could, and then just went out and did them.

"Now, I want us to start right here, right now. I want you to turn to your neighbour. It doesn't matter whether you know each other. I want you to think of ten things you can work on right away that will make things better, and then think of ten new people you can talk to tonight or tomorrow and tell them about this, and then think of ten ways you can reach out to young people like yourselves in other parts of the world and how you can reach them by telephone or letter or on television, any way at all, and tell them about being a Visioneer.

"I want you to see this like a great big wave spreading out from here in Vancouver in all directions, across the Pacific Ocean to China and Japan and all of Asia and down to Sally's country of New Zealand and Australia, too, and south to the United States and down into South America, and east across Canada, and further east across the Atlantic Ocean to Europe and Africa, and north up over the North Pole to Nick's country, Russia—until all the world is touched and young people everywhere are talking to each other about how the future can be better. They're not listening to words of hatred and anger from their parents or older people about old problems and wars and fighting from the past. They're saying that the future is different because we can see in our minds how we can work together without violence and hatred and jealousy and greed, because that's the way we want the world to be.

"Can you see all this with me, my bambinos? Turn to your neighbour and tell him or her what you see, and what you can do, and how you can be a Visioneer."

As Theresa finishes speaking, a restless wave of energy sweeps over the audience as 10,000 conversations break out simultaneously. On stage, all the lights come up and musicians appear and a fast, beating rhythm pulses out as backdrop. Then, the performers from all of the previous acts from the past two days, come up onto the stage. They're all engaged in animated conversation, and soon they've joined hands in circles of energy, swaying to the music. Then the audience, too, is on its feet, everyone joining hands wherever they can, climbing over seats, embracing, nothing disorderly, everything in motion, reaching out, reaching out, the music rising, the energy building, the centre of the wave forming, building to sweep out in force to touch the world.

On stage, Theresa, Sally and Nicholai have linked hands with the six members of Men at War, while behind them in rows the other performers do the same until all the stage, and all the audience, filling the stadium, is a sea of endless motion.

And a new beat comes up over the sound system as Theresa, arms extended, head back leads 25,000 voices in the *Song of the Visioneers*, first heard in the Visioneering Room when her own children and friends showed the way.

> "We are the ones, going to the fore.
> Big ones, little ones—all of us are here.
> Small world, big world, reaching out to all.
> Up, up and upmost—the mighty Visioneers!"

Over and over the words are sung, until with Theresa leading the way, the performers walk off the stage, and the house lights come up and 25,000 young Visioneers march out into the streets of Vancouver and into the consciousness of the world singing their new song:

> "We are the ones, going to the fore.
> Big ones, little ones—all of us are here.
> Small world, big world, reaching out to all.
> Up, up and upmost—the mighty Visioneers!"

At the Grampian Arms

Irene Henshaw and Jeremy Hiscox stand silhouetted in the car headlights as the lead vehicle draws closer and stops five metres from them. The second car halts further back. There's no other traffic on this quiet Scottish road.

The front passenger door opens and a man gets out. He's wearing a black trench coat with collar turned up against the chill of the night air.

"Good evening," he says, "MIss Henshaw and Mr. Hiscox, is it?" His voice has the unmistakable polite authority of British constabulary. "Would you mind showing me some identification?"

Quietly they comply, standing a little uncomfortably in the glare of the headlights. He examines their documents carefully, then satisfied, hands them back.

"Very good," he says. "Will you get in the car, please."

He leads the way to the car and opens the back door. Away from the dazzling beams, they can now see that it's a luxurious Jaguar limousine.

Rich black leather upholstery shines in the interior car light. As Irene Henshaw slides in, a male voice calls from the second car.

"Henson!"

Jeremy Hiscox pauses before entering.

"Yes, my lord?" the man in the trench coat replies to the call. Nothing can be seen against the glare of the second car's headlights.

"Is everything in order?"

"Yes, sir. Just as we were told to expect."

"Very good. We'll follow you to the Grampian Arms."

Jeremy gets in. Henson closes the door and comes round to sit beside the uniformed driver. The car glides off quietly into the evening. Jeremy feels Irene's hand squeezing his arm. He returns her touch and relaxes back into the soft comfort of the upholstery.

"We'll be stopping at the Grampian Arms," Henson informs them, turning slightly so they can hear. "It's a small country inn about twenty minutes from here. His Lordship has arranged accommodation there for you. He and Lady Pamela will dine with you there this evening."

"That's very kind," replies Jeremy. "I'm sorry if this seems somewhat cloak and dagger stuff to you, but it's important that we meet with Lord and Lady Feversham this evening. When we heard that they'd been staying at Balmoral Castle and would be leaving this evening, we thought this would be the best way to arrange the rendezvous."

"His Lordship has a bent for the mysterious, sir. I expect in part that's what got his attention. Your fax message said you were part of an international visioneering project. That was a new one on me. However, you come with the very best references from Cambridge. So you have our attention."

Irene Henshaw speaks for the first time. "I'm sure when you hear the details of our venture, Mr. Henson, that you'll be very excited by its possibilities. What about my credentials? Did they check out?"

"Exactly, so, ma'am. Your headmistress described you as enterprising and adventurous and a wonderful model for the girls at your school. She would also appreciate a telephone call from you. She seems a little uncertain as to how long you'll be absent from classroom duties."

"Of course," says Irene. "After this evening's meeting, I'll be able to speak more freely. In fact, the whole world will quickly know what this is about."

"Indeed, ma'am. That's most intriguing. " With that, Henson settles back into his reserve. He has served as Chief of Security for Lord Nigel Feversham for many years and respects his employer's rights for proprietary information. The car and its occupants cruise into the darkening evening along the winding road. The headlights of the vehicle following maintain a steady distance between them.

Twenty minutes later, precisely as Henson had predicted, they pull up in front of the Grampian Arms. It's a two-storey, standard, unpretentious country inn, such as one finds on backroads throughout Great Britain. Henson opens the door for them and escorts them into a dimly lit, oak-panelled lobby with large overstuffed chairs.

"If you'll be so good as to wait here," he says, "Lord Nigel and Lady Pamela will join you directly."

A few minutes later, their hosts enter. They are young, mid-thirties, well-dressed in stylish travelling clothes. Lady Pamela has short blonde hair framing her attractive open face. She's wearing a white silk blouse and long black skirt. A black and white check jacket, gathered close around her slim waist completes her presence of casual elegance. Her husband, a little more formal, in grey suit and black mohair top coat, stands easily beside her. His face is long and thin with dark inquisitive eyes, already probing his two strange guests, looking for explanations. However, he sees little at first to suggest that he's meeting with anyone other than a slightly rumpled Cambridge professor and attractive, energetic school mistress.

"How do you do," says Lord Nigel, extending his hand. "I'm so glad to meet you. Allow me to present my wife, Lady Pamela—Professor Hiscox and Miss Henshaw. I must say you've certainly captured our curiosity. Will you join us for dinner? They have a very respectable dining room here for a small place, and on a Sunday evening I'm sure we'll have it mostly to ourselves."

Within a few minutes, the four of them are seated in a private alcove off a paneled dining room. Over drinks, Jeremy Hiscox begins to explain the enterprise that has brought them together.

"As one who professes the study of history, I'm attracted to the idea of watersheds," he says. "By that, I mean times or epochs which rise like mountain ranges in the landscape of human development and affect the future course of affairs—at least until the next watershed emerges. The time of Christ, the sixteenth-century renaissance, the birth of industrialism—all were watersheds of history. I'm now intrigued by the notion that we have come to the next and possibly most portentous watershed. Those of us alive today have the potential to substantially influence the flow to the future in a way not open to previous generations. We have the opportunity to change our minds about where we're going, and therefore arrive at a different place. The visioneering project is designed to give people worldwide—irrespective of age, nationality, ethnicity, location, education, religion—the opportunity to do that."

"Inspiring, Professor Hiscox," responds Lord Nigel. "Who is the 'we' in your scenario?"

" 'We' is everybody. It's people thinking and acting together to build the future they wish to live in."

"There are several limitations to that in many parts of the world."

"Exactly. That's what the vision will change."

"But how do you do that?" Lady Pamela has entered the conversation, leaning forwards, elbows on the dinner table, chin cupped in her long, white hands, intense blue eyes searching Jeremy's face. "I mean, people are in prisons everywhere. Either in fact or in their minds."

"Yes," he replies, "and we must set them free by taking away the idea that they can't be."

"And the Visioneers will do this?" Lady Pamela again

"Yes, with help from people like yourselves."

"When?" asks his Lordship.

"Beginning now with substantial progress over the next six months." Silence.

"But who are the Visioneers?" Lady Pamela has finally asked the central question. "This is really most strange. I mean, appearing out of nowhere on a lonely country road. It doesn't seem, well, very real."

"Something like three wise men following a star in the sky," ventures Jeremy, with a twinkle in his eye.

"Oh, I say, that's one for you Pamela," Lord Nigel has caught the implication. "We need a little bit of faith, eh?"

"Quite a lot of faith, actually," Irene Henshaw speaks for the first time. "But we do come with good credentials."

"Ah, I see Henson has tipped his hand. Sorry about that, but he does look after us."

"Faith or no," Lady Pamela is back, "I would still like to know more about the Visioneers."

"And you're certainly entitled to, ma'am," says Jeremy. "There are twenty of us, various backgrounds, just like the 'we' of the larger world I was just mentioning. We've come together around the vision of a world in which people are using their educated imaginations to create a preferred future. We're now dispersed worldwide to trigger a series of cumulative events to make that happen. There's one occurring tomorrow at Unesco headquarters in Paris. That's the immediate issue on which we need your assistance."

"Oh, and how can we help?" asks his Lordship.

"Prince Rupert of Wittenstein is scheduled to speak to the General Assembly at 10:30 a.m. We'd like him to create the opportunity for our General Francois Soulière to speak to the delegates. General Soulière has already arranged to meet with Prince Rupert at 9 a.m. tomorrow to request his assistance. A phone call from you to the Prince tonight would be very helpful."

"Knowing Prince Rupert, he won't like being upstaged."

"There's no question of that," Jeremy has become very intense. "He's actually in a pivotal position to effect the most significant intervention in the history of Unesco. As head of a non-aligned, tiny principality, he can lend considerable prestige to a movement designed to shift the world in the direction of equity and general well-being."

"If that's the case, why don't you go directly to him with the proposal?"

"General Soulière will do that tomorrow. We have an additional reason for meeting with you tonight. We'd like to enlist the support of both of you for the visioneering project from the network of royal families and the foundations they serve throughout the world. Your reputations as friends of the Earth are substantial. That's why a word from you to Prince Rupert tonight can trigger an immediate ripple effect through the education and scientific communities of Unesco. If it's followed by a message through the network of foundations and non-governmental organizations, the synergy will build. The world has too many times suffered from the force of the big lie. Now for the first time in history, it'll experience the power of the big truth."

"And what, Professor Hiscox, is the big truth?" Lady Pamela was almost devouring him with the width and depth of her searching gaze.

"The big truth, ma'am, is that people can choose to become connected through their minds to the energy of universal creative intelligence. If enough do so, they can set in motion a wave of creative initiative to usher in an era of unprecedented harmony and collaboration worldwide."

"It sounds rather like the big dream," replies Lady Pamela.

"That, too, ma'am." Jeremy's answer is quick and sure. "All great accomplishments begin as dreams in the human mind. If we can allow such a dream to grow in the minds of enough people, the means to accomplish it will be quickly found."

"By gosh, Professor, I like your style," Lord Nigel has come to a conclusion. "I'm going to call Rupert right away and get him to do his bit. Now I need some more details from you as to what this is all about."

With that, the next piece of the visioneering project is set in motion. The phone call to Prince Rupert in his Paris apartment is made, and before the evening is out, Lord Nigel and Lady Pamela have laid plans to spread word of the project throughout their networks. Irene Henshaw is to return to her school to launch an initiative though the Association of Independent Schools. Jeremy Hiscox will proceed to Cambridge to establish the European base for the Visioneers. The big dream is beginning to form and hangs breathless in the space around the Grampian Arms. The rest of the world works or sleeps, unaware as yet of what is about to happen.

In the Spirit of Terry Fox

Sally Hearst is caught in the crush of several hundred teenagers on the street outside the entrance to B.C. Place Stadium in Vancouver. Nick Andropov still at her side, looks decidedly bewildered by what's happening. They've become separated from Theresa, who after her sensational performance on stage has been swallowed up in the press of activity.

Sally and Nick are recognized by the group around them.

"Hey, you two were up there on the stage with that lady," says someone. "Who is she? What's going on? What are we supposed to do?"

"Just do what she said," replies Sally, "go out and spread the word. You've all got projects and dreams. Go and get them started. And get yourselves organized, so you can keep in touch and help one another."

"But how? What do we do?"

"Let's begin right here." Sally is shouting to make herself heard. Someone pushes a megaphone into her hands. She climbs onto the base of the Terry Fox Memorial and speaks to whoever's listening.

"Look," she says, "look where we are. Right here at the Terry Fox Memorial. Look at the impact he had without really having a plan or knowing what the outcome would be. He just wanted to focus people's attention on beating cancer. He did it the only way he knew how; by putting himself to the test to run from sea to sea across Canada, one of the largest countries in the world, with one artificial leg and the cancer still inside him wearing him down as he ran, until he made the supreme sacrifice of his life. But his spirit and courage lives on, and every year in the Terry Fox Run, thousands of people participate, and money pours in to find a cure for cancer.

"Well, we're going for an even bigger prize. We're out to change the way people think about the future. Instead of accepting the old ways, we're going to say people are better than that. We're all human beings, part of the life force on the planet, and we can lift our minds to make love and cooperation the way of the world. All the rest of the hatred and violence are unnatural and can be avoided, if we just change our minds and say that the future isn't going to be like that.

"But we can do it only if we have some wonderful exciting visions to aim for. Visions of young people like ourselves, working together in hundreds and thousands and millions across the world, in every corner of it, and not allowing our parents or our leaders to say we're naive children and that it can't be done. Because it can be done. It must be done. That's what the Visioneers are about. We can all be Visioneers together, to build the new millennium. What do you say? Are you ready for that?"

Shouts of "Yey!" "Right on!" "Let's go!" reverberate around the group, growing larger by the minute. Several police officers attracted by the noise have moved in on the fringes. Nicholai takes the megaphone to speak.

"Excuse me!" he shouts. The noise subsides a little. " My name is Nicholai Andropov. My home is in Moscow in Russia. I just want to say I believe what Sally says is true. We're having terrible times in my country because we didn't have a good vision. We allowed ourselves to be misled. Now we have to begin again. It'll be hard times, and so it will be every-where. People will become impatient and expect too much too soon. But we mustn't become discouraged, and if we keep working together to build the vision, we'll find what we need to do to make it happen. I just want you to know that the young people in my country want nothing more than to be friends with you. Send the message out that you've heard here this evening and it will rush around the world like a, like a firestorm. If that's a good English word."

Sally takes back the megaphone. The crowd is growing larger, several hundred now, filling the space around the memorial and spilling out onto the street. Cars are being held up, horns starting to honk. The police officers are looking nervously at each other, wondering what to do.

"Firestorm is an excellent English word, Nick. And to all of you here I say go out and start the firestorm. And let me tell you the one simple thing to do to get it started. Call your favourite radio station. Tell them about visioneering. Keep it up, one after the other of you calling in, across the country, across the continent. Get on the radio waves, on the news. Leave your names, and telephone numbers. Get other kids to call you and pass the word. All of us will be the New Kids of the World. Nick and I will be setting up the headquarters here in Vancouver. Keep listening to your radio stations. You'll hear about us. Keep singing the song."

With that, Sally leads them in the *Song of the Visioneers* and they all march off singing, smiling good naturedly at the police officers and the irate car drivers, and the chorus of the song reverberates through the streets:

"We are the ones, going to the fore.
Big ones, little ones—all of us are here.
Small world, big world, reaching out to all.
Up, up and upmost—the mighty Visioneers!"

At Unesco Headquarters

General Soulière shows his identification to the security guard outside the V.I.P. lounge at Unesco headquarters. It's 9:10 a.m. There are just fifty minutes before the General Assembly convenes. He hopes that Boris Gunther and Junichi Yakasawa have got their strategies underway.

"His Royal Highness is expecting me," he says to the guard. The man studies the identification card and looks carefully at the general. Satisfied, he nods and opens the door for the visitor to enter.

Inside, he's met by a short, slight man in his middle fifties with wispy grey hair brushed back along his temples.

"Ah, good morning, general," he says affably, "I'm Marcel Lafayette, principal secretary to his Royal Highness. Will you come with me, please."

They pass through a curtained doorway into a larger room elegantly furnished with period French pieces from the eighteenth and nineteenth centuries. Prince Rupert is standing by the window, looking out over the misty skyline of Paris, sipping from a small cup of strong espresso coffee. He is short and plump, dressed in a pin-striped grey business suit. He turns as they enter. He has a small, bushy black moustache and a full head of curly dark hair. His smile is friendly as he greets his visitor.

"Ah, good morning, General Soulière. Will you join me in coffee while we chat? Marcel, I would like you to stay to make notes, please."

The three men sit together. Prince Rupert pours coffee while he continues to talk.

"I had a very interesting telephone call last night from Lord Nigel Feversham in Scotland. It appears that two of your compatriots have spoken to Nigel and Lady Pamela about your project. I must say Nigel was most insistent that I pay close attention to what you have to say this morning. I'm ready to do that. We have limited time. The floor is yours, general."

"Thank you, Your Royal Highness. As I said in my communication with your office a few days ago, I would like your assistance in introducing the visioneering project to Unesco's General Assembly. As you've been asked to deliver the opening address to this Extraordinary Session on New Directions, you have a unique opportunity to launch an enterprise that captures the essence of what Unesco was established to do. It's been truly said that wars begin in the minds of men. Equally true is that peace and prosperity take root in the visions that people have of the way they wish to live their lives. If we speak of peace, but see ourselves fighting to achieve what we want, then there's no truth to our words.

"I'm a survivor of many campaigns. I fought always for peace, but we never found it, for in the fruits of every victory lie the seeds of the next conflict. It's past time for us to replace destructive thinking with creative thinking. That's the essence of our project."

There's a pause while Prince Rupert considers his reply.

"One cannot, of course, disagree with what you say, general. But you and I both know that it's not the way of the world."

"It's not the way of the old world, Your Highness, but it can and must be the way of the new world."

Another pause while the Prince considers.

"You are a military man, general. I presume you have a strategy in mind, some outcome you want to achieve from today's events."

"Indeed, Your Highness, I do. Our project is set to burst onto the world scene in many different ways. A few hours ago in Vancouver, in Canada, a wave of excited teenagers were sent out. In South America, the television networks were interrupted. Reports on that are already starting to come in. Foundations and non-profit organizations will be used to spread the message. Many other initiatives are underway. By the time the delegates return home from this conference, the world will be buzzing with the news.

Because of the stature of the people present here in the education, scientific and political communities, their endorsements will be key. A resolution from this conference supporting the visioneering project would have a tremendous impact."

"But it's not even on the agenda."

"Precisely. That's why we're asking you to put it on."

"It would be most extraordinary."

"This is an extraordinary conference."

"Why not ask the Director-General to deal with it?"

"The Director-General has worked hard to set the agenda. He's not going to initiate changes at this stage. But you're above the agenda. Two of my colleagues at this moment are speaking to the information groups of the different Unesco geographical regions. If you decide to support us, you'll find a receptive audience. Your direction, your remarks, in support of us, will be key."

"In that case, general, you had best convince me. You have fifteen minutes to do so. Then I must go and meet with the Director-General for the opening of the conference."

Broadcast by Satellite

George Cardinal makes a final adjustment to the small television camera, then looks directly at Luis Valdez.

"One minute from now you're going to be the most famous Roman Catholic priest in South America," says Cardinal. "That's a very dangerous reputation to have in some quarters. It's not too late to choose a disguise."

Father Luis smiles and shakes his head.

"If I can't stand full face in declaring our beliefs, the project will be the weaker for it. It must be this way."

"Okay, but let's hope that captain isn't watching. Stand by for cue: five, four, three, two, one, you're on."

Speaking softly in Spanish, the sad-eyed priest begins to transmit his message. It's going out via satellite from which it can be picked up and rebroadcast in a thousand different ways across the continent. They've made what arrangements they could for the broadcast to be transmitted by networks in various countries, but there are no guarantees or controls on what will happen.

"My friends, if you're watching this, it will be because someone with a little power or influence believes you should. Perhaps before I'm finished, the transmission will be interrupted. If that happens, I hope you'll be resourceful to find out what someone else believed you shouldn't hear. I don't know when or how I may speak to you again, but I can assure you that what I'm about to say will soon be a force abroad in the world, and if you seek actively to become a part of it, the opportunity for you to do so will be found.

"My name is Father Luis Valdez. I speak to you on behalf of the Visioneers. We are a group of twenty ordinary people from many countries who have come together on an enterprise to change the future of the world. That may sound like a bold and ridiculous statement, except that all actions from the past which have changed the course of history, began in the minds of a few people who decided to act on their ideas. In some cases, those ideas were wicked and corrupt, and they brought misery and death to countless millions of people. In most cases, the ideas were magnificent and the world prospered greatly from them. In all instances, vision preceded action, and action was carried forward through courage and determination.

"I'm speaking to you now as a consequence of all the ideas and actions that have gone before. The challenge for us now is to take the future into our hands, to care for it as something to be nourished and enriched. Fine, you say, it's all right for you, well-fed priest, with all the power and wealth of the church behind you, to speak of caring for the future. For me, you say, it's not so good. The only future I know is getting up every day to grinding poverty and fear for my life. The future for me is a fearful place. You have to be fat and well-fed with a decent roof over your head before you can have the luxury to think about the future.

"And you would be right, my friends, to castigate me so. For if your future is like that, it's because those of us who could have done better chose not to do so. Not necessarily out of maliciousness, though there's often a lot of that, but because of ignorance, and there's much of that. It's a particular kind of ignorance. It lies in not understanding that all life is interconnected, not knowing that if you have a problem, then it's also my problem, and if I have a problem, it's also your problem. My prosperity depends on your prosperity. If either of us acts as if this isn't so, we work against the basic law of the universe. We ultimately bring destruction, if not on our own heads, then on those who follow, who will eventually suffer when the slack that's in the system, which preserved me from the consequences of my actions, is all used up.

"My friends, the world is now coming dangerously close to running out of slack in the system. The human race is now multiplying too rapidly and acting too aggressively for the natural system, of which we're all a part, to continue to support us. We must now take care and learn new frames of mind for the new millennium.

"The Visioneers are calling upon you, wherever you are, whatever your status, to come together with whoever you can to build shared visions of the future. Begin small, with your family and your neighbours, in your community. See in your minds the condition in the future that you wish to create, and then begin to widen it out, to test it against the visions of others, to refine it, to change it, and to continuously learn how to do this, because we have no choice now but to learn how to create a sustainable future for all of us.

"You must demand from yourselves first, then from your employers, your authorities, your teachers, your priests—from everyone, you must demand the right to think in this way. It's a new kind of learning. It's creative learning. It's the only kind of learning that can save us from ourselves.

"My time has almost gone. If you have seen this broadcast, act now. Call your television station. Ask them to repeat it. Take responsibility for acting to begin the process. Don't accept the old ways of conflict and agression. My friends, the future requires that all of us work together to win, or ultimately we will all lose together. We have beautiful and miraculous minds, which, if we choose to use their potential, can touch the mind of God. The time for us to do so is at hand. Go forward, my friends. Join us as Visioneers and look for the signs of the transformation all around you.

"God bless you and good-bye until I can speak to you again."

As he finishes speaking from the cramped transmission room in the Mission of the Holy Virgin, high in the Andes, Luis Valdez looks across to George Cardinal. The burly Cree Indian chief had automatically flicked the switch to end the broadcast and now sits staring at his friend in silence.

"Well, ," asks Valdez, "What do you think?"

"I think," Cardinal's voice is choked with emotion, "you may have started the rebirth of civilization. You were inspired. If only the whole world could have heard it . . . "

"The world will hear it," says Valdez. "The play's begun, and the curtain will never come down again. Now I have a great need to pray. Will you come with me to the church?"

Silently, the two Visioneers leave the house and walk over to the church standing square and firm against the Andean skyline.

An Extraordinary Session at Unesco

It's 9:55 a.m. and most of the delegates have already assembled in the main hall at Unesco headquarters. General Soulière waits impatiently outside the entrance for Boris Gunther and Junichi Yakasawa. Presently, Gunther arrives.

"How did it go with Prince Rupert?" he asks.

"I'm not sure," replies Soulière. "I think it's 50-50 as to whether he'll back us. We'll have to wait to see what he says. How did you make out?"

"I spoke to the Europeans and Asians. I think they're a bit confused. Most of them don't have much expectation for anything to come quickly out of Unesco. They'll need a good push from Prince Rupert if they're to do anything."

"So it hangs in the balance," replies Soulière. "I wonder what's keeping Junichi."

At that, Junichi arrives, breathless from running up the stairs from the conference room at the lower level. His normally passive oriental features show unmistakable signs of excitement.

"Something's up," he gasps. "Have you heard?"

"No, what?" asks Soulière.

"Luis Valdez made a pirated broadcast by satellite last night and several of the South American networks put it on the air. One of the delegates had a copy transmitted to him. He's got it with him. I gather it's causing something of a sensation in many of the delegations."

"What's the reaction?"

"Rather mixed, I think. The non-political people are excited, but some of the government people are pretty nervous."

"Good for Luis. I hope he's safe," says Soulière. "I wonder if Prince Rupert has heard. Let's go in. It's 10 o'clock."

Inside the assembly hall, they take three seats at the back among the non-governmental agencies. The official delegations have filled all of the seats in the main body of the hall behind their country names. On the platform at the front, the Director-General and several of his officials are already seated. Beside the Director-General, Prince Rupert sits quietly reviewing his notes.

The ceremonies begin exactly on time at 10 o'clock. The ambassador from Zimbabwe is quickly elected to the chair as President of the conference and takes control of the meeting. The Director-General presents a fifteen-minute report outlining the accomplishments of Unesco and giving the background for this extraordinary session. He mentions the growing uneasiness in the world about environmental issues and the seemingly intractable problems of development and inequity among member nations. There are the usual admonitions to delegates to come up with new ideas, but no hint of any way in which such ideas might emerge.

General Soulière is watching Prince Rupert. As the Director-General speaks, the Prince becomes perceptibly agitated. He drums his fingers and shuffles his papers. When the presentation is over, he nods, but doesn't smile. Now it's his turn. The President introduces him. The delegates applaud warmly as he goes to the podium. The Visioneers wait expectantly.

The Prince speaks for twenty minutes from his prepared text. It's an elegant, forceful appeal to the delegates to take bold initiatives in their deliberations. Then he pauses, closes his notes and speaks directly to the audience.

"What I've just said you all have heard a thousand times before. Now I'll tell you something new. There's action afoot to shake the world and all of us in ways we can hardly imagine."

He pauses. General Soulière sucks in his breath.

"I was informed last night of the existence of a group of people called the Visioneers. This morning I spoke with one of them. I believe he and his associates are in this assembly. Their intent is to excite worldwide passion for people to ask: 'What kind of a world do we intend to create?' They have already begun to make their move. Last night, one of their colleagues broadcast a message via satellite across South America. This morning, as I walked into this hall, I was handed a copy of that message. I have it here."

He holds up a videotape.

"The question is, Mr. President and ladies and gentlemen, do we bend the rules of this assembly to consider a new kind of intervention that just might do our work better than we ever could do it ourselves. I've already answered that question for myself. If a man is brave enough to risk his life by making such a broadcast, I'm willing to give him the balance of the time I would have taken to receive your polite attention. With apologies to the translators, who are as surprised as you by what I'm about to do—for they must translate from the Spanish of the broadcast—I'm now going to show you this tape."

There's a moment of silence, then the assembly breaks into an excited hubbub of conversation. On the platform, the Director-General speaks animatedly with the President, who finally smiles broadly, and sits back to await developments. During this time, the Prince has passed the tape to a technician. He calls for order.

"Ladies and gentlemen, all of us will now see what the Visioneers are bringing to the world."

The lights are dimmed and on a large screen at the front of the assembly hall, the face of Luis Valdez appears. The tape is poor quality, fuzzy and streaked, but to the three Visioneers in the room, their friend is clearly recognizable. As he begins to speak, the halting voice of a translator captures in their headphones the essentials of his message. Within the hall, the original Spanish of the transmission is played over the sound system. The attention of every delegate is riveted on this extraordinary presentation.

. In a few minutes, it's over. The lights come up. Prince Rupert is still at the podium. He speaks to the assembly with hushed urgency.

"Ladies and gentlemen, you have now seen and heard the real agenda of our work. One brave man has stood up to say that what we're now doing as a global community doesn't work for the ultimate benefit of life on the planet. He's asking all who will listen, to move our minds into the future and build together there the visions we need, to lift us beyond the slow grinding clog of our interminable impasses. This message is going directly to the ears of people who've never before been encouraged to think this way. I was told this morning that within weeks, the same message will be heard in a hundred thousand different ways by millions of people across the face of the planet, from parliamentary assembly to mud hut, from palace tea parties to jungle guerrilla camps, from boardrooms of industry to starving peasant farmers, from teenage gatherings to conferences of elders.

"What they will hear, ladies and gentlemen, is an appeal to their creative intuitive minds, to reach out and fashion new relationships, new ways of being, new and powerful visions of what can be accomplished when human minds meet at the level of creation, rather than at lower levels of confused arguments and conflict. For us here the question is whether we, as the trained intelligentsia of the civilized world, are prepared to support in spirit and in deed such a simply conceived initiative.

"We have a choice in these matters, ladies and gentlemen. I made mine this morning when I decided to put aside my prepared text, and with it my comfortable intellectual musings, and join with the Visioneers on their mission of creative human enterprise.

"Mr. President, I thank you for your tolerance and judgment in allowing me to do what I have done. I now hand the assembly back to you."

Prince Rupert steps away from the podium. A deep hush has settled on the assembly. Then, from the back of the hall, someone stands up and shouts, "Bravo!" Within moments, a wave of applause breaks out, beginning slowly as puzzled delegates try to decide their reaction, then swelling, and finally building to a crescendo as people come to their feet in a standing ovation for an act of courage. It continues for five minutes before the President can bring the assembly back to order. His large, round, black face is alive with the broadest of smiles as he speaks.

"Your Royal Highness, allow me on behalf of my colleagues, to thank you for including us in a moment of history. Now it's for us to decide what to do. We have an opportunity now as we break into separate commissions to consider what you have placed before us. You departed from orthodoxy to present us with a challenge. Now, we must decide what to do with it. You mentioned, too, that there are in this assembly three members of the company of Visioneers. I, too, would like to depart from orthodoxy by inviting them to come to the platform to be recognized."

Another breathless hush. The three Visioneers look at each other, then as one man they rise from their seats at the back of the hall and pass from anonymity into prominence. Every eye turns as they make their way down the long aisle. They are halfway along when the applause begins. The President stands and with him the whole platform party, applauding. The assembly stands, the applause swelling. They reach the platform. Prince Rupert greets them, shaking hands, likewise the President and the Director-General. Chairs are found and the three Visioneers sit between the President and Prince Rupert. The President waves for silence.

"Ladies and gentlemen, fellow delegates to this extaordinary session of Unesco, I would like to introduce to you our three guests whom I have just this moment met for the first time: General Francois Soulière from France, Mr. Boris Gunther from Germany and Mr. Junichi Yakasawa from Japan."

Applause breaks out again. The President waves for silence.

"We have now completed an extraordinary beginning to our extraordinary session. When you reconvene after the break in separate commissions, we will place before you a revised agenda to accommodate these new developments. This session is adjourned."

A strike of the gavel, the session ends, and the merging of the visioneering project with the agenda of Unesco has begun.

Watching Developments

"Brilliant!"

"An absolute first-rate coup!"

"Oh, we're really on the way!"

"That's put the fox among the chickens!"

They're all here with you in the thinking room—President Kennedy, Charles Dickens, Winston Churchill, and Anne.

Mark Venture's face comes on the screen.

"What's happening?" he asks. "Have you heard anything?"

"Mark," you reply, "our team has just made it into worldwide prominence on Unesco's program. Within hours, every major news outlet will be buzzing with word about the Visioneers."

"Ah, that's great! Old Soulière pulled it off. What about Valdez and Cardinal? Any news of them?"

"Not since the broadcast. They could be in considerable danger now. There are many interests in South America that won't like what just happened in Paris."

"I know. Listen, I need to get back to the Visioneering Room so I can keep developments on track. Things will be all right here in Australia for a bit. Can you arrange to get me there right away?"

"Of course."

Churchill raises his hand and whispers gruffly in your ear.

"Oh, and Mark," you say.

"Yes? What?"

"Winston says you're doing a fine job.'"

The screen clicks off, your companions disappear, and you go to meet Mark Venture in the Visioneering Room.

CHAPTER SEVEN

Adding
the
Next Pieces

T HIS IS GETTING COMPLICATED."

Mark Venture is poring over a time chart, trying to establish the time of day in the various locations around the world in which the Visioneers are operating.

"It's 11:00 a.m. on Monday in Paris," he says, "but I haven't heard yet what happened on Sunday in Russia, China, India, or Africa. We need to revisit them to find out."

"Of course," you respond, "where would you like to go first?"

"To Bill Bates and Daniel Thomas in Russia," replies Mark.

Instantly, the globe in the centre of the Visioneering Room dissolves into a three-dimensional view of the two men in the rowing boat pulling towards the shore of Lake Radovichy.

Putting the Russian Connection in Place

Even before the prow of the boat has run up onto the sand of the lake bottom, the red-bearded giant has come splashing into the water, shoes and all, to grasp the boat and haul it precipitously up onto the beach. Not anticipating this sudden assistance, Daniel Thomas makes one final pull on the oars, digs deep into the sand and winds himself severely as he punches the butt ends of the oars solidly into his stomach.

"Oof!" he cries. "What in thunder . . . !"

"Oh, well done, Daniel," chortles Bill Bates from the back of the boat, "a pair of beautiful crabs for the Welsh rowing team."

Daniel glares at him furiously as he sucks in great gulps of air. But they have no time for further patter as the big Russian, having hauled them up onto the beach, is now slapping them on the back and pulling them out of the boat.

"Welcome, welcome," he says in guttural English. "I am Vladimir Rostov. What are you doing rowing across the lake? Why don't you come by motor boat like everyone else?"

"We tried that," says Bates, "but we couldn't get it started."

"What do you say?" roars the giant, pushing his thick red beard into Bates' face. "Do you imply our fine Russian motors are inferior? Perhaps you should bring your own, hey!" His eyes are slits of mock anger. Then he laughs uproariously. "Even if you did, you couldn't get it to run on the sludge they sell here for gasoline." Then serious again. "But you better not let my friend, Boris here, know that you're critical of our Russian products. He used to be a member of the KGB, you know. Kind Good Brothers, we call them in English." And again, he laughs uproariously at his own joke.

"Vladimir, get off with you." His bulky female companion has intervened. "Our guests will think we're all crazy. Hello! I'm Anna Borodino. Don't mind Vladimir. He likes to play the fool."

"Oh, I just thought it came naturally to him, like dung in the cow yard." This time it's Daniel Thomas' turn to shoot in a barb. Both Russians look perplexed.

"That's a Welsh joke," Bates hurriedly intervenes. "They have a colourful turn of phrase, you know. Worse still, Daniel is a poet. Try not to get him started, or we'll all drown in a sea of rhetoric. I'm Bill Bates from Los Angeles. Who's the third member of your group?"

"I'm Boris Dubrovsky," the other Russian replies. He is as slight and lean as the others are tall and stout. His clear blue eyes shine with the glow of a keen intelligence. "I was never with the KGB, but I have excellent connections of other kinds that will prove helpful to your cause. I'm anxious to discuss the project."

"Yes, he's the serious one," says Anna, "but there's to be no more discussion until we get up to the cottage. What equipment do you have to carry?"

"Just a portable computer and transmitter," replies Bates.

"Here, I'll take them," says Vladimir as he gathers one heavy piece under each burly arm.

"Well, wouldn't you know," sighs Daniel. "I row clear across the lake and now you get a porter to carry the gear. There's no justice."

"Oh, yes there is," replies Bates. "It's called staying positive. As a good Visioneer, you'll soon learn the trick of it."

He puts his arms around Daniel's shoulder and they follow their new friends across the sandy beach into a line of aspen and pine trees. They continue up a gentle incline until they reach higher ground in a clearing overlooking the lake. Here they come to an old cottage, built of rough hewn logs with a roof made of thatch from lake reeds.

Inside, the cottage is comfortably though sparsely furnished. A meal waits for them on the large kitchen table. Within minutes, they're eating well of juicy ripe tomatoes, red caviar, a wide variety of green vegetables, many not recognizable to the Western guests, baked chicken, veal, and Russian beer.

The conversation soon becomes as expansive as the meal. The Russians eagerly press their visitors for details of the visioneering project. In planning the Eastern European front, Mark Venture had selected these three for their links to the rapidly expanding networks to establish democratic free enterprise in Russia and the other former Soviet republics. This movement has been underway for some time, but clawing its way forward on the back of several generations of a repressive, controlled economy is proving to be very difficult. Everywhere cynicism and despair abound.

"You mean to say you Visioneers expect to change the world, poof! Just like that?" Vladimir is speaking as he gnaws on a chicken leg. "Obviously, you haven't yet pushed the flab of our magnificent bureaucracy. It is like a great fat sow rolling around on top of its litter of piglets. Every time we get our heads out to gasp the air and glimpse the sunshine, this mass of lard rolls over us again."

"Well that makes it clear, then," replies Daniel Thomas. "All you have to do is put some life into the piglets and slim down the mother and you'll have a happy family. We're here to get the wee little pigs jumping."

"And how do you propose to do that?"

"Ah, now there's the rub. They have first to see pictures in their minds of green grass for them to run in, and to smell the good smells of the earth with the dust up their noses, and the soft rain drumming down forming delicious mud puddles for them to root around in. After that, when the sun comes out again, there will be sweat steaming off the soil, and the smell of the daisies and the buttercups, and the chasing of the butterflies until all the blue sky is filled with the flutter of their wings. The little pigs can lie down in the warm sun and feel the goodness of it soaking into them, while they watch the waving of the grasses and hear the songs of the birds up in the trees. Ah, it's a beautiful life for the living when you can dream the dreams and let them lead you forward to where you want to be."

"That's fine for a Welsh poet," Anna Borodino cuts in, "but we Russians are not like that. We need someone to lead us, whether it's a Czar or a Lenin or a Stalin. True, we know of the atrocities committed under all those regimes, but still, we look for the leader who will take us forward into the good life."

"You can still have your leaders," Bill Bates intervenes, "but what

Daniel is saying is that the people too must clarify what they want in their minds, and find the ways to make it happen. What we need here is a vision, across this vast complicated country, of people working together, building the future, not out of fear or selfishness or greed, but because they feel deep inside them that they have the power and the freedom to be part of a larger human family that's caring for the future of the world."

"And just think," Daniel adds, "if Russia can do that with all of its history of repression, what a symbol that would be for the world. People would want to come here to find the secret for building the future. Russia, the great mother country, would stretch out her arms to welcome the world.

"All of her riches in story and poetry and song and dance and art would be there, open to the heart, touching the soul. Russia will lead the world in a new flowering of the nobility of human endeavour. Freedom, and dignity, and justice, and above all, hope, would flower again in the new millennium."

Vladimir Rostov leaps to his feet. "Yah, you funny little Welshman," he shouts. "I don't understand half of what you're saying, but the other half sounds so good that I'm proposing to celebrate it now before I forget it."

As he speaks, he takes down a half-empty bottle of vodka from a kitchen cupboard and splashes liberal quantities of the colourless fiery liquid into their glasses. Demonstrating how to do it, he shouts something like "Up to the future!", throws back his head and drains his glass at a gulp. Not to be outdone, Daniel leaps to his feet also, and with a cry of "Up the Visioneers!", attempts to snap off his drink too, only to end in a fit of eye-streaming coughing and spluttering as the vodka sears the back of his unsuspecting throat. The table erupts in uproarious laughter and toast after toast is drunk to peace, prosperity and vision until the bottle is quite empty and the cheeks of the company are as flushed as the red splash of crimson in the autumn leaves outside.

It's Boris Dubrovsky who finally brings the conversation back to the real business at hand.

"From what you say, it seems that the essential issue for people in our country is to learn this skill of visioneering. Do you have some proposal for teaching it?"

"You bet," replies Bates, "but first, we have to set up the communication systems. That's where you three come in. We want to set up our base here on Lake Radovichy, just far enough off the beaten track not to draw too much attention. Then it's up to you to activate networks to get it to people wherever they live across the length and breadth of Russia and the other republics. At the same time, there'll be initiatives getting underway across the rest of the world. Tomorrow, some of our people plan to get it on the agenda of a Unesco conference. Once the Western press picks it up, there'll be no stopping it, though then the problem will be to keep it from being distorted.

"It won't be easy and nothing is certain, but we're going ahead and doing it. We know that you're with us, otherwise, we wouldn't be here. It's exciting work. It's the greatest venture undertaken in the history of civilization. Russia's successful involvement is a key factor for its success.

"We have a lot more to tell you. That will come in time. Today, we've made a start. The company's good, the food's excellent, and the spirits are high. We welcome you to the band of Visioneers."

With that, there's further handshaking all around and a sealing of the bond of friendship in an enterprise of great worth. The Russian connection is in place.

◆ ◆ ◆

"That seems to be going well," murmurs Mark Venture as he watches the last scene in the cottage on Lake Radovichy. "But we'll have to take Bates out of there and get him back to the United States before the end of the week. Daniel should be able to look after things in Russia. He has them mesmerized with his Welsh loquacity."

"So much to do with so few people," you say.

"Yeah, well, we're off to a thundering good start," Mark replies. "We've put on a pirate satellite transmission in South America, been recognized on the agenda of a Unesco conference, hooked into the European royal families and their worldwide foundations, and primed the pumps for communications in Russia and Eastern Europe. Not bad for a couple of days' work. Now, let's see what's happening in China."

The scene in the Visioneering Room dissolves from the Russian countryside to the steps at the entrance to the Great Hall of the People on Tiananmen Square in Beijing.

An Old Man's Vision for China

Lin Yuen and Mohammed Hussein are ushered into one of the smaller reception rooms of the Great Hall. Even so, it's huge by conventional standards, with ten metre high ceilings, large oil paintings and tapestries on the walls, and a deep-piled, intricately woven carpet on the floor. Seated alone in a high-backed plain chair by the window is a very old Chinese gentleman. He is dressed in a simple, though well-cut, Mao jacket and pants. His hand as he extends it to his visitors is trembling and as fragile as a leaf. Wrinkled parched skin is stretched over an ancient face. Eyes that have seen the sun rise more than 30,000 times over turbulent Chinese history survey them quietly. This is Zhao She Yuhan, a former Vice President of many portfolios, now retired from most official duties, but well-respected among China's ruling elite, and a benevolent supporter of Lin Yuen among many hundreds of senior secretaries in the central administration.

The old man doesn't speak English and the conversation proceeds with Lin Yuen translating into English for Mohammed.

"You're welcome here," says Zhao, and his voice is soft like the whisper of wind blowing across the rice paddies of his ancient land. "I have heard from my friend, Lin Yuen, of your vision for the future of the world. It is good to have a vision. I have seen many days and always I have been led by something lying just beyond my grasp. In my life time, our great challenge has been to move this vast country with all its people forward by holding out just such a vision."

"Six hundred million people, strong in unity, firm in principle can shore up the falling heavens . . . " Mohammed has spoken in English the lines he remembered from the poetry of Mao Tse-tung as he was walking through the Forbidden City earlier this morning. As Lin Yuen begins the translation, the old man's face lightens perceptibly and he completes the poem aloud with the translator. He looks at Mohammed with renewed interest.

"I see you know the poetry of our former great Chairman," he says. "They were hard, grand days of vision. Much went wrong after that, but there was much good. And we have it today in our fine educational system and our technology and all of our people eating with enough food in their stomachs to do the next day's work."

When he finishes translating, Lin Yuen speaks to Zhao in his own language.

"You're right, sir," he says. "We've accomplished much, because we were so far behind. Now we stand shoulder to shoulder with the rest of the world at a time when there's need for new direction, not just for China this time, but for all humanity, otherwise we'll overwhelm the Earth, and all of our progress will be as ashes on our lips."

While the old man ponders, Lin Yuen explains to Mohammed what he has just said. Mohammed indicates that he wishes to add to the comments. Zhao nods and opens his hands in a gesture to continue.

"We're members of a band of Visioneers. We've already spread across the Earth to act as catalysts for life-supporting initiatives to spring forward in the minds of people everywhere. It's a grand dream. But it's also a possible future. Our task as Visioneers is to show how to move the possible to real. China will play a very large role in the success of our venture. The whole world waits with bated breath to see where China will go next. It's of utmost importance to the future of humanity that it moves with dignity and certainty to the freeing of people's minds to first see and then create their own destiny. We ask that you will help us with this great enterprise."

After he has heard the translation, the old man sits silently for a few moments. Then he beckons to Lin Yuen to help him to stand and assist him to the window overlooking Tiananmen Square. He motions to Mohammed to join them at the window. He draws the curtains and the three men look out on the huge open space, almost empty now save for small groups of sightseers, clusters of military personnel, and classes of school children forming up to spend the day visiting the monuments of the city.

"Not many years ago," Zhao speaks, Lin Yuen translating slowly, "we witnessed a terrible scene out there on the Square. Thousands of young people were demonstrating for what they claimed to be democracy. A nervous administration and over-zealous military commanders brought an end to it with blood staining the stones and sullying China's image across the world. I didn't agree then with either side. The students were too vociferous and unreasonable in their demands. The leaders were too ruthless in their response. There was no meeting of minds, no shared vision, only two sides battling it out; and the outcome hasn't worked well for either side, but particularly, it hasn't worked well for China.

"I understand what you're saying about vision and what you call visioneering. Now I'll share with you an old man's vision. I want you to look out there on that Square and see two hundred thousand Chinese citizens, of all ages, but more young than old, and many of them school children, just like we see the ones out there today. All of these people have come together for a celebration. They're smiling and moving easily. They've brought their lunch, for they intend to make a day of it, and families are sharing their food with each other and with other families that they don't know. There are street musicians, and some acrobats and clowns, and people are laughing and the sun is shining, and there's not one soldier or any sign of authority or force among the whole two hundred thousand people.

"In the centre of the Square, there's a huge platform with banners on it saying, 'The People Share their Vision'. And there's speaker after speaker for several hours telling of what they have done in their districts, in their factories, in their schools, everywhere, telling what they've done to build a cooperative vision. Sometimes instead of speaking, they put on little dramatizations, and they tell their story that way, and sometimes in song and dance, and the loudspeakers are booming out the messages all around the Square so everyone can hear. The television cameras of the world are there and it's all being shown to the world as the way China is caring for its people and helping them to invent the future.

"At the end of the day, there's singing and dancing in the Square and fireworks and food for everyone and more than enough to go around, because people are sharing everything as they celebrate their vision.

"This is what an old man sees, and it will happen soon. I have been waiting in my heart to see it come forward. Now both of you are here, sent from somewhere to make it happen. We must sit together now and plan how to begin."

As he finishes speaking, and when Lin Yuen completes the translation, the old man grasps each of them by the hand, and together they lead him back to his chair. He orders tea served in fine porcelain from one of the attendants at the far end of the room, and together the two Visioneers, plus one, sit and begin a strategy to bring China into full play in the visioneering project.

◆ ◆ ◆

"Beautiful!" exclaims Mark Venture, "that's really beautiful! I think that old man will do it. If anyone can bring China along, then he surely can. We'll work with him to make his vision come true. Lin Yuen will stay to help. I'll have to move Mohammed out soon to the Middle East. I'm anticipating we'll need all the help we can in that quarter."

"Where to next?" you ask.

"India," he replies. "This next piece is critical. The success of our whole venture depends on the ability of people to come together across all the differences that currently divide us. To do that people will need to touch deeper levels of spirituality than we've managed to reach to date. The world's great spiritual teachings emerged in India over 2500 years ago. We must go back there now to enlist them in our project. Let's see how Indira and Carmen are making out."

The scene in the Visioneering Room dissolves from China's Great Hall of the People to the dusty track leading to the ashram of Baba Satyananda near the village of Ventagiri in southern India.

A Great Teacher Emerges in India

Indira Murti and Carmen Santander are quite unprepared for the sight that meets their gaze as they come over the crest of the hill and look down into the valley of Ventagiri. They have spent more time on the road than anticipated, and when they look down from the hill on the ashram, the sun over their shoulders is beginning to set, and the warm glow of its long rays bathes the buildings below.

But more outstanding than anything else is the huge crowd of over a thousand people sitting on the green lawn in a large semi-circle in front of a low, white stucco building with a wide verandah and a large glass dome in its roof. On either side of the central building neatly kept two-storeyed guest homes stand out prominently, while further back along paths winding among trees and flower gardens more guest houses peek out shyly, seeming to enjoy their privacy. The whole aspect is one of a quiet sanctuary among the otherwise rock strewn, barren, red-tinctured countryside.

Adding to the sense of peace and serenity is the beautiful chanting floating up to the visitors from the crowd gathered on the lawn. It rises and falls in rhythmic patterns, touching the ear gently, but somehow going deeper, soothing the mind, calming the spirit, seeming to be a preparation for something deeper and more profound. Indira and Carmen are captured by it. Silently, they come down through the gates of the ashram and sit on the ground at the edge of the crowd.

Presently, the rhythm of the music changes, slightly faster, a little more urgent, presaging a change, a new development. Then, out of the doorway of the white building, onto the spacious verandah, into the golden glow of the setting sun, comes a tall male figure, moving graciously and easily, dressed in a long saffron-coloured robe, falling simply from his shoulders to his feet.

He pauses for a moment on the steps of the verandah, singing with the people. He raises both arms in a gesture that seems to embrace the whole assembly. The spacious sleeves of his robe fall away from his arms like waves of liquid sunshine. He steps down from the verandah and moves among the people as they sing. A ripple of movement passes through the crowd where he walks as if his presence somehow breathes a life beyond the life already there. Heads bow, faces turn up to his, smiling. There's no pushing or grasping or frantic disturbance of any kind, just quiet passage of this gracious figure through the throng. Then, as he passes, people begin to rise, still singing, and move up the steps of the verandah into the white building. As they move, the sound of their singing goes with them, until it becomes a muted cadence, drifting into this space from another source.

By now, the saffron-robed figure has moved to the edge of the crowd nearest Indira and Carmen. The people move off. Only about fifty remain seated when he comes to the two visitors and stands smiling down at them. His face is slim, clean-shaven, with high cheek bones, and soft, brown luminous eyes. His skin is light brown, his hair dark and curly, but well groomed. His features are unmistakably Indian, but they glow with an inner light that transcends any cultural or ethnic origin. Both Carmen and Indira instinctively feel that they are looking into the face of spirit and are unmistakably touched by the energy surrounding him.

"Hello," he says. His voice is deep and warm. "You're welcome here at our Place of Peace and Serenity. I am Baba Satyananda. I know of your work and am glad you've come to me to speak of it. Please go now with my friend Nirmalananda. She'll show you to your room and after dinner, I'll come and speak with you."

With that, he's gone, walking with the last of the group back towards the white building, where the chanting is now so soft that it can scarcely be heard above the rustling of the wind in the trees and the beginning calls of crickets and other night sounds, as darkness quietly settles over the ashram.

One of the group has stayed behind. This is Nirmalananda, a slight wisp of a woman in a white robe. She's full of conversation and questions as she takes them to a guest house down one of the paths branching away from the main building. Their room is comfortable, but simple, with two beds, a writing desk and several easy chairs. There's no sign of plumbing, obviously a luxury to be shared with other guests in a communal bathroom.

Nirmalananda leaves them to freshen up and change for dinner. Carmen wears a simple white evening dress and Indira, a golden silk sari. Nirmalananda returns and takes them out through the cool evening air to another building with a large dining room of long wooden tables and benches. They share a simple vegetarian meal of salads and spiced dishes with crusty home-baked bread and copious quantities of weak tea. The other guests are all Indian, but from many parts of the vast country. They're eager to share stories of their meetings with Baba, his miraculous healing powers and his teaching concerning love and self-realization. Each person has come individually to spend what time he or she can in the presence of the great man, and then return to their regular life, spiritually enriched and sustained by the encounter. Of the origin and nature of their spiritual leader, they have many opinions, but all unquestionably believe that he is a divine incarnation. Carmen and Indira return to their room in eager anticipation of what might happen next.

They don't have long to wait. Within a few minutes, a tap on the door signals Baba's arrival.

He glides into the room. His presence is overflowing, somehow giving the impression that he had entered the room before he knocked on the door, which announcement was merely a courtesy to the guests, lest they be startled by a too sudden appearance. He sits in one of the easy chairs by the open window.

"You're engaged in a great work," he says. "Your friends are about to create some extraordinary changes in many ways. By the end of this week, the world will be humming with it. That's truly exceptional. It's driving from a deep source, and you'll have great success."

Indira replies: "I didn't know you were so well informed on our enterprise. We came to tell you about it. It hardly seems necessary now. How did you know?"

His smile embraces them.

"Let me just say that I have my ways," he replies. "The world and its future are of great concern to me. But it begins in the hearts of the people. That is where I move. And you're wondering if I can help you. The answer is yes, but first you must understand the teaching."

"We have come to be taught," says Indira.

"Ah yes, and it comes easy for you, my dear. You're from this land. You know the spiritual traditions. But what about Carmen? You come from Spain. Do you find it strange here?"

He has turned his full brown eyes on Carmen.

"Well, yes, a little," she replies. "But I'm ready for it. You cut quite a presence. I felt that at once. I'm an entertainer. But, I'm sure you know that.

You seem to know everything else. But, anyway, I can tell another performer when I meet one—and there's no question, you're a great performer.
But I would like to know more about what you do."

"I speak to men and women in their hearts. And you're right, it is a
performance. But only at the beginning. Soon, the performer and the
spectator become one in the performance, and then there's only the act of
being. Being one with the flow of divine goodness that comes from listening
deeply, not with the ears, but with the mind turned inwards, searching."

"Searching for what?" asks Carmen.

"Searching for truth," replies Baba. "For truth is foremost among the
qualities that men and women must embrace if they are to build the visions
you would have them create for the future. The world has lost its way in
the search for truth, which was first revealed in the scriptures of the
Upanishads almost 3000 years ago. People were considered ready then to
receive the truth, or at least to know the path to the truth, in preparation
for this later time when other knowledge might lead them away. And so it
has happened. Humanity has embraced the knowledge of science, but it's
not truth. It's only the outer part of truth, the thinnest part of the outer husk
of knowledge. Within is the kernel. But that remains unknown and unknowable to those who search only with the senses and the intellect. I've
come to lead the world back to the search for truth.

"Others have come before me, each one showing the way, but their
teachings have not been heard deeply enough, or they've been set aside or,
what is worse, reinterpreted. So now we have nations arming themselves
for mortal combat, just as they always have, but now with weapons too
horrible and destructive to be imagined, and impoverishing themselves to
do it. And what is the basis of it? The base is the false sense of truth.

"The truth of the world is that happiness comes from the pursuit of
pleasure through acquiring material goods. But that's not the truth of the
universe. The truth of the universe is that happiness comes from loving. It
begins with loving God, who is the flow of the universe, from whence all life
derives, and understanding that God is in us because we're part of the spirit
of the universe, and that we are first and foremost spirit, and only second-
arily body. We are spirit housed in body. We call it *Atma*. Because everyone
is *Atma* we are all of one being, one spirit, and that one spirit is God.

"If people were to understand, that they are one with God, then they
would know that we are all one, and that in loving God, we love ourselves
and our neighbours, and we wouldn't seek to harm or ill use any of our
fellow human beings because we are, all of us, manifestations of one divine
spirit. That's the truth I've come to teach, and it's the truth that underlies
what you call visioneering. Once people understand that we're all one in
God, and that it's the same God for all, then they can build the shared
visions of a world moving forward in harmony and peace."

"But if, as you say, this truth has been revealed to human beings for thousands of years, why haven't we heard it?" Carmen asks. "Surely, it's the same teaching that Jesus brought, which is the foundation of my faith, the Roman Catholic Church, which has spread across the whole world, along with other branches of Christianity. But still, we have no end to conflict and war and hatred and greed and all of the other abominations that Jesus condemned in his own day, and the prophets before him, and, as you say, the teachers of other religions before that. Why don't we learn? Why doesn't the world learn?"

"Because people keep looking in the wrong place," replies Baba. "They search with their rational minds for order and truth. They say that this is out of place, so we'll fix it; or that this is not working to my advantage, so I'll change it; and if you complain, then I'll control or punish you, because I'm stronger, and I am right and you are wrong. So it goes on to the absurdity and tragedy of world wars and unmentionable atrocities. All of this happens because the world is focusing on the pursuit of happiness through pleasure, failing to understand that what humanity really is, is spirit. Until people turn to loving the spirit within, they'll see nothing but the warts and carbuncles of the body without, and they'll fight and argue and condemn right up to the end of the world."

"But there is hope," Indira intervenes. "The very fact that we have the scriptures and that you're here revitalizing them for all: Hindu, Christian, Jew, Moslem, no matter who. That's a sign. The fact that we have people everywhere beginning to realize that unrestrained material consumption will destroy life, that's a sign. The fact that we have millions of people worldwide who have ignored or been forced to abandon their spiritual life, and are now turning back to it, in some form or other, that's a sign. And our visioneering project starting now and gathering force because people are truly searching to create a better future: all these are signs. I believe they're signs that human beings are making an evolutionary leap in human consciousness, just as they did when the 'goodwill religions' which you describe were introduced into human thought.

"And I'm hopeful, too, because I'm seeing the best of our science turning away from mechanics toward spirit and looking at the holoverse within and seeing there a complexity and beauty as astonishing as anything in the world or universe without. And so we're beginning to say this marvellous creation of human life is sacred and holy, and so we must build a world where that's respected in all quarters and sustained indefinitely into the future, because anything else is in the end unthinkable.

"That's our project, Master Baba Satyananda. We know that you're a great spiritual leader in India. We ask that you nourish it here so that it can spread and touch the other great spiritual traditions of the world. We can't tell exactly how that will happen, but we know you come from God and when the time is right, it will happen."

He smiles at her and the room fills with the energy of their exchange.

"You're already a great spirit, Indira," he says. "What we must seek for are many millions across the world who lead like you with their love. Not love framed by the ego, which says that I love because I feel better for loving, but love which is pure and unconditional and has its greatest sense of fulfillment in the spread of loving.

"The world will not learn that lesson easily, but it starts in the individual human heart. You're right, humanity is now taking a step forward in evolution. The separation and division of many millennia are coming down. The Earth has entered a new relationship with the heavens, and is beginning to be bathed by cosmic forces that have not been present for thousands of years. Many men and women of science are coming under the influence of these forces, as indeed are other leaders in our communities. All are seeking for the spiritual understanding behind what is otherwise incomprehensible to them.

"Your visioneering project is a bold and audacious leap forward. It's the pathway of *karma* to the greater light. That's the pathway of action. You're right to ask people to set up their visions and act toward their fulfillment. But people need teachings of the other pathways. They are *jnana* or knowledge, and *bhahti*, devotion.

"You have come to hear my teaching and this is the essence of it. People must seek first the spirit of God that is within them, giving up thoughts of themselves, searching each day with devotion for the higher good, and working with others in acts of continuous learning together. Only in this way can they find the peace of mind to build life here on Earth satisfying to the divinity within them.

"Now I must go. Please stay as long here in the ashram as you choose. We'll speak some more. I am with you in your enterprise. It's a good thing you seek in your hearts, and it will be sustained."

He stands up. Carmen, who has been silent for most of the time, looks up at him with wide, beautiful tear-filled eyes. Indira bows her head. He touches both of them lightly on the cheek with his hand, then glides quietly out of the room. Alone, they look wordlessly at each other for several moments, then Indira takes the hem of her sari and wipes the tears from Carmen's eyes. The spell is broken. They embrace, each filled with the glow of a rich spiritual encounter, then sit together talking long into the night of Baba and his teachings and what they mean for the work of the Visioneers.

◆ ◆ ◆

In the Visioneering Room, Mark Venture sits silently staring as the scene from the ashram fades from his view. After several long minutes of contemplation, he turns to you, still lost somewhat in his thoughts.

"I'm thinking," he says, "that somewhere between that divine concept of the human being described by Baba and the world's current angry divisions, lies the path of our project. He's right on so many counts. We've certainly lost our way in fragmented knowledge and unbounded scrambling for material things. The planet can't sustain that escalating level of pressure. And we have very little sense of the spiritual. Most of our religious activity is vacuous mumblings of words we don't really believe or pay attention to. He's right to pull us back and hold out a divine image for us to reach for. He's a great spiritual teacher. But we can't be totally spiritual in this world. We have to drive somewhere down the middle. Somewhere between grasping opulence and grinding despair. We have to push for balance. And that's what our project will do. We'll set people in their minds to see that there can be no happiness or satisfaction in grasping always for more at the expense of others around us, and at the peril of destroying the best of the very Earth on which we stand. That's where we must come down! That's the basic understanding that must settle into every corner of the world. That's what people must feel in their hearts so that they can then see in their minds the visions they must build. Visions of people working together in enterprises of great good and service without rancour and violence. That's our project! That's what we must do! Do you follow what I'm saying? Do you see it that way, too?"

His face is glowing with the energy of his concentration, intensely searching. He's reaching deep inside himself, looking for the path. His inquiry to you is strong and compelling. You search for a reply.

"I think," you say, "that we're just beginning to probe the depths of what this is about. Baba has thrown out the ideal of what to push for. No one expects to get there tomorrow. The direction is what counts. Indira can see that. I thought she was magnificent. She has the sense of it. And the old man in Beijing. His vision was pure selfless love for his country. We can move from there to the world. Baba's teachings are hard, but there are people out there who can live up to them."

"Yes, and we need to think about how to get his message out more effectively. It's an incredible challenge, a magnificent opportunity. Baba has given us a lot to think about."

"And the assurance that we'll be successful," you add.

"Okay," Mark replies. "Now, we need to look at Africa. There's a land crying out for vision and hope. Let's see what President Mutsandu and Karl Ibsen are putting together. Can you take us there, now?"

"Of course."

A Vision for Africa

At approximately the same time on Monday morning as Prince Rupert is showing the video of Luis Valdez at Unesco headquarters in Paris, President Mutsandu and Karl Ibsen are planning the visioneering strategy for sub-Sahara Africa. They are sitting on the shaded front porch of Mutsandu's modest country home in the Yarawi Hills, overlooking the green savannah they had crossed the previous afternoon in the President's Land Rover. Beyond, in the far distance through the sharp clear air, Lake Mbale gleams in the brilliant sunshine. Spread liberally over the cane tables and chairs of the porch furniture are innumerable charts, maps, reports, books, photographs and dossiers of every description.

Mutsandu points to a tiny cloud of dust moving slowly along the red-dirt road snaking across the flat land below.

"That will be our team now," he says. "They should be here within twenty minutes. Then we'll have first-hand information on what's been accomplished and where we can best exert leverage."

Karl Ibsen nods. He's working on a large sheet of architect's drawing paper, mapping out in diagram, symbol and text, an intervention in more than forty countries. He looks up from his work, frowning angrily.

"These are the most incredible statistics," he says. "I had no idea Africa had suffered like this. More than 300 years of rape, pillage, slave trading, and colonization, first by the Europeans and later by the Americans. Now in all the years since independence, nothing but a procession of savage military dictatorships, corrupt administrations, and the scourge of apartheid in South Africa. On top of that, grinding poverty, fourteen out of twenty of the poorest countries in the world, none with a per capita income above $300 US, and half of them sliding backwards rather than gaining. Their debt owed to rich countries is as high as their gross national product, while they're spending billions of dollars on useless civil wars fought with weapons supplied by the same rich countries who are lending them the money. Ten thousand children dying a day from malnutrition, more than a hundred million in total suffering from chronic food shortages, plenty of agricultural land going unused, importing 40 per cent of their food when less than fifty years ago they were self sufficient. Only a few countries out of fifty with a democratic government and a free-press. Some African Heads of State are among the richest people in the world. There are government officials with Swiss bank accounts. It's an abomination! How could the world let this happen?"

Mutsandu looks sadly at his guest. As he replies, the rich music in his voice is all the more poignant in the face of the bitter reality he describes.

"When you reject the idea that you are your brother's keeper; when everything is business and nothing is kindness; when you give guns to men with the minds of cretins; when you teach hatred and practice genocide; when you do all this and more, then you have a land that weeps blood for tears and never rests at ease for fear of the dagger in the night."

He pauses, then shakes his head, and smiles gently.

"But it would be wrong to think it's all like this—that there's no cause for hope. The road ahead will be long and hard, just like the road behind.

We've been there, you see; so we know how to travel that way—with hope in our hearts, and vision in our eyes. We Africans may be short of many things, but courage and determination we have in abundance.

"You'll see shortly. My friends, there, you see, they're coming. They've already begun the long trek back. They can be first now among our Visioneers."

He gestures at the cloud of dust coming along the road, now much closer. Karl Ibsen strains his eyes. Finally, he makes out the detail of a large old-fashioned bus, green and gold. It disappears among the trees, then comes into view again, labouring up the hill towards them. It's close enough now to read the plain black lettering on the side—GOVERNMENT OF YARAWI; then another sign, hand-painted, fastened above the wind-shield—VISIONEERS EXPRESS. Karl Ibsen looks at Mutsandu, who slaps him on the shoulder and throws back his head and laughs. The bus rolls up noisily to the front of the house, then stops with the dust drifting lazily up from around its wheels.

As the people step down from the bus, Karl's eyes open wide with wonder. They keep coming, stepping down out of the bus, more than twenty of them, perhaps thirty, men and women, laughing and jostling each other, stretching their arms and legs, rubbing their backs, shaking the dust out of their clothes. Oh, and what clothes! The colours: the reds and golds and purples and greens; the flowing robes, and the uniforms, and the medals; the scarves, and the straw hats, and the turbans. But above all the faces, the smiling, laughing, friendly, all shades of chocolate, brown faces; beaming at Karl and Mutsandu as the two men come down from the porch, shaking hands, not waiting for introductions, embracing, greeting one another with jokes and laughter. And the voices, all the rich tones of the land, like songbirds, filling the air, a winderful festival of colour and sound and rich human fellowship. Karl laughhs out loud: the VISIONEERS EX-PRESS! This is a likely group of travellers to set their feet on the path and take the journey towards the vision gleaming in their eyes.

By the time everyone is out of the bus and they've gathered up their belongings, it's noon and time to eat. The meal has been prepared by Mutsandu's servants on the lawn at the back of the house. It's spread out on tables, another festival of colour, but this time adding taste—all the tastes of market and garden; of red watermelons, radishes, pepper, and tomatoes; of green beans, cabbage, lettuce, peppers, avocado; of yellow corn on the cob, mangoes, pawpaws, bananas and pineapple; along with potatoes, squash and pumpkin, thick slabs of wholegrain bread, and many dishes of spiced vegetables of extraordinarily exotic creation. Whatever the depriva-tion of the land, or the limitations of his treasury, Mutsandu has not spared this day to feed his guests well. They move in colour and animated conversation among the tables, piling their plates high, returning again and again to a never-ending supply of delicacies, continuously replenished by

Mutsandu's servant boys in their crisp white shirts and shorts, padding rapidly from kitchen to table and back again on large bare feet more suited to the wide savannah than the domestic country garden.

President Mutsandu and his wife play the congenial hosts. She's a large, comely woman wearing a pink hostess dress, belted in neatly around her ample over-flowing bosom. Her hair, dark and flecked liberally with grey, is gathered on the top of her head and bound with a bright pink bandana, the tails of which dance merrily around her ears as she mingles with the guests.

Finally, the meal is done, the dishes cleared away, and the tables arranged on the lawn in the shade of several large eucalyptus trees. The people sit in a large square with Mutsandu and Karl Ibsen at the head table. Mutsandu addresses the group.

"My friends, this is a wonderful day for us. Thank you for coming, some of you from great distances. All of the countries of sub-Sahara Africa are represented here to join in the most exciting project that our land or the world has ever seen. My friends, we are turning the tide of history. Here, in this place today, we symbolically begin the journey back from our troubled past to a prosperous future. I've prepared a symbol of the occasion for all of you and would like to give it to you now."

He waves to the servant boys who have been standing in the background smiling broadly and holding several small cardboard boxes. They run to the tables and hand to each person from out of a box a small blue flag with a large white circle in the middle of it and a bold white V inside the circle. It's the flag of the Visioneers, first seen in the Visioneering Room when Theresa's children ran through the streets of Naples. Now it's handed out on this sunny day in Africa as the official symbol of the Visioneers in that vast land.

"My friends," Mutsandu is saying, "take your flags and from them make thousands more to wave proudly among those who'll work with us as Visioneers of Africa's new future. You've been brought here because of who you are and what you've already begun to do on many fronts. Some of you, I know, are in great danger of imprisonment, or even death in your own country because of what you do. Even I, here in my own more gentle place, can't escape from that reality, for what I do isn't always popular with the heads of some other African states. But I must follow my heart and let my actions speak for me, because I see Africa as the best hope for the world. We're rich, my friends, with many resources of minerals and products that the world needs. But we're richest most in the wonderful spirit of the people, represented by all of you here today—millions of us throughout every region, ready to learn, ready to work together, ready to apply ourselves to building a shared vision of a land that can take the best of industrial technology and apply it with a new spiritual understanding. And it won't be hard for us, because the new truth is more old than new. It's in the scriptures that some of us have studied, and in the traditions that all of us know, that we are brothers and sisters working together as stewards of the land God has given us to care for in our lifetime and to pass on to our children richer for our being here.

"We'll build this, my friends, in the sure and certain knowledge that we're not alone in the creation of the new vision for the world. Because we're part of a network of Visioneers beginning now, even as we meet, to spread out to embrace the world. We'll tell you more about that as we continue our discussion. But most important, you must know that you're here because of who you are and because of the stories you can tell already. And I want us to begin now by sharing those stories, telling each other who we are and what we see in our hearts of who we can be together."

There then follows a most extraordinary energetic sharing of experiences. David Mboto from Zimbabwe tells how he grows beans for sale and sows maize among the beans for his family, and plants trees for firewood and spreads beehives among the trees for honey for the bread from the maize—and all of this on five acres of stony soil. Elizabeth Kuyhan from Kenya recounts how she and other women from her district learned how to grow vegetables and irrigate their land to feed their starving children, when all around, their cattle and goats were dying because of drought and overgrazing. And there are stories of new resistance councils that have grown up over the bodies of hundred of thousands of people slaughtered in Uganda and how they're putting power back into the hands of ordinary people. There are the plans for new political structures in Southern Africa when the tyranny of apartheid has passed. Stories, plans, dreams—they pour out around the table. They tell how ordinary people make extraordinary accomplishments when their minds are enlivened with vision and a passion for achieving what they must do, no matter what.

Karl Ibsen has been listening, making notes, adding details to the charts before him on the large sheet of architect's paper, which has now grown into a giant map of what he's beginning to see as a strategy for action. With every story he has become more excited. The ideas are coming almost too fast to grasp. He's on his feet moving around his table, adding details, extending branches, connecting points. Some of the participants, fascinated by what he's doing, are also on their feet, peering over his shoulder, whispering to each other about the strange patterns of words and symbols that are growing on the paper. Finally, Karl can contain himself no longer and he asks Mutsandu for the floor to speak.

"Mr. President, ladies and gentlemen, friends," he says. "I'm excited. I'm really excited. I came here last night and I was reading then and this morning about all the tragic past of this land of yours. And I was saying to myself and to President Mutsandu, 'How can this be? Doesn't anyone care? What can anyone possibly do to make a difference?'"

"And now, here you are telling how it can be done with your stories of how you've already started. And I'm marking it all down and saying to myself, 'Yes! That's right! These people know the way. All they need is some help and encouragement and some teaching of how to add small visions together to build bigger shared visions and how to put the action to the vision.'

"My good friends, I'm so excited that I can hardly contain myself. Poof! The ideas are everywhere. And the strategies, there they are, plain to see: give priority to food production and train millions of David Mbotos; empower the women like Elizabeth; build the resistance councils; bring in aid from the rest of the world but only for countries who respect the rights of the people; get the world to share in building the prosperity of Africa, instead of exploiting it; cut the arms shipments; restructure the debt. All this and more—so much more. Poof! We must get started. This is wonderful. Within a few years, Africa will be the jewel in the crown of the Visioneers. You'll see. It has to be! Because you have the energy and the hope for the world to see. And the world will see it, because we're here to help them see it, the Visioneers, worldwide, opening up the doorways, changing the minds. You'll see, it'll be like that, I know it as sure as I know I'm a crazy Swedish architect who's just seen something greater to build than homes and office towers. My friends, I'm proud to be your fellow Visioneer!"

With that, there's a spontaneous outburst of applause, with people standing up, some beating on the tables, and the ones closest shaking Karl by the hand, and everyone shouting out words of encouragement. Then President Mutsandu is on his feet, waving his arms, calling for order. Finally, the energy level subsides enough for him to be heard.

"My friends, my African friends, and our dear Swedish friend, Karl Ibsen. Friends, I was searching for what I could say to follow Karl, because he seems to have said it all. But now, I have it. It's just been handed to me as news." He waves a piece of paper. "It's wonderful news for me to share with you. It has come in from Unesco in Paris. This morning, just a few hours ago, our visioneering project was introduced to the general assembly by Prince Rupert of Wittenstein. It came right out of the blue. Nobody was expecting it. Then he showed a video which had been broadcast last night over the networks in South America by Luis Valdez, one of our team, announcing the visioneering project for South America. Now all of Unesco is buzzing with it. Public news reports are probably coming out now. The world's beginning to hear about the Visioneers.

"And I'm going now to send out our own news release. I'd like two or three of you to work with me on it. We must move quickly for maximum effect. We'll have a draft for you within the hour for approval. By the time the world watches the evening news tonight or the morning news tomorrow, it'll know about the Visioneers and what we've begun to do in Africa.

"My friends, we've started our brave important work. We have a little time together now to plan the next steps. Karl will be the coordinator at first. I'll work closely with him. This will be our headquarters for the time being. Wherever you go to work after our time here has ended, this will be your contact point. My office and my staff are at your disposal. God speed us in what we do."

Mutsandu leaves to prepare the news releases. Karl Ibsen takes over the group to begin to train them in the creative thinking they will need for the work ahead. Visioneering in Africa has begun.

The World Pays Attention

"There's the balance I was talking about," Mark Venture speaks excitedly as the African scene fades from view in the Visioneering Room.

"Do you see?" he continues. "Those practical, hope-driven projects carried out by ordinary people—that's what will build for the good. It puts people back in charge. It's the middle ground between Baba Satyananda's spirituality and the cynical rationalism of the rest of the world. If we can get ordinary men and women across every culture, country, and division in the world to work together on projects like those Africans, then we'll have taken a giant step forward.

"And with it, we can reduce this insatiable drive for more and more material things. People don't need great quantities of stuff that's just filling up the garbage dumps around the world, and polluting the rivers, and the land, and the air with its toxins and its side effects. What people need is hope and a vision of themselves moving forwards. And if they can learn to build those visions together, then we'll begin to see some real progress— instead of this lopsided, so-called development, built on exploitation and violence. Shared vision is the great hope for the world. I can see that so clearly now. We've just got to make some progress on that and quickly!"

"I think we are," you reply. "Here, take a look at the news broadcasts."

You, too, are caught up in the excitement of Mark's vision. Your mind is working at fever pitch to move it forward. Into the Visioneering Room you bring, in rapid succession, three news reports of the fallout from the work of the Visioneers.

The BBC announcer is speaking on the Monday evening news from London, England.

"On the international scene, we have a rather extraordinary report from a Unesco conference in Paris. Unesco is the United Nations Educational Scientific and Cultural Organization. Speaking at the opening of its general conference in Paris this morning, Prince Rupert of Wittenstein made an unexpected departure from his prepared text to tell the delegates of the existence of a group of people calling themselves Visioneers. He then ran a short video presented by one of the Visioneers, Father Luis Valdez, a

Roman Catholic priest in Chile. This presentation was made last evening, Chilean time, via satellite, and picked up as an unscheduled broadcast on several South American networks. Our sources in South America say that it's already producing a lot of reaction in political circles in several countries, though there's considerable confusion as to its origin and purpose. We have a short clip from the presentation as shown to Unesco delegates this morning."

The scene dissolves to Luis Valdez speaking:

"The Visioneers are calling upon you, wherever you are, whatever your status, to come together with whoever you can to build shared visions of the future. Begin small, with your family and your neighbours, in your community. See in your minds the condition in the future you wish to create, and then begin to widen it out, to test it against the visions of others, to refine it, to change it, and to continuously learn how to do this, because we have no choice now, but to learn how to create a sustainable future for all of us.

"You must demand from yourselves first, then from your employers, your authorities, your teachers, your priests—from everyone, you must demand the right to think in this way. It's a new kind of learning. It's creative learning. It's the only kind of learning that can save us from ourselves."

The scene cuts back to the BBC announcer.

"The content of the Valdez broadcast appears less controversial than the way it has suddenly arrived on the world scene. Three other members of the visioneering group were on hand at Unesco in Paris. The BBC has secured an interview with them and Prince Rupert and this will be broadcast as part of our International Affairs program tomorrow evening.

"In the meantime, an apparently related development has been reported from Yarawi in Southern Africa. In an official communique, President Mutsandu from that country announced that a group of people whom he is calling Visioneers will be leading a series of community-based development projects in more than forty countries in the sub-Sahara portion of that continent. An interview with President Mutsandu will be included in our item on this topic tomorrow evening."

The scene dissolves to a radio announcer on CZFT-FM in Toronto, Canada.

"Wow, we have a wild one going here boys and girls! That's the third phone call we've received from someone who was at the Marathon Miracle show in Vancouver at the weekend. They're all reporting a weird, and I mean weird, conclusion to the program. Apparently this strange gal, calling herself Theresa, somehow got onto the stage and led everyone singing *Amazing Grace* and then told them she wanted them all to be Visioneers. Now that's a new one on me. I mean, I've heard of engineers and mouseketeers, but not Visioneers. Anyway, this gal Theresa apparently brought the house down and sent everyone out marching to this new song about the mighty Visioneers. What a scene! Weird, definitely weird.

"Now, I'll tell you what, boys and girls, we're going to open up the phone lines again and if there's anyone else out there who was at the show, just call in and tell us about it. Wow! Will you look at that! Every phone light lit up right away. This is wild. I'm going to Line 1 right now. Hello! Who's this?"

A young boy's voice comes on the air, speaking over the telephone.

"Hi! This is Brett."

"Hello, Brett. Were you at the show in Vancouver last night?"

"I sure was."

"Tell us about it."

"Well, it was like you say kinda weird, but something more than that. We'd just heard this big number from Men of War and they finished with this great explosion, smoke and lights and this great whooshing sound—I mean, like we thought we'd just been blown clear away. the girls next to me were just screaming their heads off."

"But not you, Brett, you weren't screaming, were you?"

"Well, I dunno, maybe a bit. I mean, like those guys really poured it on. Anyway, right out through all of this smoke and stuff steps this lady all in white, like as if she might have been, I dunno, maybe the Mother of God or someone. Anyway, she starts to sing *Amazing Grace*, no back-up or anything—just her singing. And you could've heard a pin drop in the place. Then she taught us some new words to it and we all sang it through a couple of times and we felt really great."

"But what about this visioneering stuff? When did that come in?"

"Well, then she told us she was a Visioneer and she wanted us all to go out and be Visioneers too and start people thinking positively about the future by doing good projects and stuff like that."

"That sounds like good advice. What happened?"

"Well, I dunno, she just got us all so excited, and then everyone came back onto the stage and they were all holding hands. And then the whole audience gets up, holding hands. I even held onto this guy next to me and I'd never seen him before. Then she taught us this new song and we all marched out singing it. You shoulda seen it. It was something else. Thousands of kids marching out singing. The cops and all those security guards looked at us, but they didn't know what to do."

"What was the song, Brett? Can you sing it for us?"

"Well, geez, I dunno. I'm not a very good singer."

"Come on, give it a try."

"Aw, okay. Theresa called it the *Song of the Visioneers*."

With that, Brett gives a slightly off-key, trembling rendition of the song, gaining confidence as he goes.

"We are the ones, going to the fore.
Big ones, little ones—all of us are here.
Small world, big world, reaching out to all.
Up, up, and upmost—the mighty Visioneers!"

"Say, that's great, Brett. You should see the guys here in the control room. They're marching up and down. That could be a big hit. What happened after that? Have you started to change the world?"

"Well, we were all a bit confused, but then we saw Sally—she was with Theresa, you know. And she was standing up on the Terry Fox statue right outside B.C. Place Stadium and she was reminding everyone about how Terry did so much for finding a cure for cancer by just going out and running with his artificial leg and cancer and all, until people paid attention. Well, Sally said it could be like that with the Visioneers too. She called us the New Kids of the World. She told us to tell everyone about what happened in Vancouver and to call the radio stations and to get things started, because it could be like a firestorm and sweep across the world."

"Well, you've certainly done your bit. Thanks, Brett. We have to go on to another call now."

"Oh, one thing more."

"Yes."

"Sally said we should leave our telephone numbers so all the kids listening would call us back. Can I give my number?"

"Sure, go right ahead."

Brett leaves his number and rings off. The announcer takes another call.

"Hello, this is Caroline. I just want to say I wasn't in Vancouver, but I've been hearing this all day and we've been talking at school, and we've already got a Visioneering Club organized and we're going to start tomorrow by sitting down together and really start to describe the kind of future we want—you know, in the school and where we live and we're just going to figure out how to do it. And if anyone wants to know more, I'll leave my telephone number and they can call me, too."

And so it continues, more calls, more phone numbers, a wave of enthusiasm breaking out, in one place, in Toronto, but repeated, in countless locations across Canada, into the United States, reaching out around the world—the wave of the young Visioneers.

The scene changes to the Thursday morning CBS news hour from New York. Jennifer Harris is anchoring the show. She's talking to a reporter.

"Well, Mike, what's the latest on this visioneering business? It seems to be taking the world by storm."

"Well, maybe it's a little bit like that. Though as far as we know, the main activity seems to be in Africa and South America, except for what we're hearing about some kind of kids network here in the U.S. and in

Canada that started at a rock concert in Vancouver last Sunday. Whether there's any connection between all these things yet, we don't know."

"But Unesco seems to be treating it seriously, aren't they?"

"Yes, well, it seems so on the surface. As you know, the U.S. government hasn't been too impressed with Unesco in the past. However, the Paris conference has apparently adopted a resolution endorsing this idea of creative learning that the so-called Visioneers are promoting. We're trying to get more details on that right now."

"Thanks, Mike, we'll check back with you later."

The scene fades from view in the Visioneering Room. Mark Venture has watched all three sequences with keen interest.

"It's time to move on a U.S. initiative," he says. " I need to talk to Bill Bates in Russia."

Instantly, Bill Bates appears.

"Hello, Bill," says Mark. "Is everything okay there?"

"Yes, we're fine," replies Bates. "Our Russian hosts are incredible characters. But anyway, we've got a strategy worked out on how to move things forward. We've got to be careful. This country might not be as secretive and closed as it used to be, but there's plenty of the old guard still around and we have to make sure they don't close us down before we get started."

"After tomorrow, there shouldn't be much fear of that," says Mark. "You probably haven't heard, but Unesco has adopted a supportive resolution. Listen, I want you to leave things there with Daniel. It's time to get moving on your home front. I want to meet with you and some others in your office in Los Angeles tomorrow. I'll take care of the details. We'll meet at 5 p.m. Los Angeles time. I'll see you there."

With that, Bill Bates is gone.

"Now I need the Unesco team," says Mark.

Instantly, General Soulière, Boris Gunther and Junichi Yakasawa appear.

"You guys have done great," Mark smiles at them warmly. "Now we have to keep things moving. Francois, I want you to stay on in Paris to keep the Unesco Secretariat on side. You should also get in touch with Jeremy Hiscox at Cambridge to coordinate the European initiative. Boris, you can help with that for a while, particularly in Germany. Junichi, we have to get something moving in Japan. I want you to go to Tokyo to get that started. All of you have done a great three days' work. Give us another couple of weeks and we'll have the whole world buzzing with activity. Then the hard work begins. It's one thing to tell people to be creative about the future. It's another to give them the skills to do it. But we've made a great start. You fellows go out and celebrate. You've earned it. I'll talk to you again soon."

Alone again in the Visioneering Room, Mark turns to you and winks.

"They're a great team, all of them. And look at the others out there coming on side: Zhao in China, Baba in India, Prince Rupert, Lord Nigel and Lady Pamela, the whole group in Africa, the Russians, even Brett and Caroline in Canada, and all of the other Bretts and Carolines around the world. We've got this thing moving now. God grant that we can keep it going without mishap to our people."

"Amen," you say quietly to yourself.

CHAPTER EIGHT

The American Team

As HE STANDS LOOKING out of the fifteenth-floor window at the smog-smeared Los Angeles skyline, Mark Venture's thoughts are on Esther Fisher in Jerusalem. Before leaving the Visioneering Room, he spoke with her briefly. She's safe with friends, still searching for an opening to bring the message of the Visioneers to that hate-torn area of the world. There Arabs and Jews kill each other with inhuman viciousness, and children learn to hate everyone on the other side as deeply as they learn to love their own. Between the two lies a seemingly unbridgeable gulf, festering place for masked terrorists to commit their atrocities, and for strident fanatics to cry out for a Holy War of extermination.

In this terrible space, the quiet and lonely spirit of Esther and her like, on both sides, wanders grieving, looking for a solution. Mark has an uneasy feeling of foreboding and has promised to join Esther by week's end.

And Luis Valdez is never far from Mark's thoughts. The plucky little priest has undertaken a courageous initiative. He has catapulted the name of the Visioneers onto the world stage, but he remains dangerously exposed to the violent backlash that would wish to quiet his voice. Mark has had no contact with Valdez since the original broadcast five days ago. He makes a mental note that after this meeting, he must try to find out what's happening in South America.

But there's no time for further thought now. The door opens and Bill Bates comes in, escorting the other guests. The meeting is being held in the boardroom of Bates' executive suite. A long, broad marble-topped table occupies most of the space. Fine statues and paintings convey the atmosphere of comfortable success. It seems a far cry from the dangers of the Middle East and Latin America.

"Now then, Mark," Bill is saying, "I want you to meet our guests. I know you've spoken to them all by phone, but here they are in the flesh."

First comes Julia McCarthy, Chairman and majority stock holder in McCarthy Broadcast Systems, a network of television and radio stations across the eastern United States. Julia is fifty years old, neat, well-groomed, her steel-black hair flecked with grey. Sharp, intelligent eyes search for every nuance from behind designer eye-glasses in thin ebony frames.

Arthur Rhinegold is an independent film producer from Los Angeles. He presents himself as the casual bordering on flamboyant in white cord slacks and a bulky pink and gold sweater. At thirty-six he still has a very full head of curly brown hair, which he wears a little longer than careful grooming would require.

Diane Koplitz appears in marked contrast. She's an author, lecturer, and academic living in Sausalito, just across the Golden Gate Bridge from San Francisco. A big-boned woman, she is dressed functionally in a slightly rumpled navy blue suit and white blouse. She makes no attempt to disguise the thinning, grey hair of her middle fifties. However, her face is alive and glowing with the youthful vigour of one who finds great joy in what she's doing at this moment in her life.

George Walker brings another dimension to the gathering. He's a businessman, chairman and chief executive of Advanced Systems Incorporated, the umbrella organization for a group of companies operating in a variety of fields, ranging from energy to advertising, and acquired by Walker as underperformers. Slim, athletic, and still in his early forties, he has already achieved a national reputation for transforming organizational performance through empowering employees to develop their creative potential, and by tearing down the boundaries to open communication. He is dressed in a light grey business suit, white shirt and burgundy tie and moves easily in the boardroom setting of the executive suite.

The last member of the group is Senator Wilfred Brown, from North Carolina. He is tall, with the big frame of a college football player, now slipping to fat, but still athletic and strong. His large, round, black face smiles warmly. His age is indeterminate, but probably lies well on the far side of sixty. He has many years behind him in the U.S. Senate and carries a solid reputation for support of human rights legislation and a program for the reform of public education.

Mark Venture greets the new arrivals and motions them to join him around the end of the large table.

"Friends," he says, "thank you for coming. Our time together is short, but we can make it powerful and productive. I'll begin by telling you more about the Visioneers. We're a group of twenty concerned with empowering people worldwide to redirect the future of the planet. We're proceeding with initiatives on every continent. Our aim is to create a ripple effect to bring about change. We're speaking to the hearts and minds of people, to ask them to see visions that can, when realized, make every corner of the world a decent and comfortable place to live.

"It's an enterprise fuelled by human energy, which is the most plentiful and powerful source of energy in the world. However, it consistently gets dispersed through conflict and confrontation, The Visioneers are out to change that. We know it can't be done overnight, but we believe small gains can be made immediately in millions of situations across the planet. From that will come a cohesive central vision. As it grows, it'll be the force that keeps people working together, across their divisions and historical conflicts and prejudices, simply because in the final instance, such cooperation and synergy are the only hope for the future."

Mark pauses and searches the faces at the table. He has their close attention.

He continues. "If the vision is to be built for the world, people must be able to do it first in their own space, where they live. Which brings us to the reason why we're here. America and her people are a powerful force in the world. Her own dilemmas and internal struggles lie at the heart of the world's dilemmas and struggles. If the world is to create a planetary culture, Americans must learn to build and share a new vision for their own country that takes into account the new and emerging world order. We're asking you to be the first of the American Visioneers to show the way.

"Now, in case you think that this is all a strange delusion from someone down-under with a funny accent, I'm now going to ask Bill Bates to add his comments."

Bill is quick to respond.

"Funny accent, or not," he says, "that's the best speech I've heard you make yet, Mark. I should tell you other folks that when the Visioneers first met, Mark was as green to these ideas as any of us. Now he's really got his mind to it and he's sent all the rest of us out into the world to get things moving. I've just come back from Russia where we've set up shop in this little country cottage not that far from Moscow. It'll certainly move more slowly there than here because of all the state controls, but I can tell you there's a thirst and a hunger there among so many people for a new vision that there'll be no containing it.

"Now here it's different and I want to be frank with you folks. You all know I'm a newspaper man, so I have a nose for a good story, and I can tell you that this is going to be a blockbuster before it's done. So far, I haven't said anything to my people, but that's about to change. As soon as we get some strategy worked out at this meeting, then it's away to the presses to give Mr. and Mrs. America something new to read about over their morning coffee.

"But why are we all here, and why you folks in particular? Well, Julia and Arthur, the three of us go back quite some ways and I figure that between us, we've got a pretty good handle on the communications business in the U.S. in television, radio, film, and print. This whole thing is really a huge exercise in communications, so if we get together on this, we can really make things move.

"Now, Senator, you're here because we need some good political savvy. You've got good horse sense. I'll admit I thought you were a bit too liberal in the past, but as I begin to look at things now, I think you've been on the right track all along. So, welcome aboard the VISIONEERS EXPRESS, and we'd like to have you up front driving this thing.

"And George, you've been invited because we see you already in the front ranks of new business thinkers who are going to turn this country around. I know you've also been appointed as Chairman of the new Planetary Business Network and that can link effectively with the visioneering project.

"Now, Diane, ma'am, I'm not too sure where you fit in. You'll have to excuse a plain newspaper man who doesn't know as much as he should about most things, but I'm not familiar with your work. But Mark is, and that's good enough for me."

"Perhaps that's where we should go next, then," Mark intervenes. "Diane, why don't you give us your perspective."

Diane Koplitz fidgets nervously for a moment, then speaks slowly and distinctly, her voice rich and mellow and still carrying some of the trace of her native Poland.

"Yes, well, when I listened to you, Mark, speaking about how people can fashion a new vision of a future of cooperation and synergy, I said, 'Yes, of course' because that's exactly what much new research in many disciplines is saying. The only reason why people don't see it is because they're locked into their own paradigms or views of reality.

"For instance, what if we believed that war and violence were unacceptable? Would all the nations on Earth then continue to spend fifty or sixty times as much money on equipping a soldier for battle as they do on educating a child? What if we believed that we are a part of nature and that every act of violence against nature is a punishment against ourselves? Would we still go out and slash and burn the forests, or pour poisonous gases into the atmosphere, or dump toxic chemicals into our streams and rivers? What if we believed that men and women are true partners in every way and that together they are co-creators of evolution? Would we then have men in positions of control and authority, making decisions about war and violence and aggressive economic domination of weaker parties? What if we placed love and caring and spiritual well-being at the centre of our value system? Would we still organize our economy around the production and consumption of vast quantities of material products and their rapid disposal until the whole world begins to look like a garbage dump?

"The answer, of course, is that we wouldn't do these things, because normal human beings always act in accordance with their values and their self-interest. Well, then, we might ask, is there anything inevitable about the way things are today that seem to lock us into patterns of violence and destruction and domination and exploitation? The answer again is no, because new research clearly shows the previous existence of cultures from pre-history that had none of the dominator characteristics of modern society.

"What all this suggests is that at various critical turning points in human evolution in the past, we went down a path that has led to the current predicament. Now we have to turn again to life enhancing models of organization and to do it quickly before the sheer volume of our present excesses and errors overwhelm us along with the natural world on which we depend for life.

"That's why the visioneering project is so exciting and so critical. It puts the opportunity for change in the hands of people who stand most to benefit, and takes it away from the leaders and the power brokers who believe they have most to lose. The truth, of course, is that in the long term everyone will gain from being in a world where love and compassion and caring are at the centre of our daily interactions.

"So I'm with you, Mark, 100 per cent—you and your band of Visioneers. And we have a marvellous opportunity in this great country to give support because even with all of our own problems, I believe we have preserved enough freedoms for people to act to turn things around."

"Why, and so do I," the warm southern voice of Senator Brown has entered the discussion. "I want to thank you, Diane, for what you just said. It points the direction for what we must do. I don't know whether you all understand the extent of our political paralysis in this country. I mean, we've got some really big messes to clean up and I'm not just talking about the environment, but drug addiction and all the crime that goes along with it, and the schools, and the banks, and housing, and all of the infrastructure in our cities that's wearing out.

"But our biggest problem is that we don't have leaders who can inspire vision, and we aren't good at following the ones we've got. We're a fractious, self-interested lot, all pressing our own agendas. We want to continue our high-consumption life styles and we seem to be prepared to sell off the farm to pay for it. There's little thought for the future. Most of our policies were made in the 50's and 60's and most of what goes on at the political level is tinkering by representatives who think they're doing enough if they stay in office by satisfying a tiresome parade of self interest groups.

"It isn't good enough and in our hearts we know it, but we haven't got the fire in our bellies and the gleam in our eyes to know what to do. We instinctively know that the old ways aren't working, but we're too tired and unimaginative to invent the new, so we just let things roll on and the mess gets deeper and deeper.

"Now, along comes Diane who says, 'Hey, what if you stopped believing all that stuff that's making everyone so nervous?' And along comes Mark who says, 'Hey, we've got this band of Visioneers who are going to fan out across the land and across the world and get people to sit down together and just plain invent a better future.'

"Well, I tell you, I'm with you folks. And I'll tell you something else, there's a whole dang crowd of young people out there—and a lot not so young—that are just waiting for someone to tell them that it's okay to do that. If we can find a way to rush this way of thinking right over the top of the cynical do-nothings, then I tell you we could light a fire under this country that wouldn't see no stopping of it from one end to the other."

As he spoke, the old Senator warmed to his ideas and by the time he finishes, his eyes are wide and sparkling and he is leaning forward, grasping the edge of the table, as if to stop himself from lifting off to fly in pursuit of the vision he longs so dearly to grasp.

"You're right, Senator, you can get that kind of transformation. But you have to be prepared to work hard at it." George Walker is speaking. He gestures to include the whole group and the quick infectious fervour of his voice holds their attention. "Friends, what we're talking about here is critical to the future of America. I'm a businessman and I can tell you, I've been out there for the last fifteen years seeing our businesses going down one after the other because they haven't understood how the world's changing, and they go running to politicians like Senator Brown, crying unfair competition and asking for special help.

"I watched this through the 70's and 80's until I finally said enough is enough, and I formed Advanced Systems to show there must be a better way. And we've been doing it ever since. What we're doing fits exactly with what Mark and Diane have said about people getting empowered. You put them in touch with who they are, and let them go flat out building their own dreams into the heart of the corporation.

"What the world needs is improved productivity through the concentration of human energy. Mark's absolutely right. Human energy is key and it's boundless, but we waste it, we squander it, we pour it out like so much waste water in apathy and indifference, or we tear it to shreds in vicious combat with no productive outcome. We look for productivity gains through smart new systems, but the way you really get leaps in productivity is in the hearts and minds of people. The new paradigm that's out there for business is to understand that human consciousness is the most important resource we've got. We have to weave it together in the kinds of new patterns that Diane is talking about. We need to put concern and caring for people first in a spirit of enterprise and service; and then just watch the rest of it begin to happen: productivity, profits, health, well-being. All of that follows from empowering people around a vision of what they believe they can really do together.

"And of course, it goes beyond the company to the whole country and to the world, and that's why I'm really excited about what I'm hearing about this visioneering thrust. What a great idea that is! A few years ago, some of us who were business associates from different countries put together the Planetary Business Network because we could see that the current world economy won't work for the planet. We were foreshadowing your Visioneers, Mark, but I like your style. It's got real pizzazz to it. What we have to do is look for the ways to get sustainable development, before the world plunges into chaos and misery. We've made a start on this. We've got a network in place. Now I see that we can tie it into a broader-based visioneering network. What an impact that'll have! I tell you, I'm just excited out of my skin with the possibilities I'm seeing here!"

"Great jumping jacks!"

This explosion has come from Arthur Rhinegold. Every eye turns to him. He has leapt to his feet and runs to a large whiteboard on the wall. With a few bold strokes of coloured pens, he dashes off an insignia featuring the world with a great arrow thrusting through it and beyond. Above the arrow, he prints in bold red letters THE VISIONEERS. Below, he writes in small black script, A Film by Rhinegold Productions.

"There it is," he beams. "This will be the story of the age; the block-buster for the new millennium! With the whole world teetering on the edge of economic and environmental collapse, a band of Visioneers zips out and turns things around, revitalizes flagging businesses, overthrows corrupt governments, sweeps away the Los Angeles smog, saves millions from starvation. Don't you think people could get just as excited about something like that as they did about star ships zapping each other out of the skies, and ghosts bubbling out of the sewers of New York City, and mutant turtle-boys beating the daylights out of thugs in the subway system?"

"More to the point," Bill Bates pounds the table, "this is the real thing. Our people are out there now doing it. Within a few weeks, there won't be a spot on Earth that hasn't heard of the Visioneers. If you get a film production going right away, it can come zinging in just when the other is picking up a head of steam, and boy, there'll be no stopping this! What do you say, George? Do you think those guys in that Planetary Business Network of yours would be backers for this?"

"Yes, I think that's a real possibility," replies George Walker.

"There you go," shouts Arthur. "We've already got the capital! And what about the story, Mark, can you get that for us?"

" Well that's easy enough," says Mark, opening up his arms in a palms-upward gesture. "We're writing it everyday. Just follow us around with a camera and you've got the story."

"Ha!" snorts Bill Bates. "Good luck on that one. The way these Visioneers are moving, you'd need a crew of several thousand on rocket-powered roller skates."

Just then, the telephone in the corner interrupts with three urgent electronic beeps.

"That has to be important," says Bates, moving to the phone, "otherwise they wouldn't put it through." Speaking into the phone, "Yes, Bates here . . . You mean it's on right now? . . . Okay, we're on the way."

He slams the phone into its cradle and turns to the others. "You won't believe this," he says. "Luis Valdez is on the air right now with another pirate broadcast from South America. We're picking up the signal on our own system. Follow me to the video room next door and we'll catch it."

He's already heading out the door as he speaks. The others tumble after him.

"Who's Luis Valdez?" asks someone.

"A very brave man," says Mark out loud. To himself, he adds, "And a good friend. I hope he knows what he's doing."

In the video room, a large flat screen on the wall flashes into life. The signal clears and shows Luis Valdez standing beside a large blue globe of the world, which he turns slowly as he speaks. His words are in Spanish, but this time, English sub-titles are running along the bottom of the screen. Mark notes to himself that Luis and George Cardinal have improved their production values since the first transmission he saw on the BBC newscast.

The group watch and follow the subtitles.

"THIS IS OUR HOME . . . IT SITS HERE BLUE AND FRAGILE . . .
EVERYWHERE IT IS BEING ATTACKED . . . BY MEN WHO
SHOULD KNOW BETTER . . . NOWHERE IS IT MORE SERIOUS . . .
THAN IN OUR OWN RAINFORESTS . . . "

He moves to a map of South America and sweeps his hand over the vast equatorial tracts of the continent.

"HERE FOR THE BLIND HOPE . . . OF A SHAKY FUTURE . . .
MEN DESTROY GOD'S CREATION . . . AND A LIFE FORCE TO
THE WORLD . . . FOR THE FEW PESOS THEY CAN EARN . . .
FROM SCRAWNY CATTLE AND STRUGGLING CROPS . . .
UNTIL THE SOIL GIVES OUT . . . AND ALL THAT MAN HAS
CREATED . . . IS A DESERT . . . WHERE GOD HAD PLANTED A
GARDEN . . . "

The backdrop fades and the camera zooms in slowly on the face of Luis

Valdez. Mark Venture catches his breath. A dry taste leaps to his mouth. In an instant he recognizes in the lines and worn face the agony he once had seen, as a young man, in a painting of the dying Christ on the cross at Calvary. The flash of recognition sears through his brain as he tries to follow the words on the screen.

"WHO PROFITS FROM SUCH MADNESS? . . . NOT THE INDIAN WHO LOSES HIS FOREST HOME . . . NOT THE FARMER WHO REMAINS POOR . . . NOT THE EARTH WHICH SUFFERS . . . A MORTAL WOUND . . . ONLY THE DEVELOPERS . . . AND THE BANKS . . . WHO LEND THE MONEY . . . AND TAKE THE INTEREST . . . AND OFFICIALS WHO ARRANGE THE DEAL . . .

"MY FRIENDS . . . IT IS TIME FOR THE PEOPLE . . . TO TAKE BACK THEIR HERITAGE . . . AND THEIR DIGNITY . . . AND BUILD THE FUTURE . . . THAT THEY WISH TO HAVE . . . VISIONEERS ARE GATHERING IN YOUR COMMUNITY . . . FIND THEM . . . JOIN THEM . . . LEARN HOW TO BUILD . . . THE FUTURE TOGETHER . . .

"I MUST GO NOW . . . I WILL SPEAK TO YOU AGAIN . . . ON SUNDAY EVENING . . . AT THIS TIME . . . IT WILL BE A WIDER BROADCAST . . . MANY MORE STATIONS ARE LISTENING . . . HERE IN SOUTH AMERICA . . . AND ALSO AROUND THE WORLD . . . I WILL GIVE YOU DETAILS . . . TELL YOU WHERE YOU CAN GO . . . WHAT YOU CAN DO . . . .TO TAKE THE POWER OF YOUR LIFE . . . BACK INTO YOUR OWN HANDS . . .

"GOODBYE AND GOD BLESS YOU."

The screen clicks blank. The tension in the Los Angeles video room could be cut with a knife.

"Sensational!" exclaims Arthur Rhinegold. "The drama of that is electric. We've got to get to work on this film right away. Bill, can I talk to you about the rights and a contract first thing on Monday morning? I'll put something together over the weekend."

"Sure, Arthur, that'll be fine." Bates is rather distracted. "I'm still thinking about what Luis said about another broadcast on Sunday. If we could get that over the U.S. networks with some introductory promo from us . . . Julia, what do you think? You haven't said a word yet. What do you think? Can we get this on to a network that will put it into the home of every American on Sunday evening?"

"You're right," Julia McCarthy replies. "I haven't said a word. It's the first time I can remember being in a meeting for nearly an hour without being able to get a word in. To answer your question, I'm sure it's, yes. If it's important enough, we can do it. But the other part is, should we do it? What can of worms are we opening here?"

"I dunno, Julia," says Bates. "I'm sure it's a great big can, but I'm not stopping to think about that now. This is news with a capital N and we've got the potential for a world scoop here. I say we go for it. What do you think, Mark?"

"Yes, of course we should give it maximum exposure. You all need to understand that Luis Valdez is in incredible danger by what he's doing. He has launched the project in a way we could never have achieved otherwise. But after Sunday, I'm going to have to pull him out of there. It's just too dangerous for him to continue."

"Where is he, anyway?" asks Arthur. "I mean, how is he doing this? He must be some kind of superman to get all this going without all the technology it normally takes."

"He's a Visioneer with a mission," replies Mark. "I can't tell you where he is. The less everyone knows about that, the better. But you're right. He is a superman. He walks with the spirit of God and a great love in his heart. That combination can change the world."

"Julia?" asks Bill Bates. "What do you say? Are we gonna go for this?"

"I'm already reaching for the phone," she replies, "but after that, you and I have got to talk."

"I'm available twenty-four hours a day on this business, my dear. Let's go to my office. Mark, anything further to do here?"

"No. I'd just like to thank you all for coming. As you can see, we're riding a rollercoaster. Bill is in charge of operations. Keep in touch with him. Thank you again for your contributions."

With that, they disperse. Alone, Mark Venture returns to the boardroom and sits for several long minutes at the elegant marble-topped table and wonders why he feels so heavy in his heart.

CHAPTER NINE

Dark Passage

A THICK, PUNGENT SMOKE HAZE fills the tiny bar in the fishing village of Lascano in Northern Chile. Besides the three soldiers in uniform, only a handful of other patrons sit at the tables. Behind the bar, a squat little man with balding head leans against the counter watching a small television set hanging from the ceiling. No one else pays attention to the television program, which is barely audible above the noisy conversation of the few but highly vocal patrons. One of the soldiers comes to the bar to order more drinks.

"Hey, Pedro," he says to the bartender, "what do you say, the same again, eh?" He glances up at the television set. "What are you watching here, eh?" Then he catches his breath, grabs the edge of the counter and squints through his alcohol-dazed eyes at the face of Luis Valdez on the television screen.

"Hey, captain!" he calls, waving his arms and shouting loud enough to catch the attention of everyone in the bar. "Look here! It's that priest we told to get out. Look now, here he is preaching on the television!"

A chair crashes back as the other two soldiers stumble over to the bar.

"So, it's our little holy mountain man, is it?" The words strain through the captain's clenched teeth. He turns to his two companions. "That's who we got the message about—since he started to broadcast his drivel last Sunday. To think we could've squashed him then! But now we've got him. I'm going to nail him up on his own miserable church."

"You know that priest, eh?" the bartender, Pedro, has interrupted. "My

119

wife, she heard him last Sunday. There's been a lot of talk about it in the village. Look, see there, hear what he's saying. He's going to broadcast to the world next Sunday."

Luis Valdez has signed off and the face of a news reporter has come on the screen. He says that no one seems to know much about Luis Valdez or where he's broadcasting from.

"Do you know him, then?" the bartender asks again. "Is he here in Chile?"

The captain leans across the bar and presses his face close to the man's ear. The alcohol slur has left his voice and it cuts like a steel knife-edge in the thick acrid air.

"Listen, bartender, listen good!" he says. "You don't ask questions, and you don't say anything to anyone about what you just heard. Do you understand me, bartender?"

Without looking further at the three soldiers, Pedro nods, and turns his attention to polishing the glasses on the bar with a dirty, beer-stained towel. The captain moves towards the door.

"I'm going to call headquarters," he says to the others. "You stay here and listen, and tell me what else is said."

The captain straightens up, glances around the room, where the other patrons suddenly resume their conversations, a little quieter than before. He walks across the room and out into the crisp evening air.

Saturday Morning in Jerusalem

The sun has risen sharp and clear into a brilliant blue sky over Jerusalem. It's early morning on the Sabbath and the streets are quiet. Esther Fisher stands in the covered entrance-way to the small apartment block where she has been staying with her friends, David and Mina Roth and their two teenage children, Joshua and Sarah. The air is fresh and the gentle calm of the ancient city seems to spread like a comfortable shawl for those who will be setting off soon for prayers in the synagogue.

The Roth family is not deeply religious. They keep the Sabbath quietly at home, reading (studying for the children), doing the simple household chores that have built up over the week. David is a government official and works as an administrative officer for social welfare programs. Mina teaches in the local elementary school three blocks away. The children are showing promise of becoming talented musicians, Joshua as a pianist and Sarah on the cello. Later in the day, as the Sabbath draws to a close, they'll gather in the small living room of their first floor apartment for a small recital. It has become a custom for them. They'll be joined by friends, adults and children, for these few hours of peaceful family time at the end of a busy work week.

Esther won't be joining them today. She has plans to spend the next two days in a kibbutz not far from the city. She has arranged for a small conference of a hundred young people drawn from all over Israel to meet there, where she'll tell them about the Visioneers. Her reputation as one of her country's leading artists has been a strong drawing card. In addition, interest in the event has increased dramatically over the past few days, with the word coming out of Unesco in Paris of the broadcast in South America by Luis Valdez, and the adoption of a resolution to support the work.

Even this early in the morning, the entire Roth family has gathered to say goodbye to Esther. She's waiting in the cool entrance-way with her packed suitcases for a friend to arrive to pick her up. Joshua and Sarah in dressing gowns shiver a little. David and Mina are chatting animatedly with Esther. A small red car swings into the driveway. Esther loads up her suitcases, embraces everyone and gets into the car. As they leave the entrance way, she glances back and waves to the four smiling figures standing in the doorway. She looks back for a long time, even after they have entered the street, etching the memory of that smiling family group strongly in her mind.

Friday Evening in the Visioneering Room

Mark Venture is back with you in the Visioneering Room. It's been less than an hour since he watched the Luis Valdez transmission in Los Angeles. Tired and anxious, he attempts to unravel what's happening.

"Look," he says, staring hard at you, "I knew when we started this that some of our people would get into danger spots. I'm uneasy now about Luis Valdez. You're running this show. Is there anything you can tell me about that situation?"

"No, Mark," you reply. "I'm not running the show. I'm merely the channel through which it's happening. All of you are taking it where you will. I can't tell you any more about Luis Valdez than you already know."

The irony of your situation is beginning to haunt you. Like Mark, you wish to intervene. But it's out of your hands. You know of the events, but you're not controlling them. The actors themselves are doing that. You realize only too well that Mark knows nothing about the three soldiers in the small bar in the Chilean fishing village.

"Okay," Mark sighs. "I want to talk to Luis. Will you get him for me?"

Instantly, Luis Valdez and George Cardinal appear in life form in the centre of the Visioneering Room. They're relaxing in the small living room of the house at the Mission of the Holy Virgin.

"Mark, my friend," Luis gestures warmly, "it's good to see you. We've heard nothing of the other Visioneers since we left you there over a week ago. Can you tell us what's happening?"

"In a nutshell, Luis, *you* are what's happening. Your first broadcast got picked up and debated at a Unesco conference. Then with good inside work from General Soulière and Boris Gunther and Junichi Yakasaywa, the conference adopted a resolution in support of what we're doing. In addition to that, we've got activities underway in Russia, China, India, Africa, and the United States. But you've become the unifying force. The world's hearing about you. I watched your second broadcast an hour ago in Los Angeles. They're already making plans to put your transmission next Sunday over the national networks."

"Ah, that's very good news." Luis Valdez allows himself a small smile. "We're in touch here with good friends in some of the South American networks. I'm sure they're going to arrange for a worldwide broadcast."

George Cardinal smiles broadly. "That's not bad for a poor parish priest and a simple Indian chief, eh, Mark?"

"No, George, that's not bad at all. But I want to tell you, I'm concerned about your safety. A lot of violent people in that part of the world would want to get you off the air. Have you seen any sign of trouble yet?"

"Not really," George replies. "We had a visit last Sunday before we even got started from three soldiers on some kind of patrol up here. They're unsavoury types, but they had no idea about what we're doing. We're sure they don't have any official orders to interfere with us. They'll probably be back, but not before we pull out of here."

Mark Venture absorbs this new piece of information.

"That makes me even more concerned," he says. "Look, my gut tells me you should get out of there right away. But there's so much interest building up around your Sunday broadcast, that it would be good to do it. Is there any way you can set up some place else before then?"

"No," says George. "We're finally getting the technology to work well for us here. Don't worry, Mark, we've got good communication links to the outside world, now, and while no one knows exactly where we are, we can get the word of any trouble out very fast. Faced with that kind of reaction, I don't think any official source is going to try anything extreme."

"Yes, but there are other elements that might. You're stepping on a lot of toes."

"Mark, my friend," Luis Valdez is speaking again. "You're a fine man and a good leader. Deciding to send us here was a stroke of brilliance on your part. We're pleased it's working so well. You have to remember that God is with us. He's telling me I must make this broadcast on Sunday. After that, if you think we should move, then we'll move. Is that agreed, my friend?"

There's a long pause before Mark replies.

"All right," he finally says. "You do the broadcast on Sunday evening and then get out of there right away. But keep up your guard between now and then, and if there's any sign of trouble, your safety comes first. Do I have your word on that?"

"Yes, my good friend," says Luis. "You have our word. We're going to rest now. It's getting late for an old man to be still awake. God bless you, Mark. You're doing a great thing for the world."

"God bless you, Luis, both of you. I love you like my brothers."

With that, they're gone, and Mark looks across to you with deep concern in his eyes.

On the Road to the Kibbutz

"Hello, Mark," Esther's voice is cheery and bright. "It's lovely to see you. This is really nice. I certainly wasn't expecting to hear from you before breakfast."

"I just wanted you to know that I'm thinking about you. Who's your friend?"

"This is Jenny Lovicks," Esther replies. "She's a good friend. She's driving me to the kibbutz."

"Hi, Mark," says Jenny. "I must say, you have an impressive style of communication. Just zipping in on us while we're driving along in the car. Does he always drop in on you like that, Esther?"

"Not nearly often enough," laughs Esther.

Mark is talking to them from the Visioneering Room, as if he were riding with them in the car.

"Is everything going well for the conference?" he asks. "I expect to be joining you on Sunday afternoon your time."

"Everything's fine," replies Esther. "I'll have everyone well briefed by the time you arrive. Are you sure you'll be able to find us?"

"That, my dear, is the one thing I am sure about. Now, take care. You look after her, Jenny. She's very precious cargo. Goodbye for now."

With a cheery wave of their hands, the two women are gone. It's dark in the Visioneering Room as the sunny Israeli morning disappears from view. Friday evening—the end of a long week. Mark closes his eyes briefly to rest.

Saturday Evening in Chile

The telephone lines between Santiago and Bogota are surprisingly heavy with traffic for a Saturday evening. Elmiro Perez has been careful to put the call through the scrambler so there's no possibility of a third-party wire tap on his conversation. He's been cooped up in his office all day, waiting for calls to go back and forth on this Luis Valdez business. Ever since he'd received word last night that an army captain knew of Valdez's whereabouts, he's been seeking instructions on what to do about it.

Perez is a small-time businessman in Santiago, but a bigger-time link in a variety of underworld activities networked across South America. He was not sure at first where Valdez fitted, but as the hours and phone calls have worn on, it's become increasingly apparent that Valdez has caught the attention of people of prominence on the darker side of Perez's activities. He hopes that this last call to Bogota will clarify the matter. A thickset man, overweight and asthmatic, he breathes heavily and irregularly as he listens to the phone ringing at the other end of the line. Someone answers.

"Hello." A woman's voice.

"Cordoba for Carcuta," he says.

"One moment."

"Carcuta." A man's voice.

"Instructions concerning insecto," says Perez.

"El olvido," is the reply. "Take care of it."

"What status?" asks Perez.

"El Condor. Goodbye."

Perez hangs up the phone and sits staring at it. El Condor! The persistent parish priest has ruffled feathers at the highest level. And the instructions are el olvido—oblivion. It must be handled well. He looks at his watch. Almost midnight. Twenty hours before Valdez is scheduled to make his broadcast. There should be plenty of time to take care of it. He picks up the phone and makes another call.

"Hello," a tired voice answers.

"Concerning insecto," says Perez, "the instructions are el olvido from El Condor."

There's a whistle at the other end of the line.

"You know what needs to be done?" asks Perez.

"Yes, of course."

"Before 8 p.m."

"Yes."

"Is that captain reliable?"

"Yes."

"All right, tell him to proceed. And one more thing."

"Yes?"

"This is not a military matter. Do you understand?"

"Of course."

"Good."

Perez hangs up the phone, turns out the light in his office and goes home. Before he has reached his car parked in the street, the captain in the dirty little hotel in Lascano has received his instructions: "Take care of the priest, incognito." The captain rouses his two henchmen and they stumble sleepily out to the army jeep to begin the long 600 kilometre drive over slow, rough roads to the Mission of the Holy Virgin.

Saturday Evening in Los Angeles

It's 9 o'clock Saturday evening in Los Angeles. Bill Bates, still in his office, reviews the activities of the past twenty-four hours. Following the break-up of the meeting with Mark Venture last night, he and Julia McCarthy had spent most of the evening speaking to network executives about taking the Luis Valdez broadcast on Sunday evening. They had dealt with the full range of ignorance, enthusiasm, and greed. "Who is Luis Valdez?" "Do you think this can really be the start of a new wave of decency in the world?" "What's in it for us?" "Visioneers! Who are they, some bunch of boy scouts lost in the woods?" "Listen, I've got sponsors. How do I know they'll go for this visioneering stuff?" "Yes, I've been following this story, we'll do our best to cover it." And so it went, long into the evening. Julia had returned to New York early this morning to continue to work on it. Bill is expecting a call from her at any time now.

The other activity was getting the story into his Saturday morning newspapers. He had written it himself, just in time to catch the presses and his editors had run it as the second item on the front page. He has a copy of the Los Angeles paper in front of him.

"VOICE OF THE VISIONEERS. At 6 p.m. Friday, Los Angeles time, a Catholic priest broadcasting by satellite from an unknown location in South America, stole air time on major news networks to bring a message of vision and hope for people and the Earth.

"It was the second time in a week that Father Luis Valdez has put out his simple message. It's now catching wider attention and was picked up by many independent satellite listeners around the world. Valdez announced that he would be broadcasting again at the same time on Sunday evening. News networks in North America are now scrambling to see if they should pay attention and bring the Valdez broadcast to their viewers.

"Valdez hits bluntly at land barons, industrialists, and officials who, in his opinion, are despoiling the environment and exploiting the people for their own profit. His appeal is to people everywhere to band together as what he calls Visioneers to create a better future for themselves.

"The Visioneers are a previously unknown group who have come to world attention in the past week. A Unesco conference in Paris surprisingly adopted a resolution in support of their efforts to get people more actively involved in creating the future for themselves and their communities. This was an unusual move for this government-funded organization, given that it could be perceived to be supporting activist initiatives contrary to the interest of the governments of many member states.

"Little more is known about the Visioneers at this time. However, this paper can report from inside sources that small initiatives are underway on all continents. In the United States, preliminary discussions have been held prior to the announcement of a full scale program of activities.

"We can also report that the leader of the group is an Australian named Mark Venture, who has chosen at this time not to make any public announcements. He prefers to see the country initiatives develop on their own. He's looking to the broadcast by Luis Valdez on Sunday evening as a significant indication to the world of what can be achieved by people acting together to bring a more positive future for themselves."

That had been enough to set news networks buzzing. All day his office has been besieged by demands for more information about the Visioneers and Mark Venture and Luis Valdez, in particular. As a newspaper man, Bates is enjoying the situation. He's playing it for effect, deliberately minimizing his own involvement and building interest in the Luis Valdez broadcast.

The other significant issue of the day had come from George Walker, who at the meeting last night had spoken of the link he saw between the visioneering project and improved business performance in America. At 9 o'clock this morning he had called Bates to pursue the point.

"Bill, I've just read the story in your paper this morning. I'll bet it's stirring up some interest."

"Yeah, but it's nothing to what's coming."

"That's what I want to talk to you about. One of the big problems we have because of our fantastic communication systems is that we create interest and expectations way beyond our ability to follow up."

"What do you mean?"

"Well, look, millions of people in this country, not to mention the rest of the world, are going to hear over the weekend about something called visioneering. They'll be told that by working and planning together they can build a better future. Now, you and I both know there's a lot more to it than that. If it was that simple, we'd already be doing it. The problem is that people haven't learned how to build shared visions. We haven't concerned ourselves about the future. It wasn't on the agenda. Our schools and colleges don't teach students how to use their creative imaginations to build enterprises. We've taught them to be conforming consumers. That's why business is now being caught flat-footed, because everyone running it has this conformist mentality when what we need is entrepreneurship. We have a great myth in this country about the American way as being bold and enterprising. The truth of the matter is we're so conservative and protectionist that we're rapidly losing our ability to hold our own."

"So?" Bates had asked, his interest firmly caught. "What's your point, George?"

"My point is that we have a bad educational and attitudinal problem on our hands. We aren't going to be able to deal with it through the existing institutions because they're caught up in the problem themselves, and we can't wait while they try to reform. We have to get something else going. Something coming in from the side. Something created in the same spirit as the Visioneers: informal, decentralized, networked, pushing the limits of learning about how to vision and create; a creative learning initiative, if you like."

"And you have some ideas about how to do that?" Bates had asked.

"Yes, well, some principles anyway. It has to be business-based, entrepreneurial, something that grows because it's successful and not because it's pumped up with government dollars. Second, it has to be networked so that people in every part of the country can hook in quickly and get the help they need when they need it.

"Now, I mentioned last night that there's a number of business people around the world who've formed the Planetary Business Network because we see business as the institution most likely to pull the world into a decent future. There's only a couple of hundred of us so far, but we're growing every day, and more than half of the members come from the United States.

"So far, we don't have any particular program. We're mainly a forum that meets from time to time to share ideas. What I suggest is that the Planetary Business Network link up with the Visioneers to develop a curriculum and a program for teaching creative learning throughout the length and breadth of this country; and around the world. We could put the best minds in the world at work to develop workshops and teaching programs for people and organizations in creative learning."

"I like it, George," Bates was enthusiastic. "I suggest you go to work on that right away with your contacts and next week, we'll sit down with Mark and work on the details."

As he reflects now on that conversation, Bill Bates has a sense that in the end, it might turn out to be the most important event of the day. But he has no more time to think about it now. The video phone on his desk has lit up and he sees that Julia McCarthy is calling him. He punches the line button and her face appears on the screen.

"Hi, Bill," she says. "How are you doing?"

"I'm doing great, Julia. What'd you think of my scoop in the papers this morning?"

"Well, it's creating as much of a sensation here in New York as you can expect from anything coming out of Los Angeles."

"Yeah, a real pain in the neck, right, from trying to run the other way and look back over your shoulder at the same time."

"Something like that," laughs Julia.

"Well, I'll tell you what," says Bates. "By this time tomorrow night, any of those Eastern prima donnas who chose not to dance in this ballet will be begging for a part in the next performance. What luck have you had with the network types?"

"Oh, it's coming along," replies Julia. "You know, it's only midnight here, and we've still got all day tomorrow to put it together. Is there any further word from Valdez or Mark Venture? I mean, is this thing really going to happen?"

"Julia, dear, don't worry. Uncle Bill will bring the candies."

"Don't patronize me, Bill," Julia shoots back. "I've gone way out on a limb on this one and you'd better not saw it off on me."

"Sorry, Julia, no offence meant."

"Okay," she replies. "Oh, and there's one more thing. The news coming out of Israel today is starting to grab a lot of attention here."

"You mean the terrorist attack this morning?"

"Yes. You know, that could be used as a link to create interest in the Valdez broadcast."

"What do you mean?"

"Well, it's another example of the kind of thing that Valdez and the Visioneers are trying to overcome, isn't it? Say, do you know if there are any Visioneers in Israel that we can tie into the story?"

Bates remembers Esther Fisher, but he's not sure where she is. There's also something in Julia's tone that's beginning to irritate him, the sense that it's only the story that's important, rather than what lies behind it.

"I'm not sure," he replies. "I'll look into it. Now, it's been a long day, Julia; more so for you than for me. Let's call it off, and I'll be in touch again tomorrow before noon your time."

"Okay, Bill, goodnight—and think about how we can connect those two stories together."

"Yes, Julia, goodnight."

With that, she's gone. Suddenly, the excitement he was feeling about things has subsided. A terrorist attack on an Israeli family is seen as another piece of news. He hadn't paid too much attention to the story when it had come in this morning. Now maybe he should. But for what purpose? Because it's part of a troubled world that must be changed, or because it's good promotion for Valdez. And what about Esther Fisher? Is she in Israel? Should she be brought into this?

He decides to call Mark Venture.

Esther's Dream

Esther Fisher looks around at the group assembled in the recreation centre of the kibbutz and wonders whether this is, indeed, the best way to launch the visioneering project in Israel. In a country so fixed on hope for the future, but so besieged by hatred and violence from the past, it's difficult to know where to begin. It's early evening and the end of the Sabbath. People have been resting all day. They have just eaten together: simple food and plentiful, mountains of fresh vegetables from the garden, bread, cheese, and fish; all spread out on large tables, people helping themselves, buffet style, families eating together, plenty of laughter and energetic conversation. The younger children have left now, but some of the teenagers have remained, joining their parents and the visitors who've come to hear Esther. It's a mixed group, predominantly younger than thirty-five, but with a few grey beards and bald heads, and at the back, unobtrusive but noticeable, a dozen young men and women in uniform, members of the Israeli army, on duty at the kibbutz, ever mindful of violent and sudden attack.

Esther has mingled well. She has met most of them. About a hundred people are gathered in the room. She stands up to speak.

"*Chaveyreem*, friends, *shalom*," she begins quietly. "It's good to be here with you this evening. I have just a few brief remarks. Tonight is for relaxation. Tomorrow we'll have a workshop and be joined by Mark Venture, the leader of the Visioneers, and you'll hear about how that movement is gathering force to change the world. Tonight, I want to share a dream."

The room is hushed. All attention is focused on this young woman who they know and respect for her contribution to Israeli culture. She's wearing a long, autumn-toned skirt, which she gathers around her now as she sits perched on a high three-legged stool in the middle of the group. She picks up a simple wooden guitar which was leaning against the stool and begins to play.

She sings to them softly, songs that they know, songs of peace and hope. Her voice is clear and tremulous, pitched to the tone of a distant bell ringing across the land. *Hevenu Shalom Aleichem*—let us bring peace, peace to all of us. *Hallelujah*—glory to the world, heart to heart, each to each, hallelujah to the things that were and to the things that have not been, hallelujah to yesterday and tomorrow. *Heeney Matov*—here's what's good, people sitting together, all of us here. The voices are rising now, joining with Esther. *Osse Shalom Alenu*—let Him make peace among us. Everyone is singing, getting to their feet, joining hands, swaying to the music. *Osse Shalom Alenu*—let Him make peace among us, and to all Israel, and to that let us say, Amen. Everyone is standing, Esther too, standing as they reach into their hearts and sing. Heads are high, everyone standing tall as the passionate music resonates in their hearts, then ends, and the room settles into a hushed stillness as full of hope and longing for peace as the songs they've just sung.

"My good friends," Esther is speaking again, walking among them, her voice warm with the energy of what she feels in her heart. "I said I wanted to share a dream. It's a dream I've carried in my heart since I was a small girl. I'm walking in a garden. It's a beautiful garden, full of flowers and fruit trees, and the sun is shining, warming the earth and making the leaves sparkle with rainbows as the sunlight catches the large clear drops of dew that have settled on them overnight. There's no one in my garden but myself. I'm walking there alone, hardly daring to breathe lest I disturb the beauty and the stillness.

"I come to a wall. And it seems to me that this must be the end of the garden, for it's a very high wall, much taller than I am, that someone has put there to say, this is the end of the garden. I touch the wall with my hands. It's cool and rough, and I see that it's a very old wall and that there are cracks between the large flat stones where the mortar has fallen out. I look more closely and I see, peeping from one of the cracks, a note on a tiny piece of paper, crumpled and a little dirty and bent over a little, as if it's been pushed there through the crack, coming from the other side of the wall.

"I reach up and take down the note and read it and tears come to my eyes. It says: 'Hello, I live in a garden on this side of this high wall. I used to think that the wall was the end of the garden, but one day I climbed a tree and I could see over the wall and I saw that on the other side there was another garden and I saw you there walking alone. And the thought came to me that perhaps the wall wasn't really the end of the garden after all, but maybe it was the middle and that someone had built the wall there dividing the garden in two, but really it was one garden with a wall down the middle of it. Do you think that's a funny idea? I'm writing this note to tell you what I think. I hope you won't laugh at me, and that you'll write back to me and tell me what you think.'

"The note wasn't signed, so I didn't know who sent it. I turned it over and quickly wrote a reply on the other side: 'Hello,' I said, 'what an interesting thought! Perhaps the only way we can tell is if we visit each other. I'm too tiny to climb over this high wall, but if you could throw a rope, maybe I could do it and meet you on top of the wall.'

"I pushed the note through the wall and waited. Within a very short time, I heard a whooshing sound, and the end of a strong, brown rope came over the wall. I grabbed hold of it and began to climb. I wasn't very good at it, and it was taking me a long time to get to the top, and I was getting very tired. I was near the top and my arms were aching and I felt for sure I would fall back and hurt myself when I looked up and saw a hand reaching down towards me. I'll never forget that hand. It wasn't large, but it looked strong and it was dark brown, as if it had been tanned a long time in the sun. I reached up and grasped it, and straight away felt new energy in my tired arms. And soon, I was sitting on top of the wall facing my new friend.

"He said his name was Ali and I told him I was Esther and we looked on both sides of the wall and sure enough, it seemed to both of us from up there that both sides looked very much the same and that perhaps it really was all one garden with a wall down the middle of it.

"And do you know that as soon as we began to think that way, we felt the wall begin to shudder and we could see it suddenly breaking down, piece by piece, in the distance and travelling toward us. Ali gave me his hand again and we barely had time to scramble down on his side of the wall, before the whole thing crumbled and lay in a big pile of rocks stretching away as far as we could see.

"We stood there and looked and after a few minutes, if it hadn't been for the pile of rocks, we couldn't have said that there ever was a wall there at all. After that, I played with Ali on what had been his side of the wall, and he played with me on what had been my side, and we found that we both knew most of the same games and songs and what we didn't know, we taught each other quickly."

Esther's voice had grown very soft, but every person in the room was listening intently.

"That was the end of my dream," she said, "but I've carried it through all my life in Israel, through all of the bombings, and the wars, the hijackings, the missile attacks, the hatred, and the violence, the strikes, and the counter strikes.

"And I find myself saying now, more than ever, what if all of us—Jew and Arab, Palestinian and Israeli—came to see that what we have is one land with a wall down the middle of it. But if we take down the wall, then there are ways that we can learn to live together and find that we already know most of each other's songs and games and from there it's only a short step to learn to sing together Hallelujah for the things that are still to come.

"That's the message of the Visioneers, my friends. It's the thought— and the dream—that I want to leave with you tonight. Tomorrow we'll talk about it together."

Esther then asks everyone to stand and sing with her *Hatikva*, their national anthem—Hatikva, the hope, the hope to be a free people in their homeland. The bewitching melody tugs at their hearts while Esther's dream stirs in their minds. The song ends and Esther smiles at them, then turns and steps quickly out of the room, out into the fresh evening air to walk by herself for a while under the clear star-filled sky.

Jerusalem Nightmare

At the same time as Esther is telling her dream to the people in the kibbutz, her friends, David and Mina Roth, are hosting their customary gathering at home for several guests in their apartment in Jerusalem. The children, Joshua and Sarah, have been entertaining, Joshua with two Chopin impromptus and Sarah playing Albinoni's *Concerto a cinque B-Dur in B flat major*. The room is relaxed, coffee is served and Sarah and Joshua are bringing around trays of sweets.

Downstairs, Peter Kardous, a colleague of David's from the Ministry, is just arriving. He had been delayed by another appointment. He buzzes the intercom and David lets him in. As the Roth apartment is on the first floor, he decides to take the stairs rather than the elevator. Halfway up, he is struck by a sudden overwhelming apprehension. As he came in, he had barely noticed the small car parked in the entranceway. Suddenly, he realizes that the car should not be there. Isolated parked cars in Jerusalem are a danger sign. He turns and dashes back down to the street. The car is still sitting there. Something in the back of his mind processes it as a small white, two-door Chevrolet. He tries both doors. Locked. The car is on a slight incline with its wheels turned into the curb. Well-parked, one part of his mind says, while he searches for a solution. He sees the rock border of a flower garden, a few metres away. He rushes over, picks up a large rock, runs back to the car and smashes it against the driver's side window. Jagged glass cuts his hands. He reaches in, searching for the gearshift. It's an automatic. He knocks it out of park and searches for the hand brake. He releases it and pushes the car, but it doesn't move. Its wheels are turned firmly into the curb. The jagged glass from the shattered window cuts deep into his arm as he makes a superhuman effort to turn the driving wheel and push the car with his shoulder to get it moving. Nothing happens. He tries again, stronger now, a dreadful conviction driving him. The car moves, just slightly, then more, the wheels turning, coming away from the curb, starting to roll down the incline.

At that moment, the bomb goes off.

Upstairs, the whole front wall of the Roth apartment is blown out. The small grand piano where Joshua had been seated a few minutes earlier spins crazily around, then topples forward and hangs precariously at the point of balance without falling into the street. Chairs, coffee tables, a stereo player, all are blown clear out of the building and one of the chairs lands strangely intact in the branches of a tree fifty metres away.

Four people have been killed in the blast. Peter Kardous, bravely seeking to avert the tragedy is blown to pieces. His efforts unquestionably prevented many more deaths upstairs. An elderly couple, the Horchberg's sitting by the front window, were crushed by the concussion and died instantly. Joshua Roth, beautiful young man and promising pianist, dies in his mother's arms a few minutes later, herself cut and bleeding profusely. David Roth had been at the back of the apartment in the kitchen and has escaped without a scratch. Sarah was thrown hard against a wall and is sobbing hysterically as she looks down helplessly at her crushed and broken left hand which a few minutes earlier had fingered Albinoni so delicately on the cello. The remaining guests are all in various states of injury and shock.

Somewhere out in Jerusalem's dark streets, the sirens begin to scream. Somewhere out there, as well, two young men in sneakers and black jackets hurry away from their ghastly handiwork. As they jump into a compatriot's car and speed off, their minds are closed to the horror and the rage that screams out from the twisted building with its gaping black hole of death. Too many times, O Jerusalem, have you seen such butchery and horror! Too much death! Too much hatred! Too much mindless revenge that does nothing but keep an ugly score! As the sirens draw closer, keeping their frenzied appointment with the latest dead and injured, there's a whisper somewhere out in the universe saying, "This cannot be." Quietly, it gathers the force that it must find to break the tyranny of the dark minds that infect the human condition.

Is There No End to It?

Esther is returning to the kibbutz when she hears Jenny Lovicks calling to her frantically in the dark.

"Esther, Esther, where are you? Oh, Esther, please answer me! Where are you?"

"Here, Jenny," calls Esther, running. "What is it?" What's wrong?"

"Oh, Esther," Jenny runs up to her, barely able to speak. " Something terrible has happened. There's been a bombing in Jerusalem. Oh Esther, it was at your friends' apartment, the Roths. David just phoned. He wants you to come right away!"

Esther feels a light go out of her life. Her dream, the garden she longs to share—all gone in the blinding flash of a terrorist bomb. Oh Mark! Where are you? Come quickly now, not to the celebration we planned, but to bring some hope to this new horror.

To Jenny, she says, calmly, "I must go. Will you take me?"

Sobbing, Jenny indicates she already has her car keys in her hand. They run to the parking lot and within a few minutes are speeding towards Jerusalem.

But they never arrive at the scene of the tragedy. On a quiet stretch of road, a car suddenly swings in behind them, its lights bright in the rear vision mirror. It follows very close for a few minutes, then abruptly pulls up beside them. With a quick twist of the steering wheel, the other driver catches a surprised Jenny and cuts in front of her. She screams and panics and her small car ploughs at high speed into an embankment, ricocheting, careening, and bouncing until it comes to a stop, perilously close to a steep drop off. Within moments, the two young women are dragged out of the car. Bags come down over their heads, and they are shoved unceremoniously into the back seat of the other car, which turns and heads away at high speed into the darkness.

It's a Pretty Bad Scene . . .

Mark Venture is already in the Visioneering Room when you arrive. It's 9 o'clock Saturday morning, Pacific Coast time in North America.

Mark has set up an operations station at the open end of the room. The rows of chairs where the Visioneers had sat on their first meeting are empty. The large globe of the world glows iridescent in its space in the centre of the room. Mark is sitting at a desk facing the globe. To one side is a printer chattering out news events from around the world in a continuous roll of paper which Mark periodically tears off, scans, sometimes making notations, then pushes to one side while he reaches for the next bulletin.

He doesn't notice you at first. You sit quietly in one of the empty chairs watching him. Suddenly, he stiffens and sits bolt upright. He looks up, sees you, and slaps the paper he's holding with his hand.

"You know about this, of course," he says. "Some terrorists have bombed an apartment block in Jerusalem."

You nod.

"What about Esther?" he asks. "Is she involved?"

"She wasn't there," you reply. "It's her friends' family who was hit. But she hasn't been hurt."

"Where is she then?" he senses you're holding something back.

"Mark, you have to prepare yourself for some bad news. Things are starting to become difficult to manage."

"What do you mean? What things? Has something happened to Esther?"

"She's all right for now. She's been captured by terrorists, but they haven't harmed her. It's not the same ones who did the bombing, but the incidents are related."

"What!" He's on his feet. "Esther's been captured! Show me."

The globe dissolves into a scene in a small room with white plaster walls and a tiny window. Esther and Jenny are sitting on chairs, tied loosely to them, and blindfolded. It's evening and the room is poorly lit by a single light bulb hanging on a cord from the ceiling. A slight young man sits in another chair by the door, smoking and reading a newspaper.

"The swine! " Mark explodes. To you he says: "Tell me quick. What's going on?"

"Esther and Jenny were run off the road on their way back to the Roth apartment after the bombing. They're being held in an Arab village on the West Bank."

"Tell me where. I'm going to get them out."

"You'd better think it through, Mark. There are things going on in that situation you don't know about. You could end up getting yourself and the women killed."

Mark is quiet for a moment.

"I'm going to Israel," he then says. "You can tell me where they are so I can get them out when the time is right. I'd like to speak to them, but I can't with that guard in the room. Can you get him out of there?"

"Mark, I'm not controlling the events. I can just show them to you."

"All right. Well, show me where David Roth is. I want to start there."

"He's at the hospital with his wife and daughter. They were badly hurt in the blast. The police are on the scene there. They've got all the injured out, and they've removed the dead bodies to the morgue at the hospital. David's son, Joshua, was one of the four killed. It's a pretty bad scene, but I can take you there, if that's what you want to do."

"Yes, I want to go now."

An Eye for an Eye

From this time on, Mark, the chosen leader of the Visioneers, is to leave the Visioneering Room and join his compatriots. He will now move with them in the flow of the action that follows. He can communicate with you when necessary; otherwise, his decisions will be determined by the circumstances as they unfold. You send him now, as he requested, to join the action in Jerusalem.

At the hospital, Mark finds David Roth in a small anteroom where he is waiting while Mina and Sarah are in surgery. He's alone for now. The police have just finished their questioning. Friends and relatives of the casualties from the blast have gathered in other parts of the hospital and David has a few minutes alone to begin to confront his grief and guilt.

When Mark enters the room, he sees a man haggard and shaking, the unmistakable red smears of blood staining his grey sweater.

"Hello, David. I'm Mark Venture."

"Oh?" David's face is blank. "You're Esther's friend, aren't you? Is she all right? I called her, I think, but I can't remember seeing her. I'm sorry. I'm not doing very well right now."

"I understand," replies Mark. "I don't have the words to say to you at a time like this. But I do understand. I wouldn't bother you now if I didn't have to. It's about Esther. She's in terrible danger. She's been taken by terrorists. I know where she is, but I don't know why they've taken her or who they are. I need some help with that before I make a move. I was hoping you could shed some light on it."

"Not Esther, too!" David collapses on a chair and buries his face in his hands. When he lifts his head, he looks at Mark through eyes tormented by a hundred thousand demons. His voice is a hoarse whisper. "It's me they were after. And look, not a single scratch! And Joshua, poor Josh, dead; and little Sarah, her hand. Oh, you should have seen her hand! And Mina, she still thinks she's holding Josh in her arms. Now Esther, too! And here I am—not a single scratch."

"David," Mark's voice is rock steady as he drives straight at a target, "why did you say they were after you? Who are they, and why did they want to kill you?"

"I don't know who they are. There's so many of those cells out there. They fade and change every night. But they're after me because of my group. We call ourselves the *Nohkamim*, the avengers. We've been striking back at them. It's *ahyeen beshveel ahyeen*: an eye for an eye."

David's voice trails off. Mark stares at him dumbfounded. A mild spoken civil servant, father of two lovely young children—and head of a group of vigilantes! How can anything ever make sense in this tormented land? "An eye for an eye." The same brutally simplistic law operating on both sides, when everyone has long since forgotten who took the first eye. How many sweet Joshuas are to die because of this, and how many young Mohammeds?

"Do the police know?" Mark asks.

"Yes, I told them. They suspected it anyway. I don't care anymore. I'm just sick to my heart of all of this."

"And Esther, is that why they would've grabbed her? Do they think she's involved with your *Nohkamim*?"

"I don't know. I think it's more likely she's being held as security against reprisal."

At that moment, the door opens and a female police officer comes in. She looks at Mark and speaks to him in Hebrew. He shakes his head and says, "English."

"Who are you? How did you get in here?" she repeats in English.

"I'm a friend," replies Mark, ignoring the second question.

She looks hard at him, then turns to David and continues speaking in English.

"I'm sorry, Mr. Roth," she says, "but there appears to have been another development. Do you know Esther Fisher and Jenny Lovicks?"

David nods sadly.

"We've found Jenny Lovicks' car abandoned on the outskirts of the city. We understand they were on their way to see you. We think they may have been abducted."

Mark decides to leap in, the outline of a plan suddenly flashing through his mind.

"Officer, Esther Fisher is an associate of mine. I know she's missing. If you have any idea of where she is, I would like to know."

"And who exactly are you?" She has fixed him again with another searching look. "You're obviously not Israeli."

"No, I'm an Australian citizen. My name is Mark Venture. Esther Fisher and I are members of an international group of Visioneers."

"A group of who?" Curiosity is now giving place to hostility. "Is this another self-styled group of avengers? I think we've seen enough of what comes of that for one day."

"No, we're not avengers. I'm prepared to give you a full statement."

"Yes, I think you'd better do that." She turns back to David. "Then we have to deal with the media, Mr. Roth. I can't keep them at bay much longer. There's no need to say anything about the *Nohkamim* at this time. I'll stay with you and help field the questions." She turns back to Mark. "Now, Mr. Venture, let's hear your story."

We Will Speak Again

The telephone jerks Mark into consciousness at 9 a.m. next morning, Sunday, in his hotel room in Jerusalem. It had been a long night of interrogation by the authorities and interviews with the media. At 4 a.m. he had finally managed to escape. It was then he'd called you, for the third time that evening, inquiring about Esther. You could report that she and Jenny seemed to be getting good treatment and had been allowed to sleep in two bunk beds in another room in the house where they're being held. Satisfied on that score, he'd finally got to bed around 6 a.m. to try to grab a few hours sleep. Now he's awakened by the strident ringing of the telephone.

"Hello, Mark. It's Bill Bates in Los Angeles. I finally tracked you down."

"Hello, Bill. What time is it there?"

"It's 10 o'clock Saturday evening. I've just come in from the office. I've been working on the Valdez promotion all day—I think it's going to fly. Then Julia reminded me about the bombing in Jerusalem as a possible connection to Luis Valdez and the Visioneers, so I thought I'd check with you. But I didn't know you were there on the spot yourself. What's going on?"

"The bombing is a horrible business. I saw the place myself last night. It's hard to believe that human beings can do this kind of thing to one another. Worse still, Esther's been caught up in it. She and a girl friend have been abducted by terrorists. I know where they are, and I'm working on a plan to get them out safely, but I'm worried sick about it."

"Yeah, I guess so. What a mess! I'm really sorry to hear that about Esther. I know the two of you are close. Are the police involved? What about the media? Do they know what's going on?"

"Yes, in part. That's my strategy, to use the media to get to the terrorists who are holding Esther, to see if they'll negotiate with me."

"Mark, those people don't negotiate. The only things they understand are bombs and the barrel of a gun."

"Well, I'm going to try."

"Okay, good luck, for Esther's sake. I'm going to see what we've got coming through here on this story. Then I'll get to work on it myself. This is sure going to be a great build-up for Valdez tomorrow night. Does any of this make sense to you, Mark? I mean, there's Luis risking his neck to preach about brotherhood and vision, and there's Esther being held by a bunch of thugs who go around blowing up innocent people."

"I'm not sure what makes sense, Bill. We're too much in the thick of it at the moment to see anything clearly. One thing's certain, though, the Visioneers have got to come through this with a consistent message that this kind of violence is no solution to anything. Human beings have to do better than that to manage the kind of world we're already living in, let alone what's coming. Keep that in mind in whatever you write."

"You bet. I've got some buddies over in Russia who are treading a pretty fine line, too. The whole world's listening now, Mark. We're going to do good on this, you'll see. So long now. I'll talk to you later. Take care of yourself—and Esther too."

"Yes, Bill. Thanks. Goodnight."

Before Mark has finished shaving, the phone rings again.

"Mr. Venture." It's a thick voice, male, obviously disguised.

"Yes, who's this?"

"It doesn't matter. If you want to see your friend Esther Fisher alive again, you will listen."

Mark stiffens. Is this Esther's captor on the other end of the line?

"I'm listening."

"I have read in the paper what you say about your Visioneers. We Palestinians have a vision, too. It's to be free in our homeland. What do you say about that?"

"I think that's a fine vision for a group of people to hold."

"Our vision does not include the State of Israel."

"Well, there I think you have a problem."

"No, you have a problem, Mr. Venture. You have a group of Visioneers to represent the world and you include someone from a state we Palestinians do not recognize. That is not acceptable to us."

"The Visioneers are not a formal body put together by governments. They are a group of people talking to each other about a future vision of the world. They come from every continent. They're working now to encourage people in all communities to build visions and share them with each other around a common vision for all of us, the future of the planet. That's what Esther was here to do."

"And she begins with her own people. That is not very credible to us."

"We always begin with our own people. Where would you begin?"

"You didn't ask me."

"I don't know you. I began where I began. Esther was here to widen the circle. Inadvertently, you may have helped to do that, but your methods are crude."

"No one is asking you to approve of my methods, Mr. Venture. Miss Fisher was taken because she's an associate of that murderer, Roth."

"I don't believe Esther knew anything about what Roth was doing."

"It doesn't matter. We have her now so there can be no retaliation or she will be sent back with her throat cut."

Mark feels his own throat tighten as he hears the hatred in the voice and knows that Esther is there, vulnerable to it. But he keeps his voice steady.

"You have a much better opportunity now than anything you can achieve by such savagery. We don't know each other. We're just two voices at two ends of a phone line, talking about one of the world's most intractable problems. But we're talking and not killing. A week ago, no one had heard of the Visioneers. By tomorrow morning, our work will be known throughout the world, and millions of people will be talking and starting to look at many things in a new way. You have an opportunity to be a prominent part of that."

"Yes, and to find myself rotting in an Israeli prison for the rest of my days for my trouble."

"I don't know what you've done already that you might be held accountable for, other than abducting Esther, but you have a chance now to turn that to your advantage by bringing her back."

"Just walk into your camp, eh, Mr. Venture? Where would I see a friendly face there among Jews and Christians. You have no sense of who I am and what I see."

"We have a Jordanian on the Visioneering team."

There's a pause. Mark holds his breath, waiting to see if this has scored a point.

"Who is that?" the voice finally asks.

"Mohammed Hussein. He's an official at the United Nations headquarters in New York."

"I know of him. He's a good man. Is he there with you?"

"No, he's in China."

"Why is he in China when his people are here?"

"A fifth of the world's people are in China. I had need of him there. But he can be here by tomorrow morning."

Another pause.

"You bring him here, Mr. Venture, then we can talk again."

"Good. Now I have something to ask of you."

"What?"

"Let me speak to Esther."

There's a pause and some scuffling sounds on the phone. Then Esther's voice is there, unmistakably clear and brave.

"Mark? Oh, Mark, is that you?"

"Yes, Esther. Oh, your voice sounds wonderful. Are they treating you well?"

"Yes, yes, we're fine. I could hardly believe it when they showed us the paper this morning and let us listen to the radio. You seem to be the big news in Israel today."

"I haven't seen any of that myself yet. Listen, we can't talk long now. I'm working to get you out of there. I know I can count on you to do what you can. I love you, Esther."

But she's gone.

"Enough," the voice is back. "We'll speak again, Mr. Venture."

And the line is dead. Mark looks at the receiver and hangs it up. He notices for the first time the streams of perspiration running down his face and the tight knot in his stomach.

New Vision: New Prospects

On both sides of the world, straddling almost a dozen time zones, the events of this fateful day move on apace.

The American and European press report the horror of the Jerusalem bombing. Added to it now is the strange reoccurrence of this Visioneers group, first mentioned earlier in the week as a minor item coming out of a Unesco conference. Now the leader, an Australian, has appeared in Israel, claiming that one of his associates, an Israeli woman, has been abducted by a Palestinian terrorist group. Meanwhile, out of South America, there's the continuing bizarre story of another alleged Visioneer, a Roman Catholic priest, broadcasting from some unknown location by satellite and being picked up by an increasing number of news networks around the world. There is word, too, of Visioneers operating throughout Africa and rumours of other activity, including the strange story of a woman dressed in white taking over a teenagers' rock concert in Vancouver in Canada. It all makes interesting reading in the Sunday newspapers.

At noon Sunday, in Jerusalem, Mark Venture receives a call from the American-based ZNN news network for an interview to be broadcast Sunday evening in the Middle East and Europe and Sunday morning in North America.

The interview is to be conducted in the lobby of the hotel. As the film crew moves in, curious bystanders gather around. The interviewer is a tall, attractive American, Pamela Barrett, from Minneapolis. Mark Venture sits casually facing her, his deep Australian suntan making for good colour under the bright lights of the hastily erected set. Pamela takes the interview through the background material of the week's events, then asks the central question.

Pamela: *"Mark, what do your Visioneers see for the world? I mean, what's your vision?"*

Mark: "Our vision is clear. We see people everywhere throughout the world sitting down talking about what they would like to see for the world. We talk about a WE future, which means cooperation, participation, sharing—seeing things as a whole acting together. If we look at the history of human endeavour, it's a dismal record in practically every culture: conflict, aggression, war, conquest, destruction. The world doesn't have a future if we continue like that. There are too many of us now and we have too much destructive power. We simply have to change our minds about all that by visioning together something that'll be a whole lot better. We have to pursue a new kind of learning; creative learning. It's learning that helps empower people to understand complex relationships, to listen deeply to one another so they can build something they can all feel good about. It's a long answer, Pamela, but it was a big question."

Pamela: *"Well, yes, on both points. But what are the implications here for us in the Middle East?"*

Mark: "The neighbours here have to create a better neighbourhood. The world can't afford another major war. People can't give up power to despots, either self-styled or elected, and they can't live by the sword and traditions from the past. They have to create together new traditions for the future. They can learn to do this. They just have to know how to use their minds differently."

Pamela: *"But there are people out there with black visions of personal power. What do the Visioneers say about that?"*

Mark: "They are the enemies of the people; the evil presence in the world. That can only be controlled by powerful collective visions of something good. Luis Valdez will be speaking about that tonight."

Pamela: *"Now what about Luis Valdez? He's really got the world intrigued. Who is he? Where is he?"*

Mark: "Luis Valdez is a good friend of the world. He began with his personal mission to speak to the people of South America, but the world started to eavesdrop. It just shows how open the skies now are to words and ideas. So the whole world can hear directly in a few hours from the heart of a man who has no fear and speaks with great passion about his beautiful vision."

Pamela: *"When is this going to happen? How do people tune in?"*

Mark: "He'll broadcast at 5 p.m. tonight, Sunday, Pacific Coast Time in North America. I think that's 4 a.m. Monday morning here. Various networks are still scrambling to see whether they'll broadcast it live. I'm sure ZNN will."

Pamela: *"Well, of course. I take it you're not going to tell us where he's broadcasting from?"*

Mark: "No, I can't tell you that."

Pamela: *"Well, what about your associate here, Esther Fisher? We understand she's being held by Palestinian terrorists. That's a rather dark vision for her, and for you, too, I expect. What can you say about that?"*

Mark: "I think we have to appreciate the power of the media to impact on delicate situations. I can't discuss Esther's future here. I can discuss it only with those who are immediately controlling it. If they've heard anything in their hearts in what I've already said, and if they listen to Luis Valdez tomorrow morning, then hopefully we can begin to show the power of a new vision at work here right away."

Pamela: *"Is that your message to the terrorists?"*

Mark: "I've said what I've said."

The interview continues for several more minutes, but in those few words, Mark has directed the attention of the world toward the prospects of a new beginning.

One Steadfast Hope

Thirteen thousand kilometres away, across two continents and the Atlantic Ocean, the impact of Mark's interview begins to take effect. Like a small snowball rolling down the slopes of the snow-capped Andes in the distance, there's a gathering together of the forces of mass and motion, until a sweeping, unstoppable avalanche of energy is unleashed.

It's 6 p.m. Sunday evening in Chile: two hours to broadcast time for Luis Valdez. George Cardinal is finalizing what he knows about the networks that have agreed either to take the broadcast live, or to replay it as soon as possible in their schedule. He estimates a viewing audience of several hundred million people on every continent.

The presentation has been carefully prepared. Given the global audience, it will be presented by Valdez in two languages, English and Spanish, alternating between speech and sub-titles. The production remains simple, though Cardinal has brought in two technicians to assist. If their space was cramped before, it's now packed to sardine-tin congestion. Once each player is wedged into place, he'll stay there for the duration of the broadcast. One of the walls of the studio has been taken down so that the operation is now open to the house. The time for secrecy is past. This will be the final act on this particular stage. After tonight, they'll leave quickly as agreed to with Mark Venture. All energy is now focused on the final preparation.

Luis Valdez is ready in his mind, but he seeks consolation in his heart. He has left the bustle of the studio with its continual checking and rechecking of technical systems. He kneels quietly in the sanctuary of the Mission of the Holy Virgin and prays quietly to his God.

"Heavenly Father, I am here simply as your servant, Luis Valdez, priest and sinner, full of love in my heart for my Saviour, and troubled in spirit for what the world has made of His loving sacrifice. We have heard, but not listened; we have preached, but not empowered; we have seen, but closed our eyes. And we come now to this turning point in time, aching with the burden of our own willfulness, inflicting our own tortured cravings on the gentle loveliness of our world, which you gave to us for safekeeping. I am not blameless in this, my Father. None of us are, but I seek now with your help to find the words to touch the hearts and minds of enough who will listen, then say: Yes, we must change. We must turn away from what we have seen only with the limited vision of our conscious thinking, without reaching deep within to hear your voice.

"It is time now for me, my Father, to do what I can. May I serve you well in this. May I love in my heart as you have loved: for the beauty of the world, for the loveliness of the unselfish spirit, and for the forgiveness of those who may wish me harm. In all this, I pray to you my God, my Saviour, my Redeemer, and my one steadfast hope for all that yet can be."

He continues to kneel and pray silently in his heart, as the darkness outside gathers, as the minutes tick away, as he waits for George Cardinal to come and tell him it's time.

Their Terrible Assignment

A hundred kilometres away, three men hunched over the hot engine of their stationary jeep curse loudly at the futility of their repeated efforts to get it started and continue on their way.

The captain and his two soldiers have taken off their uniforms and replaced them with leather jackets and dungarees. They look like roughneck hunters out for the kill. Powerful semi-automatic rifles are thrown carelessly in the back of the jeep. Their efforts at disguise have not extended to the vehicle. They had planned to park the military jeep near the village and the mission and cut through the forest on foot for the remaining distance. After killing Valdez, they could then return to the jeep, resume their military roles and arrive officially to investigate the incident. It was a simple, crude plan formed by simple, crude minds. Now, however, it's coming apart. The jeep has been badly overheating for the last hour on the rough roads. Now it has stopped completely. They're losing valuable time while they wait for it to cool.

To bolster their zeal for the mission, two large bottles of cheap whiskey have already been dispatched. The third is half finished. Alcohol, combined with frustration and fear of failure has made them aggressive and violent.

The captain storms around the jeep kicking every wheel, abusing road, vehicle, and occupants with a flood of invective and crudity.

Finally, their despairing efforts to get started again bear fruit. The engine fires into life, and after a half hour's delay, they clamber into the jeep and head off on their terrible assignment.

The World Prepares

Around the world, the Visioneers are preparing to capitalize on the interest being generated by Luis Valdez. Bill Bates has notified everyone and asked them to spread the word.

In Africa, President Mutsandu from his office in Singula in Yarawi has telephoned all members of his visioneering team to promote the broadcast. Even in countries where the media is state controlled, private viewing is being organized where satellite dishes are available to pick up the signal.

From Cambridge, in England, Jeremy Hiscox has asked Lord Nigel Feversham to pass the word down the network of royalty supported foundations. The BBC is already responding by carrying Mark's ZNN interview. Rapidly placed phone calls to people in the academic community are also stimulating interest there. Similarly, from Scotland Irene Henshaw has done what she can to activate the independent schools.

In Paris and Berlin, General Soulière and Boris Gunther are working on the media. Through Prince Rupert, Soulière has also managed to unofficially activate the Unesco network so that in the time available, word is going out to member countries.

In Russia, the task is more difficult. Daniel Thomas and his team at Lake Radovichy have alerted contacts in each of the nearby republics, but it's uncertain what the state controlled news networks will do. At the very least they'll monitor the broadcast and may decide to replay it in whole or in part at a later time.

In China, the situation is much the same. Even with the cooperation of Zhao She Yuhan, Lin Yuen can't expect more than official monitoring at the time of broadcast. However, interest has been created and the possibility exists for hundreds of millions of Chinese to see an edited version at a later time on either the educational or news networks.

Junichi Yakasawya is now in Tokyo and he has caught the interest of several news networks. He has also received a call from Ahiro Morita, a wealthy industrial recluse, who has invited him to his estate in the mountains on the Island of Hokaido to talk about the Visioneers and their work. Junichi plans to watch the Valdez broadcast from there on Monday morning.

In the United States, Bill Bates and Julia McCarthy now seem to have the major networks convinced that they should take the broadcast live. Mark's interview on ZNN, reported several times throughout Sunday morning, was the clincher.

The interest in North America is also being fanned by the continuing wave of excitement created by Theresa Romano, now being called "Momma" Theresa by disc jockeys across the United States and Canada. When Bill Bates tracks her down, she is being interviewed on a New York radio station. She takes his call live and within a few minutes, the whole listening audience hears about terrorism in Israel and its link to the Luis Valdez presentation scheduled for broadcast out of South America in just a few hours time. It's not many more minutes before the word starts to spread across pop radio stations on the continent so that by mid-afternoon on Sunday, a potential audience of several million teenagers and their families has been assembled for Luis Valdez. The word is also telephoned to Sally Hearst in New Zealand where the time is already 3 a.m. on Monday. By the time the kids are having breakfast and listening to their radios, the word is out across New Zealand and Australia, and a few hours later, schools are finalizing arrangements to catch this extraordinary broadcast from South America.

But perhaps the most significant contact is made by Mark himself with India. When he calls, it's early Sunday evening. Indira Murti and Carmen Santander are excited to hear from him.

"Hello Indira, hello Carmen. It seems so long since we spoke. How are you?"

"Oh, Mark," replies Indira, "This is a wonderful place. We've been here a week and it's going to be so hard to leave. We've made marvellous contacts. Word about the Visioneers is spreading all across India. But this is a tortured country. We'll have so much to do to encourage people to build vision and hope for the future. But Baba is magnificent. He'll help us so much. I truly believe he is from God."

As Indira says this, she gasps a little.

"What is it, Indira?" asks Mark.

"Oh, Baba has just come in," says Indira. Another pause. Then Indira adds: "Mark, Baba would like to speak with you."

"Hello Mark," says Baba. "Welcome back to our Place of Peace and Serenity."

"Then you know I've watched you before," says Mark, recalling clearly the image of the saffron-robed figure he had seen from the Visioneering Room.

"But of course," replies Baba. "You and I both have a way of coming and going in the world. Yours is to manage a grand project, mine is to speak in people's hearts. Soon we'll work together."

"I would like that," says Mark.

"Indira and Carmen are great souls," continues Baba, "They are wonderful Visioneers. They will achieve much, especially after the events of tomorrow. Now, I must go. Goodbye, Mark. We'll speak again soon. Be of good cheer. What happens with Luis and Esther will be of great importance."

With that, he's gone.

Indira comes back on the line.

"What did he mean, Mark? What's happening with Esther and Luis?"

Mark tells her, sensing all the while that Baba knows much more than he does.

Waiting in Jerusalem

In Jerusalem, Mark calls on David Roth as he sits beside the casket of his dead son, Joshua, in the Beth-Judah Funeral Home. It's almost midnight on Sunday evening. Mina Roth is there too. She was released from hospital earlier in the day. Her face is swollen from cuts and bruises and her heavily bandaged right arm is supported in a sling. Husband and wife are keeping their lonely vigil with their son before he is to be buried tomorrow.

Mark sits with them for an hour and they say together the prayer in memory of a son and the Mourner's Kaddish: *Veyischor Ehlohim nishmat benee moiree*—Remember God the soul of my honoured son—*sheh halach le ohlamoh*—who has gone to his eternal rest. *Yisgadal veyiskadash shmay rab boh*—Glorified and sanctified be God's great name.

Then Mark asks quietly, "David, I would like you to come with me for a few hours. I need your help to free Esther."

David looks at Mina. She nods gravely.

"Yes, you must go," she says. "I'll be fine. There are many to help. Go now and bring Esther back."

An hour later, Mark and David are at the Ben Gurion Airport waiting for Mohammed Hussein. Since Mark contacted him, Mohammed has been travelling continuously to get there. Security is intense. Mohammed is closely interrogated, but his United Nations credentials get him through quickly. Mark greets him, introduces David, and they head back to Jerusalem.

It's after 3 a.m. Mark has made arrangements with ZNN to watch the Luis Valdez broadcast at their studios. When they arrive, Pamela Barrett, who had interviewed Mark sixteen hours earlier, is there.

"Hello," she smiles cheerily enough for the early hour. "You see, you convinced me that this is one broadcast I shouldn't miss. We're recording it and will broadcast it at 8 a.m. Who are your friends?"

Mark introduces David and Mohammed. Pamela's journalist's instincts are immediately aroused when she realizes what the three of them together represent.

"Why do I have this feeling that I'm standing at the edge of history with you fellows?" she asks with a wry smile. "Can you fill me in?"

"There'll be no interviews now, Pamela," says Mark. "Maybe later. I'll let you know. Thank you for arranging this part of it."

"Okay, Mark, but I know a good story when I smell one, and I'm sure picking up the scent here."

With that, she leaves them to talk over coffee in the studio lounge, while they wait for Luis Valdez.

CHAPTER TEN

A
Light
Goes Out

THE MOUNTAIN AIR IS CRISP and sharp and the stars stand out like zircons in the dark, moonless sky. Luis Valdez puts his hand on George Cardinal's arm.

"Look up there, George," he says. "Look there. Have you ever seen such a sky? The good Lord has sent a hundred trillion fireflies to light the heavens tonight for the safe passage of our words. Soon they'll be dancing on one of those smallest lights, the satellites sent by man to encircle the world. Oh, this could be such a wonderful universe if we could just take the evil out of it."

"We will, good friend," says George. "Tonight with the world listening, you take another step. Now we must go in. It's fifteen minutes to time."

"Yes, I'm ready. Let's go."

Inside the house, the preparation for the transmission is done. The whole back end of the building has become a studio. The set remains simple and cramped with a few visuals added. The lighting is stronger and a second miniaturized camera has been added that can be moved around to catch best angles. The other camera is fixed on the set. Two assistants double as camera operators and technicians, leaving George Cardinal free to direct and monitor the production.

Luis Valdez goes to the set. He's wearing a simple white cassock. His face is composed and serene. He settles himself beside the blue and white globe of the world that he shares as the dominant visual. He smiles at everyone and nods that he's ready. George Cardinal counts down the seconds. A technician brings up background music. The camera focuses on a simple text, the same in English and in Spanish, to announce the broadcast to a waiting world: "Luis Valdez—Vision." The signal goes out to the satellite, technicians around the world scramble to bring it in as audiences on every continent, in every time zone, curiously wait to see what this is all about.

Vermin

Five kilometres away, Luis Valdez's would-be assassins drive recklessly along the last stretch of the rough and twisting mountain road that leads up to the mission. Knowing already that he has failed in his assignment to silence the priest before the broadcast, the captain has abandoned all thought of caution.

"Ayee!" he shrieks into the wind as he sees the hour come and go on his watch. "Faster, drive faster!" he yells at the driver. "What's wrong with you? What are you doing? You're dead, you hear me, you're dead! We're all dead! Faster! Don't you know the time? They're out there watching. The whole world's watching this miserable priest, and you drive like your head's on backwards. Dead! We're all dead! We could've stopped him. We had the chance. We were the only ones who knew. We could have retired rich for life. Don't you see? This was El Condor business. No one messes up with El Condor. We're dead! All of us are dead."

"We can still stop him," this from the third soldier, in the back seat, leaning forward, shouting into the wind, gripping hard to the seat against the bone-crushing bouncing of the jeep. "We'll be there in five minutes. What can he say in five minutes? And then he's gone. Pssfit! Snuffed out—off the air, forever. Goodbye priest!"

"Maybe he hasn't started yet," adds the soldier doing the driving, struggling hard with the steering wheel and gears as he drives the vehicle mercilessly over rocks as big as footballs and in and out of half-metre deep potholes. "How could a stupid priest up here know what time it is?"

"Shut your face and drive!" bellows the captain. "He's not so stupid that he hasn't done this before. But we'll stop him before he's done. If I'm dead, then he's dead, the snivelling little holy freak."

The jeep roars on into the night, its headlights bouncing like the crazed eyes of a lunatic stumbling in the dark. The lights of the village come into view, very faint, and above them fainter still, the one flickering light at the mission. The road straightens a little. The driver pushes the accelerator to the floor. The jeep leaps forward with a surge of power. Too late, they see the huge pine tree fallen down across the road. With a sickening crash, the jeep ploughs headlong into the heavy trunk. The fan blades tear a screaming gouge into the radiator, shooting spouts of boiling water into the air.

The occupants are flung about like corks. The captain catapults over the windshield and lands heavily among the branches of the pine tree. The roaring of the wind, the racing of the engine, both are gone. The silence settles back upon the scene as quickly as it was shattered. Darkness rushes in, and all trace of the mishap disappears, save for two twin beams of light stabbing upwards from the headlights and the low moaning of the captain among the branches of the pine tree.

Vision and Violence

When Luis Valdez speaks, he begins in English in recognition of his international audience. Spanish sub-titles run for his South American viewers. As the transmission continues, he will reverse the use of speech and subtitles in English and Spanish.

"My friends around the world," he begins, "how swift the arrow flies when it is released! Only one week ago I looked for a way to bring words of hope to my brothers and sisters of Latin America, who too long have suffered under the burden of oppression and violence. What I said then mysteriously found its way to other lands and touched hearts in many places. Even when my words were not completely understood, they played upon a deep and powerful longing across this planet for peace and respect among a single human family. That so many more of your have come this time to hear, not only touches my heart with deep humility, but also empowers me with the hope that we truly now are reaching beyond all bounds of previous limitations to forge on Earth a universal fellowship that can endure forever.

"I want to take you now, my friends, with me in the rich creative power of our marvellous human minds to see the world that we were truly born to know. It's not the world we see today, but it's the world that we together could build tomorrow. Nor is it a world that waits on the other side of the pain and suffering of this one. No, it's the world that we live in now which we claim for our own and give as a heritage to all who follow. It's a world that flowers first in the fertile gardens of our minds, our inner selves, where God has placed his own universal spirit to be a sure and certain guide if we allow ourselves to listen and to see.

"I want you to close your eyes now, my friends, to see this other world. You will not see it here in my face or on your television screen or anywhere around you. You will see it only in the rich tapestry of your mind. Close your eyes now and follow my voice.

"Imagine with me the blue sky, arching over all the Earth in a great blue dome, gathering all of us together, in this one great fertile garden where we live. Imagine the green fields and the orchards, the rich harvests, and the markets full of food and busy smiling people. Imagine the forests and the lakes and the rivers. See the wild creatures that live there as part of the life of the planet. See yourself moving among them, recognizing all of them as co-inhabitants of this rich and fertile place. Imagine the great oceans swelling and heaving through all eternity, teaming and rich with fish life and huge whales that roam free and magnificent. And see the mountains everywhere reaching skywards, snow capped, rocky, standing bold and resolute against time and change.

"All of this you see under the great blue dome of the sky. You see yourself a part of it, intimately woven into the fabric. And you stand back further now and see the Earth as a planet swimming blue and white in the immensity of space, and within that, the other planets and the stars of the galaxies—galaxy folding into galaxy, all expanding out into the immensity of the universe.

"You see people around you, of all races and cultures, everyone an individual, old or young, strong or weak, each one part of this energy, part of this life force, part of the same universal spirit that moves in you. They are a part of you, and you are a part of everything and everyone around. It is one great vision of a single whole, undivided universe that flows in you and through you to every other part of it.

"Look, my friends, look in your minds, and see yourselves living in such a world. How is it different from what we know today, from what we know of history? See there, see how we would hold in great respect the sanctity of human life. We would not kill or slaughter in battle or allow to perish in hunger or neglect any one of these our brothers and sisters. Each one is the most marvellous being of a supreme and wonderful creation, whose mind and soul is alive with the same universal energy.

"Our minds would know nothing of destruction and violence against a fellow human being. There could be no thought of that, no badge of honour for taking human life, no comfort in material riches while others suffer in the agony of despair and deprivation.

"How would we build our economies if our first thought was for our brothers rather than ourselves? How rich would we find ourselves in resources if we turned away from building weapons of destruction? How much energy and wealth would we find if we put aside the conflict of legal battle and fierce aggressive competition?

"And where, my friends, in such a world would there be a place for the villains that we know today? Where would be the overlords of crime who swell and bloat on threat of violence? Where would we find the dealers in arms and munitions and the manufacturers who grow rich today in producing such affrights to human decency? Where would they be, my friends, in our world if we did not write them in? Where would the monsters be if we took away from them all their power to be so, by taking out of our own minds all thought of hatred and violence?

"I know, my friends, that these thoughts are not new. The questions have been asked by people of good will for hundreds of generations. And always they have sought to answer them in one way, in every culture, the one way, and it has failed. It has failed consistently to bring the peace and the decency to the world that so many long to see.

"The one way has been the book of rules, the commandments, the code of ethics, the tablets of stone—and always they failed, not completely, but failed enough to bring the world in our day to the brink of destruction.

"Why do they fail, such noble and well-intentioned codes and rules of conduct? They fail because we have not understood the full nobility of the human mind as a supreme creative force. My friends, you and I, each one of us, can only be what we imagine ourselves to be. And we cannot imagine a negative. Oh yes, we can be fearful and see ourselves as failures, but even then we are imagining a concrete outcome, a negative which we have chosen to make positive. We cannot have a world without crime or bloodshed if all we do is say, 'Thou shalt not steal' or 'Thou shalt not kill.' All that such rules lead us to are images of stealing and killing, and finally a conviction that there can be no other way.

"But now, my friends, we know that there can be another way. Because swelling up across the whole vast richness of the human minds on this planet is a revulsion at our failure as the most noble creature on God's Earth to live up to our nobility. And out of this moment of crisis, we are poised to take the great leap forward, to turn inwards in our minds to discover there the bold and beautiful images of another world, and to raise them clear and shining, and to strengthen them every day by each rich mind adding its piece of positive creation, daring to imagine what we can be, what the world can be, what life on Earth can be, because we, as its co-creators, have seen it, and decided that this will be so."

With his words, energy and passion have flooded into Luis Valdez's face. Those watching in the studio are transfixed with the power concentrating around this slight man. And beyond the studio, the energy projects through the harsh and critical scrutiny of the television camera, transforming the medium, overcoming its limitations, because deep in the soul of this one man is the burning desire to move the world to see what he can see and bring it within the grasp of enough to make it happen.

He continues without pause, spinning out image upon image of the possible, in every setting, in every land, challenging, provoking, calling upon everyone to see and to act and to come together in a surging wave of visioneering across the face of the Earth. Minutes tick by unnoticed as this one man calls up across every time zone the latent yearning creativity of humankind for peaceful, empowering co-existence.

"If we understand, if we truly see that in each one of us on this planet is the energy of the universe, the spirit of God, running freely, then how can we raise our hand against our brothers and sisters? In destroying the least among them, we destroy part of creation and part of ourselves.

"My friends, it's time now for us to take back into our own hands the responsibility for building a vision of the future that's full of the joy of human cooperation and caring.

"To those out there who are calling us to hate and kill, we must say, 'No more! That does not fit our vision.' To those who have gathered around them, power bases of evil and terror, we must say, 'Enough! Your wickedness cannot be tolerated.' To those who drive with passion and greed to enrich themselves at the expense of others, we must say, 'No, you cannot do this. Our vision sees all of humanity living well with dignity.' To those who prey upon the poor and disadvantaged and destroy their minds with drugs and malnutrition, we must say, 'You are finished. We will care for our own and restore them to the dignity of the godliness within them.'

"My friends, the world is about to transform to a new age of enlightenment, gathering together around the powerful visions for good that lie in the hearts of the overwhelming majority of human beings on the planet. Those visions will now come forward and wash over the ugly, scarred remnants of a violent past, which we will not accept as the future. We are taking the future into our hands. We are enlivening our minds with visions of the possible. We are taking away the power from those who too long have held us back from all that we can be.

"Tomorrow I ask you to go out and form yourselves into bands of Visioneers. Put up your dreams. Talk to each other and listen. Listen deeply to the wisdom of your collective minds at work, building something strong and rich and beautiful for all.

"This is our heritage. This is the nobility of our human spirit. This is the time of new and wonderful beginnings. This, my friends, is . . . "

But Luis Valdez does not finish the statement. At that moment, a resounding crash reverberates in the studio. The priest turns, on camera, and sees what the watching world cannot see. A blood stained figure, his clothes ripped and half torn from his body, has stumbled wild-eyed and ghastly into the studio. In shaking hands, he levels as he comes a heavy 45-calibre revolver, aiming it directly at Luis Valdez.

"Now, priest, die for El Condor!" the words spit out as excrement of hate. The revolver explodes, once, twice, three times and the heavy slugs slam into the priest's chest, flinging him with their dreadful impact against the back wall of the set.

Transfixed and immobile with horror, the camera operator keeps his camera trained on the priest, and as a gasping world watches, blood spreads over the simple white cassock. With a howl of rage, George Cardinal launches himself forward around the set moving on the intruder. The revolver turns toward him. He weaves. The shot rings out and he feels its hot breath sear his cheek. A second shot also passes harmlessly. Then, he's upon the man, whom he recognizes as the army captain he had first watched through binoculars only a week ago. The fury of Cardinal's attack carries them crashing against the far wall of the room. The revolver spins free from the assailant's hand as Cardinal pounds the man's head incessantly on the floor. In a moment, all resistance is gone and the captain lies twisted and senseless by the door.

It all happened in less than thirty seconds. The second camera operator also acted instinctively and followed Cardinal's attack. His co-worker, recovering slightly, switches the image being transmitted to the world away from the dying priest to the shaking picture of Cardinal hammering the attacker senseless. The camera continues to roll as Cardinal now leaps to his feet and rushes back to Luis Valdez. What the camera shows is then etched indelibly into the minds of millions of viewers across every continent.

The burly Cree Indian chief, tears streaming down his face, tenderly takes the head of his friend in two huge hands and presses his lips to the now lifeless face. His body shuddering with uncontrollable grief, Cardinal gathers the crumpled figure in his arms, comes slowly to his feet and turns to face the camera. The world sees the slight figure in blood-stained cassock, who only moments earlier had spoken so passionately about a future vision of peace and love, lying lifeless in the arms of his friend. The head hangs back and one arm falls loosely towards the floor. For those who can recognize it, it's the very image of the Pieta—the crucified Christ cradled in the arms of his mother. For others, it sears into memory as a testament of the ruthless violence the victim had denounced and which the world can no longer tolerate.

George Cardinal speaks into the great hush that has settled in the studio and around the world.

"In his closing words, he was going to talk of love. There was no one more qualified to do it. Lying here in my arms is a man who had more love in his heart than it seems the world can hold. He was going to say that the world cannot continue in senseless conflict. He could see in the hearts of his fellow human beings something better than that. Now here he is, struck down by the very violence he sought to replace with love.

"Was he right? Was he right, this sweet and gentle man, to have such hope and vision for the world? I swear at the moment I cannot tell. My heart howls out in anger that the world could take his life like this. He did his best and now he's here, broken and bleeding for it.

"He couldn't even finish the broadcast, and I must do it for him. So he might have the dignity of a decent closing. The world at least owes him that much, a decent closing."

George Cardinal is struggling for words. He wants desperately to end the whole horrible nightmare.

"Luis Valdez is signing off, for the last time—not in the way he would have wished, but as the world has chosen to give him. God grant that the world may now be the better for it."

With that, George Cardinal turns and carries his friend abruptly off the set. The camera continues to run for a few moments, recording only the blue world globe and the empty space beside it. Then, a confused and still terrified technician cuts the lights and ends the transmission. Around the world, a stunned audience continues to watch while local stations struggle to find their own ways of interpreting what has happened.

You Must Go On

For Mark Venture watching in Jerusalem, the impact is electric. Gasps of despair and amazement burst from the small group of viewers in the studio during the last thirty seconds of the telecast. Mark has sprung to his feet. To Mohammed and David, he snaps, "Wait here for me!" and brushes past a still reeling Pamela Barrett to the door of the studio and out into the hallway.

Watching everything from your thinking room, you know that Mark must speak with you. In a moment his face, haggard with despair, stares out at you from the television screen.

"He was my friend and brother," he cries. "I had a premonition that something like this would happen. Why didn't I get him out of there?"

"Mark," you say, "I think he knew it, too. There was no stopping it. Now we must go on. You must go on. The world is waiting for you."

"You must speak to George," he says. "Don't leave him there like that, all alone. I can't reach him from here. Tell him to carry on for Luis, for all of us. I'll be in touch with him as soon as I can. Right now I have to go to Esther to prevent another tragedy. Will you tell him that from me? And tell him, please tell him, that I'm sorry. Will you tell him?"

"Yes, Mark, yes," you reply, "I'll tell him."

"Mark! Mark! What are you doing?" Pamela Barrett has come out of the studio in Jerusalem looking for him. "You've got to come back. The whole world's going crazy."

Mark re-enters the studio. Pamela Barrett is almost incoherent with excitement.

"Mark," she cries. "You've got to make a statement. We've got calls coming in from all around the world. This is a mind blower! People are already saying it's a second crucifixion—this time done live on television with the whole world watching. Do you know the implications of that? If you don't, ask your friend, Bill Bates. He's on the phone from Los Angeles."

She pushes a handset at him.

"Hello, Bill. It's Mark."

"Mark, thank God I've reached you!" Bates' voice is shrill with excitement. "What a thing to happen! This country's going crazy. I swear the phone lines of every television station from here to New York are jammed with people trying to find out what they just saw. I'm sorry, Mark. What can I say? Luis was just incredible, but to be gunned down like that! It makes me sick to the stomach. Do you know anything more about it?"

"Not much," Mark replies. "We've got to be careful how we react. Esther's still out there in the hands of terrorists. We can't say anything they'll misinterpret."

"I understand. But Mark, you need to make some kind of statement right now. Just give me a minute and I'll put you on air and they'll hook you into the networks across the country. They're all still open with commentators trying to think of something to say."

"All right. I'll make a brief statement."

"What's that?" Pamela has been listening and explodes, fearful of losing a scoop. "Are you going to make a statement for him while you're sitting right here in our news studio?"

"Come on, Pamela," Mark is exasperated. "This isn't a competition! One of the world's most decent men has just been brutally murdered and an equally brave and sensitive woman is being held here right under our noses. I'm not interested in whose scoop it is. I just want to get Esther out safely and avoid any more tragedies. After that, I'll come back here and give you the full story."

"Okay," says Pamela, "that's a deal."

"Mark?" It's Bill Bates again. "Are you ready?"

"Yes."

"Okay, we're live now . . . This is Bill Bates in Los Angeles, speaking with Mark Venture in Jerusalem. Mark is the leader of the Visioneers and like the rest of us, has just witnessed the tragic murder of Luis Valdez while he was broadcasting his vision of peace for the world. Mark, can you help us to understand what's going on?"

"What we've just seen is brutality at its worst." Mark's voice is trembling with emotion. "Luis Valdez stood for decency and love in the human family. He believed that people are good. He was gunned down, for whatever reasons, by a brutal minority who think they have the power to behave like that. The world can no longer tolerate such wretched wickedness.

"And that's the basic message of the Visioneers. Luis Valdez spoke of it with all of the passion of an eloquent and committed human being. The way he died speaks with equal clarity of the alternative. Now people must choose which kind of future they want to have. As Visioneers, we're confident that the overwhelming desire for decency and peace abroad in the hearts of people in every land will win the day.

"That's all I have to say for now. I'll speak again soon. May I ask that everyone listening say a prayer of thanks for the life of Luis Valdez."

Mark puts down the phone and signals to Mohammed Hussein and David Roth that they must go. He nods to Pamela and the three men leave the building in the darkness just before the dawn.

CHAPTER ELEVEN

Making Room
for a
Miracle

T HE THREE MEN HAVE BREAKFAST in a coffee shop near the studio, then drive a few kilometres south of the city in David Roth's car through the occupied territory towards Bethlehem. Despite strict surveillance by Israeli soldiers, they have little difficulty in entering the occupied territory because of David's pass as a government official with frequent business there. First light is just touching the Judean Hills when Mark tells David to pull off the highway onto a dirt road winding through terraced hillsides near the ancient birthplace of Jesus of Nazareth.

Bringing Esther Home

"Stop! Pull over right here!" Mark says suddenly.

They have stopped under an embankment about 200 metres from a group of squat, red-earth buildings, tucked into the terraced hillside in a grove of olive trees.

"Down there, in that house a little apart from the others. That's where they're holding Esther and Jenny," he says.

"Come on, Mark, how do you know that?" asks David, incredulously. "Look, here we are, just a few miles from Jerusalem, near one of the busiest tourist sites in Israel. Why would terrorists be holding their hostages here?"

"I don't know," replies Mark, "but that's where they are. Now we have to get them out."

"If you're sure that's the place," continues David, "then all we've got to do is go back and get an army patrol and we'll have the place surrounded in a few minutes."

"Yes, I know, but I don't think that's the way to do it."

"Do you have a better plan?"

"Maybe. I'm not sure. I want to take a closer look. Will both of you stay here and wait for me?"

David Roth is clearly very nervous.

"Look, Mark. I've got a great respect for who you are and what you seem to be able to do. But this is my country and we're sitting here unescorted and unarmed in occupied territory and you say there's a band of terrorists down there. If that's true, then the last thing you want to be doing is walking around in full view. They've probably already spotted the car which makes us sitting ducks. I tell you the only sensible thing to do is to let the army handle it."

"Given conventional wisdom, I'm sure you're right," replies Mark. "But conventional wisdom so far has resulted in bombing and hostage taking. I'm not interested in more of that. We have Mohammed with us. I told them I would bring him and I have. I want you here, too, David, because you've been the catalyst in this tragic episode. We have to take a different tack from bombing and killing. I can't ask you to stay. I know what you've been through. And there's Luis Valdez, shot down in cold blood before our eyes. And Esther, the dearest person in the world to me, caught up in violence, too. More of that is not the way to go. But, you're right, I don't know that for sure. I may get us all killed or taken hostage, but then again, we may pull off a miracle—and the world could use a few miracles about now. What do you say Mohammed? You've been very quiet. What do you think we should do?"

"I'm an Arab," replies Mohammed. "I'm not in danger here. I believe I can help you, but you must follow your wisdom on this. I could go down there and try to negotiate, but not many miracles ever happen through negotiation. If you want a breakthrough, you need a bolder initiative."

"David?" Mark asks. "Will you trust me a little on this? I need some time to reflect alone. Will you wait for me?"

There's a pause. David puts his head down on his hands as they tighten their grip on the steering wheel. White pressure points show through his knuckles. Finally, he says softly, "Go ahead. I'll wait."

Mark gets out of the car and walks slowly towards the houses, staying in the shadow of the embankment and being careful to keep a line of olive trees between him and the buildings. He skirts the main group, then pauses on the crest of a hill overlooking the one where he knows the women are being held. It's only a hundred metres away now. He could easily be seen if he stepped out from behind the cover of the trees. On his stomach, in the soft sandy earth of the road, he crawls to a good vantage point, and lies there motionless staring down at the building. Somewhere a cock crows, breaking the stillness of the morning, while the tinkle of bells comes intermittently from a small group of goats feeding on the coarse, short grass further down along the roadside.

As Mark lies there looking at the place where Esther is being held, his mind is a torrent of questions. Was David right? Are men who would drag innocent women out of their car and hold them hostage likely to understand any language other than violence? Is this any different from the hideous spectacle he had just seen on television? Sweet, trusting, passionate Luis Valdez gunned down by a savagery he didn't understand. Or perhaps he did understand it only too well, and knew he had to push it to the final limit to make a breakthrough. But Luis Valdez was gambling with his own life. Here, Esther's life is at stake. Something grips tight in Mark's throat as he thinks about the time they spent under the star-filled sky in Australia less than two weeks ago.

He stares hard at the house, wanting to see past the drab exterior, to be inside, to be with Esther, cutting her free from her bonds. Revulsion rises in him stronger now. What wretches they are, these men who capture innocent women and gun down helpless priests! Perhaps Bill Bates and David Roth are right. The only justice they understand comes out the end of a barrel. If so, then he should get the army now and let them take over.

But somewhere deep inside his mind, another voice is talking. It's very faint, as if a long way off. There are no words, only a feeling, a sense that he must try another way. But what? He goes over in his mind word for word his telephone conversation with the terrorist almost twenty-four hours ago. The man was belligerent and crude, but in the end, he wanted to talk. When he knew that Mohammed was part of the Visioneers, he wanted to talk. Now Mark could go one better. He could arrive on their doorstep with Mohammed, clearly showing he knew where they were hiding. And what would they talk about? As Mohammed said, he could probably negotiate something, but there are no breakthroughs in negotiations, only tactical gains and losses—and the world needs breakthroughs. More than ever after tonight, after the murder of Luis Valdez, the world needs breakthroughs.

Nor does the irony escape him. Lying here in the dirt outside Bethlehem, birthplace of Jesus, who was to be called the Christ, Saviour of humanity, bringing his message of inextinguishable love. But in the end, they extinguished his life, just a few miles from here, at Calvary, with the greatest possible brutality on a wicked cross of rough timber, driving nails with searing pain through his hands and feet, while the crowd looked on. And two thousand years later, Luis Valdez, is shot three times through the chest with heavy calibre bullets, thrusting the life out of him, again while the crowd looked on.

And here in this dust, the very same dust that Joseph may have walked in to bring his pregnant wife to Bethlehem, lurks the same violence, unabated, for two thousand years, in the face of the most extraordinarily loving life the world has ever seen. It's the same bloody violence that takes the lives of innocent people in bomb blasts, and puts the knife to Esther's throat, and guns down a gentle priest; the same bloody, useless, wretched violence, while the crowd watches.

But this time it's the whole world that's watching, not just a mob on a hill outside Jerusalem, but the whole world. And it's the same world that has come through the most violent century in human history, and seen at the beginning of its last decade, on these same desert sands, only a few hundred kilometres from here, at the Persian Gulf, the most incredible display of precision violence raging against incomprehensible savagery and brutality.

How long can the world watch all this until it says with one voice, swelling louder than all the bomb blasts in hell: Enough! Stop! Now! How long? Dare one hope, lying here in the dust just outside Bethlehem, that the answer might be, "No longer. This is the time when we turn away from all that wretchedness and embrace the other side of life."

Filled with this torrent of thoughts, Mark looks away from the hostage house and glances down the road where the rising sun sends shards of long light slanting down through the trees onto the dusty surface. He catches his breath. Walking towards him, no more than fifty metres away, is a tall figure in a saffron-coloured robe, a man, coming slowly down the road, looking directly at him.

Mark springs to his feet, unconsciously taking care to remain screened from the buildings on the terrace below, but focusing intently on the man coming towards him. There's something very familiar in the stance, in the way he moves, effortlessly, almost gliding. Mark has seen him before. But where? Could it be, that here, at Bethlehem, in this holy, tragic land, that two thousand years later . . . ? Could this be, coming towards him, bathed in the glow of early morning sunlight . . . ? Could it be, images from his childhood in Sunday school, the figure of Jesus gathering the children around him . . . ? Could it be, here, the figure of Christ coming towards him, on this dusty road, a transfiguration . . . ? Too absurd to imagine, but, perhaps, so familiar . . . ? Could it be, Jesus?

He's less than twenty metres away. Mark moves towards him. The man steps into a pool of shadow, his face not quite clear, but slim, clean shaven, long curly hair. He stops, waiting, watching. Mark moves closer. They're close enough to speak easily.

"Hello, Mark. I said we would talk again soon." The voice is soft and melodious, speaking in perfect English. His face is clearly visible now, high cheek bones, luminous brown eyes, a clear white smile, features unmistakably Indian.

"Baba!" exclaims Mark. "For a moment I thought you were . . . " He breaks off.

"Jesus?" smiles Baba. "It would be appropriate, wouldn't it? Do you know Jesus, Mark?"

"I thought I did there for a bit, a lot of Sunday school stuff comes to mind. I expect it was quite different in reality. But you, Baba. I think I know more of you. I've heard you speaking to Indira and Carmen at Ventagiri. What are you doing here? Is this your place, too? Are you Jesus and Buddha and Baba all in one?"

Baba smiles. "Ah, Mark you've come directly to the point. But it doesn't really matter who I am. It's how I can help you now that counts. You have lost Luis, and I grieve with you for that. He was a great man of peace and love with much wisdom for the world, and strangely he will touch the world more in his dying than in his living.

"But you, Mark, your work is for the living. The world is waiting breathless this morning, part stunned, mostly still unknowing. How you move now will make a great difference. Luis prepared your way. Now you must follow through.

"And it begins, down there in that house, where hate-filled minds are holding Esther, your Esther. You must free her, but in the way you do it you can either move the world a little or lose the chance. Your heart is full of anger against the brutality that seems to run unfettered. But, Mark, what you must know, and this is what I have come to tell you, you must know that the brutality has almost run its course. It has taken the world to the brink. Now you and your Visioneers, and many millions of like-minded souls across the planet, are moving to take history away from the brink, toward the horizon.

"And it always begins here in the present, with the next step. It depends on how you act, either with an open heart, filled with the love of God, knowing the oneness, the ocean of the universal *Atma*, the connection of all things in love; or whether you act in stubborn, perhaps violent opposition, repaying brutality with brutality, an eye for an eye. Sometimes leaders don't seem to have a choice. Even to do good they have to act brutally in a brutal world. But your leadership is not of that order, Mark. You have chosen a different path. Your Visioneers are out there as beacons of light for a possible future most people haven't dared to imagine. In the last forty-eight hours, the forces of evil have been lining up to take the initiative away from you. Now you have the opportunity to take it back on a world stage of unprecedented possibility.

"And it begins now, within the next few minutes, when you go to bring Esther back. The world is watching, Mark. I've come to tell you that, and to give you courage. You are not at the beginning. The world, the universe, is primed for a breakthrough in human consciousness. You're at the eye of the hurricane. Go and act now, with your heart, with your inner wisdom, and you'll see a glorious movement, still small, but moving, the source, the essence of the powerful forces for change ready to sweep the Earth."

As he finishes speaking, Baba smiles the same enigmatic smile as at their last meeting. He embraces Mark warmly and looks deep into his eyes.

Mark nods, knowing that Baba will leave now.

"Thank you for coming," he says. "I hope I might see you again soon."

"When you've done what you must do," replies Baba, "we'll meet again. In the meantime, I am at hand. Goodbye for now."

He moves off swiftly, walking back the way he had come. Mark watches for a moment, then turns away and sets off for his companions at the car. He doesn't look back, for he senses that the road is empty, that Baba is gone, if, indeed, he was ever there.

At the car, Mohammed and David greet him anxiously.

"Thank God, Mark," says David, "you've been gone almost thirty minutes. We were getting concerned."

"I'm sorry to keep you waiting," replies Mark, "But I'm ready now. Did you two take the time to talk?"

"Yes," says Mohammed, "we're strange bedfellows, Jew and Arab, but we come together on one point, love of family and homeland, and the desire in the end to live in peace."

"When you can each see the other's peace and work towards it, then we'll all be moving to a better time." Mark looks each man closely in the eye.

"I want both of you to come with me now to meet these men and bring Esther back. Will you come?"

"Just like that? Walk up to their door?" asks David, again very nervous.

"Yes, David," replies Mark. "I know it's dangerous for you, but, please trust me, a lot depends on your coming."

"Did you discover something out there that gives you confidence for such a course?" asks David.

"Yes, I did," replies Mark.

"Can I ask what?"

"You can ask, but I'm not sure I can tell you, other than to say that I believe if we go down there together, we have a chance to make a great difference."

"And what about Mina and Sarah if you're wrong? In a few hours, we're going to bury Joshua. And these may be the criminals that killed him. How can you ask me to walk in amongst them? There's no sense to that."

"There's no sense to any of the conflict here, only hatred. I'm asking you to put that aside and come with me. I think Mina understood that when she let you leave with me from the funeral home. I'm looking for a miracle, David, and to find it we have to make room for it to happen. Will you come?"

At that moment, Mohammed puts his arm around David's shoulders.

The three of them stand silently together. A minute passes. David breathes heavily. He searches with agonized eyes the faces of his two companions, then bites his lips and nods. The three of them set off along a path leading to the building on the terrace below.

The sun is well up now and when they come out onto the road leading up to and past the buildings, they're in full view of anyone who might be watching. The road is empty. At first there's no sign of movement anywhere. Then, as they come to the first house and walk close by the front door, they see activity inside: children's faces pressing against window panes, staring out. A dog howls at the second house and comes trotting around from behind, a strange three-legged tawny mongrel, looking at them, shaking his head and growling a little. Chickens scurry across the road ahead. They're at the fourth house and an old man stands in the doorway. He's wearing a checkered Palestinian headdress and tattered black robe. He spits heavily in the dirt as they pass, but says nothing. The fifth house, where they're heading, is about fifty metres off, tucked further back into the terrace. A battered black car of indeterminate make and vintage is parked at the side. Mark glances over his shoulder. The road behind them has suddenly filled with people, children and adults, but there's no sound, only a sea of eyes staring at the three tall strangers: one an Arab in headdress and casual shirt and slacks, another Caucasian, brown-haired and suntanned, the third, Semitic, not an Arab, probably Jewish.

The three men have arrived in front of the fifth house. Heavy curtains drape the windows. The door is firmly closed. Mark Venture knocks loudly. There's no answer. He knocks again, rapping a little. Still no answer. He tries the handle. Locked. He knocks again and when there's still no answer, he turns to the others and signals that they should try the back.

At that moment, two men rush out from each side of the house. They're carrying automatic weapons slung over their necks and trained directly on the three visitors. Over their heads and across their faces they wear blue checkered headgear, so that only their eyes, cold and intense, are visible. They shout orders in Arabic, and wave the guns menacingly. Inside, one of the curtains is suddenly dashed aside and a man looks out. For a moment, he surveys the scene outside, then leaves the window and throws open the door, standing arrogantly in the doorway.

He seems young. His clothes are black, all black. It's the most noticeable feature about him: black shirt, black pants, and black running shoes. His headdress, like the others, is checkered blue and drapes over his shoulders and across his face as a mask. His eyes, rock hard and cold, stare at the three men before him. In his hand, he holds a heavy, long German pistol, pointing directly at Mark. More threatening than that, however, is an intense, black energy emanating from him.

"I'm Mark Venture." Mark's voice is strong and confident, confronting the other's energy, and resonating to carry into the darkened rooms inside.

"This is Mohammed Hussein and David Roth. We've come for Esther Fisher and Jenny Lovicks."

A flicker passes across the cold eyes, but he says nothing. He stands in the doorway, feet planted firmly apart, watching them intensely and waiting for something. There's a scuffle of sound at the side of the house and another armed man comes sliding in a shower of small stones down the embankment. He says something in Arabic to the man in the doorway and holds up a black plastic object with wires trailing from it, waving it in the air for everyone to see.

Mohammed speaks out angrily in Arabic. To Mark and David he says in English, "They've found the car and torn out the distributor. I told them there was no cause for that. We have come alone."

Mark nods. To the man in the doorway he says, "I spoke on the telephone yesterday with someone. Was it you?"

The man almost imperceptibly moves his head up and down. He's obviously trying to assess the situation of three apparently unarmed men on his doorstep asking for the return of the hostages.

"Good," Mark continues. "I said I would get Mohammed Hussein to speak to you. Now, I've gone one better and brought him directly here. He's already told you we're alone and unarmed. There's no need to wave all these guns at us or interfere with our car. We've come in peace to collect our friends."

The three Arabs outside the house all speak at once to the man in the doorway, waving their weapons and fidgeting nervously. He snaps an order and they quieten down. Silence settles, uncomfortable, tense.

"Look," Mark intervenes, "if you're wondering how I knew where to find you, I can simply tell you I have a way of knowing always where any of my Visioneers are. I've known where you were holding Esther from the start. I could have been here yesterday with a truckload of soldiers. I didn't want to do that. We've come to talk, not to shoot, but above all, we've come to bring our friends home. Now, will you put your guns down, so we can feel easier, and between us we can work out a deal to settle this."

"So," the man finally breaks his silence, "you want a deal. You're a fool to come here with so little to bargain with."

"No," replies Mark, "I'm not a fool, and I have a lot to put on the table. You have a chance in dealing with me to do more for your cause than all of this force and bravado will every accomplish. Can we come in and talk? What's your name? You know who we are. We would like to know who we're dealing with."

"You want to know who I am. Ask your Jewish friend there. I suspect he knows well enough. He has carried out enough murderous raids to know who'll stand up to him."

David Roth speaks up. "I believe you're Kamal Rashid," he says. "At least I've heard of someone like you with that name."

"Perhaps," the man replies, "and perhaps that is not my real name. And perhaps I had a brother, Abdullah. You might remember him, Jew. He was only seventeen when you and your crew gunned him down in Jerusalem last year. Now you come here like this. Do you have a death wish, Jew?"

"My son, Joshua, will be buried today," the words are catching in David's throat. "My life doesn't matter much after that."

"Wrong!" Mark's voice is furious with its intensity. "All lives matter and there have been too many of them wasted. I've come here to stop the killing. At least here in this one small space we can stop the killing."

"What do you know?" snaps Kamal, furiously. The full fury of his anger surges to the surface. "You're not an Arab or a Jew. You know nothing about who we are. If all the days of recorded time were laid end to end, there wouldn't be enough for me to hate and despise this man and all he stands for. You come here and tell us to stop the killing. Well, it will stop when every last one of his murderous race is driven out of our lands."

"Enough!" Mohammed has intervened. "How many times have I heard such useless words uttered by fools who would rather walk in a sea of blood than a field of grass! I am an Arab and I will use all my energy up to my last breath to stop the killing, not to prolong it to the end of time. And let me tell you, all of you here, that now we have a chance for that. Here, standing right here amongst you, you have a man, unarmed and unafraid, not a diplomat or a politician, but a man of the people, leading a group of ordinary people, and I'm one of them, and you have another one locked up there inside, ordinary people, who are working tirelessly, fearlessly, to bring the world to its senses before it becomes such an abomination that no one can live on it, Arab, Jew, or anyone else. You have a chance here with this man to do something that in all your assaults and bombings you couldn't do in a thousand years. Listen to him, put aside your guns, and listen to him, and you'll do more this day than in any since you picked up the first rock to throw or gun to shoot."

The intensity of Mohammed's words cuts through the raw anger of Kamal's tirade and a momentary hush settles on the group. Into that space, Mark Venture steps, sensing that this is his one chance to do what he has come to do.

"Thank you, Mohammed, good friend. Kamal, I'm sorry about your brother. I didn't know about him. But Mohammed is your brother, too, and he's speaking for your good. I would like to be your brother. I know it's too soon for that, but I want you to know that when you're ready, I'm here. This morning, I lost my own spirit brother. It was a great tragedy for the world. His name was Luis Valdez. He was a Visioneer. He was speaking to the world about peace and love and he was cut down by bullets in full view of the television audience of the world. It seems now in the midst of all this torment here almost too much to bear.

"I want you to know, Kamal, that I've come to try to end such madness.

I told my friends up at the car before we came down that I wanted to make room for a miracle to happen. I'm looking past your guns, past the hatred in your eyes. I'm searching for that inner part of you where I know there's a longing for something better. I heard that in your voice on the phone when we spoke. You're a young man and a leader. You have the time and the space to lead your people to a better place, not by bombs and bullets, but by the power of the vision in their minds, a vision for a future which they can share with the rest of us on the planet: Jews and Christians and Hindus and Buddhists, and members of every nation.

"I want to tell you about the Visioneers, about what we've begun to do, about the changes that can happen so quickly now because we've made a start, and because people are ready as they've never been before, to reach out, to listen and to learn.

"Can we come into your house now, Kamal, to talk? Can we see our friends? Can we embrace them? Can we tell you about what we're doing and the great hope that lies in the future for you and your people and for all of us. Can we do that now?"

Mark stops speaking. It's not his words that are important. He knows that he must break through the dark force-field of the man before him. He is consciously projecting his own energy outwards. He feels Mohammed beside him doing the same, and David, too, weaker, much weaker, but trying. All of them seeking to touch this man, to break through just a little, to make space for something more to grow.

The silence seems endless. Kamal Rashid searches their faces. The pistol wavers a little, then suddenly he nods, tucks the gun into his belt, and steps away from the door, motioning them to come inside.

They enter a sparsely furnished room with a few old carpets on the floor, and several cheap chairs with frayed upholstery. A television set stands in one corner. Kamal motions them to sit down. He speaks to his men who lower their rifles and stand at the back of the room, watching. Kamal leaves. The others sit in silence. They hear voices from the back of the house. Mark stares at the doorway through which Kamal had left. Suddenly he sees Esther standing there, looking small and dishevelled, but incredibly, incredibly beautiful. In an instant, she's in his arms. The close touch of their bodies sweeps over them in waves. He buries his head in her long hair and feels small hands gripping tightly against his back, her body folding into his, clinging closely, more closely than he can ever remember holding a woman in his life. He looks in her face and sees the tears streaming, and the tiny round mouth quivering as she bursts into heavy sobs of relief from long stored up tension and fear. Reluctantly, he lets her go and she moves to embrace David and Mohammed. Jenny Lovicks is there, too, equally emotional, a slight trembling figure, embracing the three men and trying hard to stifle her sobbing.

Kamal has returned behind the women and stands in the doorway watching. If he is touched by the reconciliation, he shows little sign of it. The other armed men shift uneasily from foot to foot, watching, taking their cues from Kamal.

"Thank you for this," Mark says to Kamal. "Now, perhaps we can talk."

For more than an hour they do, Mark telling the story of the Visioneers, Mohammed interpreting, bringing in his perspective from the United Nations and telling of his meeting with the old Chinese leader, Zhao She Yuhan, in the Great Hall of the People, looking out on to Tiananmen Square. He compares the old man's vision of a new China to his own vision of the Middle East, where Arab neighbours and a strong Jewish state will exist side by side, prosperous trading partners in a world growing rich from the knowledge and the vision of people's minds, searching beyond the old enemies and hatreds, putting their hopes in a future of trust and cooperation.

Kamal listens well, but clearly doesn't trust, even in the words of Mohammed. He hears, but doesn't believe. His mind is too seared with the hatred and violence of too many sorties, too much application of the holy law of reprisal and persecution.

Mark looks at his watch and sees that it's coming up to 8 a.m. He makes a proposal.

"Kamal, I said outside that this morning I lost a brother. I would like you to meet him now and hear his words. He died this morning because he dared to speak too prominently of the future we've just described to you. I think you might see through his story more clearly what you must do than in anything we can say. The entire episode was recorded by ZNN at 4 o'clock this morning. They're rebroadcasting it at 8 a.m. Will you watch it with us now?"

When they tune in the channel, Pamela Barrett is already speaking, preparing the viewing audience for what she calls one of the most extraordinary and tragic events in television history. Then Luis Valdez is on, and Mark feels a lump catch in his throat. His body stiffens and Esther sitting beside him senses the change. She takes his hand. He smiles and gently returns the pressure.

Seeing Luis' presentation for the second time in a few hours, Mark struggles with mixed emotions. He sees the masterful weaving of condemnation and image and the call for people to take back into their hands the power to create a future founded on the sanctity of human life and peaceful cooperation. They come to the final moments as Luis is brought up close on camera and speaks of the transformation of the world to a new age of enlightenment, "gathering together around the powerful visions for good that lie in the hearts of the overwhelming majority of human beings on the planet . . . Tomorrow I ask you to go out and form yourselves into bands of Visioneers. Put up your dreams. Talk to each other and listen, listen deeply to the wisdom of your collective minds at work, building something strong and rich and beautiful for all."

And then he is gunned down. The impact in the room is electrifying. Esther and Jenny scream with shock. Even the Arabs who have barely been able to follow the words in English gasp and stiffen in surprise at the viciousness of the attack. When George Cardinal faces the camera with the dead body of the priest lying in his arms, the tension in the room is stretched to breaking point.

Mark switches off the television set and turns to speak to the group.

"When the life of a Luis Valdez is taken by an assassin's bullet, it's an affront to the rest of us as members of the human race. But such violence is bred by the minds who would kill Abdullah and Joshua and all the thousands like them throughout the world.

"I would like us now to take Luis at his word, to part if not as friends, at least no longer as enemies bent on each other's destruction. Kamal, with your permission, Esther and Jenny will come away with us. There will be no report of this to the authorities and no recriminations. You have my word on that. May we go now?"

The young Arab leader takes the pistol out of his belt, holds it for a moment, trained on Mark, then sets it aside on a table.

"You're a brave man, Mark Venture, to have come here like this. And your friend there on the television, he was a brave and good man. We have no quarrel with such as you. Yes, you may take your women. I do this as a token. They're of little value to us here. I will test your word, Mark Venture, and hold you accountable. You may go, all of you. My men will repair your car."

David Roth comes forward to speak to the young Arab.

"Kamal, let me say, for what it's worth to you, that what you do now will rebound a thousandfold to your stock among the Israeli community. I'm sure that Esther and I can see to that. I also want to say that I'm deeply sorry about your brother's death. If I had the power to undo it, I would. But I'm going now to bury my son. Perhaps you will think of us. I know that when I see his casket lowered into the ground, I'll think of this meeting here this morning, and you have my word that David Roth will not be leading any more reprisals."

Without waiting for a reply, David nods to the young man and walks outside. Mohammed embraces Kamal and they speak animatedly for a few moments in Arabic, then Mohammed follows David, taking Jenny with him.

Mark and Esther face their former captor. Mark extends his hand, but Kamal shakes his head. They look hard at each other across a gap still too wide to bridge. Esther gently touches the young Arab's sleeve.

"*Shalom*," she says quietly, then takes Mark's arm. They walk outside and follow the others who have already set off for the car, through the much larger crowd of children and adults who have gathered to stare curiously at the strange parade of foreigners passing through their midst.

Outlining the Vision

The difficulty for them begins when they reach a checkpoint on their way back into Jerusalem. The soldiers recognize the two women immediately as the hostages taken, presumably by terrorists, two days earlier. Hard questions are asked about how they came now to be suddenly released and where and by whom they had been held.

After an hour's questioning, David Roth is allowed to leave to go to attend to the business of his son's burial. The rest of them are taken by military vehicle to an interrogation centre in Jerusalem.

They find themselves in the presence of an officer who introduces himself simply as Colonel Greenberg of Special Services. He is a short, stocky man with thick black hair and a heavy black moustache. His voice, as he speaks in English, has a thick accent.

"Now tell me again," he says, gesturing to all of them, "what's going on here? We have a very serious bombing, four people are killed, many other injured. You two women are taken hostage, presumably with some connection to the bombing. Now you turn up with these two men, coming out of Arab occupied land, apparently uninjured, and you say freely released by captors whose faces you never saw. Now, come on, ladies and gentlemen, things don't happen that way, and even if they did, I still want to know who these murderers are, so we can round them up and put them away."

"Look," says Mark, "I appreciate where you're coming from, colonel. But there's no clear connection between the bombing and the hostage taking. I believe there were different people involved. They might know each other, but we dealt only with the hostage-takers, and they've acted in good faith in letting Esther and Jenny go. We've assured them because of that, that there'll be no reprisals."

"Listen, Mr. Venture, you have no authority here to make deals with these criminals. All right, you might have got these two women out, but what about the next ones, and the ones after that. You won't be around to deal with those, but I will, and I want to know what you know about this lot, so I can move on them now, before they do it again."

"And where's the end to that?" asks Mark. "There isn't any. You have to make a different intervention, if you're going to get a different outcome. We've made a start on that this morning. The most valuable thing you can do is keep it going. This is much bigger than Israel and the Palestinians. I have the world media waiting for me as soon as I get out of here, and what I say to them about the reaction of Israeli authorities to this incident will have a dramatic impact, not only on what happens here, but on reducing the power of terrorism and conflict around the world. Things are happening very quickly now, colonel. You don't realize it yet, but you've suddenly been thrust into the centre of a movement that's going to sweep the world.

I don't fully understand it myself, but I'm running with it because I sense the outcome is going to be a major breakthrough. All I ask of you now is don't get in the way of it. You can't stop it anyway, but you can do a lot to help it move."

"Mark is right, Colonel Greenberg," Esther has intervened. "If anyone has the right to say something here, it's me and Jenny. We're Israelis. We were snatched out of our car and hauled off in the dark to we didn't know where. We were terrified. We expected to be raped and killed at any moment. But we weren't. They treated us decently under the circumstances. And then when Mark and the others arrived this morning, you wouldn't believe the change that took place. There was movement. There was real movement, because these men came right in unarmed, no soldiers, and said we want to take our friends home. And David Roth was there, his own son lying dead in the funeral home, and there he was walking openly into the enemy camp with Mark and Mohammed. I mean, you have to understand what kind of a powerful statement that was. And then we all listened to Luis Valdez and saw him cut down in the middle of his beautiful vision by the same kind of violence that tore the life out of Joshua Roth. Do you know about Luis Valdez, colonel? Have you heard what happened? If you haven't, then you will. Before the end of the day, the whole world will know about Luis Valdez, and through Mark they'll know about what happened here in Bethlehem, and people will see that it's all part of the same miracle that will change the world.

"Now, Jenny and I are very tired and very dirty. We've been held as hostages for over thirty-six hours with no chance to clean up and frightened out of our wits. We just want to leave now. We've told you all we can. We don't really know who our captors were or what they may have done in the past. We just sense that because of everything that's happened, they can help change the direction of the future for the better.

"Now, could we please leave and go and have a hot bath?"

After that, Greenberg backs off. He agrees that they can leave while he completes an initial report. Jenny is taken home, while the other three go to Mark's hotel. Pamela Barrett of ZNN is sitting in the lobby when they come in. At sight of Mark and Mohammed, she's on her feet in a flash.

"Chalk one more up for woman's intuition," she says. "I figured you two would turn up here pretty soon, so I decided to come down and wait." She looks at Esther. "Now, if this is who I think it is, I know I have the scoop of my life!"

"Hello, Pamela," says Mark. "I'd like you to meet Esther Fisher." To Esther he says, "I promised Pamela an interview when we got back."

"Esther, it's such a pleasure to meet you," says Pamela. "I've admired your work as an artist for a long time, though we haven't met before. When I heard that you'd been kidnapped I couldn't believe it. Now here you are free as part of this group of Visioneers. The world is just waiting to hear your story. Could we do a short interview?"

Esther smiles a little ruefully and nods. "All right," she says, "But you'll have to excuse how I look."

"Don't worry about that. For someone who's been through the ordeal you faced, you look just fine. What about your friend, Jenny? Where is she?"

"She's safe at home," Esther replies.

"Oh, I'm glad to hear that. All right then, can we get started?"

Pamela Barrett quickly organizes and her cameraman begins shooting. A crowd of interested bystanders is beginning to gather. Pamela speaks first, setting the scene.

"From time to time in the life of a news reporter, one has the sense of being present at events of great importance: royal weddings, world conferences, space launches, presidential inaugurations. I've been to my share of them. But never have I felt more excited than I do at this moment. A few hours ago, I sat in the darkened studios at ZNN with a few others and watched an extraordinary telecast coming in by satellite from South America. It was a simple Roman Catholic priest, Luis Valdez, describing his vision for the future of a world run on cooperation and love, and built from the ground up, so to speak, by ordinary people putting out their visions for the future. As we sat and watched, we were horrified to see this lovely man cut down by an assassin in front of our eyes.

"Since then, over the past six or seven hours, the telecast has been replayed on thousands of channels all over the world. People everywhere are asking the same questions: What was this all about? Is this a new 21st century crucifixion? Was this Christ held up before us again, and cut down by the violence his teachings from two thousand years earlier had not overcome? What are we to make of this? Who was the killer? We don't have answers yet.

"But now something else extraordinary has just occurred here in Jerusalem. The well-known Israeli artist, Esther Fisher, was captured two days ago by terrorists along with her friend, Jenny Lovicks. Now I have Esther Fisher here with me safe and sound and Jenny is fine too. Their release was secured by Esther's friends, Mark Venture and Mohammed Hussein, and both of them are here, as well. All of these people, including Luis Valdez, the murdered priest, are calling themselves Visioneers. Judging by events to date, they seem to be miracle workers. Now, we're about to find out."

While Pamela was speaking the camera covered Esther, Mark and Mohammed. The crowd in the hotel lobby is growing larger. Hotel staff have moved in to keep order. Pamela Barrett thrusts her microphone towards Esther. The camera covers both of them.

"Esther, let's begin by saying, how relieved we are that you're safe and fine. What happened? Tell us the story."

"It's hard to tell everything about something like this," says Esther. "I haven't really put it all together for myself yet. But the main point I'd like people to understand is that Jenny and I, just a few hours ago, were captives in fear of losing our lives, and now we're free. And it is a kind of miracle. Mark and Mohammed and David Roth, whose son was killed in the bomb blast last Saturday, just came to where we were being held and asked to take us home. Just like that. They came unarmed and asked to take us home."

Pamela turns to Mark.

"Mark," she says, "that's incredible. How did you know where to find Esther? Why would you go unarmed without soldiers?"

"It begins with understanding what the Visioneers are trying to show," Mark replies. "You heard it from Luis Valdez. The fact that he was brutally murdered doesn't make what he was saying any less true. It just underlines the importance of paying attention to what he said."

"And, in fact, that's what happened," Esther interrupts. "Mark got our captors to watch a repeat of Luis' telecast. And that's when I saw it for the first time. It began so beautifully and ended so tragically. It seemed to make our own situation, as bad as it was, somehow less terrible. But the effect on our kidnappers was more important than anything else. After watching that and listening to Mark and Mohammed they just let us go. Even for those violent men, more violence didn't make sense."

"But terrorists don't behave like that," Pamela interrupts.

"That's our whole point," Mark replies. "If you start to shift the way people think about violence and conflict towards the model Luis Valdez described, then you can see some amazing transformations. What we've seen here today in Israel is just the beginning of a change that's going to sweep the world."

After that the cut and thrust of questions and answers continues apace. Who are the Visioneers? What are they trying to do? Who were Esther's kidnappers? What's happened to them? What are the police doing about it? Who killed Luis Valdez? Why was he killed? What's going to happen next?

Throughout it all Esther and Mark keep making their point: the old ways of conflict and retaliation will not work in the future, just as they've never really worked in the past; but now they have the potential to destroy the Earth as the one planet in the universe which we know can support life. Human consciousness cannot accept that outcome. The change to a new consciousness for peace and cooperation is building, and the Visioneers have come as catalysts to help speed the transformation.

Pamela Barrett plays her role fairly. It's clear that she wants to find truth in what Esther and Mark are saying, but she can't let go of the past. She turns to Mohammed and asks the obvious question:

"Mohammed, you've been in the centre of Arab and Israeli conflict for a long time. You've got an important role at the United Nations. What do you say about this. Can the Visioneers bring a new kind of thinking to the world?"

"Yes," Mohammed replies. "I want you to know that I subscribe with all my heart to what my friends, Mark and Esther, have said. I am an Arab and I grieve that we haven't found the brotherhood among ourselves to enjoy peace and prosperity. We're a deeply religious people and our belief in Allah is absolute, but still we seem to wander, century after century, unable to separate illusion from reality, all too ready to follow power figures who promise greatness, but who mostly bring sorrow and suffering on our heads.

"We indeed need to learn the skills of the Visioneers and I'm here to work with my people, in all of the Arab states, to find that vision of the future that can forge our brotherhood as Arabs and our joint citizenship on the planet with all of our fellow human beings.

"To do this, we'll need to look deep into our hearts, to put aside grievances and old sores. The sands of the desert have run too deep in blood for too long. It's an immense task, the building of brotherhood, not by the sword, but by the mind, seeing our success in our brother's progress. We must reach for that, each helping each.

"And those who say that this is too naive or simplistic should remember the dismal record we've had to date by following the other path of violence and deceit. The path of the Visioneers calls for all good men and women to step forward, to step forward in such numbers that no power on Earth can stop them, in their intent to build a future that is good and true and decent.

"That's what I wanted to say, not only to my brother Arabs, but also to the Israelis, and to all who have love in their hearts for this Earth and a sense of what we can build of it together."

As he spoke, it was clear that Mohammed was moved by great passion. The camera zooms in on him. Tears stand out large and overflowing in his eyes, until they run down his cheeks and he fumbles for a tissue to brush them away. Esther and Mark move closer to him to give support.

At last the interview is over. The bright lights are turned off. The camera stops running. Pamela Barrett thanks them all and leaves. But the crowd of onlookers who had steadily gathered in numbers as the time went on, doesn't leave. People press forward smiling, hands outstretched to touch the Visioneers, to wish them well, to thank them for what they're doing. As they look into this small sea of friendly, smiling faces, Mark, Esther, and Mohammed catch a glimpse of the future world of their vision, far removed from the blood-stained studio of death in northern Chile and the gaping ruin of a bombed-out apartment in Jerusalem.

A small girl comes forward and throws her arms around Esther. Her childish face open and unafraid, she says, "I want to be a Visioneer. Will you teach me how?"

Had Pamela Barrett stayed to hear it, she may well have noted that this was the most important question of the morning.

Grief and Hope

In the chapel of the Beth Judah funeral home, a large crowd of mourners are already gathered when Mark and Esther arrive. In the front row David and Mina Roth sit only a few feet from the plain casket where Joshua's body lies waiting to be buried. Sarah isn't with them, for she still remains in hospital recovering from her injuries. The chapel is plain, austere, and dark, contrasting markedly with the bright sunshine outside.

Rabbi Ruvain Ben Sabbath, a tall thin man with a brooding, sombre face, presides. Respecting the large number of English-speaking people among the mourners, he delivers his words on Joshua's life in an alternating flow of Hebrew and English.

"*Chaveyrim*, friends," he says, "We're gathered to honour the short life of Joshua Roth, a good son to David and Mina, kindly brother to Sarah, and cheerful friend to his many schoolmates. We are all keenly aware of the tragedy that overtook Joshua and cut short his future of unachieved possibilities. He was a good student, a sensitive and talented musician, and a generous spirit to others. The world needs boys like Joshua to grow into men who will lead us into the future. For Joshua, that wasn't meant to be; why, we don't know, except that it was God's will, who now has taken this young soul into His safe keeping.

"We have come together to honour Joshua's life, and we are outraged at the way it was snatched from him. To men who would commit such a wicked atrocity against defenseless people, who would slaughter and maim with malicious intent, who would take the life of Joshua at the fresh promise of its unfolding; to such men and against their wickedness we bring the most fervent condemnation. We are outraged and we will not tolerate such assaults against our family lives.

"Our anger this day can be exceeded only by our grief and in the affectionate sharing of our passion with the family. Joshua's was a life already of great worth, but stretching forward it held unlimited possibilities for service to our people. That such a life should be extinguished with so much more to be accomplished, is a tragedy of great magnitude. Our grief for such irrecoverable loss can know no bounds and swells up here as a great wave of human emotion that touches the very depths of our being. In the fullness of our hearts we offer our support, our love, and our enduring friendship to David and Mina."

The rabbi goes on to speak long and affectionately of the contribution of the Roths to the community and especially of Joshua's stature and accomplishments among his peers as a student, friend, and talented musician. The outpouring of grief for his senseless sacrifice in the bitter conflict of politicized violence is deeply moving, as every mourner identifies with the loss and links it in memory to the vicious assaults of centuries of hatred against the Jewish people. When he comes to the subject of the terrorists who planted the bomb that took the young man's life, the rabbi's voice is shaking with emotion.

"What can we say about monsters who would commit such a crime against our families? Our minds are revolted by their actions. Every fibre of our humanity is violated by what they've done. Our voices choke with outrage as we shout out until the very hills reverberate with our anger that such wickedness clothed in human form should walk the Earth. There is no judgment too severe that could be passed against such abomination and we cry out to God that in His infinite wisdom He will deal with them as they deserve.

"But, my friends, what of our own actions here and now in the face of this cruel and senseless assault against us. Do we turn with vengeance and seek for retribution against these criminals? To act as they have acted is to debase ourselves to their level. We seek justice, not retribution, and we must leave it to our authorities to find these criminals and bring them to trial. We are angry. We are outraged. But we must channel our outrage and our anger to search for the solutions to the problems that bring such tragedy and atrocity into our midst."

The rabbi pauses as he looks to the family in the front row.

"David has asked to speak to you of this. You may have heard that in the midst of his grief, he was party this morning to the rescue of two of our Jewish women who were taken as hostages shortly following the bombing on Saturday. What happened this morning seems like a small miracle, a glimmer of hope in the otherwise dark night of our despair. David, do you wish to speak now?"

As David Roth stands and turns to face the mourners, Mark sees in his face the torment of their time on the country road outside Bethlehem this morning. His voice as he speaks is firm though never far from breaking.

"My friends, thank you for coming. You will understand that I don't wish to speak of Joshua. I don't have the heart for that right now and Rabbi Ruvain has already been most eloquent and moving. I just wish a few moments to share what is in my heart about the future. The grief, the anger, the passion, all the hostility and rage of which the rabbi spoke, I feel them as a torment in my soul. They weigh on me like a burden of great weight, and I feel hatred stirring in my heart against those who have perpetrated this awful wickedness and all those in any way associated with them.

"And yet I have to say, indeed, this is all I wish to say, I feel a faint glimmer of hope that out of this time of unspeakable sorrow, we will see a change. This morning, under duress and persuasion from others more hopeful than myself, I met with terrorists and caught a glimpse of distress not unlike my own. Following a most remarkable time, there in their house, completely at their mercy, we came away bringing our Jewish women with us. My friends, there is a stirring in my heart that in this we may see the first faltering step toward a peace that will preserve the lives of our loved ones against the kind of tragedy that has overtaken my family. I can only say that with all my heart I wish that this may be so. I know that Mina joins with me in this and she would like to add a word."

Mina Roth, grieving greatly, but resolute and strong, stands up beside her husband.

"Friends, what can a mother say at a time like this, when she feels that half of her life has been taken away. My anger against the criminals who did this knows no bounds, and yet, like David, I am looking now for the answer that lies beyond the agony of our loss. If David caught a glimpse of it this morning, I swear I will with all my heart support him in trying to make it grow.

"Joshua was our child of love. He had a deep longing even in his young years for a lasting peace in the world. For Joshua and for all of us, David and I would now like to say the prayer for peace."

Together with bowed heads, husband and wife, father and mother, standing beside the casket of their dead son, offer the prayer for peace:

"May we see the day when war and bloodshed cease,
when a great peace will embrace the whole world.

Then nation will not threaten nation,
and mankind will not again know war.

For all who live on Earth shall realize
we have not come into being to hate or to destroy.

We have come into being
to praise, to labour, and to love.

Compassionate God bless the leaders of all nations
with the power of compassion.

Fulfill the promise conveyed in Scripture:

I will bring peace to the land,
and you shall lie down and no one shall terrify you.

I will rid the land of vicious beasts
and it shall not be ravaged by war.

Let love and justice flow like a mighty stream.

Let peace fill the Earth as the waters fill the sea.

And let us say: Amen."

Amen, again, Mark says silently to himself, but not to wait for a God, however compassionate, to act; but to take the reins of future peace and prosperity firmly in hand ourselves, and to fire up our minds with visions of what such peace will be like in every land, and to commit, now, to act to secure it in our lifetime. And to that, let us truly say, Amen.

Time to be Together

Early evening has settled over Jerusalem. From their hotel balcony, Mark and Esther can see spread out below a tapestry of soft lights. They feel the cool edge of the air brought on the breezes blowing in from Judea and Samaria, sensing in their motion the deep and steady breathing of the ancient land that lies beyond this faint glow of human presence. Overhead, the stars are as clear, brilliant, and timeless as when Moses first looked out over the promised land that he would never enter.

In this quiet space, the two seekers for a gentle future time feel, at last, alone, however briefly, cherishing the moments against the press that must come again tomorrow. A few hours earlier at Beth Judah cemetery they had, with David and Mina Roth, spread a few shovels of red earth on the casket of the young Joshua. Since returning from there to the hotel, they've had little respite from the probing of the world. Reporters, telephone callers, officials, Esther's friends and family in Tel Aviv: all had crowded in, a wave of surging enquiry about what had happened, was happening, would be happening with the Visioneers and the world in the aftermath of Luis Valdez's death and Esther's release from her captors. There had seemed no end to it, until finally they retreated behind the closed doors of Mark's room with all calls and callers being intercepted by the hotel staff. Dining together in the room, they have begun to catch a glimpse of Mark and Esther. Now on the balcony sipping the last of their wine, they gratefully embrace some peace for themselves.

"Oh, Mark," Esther says softly, "What a time this has been! Do you remember when we first met in the Visioneering Room with the others? That seems so long ago now. Do you remember, I spoke of how the artist is filled with energy before she begins to create and then out of the energy field the image of what she's painting comes tumbling and suddenly you're filled with the power to capture it to get it down in oils so that it's there forever? Well, I think that's where we are now in our work. There's an energy field building up and we're in the middle of it, you especially, because you've been called to be the leader. I remember you spoke that same day about leadership. You were the first to see what a Visioneer is. Someone who can work to build a better future. And now it has started. It really has, and you're here to keep it going."

Mark looks across the table into the glowing beautiful face of this lady who has swept so suddenly into his life. He touches her hands and she responds, grasping his firmly.

"Whatever's happening, Esther, I know one thing: I want us to be part of it together. There's been so little space for that. One snatched day in Australia before you came here, and now this evening, before we both have to leave again and go separate ways. You're very precious to me. I didn't know how much until I first heard you'd been captured. You speak about a life force. I understand that better now. When you were taken, I felt a powerful thrust of energy, and I knew that somehow out of that energy field we were going to find a way to be together again."

His strong hands tighten a little more on hers.

"It seems I'll have to be in the thick of things for a while, but I tell you, right now, I feel very uncertain about it. All I really want to do is be here with you, to learn to know you better, to understand who you are and what your Jewishness means. Before all this started, I was a very ordinary fellow from Brisbane with a good Church of England background. I knew a bit about building bridges and roads. I had a marriage that went wrong, and I was out on my own, and pretty wary of any further involvement.

"Then suddenly I'm catapulted into this visioneering scene, and there you are, pink sweater and white unicorn, and saying the most incredible things about creating a vision for the world. It was you who got me fired up. I was saying to myself, 'Who is this woman? She's Jewish. Hold on, Mark, you don't know anything about that.' But I couldn't hold on, and suddenly, I was talking about Moses and the Exodus and all the rest of it. And I've known since then, that if I was meant to be involved with this visioneering movement it was going to be with you. Now, things have started to move, but there's been so very little time for us—and even now there's only tonight. So I must tell you, now, Esther, while I can, that I've fallen very much in love with you, and you're more precious to me than anyone I have ever known or anything I might ever have."

She is looking across the table at him, her eyes moistening, catching the glow of the soft light on the balcony. Her lips move a little, but no voice comes, only her breathing, a little rushed, flooding her cheeks with colour, while her mind swims with the feeling of his words, knowing their truth, sensing how hard won they are to come from this man, whose emotions and feelings are kept very close to himself.

Finally she finds her voice and replies with the full spirit of one questing soul responding to another.

"Thank you, Mark," she says. "Thank you for knowing and seeing in me who I really am. Thank you for saying you love me. I understand how strong men love, and I sense that in you, a strong man looking for his partner. You'll find in me that I, too, know how to love from strength. I feel that love growing towards you. But I need a little more time. It takes time to move from alone to together. But I'm coming. For tonight, Mark, darling, I would just like you to hold me."

Her lip is trembling a little as she feels herself drawn to this man who has come so suddenly into her life out of another world. She has grown up in Israel and though she has travelled widely, her spirit, the deep inner part of her, is still defined by her homeland and its traditions. She was married as a young woman to an officer in the Israeli army. Eight years ago he was killed in a border incident in Lebanon, and a light went out in her life. She hasn't felt it rekindled until now—until she met this tall, strong man from another land who seems to feel as deeply as she that life is meant to be lived with meaning and purpose. Looking across at him now in the stillness of this time together, she's not sure yet whether she can trust herself to love. She knows only in this moment that she wants to feel his arms around her, and to move with him in the energy of their exchange.

In a moment, she has slipped around the table and he has risen to meet her. She folds herself to him, tipping back her head, parting her lips to be kissed. As their lips meet, the longing of the two souls in search of a union comes flooding forth. Wave after wave of passionate desire ignites them as his strong arms pull them closer together. Her voice is murmuring, trembling and low.

"Oh, Mark, hold me, yes, hold me, tight. Hold me, now, my darling and love me, please, love me, now."

The quiet evening in Jerusalem slides slowly into time, unrocked this night by bomb blasts or rifle fire, the city catching its breath against the tensions that engulf it. In the intimate space of their own precious time together, Mark and Esther move like wind across the grass, flowing gently in one sweet motion, two minds, two spirits, two bodies committing to growing towards each other. In their union this evening, in the loving that transfuses their physical longing, in the quietness of the aftertime as they lie tenderly in each other's arms, in all of this, Mark and Esther gather their strength for whatever lies ahead. Tonight, they embrace their time together. Jerusalem enfolds them. And at the dawn the world lies waiting.

CHAPTER TWELVE

The
Chapter
Closes

Y OU REST A MOMENT in the Visioneering Room. The images have cascaded through your mind in a ferment of activity as the events have swept you and all the players into a spiral of interlocking motion. There are so many pieces out there now that your mind begins to swim with the complexity of it. And yet, it's all building toward an outcome. You're not sure what. You think briefly of your mentors: Winston Churchill, John Kennedy, Charles Dickens, and Anne. Where are they? There's been no time to consult with them since the Visioneers went out. You must make time, but not now. There's too much crowding in.

Enter El Condor

While the events have unfolded in Jerusalem, George Cardinal has taken charge in Chile. He has moved quickly to abandon the Mission at Santa Maria, taking the sad burden of Luis Valdez's body back to Santiago, where he's plunged into the turmoil of officialdom and the news media. The crazed army captain is handed over to authorities, and as news leaks out of who he is, the speculation of conspiracy and corruption spills into the world headlines. It's an embarrassing situation for the government, even though the captain was acting outside his official capacity. Throughout it all, George Cardinal plays a solid central role, just getting the job done of seeing to his friend's last needs for a fitting farewell. The church and the

Valdez family come to his aid, and a quiet funeral is arranged for Wednesday afternoon in the Valdez home village of Casilda just a few kilometres into the foothills of the Andes from Santiago.

Early Tuesday morning in Jerusalem Mark Venture succeeds in reaching George Cardinal by telephone in Santiago. It's early Monday evening there, the end of a long and harrowing day for George, in which the constant interrogation from the police and reporters weighs heavily on him along with his grief over the cruel death of his friend. George advises Mark not to come to Santiago for the funeral. Reluctantly, Mark agrees. The Visioneers have become too high profile for him, as their leader, to be personally embroiled in the intrigues going on in Chile. He is, however, concerned about leaving George there to handle the situation alone. Through Bill Bates, he arranges for the United States and Canadian embassies to get involved to ensure that George is able to leave as soon as possible after the funeral. Mark's strategy now is to hold a memorial service for Luis Valdez in a more friendly location, where the man will not only receive the tribute due to him, but also the work of the Visioneers will be advantaged.

Not that the world is by any means ignoring them. Luis Valdez's tragic last telecast continues to be played and replayed on networks in more than a hundred countries. The interviews given by Mark along with Esther and Mohammed, reach almost equal prominence. Partly to escape some of the glare of publicity, Esther leaves Jerusalem on Tuesday morning to go to her home in Tel Aviv. She joins her parents there, who haven't yet seen her since her release by the terrorists. Mark remains in the hotel, trying to deflect most of the media probing to Bill Bates in Los Angeles, who is emerging as the master communicator for the Visioneers. While still considering his next move, Mark receives an unexpected phone call from the man who calls himself Kamal Rashid. Mark recognizes the voice immediately.

"Mark Venture," says the voice, "I call to tell you that I respect what you and your friends have said about the hostage taking. I know the Israeli authorities will have pressed you hard for information about us, but so far they've made no move, and I can only assume you have kept your word."

"Yes, we have. We wish you no harm."

"I believe you, Mark Venture. For the others, we will wait and see. But for you, I have a message. It concerns your friend, Luis Valdez."

Mark's spine tightens.

"Yes, go on. What about Luis?"

"The man who killed him, he shouted something. It was hard to hear at first, but I have watched that piece several times now and I believe he said, 'Die for El Condor.' Do you know what that means?"

"Only that El Condor is an eagle."

"I think you may find him to be an eagle with human talons. El Condor is the code name for a man I met last month in Amman. He has many names.

This one is new and few know it. It appeals to his sense of power. We were discussing arms shipments for the Palestinians. He's a dealer in such things, but I didn't like him. I think he would just as readily supply weapons to Israel as to us. I believe he's also involved in the drug trade in South America. That's another reason I don't like him. I have no time for that business, when we have such real injustice to correct as we suffer here. I suspect he saw your friend as a threat to his ventures and gave word for him to be killed. I thought you might like to know this. Now I must go."

"Wait a minute," Mark says. "How do I find him? Where does he operate from? What more can you tell me?"

"Nothing. This much I give you out of respect for your grief and your honest dealing with me. The rest you must do for yourself. Goodbye, Mark Venture. Perhaps we shall meet again."

Mark is still pondering these words when the phone rings a second time. It's Mohammed. Mark tells him about the other call.

"Yes, I was calling to tell you as much myself. Kamal had said something about it to me at the house in Judea after he had let the women go. I've been checking with my contacts at the United Nations. There's speculation that El Condor is the code name for Carlos Palmira who started out about ten years ago as a drug trader in Colombia, but is now generally understood to be involved in arms dealing and espionage in various parts of the world. He lives in Switzerland in the countryside somewhere. At least that's what he says officially. By all accounts, he would be the arch enemy of the Visioneers. He would stand to lose a lot of business if people started to take more personal responsibility for the way things are in the world. There's no question he's been actively dealing with Palestinian leaders and some Arab states in this part of the world."

"It's a tangled mess," Mark muses aloud. "What do you think the chances are of a thorough investigation in Chile, to see if this is the El Condor responsible for killing Luis?"

"It's hard to say. He probably covers his tracks well. My guess is this fellow who did the killing will get put away and that'll be the end of it."

"Not for me, it won't. We have to show that there's no place in a Visioneer's world for El Condor or any of his like. I'll need your help on that, Mohammed. We have to look to the United Nations to play a stronger role in dealing with international criminals."

"You know you have my commitment. What do you want me to do next?"

"For now, I want you to stay here and work with Esther and David to get some grassroots dialogue going between the Israelis and the Palestinians. We need to make that a lighthouse of hope for the world. I'm going back to North America to work with Bill Bates to put together a memorial service for Luis Valdez that will make the world really pay attention to what he had to say. I want the United Nations involved up front. That's another way you can help. I'll be in touch as soon as I can. Goodbye, Mohammed, and thanks for everything you've done here."

Moving towards Spectacular

By Wednesday noon Pacific time, Mark is with Bill Bates in his office in Los Angeles. Mark notes with pleasure the friendly, solid square face of the man he has come to respect as a force for getting things done.

"Bill, it's good to see you again," says Mark. "Bring me up to date on what the world is saying about us."

"I've never seen anything like it. I tell you, the pump is primed out there. We've got calls coming in from kids in Caracas, diplomats in Delhi, scientists in Sweden, journalists in Jerusalem. I've put half a dozen people on to just monitoring the world media, and I tell you, it's incredible. You'd literally have to be a hermit in a cave in Botswana not to have heard about Luis Valdez, and Mark Venture, and the Visioneers. That escapade you pulled off with Esther, freeing her from the terrorists by just talking to them, that's blow your mind stuff. I was the first to warn you to watch out for those people, and there you go. You walk in without a weapon and you walk out with Esther. Oh, and on that score, I'm starting to get calls about you and Esther—the romantic touch, you know. What are you saying about that, you two? What's the story on Mark and Esther?"

"For the world," replies Mark, the colour rising a little in his cheeks, "we're very close friends. For you, Bill, we're very much in love."

"Yeah, I thought as much—and so do a few hundred million people around the world. You and Esther can expect the newshounds from every country to be after you about that."

"I'm sure you're right, but at least it'll bring more publicity for the Visioneers. Now, Bill, I want to know how we're doing on the memorial service for Luis. What are your thoughts on that?"

"Well, it's got two main thrusts to it. First, it's an international story, and second, Luis was a Roman Catholic priest. Therefore, I think we should tie it closely to the United Nations and the Vatican. The fact that the work of Luis and the Visioneers got an endorsement from Unesco is a good leg up with the U.N. On the Vatican side, you should know I got a call this morning from a Cardinal Claudio Vachiano, a close advisor to no less than the Pope, himself. It seems that His Holiness has been particularly struck by what has happened, not only to one of his priests, but by the reaction of the world, and to what they've heard about the Visioneers. They're obviously feeling us out, but they could possibly be brought on side. How do you feel about a quick trip to the Vatican to talk to the cardinal?"

"Of course." Mark's response is immediate. "It's a natural connection for us. Similarly, with the U.N. I'll ask Mohammed to set something up there right away with someone who has the ear of the Secretary-General. Just imagine, if we get the power of those two international bodies behind us, how quickly we can move. We can draw on their resources and influence, but still stand apart from them so that we aren't bound up in their structures. We can give new life to their humanitarian and spiritual work, as well as to all of the other international agencies doing similar things. The framework is there. It's been building for generations, but it needs a catalyst, an energy source that comes right from the hearts and minds of people. That's the work of the Visioneers, Bill, and we're on our way to do it. I'm off to the Vatican and the United Nations. You keep the fire burning under the media, and we'll talk again in a few days."

At the Vatican

Mark follows the stooped and wheezing frame of an ancient Dominican monk through the chilled marble corridors of a Vatican palace. All around, the sumptuous wealth from centuries of endowment overwhelms the senses: statues in bronze and stone of saints, popes, warriors, and poets; huge paintings, crowded with figures, in patches of dark and light, playing out the themes of Botticelli and Fra Angelico; tapestries, wall hangings, ornately carved ceilings and pillars. The opulence, wealth, mystery and faith, crowd in, symbols of what one of the world's great religions attempts to say about human aspirations for the eternal. Mark is impressed and troubled. He searches in the reality of such magnificence for hope to avert the bullets that pour the life-blood of a great man onto the floor of a mission in South America, or the bomb that tears a gaping hole in a Jerusalem apartment and with it wrenches life from a fifteen-year-old boy.

His musings are cut short. He finds himself being greeted by a smiling, scarlet-robed man, extending a delicate, fragile hand with its ruby ring almost glowing in the half light of the huge, high-ceilinged room. Mark takes the hand. The monk is dismissed and Cardinal Claudio Vachiano motions Mark to join him in a small vestibule where four-metre high arched windows pour welcome light onto the marble floor, partly covered with French carpets. They sit in high-backed comfortable chairs from the 17th century and sip the tea poured by the Cardinal into the finest china enlivened with glazes of crimson and gold.

"It's good of you to come, Mr. Venture, at such short notice." The cardinal's voice is mellifluous and clear, his English rich with the cadence of an Oxford education.

"I'm honoured that you asked me, Your Eminence," Mark replies.

"You're doing great work for the world of which I would like to know more," the cardinal continues. "We have been deeply troubled by the loss of our brother Luis, but we are astonished and humbled by the way in which his message seems to have excited people in every country.

"But the Church must be circumspect in its commentary on such initiatives. We are a conservative institution, Mr. Venture, and we are expected to be so by the many millions of our faithful around the world. Our brother, Luis, undertook his work with you without either our knowledge or approval. Had he sought it, it would almost certainly have been withheld. We could say that his tragic death was a consequence of ill-considered impetuosity, which is the reason why we would have forbidden him to do what he did."

"And yet," Mark intervenes quietly, "we now have several hundred million people paying attention not only to the violence of his death, but to the spirit of his message and life."

"Exactly. And so we seek to honour him with you, and the Holy Father has expressly asked that I speak with you of this. But first, you must forgive my curiosity but I am deeply intrigued about who you are, Mr. Venture, and what your organization of Visioneers seeks to do in the world."

The two men continue their conversation long into the afternoon. Twice the ancient Dominican monk appears with hand-written messages of other appointments. The cardinal waves them aside and orders more tea and biscuits as he engages with rapt attention in a conversation that he has astutely grasped to be one of the most important in his life. Finally, the time has come when the pressure of other responsibilities must be attended to, and the cardinal indicates that the meeting is at an end.

"I am touched and humbled by all that you have said, Mr. Venture. We shall indeed participate fully in a fitting memorial service for Father Luis. I plan to attend personally to represent the Holy Father. The ceremony will be held, as we have discussed, in a small country parish within easy access from the United Nations in New York, but still open to the natural beauty of the Earth that held such great importance for Father Luis. The date and details we will confirm in a few days.

"Go with God, Mr. Venture, and the blessing of our Lord Jesus be with you and amongst all those with whom you work."

The smooth white hand is extended once more. Mark, then follows his ancient guide back through the labyrinth of treasures into the fading autumn sunlight in St. Peter's Square. Above him, the massive dome of the basilica rises as an eloquent symbol of man's rich creative heritage. Encompassed in that metaphor, Mark catches a glimpse in his mind of a larger, world-size spiritual dome of tolerance, justice and eternal hope in the future of an evolving human presence in the splendour of God's creation. He turns away and sets his thoughts on the next step along that path.

Lunch at Woodlands

The restaurant is already crowded with its usual lunch trade of business people and tourists when Mark Venture arrives. From the street, Woodlands is an undistinguished hole in the wall in a decaying warehouse district, ten minutes by cab from the United Nations Plaza in New York City. Inside, the refugee from the snarl of traffic and littered streets is treated to a sparkling vista of green shrubs, flower gardens, small trees, hanging ferns, miniature waterfalls, and a tiny pond complete with lily pads and huge goldfish prowling the bottom among reeds and stones.

It's a far cry from the Vatican palace, Mark says to himself, as he follows an attractive hostess in peasant blouse and denim skirt along a meandering path of cobblestones, past happily dining patrons, down to the pond and a table under a three-metre high umbrella tree.

A trim, medium-framed man, fortyish, in grey, pinstriped double breasted business suit, crisp white shirt, and red tie with matching pocket handkerchief, is waiting for him.

"Hello," he says affably, standing and extending his hand. "I'm Peter Hemphill and I know you're Mark Venture because I've seen your photograph in practically every national newspaper from more than a score of countries that I've looked at over the past week."

"The same story repeated many times creates the illusion of prominence," smiles Mark, sliding into a chair at the table.

"True," replies the other, "but it's an impressive story all the same, and destined, I'm sure, to be only Chapter One in an unfolding epic."

Peter Hemphill is Under Secretary-General for Political Affairs at the United Nations. He is a twenty-year career diplomat of British origin. His skills of friendly communication sit easily with his guest.

"I hope you like my choice of restaurant," he continues. "It's my periodic escape from the tyranny of skyscrapers, traffic, and sunless, windy streets."

"Yes, it reminds me of the rain forests in north Queensland. I'm surprised there isn't a by-law in New York against eating food in such thick foliage."

"Oh, no," smiles his host, "believe me, we're better off to take our chances in this jungle than the one outside."

"Are you referring to New York or the world in general?" asks Mark.

"Both, now you come to mention it. In my line of work, just as in yours, I expect, we see a little too much of the human claw and fang. But that subject is too heavy before lunch. Shall we deal with the essentials first and order? They have a wonderful Wild Garden Buffet here, complete with all the exotica of vegetables and fruit that we United Nations types thrive on. Would you care to join me in that?"

"Absolutely. What else would one eat here but fruits from the Wild Garden? Go ahead. I'll follow your lead."

The buffet is true to its name with all manner of fruits and vegetables as hot and cold dishes. The whole display is spread around in a meandering pattern of earthenware serving dishes placed on tree stumps, rocks, swinging baskets, all clustered together in a haphazard arrangement where patrons weave around, jostling one another in polite good humour as they stoop and sample and stretch for the fruits of the Wild Garden. Mark quickly catches the spirit of the place, selecting among items while he winks and smiles with fellow guests of every race, colour, and costume. After a while, he realizes that he has completely lost sight of Peter Hemphill and has absolutely no idea of where he is in this maze of people, plants and produce. Then, a touch at his elbow reveals his host good naturedly smiling at him, rolling his eyes, and motioning him to follow as they weave their way back to the table under the umbrella tree.

"Well, there's a new story for the press," laughs Peter as they slide into their chairs. "The intrepid Mark Venture, leader of the Visioneers and rescuer of damsels from the hands of terrorists, lost in the Wild Garden Buffet at Woodlands in the heart of New York City."

"Yes," rejoins Mark, "and the whole thing craftily engineered by the United Nations as a diversionary tactic to prevent me from discovering the extent of their own confusion in the real wild garden of human affairs."

"Ah," sighs Peter, "I see I am discovered, and I thought I was being clever. But you're right. I wanted to meet you here rather than in my office, because everything there is over-burdened with reports and statistics and here there's a chaotic flow of life with a spirit of congenial good will. I thought, from what I've heard of the Visioneers that perhaps that's what you people are trying to bring to the world, building a Woodlands out there for people to enjoy. Have I got that right, Mark?"

"Yes, I think you have. It's a good image. I'll keep it in mind. Now, let me tell you about us and how the United Nations can help."

Mark tells the story, sensing in this new contact, a kindred spirit who would like to break free of many bands that bind him in the perennial dance of diplomacy. He sees Peter's eyes warm with interest as he hears about President Mutsandu's busload of Visioneers rolling in across the grasslands of Yarawi; of Bill Bates and Daniel Thomas planning the revitalization of Russia in a boisterous vodka-laced celebration in the cottage at Lake Radovichy; and of Indira and Carmen captured by the spiritual wisdom of Baba Satyananda at his Place of Peace and Serenity at the ashram at Ventagiri. Seeing Peter's deepening respect for the scope of what he's hearing, Mark continues on with the rest of the story: Zhao She Yuhan's vision for the rebirth of China; the spell-binding performance of "Momma" Theresa at the rock concert in Canada; Jeremy Hiscox and Irene Henshaw waylaying Lord Nigel and Lady Pamela Feversham in Scotland; and General Soulière's successful appeal to Prince Rupert to introduce the mission of the Visioneers to a Unesco conference in Paris. The account ends with the triumph and tragedy of Luis Valdez's brief ministry in Chile.

"Concerning the man who killed Luis," Mark is saying, "I've been told he was acting for someone called Carlos Palmira who goes under a code name of El Condor. Do you know anything about him?"

A shadow passes over Peter Hemphill's face.

"Mohammed Hussein told me you would be asking about him. Arms deals, espionage, drug trafficking: they're not my stock in trade, you know, but I've made a few preliminary enquiries. Palmira is into all of that. He's never been convicted of anything but the dossier on him is apparently pretty thick. If he was behind the killing of Valdez, you can be sure someone else will take the blame for it."

"We've got to deal with people like that!" Mark feels the anger building inside him. "The whole world is just too accepting and cynical of that kind of thing. Well, the costs of continuing like that now and into the future are way beyond anything we can imagine. We have to deal with it head on. People have to deal with it; not just the authorities, who might or might not through the process of law and political manoeuvring, cause something to be done; but people out in the street, in every country, looking around and saying, this is unacceptable, and moving to do something about it.

"The way they can do it is by coming together in small, human-scale, community groups, building visions of what they want in their communities, and going out and seeing that it happens. This is the way they will take the power from El Condor and his like.

"Do you understand what I'm getting at, Peter? It's the difference between reacting to the dark side of what people do, as compared to looking out at a vision of what it is possible to do on the good side, before the evil begins to take root."

"And that's what your Visioneers are doing?" Peter asks

"Yes, the Visioneers are acting," Mark replies. "They're out in the world. They're grabbing attention. They're pulling up the blinds. They're throwing open the windows. Today, we're a curiosity. Tomorrow, we'll be a force so strong that the El Condors of the world will tremble in their eyries for fear of it.

"We're empowering people to work together to find what needs to be done; to learn what they need to know, and do what they need to do. And the key to it all is shared vision: millions of people around the world overcoming barriers of language and culture and economic differences, to build a vision in which each of them can see something for themselves that they prefer, something better than they or their children will otherwise have.

"We need models, lighthouses, beacons, and we need them quickly. The United Nations, Peter, can be an organization that will nourish the flowering. With its member agencies, it can be a powerful proactive force for the future. The Visioneers are out to make a difference and I'm here to ask you to come on board, to do whatever you can to nourish the enterprise.

"It's a long speech, Peter, but it's a simple and powerful idea. Are you willing to help us act?"

A long silence settles at the table under the umbrella tree. His food untouched, Peter Hemphill is staring hard at his lunch guest. He had arranged the meeting partly as a courtesy to Mohammed Hussein, who had asked him to do it, and partly out of curiosity to meet this man who was grabbing world headlines as the leader of the Visioneers. Now he is caught by the intensity of the man, the flash of passionate excitement in his eyes and the eager, knife-edge urgency in his voice. Nothing could be a greater contrast with most of the grinding diplomatic negotiations and interminable delays that dominate Peter's own work at the United Nations.

Unfettered by political considerations, the Visioneers are by-passing governments and going straight to the minds of people. Where that might lead, Peter Hemphill has no idea, but the sheer audacity of the enterprise, and the compelling persuasiveness of its self-styled leader now across the table from him, induces him to take a chance. He leans forward and replies to Mark Venture's question:

"You've got my attention, Mark. I'm certainly prepared to help. What do you have in mind?"

"First of all, it would be good to see a large turnout of the U.N. permanent delegates to the memorial service for Luis Valdez. The Pope's personal emissary is working with us to arrange for it to be held in a rural parish not too far from New York within the next two weeks. As soon as the place and date are set, we'll be inviting all of the permanent delegates to attend, along with representatives from all of the U.N. agencies around the world. It's important to us to have the United Nations and other humanitarian bodies well represented. We haven't had time yet to become well known in all those circles. You have a powerful influence on the inside and could be a big help to us."

"Consider it done," replies Peter.

"Thank you," says Mark. "Secondly, I would like to receive whatever information and advice I can on how to deal with El Condor."

"That's a different order of things, and it could be dangerous, too, but I'll put you in touch with the best contact I can. I hardly dare ask if you have any other requests."

"Only one. So far, our approach has been to go directly to the people on every continent to get large numbers recruited and active as Visioneers. We have an immense amount of work to do there. I'm giving us a hundred and fifty days from the date of the Luis Valdez memorial service to get that well launched. Then we'll be ready to go after the political leaders. I'd like your help in doing that."

"It's good to see you keeping the issues simple," smiles Peter. "You know, of course, that the U.N. has a conference of world leaders scheduled for just about that time in New York. I don't suppose there's any coincidence in your timing, is there?"

"I see you're quick to grasp my drift," replies Mark. "Yes, we intend to target that conference directly. That's where I think you'll be able to help."

"Anything particular in mind?"

"Yes, but it's too soon to say. One thing you can be sure about, though. It'll be spectacular."

"No doubt."

"Are you ready for that?"

"Why not, though I hope you'll do me the courtesy of defining spectacular before we reach a deal."

"Absolutely. Now, do you know what I think?"

"I hardly dare ask."

"I think we should eat our lunch."

The People Come Out

The early morning fall mist has lifted, burning off in the warm sunlight now touching fields, trees, and roof tops of the quiet countryside. Less than two hours away by car the megalopolis of New York and its surroundings, discharge their daily discourse, engaging countless millions of people in every corner of the globe. But here in the rural parish of St. Paul, that world barely exists. Tucked into the lower reaches of the Catskill Mountains overlooking the wide sweep of the Hudson River valley, the church sits quietly in a sea of blazing autumn colours of red, orange and scarlet. A wide paved driveway lined with towering elm and maple trees winds up the hill to the stone buildings and their carefully groomed lawns and flower gardens. All is quiet and deserted, a retreat lying at rest, hanging motionless in time at the edge of a day in its life unlike any that has gone before.

For the Roman Catholic parish of St. Paul's has been chosen by His Eminence Claudio Vachiano, personal envoy of His Holiness, the Pope, to be the site of the memorial service for Father Luis Valdez. Today, the restful solitude of this place will be caught up in the surge of worldwide interest in the last tragic moments of this man's life and its portent for the future. The church, the setting, the morning catch their breath preparing for the approaching glare of attention.

The first signs are the arrival of the vans from three television networks, preparing to carry the event live to a watching world. Heavy electric cables seeking outlets for power soon stretch from parking lot across the lawns. Chairs by the hundreds disgorge from the parish hall. Powerful lights are set up inside the church from nave to sanctuary. Microphones, sound equipment, outdoor speakers, all spring quickly into place, preparing for the ceremony and anticipating a congregation that will spill outside the church into the grounds and gardens.

But no amount of preparation could have foreseen what begins to happen by mid-morning. The people start to arrive. These are not invited guests or officials, but ordinary folk driving in by car and camper van, all manner of recreation vehicles from huge motorhomes to cut-down Volkswagens, with license plates from practically every American state and all ten provinces in Canada. They come in a steady stream, turning off the freeway, hesitantly looking for directions along the side roads, then finding the church grounds, confidently coming up the driveway, filling the parking lot, while officials hastily arrange for an adjoining field to be used, which soon begins to fill as well with hundreds of cars coming in.

Then the buses start to arrive, chartered tour buses, the names of their cities of origin in the front window beside the driver: New York, Boston, Chicago, Philadelphia, Washington, Cincinnati, Buffalo, Toronto, Montreal, and dozens of others. And the school buses, too. First there are only a few, sprinkled conspicuously like bright yellow squat beetles among the other vehicles, but by noontime they begin to come in convoys, disgorging hundreds of children of all ages with teachers and parents, scurrying to find places on the lawn for the ceremony, carrying their box lunches, many wearing black armbands, some in uniforms of scouts and guides and church groups and private schools.

And it seems that each group of children has a banner, all shapes, sizes, colours, unfurled, blowing gently in the light breeze. Each banner has its own design, but on all, emblazoned in bold letters of gold on blue or bright red or emerald green, the word VISIONEERS, or a huge V. All of these banners are dancing and bobbing around above the heads of the children who brought them, mixing in with the other people, nothing organized, but nothing disorderly, everyone quietly expectant and respectfully subdued in greetings and conversations, finding places to sit and wait for the start of the ceremony.

Pamela Barrett of the ZNN network has taken up a position on a small platform erected beside the front entrance to the church. Beside her, the technical crew is setting up its cameras and sound equipment. As the congregation grows, she watches in mounting amazement at the size and diversity of it. She remembers clearly her last contact with the Visioneers in the small hotel lobby in Jerusalem when Mark Venture, Esther Fisher and Mohammed Hussein were interviewed. She was intrigued then by the way in which the spirit and events surrounding the Visioneers were attracting world attention. She had requested permission to stay with the assignment and when the time and place for the memorial service for Luis Valdez were announced, she was among the first of the news teams to secure rights for coverage. Now, with one hour to go before the ceremony is due to start at

2 p.m., she is on the air sending in bulletins, preparing the network for what she is now sensing as a major event, beyond any previous expectations even she had held.

"I can't believe what we're seeing here," she is saying on air. "We had some sense that people had been touched by what happened to Luis Valdez and by the whole spirit of the Visioneers. But what's happening here is truly extraordinary. I must be looking down now at a sea of four or five thousand people, and back along the road as far as I can see there's a steady line of cars coming. I don't think the organizers had any idea this would happen. The people I've spoken to say they're here out of respect for a man they didn't know, who was snatched from them at the very moment when he was opening up hope for the future. They seem to be here to make a statement about that.

"Now, that's the general public who are all gathered outside the church. Inside, there are about 300 seats for the official guests, and many have already arrived. I've seen several black limousines with diplomatic plates pull up, and there are more coming up the drive, mostly delegates from the United Nations in New York. There's quite a few church people, too: sisters and brothers from various orders and senior clerics, but not all Roman Catholic or even Christian. According to the list I've got here, the whole spiritual spectrum is represented: Jews, Moslems, Hindus, and many others I don't recognize.

"The service will be conducted by Cardinal Vachiano from the Vatican representing the Pope, and he'll be attended by the Archbishop of the Diocese and I see several other bishops on the list, quite a display by the Church for one of its own. On the political side, the Secretary-General of the U.N. will be represented by Under Secretary Peter Hemphill, and the Director-General of Unesco has his representative here, too. The list goes on and on: all of the U.N. ambassadors I mentioned before, but I see some Senators and Governors, too, and a whole long list of non-profit groups, and foundations, and peace groups. This is really quite amazing: all of this attention for a man no one had heard of a few weeks ago.

"But, of course, the group everyone is most interested in are the Visioneers. Apparently they're all coming, about twenty of them from the original group, but almost a hundred, counting others coming from various countries who have been recruited as leaders. This is the first time the world will have seen them. Who are the Visioneers? Where did they spring from? No one seems to know. I've spoken to the leader, Mark Venture, a couple of times in Jerusalem, but I'm still not sure how they operate. And he's quite a remarkable man, too. I think we've all heard how he sprang his friend Esther Fisher free from the terrorists. I'm sure everyone will be looking to see both of them here.

"We've got absolutely no information on how the Visioneers are going to arrive, or how we'll even recognize them when they do. It's really quite intriguing; no wonder the world's paying attention. I'll keep you posted with bulletins from time to time, until we come back for the start of the ceremony in about an hour from now. This is Pamela Barrett from ZNN at St. Paul's Church."

When Pamela comes back on air fifteen minutes later, she can hardly contain the excitement in her voice.

"We've just got the official word: the Visioneers are coming! There are three bus loads. They've just turned off the freeway and are on their way up to the church. I can't see them yet from where I am, but there are still dozens of other cars coming in. I don't know how anyone is going to get through. There must be seven or eight thousand people now. Where are they coming from? And, just look at all these children in their uniforms with their VISIONEER banners.

"As you can see on your screens, there are no more cars coming up the driveway except those bringing official guests. The rest are being held back in some outer parking area and the people are walking in. Just look at them on your screen. Thank goodness the grounds are large. They're all finding seats somewhere on the grass, under the trees. It seems that everyone has a blanket or cushion to sit on; just like a picnic, but it isn't a picnic. They're all conscious of that. It's all so incredibly orderly and quiet, thousands of people, just finding a place to sit and wait for the ceremony to start.

"Here's a police escort coming up through the crowds on the driveway. It could be the Visioneers; but no, there's no buses, just three black limousines. I expect it's Cardinal Vachiano. Yes, there's the scarlet robes. He's getting out, acknowledging the people, going over and speaking to some of them. I think he's as surprised as the rest of us to see the numbers. Now you can see the others in the Vatican party, and the Archbishop. And now the United Nations group: Peter Hemphill representing the Secretary General and several others there. I'm not sure who they are, possibly the Unesco delegation.

"Here's another escort coming, and two more limousines. Now this is quite extraordinary. It's His Royal Highness Prince Rupert of Wittenstein and Princess Christiana. The Prince was speaking at Unesco when the first word of Luis Valdez came through. He was responsible for bringing Father Valdez to the attention of the delegates and to the world. Now here he is a few weeks later, attending a memorial service for the man. I doubt if they ever met. This is certainly an acknowledgment of the influence of this simple priest and his witness to the world from Chile. I believe the other couple there with the Prince and Princess are Lord Nigel and Lady Pamela Feversham from England. My notes say that Lord Nigel is the President of the International Foundation for Friends of the Earth. I believe that's an umbrella group or network for a whole host of foundations with environmental and peace missions, many of whom are also represented here separately by their own officials.

"There they go now, joining Cardinal Vachiano and his group, up the steps and into the church. Still no sign of the Visioneers. I expect they're making slow progress through the cars and people down there on the road. There's the scene inside the church on your screen. It's pretty well full except for a block of seats for the Visioneers. The Cardinal has gone for robing. There's Ramon Valdez and Maria Esteban in the front pews. They're Father Luis' brother and sister. They've come in from Santiago. I suspect they never dreamed their brother would attract so much attention.

"Now, there's something beginning to happen out here. It's another police escort. Yes, and I can see the buses, three of them, big coaches, land cruisers, and, would you believe, they've got VISIONEERS in big block letters on the front of each. The people are standing up and moving forward to get a better view. It's the first sign of any pressing, but everything's still quite orderly, almost like a movie in slow motion, particularly with those children out there. You have the sense that they'd all like to break out cheering and rush forward, but they won't because this is a solemn occasion. But what energy and interest there is! The air is electric with it!

"Now, here's the first bus, coming right up to the steps of the church, the others pulling in behind. I can't really make out any of the passengers, the coach windows are tinted, so we'll just have to wait. There's the door opening on the first bus, no one coming out yet. Yes, here we go. Let me see, is it? Yes, it's Mark Venture. I'd recognize him in an instant: tall, handsome, suntanned, wearing a formal, dark business suit, looking out to the crowd, nodding to them. He seems to be saying, thank you for coming, looking every inch a leader. Now, there's Esther, right behind him. She's wearing a simple black dress under her coat, and a tiny black hat with a wisp of veil at the front. She's joining Mark by the steps, just a few feet from me here. They're a stunning couple, even on this sad occasion. The crowd is pushing forward a little now. They really want to see Esther and Mark.

"But now all the buses have pulled up and the passengers are getting out. Will you look at these people! I have names here, but I'm sure I don't know who anyone is. Now that has to be Mutsandu, President of Yarawi: tall, black, impressive man in long, white robes, and it looks like he has his whole African contingent with him. They keep on coming out of the bus, in beautiful clothes, all the colours of the rainbow.

"Now will you look there, coming out of the third bus! Have you got that on the screen, guys? Who is that man? He's just so striking: tall, saffron robe, but he glows. He's positively glowing. And there's an Indian lady with him in a beautiful blue and gold sari. It's extraordinary. These people are just glowing with energy. And I'm sure the crowd can sense it, too. Everyone's just staring spellbound. And the man in the saffron robe is smiling at them. Now Mark and Esther are going over to join him and the Indian woman, and the four of them are moving out among the people, greeting them. Oh, what a nice touch, the people are really appreciating this. And there goes Mutsandu and his group, they're just going over to mingle. Oh, the people are really loving this. The whole atmosphere is just charged since these people arrived.

"Now, what's happening? The children in the crowd are getting excited. Yes, look, coming out of the second bus: this lovely, motherly woman, with her round face positively beaming. It has to be "Momma' Theresa. She obviously can't restrain herself. She's over amongst the nearest group of children and they're all pushing around her. She's moving through them and it's like a wave.

"And there are still people getting off the buses. Oh, and here's someone I know. It's Bill Bates from Los Angeles. Bill's one of the Visioneers, but he's also in the television business. Maybe he'll come up here and help me with some names.

"Oh, Bill! Bill Bates! Hi, it's Pamela Barrett. Will you come up here and help me with some names?"

"Hello, Pamela," Bill calls out. "Sure. I'll come up. Just give me a bit of room. There we go. Well, that's quite a scene, isn't it? I hope your cameras are getting it for the world. The Visioneers create quite a stir, don't they?"

"Oh, Bill, you have to tell me, who is that man in the saffron robe? He's electric. The people are just melting around him."

"That's Baba Satyananda. I think he's probably the most spiritual being on Earth. Now that the Visioneers are in motion, the world's going to learn incredible things from Baba.

"But look here, this is our American group just getting off the bus. That's Julia McCarthy, Chairman of McCarthy Broadcast Systems; and next to her looking rather uncomfortable in his formal suit is Arthur Rhinegold, a film producer from Los Angeles; then Diane Koplitz, probably one of the most original minds in the country; and George Walker, he'll revolutionize business in the 21st century; and lastly, Senator Wilfred Brown from North Carolina, the old war horse for human rights. Maybe they're not as colourful as some of the others, but they're great team players, and they're going to make a big difference to this country and the world.

"But look back there, just getting out of the third bus, the giant with the red beard. It's my Russian buddy, Vladimir Rostov. If anyone has got the spirit to put that country in order, it's Vladimir. And the big woman with him is Anna Borodino. She's a powerhouse, too. And the serious looking fellow with her is Boris Dubrovsky. The other fellow with the long hair is Daniel Thomas, Welsh poet extraordinaire, and by now, I think, probably more Russian than the Russians.

"That's some of our folk, Pamela, for your viewers to meet. It's really staggering to see all these people here. Luis Valdez certainly had an impact. I think Mark is a little overwhelmed. That's why he's walking around out there among the people. He wants to show his appreciation to them for being here. But this day is for Luis. Now we're going to honour him. I'll talk to you later, Pamela."

"Thank you, Bill." Pamela is surveying the scene below her. "Now, this is strange. I think everyone is off the buses, but they're all coming forward to group around the lead bus, and here are Mark and Esther coming through to stand at the door of the bus, looking up, as if they're waiting for someone.

"Oh, my stars! In the excitement of all this, I'd forgotten! Look at this man coming out alone, wearing his buckskin jacket. It's George Cardinal. The last time the world saw him, he was holding Luis Valdez, dying in his arms. What a magnificent stamp of a man! He looks so strong, but sad. Luis Valdez was his great friend and hero. I think this day must be for George, too. Mark is showing him great respect. There they go up the steps now into the church, George Cardinal leading the way. Mark and Esther are following, and all of the others, the Visioneers. What an incredible group of people! Somehow, I don't know, I have this strange feeling, as if, I'm not sure what. As if, something has changed in the world, as these people walk by me, almost close enough to touch, going to pay honour to the memory of their friend. I have this sense, that somehow the world is listening in a way that it's never listened before; and that if someone, today, speaks the right words they'll be heard, and the world will have turned a corner.

"I'm sorry, I can't continue now. Let's go in silence with the Visioneers into the church."

As she stands there quietly on her platform, head slightly bowed, watching the figures below her file past, Pamela feels a warm wave of peace pass over her. She turns and looks down into the smiling eyes of Baba Satyananda. He raises his hand to her in the gentlest of motions and she knows at once that he has slipped into her mind and seems to linger there as he passes by and steps slowly with the others up into the church.

Remembrance, Celebration, Triumph

The memorial service for Father Luis Valdez is elegant and filled with the ritual and ceremony of the church founded on St. Peter, the rock, in Rome. Now it's played out here today, almost two thousand years later, in the New World of the Americas, in the parish church named for St. Paul, first among Christian missionaries. With His Eminence, Cardinal Vachiano presiding, the service is rich with symbol, pageantry and music. All members of the congregation, whatever race or religious affiliation, are gathered up into a spirit of thankfulness and respect for a life devoted to the service of God, and laid down in striving, without fear, for human well-being.

When the cardinal rises to speak to the congregation, his voice is filled with the emotion of the time and the occasion. He is conscious that in this place, as in no other that he has ever been, a spirit of search and renewal is moving. Luis Valdez was its first spokesman to an apprehensive, but hopeful, world.

"I speak to you, my friends, for the Holy Father and the church, in loving and sorrowful memory of our brother Luis. In his life and death, we have seen again the play of forces which those who witness for good against evil have known since our blessed Lord walked upon the Earth.

"When the Christian Church was in its infancy, it suffered greatly at the hands of those who didn't wish to hear its scathing denunciation of the hardness and sterile complacence that had settled in men's hearts and minds. Our blessed Lord was first victim of that hardness, and he gave his life on the cross in a sacrifice not understood by those who witnessed it. Perhaps we don't fully understand it today, for only God can know His plan for the human family and our earthly home.

"In those early days, we are told of an incredible power that settled on and moved in the hearts and minds of the followers of Jesus. This was the Holy Spirit that gave ordinary men and women power of speech and action to touch the hearts and minds of others and bring the gospel of Christ to a world that had never before heard such teachings.

"And we are told in those early days of the words and actions of one man whom it seems fitting to remember today, as we mourn the cruel death of our beloved brother Luis. This man was Stephen, chosen among the disciples for special service, because he was recognized as a man of great faith, filled with the Holy Spirit.

"We are told that Stephen performed many wonders and signs among the people. But he soon clashed with those who didn't wish to hear his teachings, or know his criticisms of how they had turned from the path of God. He finally spoke out, perhaps too boldly, filled as he was with the wonder of his own contact with the Holy Spirit. His opponents turned their vengeance on him. And we are told how this lovely and gifted man of gentle spirit was dragged out of the city and put to death by one of the most cruel and barbarous punishments of the day. The life was savagely crushed out of his body by stones, thrown by those who couldn't bear the scorching of his tongue or the vision in his eyes. And he died, we are told, gazing intently into heaven, where he saw the glory of God and Jesus standing at the right hand of God. As the stones rained down upon him, he called out, 'Lord Jesus, receive my spirit!' And his last words, as he fell unconscious under the brutal barrage of hate, were of forgiveness for those who were taking away his life: 'Lord, do not hold this sin against them.'

"Stephen was the first martyr of the Christian church. Our brother Luis is among its latest. We would wish with all our hearts that he might be the last. Yet we know that time has not yet come. Nevertheless, his brave act puts such a time so much closer within reach, if those of us who heard and saw it move now to act against the evil in the world, and say, 'Enough, no more. Such acts are an abomination in the eyes of God and of his people and we will have them no longer on this Earth!' If we do this, then our brother Luis will not have laid down his life in vain.

"When Stephen died, there was one man there witnessing and approving of the violence, whose name was Saul. He went on to be one of the most powerful persecutors of the church, ravaging its congregations, entering house after house, dragging off men and women and putting them into prison. And because of the fierceness of Saul's persecution, the disciples were scattered, but they kept preaching, and the Christian faith was taken out from Jerusalem into Samaria and then to the gentiles and out into all the nations of the world.

"And that same Saul, first and strongest among the persecutors, himself became an apostle, when, only a short time later, the Lord Jesus came to him in a vision on the road to Damascus and said: 'Saul, Saul, why are you persecuting me?" From that moment on, Saul of Tarsus, the persecutor of Christians, became Paul the Apostle, and was given the mission to take the teachings of Jesus to the gentiles, and no one since has done it with more power and spirit.

"So it is indeed fitting that we hold our memorial service for our brother, Luis, today in this church named for St. Paul, here in this beautiful countryside that represents so clearly the beauty of the Earth that Father Luis spoke for and sought to reclaim from the ignorance and greed of our age, which is destroying it.

"There is no simple message in the life and death of Father Luis Valdez, for it is not a simple world that struck him down. He stood for the core principles of love and faith, and a sense of awful wonder in the supreme beauty of God's creation, which we have no right to destroy, whether it be the land or the air, or the precious human life breathing in the body of each one of us on the planet. For we all are part of one great creation, which is born and reborn every day, and will be for eternity.

"The message of Father Luis' life and death was his proclamation of this awesome wonder of the universe, and his insistence on our duty as its intelligent and spiritual stewards to bestir ourselves now in these days of great peril for the future. He asked us to find within ourselves visions of wonderment and power. He called us to use our God-given gifts for positive acts of creation and loving care. If we do this, we will not only honour the memory of his name and life, but we will usher in the millennium of hope and fruitful purpose which he envisioned so clearly and longed with all his heart to see come to pass.

"May the spirit of God in the universe be with us all as we go forward with this great work."

The cardinal concludes his remarks and the ceremony in the church quickly comes to an end. But for Mark Venture, this doesn't seem enough. Sitting beside George Cardinal in the front pew, he is conscious of the enormous grief the Indian chief feels for his fallen friend. Mark is conscious, too, of the great crowd of people gathered outside who have come not only to honour Luis, but to show support for the work of the Visioneers. Though the ceremony inside the church has been carried to them by loudspeakers, Mark senses that they must be included more fully as participants in this first public gathering of the Visioneers.

He stands and makes an announcement that is carried to those outside.

"Friends, this is Mark Venture speaking. We are deeply touched that so many of you have come here today. This is also the first time the Visioneers have been together in public. If you will bear with us for a few minutes while the congregation leaves the church and joins all of you outside, we will then speak with you further."

Mark rejoins George Cardinal and asks softly, "George, would you like to say something?"

"Yes," replies the big man, "thank you, I would like to speak."

The congregation files out slowly into the bright autumn sunshine. The crowd outside seems to have grown even larger. Perhaps ten thousand people are now packed into the church grounds, quietly standing or sitting as the official guests come out and join them. Mark motions the original Visioneers to join him and George Cardinal on the steps of the church.

Pamela Barrett has resumed her position on the television platform. Tense with excitement and expectation, she adds her commentary to the scene being broadcast and recorded for worldwide distribution.

"This is completely spontaneous," she says. "No one was expecting anything like this show of interest from the public. Mark Venture is reacting off the cuff. He's gathered all the Visioneers together. You can see them there with him on the steps. The cardinal is there too, and Baba Satyananda, the mystery man from India in that striking saffron robe. Here's Mark Venture now. He's going to speak to the crowd. Just look at all those people! And they're all so quiet and orderly. I've never seen anything like this."

"Friends," Mark is speaking, "thank you again for coming. There's much I'd like to say to you, but no one among us has more right to speak this day than Chief George Cardinal who was with Father Luis Valdez when he died. George, would you like to speak now?"

The tall Indian Chief steps forward. His voice carries the rich resonance of the Earth. His hands held out to the crowd seem to embrace the sky.

"If I had the words, I would speak to you of the grief that is in my heart. But I do not have such words. My mind turns away in anguish from the memory of my dying brother. It refuses to accept the thought that such treachery can exist in this world that would strike out like a viper and steal a man's life only for speaking good. I do not understand such things. My mind cannot comprehend them.

"I am a man of the Earth. The rivers and forests are my brothers. The sky and the sweet fresh air that blows from it full of the scent of the rain shower—these are my companions. Luis Valdez was my brother also. Sitting on days like this in the sunshine with the great towering snow caps of the Andes above us, we would speak softly and listen to the wind moving gently across the grass and into the trees.

"And my brother Luis would speak to me of his God and of the life and work of his Lord Jesus. And I would speak to him of my God whose breath is in the wind of the forest and whose kiss is in the touch of the morning mist on the face. And we would know that his God and my God were the same.

"And as we sat there in the sunshine, we would know that our God was connected to us in the land and that we were connected to Him and to all people everywhere. For everything is connected to everything else.

"And we could not understand why, just a few kilometres away, men who were connected to God, were destroying the forests which were also connected to God and to the men. And we could not understand why the men would be destroying themselves.

"We thought it must be because a terrible sickness had come upon the men which had stolen away their minds. And we wondered how all over the world people could be doing such things. We could hear the Earth crying out in pain.

"And Luis' God said to him, 'You must speak out against such wickedness and touch the minds of men and women who have not yet fallen fully under the curse of such sickness.' And my God, speaking through the mountains, and the eagles that soar among them said, 'Yes, you must speak out against this.' Because my God was also his God. He is also your God, and we must all speak out against such evil.

"But then the evil came striking back savagely against us out of the barrel of a gun and took away the life of my brother, Luis, even while he was speaking out to save the Earth. And I did not understand that such a thing could happen. And I did not protect my brother from it, and now he is gone.

"But I am still here, and I have been asking myself what do I do now. And the answer was not coming, until today, until I saw all of you here, and knew that you would not be here if the evil was in your hearts. And if so many of you are gathered here in this one place, how many more of our brothers and sisters are out there in the world, seeing us and listening to our words and joining in our sorrow? How many more out there will be ready to gather like you and take strength from each other to act against the great evil that has settled over our world?

"I don't know how many, my friends, but I think it must be like the leaves of the forests or the grains of sands on the beach. I think it must be a very great number. And I think they must be learning from each other, and together they will build visions of what the world can be like again in the future, and from their visions they will act to make the world be like that. And the few, the very few truly evil ones amongst so many others, those few will not be allowed to triumph. Because many who might otherwise have followed such evil will turn away, because they will have seen in their minds that no good for themselves or their children can come from allowing such evil to move on our Earth to destroy its precious life and the lives of the people and animals on the Earth.

"This is my vision. It is full of hope. It is strange that in the time of my great sorrow, I can also be full of hope. But I am a simple man. I love the Earth. And I love you, my brothers and sisters. I do not think that you will allow the Earth to die. It is my vision. It was my brother Luis' vision, also. We offer it to you to be your vision, too."

As George Cardinal finishes speaking, a profound hush has settled over the crowd. A ripple appears in the ranks of the Visioneers on the steps of the church. Into the space of silence moves the motherly figure of 'Momma' Theresa, rolling up beside George Cardinal, embracing him, then taking the microphone, and in the same magnificent voice that rang out on the stage in the stadium in Vancouver, she sings to the crowd the same haunting melody of *Amazing Grace*.

Ten thousand voices spontaneously pick up the words of this song of ages. The sound of the singing rises up and floats out over the open countryside. Theresa now calls out to them to sing the melody with the new words she taught to the young people first at the concert in Vancouver. Those at the front of the crowd, along with the television cameras, can see her round face shining with the absolute joy of the performance, yet still sombre with the spirit of the day.

"Sing it with me now, with new words for the hope and the vision in our hearts. I will teach you, follow me:

"Amazing Grace, how sweet the sound.
That calls to us to hear.
We once were lost, but now we're found;
The time to come is near.
Amazing Grace, our hearts inspire,
Show us the way to see.
Our dreams, our hopes, our great desire:
To grow, to live, to be!"

With Theresa leading, they sing it through again and then again, each time the volume swelling as more people pick up the melody, and the words stir their minds to see and to feel the vision that George Cardinal has held out to them.

As the singing sweeps through the third time, a new figure joins Theresa and George at the microphone. It's Baba Satyananda. He embraces the others, then they stand back, and as the last words of the song float out over the land, Baba speaks, his voice as warm and gentle as the soft afternoon sun bathing the people below.

"It's good for us to sing, my friends—to sing with all our heart for the coming of the vision that George has placed before us. I am Baba. You may not know me by that name, but each of you knows me by the name that your faith speaks to you of love. I come from India, but I live also in every land where people of good will are reaching out to create a better time.

"I am here today because at this moment the world is taking a very big step towards the time which, His Eminence, the Cardinal, spoke of in his address. The time when men like Luis Valdez and Stephen, the disciple of Jesus, will not be stoned to death or shot down for speaking the truth. For that, my children, will be the time of truth, the time of universal truth—truth formed from the flowing together of all the truth that is in the minds of all people from every land—separate truths flowing together like all the rivers of the Earth, forming a mighty lake of universal truth from which we all can drink and be refreshed.

"And when we drink of that lake, we will know that everything is love, and that love is spirit, and that, therefore, all of us are love and spirit, and that love and spirit are God, and that all of us therefore are God, and God is everything and that we therefore cannot destroy or take away life because when we do, we destroy ourselves.

"This is the great and universal truth, and today the world is taking a step towards it, as we here in this place feel it in our hearts, and as those millions of you who are watching on television also feel it in your hearts and begin to turn towards it.

"And you will move towards it, as you begin to pay attention to those who need your help. Those who are not here or are not watching, because they know nothing of Luis Valdez or the Visioneers or the love of which I speak. Those whose lives are consumed by the agony of fear and pain and suffering—in the ghettos, on the streets, in refugee camps and prisons, in hospitals and institutions, begging in poverty, starving in the midst of plenty, destroying their minds and bodies with drugs, living continuously in fear and torment.

"The time of universal truth cannot come, until we care for these, our brothers and our sisters, with all the love and care we feel for ourselves and for those closest to us. The time of universal truth is the time of the meeting of the minds of all men and women everywhere, putting aside the enmities and hatreds of the past, knowing now that everything is spirit, that all of us are connected in spirit, and that none of us can be whole unless all of us are striving to make all of us whole.

"This is the great learning that we are here today embracing in the memory of our brother Luis, in the words and vision of our brother George, in the song and spirit of our sister Theresa, in the great and eternal goodness of the love of God which flows in us and through us to all things and all people everywhere.

"Let us sing again, with all our hearts that great song of Grace that Theresa has taught us."

Stronger now, much stronger, as if reaching out to embrace everything in the universe, the voices of the ten thousand people rise in a great crescendo of song:

"Amazing Grace, our hearts inspire,
Show us the way to see.
Our dreams, our hopes, our great desire:
To grow, to live, to be!"

Mark Venture comes forward with Esther, hand in hand, standing at the front with George, Baba, and Theresa, while the other Visioneers cluster close behind, their faces wreathed in smiles, glowing with the spirit of this great moment.

"Friends of Luis," Mark speaks out, "friends of the Earth, friends of the future—thank you for being here. Go now with peace and love. Go from here knowing that the time of which Baba has spoken is not far away. Go knowing that the vision George has described can be achieved. Go out into the world from here knowing that this can be done. Under no circumstances should you go from here thinking that it can't be done—because it can. If we dare to imagine that it can be done, then it will be done, because you will make it happen.

"Of course, it will take tremendous effort. Of course, it will require sacrifice. Of course, it will involve risks and danger, and at times you'll be afraid, dreadfully afraid. But none of that will change the fact that it can be done. Because if it is in your minds to do it, it can be done.

"I'm speaking to all of you here today, and to all who are watching on television, in every country, especially those of you who live in countries where you are free to act and choose your future. You must act now to choose a collectively decent future for the whole world, because nothing else is good enough. Act now to help those who are not yet free to act for themselves, because they live under the terror of oppressive regimes, or because they are impoverished or illiterate and they haven't heard what you have heard from Luis Valdez, and George Cardinal, and Baba Satyananda, and Cardinal Vachiano.

"These are not just words that you have heard. They are ideas. And there is nothing more powerful than an idea whose time has come. And the time has come for the idea that we can, by leading with our visionary minds create the kind of world that we would choose to live in for ourselves and for our children, and for their children after them.

"To do this, you will need to learn many new things and to unlearn many old ones. You will have to learn to be humble and tolerant. You will have to learn the truth from your neighbour and to add to it your truth to make a better truth.

"The Visioneers are going out to help with this. You see them here in front of you, just a handful now, but down there in the crowd, already many more. And if all of you who are listening commit today to become Visioneers in your community, then how quickly this will grow.

"It's time now my friends to go, to go out and create a better future for the world. As you go, we will give you a song, the *Song of the Visioneers*, in memory of Luis Valdez. We have grieved his death: and now we celebrate his life.

"Theresa will lead us, the *Song of the Visioneers!*"

With that, Theresa comes to the microphone again. Her voice is quivering with the emotion of Mark's charge to the crowd. She sings the words, and the children in the audience, already knowing them, join her, then their parents, then everyone, singing, full voice, with energy and passion, singing as they go, Theresa leading them, singing the words over and over, the *Song of the Visioneers*.

"We are the ones, going to the fore.
Big ones, little ones—all of us are here.
Small world, big world, reaching out to all.
Up, up, and upmost—the mighty Visioneers!"

With Theresa leading at the microphone and the crowd joining in ten thousand strong at the tops of their voices, the Visioneers come down from the steps, led by Mark and Esther, and move through the crowd, shaking hands, laughing, smiling, crying, waving, moving to their buses. Finally, Theresa, too, follows, and the buses begin to move away, the crowd parting and waving, most of them still singing. Then the crowd begins to move also, a great mass of people, slowly leaving, reluctantly turning away from the magic of the moment, snatches of song still ringing out long after the buses of the Visioneers have disappeared from sight down the driveway.

On the television platform, Pamela Barrett turns to face the camera to close the telecast.

"Again," she says, "we've seen these Visioneers releasing a flood of incredible energy. If it touches each of you watching with only a fraction of the force all of us here have felt, then I have no doubt that the world is indeed setting course for a new and better future. I don't know what more to say. I'm completely lost for words. They've all been said.

"This is Pamela Barrett for ZNN, signing off from St. Paul's Church and the memorial service for Luis Valdez, Visioneer."

PART THREE

Positioning for Strength

CHAPTER THIRTEEN

Imaginary
Versus
Real

Y OU'RE ALONE IN YOUR THINKING ROOM. The fire crackles with its customary coziness. Outside, the first snow flurries of winter spatter against the window panes, breaking in crystalline stars of moisture, quiet messengers of a coming turbulence.

You sit back deep in the comfortable leather chair and call to mind all that has happened since first you dared to imagine that vision could change the world.

You began in the waves, great towering mountains of liquid energy, gathering you up and almost crushing the life out of you as you struggled with them. And there you found your metaphor for the future: arching, swelling, crashing waves in endless motion, an ocean of limitless possibility, but great danger, where people, all the people of the Earth, are swimming and struggling to ride the waves to their personal success.

And then you sought to change the metaphor, to give people the sense that this ocean and these waves are of their own making, and can, therefore, be shaped by their actions into something harmonious and controllable, but only if all minds are working together to do it. Over the ocean, you put the blue dome of the sky as the symbol of the unity of mind needed to fashion a preferred future. And across the sky you put a silver bridge, gleaming, magnificent, where people can travel on a moving sidewalk into a future filled with the richness of their own creativity.

To help you build the framework for this possible future, you called from your imagination four large minds and spirits from other times and places, excited now with the prospect of creating a new millennium of hope and superb human enterprise: Winston Churchill, Charles Dickens, John Kennedy and Anne Shirley of Green Gables. Together you and your mentors created the band of Visioneers, and sent them out into every continent where men and women struggle with limiting beliefs and wreak havoc against themselves and the great natural biosphere that sustains their life, which, in the final instance, is their only hope for the future.

And the Visioneers have begun to stir that great sea of humanity into awareness of their potential. They have found in themselves power and energy that hitherto they had no sense of, discovering along the way others of like mind and spirit. Together they have launched a venture which already has achieved spectacular results.

They've become your friends, these Visioneers. For you, they are real human beings with a passion and energy for life that leaps out and engulfs all whom they touch, giving them new hope and determination. You have seen them grow in spirit as they rise to the challenge, each one leading and following as the situation demands. You have seen them confronted by the worst of the devils that can infect the human mind, striking down Luis Valdez, snatching life from Joshua Roth, plunging Esther Fisher into grave danger.

Through all of this activity, you now have come, you and your Visioneers, to the threshold of the opportunity you sought to create. You are at Day One of the hundred and fifty days Mark Venture has set for the Visioneers to make a difference, a difference so strong that from there it will move with its own momentum into a future of promise for all humankind.

You're now deep inside your mind imagining the possibility of such an enterprise, where the characters you've created will go out and transform the future of the world. It's a prospect of such exhilarating potential that you're trembling with the excitement of it. And yet, at the same time, you know that so far all this is in your mind, and that even if you and your comrades travel the hundred and fifty days, there will be another world running in parallel, a world untouched by the spirit of the Visioneers, and which you must, at some point, confront. You've set yourself in a force-field of creative tension: tension between the future you can so vividly imagine, and the current reality of a world locked into the helplessness of old ways of thinking. In this force-field lies the potential for you to move to your own future reality that will transform your life.

One Hundred and Fifty Days of Change

The hundred and fifty days begin in grand style. Mark Venture is true to his word to provide support and encouragement to those who seek to be intentional about the future in a world so complex that no single mind can begin to comprehend it. The framework is elegant and comprehensive.

Following the memorial service for Luis Valdez, while the *Song of the Visioneers* is still ringing out on the air waves of a curious world, an announcement is made that a global headquarters for the Visioneers has been established in Los Angeles. Bill Bates is in charge of it. Money pours in from corporate sponsors, attracted by the notion that employees can be empowered with a sense of vision that will greatly enhance the productivity and performance of the corporation.

A new program of creative learning is established. George Walker, Bill Bates' business associate from Advanced Systems, takes the lead on it. He had first suggested the idea to Bill before the ill-fated final telecast by Luis Valdez. Now, George moves quickly with approval from Mark Venture to set up an educational branch of the Visioneers. Through the Planetary Business Network, the program is quickly made available to the business community across the world.

While this is happening, Mark is equally insistent that teachers are encouraged to enliven the minds of children to become what Winston Churchill called "Visioneers of the future possible." The pressure for this also pushes vigorously upward from the children themselves. Fired with the concept of Visioneers, children around the world form clubs, music groups, adventure teams, and all manner of business enterprises of their own. Everywhere, the blue flag of the Visioneers with its white world and big V waves boldly over club houses, dens, and secret hideaways where bold adventurers dream their dreams of high achievement.

But nowhere does the Visioneering movement gather force more quickly than in the community. The driving energy comes from women who push beyond earlier moves for equality and equity to take the role now as full partners with men in providing leadership in every aspect of community life. Diane Koplitz from Sausalito, another one of the American team of Visioneers, assumes the lead on this. She is skilfully promoted by Bill Bates as a transformational leader of women worldwide to demonstrate what can be achieved when they work in partnership with men around values of love and caring rather than aggression and power. She is joined in this by Esther Fisher, Indira Murti and Carmen Santander. Together and individually, the four of them become as well known on television talk shows and in the popular press and magazines as any Hollywood star or popular singer. At the same time, their ideas on the leadership role of women in cultural transformation receive ready acceptance in intellectual circles on both sides of the Atlantic and Pacific Oceans. When the work is picked up by George Walker and incorporated into the programs of the Planetary Business Network, the new ideas of men and women working in partnership begin to penetrate the thinking on Boards of Directors and executive teams of major corporations.

As anticipated, government is the area slowest to respond to the empowering ethos of citizen-driven visions. Conflicting pressures and heavy inertia make it difficult for public bodies to initiate change. Institutional forces seem to cause policies and procedures to become ends in themselves, rather than being what they are always created to be, tentative and flexible means to accomplish a public good.

Mark understands this, which accounts for the priority he has given to moving first on community initiatives supported by business and education. The intent is to build up a momentum of citizen-based projects where people get the sense of what they can accomplish when their minds search freely and creatively for what needs to be done. Driven by vision they become centres of energy that recognize no boundaries or limits.

Part of the strategy here, too, is to involve public officials in visioning as citizens themselves, in projects where they can be full participants and beneficiaries of a mission accomplished. In this way, they can learn the skills of visioneering and the likelihood is increased that they will bring the process to their own official duties.

Officialdom in every country is gradually exposed to the spirit of visioneering over the course of the hundred and fifty days. In the democratic countries the media plays a key role and Bill Bates and his team skilfully keep the Visioneers as the darlings of the media, providing them with stimulating copy to attract the attention of readers and viewers. Stories of dramatic accomplishments abound: children banding together to clean contaminated swimming holes; senior citizens coming out of retirement to build and manage their own housing complexes; displaced workers creating self-help communities where their different skills and talents are brought together in new enterprises; middle-class suburbanites venturing into the inner city and ghettos to develop a shared vision with the residents of what their community could be, and beginning the action plan to accomplish it. Success stories and positive accomplishments assume growing importance as news with the violent and the bizarre and, indeed, begin to become the reason for increased sales of newspapers and periodicals.

One particular visioneering event steals the media spotlight. True to the idea that gripped him in Bill Bates' office at the first meeting of the American team, Arthur Rhinegold pushes ahead to make a film telling the story of the Visioneers. With Mark and Bill continuously keeping the work of the Visioneers in the public eye, the interest in what they're doing is maintained. This provides Arthur with an opportunity to make a docudrama, using real footage as much as possible from telecasts, but heightening the drama by using actors on location in key episodes around the events in Chile and Israel. The project moves very quickly as a three-part series. Part I will tell the story up to the memorial service for Luis Valdez. This is targeted for early release. Part II will cover the hundred and fifty days of growth and development. Part III will recount how governments respond once the impact of the Visioneers has reached the point where they are forced to pay attention.

The film comes in on schedule and Part I has its North American premiere just eighty days into the hundred and fifty. It is heralded with great fanfare and Mark, Esther and several of the other Visioneers are on hand in Hollywood for the event. An immediate hit, it reawakens the initial interest in the extraordinary accomplishments of this group of people. Released simultaneously in almost every major English speaking community in the world, it is quickly rushed into production for release with subtitles in several other languages. Again the world is caught up in the exploits of Mark Venture, Luis Valdez and the others, and a surge of interest is created in what the Visioneers have been doing since the stirring close to the ceremonies at St. Paul's Church almost three months earlier.

And there's much to report. Activity has spread across every continent as the Visioneers have fanned out into the world. The work has spread most quickly where democratic structures and high quality communication systems have facilitated it. The United States, Canada, the European Community, Japan, Australia and New Zealand—all have seen solid initial development. The spirit of visioneering has caught on in business and fostered greater creativity and initiative among managers and workers. Similarly, the women's initiatives led by Diane Koplitz and her team have focused attention at the community level on non-violent approaches to securing peace as a permanent condition of international relations. This thrust is given a significant push when Jeremy Hiscox, working with Lord Nigel and Lady Pamela Feversham in England, sponsors an international exposition for peace. More than a hundred thousand people gather for three days on a former airstrip in southern England used by British fighter pilots in the Battle for Britain in World War II.

Led by Diane Koplitz and Esther Fisher, participants of every nationality and of all ages from eight to eighty engage at this exposition in visioning what the next fifty years on Earth would be like if lived in peace, real peace, without production or sale of arms and without civil or cross border wars. More than thirty thousand separate workshops are held with people convening and reconvening, sharing their visions and hopes and dreams, learning from each other. As well as the exposition in England, ten thousand other smaller gatherings are held in every part of the world that had been a theatre of the century's terrible wars: from Calais to the Coral Sea, from North Africa to Northern Europe, from Korea to Vietnam to the Persian Gulf. On the final day, every available communications satellite orbiting the Earth is brought into play so that people in the different locations can talk to each other, sharing their visions, and making commitments to keep their countries out of any further conflict. The whole event is held as a New Year's celebration, midwinter in the Northern Hemisphere, demonstrating the willingness of people to come out in hard conditions to make their commitment to a world of peace.

The exposition is followed a few weeks later by another satellite link-up of schools around the world, so that children of practically every country can tell each other of the visions they have for life in their community when they are old enough to be in charge. This Edu-Expo is organized by Irene Henshaw, one of the team of original Visioneers, from her school just . outside Edinburgh in Scotland.

Shortly following the two expositions, Arthur Rhinegold's film on *The Visioneers Part I* is released. The juxtaposition of the visions of peace and cooperation from the expositions with the brutal slaying of Luis Valdez from the film, and the still unexplained involvement in the murder by the mysterious El Condor, dramatically shows the distance many millions of people in every country have come in the eighty days that the Visioneers have been about their work.

Most of the activity has occurred in the democratic countries already mentioned, but initiatives are underway also on every continent. In South America a self-formed coalition of representatives from each country has sprung up and approached George Cardinal to work with them, to continue the initiative in the spirit and memory of Luis Valdez. Stung by the violence associated with them through the slaying of the Catholic priest, they are anxious to show results. Some encouraging projects have occurred at the community level in each country, but in general, repressive regimes are in power in this land and progress is slow.

A similar story can be told for Africa, the former Soviet republics, and China. The Visioneers are there: President Mutsandu and Karl Ibsen in Africa, Daniel Thomas with his team in Russia, Lin Yuen working with Zhao She Yuhan in China. Project teams are being set up, but, again, the watchful eyes of authority are everywhere.

India, on the other hand, lies like a sleeping giant, aware of the undercurrent stirring in other places and nourished by its own spiritual leaders, including Baba Satyananda, but still seemingly unable to raise a passionate energy to give its teeming multitudes a better hope for the future.

The Middle East and other Moslem states remain fractured and suspicious of the visioneering movement. Mohammed Hussein is leading a vigorous personal initiative, but progress is limited by too great a willingness of most people in the region to place their hopes for the future in national leaders. The tension with Israel remains strong, though enclaves on both sides have begun to form around what Esther Fisher and Mohammed have been able to build on the goodwill generated by Esther's release by the terrorists.

In other countries in Asia, visioneering projects are sporadic and isolated, but nevertheless real. Touched by various communication links and a variety of international non-governmental organizations, many people are aware of what is happening elsewhere. They participate to some extent in the peace and educational expositions; they know about Luis Valdez; and they follow the gossip about Mark and Esther's romance. Some of them get to see Arthur Rhinegold's film. It's a small start in a long process, but a start nonetheless.

During the hundred and fifty days, no substantial activity has been initiated by the United Nations, or Unesco, or any of the other specialized U.N. agencies. Bound as these organizations are to governmental decision-making, they don't move quickly or easily, and while many of the people within their enclaves may be sympathetic, their ability to get things moving is limited. At the end of the period, the balance of visionary initiatives is with individuals. Governments and their agencies continue to look with unseeing eyes at the possibilities for difference, accepting the status quo as appropriate and inevitable until some incremental change forces an accommodation, which then becomes the new limiting factor on future possibilities.

From Alone to Together

The unfolding of the Visioneers' accomplishments stirs up a spirit in the world for hope and belief in the future. It's a tale of adventure, courage, determination, and purpose: all that distinguishes spectacular from ordinary, and superb from adequate. It's a movement of both heart and mind, where the two come together in visions that release the energy to achieve them. It leads those who come under its spell to rediscover the simple joy of being alive, and to live each day as a quest of spirit.

With this awakening comes the search in people for something beyond themselves, some higher point, the longing that yearns to be fulfilled, and which knows that ultimately this can come only in a relationship of meaning with another responsive spirit.

Such longing is the highest expression of what it means to be a Visioneer. Little wonder then that as the world begins to pay attention to the stories coming in, the spotlight settles on the two people who best exemplify that spirit. They are the ones whose lives have come together in events tinged with fear and courage, and who rapidly grow in the eyes of the world to be larger than life itself. Their relationship gives promise of the age-old love story, which a fractured world, despite its cynicism, so desperately wants to see. Mark Venture and Esther Fisher, together, become the symbol of the Visioneers and the centrepiece of a fairy-tale romance for the watching world.

For themselves, caught in the glare of such publicity, it has been no easy task to pursue a developing relationship. Pressed on every side, there never seems to be enough time to be together to learn to know each other. For Mark, it has been easier than for Esther. From the time of their first meeting he has caught her spirit, and feels it grow around him, until he is sure he has found the partner for his life. He feels no possessiveness, just a certainty of his love, and that its strength will be the means for Esther to find her way to him. For Esther, the path is harder. Caught in the memory of a deep and tender first marriage and its tragic end, she keeps a veil around her generous spirit. Her former husband, an Israeli captain, had been killed in service on a bitter, nasty border war in Lebanon. The loss had been a crushing blow for Esther, and for the past eight years she has avoided a second such involvement. She has chosen service to her country and her art, using her professional and original family name of Esther Fisher, rather than believe that her heart can ever be deeply touched by love again.

Now, suddenly, here is Mark, bent on the urgency of a mission she completely shares and showing himself sure in every way that he loves and needs her as a partner of equal strength. The gulf between them, their differences of experience and tradition, which, for Esther, seemed at first unbridgeable, begins to appear less forbidding. Slowly she sees the sunlight peeping through the shutters she had closed around her heart.

It is at this stage of their relationship that in early February they come to the Costa del Sol on Spain's Mediterranean coastline. They have stolen time away from appearances on behalf of the Visioneers, and driven down by rental car from Madrid. In grateful anonymity as just another "English" couple, they check into a small hotel, then make their way to the beach to catch the last hour of sunshine on a cool February afternoon. Warmly dressed in duffel coats and sweaters, they have the beach to themselves, save for a few seagulls wheeling and dipping just above the surface of a calm and easy sea. At this part of the shoreline the beach swings around in a gentle arc, up to a headland of jumbled rocks, creating the effect of a secluded lagoon edged with pure white sand. Hand in hand they walk along the empty beach until they come to the rocks, then sit in a sheltered spot beside the largest boulder to watch the sun setting over the headland on the opposite side of the lagoon.

"Do you know *The Captain's Verses* of Pablo Neruda?" Mark asks.

"No, tell me," Esther replies.

"They're love poems, written in Spanish, though not from here. He was Chilean, I think. They come to mind in this beautiful place. He wrote forcefully in brilliant, earthy images of his fiery love for the woman who later became his wife; but he kept the source of the poems a mysterious secret for many years, before he claimed them as his own. He wanted, he said, to be loyal to the ecstasies of love and fury."

"By keeping the poems secret?"

"Yes, they were too close to his heart to share."

"Except with the loved one?"

"Yes."

"I understand that."

Silence. Then Mark says:

"I have a new poem for you."

"Yes, I thought as much. You've written me so many; they quite blow me away."

"Would you like to hear it?"

"Of course."

"It's a bit crumpled, I'm afraid. I wrote it last night in Madrid and stuffed it in my coat pocket. I thought I might find the right place to read it to you."

He pulls a sheet of paper out of the inside pocket of his coat.

"The crumpled love poem," says Esther, smiling.

"It's called *Daring*," he replies.

"How much to dare and why?
Good questions for all who seek to act.
It's not enough to blindly venture forth,
As many have done, with multiple regret.
Neither is it right to withdraw
From playing in the main event,
To which you have been called.
Knowing how to tell is the main issue:
To be sure you have heard correctly
The higher, inner voice,
And are not deceived
By some lesser part of ego.
Usually such decisions touch others in your life,
Which calls for planning to accommodate.
And when the decision involves another
Who is pursuing an equally urgent quest,
How much more important to be right.
If involvement grows to love,
And the deep bonding of two spirits,
A change ensues.
How much to dare becomes
Less a question
And more a search
For that higher part of self
Found only in the other.
If that's discovered, and grows in strength,
Then daring becomes attaining.
New levels of experience are reached,
As old boundaries are crossed,

And fresh horizons sought.
Questions of how much to dare and why
Are answered in the daring.
And the whole world opens
Because two people dared
To find the passage for their love."

He finishes reading and looks across at Esther, who has tucked her legs under her and sits staring intently into his face. He sees her eyes shining in the last rays of the setting sun.

"It's beautiful, Mark," she whispers, "and true. Your truth."

"It can be our truth, too," he replies, "if we dare to take the path together."

Silence settles again. A lone gull in the fading light seems to notice that his mate has left, and calls raucously, wheeling up into the air and heading off across the water in search of the other.

Esther takes an envelope carefully from her purse. It's not crumpled. She withdraws a card. In the soft light Mark sees on its cover the picture of a red rose, fully opened.

"I have one for you, too," she says.

Mark waits, silently. She reads the inside of the card, though hardly needing to look, the words seeming fresh in her mind.

"It's called, *Yes*.

"Yes is an affirmation
        built on a thousand noes.

No to
        death, pain,
        sickness,
        sadness,
        and bad compromise.

No to
        lethargy,
        fuzzy thinking,
        mediocrity,
        and boredom.

Yes begins
        with intention
        to take little yes steps.

Yes to
    vigour,
    to strength
    and striving,
    to hard work
    and homework,
    to study
    and learning,
    and thinking,
    to writing,
    and being.

Yes to
    embarking on journeys,
    to questing and questions.

Yes to
    dancing
    and singing,
    to poetry,
    music,
    and laughter.

Yes to
    feeling
    and friendship,
    to well-being,
    to good food,
    and good drinking,
    to beach walks,
    to popcorn and movies,
    to fireside chats
    and pillow talking.

Yes to
    fun places,
    to wilderness spaces,
    to mountains and climbing,
    to playing and dreaming,
    to planning and deep seeing.

And when the chorus of yeses
    rings out in celebration,
    fueling the heart with wild courage,

It's easy
>to take giant leaps
>to say:
>>YES
>to growing,
>to being,
>to soaring,
>to living,
>to loving,

>to me
>to you
>to us.

So
>I can,
>I will,
>and I do!

Looking across the tiny space between them on the beach, their eyes lock in a soul embrace. The poems flutter from their hands onto the sand as they come together, man and woman, in the full and long lover's kiss of a forever consent to be together. They gather up the poems from the sand and walk slowly as one back along the beach to their hotel.

The Announcement

Before making an announcement to the expectant world, Mark and Esther go first to Esther's home in Tel Aviv. She is eldest of a family of three daughters. Her sisters are Judith and Deborah. Her father, Tevi, is a lawyer, and her mother, Rivka, a teacher. It's a close-knit Jewish family, well-respected and active in their community and synagogue. Esther's meteoric rise to world attention, first as a victim of terrorists, second as a Visioneer, and third as a romantic partner with a Christian, has left them somewhat gasping. Her first marriage had been short and tragic. Now this sudden, new blossoming of romance and adventure is such a transformation that the family stands in awe of where it might lead. But they are, nonetheless, as one, joyful and excited for her in her happiness.

A similar visit to Mark's family in Brisbane is taken in stride by his retired parents, living quietly in the suburbs, seemingly well-removed from world attention. His father, Bob, had been a farmer and still maintains a small interest in the property now managed by Mark's brother, John. Their mother, Alice, is an enterprising and busy woman who is now thriving in a second life as suburban promoter of many causes within her church group and other organizations. There had been no children from Mark's brief and unhappy marriage which ended a few years earlier, and to see him now with prospects as a world figure of prominence with a beautiful foreign lady as companion, is stirring grandmotherly instincts in her open and friendly heart.

Mark and Esther choose to make the announcement of their engagement on the hundredth day of the Visioneers one hundred and fifty days of world awakening. They do so from Visioneer Headquarters in Los Angeles. Bill Bates organizes a press conference and the announcement drives most of the other news in the city of stars and celebrities from the major front page headlines. Around the world, other prominent dailies pick it up, while feature writers immediately go to work under banners such as MARK AND ESTHER SHARE THEIR VISION and CUPID JOINS TOP VISIONEERS. They set the wedding date for the middle of April in Jerusalem.

The wedding is cast as a celebration not only of love, but also of the worldwide spread of visioneering spirit. With it will come the culmination of the first wave of effort to awaken the world. The one hundred and fifty days will be over and you'll stand ready with your mentors and the Visioneers to implement Winston Churchill's bold audacious plan.

An Audacious Plan

You are in your thinking room. The drama of the hundred and fifty days has been played, and you find yourself clearly now in the force-field of creative tension that you have anticipated. It has two dimensions. In one, you've created in your mind a world peopled by Visioneers who are out and about acting as catalysts to move people to create a shared vision of a future world of decency and tolerance. By now they have gone a long way, and many parts of the world are crackling with the energy of their initiatives.

In the second dimension, you come out of your imaginary world and look squarely again at future prospects. You say "again", because this is where you began, in the turbulent waves of crushing uncertainty and danger. Here, there has been no change. You can read the newspapers, watch television, interact with colleagues, and the same pessimism colours every thought and word. This is the real world where real people are uneasy about the future. They have little sense that they can act to change it. Here, there's no Mark Venture, or Luis Valdez, or Baba Satyananda, no one to push away the smothering inevitability of deteriorating prospects. The creative tension stretches between the glimpses of the possible in your imagination and the way you perceive the world really is.

Both dimensions are coming together now in a single event. In the real world, the United Nations has scheduled a conference of world leaders to consider future prospects for the 21st century. This is the conference that Mark Venture discussed with Peter Hemphill. It's the same conference that Winston Churchill had raised four months ago. His proposal then was as audacious as it is extreme: to kidnap the leaders and let them see a new reality.

Everything the Visioneers have done to date is preparation for this event. You're ready for it now. However, the meeting at the United Nations is also a real event. It begins tomorrow. The delegates have all arrived in New York: more than 150 world leaders. Security has never been tighter.

You now face the creative tension between what can happen in your imaginary world of Visioneers, and what is likely to happen in the real world of international politics. How will this be resolved? Are you destined to go now this one last step with the Visioneers, only to find yourself anchored in the final instance to a reality you can't change?

These are disturbing questions for you. You turn now to the mentors who brought you here. You will be pushing them for answers. Will there be any, or are you heading for a disappointment, potentially more disagreeable than the frustration and fear for the future that first set you searching for answers?

CHAPTER FOURTEEN

Enter
the
World Leaders

Y OU ARE DUMBFOUNDED. It's the second day of the conference of world leaders at the United Nations. Called together by mutual consent to chart a new direction for the world they are locked into soul destroying debate. The tired ideologies that people across the world are trying to escape from are dragged out here like smothering blankets. Accusation, protestation, posturing—all of the old behaviours that are carrying the world down the slippery slope of decline— are there, unaffected, it seems, by the urgency of the crisis.

Amazingly, with the television eyes of the world watching, the leaders give little sense that they know what to do. True, some individual performances are outstanding. You listen to speech after speech filled with eloquence and passion, spinning out the spectacle of a world on the edge of ecological collapse, where poverty, hunger, starvation, crime and deprivation abound. You hear extraordinary, well-crafted rhetoric, prepared by the most able speech-writers in all of the nations on Earth. The case is made over and over of imminent collective collapse. The speeches fall smoothly from lip and tongue in every language, but nowhere, nowhere do you hear from any of these leaders that the collective problem begins in the policies of their individual administrations or in the unenlightened behaviour of the people they represent. Always, it's a nebulous and collective "we" who must do something different. But what? How? When? Nothing is said. Who will make the first move? Who will take the leadership? Who is prepared to follow? Who is prepared to admit that colossal mistakes have already been made, and before anything can be done, the wrong thinking that produced those errors must be changed?

You listen for someone from the developed world to admit that their science and technology have led them astray in expecting too much of the world to meet unlimited demands for material consumption. But there is no such admission. Instead, you hear the implicit belief that new technology will do what the old could not. You understand that these leaders are willing to move ahead into a precarious future with untested assumptions of meeting increasing demands. In vain, you listen for a leader from a poorer nation to describe a new understanding of the quality of life that might be reasonable for all on the fragile planet. Nowhere is there a sense that people themselves can make enlightened decisions on these matters if given the means to do so. All solutions are couched in a continuation of conflict between have and have-not for a dwindling supply.

Everywhere there are grand speeches calling for peace. Nowhere is there condemnation of members sitting in the assembly who head up regimes of terror responsible for unspeakable atrocities. All is bland. All is banal. All thinking is based on a continuation of the conflicting self-interest of sovereign states. Nowhere is there an understanding that the Earth and its ecology is a single seamless whole and that it cannot indefinitely withstand the pressures of a powerful human species that tears it apart piece by piece.

It's the end of the second day of a four-day conference. No progress has been made. The leaders have decided to go into closed session. You turn off your television set, close your eyes, and enter your thinking room.

The Mentors Return

It's early evening. You stand for a few moments gazing out at the immense skyscape of brilliant stars. A new moon has risen over the mountain ranges and its soft light catches the fresh snow on the peaks in a shimmering dance. You drink long and deep of the quiet beauty, drawing it into your heart and letting it wash your mind in gentle life rhythm. When you turn your eyes away from the window, you find you're no longer alone in the room.

They're all here, your four mentors, standing together by the fireplace. They are exactly as you remember them on the last time that you were all together. It seems so long ago, just after the first meeting of the Visioneers and before you sent them off into the world to change its future. You recall the details vividly.

At that meeting, Churchill had outlined his grand strategy for shifting the mindscape of people in every nation, beginning with sorties of Visioneers and culminating in a grand Congress of the Global Mind. Dickens had etched indelibly the images of incarnate evil which the

Visioneers would have to overcome. How right he had been, you now know only too well! Against that backdrop, Anne had painted her picture of unselfish love as the life-force that would nourish the world. Finally, President Kennedy had brought it all together in a sweeping vision of new world order of planetary stewardship, cooperation and caring. What a stirring meeting that had been! What a contrast with what you've just been listening to from the United Nations! You recall that you retreated at first, overwhelmed by the enormity of what your mentors were asking you to do. But they had prevailed, and you can still hear John Kennedy entreating you to move with courage on the adventure with your Visioneers.

Well, move you have, and here you are several months later. The venture is launched. The Visioneers have taken the world by storm. On every continent they have created networks, linking mind to mind. People are learning how to think in new creative ways, bringing into play their vision of possible futures. In your mind, the world has been enlivened with the potential for rebirth. You sense that the cosmos is holding breathless with the possibility. You're on the threshold. You're ready to raise the curtain on the next act. And your mentors have gathered again, ready to help you do it.

They come forward as one to greet you.

"Well done!" smiles John Kennedy, putting his arm around your shoulder.

Anne hugs you hard. "It's wonderful!" she says. "Oh, I'm so excited. You've put hope back into the lives of so many children. And thank you for Esther. She's my heroine—so beautiful and calm and thoughtful, and so much in love with Mark. I can hardly wait for their wedding. Let's make it a really grand event, shall we?"

"I'm sure we will, Anne," laughs Charles Dickens, now also embracing you. "As a story teller, my friend," he says, "you're among the best. You have held me riveted all these months. My only complaint is that I'm forced to get it in episodes. Now, I know how my readers must have felt when my books came out like that. I'm sorry about Luis Valdez. I know that losing him hurt you very much. But you were true to your craft, and what an impact his death has had. Bravo, I say! Just keep it up and you'll carry this off to a grand conclusion."

Dickens steps aside and you find yourself face to face with Winston Churchill. Behind the bulldog scowl, you see a merry twinkle in his eye.

"Hrrumph," he says, trying to growl a little. "So you thought you couldn't do it? What do I know of the ways of the world? you said. Well quite a bit, I'd say. It's no small feat to get a measure of the world and push it in the direction it needs to go. But you've got the Visioneers out there now, well positioned to do it. I told you Mark Venture was a natural for a leader, didn't I?

"But now the real drama begins. We've got the horses lined up at the starting gate in New York and soon we'll let 'em run. They're a mixed bunch, too: a few thoroughbreds, but a lot of hacks, not to mention the scrawny mountain ponies, and a few western cow horses. They're all acting pretty true to form, too. What did I tell you about that? It's the same old stuff: grand rhetoric, and most of it not up to the standard I set in the House of Commons. None of it's likely to lead anywhere, because their heads are still stuck in the sand somewhere in the middle of the 20th century. Well, now we're going into a special session away from the television cameras, where they can fight and call each other names without anyone hearing. Are they ever in for a shock! Today, New York; tomorrow, the Visioneering Room! Oh, I'm looking forward to this!"

With that, the old warrior looks around the room, beaming audaciously at everyone.

"Friends," you say, "it's good to see you all again. I've missed you very much. There were many times over the past months when I wanted to bring you back. But I knew I had a job to do first. Now it's done, and we're ready to move forward.

"I'd be less than honest if I said I'm not apprehensive. You're my friends, but I know you exist only in my imagination. The real world is outside this quiet place of ours. That's where I live with more than five billion other people, and we're running into grave danger. Every day conditions get worse. When you're on a downhill slide, then every minute you stay there takes you further from where you want to be.

"I'm enormously discouraged by what I hear in New York. There's no progress. There's a complete inability for the leaders of the world to move it off its perilous path. We have shown how the Visioneers can work miracles, but now that spirit has to be brought into play to deal with this situation of deadlock and confrontation. Tomorrow it begins, and I don't mind saying I'm afraid that after all this work, it won't make any difference, and the prospects for the world will be no better than when we started."

"Okay, now listen, and let's get one thing clear." It's John Kennedy who has spoken. "It's all right to be afraid. That's normal, but under no circumstances must you doubt that this will be successful. You're going to change the future of the world by what you're doing. You're putting your mind to work to shape the future. You're doing it with so much passion and energy, moving with people like Mark and Esther, Luis Valdez and George Cardinal, Baba, Indira, Theresa, George Walker and Diane Koplitz—all of these people with such powerful ideas for charting a new direction. When you do that, you're creating a force that will begin the change. And it will link up with the force being generated by other powerful minds out there in the real world who are thinking the same way, and together all of you acting together, will make the difference. But you, with your Visioneers, have a very special role to play. You're bringing a great hope to those who will make the change. So don't doubt, don't ever doubt that you can do it.

Because you can. You're already well along. You're already making a difference."

"Yes, that's good advice." Charles Dickens is speaking. "And the next piece will be stupendous. We're going to put these world leaders through a Scrooge experience. I mean to say, if the ghosts of Christmas past, present and future could transform that quintessential most miserable of misers, that 'squeezing, wrenching, grasping, scraping, clutching, covetous old sinner' (if I may quote myself); if the spirits could transform him into 'as good a friend, as good a master, and as good a man as the good old City knew, or any good old city, town or borough in the good old world' (to quote myself again); if that could be done for the good of everyone who reads the story, then think of what we can do here, by showing the leaders what lies in store for them and the world if they don't change their ways. By Jove, I can hardly wait to get at them."

"All right, all right!" You're laughing despite your anxiety. "I hear you. I know you all well enough now to believe that with you on my side, we can do anything. So I'm ready. Tonight, we rest, and tomorrow, we bring the world leaders to the Visioneering Room."

With that, they're gone. You're alone. You sit quietly, gathering strength.

The Most Powerful Force on Earth

It's 10 a.m. Eastern Standard Time in New York City. The doors of the General Assembly at the United Nations have just closed on the 150 heads of governments attending the special conference on The World in the 21st Century. As you watch by television, most of the news networks cut away to other programs, content to leave the fate of the world for a few hours while the leaders debate it. Those that continue the coverage do so with prognostication and hyperbole, bringing forward commentators with specialized points of view on the environment, on the global economy, on geopolitical relations, on world hunger, on peace, on a hundred other fragments of the great interlocking puzzle of the global future.

None of them know what to do, but they all have a point of view. Frustrated, you too, are about to turn away, when suddenly your attention is caught by the words of a small white-haired gentleman whose name you didn't catch, whose work you do not know. But he is speaking about a spiritual mind change that's taking place around the world. Like a giant ripple spreading outwards from an epicentre of thought, he says, this change of view is touching the minds of people everywhere. Mind change of this order is a mutual affair and doesn't occur until people make a commitment to listen sincerely to the other person's point of view, and together come to an understanding of what needs to be done.

Yes, you say, that's right, that's what the Visioneers are about. Now you must see to it that the leaders of the nations understand also. Then the speaker makes one last riveting point before he, too, is gone, swept aside by the irrepressible urgency of the network schedule.

"Human minds are interconnected in mysterious ways we don't understand," he says. "They can share images of hatred and war just as vividly as they can share images of love and peace, and the images most strongly held determine what happen. Knowing this, we must enjoin, with all possible haste, a worldwide visioning of peace and cooperation with the greatest possible clarity of the specifics for action. Such vivid communal imagining of positive images for fruitful coexistence with each other and the Earth, will do more to ensure its coming to pass, than all the most brilliant policies or profound scientific theories. Millions of people affirming a positive vision is the most powerful force on Earth."

"What if those world leaders knew and understood that!" you say to yourself. "What if they bent all their efforts to freeing people's minds to invent a positive future for all of us!"

You're galvanized into action to make that happen.

The Leaders Arrive

The silver bridge arches across the sky of a brilliant, sunny day. When the Visioneers had come this way to the Visioneering Room a few months ago, the mountain slopes had been green and grassy. Now, in early April, a solid base of snow packed hard runs down to the foot of the bridge. Over it a red carpet stretches full length from building to bridge. Around as far as the eye can see, the dazzling white cover of a new fall of snow on top of the old, sparkles and dances in the sunlight.

Into this pristine wonderfest come tumbling, along the bridge, the leaders of almost every nation on Earth.

Plucked from the heated comfort of the United Nations General Assembly, they come in light jackets, shirt sleeves, cotton dresses, saris, business suits, and African robes. On every face, wide-eyed disbelief and panic mirror confused shouts, imprecations, prayers, and profanities in every tongue.

"Hello, hello!" you call out, running to greet them. "Welcome, welcome. Please come along inside. There's steaming hot coffee and tea waiting. We are most honoured to welcome you here. Please, come in out of the cold."

The first group of a half dozen men have reached you, hurrying along the red carpet as fast as they can. Behind them two women, expensively dressed, are shivering a little, and hobbling uncomfortably in their high-heeled shoes on the uneven red carpet.

"Say, what is this?"

"Who are you?"

"What's going on here?"

"Have we all gone crazy?"

"Who's responsible for this?"

"It's an outrage!"

"Where are the guards?"

"Do you know who we are?"

"If this is an American idea of a joke, it's in very poor taste."

Almost everyone is muttering something as they come up to you. Much of it is in languages you don't understand. You keep smiling and greeting them in English and motioning them to go inside. No one argues or delays. It's too cold for that. Some of the looks you receive are as black as thunder. But the people move on, pushing, jostling, gesticulating. Others proceed erect and dignified. Three or four half smile at you and nod. Two in wheelchairs, assisted by others, are huddled against the cold. They keep on coming for fifteen or twenty minutes, until all 150 of them have passed by and entered the Visioneering Centre. You follow along behind and step into the Visioneering Room.

It's a truly amazing sound and sight spectacular. The room is in an uproar. Everywhere you look there are defiant people, their anger increasing with the warmth. Most are convinced it's all a hoax, though they can't see how it's been done. Clearly, you can expect little tolerance from this group. Collectively and individually you have in this room, 150 of the most powerful people on Earth, sensing that they have somehow been stripped of rank and privileges and thrown together in a melee of confusion and indignation.

In the centre of the room, as always, the iridescent world globe is turning, glowing with light in rich earth tones of brown, green, white, and blue. Some of the leaders are gathered around staring at it. Others have settled into the high-backed white leather chairs. Most are gathered around the perimeter of the room in clusters of vociferous commentary on what has happened.

You move quickly down to the centre of the room beside the globe. You raise your voice to speak, activating the automatic sound system that carries your voice above the hubbub in the room.

"Your Excellencies! If you'll please be seated, I'll explain what's happening. There's no designation by country, so please find a seat wherever you can."

"This is an outrage!" someone shouts. " We are heads of government. You can't treat us like this."

"Oh, shut up!" shouts another. "Let's find out what's going on here."

"Friends," you try again. "You're honoured guests here. Please take a seat and I'll explain everything."

It takes a full five minutes, but finally there's enough order in the room for you to proceed. You note to yourself the contrast between the fractious combativeness of this group compared with the enthusiasm and excitement when the Visioneers had first assembled in this same room. But the energy here is strong, very strong. Grouped before you are the 150 most powerful political leaders in the world. How could the energy not be strong? Whatever their beliefs and ideologies, regardless of their personal biographies, these are people of extraordinary accomplishment with enormous resources at their disposal to affect the future direction of the world. What are you to say to them? You've been thinking about this moment for many months. You've already undertaken the most elaborate preparations for this occasion. In your mind an entire alternative world has been created and filled with characters and events of superlative accomplishment. They're out there now. The Visioneers are at work in every country represented by the leaders now before you. They're showing what can be done to make a difference, and they're doing it. You know that. You have experienced it in your mind so vividly that it's become more real to you than reality itself. It's your reality. In your thinking room, and here in the Visioneering Room, it's your world, your creation, and it's an enterprise of great worth led by people of spirit, each one filled with a passionate desire to create a better world, and working together to do it.

Now, into this world you've brought the real leaders of the real world, plucked out of their litigious and politicized debate at the United Nations. You have them before you. You can look into their eyes. The leaders of nearly every nation on Earth are seated before you—angry, indignant, powerful people. What are you going to say to them now that can begin to close the gap between the world as it is and what it could be?

"Leaders of the world," you begin. "Welcome to the Visioneering Room. I apologize for the lack of ceremony to which you're normally and rightly entitled. But this is not a place of ceremony or an assembly of rank or entitlement. It's a place of learning and creativity, focused on the enterprise of the greatest importance in the known universe. We're concerned here with the evolution of human consciousness as the force that will determine the future of our species and our planet. It's enterprise of the most high-minded endeavour, and you've been brought here to see your role in its accomplishment.

"In this great learning on which you are about to embark, I will play the modest role of your medium of passage, but I will not be part of your journey. Others are now at hand to be your guides and mentors. Some of you will know them well. They understand the penalties and potential of your office. They also know, like you, the manner of your coming to it.

"For those among you who have secured your power through terror and oppression, there's no place in the planetary future which is now about to unfold. For those of you who seek only to hold power through coalition and compromise the future is equally inaccessible. What we are searching for here is creative leadership that seeks to empower others to find within themselves visions of a common future in which the sanctity of life is paramount, and where commitment to act to secure dignity and decency for all is the hallmark of citizenship. As leaders you will be champions of such a vision and stewards of its accomplishment on our precious, fragile planet.

"The doorway of opportunity to this new beginning is now ready to open. To pass through, you all must look to your learning. I leave you now to do it."

Leaders and Mentors Engage

A profound hush has descended as you have spoken. Everyone in the Visioneering Room hears speech in his or her own language, so the full force of your words has registered in every mind. The air hangs heavy with judgment. You pause a moment scanning every eye in the three rows of seating, looking down to the centre. The silence is thunderous. Then, you leave, and with you the rotating world globe. The floor area stands empty, shimmering. Suddenly, into that space, striding out of history, come the unmistakable figures of Winston Spencer Churchill and John Fitzgerald Kennedy.

The response of the assembly is immediate. Gasps of amazement and disbelief explode on all sides. Churchill in full parliamentary attire, waistcoated and key-chained, his unlit cigar stuck in the corner of his mouth, comes to a halt full centre of the room and stands feet apart staring roguishly up at them.

"I thought, Mr. President," his stentorian voice booms out, "that we had entered the bear pit, but I see that all the bears are in the gallery."

John Kennedy is beside him, in blue, pin-striped business suit, flashing his broadest, most engaging smile.

"Oh?" he says, "I rather thought, Mr. Prime Minister, that this was heaven and the choir had assembled to sing us in."

"Some choir!" rejoins Churchill.

"Yeah, the bear country jamboree!" laughs Kennedy.

With that, the room breaks up into general uproar. The two former statesmen move down along the front row of benches acknowledging some faces they recognize. A few tentative hands reach out to be shaken, then seeing that the flesh is solid, more are extended, reaching over from the second row, and other people further back shouting greetings, and every-one talking to their neighbours until the room again is a babble of voices.

Kennedy takes an empty chair at the end of the front row while Churchill strides back into the centre of the room. Without waiting for silence, he plunges right into his address.

"I always like a noisy house," he shouts. "It obviates the necessity for close attention. However, I suggest that on this occasion you may wish to listen carefully to words that come, so to speak, from the other side."

He has their attention now.

"It's customary, I know, for every age to think that it stands at the crossroads of history, and for every political leader to see himself as the fulcrum of the balance. And so it may be. But I tell you these are extraordinary times, when people are called upon to reach far deeper into the store of human energy than they ever thought existed. At such times, they come face to face with destiny and see their lives as instruments of great purpose.

"So it was with me, when on the night of the tenth of May, 1940, I was handed the power to form His Majesty's Government to do battle with the slavering jackals of the Third Reich. It felt that all my past life had been but a preparation for that hour and for that trial.

"I saw the evil forces of that time clearly for what they were, aberrations in the course of decency, insults to the nobility of the human species, inflicting acts upon humanity so sordid, squalid, and sub-human that the very stones must cry out against the abomination of their evil.

"In the face of such wickedness, the greatness of the human race was put to the ultimate test, calling upon the eternal moral forces of the universe to turn the tide, so that people, ordinary people, became transformed into giants and heroes and drove that howling pack of savage hounds into oblivion.

"The enemy then was tangible and brutal, and when people saw them for what they were, they rose to the occasion and made every sacrifice for the ultimate triumph of the free spirit. Today, the world faces an even graver danger, for instead of evil parading itself in jackboots and loutish behaviour, it lingers in the hearts of ordinary people as indifference and unthinking self-interest. The consequences now instead of being turned upon those immediately at hand, are being moved out upon the backs of generations too young yet to understand or still unborn. But come they will, as surely as floods follow torrential rain if adequate provision has not been made to control the waters.

"And the consequences already are apparent to those who have eyes to see. They show in the poisoned soil on every continent, in the polluted oceans washing every shore, in the thickening, congested air over every sprawling megalopolis. They cry out in the anguish of the homeless and the unemployed, not only in the poorest countries, but also in the richest places on Earth. They lurk with shame in the furtive, skulking alleys of the ghettos, in the stealthy sordid dealings of the drug pushers, in the alcohol-dazed murders on the native reservations.

"But worse than all, they linger in the hearts and minds of people who are the beneficiaries of the most elaborate educational systems the world has ever known. Everywhere, such men and women go about their daily life, filled with a growing sense of uneasiness and fearfulness, but unable to catch the vision of a brighter, cleaner, better future, and powerless to act to break out of their patterns of dependence and conformity.

"The time to stir that stagnant pool is now at hand, and the responsibility for engineering the machinery to do it, lies squarely on the shoulders of every one of you behind those benches. Yet what do you do? You sit in endless debate in the United Nations and paralyse it with indifference. Those of you who hold your office as a mandate from the people, scan the polls for your re-election, and those who stand as petty dictators surround yourselves with thugs to hold your power.

"Well, we are here to tell you the time has run out for continued toleration of that state of affairs. The world is in upheaval and you will be caught and crushed in the vortex of the storm unless you act now to make a change. People are on the move and will no longer tolerate leadership of indifference or tyranny. They are banding together as Visioneers, still small in number, but growing rapidly as their minds are touched by the rediscovered power of their imaginations, to create a future different from where your policies are leading.

"This is your hour of trial. You can choose now to keep your heads buried in the sand, or you can lift them up, to find again, as we did when the hell-angels stalked the Earth, that there's one bond that unites you all. This time it's not the bond of war against a brutish enemy, but the bond of vision to see a new world order, rising out of the chaos of this one now passing. With such a vision, you will show your leadership by bringing your people to see it, too, and empowering them to act to do whatever it takes to bring it to pass.

"This you must do, and do it now. To do less is to fail. And to fail is to sink into the oblivion of a life that is no life at all."

As he finishes speaking, the old warrior stands square and formidable in the centre of the room. There's no sound, not a whisper. He stands for almost a minute, his steady gaze travelling along the row of each tier of seats, meeting everyone who will look at him in full eye contact. And many there are who cannot meet that penetrating stare that seems to look right into their soul, searching for its substance.

President Kennedy rises quietly from the place where he had sat down and moves toward the Prime Minister. The President's face is sombre and admiring as he places his arm around the old man's shoulders and looks up into the silent benches. Churchill allows a sly smile to touch his lips as he nods his head three times to the assembly, then moves off to take the seat the President has vacated. John Kennedy waits respectfully for him to be seated, then raises his hands in a wide sweeping embrace of the audience.

"My Fellow Learners," he begins. "The Prime Minister has called for you to unite in a common bond of vision for the planet. To do so is to practice the highest craft of statesmanship. To succeed is to fashion a result far greater than any plan for national development that any head of state among you now, or in any past time, has accomplished.

"For you have come now to an age surpassing in significance any that has gone before. All the past has been prelude to this event. Like the Olympian athlete seeking to clear the high jump bar set at the highest point in history, you are on the run up to the standards. Above you, towering at what seems an impossible stretch for a human being, rests the bar. In the stands, more than five billion people watch your performance breathlessly. For they are more than spectators here. They are participants in your action. On your success rests all their hopes for a future worth living.

"You are in fluid motion, moving forward to the point where you know you must plant your feet, and launch your body upwards in a curving, precision-tuned surge of energy, to lift your heels over that bar, and bring your body arching with effort to follow and soar successfully to the other side.

"And you know that to succeed you must first have seen clearly in your imagination the bar above you and your body clearing it. You will have heard the roar of the crowd, and felt the spine-tingling rush of excitement as you look back upwards to see the bar trembling, but in place. You will know before your feet have ever left the ground that you have triumphed, because you created the vision in your mind and saw yourself successful in its accomplishment.

"And so it is with the work that's now before you as an assembly of world leaders controlling future prospects for the human race.

"Let there be no confusion. You must see the vision before you can achieve it. Let there be no question that the vision must be shared in the minds and hearts, not only of each one of you here, but of every living soul in your constituencies. Let there be no doubt that this is the task of statesmanship. And let there be no fear that it can't be done, because anything less is insufficient to the high moral purpose for which the human race exists.

"Let the word go forth from this assembly that you will bend every effort, commit every resource, make every pledge, support every initiative and condemn every opposition to assure the building and the proclamation of the new world vision.

"Let the people of the world know that the leaders of the nations are united and committed to a great overarching purpose for humankind: that so long as the sun will shine on this planet, it will shine on soil that is rich with harvest and oceans that teem with life; so long as people live on the land they will nourish it and care for it; so long as life and breath flows through our human family, we shall devote ourselves to tolerance, support, friendship, and love.

"To this great vision of universal peace, fellowship and prosperity for all, I urge you now to make your stand, and never, never, never give up, until it becomes a reality in your time and for all time to come!"

Hardly before the President has uttered the last words, a sudden change sweeps into the room. The sound of a roaring wind fills the air. The President steps aside, and in an instant his place is taken by a shimmering, shifting Earthscape of cloud and sky, ocean and land, open fields, forests, and snow-capped mountains. Then it shifts again into a densely packed city square, filled with people, many tens of thousands, milling around, their faces quizzical and concerned, as if searching for something lost or beyond their grasp. The scene turns over and over, but always filled now with people searching, in many lands, many settings, different cultures, different nationalities, at work, in agriculture, industry, offices, linked by communication systems of computers, satellites, aircraft, and all manner of vehicles. Then suddenly the people are gone, and a single tall building comes into view in the distance, but zooming in quickly, until it fills the space and can be recognized. It's the United Nations building in New York, tall, glass, the plaza of nations and the flags. The scene moves inside, to the doors of the General Assembly. They're closed, security guards in place. It moves through the doors into the room.

A gasp goes up from the leaders in the Visioneering Room as they suddenly see themselves in the session from which they were brought. They are all there, each one behind the country name. But nothing is happening. It's fixed frame. There's no sound or movement. No speech or action. Everything is still. The scene moves from face to face along the rows of delegates. They are all there, but immobile, almost lifeless, seemingly without thought or energy.

Then suddenly they're gone. Papers, briefs, personal effects, all remain, but every delegate is gone, every seat is empty, every seat but one, the chair of the Secretary-General. The figure there rises. It's a man. He moves down onto the floor of the assembly, alone in that empty space. The rest of the scene fades, and he's now standing on the floor of the Visioneering Room looking up into the wide-eyed, uncomprehending faces of the leaders of almost every nation on Earth.

"Good morning," he says. "My name is Charles Dickens. I am to be your host for the remainder of your time here with us in the Visioneering Room."

He is dressed as usual: nineteenth century, casual, and slightly theatrical in grey slacks, long green cutaway jacket, yellow waistcoat, and heavy gold watch chain. His long hair and wispy beard frame the lively, dancing energy of his eyes and face. Hands in pockets, he strolls casually around the space at his disposal, using it like a stage, occasionally striking a pose, working the audience and enjoying himself immensely.

His arrival has created quite a stir among many of the people in the room, who are familiar with his name.

"Are we to understand, sir," asks one, "that you are Charles Dickens, the celebrated nineteenth-century English novelist?"

"At your service," replies Dickens.

"We must all be dreaming," says another. "Churchill, Kennedy, now Charles Dickens. What is this? What's happening here?"

"Aha! I understand well your perplexity," Dickens responds. "This is not the ordinary, everyday fare of a leader, not even a head of government, I daresay. That other scene we just saw, in the good old U.N., piles of documents, long boring speeches, good lunches and dinners, plenty of protocol, that's more the ticket, I suspect."

No one ventures a reply.

"Well, of course, there's nothing wrong with that," Dickens continues. "It's the way of the world, don't you know. Except that now there's a problem because that's the way of the old world, but all of you have gone and invented a new one. Well, not you personally, you understand, but everyone acting together over the past few hundred years, and especially over the past fifty. Now, this is where I have some difficulty myself. I'm a man of a particular age. No doubt many of you know my world through my books. If you do, you'll know that it was a lively place with some rather remarkable characters. Oh, I may have dressed them up a bit, but essentially, they were like that.

"Well, then, back to the point. The point is, I have come to your world somewhat as an outsider, which means I haven't lived through it the way you have, and perhaps don't understand it the same way. But what I do see is that everything on the outside is changing more rapidly than anyone can imagine; but on the inside, the place where people are, inside their own skins and heads, so to speak, well, things haven't changed there at nearly the same rate. The result is a very bad fit between how people think and act, and how they need to think and act if the world is going to be a decent place for people, and animals too, to live, even during the next fifty years.

"Now, you've heard some very powerful words already on this point from my good friends and colleagues, Sir Winston Churchill and President Kennedy. All of us are part of an enterprise called visioneering. That's a new word you may not know. It means engineering a preferred future, using the imagination to see the kind of world you want to live in and then working together to make it happen.

"We think it's a good idea, so much so that we've put together a band of Visioneers who are out there in the world making some very spectacular things happen. Now, when I say they're out there in the world, I don't mean your world, at least not yet, because we wanted to show how this world works first by running it through the visioning mind. So that's where the Visioneers are, and you will meet them soon. That's why we've brought you to the Visioneering Room.

"In all of this, I'll be pleased to be your host and master of ceremonies, but your guides and mentors will be Sir Winston and President Kennedy."

"Rubbish!" This was a shout from one of the back benches. "I've never heard such drivel! Who do you think you are to stand there and talk to people with our responsibilities about Visioneers in the visioning mind? There's a real world out there full of problems and all of your visioning isn't going to change that one bit. Talk to the hungry people in my country about visioning food on their plate, and see where it gets you. And what are you going to do about oppression? Tell the people to vision away the tanks rolling down the streets, or the arms dealers that supply the machine guns to the hoodlums masquerading as soldiers? Don't waste our time! End this charade now and let us get back to our real work!"

"He's right," from somewhere else.

"Yes, I agree."

"Come on, we've had enough of this."

"Oh no, you haven't! We've hardly yet begun!" This is an explosive roar from Winston Churchill who had leapt to his feet at the start of the interjections, and is now standing defiantly in the centre of the room beside Charles Dickens. John Kennedy is on his feet, too, moving towards them.

"You say you have problems now," the angry Churchill continues, "well, I will tell you, you haven't seen the like of the problems still to come! I stood alone in my time, because I could see in my mind where the course of events was taking us. And all around me, mealy-mouthed men made plaintive supplication to the most treacherous swine ever let loose in international affairs. That way of closing the mind to the real consequences of actions very nearly brought freedom to the grave. Now the hounds of hell are baying again, but this time they're hiding in the useless protracted debate by men like you, and women too, who won't open your eyes to see what must be done, before it's too late. Well we will show you here and if needs be, we'll grip you by the throat and shake your head until your brains rattle, but show you we will, and act you will, because the great and glorious energy of the human race will never be cut off from its path to destiny!"

"Well said Winston! Well said!" John Kennedy is applauding. "And where are the rest of you? If you believe in the right of free men and women to come together across every boundary and division to save the world, then I call upon you to stand now and be counted!"

"Yes!"

"Hear! Hear!"

"Okay!"

"We're with you!"

"Well said!"

And so a chorus begins to build, with some people standing now, applauding. Then it spreads like a wave along the rows, the applause building. Others, uncomfortable, continue to sit, looking away. But the applause is building, reaching to a crescendo. The reluctant ones struggle to their feet, until all three rows are standing, applauding, looking down at the three figures standing in the centre of the room.

CHAPTER FIFTEEN

The Scrooge Experience

As THE APPLAUSE SUBSIDES, quick as a flash, Dickens takes control. Churchill and Kennedy move off to the side, and the ebullient master of ceremonies moves centre stage.

" 'Marley was dead to begin with. There is no doubt whatever about that,' " he says, striking a pose with hands and eyes turned upwards to the ceiling. He changes position and points his finger accusingly at the assembly.

" 'I am here tonight to warn you, that you have yet a chance and hope of escaping my fate. A chance and hope of my procuring, Ebenezer.' " He intones these words with mournful resonance.

He moves up to the front row and stares directly into the eyes of a man sitting in the middle.

" 'Are you the Spirit, sir, whose coming was foretold to me?' "

A chuckle breaks out in the audience.

"It's *A Christmas Carol*," says someone. "He's reciting *A Christmas Carol*."

" 'Who, and what are you?' " Dickens asks of another amused head of government.

" 'I am the Ghost of Christmas Past,' " says Dickens, replying to his own question.

He's back in the centre of his stage. Laughter now breaks out all over the assembly.

" 'Long past?' " Dickens asks, quizzically.

"No. Your past," says a wag from the back of the room, and the whole assembly erupts in laughter.

"Aha!" shouts Dickens triumphantly. "I see we have a scholar in the audience."

He now has them in the palm of his hand. He waits for the laughter to subside, then speaks again.

"We may not be concerned here, my esteemed friends, with the past of Ebenezer Scrooge, but we are, or should be, mightily interested in the past history of the human race. We begin a journey now, a journey that will sweep us over time into the unexpected territory of the future. But we make our start, as all journeys must certainly start somewhere, we make our start in the swirling mists on the plains of central Europe, at the end of the Paleolithic Age, 10,000 years before the Christian era."

From Benign to Violent

Immediately, the space around Charles Dickens dissolves into an eerie scene of eddying fog patches, revealing, as they come and go, stretches of forest and rocky outcrops in open country. Dickens is part of the scene, moving around in the swirling vapours like a phantom commentator in an epic drama.

"This is still a time buried for us in mystery," he continues speaking, "but we now have increasing evidence to believe that it was an age in which men and women lived with their children in communities where peace and prosperity were the established order of things."

Into the setting come families of people, looking bronzed, healthy and happy, wearing simple articles of clothing, carrying baskets of food and spears and simple flint axes.

Dickens continues his commentary as the fog lifts and the countryside spreads out lush and green in bright sunlight.

"From what we can tell, this was an age where war had little meaning and men and women lived as true partners. The Earth was rich and bountiful, and spiritual life centred on devotion to nature. Time was not measured here at all, but passed, not as we know it in jagged bursts of uncertain years for a single generation, but as millennia, flowing smoothly on. We believe from the archaeological records that communities like these existed throughout the world."

The scene changes rapidly from community to community in different climatic zones, from cool forests to steaming jungle to fertile valleys. The people change, too, in colour and ethnic features: European, Semitic, Negroid, Asian.

Dickens continues.

"As the millennia passed from Paleolithic to Neolithic times, a growing spiritual force among these people was the worship of the Goddess. In various forms, she appeared as a transcending faith, symbol and source of nourishment, like the Earth. The apex of this way of life was the Island of Crete, where for four thousand years an agricultural society flourished, worshipping the Goddess, and embracing the arts of pottery making, weaving, metallurgy, engraving, architecture and all crafts contributing to a joyful artistic way of life."

As Dickens is speaking, the scene changes to vistas of agricultural land and cities with great palaces and villas and well made roads and seaports. Everywhere people are moving about in pleasant interaction. They are attractive people, well-dressed in colourful clothes, wearing jewelry of copper, bronze and precious stones.

The scene fades to a rocky outcrop where Dickens sits facing the assembly.

"This was the beginning of civilization, a time of seemingly endless peace and prosperity, where progress and technology flowed together to extend creative enjoyment.

"But elsewhere, outside, perhaps from marginal lands, another human element had developed. Nomadic bands of warlike marauders, discovering these great civilizations, came thrusting down upon them with another mentality. Thus began the era from which we have drawn most of our understanding of human interaction. Into the Neolithic civilizations of Old Europe swarms of invaders came from the Asiatic and European northeast, bringing with them a ruling caste of warrior and priest, worshipping male gods of war and conquest, sweeping aside the gentle partnership of prosperity in the societies where the Goddess had been central."

Dickens moves quickly aside, as if to escape from the ferocity of the scenes that follow. As he continues to speak, scene follows scene of battle, bloodshed, and destruction.

"So now we have the beginning of society dominated by male aggression, where power and force become the established order. As we survey it here from a perspective seven thousand years in the making, our stomachs must indeed be strong to witness the carnage and brutality that now spreads relentlessly across the planet.

"Even where the aggressive underpinning is modified by concepts of justice and right and wrong, wrathful warring violence is at the core. In the deserts of the south the ancient Semitic tribes of Hebrews came invading into the land of Canaan borne up and sustained by their wrathful male god, Jehovah.

"With this model of warring domination those who at one time are the conquerors become at another time the conquered, and the seeds of hatred, vengeance, and retribution are sown. People, instead of being seen as the highest order of a mystical creation, become objects and instruments, swaying with the fortunes of the battlefield from conquering hero to menial slave.

"Power and control are at the centre of this aggressive society. Principles of cooperation give way to ruthless competition and a desire for domination. And so it was that this new model of human interaction was launched, which we poets and commentators for long have called 'man's inhumanity to man.' Even the gentle interlude of one who was proclaimed the Son of God on Earth did little to interrupt the pattern. Jesus of Nazareth came preaching a gospel of love and service to his fellow man, but within a few years of his own cruel crucifixion, his message had been distorted and taken over by a church built on the same male domination model as the society all around it. And since that time, the most brutal battles in human history have been fought among nations proclaiming themselves as Christian.

"And out of Europe the model of conquest and aggression spread to what we called the New World, engulfing aboriginal populations and destroying their cultures as effectively as those of the Neolithic age almost seven thousand years earlier.

"To work the plantations of some of those colonies, free spirited and joyful people from Africa were rounded up like cattle and sold into slavery by white traders, unleashing in the world the most bitter form of racism that endures long past the time when the practice of slavery was abolished.

"With the industrial revolution, a new form of slavery was invented. Here, my own work stands as testimony to the evil that ensues when greed and avarice are put ahead of human decency. Here now, I come very close to much that tortures me still, and you must pardon me, my friends, if I falter in telling it.

"For I have walked the streets of London among the labouring poor. I have known the soul-crushing despair of being a labouring hind myself in a blacking factory. I have sat and talked with the wretched outcasts of the streets, and visited their hideous dwelling places—I could not call them homes. I have seen the poor dear children, wretched and starving, and I have gathered them in my arms, as filthy as they were, crying and shivering in the bitter cold, neglected by their mothers in their drunken stupors.

"I saw it all and it choked me until I almost could not bear it. I wanted to scream out the infamy of such a system to the world of sensibility and pleasure that rushed along apace outside of all of this. But I, poor devil too, depended on that world for my own support. I could not write about the evil as it was, but I did the best I could. I created poor innocent wretches like my Jo, the street-crossing sweeper: no father, no mother, no friends, 'knows only that a broom's a broom'. In these frail creatures I poured out to a barely conscious reading public all of the filth and poverty and ignorance and disease that infected the people on the lowest rungs of society in our great empire."

By now, Dickens is so overcome with the recollection of the images, that he is sobbing loudly. He is huddled at one corner of an abject street scene in London of the 1850's where men, women and children in ragged clothes are tottering about in filth and refuse. For a moment, the orphan Jo appears with the pathetic broom. Dickens reaches out to him, but then the scene is gone and Dickens is left alone, still sobbing loudly, unable to continue.

The Century of Greatest Conflict

Winston Churchill appears from the side and takes over the narration.

"Out of that terrible squalor we step by step emerged in Britain not only as a nation of great might, but also one of social conscience. The greatness of Mr. Dickens was that he brought his message of human compassion, to both his countrymen who were in a position to make a difference, as well as to a reading public everywhere. The result was great strides in human well-being in the industrialized world.

"And at the beginning of this century, that world seemed poised for a better time. Little did we know that all that had gone before had merely primed the pumps for something to come, more terrible than anything we could imagine. We had now moved into a century where the domain for aggression would no longer be a territory, but that military ascendancy and domination of the entire world would be the prize.

"Nationhood now became more synonymous than ever with military might. To be supreme demanded the building up of armaments. No one, not even I myself who was fully involved in the thick of it, could measure the implications of what was coming. Great war machines were swung into place as a matter of course, fed by massive resources from industrial development, and where necessary backed up by policies of conscripting young men for training. Modern progress came to be measured by the armaments in place. The human race had prepared itself for the century of greatest conflict.

"When the first main onslaught came in 1914, it proved to be long and terrible. To fight on until victory was won became the sole objective, and the capacity and determination of the nations to do so was astonishing.

"In the brutal confrontation on all the fronts of what we have called the first great war, the sacrifice of human life was enormous. The young, flowering manhood that was cut and savaged by those engagements was thrown down with absolute conviction of the rightness of their country's cause."

Scenes of battle from the trenches of the first World War come up. The slaughter of the British and Australian and New Zealand troops on the beaches at Gallipoli then explode in violence followed by a deafening silence into which the Churchillian oratory breaks again.

"It lasted for five long years. Then, in vengeance, the conquering allies enacted such a penalty against the defeated Germans that it laid the grounds for the second conflagration, which came within a generation.

"But, by then, most people had lost their stomach for such an ordeal—except for the mongrels who felt they had been denied the spoils the first time around and now had the taste of blood in their mouths for a second attack on the free world. In those long ten years of the 1930s before the outbreak of the hostilities in 1939, I often felt that I alone could see what was coming.

"I had the defiance then and the determination to do what had to be done. The advocates of appeasement all around me had had their day. They chose to sidle up to a virulent Third Reich, choosing not to see its under darker belly, rationalizing their accommodation with a criminal regime. In this way, we had come to the brink of the void, from which there was no way back, except to fight and claw and struggle, until we had beaten them off and squashed the fight out of them."

Churchill is now standing squarely facing the assembly. Behind him the hooked cross of the Swastika is fluttering on a flagpole. With terrible intensity, he now focuses every word on his audience.

"You all know the story, or think you do. But I severely doubt that anyone can comprehend the barbarism that would have prevailed had we not been victorious against these monsters."

As Churchill continues to speak, a sudden, unexpected change swoops upon the assembly. They are gripped, each one, by an invisible force and propelled out of their seats down toward the centre of the room. Cries of fear and rage erupt, but there's no resisting the force that pushes them.

"When an evil power comes in the night," Churchill's voice booms out above the shouting, "and hauls you out of your house, and herds you like animals into a waiting cattle car, and transports you away out of sight to a concentration camp . . . "

The leaders are now all huddled in terror in the centre of the room under the waving Swastika. Suddenly, they are stripped of their clothes and dressed in drab prison costume. They look at each other in abject fear and struggle to get away, but there's a force-field around holding them where they are.

"When you are subjected to beatings," Churchill continues, "and forced out into work parties . . . when you hear machine gun fire, and some members of your party don't return . . . when you hear reports of gas chambers, and some of your family and friends are taken away, and don't return . . . when you live like this every day in terror and deprivation, then you have some sense of how mad the world can be when decency and honour are abandoned: when good men and women stand by and do nothing, while evil has its way."

As Churchill finishes speaking, a volley of machine gun fire rips out. Women and men alike in the audience of world leaders scream and battle with each other to get away, but they are powerless to do so. A siren goes off, continues loudly for a full minute, then stops abruptly. In the silence that immediately follows the unmistakable hissing sound of gas under pressure is heard and clouds of vapour appear over the heads of the huddled group. For many of them, this is almost too much and they drop to the floor crying and trembling in total and undisguised panic.

Then, just as suddenly as it began, the ordeal is over. The leaders are dressed again in their own clothes, and the same force that propelled them from their place now returns them to it. Churchill stands alone in the centre of the room.

"As terrible a time as that was," he now continues, "we could perhaps have taken some solace from it, if it had seemed to end the madness. But the world has run a full half century since then, and still has not found the way to live with itself. Toward that end, you are all now allegedly engaged. What you've just heard and experienced in your own being, should tell you that you cannot do it, if you continue with the old ways of thinking still in place. Change them now, for each time the world goes to the brink is more terrible than the last, and one day there will be no way back."

As he utters these prophetic words, Churchill turns and walks away. John Kennedy takes his place. Charles Dickens sits wistfully at the side. Kennedy speaks solemnly to the assembly.

"I can see you all are shaken," he says, "but you must come with me now to another brink, which was potentially more terrible, as Winston said, than where you have just been."

The scene in the centre of the room changes to a sunny vista of Japanese children gathering together in groups, wearing simple school uniforms, boys and girls jostling each other, laughing and joking. Everyone is carrying a suitcase or duffle bag or knapsack. They are assembling to go on a journey. Amongst them, adult group leaders move around giving them instructions, keeping order. Further away in the background, other adults in work teams are tearing down buildings, gathering rubble together, burning it, hauling it away, clearing firebreaks, making wide avenues of nothing.

"This is the city of Hiroshima," says John Kennedy, "August 6, 1945, preparing for expected attack by American bombers. They're planning a long, protracted defense, to protect their homeland yard by yard. It will be the bitter legacy of their treacherous attack on Pearl Harbor three and a half years earlier, and their savage war-mongering around the Pacific Ocean in the years that followed. They will pay the consequences, but the manner in which that penalty will be exacted will forever change the course of human civilization."

Suddenly, an air-raid siren goes off. The onlookers in the Visioneering Room leap in their seats, but the people in the scene pay little attention. Some of them look up into the sky, shielding their eyes against the bright sunlight. Seeing nothing, they shrug their shoulders, joke with their neighbours and continue with what they were doing. After a minute or two, the siren stops and a deep silence fills the room.

Into this space then erupts the forces of hell let loose on Earth. Everyone in the Visioneering Room is swept into it. The onlookers, the heads of governments of great and small nations on Earth, experience everything, but without the consequences of the poor wretches in the scene portrayed.

First, there is a great blinding flash of light, as if the sun had burst in the eyeballs of anyone caught watching. Following hard comes a rushing wind, dry and searing, more ferocious than a thousand tornadoes attacking at once, sucking and tearing at the terrified spectators but not lifting them from their seats.

Down below, it's a different story. Everyone and everything is blown away. Just one great sweeping, howling bellow of sound and heat. Total annihilation! And the heat! Oh, the terrible searing intensity of the heat! Instant incineration for the people in the scene, but a life in death experience for the onlookers, feeling the blood-boiling intensity of the explosion, but still sitting there watching, unable to escape or die, while the blinding light savages their eyes, and the tumultuous roar of the wind buffets their eardrums and tears at their bodies, and a great inferno of flames and unbearable heat tries to consume them.

Finally, the scene passes, and an unbelievable stillness fills the room. Every one of the spectators, participants of this first taste of Armageddon, is transfixed by the horror of it all. Sitting in their seats, white knuckles gripping the desks, they are inwardly traumatized to the point of collapse. Some are shaking visibly, others weeping openly, still more sitting bolt upright immobile, trying to comprehend what they have just experienced.

The scene below has changed from a sunny vista of men, women and children at work and play to a charnel house of blackened desolation. As the scene moves out from the total destruction at the epicentre of the blast to the impact further away, the scenes of human suffering become even more excruciating. Collapsed buildings, devastated roads and countryside, fires everywhere, and people, dismembered, disfigured, on fire, dead, dying, and miraculously unscathed, all thrown together into a hell-hole of total senseless and incomprehensible destructive violence.

At last, the scene changes to the tell-tale, ominous mushroom-shaped cloud, billowing its awful portent for the future of humanity, six thousand metres above the chaos below.

Now a new scene comes up. It's the main deck of the *USS Missouri* on September 2, 1945. General Douglas MacArthur, supreme commander for the Allied powers, wearing his familiar sunglasses and visored cap, stands before a microphone, flanked by admirals and generals from the Allied countries, while to one side a despondent group of defeated Japanese officials in civilian clothes stand shuffling their feet, looking at the hot steel deck. Two signed copies of the surrender agreement between the Allies and the Japanese lie on a mess table beside the microphone. General MacArthur speaks of a new era coming that must avoid "the crucible of war"; that "it must be of the spirit if we are able to save the flesh."

The scene on the warship fades and President John Kennedy stands facing the world leaders.

"Prophetic words, Ladies and Gentlemen, but have we paid attention? What have we done to fill the bottomless spiritual void that General MacArthur referred to? With the atomic bomb we used technique as a substitute for reason, and we have continued down that path ever since, not turning one whit away from the kind of thinking that led us into the holocaust in the first place.

"Sick of fighting, we made an easy accommodation in Europe to the ruthless Stalinist regime in Russia, and allowed that Godless power to grow so that it started to consume not only Eastern Europe but the world at large. Extolling the primacy of national sovereignty, we turned a blind eye to the repugnance of the world's next inhuman political machine. We put expediency ahead of morality and stepped away from MacArthur's injunction for a spiritual resurgence and improvement of human character. It was as if we had no skills for that. The only skills we had were to build up armaments and begin a terrible detente, for the weapons we now could make had the destructive power to obliterate all life from the face of the Earth.

"But still we couldn't turn away from that path. As a human race, we had sunk so far into the morass of spiritual impoverishment, we had no skills for a path of peace.

"Oh, yes, we put together the United Nations, and thank God we did as much, for it has done much to make the world a better place than it may well have been by now. But we built it without a soul, because we didn't know how to build it any other way."

As the President continues to speak, the plaza of the United Nations in New York comes up in the centre of the room. The bright flags of the world's nations stand out in the brisk breezes from the East River, dominant among them the blue and white U.N. flag with its olive branches encircling the world. Behind, the lean tall Secretariat building flashes brilliantly in the sunlight.

"You know it well," John Kennedy continues. "Look at it closely, testament to our desperate search for something to keep us away from the brink, but only as an objective external instrument, and very little to do with internal love between people as brothers and sisters in a single human family. The men and women who go to those assemblies as the official representatives of their nations do so to argue and preside and negotiate, but never to practice unconditional love or self-sacrifice and in that way seek to improve the lot of their fellow human beings. No, that would be a sign of weakness, for we have been schooled well to believe that strength lies only in military and economic might.

"We dare not tempt our adversaries with weakness. Oh yes, I can quote myself in my inaugural address as President. 'For only when our arms are sufficient beyond doubt can we be certain beyond doubt that they will never be employed.'

"That was our policy and we quickly had the test of it."

The huge globe of the world comes up behind the President and he gestures broadly towards it.

"Do you know this planet?" he asks the world leaders looking on. "Your countries are there, every one of them, and in them your people, countless millions depending on you to make the right decisions.

"And look here, my country, the United States, and it's October 1962, and I find out that Mr. Khrushchev, leader of the U.S.S.R., has been constructing missile sites in Cuba right on my doorstep, with their nuclear daggers pointed at the heart of Washington. The sites are almost operational, but not quite. We have a few days in which to act to stop this. We're at the brink again, and the question is how do we stop from going over.

"You all know the story. For a few days the world held its breath while two men and two superpowers stared eyeball to eyeball, with the most incredible destructive arsenals at our hands to unleash on each other, while all the rest of humanity could only wait and pray that we didn't take them over the brink into a hell a thousand-fold worse than what you just experienced.

"Can you imagine how close we were to that? Can you imagine what it would have been like if one of us had let that juggernaut go?"

As Kennedy speaks, the roaring blast of Hiroshima comes up again. Men and women in the room cry out, "No! No! Stop it! No more!" But it doesn't stop. The blinding flash returns, the searing heat blast smashes against them, the globe trembles and shakes, the anguished screams of unseen people ring out mixing with the cries of the leaders in the room. The globe disappears in a deafening roar and a huge mushroom cloud, black, ugly, and deadly fills the room, along with the acrid smell of electrified air and the nauseating fumes from burning flesh.

The voice of General MacArthur booms in again: "It must be of the spirit if we are able to save the flesh."

The cloud is gone. Both Kennedy and Churchill are in the centre of the room. They are facing the world leaders. Churchill speaks gravely:

"The darkest scenario did not unfold, but how close we came, none of us should ever forget. Yet all of you have forgotten, because you've done nothing to change the course of things. For more than twenty years after the Cuban missile crisis, the insane build-up of nuclear weapons continued, until finally the cold war collapsed under the unbearable economic burden of keeping it going. Let us make no mistake in our judgment on this point. The threat of nuclear war today is less than it might have been, not because the leaders of the nations of the world have chosen the path of peace, but only because no treasury was rich enough to measure up to the insanity of the behaviour."

"At the end of the century," Kennedy intervenes, "civilization is still labouring under the triumph of technique over reason. It showed again in 1991 in the spectacular precision bombing of the Gulf War. There, under the aggressive banner of Desert Storm, the Allied forces displayed against a belligerent opponent the breathtaking accomplishments of intelligent weaponry."

Churchill steps in.

"Again," he growls, "it was the story of a necessary response to a blood-thirsty military machine. They claimed the right of Allah for their cause, but in their hearts burned red hot coals of hatred. The passions were allowed to grow—yes, were even fed, by the economic mentality of the industrial world, until this naked, inhuman aggression was fully exposed. Then, and the world, will forever be thankful for it, the United Nations, led this time by America, summoned the will to act and strike a death blow to the heart of this ambition. This time, it was done with supreme technique, which kept the casualties on one side low, but offered little comfort that nations had learnt anything at all about how to design a world civilization of peaceful coexistence."

As Churchill is speaking, scenes of battle come up one after the other. These are the television sequences that had been watched by millions of people all over the world, during the six weeks of war fought by Allied powers against Iraq in February and March of 1991: the spectacular bombing and anti-aircraft missiles lighting the night sky over Baghdad; Patriot missiles intercepting and destroying Scud missiles over Saudi Arabia and Israel; Allied bomb sights locked onto enemy targets showing the deadly accuracy of the weapons; the chaos of army and civilian vehicles blasted out of commission with the occupants maimed and mangled.

"In this war," Kennedy continues, "the world could for the first time watch and play along as soldier, because the technique of communications was as equally spectacular as the technique of destruction. It was short, savage, and brutal, and it made great television. But again, it showed no progress in human ability to steer a course away from conflict, to know how to resolve issues through any means other than what General MacArthur called the crucible of war."

"So, at the end of the century," Churchill summarizes, "the nations still play as keenly in the theatres of war as they did at the beginning. While there has been a mass revulsion against the idea of war, the mindframe for promoting it is still in place as surely as it has been for the last seven thousand years."

Scenes of peace marches all over the world come up. Churchill watches the parades, then waves them aside and turns back to the assembly.

"People can march for peace and leaders can make speeches for peace, but unless you take out of the minds of men and women the predilection for war, then war is what you'll have, whether it be the holocaust of a nuclear bomb, or a savage conflict on a suburban street."

An angry voice speaks up from the assembly. It's the President of a European state. Lean-faced and scowling under thick black eyebrows, he leaps to his feet and points an accusing finger at Churchill and Kennedy.

"Enough!" he shouts, his voice rasping with rage. "Who do you two think you are that you can come back from the dead and torture us with horrors we didn't create. The world is thick and rotten with infamy and you stand as guilty as any who have held the levers of power. Your triumphs may have been brilliant, but they flickered and were gone, just like your own brief moments in office, just like all of us here, poor strutting fools on a world stage that will forget us in a moment once we're out. Don't lecture us on changing how the world thinks. It's enough to keep some rule and order among mobs who would tear each other apart if we didn't keep control."

"Yes, and while you think that way," rejoins Churchill, "the mobs will continue to rage and howl, because you give them no hope for anything better. You disgrace yourself, sir, and your high office, when you stand and say you have no vision for your term beyond keeping order."

"I agree with you on that, Mr. Churchill," this time it's a woman who has intervened, a president from Southeast Asia. Her voice is soft and still trembling from what she has just experienced. She speaks with passion and a quiet energy that gathers in strength as she continues. "But the people are so divided, and everywhere you turn, the self-serving demagogues come forward to denounce your best intentions for their own gain. And the people follow the path of least resistance. They first blow this way, then the other, because they have no sense for the longer term. They know nothing of building for a future beyond their own immediate years."

"Then you must teach them, madame," Churchill replies. "If you can see it yourself, you must find the words and say it honestly to their hearts. First, you must give them hope. You must hold it up like a shining beacon. Then you must wade in amongst the naysayers, the merchants of doom, the appeasers and give them no quarter, because against your vision of what is bold and decent and true their mealy-mouthed mumblings are as appetizing as yesterday's cold pudding. Then you can tell the people what you offer, that what you and your team stand for, is blood, sweat, and toil towards the accomplishment of that vision in partnership with them, each one doing his or her piece, with everyone taking responsibility for their actions. Then you must do it, just do it, giving people the freedom they need, and what resources you have, and tell them you expect a thousand-fold in return on your investment."

"It's good war-time rhetoric you offer, Winston," someone else replies. "But we don't have a war going here with an enemy you can get in your sights. It's just a dark, impenetratable gloom where no one can see the way."

"Then for God's sake, turn on your headlights!" It was John Kennedy's turn to explode. "That's why we've brought you here. There's more than a hundred and fifty of the most enterprising minds in the world in here, and outside there are more than five billion others waiting for you to show that you can put forward a vision for life on this planet that isn't a thickening fog of despair and gloom. People want light and hope and joy in working for something they can truly believe in. The task here is to put your hundred and fifty minds together to come up with the vision you can take back out of this assembly and say to the people of the world, of every nation on Earth: This is what your leaders stand for. Now will you work with us to put it in place?

"That's the task, Ladies and Gentlemen. We've begun by showing you the inevitable outcome if you continue down the path of those who have gone before. If you persist with policies that give sovereign states the right to commit atrocities within their borders; if you allow them to build up arms to attack their neighbours and threaten the world; if you step away from your immortal responsibility to preserve life on the planet; if this is all that you can do, then may God protect the people from the future you have chosen."

An Ominous Future

At President Kennedy's last words, a clap like thunder splits the air and the room shakes violently in an earthquake. For what seems an eternity, the shuddering tumult continues, as men and women cry out in terror, grasping for whatever they can hold and diving for protection to the floor. Then just as suddenly as it came, the uproar ceases. A swirling landscape of buckled earth and lowering sky sweeps into the room. Charles Dickens' theatrical voice rings out.

"You have felt the Armageddon of the atom," he cries out, "but that's only one path of hell from the past. Now you must look to the Earth itself. If it were to gather its voice in one loud protest against what men do, then it would quake and roar with a ferocity the like of which you can't imagine.

"See here, look at it churning, churning, churning in its torment. Land, sea, sky, all in protest. We have taken the magnificence of the human mind, all of its potential for creative brilliance, and thrown it headlong into the face of nature. From a heritage of awesome wonder we have torn out with ever-growing technological power and recklessness what we have thought we needed for lives of quality.

"Look here, the magnificent sweep of forest and fertile plains; oceans and lakes alive with life; air clear and clean; night skies brilliant with stars. All this we had for countless millennia, an abundance so magnificent it had no end.

"But now look. Look here, see what we have done with it: sprawling cities, jungles of concrete, roaring traffic, clouds of fumes, all of it multiplied, and multiplied, then multiplied again, until even the immensity of the oceans and the giant membrane of the atmosphere are not large enough to contain the volume of it.

"And look, look here at the consequences, samples of what we know, small indicators of the immensity we don't know, names and scenes familiar to all of you. Because this is not the future. It's the present and the past. It's the past piled upon the past, built into the present you don't like, leading to the future you don't want to think about. Look at them now. Do you remember? Nuclear catastrophe at Chernobyl; the oil spill of the Exxon Valdez; the oil fires of Kuwait; the spreading desert in North Africa; the disappearing rainforest in South America; the thick brown air of Mexico City; the grey forests of Europe; the dead lakes in Canada; the blighted landscapes of North America; the spreading cloud over China; the depleted fish stocks in tidal waters everywhere. And more terrible still are the dangers we can't see, but surely know, of changing climate, and a depleted ozone layer that protects all life on Earth from ultra-violet radiation.

"Need we go on? This is your past-present indicating future. Six million years of heritage are being swept away in a few generations of the twentieth century. Such is the tyranny of compounding disaster. Such is the enormity of our ignorance. Such is the challenge of this generation to turn the tide before everything worth having is gone."

All the while Dickens has been speaking, the contrasting scenes of magnificence and desolation have swept across the living stage of the Visioneering Room. He pauses now and moves aside as darkness settles over everything. Then, slowly, rising steadily, the faint red streaks of a dawn sky creep in, followed by a spreading golden glow. Stepping through, coming softly, a figure in silhouette appears. It's a girl, her features lightening as the dawn sky changes to full sunrise. Her flowing red hair dancing on her shoulders, Anne Shirley steps forward out of the pages of fiction into this uncertain assembly at the edge of past, present and future. She is dressed as when she first joined the group of mentors so many months ago—high-necked, puffy white blouse and long swishing green skirt. With her comes her bright engaging smile and the special energy of one who seeks for life in full.

"Hello," she says, simply. "My name is Anne and I have a dream. It's a special dream, a golden-green, crimson-veined dream, a very dream of dreams. I would like to share it. Please forgive me if I falter a little. I'm really very nervous, but if you just bear with me I know I'll find the words, because I must. What I have in my heart is crying out to be spoken. I feel, I don't know, so afraid, and yet so hopeful. My mind is full of everything. Please, may I speak with you, all of you important people? May I tell you what is in my heart, the heart of a young person, speaking for, I think, all of the children and youth of the world, with all of our lives ahead, but feeling awfully small and afraid. May I speak to you honestly with my heart and tell you my dream of dreams? And will you listen and hear my words, I mean, really hear them, not just in your minds, but in your hearts, too?"

The light has now come fully up in the Visioneering Room. All the scenes have faded, save for Anne standing at the centre, looking so small and fragile against the memory of the juggernauts of horror that had just preceded her arrival. Charles Dickens crosses to her, takes her hand, and turns expansively to the world leaders sitting row on row looking down at them.

"Ladies and Gentlemen of great power and influence to determine the future of the world," he says to them," may I present to you Anne of Green Gables, one of our team. She lives in the pages of fiction which many of you no doubt read as a young person. She's very dear to us. I believe you'll want to hear what she has to say."

"Speak, Anne, dear," one of the women in the audience calls out. "Many of us know you well. You were the dream child of our young days. Your imaginary world was a delight to us then. Perhaps it will be so again. Maybe you can show us how to move to it from the horrors of the real world we've just seen."

"Thank you," Anne replies. "If I may say it quite simply: I think the young people of the world want to reclaim the future.

"Look, let us see here, the breathtaking beauty of our planet swimming in space. Just as the astronauts showed it when they first looked back and saw a sight no living soul had ever seen before."

The familiar blue and white image of the Earth comes up, as all of the lights in the Visioneering Room go down. Suddenly, there's a slight rocking motion as the room is transformed into a large spaceship and all of the occupants are travellers looking out to the planet, their field of vision the black backdrop of space with sparks of light from meteors and stars.

"This is our home," Anne continues. " I speak to you now as universal youth and here is our universal image, our planet home. Look carefully there, as hard as you might, and you'll see no divisions, no countries, no ethnic groups, just one vast floating orb of beautiful life. It's not until we come closer that we see that the Earth and the world are different. The one is the mystical creation of God with all of its delightful places and special creatures; the other is the fractured, tortured clashing of human beings who have built their own small world and seem to have lost all sense of what is the real beauty and truth.

"My dream is that we now have seen enough of the hopelessness that comes from the tumult of the world and that we will reach for the future of the Earth.

"I see people coming together and meeting as citizens of the planet and not as arguing representatives of angry nations. I see them talking together, laughing, joyfully planning the well-being of people everywhere with everyone living in harmony with the Earth. This is the main thing, the reason for being, to live peacefully together and protect and nourish our beautiful planet. I see peace, joy, love, happiness, honour, dignity and friendship, all of these, as the things people talk about and work for.

"I see that people are less and less interested in wealth and power and all of the material things that go along with that. I see them saying no to lives of pushing and jostling like ferocious dogs fighting over bones and scraps of meat. I see them turning towards love for fellowship and cooperation and service. I see them being concerned every day for making one another feel joyful and fulfilled and dancing with light in their lives. I see them using the richness of the human imagination to turn a divided world into a single planetary home.

"Is this too much to dream? I don't think so. Is it too much to expect? I don't believe it is. How can it be too much to expect to live peacefully on the planet created for us by God? How can we bear the thought of all that magnificent heritage being destroyed by the futile grasping of human hands and minds for their few days of life? We are greater than that. We have minds that can vision the most beautiful creations. Is it too much to expect that we can work together to build those visions and that they will all flow into one grand vision of our single planetary home?

"If we don't dream this dream now, who can dream it for us later? If you, as leaders of the world, don't move to build this vision now, who will there be after you to take up the task? If the children of the world don't ask now for their birthright on their planet, who will ask for them later when the birthright is gone?

"If I don't find the words and the passion in my heart to ask you, to convince you, to stop the killing now, who can come after me to convince whoever comes after you to stop the killing then? We are all trembling with fear of the future, because we are stealing it away, destroying it, when all we have to do is say, we will stop doing that. We will stop killing the future. We will turn from the path of death to the highway of life.

"I think people can do that. I know they can do it if they just get the right pictures in their minds. They can do it if they remember the children, all the children of the world today and the ones coming after them, and all the ones coming after them, forever into the future. Because there can be no future for the human family if there are no children, and there can be no children if people don't protect and care for the Earth."

Throughout Anne's remarks, the world leaders have sat quietly as passengers on their spaceship approaching Earth. The beautiful blue planet, gradually grows in their vision, the blackness of space dropping away, as they enter the atmosphere, and the tumbled sweep of cloud, sky, sea, and land spreads out before them. Before they realize it, they are hurtling rapidly towards the ground, coming in at breakneck speed, like travellers in a giant zoom lens, details leaping out, features of mountains, valleys, rivers, forests, all sweeping in, until the focus narrows, the pace slows, like a helicopter hovering, and an open field of green grass and wildflowers encircled by trees and bushes fills the space in the Visioneering Room.

Anne is standing there quietly waiting, the emotion of her last words hanging in the air, her expression anxious and appealing. Suddenly, from the bushes at the back of the clearing, a face peeps out, the round, wide-eyed features of a black child, peering cautiously, watching and listening, cocking the head first to one side, then the other. It's a young boy's face, no more than ten years old. He sees Anne who is looking away from him, toward the audience. Curious, the boy stares at this young lady with her long red hair. Apparently satisfied, he comes forward, the rest of his body following his face, shining black arms and legs, dressed in khaki shorts and red shirt, nothing on his feet.

In full view now, he tiptoes cautiously a little further forward. Anne still doesn't see him. He stops, glances over his shoulder, and waves first one long, skinny arm in a beckoning motion, then the other. From all around the clearing, a host of other faces pop out from the bushes, like clusters of coloured Christmas lights suddenly switched on. They are boys and girls of all ages and many colours: white, black, chocolate brown, yellow; contrasting ethnic features; all curious, peeping out cautiously, wide-eyed and interested.

Their bodies follow the faces, coming out of the bushes, tentatively at first, then more confident, about fifty of them, in all manner of clothes: dresses, skirts, shorts, shirts, pants, saris, all the colours of the rainbow, a spreading human wave of young energy, rippling out from the bushes, straightening up, growing taller and more confident, smiles spreading, taking the cue from their leader, who is now creeping forward, finger on his lips, motioning for silence, then waving both arms for them to fan out, creeping up on Anne, encircling her from behind.

The audience reacts. People nudge each other, whisper, point. Anne notices, wonders what is happening, then spins around to look behind her.

With a whoop, discovered, the children rush forward, dancing around Anne, jubilant, laughing, clutching for her dress, shouting for attention. Amazed and delighted, Anne throws back her head laughing, tossing her hair, hugging the first of the children to her tightly, then moving on, trying to touch everyone, kissing their cheeks, ruffling their hair. The childish voices have reached a crescendo of laughter and shouting, filling the room with their energy and joy.

Half crying, half laughing, Anne turns to her audience of the heads of governments of the nations of the world and cries out: "Oh, my! Look here and see the children, the children of the future. Meet them, ladies and gentlemen, they've come to say, Hello!"

As if on cue, the children turn outwards from Anne and face the audience. There's no shyness or timidity—not a bit of it. The little black boy who had led the way again comes forward and waves, both arms, at everyone.

"Hi! Hello there!" he shouts. "You can call us the Kids of Hope. We don't really know who we are yet, but we know that we hope to be. We heard that our friend, Anne, was here talking to you about us, so we decided to come along and introduce ourselves. Come on kids, let's go!"

The last words are a signal for his friends to fan out and run forward to the front row of onlookers, standing on tip toe to reach over to the bench to shake the hands of the Presidents, Prime Ministers, Kings, Queens, Generals and such, all of whom immediately dissolve into a celebration of smiles and easy chatter. There's no holding the children. Like bubbling effervescence on the top of sparkling champagne, they spill over and around the benches and chairs, rushing to greet everyone, not pausing one whit for ceremony or decorum, just a tidal wave of exuberant energy.

Anne stands at the front beaming, tears running down her cheeks as she watches the children sweep among the world leaders and sees the spontaneous, joyful reaction. The same room which moments earlier, had rocked with the horror of nuclear holocaust, now bubbles with the spirit of childish fun and laughter. The leaders nearest to Anne call her over, to shake her hand, embrace her, touch her gently, nod wisely, reassuringly, thanking her for bringing the children, saying that everything will be all right.

Then, at the height of the excitement, another change sweeps into the room. The lights go out, save for a single spot on Anne, whose smile fades and she freezes in apprehension. The children vanish. Like playthings of a magician's art, they disappear, and with them all their laughter and merriment. A deathly hush has descended.

Charles Dickens steps into the spotlight on centre stage and Anne fades from view. His voice rings out emotional and strong.

"Oh, how the world cries out for its children! Oh, where are they? Yes, where are they? Precious gifts of hope! Singing their songs of innocence! 'Suffer little children, and forbid them not, to come unto me; for of such is the kingdom of heaven.' And also the Earth. Yes, also the Earth, our planetary home, as Anne showed us. What are we doing to make our planetary home, safe for our children?

"Oh yes, the nations represented here by leaders in this room have signed the Convention on the Rights of the Child. Some of you are even the ones who put your initials on the document. We can all agree with the words: the right of children to a life free from exploitation, neglect, and abuse; the right to be well nourished, to have access to shelter and health care; the right to learn, to read and write, to imagine and create, to dream dreams; the right to a future full of hope, free from fear of war, deprivation and poverty.

"Oh yes, we can agree with the words. We can come together in high-minded assemblies and put our initials on the documents. And we can then return to our countries and put our initials on bills authorizing hundreds of times more expenditure on a soldier than on a child. We can sign conventions forbidding child labour, then turn a blind eye to hundreds of millions of children under the age of fifteen working in conditions little better than slavery. We can agree that they should have good homes to live in, and then be secretly thankful that thugs and brigands of the night round up the children on the streets, murder them, and throw their bodies in the sea. We can solemnly declare that youth are the only sure hope for the future, then mortgage their lives forever with economic burdens to pay for our own excesses, while our industries poison the atmosphere that they will breathe and destroy the soil on which their crops will grow.

"We can agree in our heads, but not believe in our hearts, or see in our minds, where all of our cumulative actions are taking us. You have glimpsed here the horrors of past and present, brought on by following a steady path of conflict and greed for thousands of years. Now, step with me into the future and see for yourselves where your policies and practices are taking us and what becomes of the Children of Hope who just ran so happily in their innocence around this room."

The atmosphere thickens. Audible groans and protests erupt from many quarters. All of the leaders instinctively know that what lies ahead will not be pleasant.

But there's no avoiding it. A force grips and holds them in their seats as Dickens, the master of ceremonies extraordinaire, dons the mantle of phantom of the future and rolls out the scenario of things to come.

It begins in the sky, looking down on an expanse of red desert, stretching away unaltered to the distant horizon, barren and lifeless. The scene moves closer, and a fissure appears, cutting across the expanse of desert, a rift, darker in texture. Patches of green appear where trees cling to the edges and where sunlight flashes on water in the valley floor. In closer still, it's an enormous canyon, five hundred metres deep, two kilometres wide, cutting across the desert as far as the eye can see. Closer still, up to the rim of the canyon, looking down into its great expanse, an incredible scene unfolds.

On each wall of the canyon, a winding trail snakes down from the top to the floor. Moving along the trails, like two streams of black ants to a honey pot, an uncountable mass of children, pours down, materializing from nowhere at the top, massing on either side of the rushing river at the bottom, spreading out, filling the valley floor to its full width of two kilometres. They move forward, a listless army of small people, all ages from babies to teens, pouring into the valley, fed from the two never-ending streams coming down the canyon wall. It's an incomprehensible and compressed mass of small humanity, moving forward, the front ranks already out of sight, far up the canyon floor, while the numbers continue to swell from behind.

The scene moves along above the heads of the slowly trudging children. The big ones carry the little ones. Everyone is in tattered rags or naked, their limbs emaciated, their faces hollow and gaunt. They come in all colours of white, black, chocolate brown, yellow, with contrasting ethnic features—just like before, a few minutes ago, in the Visioneering Room—but in every other way nothing is the same. These children move like lifeless automatons, without energy, totally without hope. The numbers are incredible, incomprehensible to the human mind.

The scene continues to move along over their heads, searching for the front ranks. Five kilometres, ten, still no end to it, around innumerable turns in the canyon's formation, fifteen kilometres, twenty, there has to be an end, but there isn't, twenty-two, twenty-three, twenty-four. Up ahead, yes, there's the end of it. The front ranks treading forward, come up to a sharp drop in the valley floor, where the river plunges over a waterfall a hundred metres high, and the drop extends across the whole two kilometre width of the valley floor, so there's no getting around it. This is the end of the journey, a precipitous drop to nowhere, and the front ranks have come up to it.

They halt, staring listlessly over the precipice, no emotion, no reaction, just standing there waiting while the numbers fill in behind. Twenty-five kilometres of children, each one taking up a half square metre of space, two children per square metre, filling an area twenty-five kilometres long by two kilometres wide: 25,000 metres by 2,000 metres, 50 million square metres, with two children per square metre. One hundred million children are massed on the floor of the canyon with no way forward while the numbers are still being fed from a continuous stream behind.

The scene hangs there in the centre space of the Visioneering Room, burning into the minds of the world leaders forced to watch. Charles Dickens speaks again, his voice now low and sharply incisive.

"In a world where the leaders are preoccupied with politics, weapons, competition, unemployment and national debt, children conceived in faith for the future quickly become the children without hope. Incremental statistics in government reports; occasional sensational copy for the media when crises develop; victims of preventable diseases, avoidable famines, unnecessary wars, unconscionable adult neglect and abuse, their numbers mount over a decade of too little caring and too much incompetence. One hundred million wasted lives, ten million a year for ten years, one hundred million lost souls, massed there in front of your eyes so you can see what the statistics mean. These are the children of the future, who have no future. They are an abomination to our sight, an affront to our conscience. Let us sweep them away!"

With that, a deep rumbling roar is heard in the distance, building slowly while the children in the canyon pack in closely, giving one another what small comfort they can. If they hear the roar, they pay no attention. Their movements remains as listless and automatic as before.

The scene tilts a little so that the onlookers can see up the valley beyond the point where the children are entering. The roar has been building steadily, reaching a crescendo that now implodes the eardrums. Then the source of the sound sweeps into view, a wall of water twenty metres high surging down the valley, churning brown and ugly in its ferocity, tossing trees and boulders around like toys, bearing down with savage intensity on the living carpet of helpless children in its path. In a moment, it has hit the back of the pack and sweeps over them and adds their tiny bodies to the boiling maelstrom of objects before it. Forward it goes, on its awful journey where even at a speed of a hundred kilometres an hour it takes many long minutes to gather and destroy such an incredible number of living souls, while the leaders of the world look on.

Finally, it's done. The wall of water has swept the landscape clean of all the children. One hundred million of them engulfed by its fury. Behind, the river settles again into its former course and two unending streams of children continue to file down the canyon walls onto the valley floor.

The scene fades. The spotlight returns to Charles Dickens standing defiantly in front of his audience.

"Suffer the little children to come into the world, then blot out their tiny lives in misery and death before they have a chance to know what they might be. Then talk in the same breath about progress and development. What progress and development can the world claim in the face of the gigantic horror of those wasted lives?

"This is the first appalling shadow of the future that lies ahead: a future where everything will be on enormous scale and the tragedies as they come will be of like proportions. This is what comes when human ingenuity is cut loose to run its own undirected course without deep and purposeful intent, when just to do is considered to be sufficient cause for doing.

"Out of the conflicts and aggressive thrusting from the past we have seen the monumental barbarities of this century just closing. Come with me now and see where continued travel down that path will take the human race within the next few years of the lifetimes of everyone present in this room."

There follows now a continuous stream of images and scenes flashing across the living stage of the Visioneering Room while Dickens' voice proclaims the telling commentary.

"First will come the consequences of continuing investment in and distribution of weapons of destruction: massive amounts of financial capital and human energy diverted to no good purpose, serving only to batter down an opponent with swift and powerful intensity. Guided weaponry, select nuclear attack, terrorist bombing with remote control, the destruction of water and power systems, the poisoning of food supplies, all possible and achievable by tyrants and military regimes intent on military adventurism. With each incursion the rest of the world gets drawn in as the model of the monolithic world war of the 20th century shifts to a new 21st century model of continuous war on many and changing fronts across the world."

Scenes of violent and spectacular conflict parallel Dickens' commentary as rocket fire, detonations, nuclear explosions, destroyed cities, charred and dismembered bodies, devastated countryside, blackened skies, hordes of homeless and starving people, all sweep in and out of view in an intense and continuous barrage of visual and auditory nightmare.

Dickens' voice continues.

"Behind this and feeding it, is the violence of the cinema, television and all other media held firmly in the control of interests who care little for decency and good, and focus on the profits to be wrung from feeding the depravity of minds disjointed from any sense of noble purpose.

"On the streets, continuous demonstrations and violent clashes erupt among people protesting the bitter struggle that their daily lives have become, as systems controlled by faltering bureaucracies break down. All of the institutions are under vigorous assault. None are held in reverence or respect because the foundation of their thinking is divisive, confrontational, and domineering. In a world of infinite connections with almost unlimited access to the means for violent destruction, divisiveness and confrontation are the powder kegs for the explosions that surely follow, rippling around the world in a seemingly endless chain-reaction of frustration and violence."

Again, the images come up of street scenes of massive assemblies, violent confrontations between people and the authorities, police and soldiers turning weapons on civilians. Buildings are set on fire, churches and synagogues are bombed, legislatures are stormed, politicians are shouted down, political leaders jostled and hassled as they try to make their way between car and office and home.

Again, Dickens continues.

"All of this is played out against a deteriorating environmental background. Indeed, much of the violence and disruption occurs when uncompromising minds fail to reach consensus on how to act in the face of punishing human impact on the Earth's fragile ecology.

"Driven by continuing belief in an economy of production and consumption, political leaders continue to support economic activity that makes the problem worse. The rich industrialized countries hold to their course of expanding production. Third world, impoverished countries battle against overwhelming odds to emulate the industrial life styles. The massive build-up of toxins and pollutants in the entire ecosystem continues. Fragile balancing systems break down. Climatic changes sweep in at unbelievable speed, as crops fail, deserts spread, coastal water levels rise, underground water tables falter, and the Earth exacts a sure and certain penalty against the pressures that afflict it."

Another set of scenes sweeps into the room: factories standing idle and dilapidated, lines of dispirited unemployed people receiving handouts from harassed government workers, thick smog hanging over cities, stunted crops disappearing into desert, stark and ghastly expanses of clear-cut forests, tractors and machinery standing abandoned in fields where the topsoil blows away, dead fish floating in the water of bays and lakes.

The last scene fades and the spotlight returns to Dickens. He now adopts his most assertive, penetrating stance, driving each word into the heart of his audience.

"Oh, cold, cold calculating Reason! How easy it is for you to justify the deeds we do, expunging from our consciousness all thought of what we could have done, had we but chosen a different vantage point from which to steer our course. Oh, poor, still, silent, unsuspecting Innocence! What a toy you are among minds that dissect and measure, testing for the way that leads to greatest self-enhancement. Oh, sweet and precious Honour! Where are you to be found in days of darkness, when dreadful forces crowd around and push strong minds along the path of least resistance?

"Come now Reason, Innocence, and Honour: form the brave triumvirate, and link forces with your cousin, Courage, to raise the colours of a brave new leadership that will not turn aside at the critical hour from the hard exacting course that must be followed to achieve the higher goal.

"Leaders of the world, you have heard, you have seen, you have experienced the path the world now is on. You have seen where that path is taking us. Is there anyone in this room who can say that you would choose willingly to go there? What, no one? No one at all? Then why in God's great name would you choose to follow policies that surely will take you there? Be very clear, the future you have seen played out before you here is as sure and certain, if we allow it to happen, for you personally, and those closest to you, as it is for any of the unfortunates who have moved across this stage. The future is uncompromising. It chooses no favourites. In these days of advanced human knowledge and power, the future will be what we choose to create. As we choose, so shall we have.

"Leaders of the world, what future do you choose for the world? What leadership will you bring to bear to ensure the best possible outcome? Will you stand tall, wise and tolerant? Will you seek with unremitting determination to search in your mind in company with your colleagues to find a vision for the future that all can share, and say, Yes, this is right for the world, because it values above all the preservation of life and the opportunity for every soul to live that life with dignity and honour?

"What you have seen here are not the shadows of what *will be*. They are the shadows only of what *may be*. But they are certainly the shadows of what will be, if you do not choose quickly to turn away from the actions that will bring them to pass.

"We have chosen here to show you where you are going, where you and your governments are taking the world. We do not like what we see anymore than you now seem to like it yourselves. Thus, we stand on the threshold of future possibility rather than future foreclosed. There is more to show you, but my part in it for the moment has been done. I leave you now with the image and the thought of what you now might do when you are returned to your own dominion of power."

With that, the spotlight on Dickens snaps off and he is gone. In his place the tall glass tower of the United Nations building in New York zooms into view and dissolves into the empty room of the General Assembly. The image sharpens in intensity, moves closer, and becomes a mirror image of the Visioneering Room, save that the General Assembly remains empty, waiting for the delegates to return. A deep, unbroken silence embraces all.

Into this space it is now your turn to move, closing this chapter with the world leaders, standing before them in your Visioneering Room, with the image of their empty General Assembly behind you.

"Political leaders of our world," you say. "You have met my mentors and heard their wisdom and their insights on the prospects for humanity. It remains now for me to close this session and prepare you for your next experience with us while your own General Assembly waits empty for your return.

"The pathway to the future is through the acts we do today. I told you earlier that we have assembled our team of Visioneers who are acting to build a preferred future for the world. It's time for you to meet them, to see there how they are giving power to the people and thereby weaving a far different scenario for the future from the tragic scenes which you have just witnessed.

"I ask you now to sit back and meet the Visioneers."

CHAPTER SIXTEEN

The World
of the
Visioneers

T HE DIE IS CAST. YOU'RE IN FOR IT NOW. This is the moment of truth. You have engineered everything preceding for what follows. The leaders of the world are watching. The people of the world are both spectators and players. The Visioneers are at centre. The very Earth itself is the playing field, as it lies open to the assaults of its most powerful and pernicious species. The balance has dipped perilously far on the side of destruction. Now you and your Visioneers are engaged full thrust in weighting the other side with enterprise and hope, to pull it back, to restore the balance, to open up the prospects for a new golden age of prosperity and cooperation unprecedented in human history.

Your mind is a living volcano, ready to erupt with a passion so strong that it will sweep all before it. It will cry out to the further reaches of the universe that human kind is noble, strong, passionate for life, a species without equal, filled with caring and enterprise and love. You will find now the images and the ideas to show it—you and your Visioneers leading the way, Mark Venture at the fore, your creation, all of them your creations, coming out of your mind to inspire the world, pushing the limits of the possible, going beyond all known boundaries. Your mind is filled with the great energy of the universe, finding the words, speaking to the people of the world, capturing their attention, giving them new hope, turning towards the light.

You bring on the Visioneers.

The Visioneers Return

Mark Venture is seated in a magnificent communications room at Visioneer Headquarters in Los Angeles. In front of him an instrument panel of switches and buttons and lights extends the full reach of both arms. Immediately at hand he has a keypad, electronic sketch plate, light pen, scanner—everything he needs to send images, voice, data, text to every part of the world. In front of him a three-metre television panel dominates the wall, while spreading around in an arc formation are two tiers of smaller screens, ten on either side of the central panel. Several cameras and a monitor complete this one-person, two-way audio-visual communications system to the world.

This is the scene that has now come up in the Visioneering Room, while the world leaders look on. Mark Venture has his back to them as he makes some final adjustments on the panel before him. He now turns and for the first time they see the man who for the past one hundred and fifty days has been leading his team of Visioneers on a quest to change the direction of the world. He looks relaxed, bronzed, and vigorous. Dressed casually in white slacks and pale yellow sports shirt, he seems ready to step out of the communications centre onto the golf course. He is joined by Bill Bates who enters with a rush, his slightly rumpled grey business suit flapping about his tall, well-built body. Mark rises to shake his hand.

"Hello, Bill," he says. "You look as if you're trying to pull the world together."

"It's all right for you," replies Bill. "The great Mark Venture just has to sit here and talk. The rest of us must make sure the world can hear you. What d'ya think of the set-up? Pretty nifty, eh? The Visioneers Conference Centre, and we've got twenty of these babies on a smaller scale at Visioneer locations on every continent."

"Pretty impressive, Bill, and now we're ready to give it a full scale test. Is everything set?"

"You bet. Everyone's standing by waiting for you to call 'em in."

"Great! Just give me a minute here, old friend. You know, this is one heck of a thing we're trying to pull off. The team out there is doing a tremendous job. We've got up a good head of steam, but we're going to need all of it and more as we pull up this next stretch. We've managed to get a lot of people excited about what they can do to turn things around, but now we've got to make them see themselves as citizens of the planet. It's one thing to take care of your own plot of ground. It's another to take responsibility for the way things are everywhere. But that's what people have to do. And we can't do it without the cooperation of the governments. They can stall and frustrate us every step of the way, or they can come on side, and then we'll see dramatic changes happen overnight."

"Yeah, but it all starts with the people," replies Bill. "The politicians and leaders are only going to be as good as the people require them to be—at least in democratic countries. In the other places, it's even tougher. When you've got a ruthless dictator in control, then he takes some shifting. We've seen that often enough."

"That's why the free people of the world have got to demand the same rights for all people everywhere, and push our governments to step in wherever blatant cruelty and inhumanity are on the loose."

"And at the same time clean up our own backyards."

"Yes, Bill, it's a big agenda. But the resources to do it are there. We've just got to start directing them around a vision of what this world can really be like."

"Enter the Visioneers!" says Bill Bates, gesturing broadly to the TV screens.

"Yes," smiles Mark, slapping his friend on the shoulder, "let's bring them in and get on with it."

Mark goes to his seat at the instrument panel. Bill Bates pulls up another chair beside him.

Within moments, half the television screens have flickered into life. The sound comes on and the room is immediately filled with the chatter of voices. Mark lets it go on for a minute or two savouring the pleasure of seeing and hearing his Visioneer friends from around the world. Each screen is bringing in a different location. The large centre screen remains blank, available to Mark to choose who to switch on there.

Finally Mark speaks.

"Hello there, you Visioneers!" he calls. "It's good to see you all."

"G'day, mate," someone quips back loudly, probably Daniel Thomas in Russia. "Ow ya goin', orright?"

The other Visioneers erupt with laughter. Mark shouts back over the hubbub.

"Yes, I'm going all right. In fact, seeing all of you again makes me feel just great. Now, we want to try out this new equipment Bill has set up for us. You all should be able to see and hear me and see and hear each other—a regular global electronic tea-party. I don't know what time it is where you are—in fact, I'm not even sure where some of you are. It's 10 o'clock in the morning here in Los Angeles. What I want to do first is call each of you in to get an update on what's going on in your part of the world. Then I've got a proposal for you on where we go from here.

"I'd like to start with our good friend, President Mutsandu in Africa. How are you M'buta? And I see Karl Ibsen is with you. Hello, Karl. Tell us, how are the Visioneers in Africa?"

Mark has switched the African centre on to the large screen and the friendly, smiling face of President M'buta Mutsandu seems to fill the room.

"Hello, Mark," he cries, "and greetings to everyone from Yarawi. We're here in my administrative offices and it's 8 o'clock in the evening, still early even for an old man like me.

"Our news is all good, and look, to show it to you, I've brought the whole team along."

With that, the screen flickers, goes blank for a moment, then comes alive again to a scene of celebration, obviously in some other part of the building, where a group of African Visioneers, at least twenty to thirty in total, are having a great time. They're dressed in the same rich colours and flowing robes as when they first met at Mutsandu's private home at the beginning of their assignment as Visioneers. The President now comes in still smiling broadly and speaks over the laughter and music in the room.

"Would that this could be all of Africa, eh, Mark! One day it will, my friend, one day it will. We've made a good start. We have projects everywhere. The word's spreading and people are searching openly to put more joy back in their lives. We Africans are good at that. Our main problems are with the governments and the bureaucrats. Democracy is still a stranger here in most places. Too many of our brothers and sisters are still dying and starving because of that, but we're building our strength. If all of you will pray for us and bring pressure to bear on our governments to allow us to grow and learn, then we'll be fine. Africa will be great. We have good spirit. Tonight we celebrate, and tomorrow we toil again for our place in the future."

"Yes, M'buta, yes you will," says Mark. "God bless you all there in Yarawi—and now we continue."

For the world leaders in the Visioneering Room looking on, there follows an extraordinary view of the world that none of them has ever seen before. The playful spirit of the Africans sets the tone. It's the energy and optimism of people working with joy in their hearts for something they truly believe in. As Mark calls in the reports from centre after centre around the world, the excitement builds, each piece weaving a unique pattern in a tapestry of hope.

First, on to Theresa Romano, who with Sally Hearst and Nicholai Andropov is reporting in from Vancouver in Canada, where they first lit up the lives of 25,000 teenagers at a rock concert in the stadium, and sent them out onto the streets of Vancouver singing the *Song of the Visioneers*. From that beginning, the visioneering movement has spread around the world more rapidly among the children than any other group. Clubs, music groups, sports teams, comics, newsletters, clothes, running shoes, school bags, balloons, kites—every conceivable assembly, object, or entity associated with children and youth in every country has been somehow touched with the spirit of visioneering a better future.

Expanding on this theme, Irene Henshaw reports in from Edinburgh, Scotland at St. Aidan's School for Girls on the curriculum developments beginning to bring a framework of anticipation and creation into class-rooms around the world. At Cambridge, Jeremy Hiscox has assembled a group of academics who comment on a reorientation of several disciplines in higher education towards acceptance for intuitive knowing and vision as central elements.

On issues of peace, spirituality and human well-being, enthusiastic reports come in from Lord Nigel and Lady Feversham at Cambridge with Jeremy Hiscox, and from Prince Rupert of Wittenstein with General Francois Soulière in Paris. It seems that foundations and non-profit orga-nizations worldwide are bringing the spirit of visioneering into the agendas for peaceful coexistence, equity, world health, shelter, food, and environ-mental protection.

From India, Indira Murti and Carmen Santander report a growing consciousness, even on that divided and desperate sub-continent, of the need for cooperation and unity of spirit. The teachings of Baba Satyananda are taking greater hold as he now moves more frequently about the coun-tryside and broadcasts to millions via satellite.

In China, Lin Yuen and Zhao She Yuhan continue to lay the ground-work for the kindling of democracy. Also in Russia, Daniel Thomas reports with his team that behind the stumbling and faltering bureaucracies, the spirit of visioneering is making ground.

The three great industrial countries of Japan, Germany and America stand out as lighthouses of promise but giants of resistance. From Japan, Junichi Yakasawa reports awareness among more and more people for a reconsideration of where their industrial strategy is taking them and the world, but they continue to hold to an isolationist position. In Germany, Boris Gunther sees fierce national pride as a growing concern, though the spirit of the Visioneers can stir strong passion in these determined people. Across the Atlantic, the American visioneering team has assembled in New York where each reports a piece of the national reaction to the work of the Visioneers. In the media, Julia McCarthy sees interest, but as yet, no deep understanding. For business, George Walker reports wide acceptance of creative learning but a continuing preoccupation with survival. Senator Wilfred Brown sees the political system as fractured and as partisan as ever. Diane Koplitz is hopeful that the women of America are hearing the message and bringing a new spirit of visionary leadership to the land. Arthur Rhinegold is well into the shooting of his film on *The Visioneers Part II*, which will tell the story of the hundred and fifty days just passed, and he believes that when this is released, Americans will catch the spirit of the Visioneers and move as a force in the world of enlightened awareness.

Across the world to another potential centre of awakened change, Esther Fisher and Mohammed Hussein report in from Jerusalem. What can they say but that the old entrenched hatreds remain firmly in place and in control of events. However, at a deeper level, the spirit of understanding and respect that lay behind Esther's release by her terrorist captors, and the weary revulsion at the tragedy of the Roths and the like, are stirring faint flickering flames of a new consensus and accommodation of interest.

Finally, in his round-up of reports, Mark calls in George Cardinal. The tall Indian chief, a leader among the people of the First Nations in Canada, appears on the centre screen as proud and arresting as when he stood on the steps of St. Paul's Church and spoke of his vision that good would triumph over evil. As he looks out now to his friends, the Visioneers, all who are watching know that standing there beside him is the spirit of the one Visioneer who won't be among those giving reports today, Father Luis Valdez.

"Hello George," says Mark. "It's good to see and speak with you again. How are you?"

"I'm well," replies George. "And I'm full of hope. I've spent these past months mostly with my people. This is a cold time of year in northern Canada, very cold. The days are short, but sunny, like the promise of summer to come. There's not much moisture in the air, but sometimes at night what there is distills out and settles on the thin bare branches of the poplar and birch trees and on the cold stiff needles of the spruce. And when the sun comes up again next morning, the world is transformed into a fantasy of white crystals, gleaming in the sunlight, cloaking those ordinary trees with a magic costume that settled out of nowhere, but was there all the time, only waiting for the right conditions to bring it out.

"As I've listened to you, my friends, call in from all over the world, each one saying that beneath an old exterior some new spirit is stirring, I'm reminded of that beautiful, gleaming hoar frost on those trees. The true beauty of the human soul is there waiting to come out. It's our work to make the conditions right for it to come. And then it will collect and grow and shine on every limb in every land. But unlike the frost, it won't be disturbed by any breeze or warming of the day, because it has come from the soul of the people, which is a very deep and rich place and gives up only qualities of great worth.

"I think we're close now, perhaps closer than we think, to that transformation. My brother Luis felt it on that night when he went out to speak to the world of the love that was in his heart. When he was cut down by the assassin's bullet, the love didn't die with his body. It has grown through you and your work, and through the millions of others who've been touched in their souls by the truth of what Luis and all of us are saying: that we are a good people; that we care for the Earth; that we care for our brothers and sisters; and that we'll turn now with new understanding to build a millennium of peace and love in the land.

"I'm speaking today from my home in Canada, but tomorrow I leave to set up a new headquarters in the land of Luis Valdez in Santiago, where I'll work with new friends from all the countries of South America to make that land, too, a place where the transformation will grow and shine more brightly as the sun rises on each new day.

"May the God of all of us bless us in the work."

"Amen to that, George," says Mark.

Similar murmurs of confirmation come quietly over the sound system from all of the other Visioneers. Mark pauses for a moment to let the mood created by George Cardinal's words settle as the backdrop to what he intends to propose.

"Friends," he begins, "your words are full of hope and pride. And rightly so. We've done much in a short time to make a difference. But we have to understand that the change so far is only on the surface. Out there we all know that the way of the world is still as fiercely destructive as the day we first met together in the Visioneering Room.

"We've come to the end of the hundred and fifty days during which we intended to raise awareness. We've done that. Now we must move to the next step. And that, my friends, is to engage people in an agenda for action. The agenda is for people to see themselves as planetary citizens. They have to see that the Earth, their planetary home, is in grave danger from the accumulated actions of all of us living on it. For this, we're all responsible. People have to come to realize that, to break out of their cocoons of local and national preoccupation and see themselves as a vital part of the living intelligence of the planet and to stop acting in any way that's not compatible with the long-term future.

"This is a punishing agenda, because it means turning away from much we're currently doing. It will touch people in their lifestyles, in their pocketbooks, in their deepest beliefs and values. It requires a massive shift of mind away from the agressive, competitive behaviour of the 20th century to the cooperative, stewardship lifestyle required in the 21st century. We have to come together as a human family on the planet. This is a big mind change, but we know it can be done, because the human mind is capable of far higher levels of achievement than we have ever asked of it.

"Now we're beginning to ask it, and our task is to find the way to do that at the level of the planet as a whole, in a great, surging, cumulative, flood of new understanding, ultimately reaching every intelligent mind on the planet. That's our task. That's our reason for coming together.

"To do it, we must now move rapidly to convene a Congress of the Global Mind. What do I mean by that? I'm not sure that I understand it fully myself yet. It means a coming together, mind to mind, at the deepest levels of intuitive understanding, engaging in the most profound levels of dialogue where we listen to each other with deep listening and hear what the other says with deep hearing.

"Our task now is to design what this Congress of the Global Mind might be, how and when it will happen, and how every citizen on the Earth might participate. That's not our agenda today. Today, I merely wished to put it to you, for you to take away, to put it in your minds, and to reflect with the others around you on how we might accomplish it.

"There's one last part, however, that's clear to me, and we've got to act on it now. Our work to date has proceeded independently of any particular cooperation with government. But that can't continue. Too much of the vast resources of the world are controlled by governments, and they're presently being largely directed towards objectives not consistent with continuing life on the planet. We must intervene on that point now, as a necessary precondition to creating the Congress of the Global Mind.

"Each of you can act locally and nationally as you best see fit to intervene with your governments. But there's a window of opportunity available to us within ten days to make a substantial intervention at the international level. The leaders of most of the countries of the world are meeting at the United Nations in New York at that time. I'm working on plans to speak with them and ask for their cooperation.

"If this initiative is to be successful, I believe we have to see it for what it is—a very large scale political and media event. It's absolutely critical that we have the full force of the media on our side. For that reason, I intend now to work very intensely with Bill Bates and through him with all of you to see that we get good and friendly exposure as we head up to this meeting at the U.N.

"That's the gist of what I wanted to say. Now I'm ready to listen. Tell me what you think."

There follows a lively interaction among the Visioneers as ideas and proposals are traded back and forth around the world. To the world leaders watching and listening in the Visioneering Room, it's a strange experience. They have heard Mark Venture refer to their meeting at the United Nations as if it is still ten days in the future. They sit as audience to a drama unfolding on the same world stage on which they themselves play such a prominent role. But the actors here are not politicians, save for Mutsandu, and he's more a man of his people than an international figure. No, they are citizen-activists, who seek to give power to ordinary people by awakening inside their minds the visions that are there, for themselves, their families, their communities, and the world. Now Mark's intent is to bring the action to the world leaders themselves. How is this to be worked out?

There will be no answer to that question at this time. Mark Venture moves to close the session.

"Thank you, friends," he says. "We're agreed that today we begin our move to bring the work of the Visioneers into the full glare of the political arena. As we do so, we must be aware that we'll encounter powerful enemies. We've tasted already the tragedy that comes of that. The murder of Luis Valdez is our constant reminder that in every step we take, the forces of evil and ignorance are at our heels. But they can have only as much power as the force for good extends to them. We're aligned, my friends, with the most powerful force in the world, the force for life and love. Against that, nothing else can ultimately prevail."

"Oh yes, Mark, that's so true." Indira Murti from India has intervened. "We're moving now to ask the central questions: What does it mean to be human? How does a worldwide community of human beings behave when they understand that they have minds that can touch the mind of God? What systems of economics and government will we build when we begin with the proposition of love for all our fellow beings and the planet?"

Indira now smiles a little as she continues.

"You've spoken, Mark of the force for life and love, but we're all waiting for you to say something more about one particular story of love. Something, perhaps, about a wedding? What about you and Esther? Here it's only two weeks away from your wedding and you've said nothing about it. And Esther, there you are on the other side of the world from Mark, and you've said nothing either. Now, come on. It's all very noble for both of you to be so busy helping the world, but we're looking for a celebration. Tell us. What about the wedding?"

Mark bursts out laughing.

"Oh, yes, the wedding! Thank you for reminding me! You want a celebration, Indira. A celebration, you're certainly going to have. But Esther's in charge of that. Tell them, Esther. What about the wedding!"

As Esther speaks from Jerusalem, Mark switches her image up on to the large screen. She is radiant. Her auburn hair cascades around her shoulders, framing her face with a lively beauty that fills the screen with energy and seems to leap out to embrace everyone watching. Her smile shines like sunshine dancing on snowy mountains.

"Thank you, Indira, and everyone for your love," she says. "Well, I can tell you with great confidence that preparations are coming along just fine. Actually, I almost believe I know less about it than the reporters who have been writing it up for weeks in magazines around the world. I get some of my best ideas by sitting down reading what someone else says I said. It's a crazy way to do things, but I love it. And everyone's so positive and helpful, sometimes a hundred phone calls a day of advice and good wishes.

"And you folks are going to have pride of place among the guests. Our own dear friends, the Visioneers, all coming here to Jerusalem to celebrate with us. The very thought makes me tingle with excitement. We're holding it in the amphitheatre on the site of the old Sultan's Pool just outside the city walls at the foot of Mount Zion. It's a magnificent setting. Everything will be outdoors. I'm sure there'll be thousands of people, and the whole world's going to be watching by satellite. I'm looking at this as our gift to the world and the world's gift to us: sharing and celebration. I can hardly wait. Make sure you all come early. I've got a special office set up handling details, but I'll always be available to meet and greet each of you personally. Thank you, thank you so much for being our friends and supporters."

"Amen to that," adds Mark. "Friends, it's a wonderful work we're about. It's a great time to be alive. If we can just take the spirit and joy that's crackling around the world through this conversation we're having, and widen it out to include everyone, then we'll have done something truly great.

"May God bless us in this and go with each of you and keep you safe! We'll talk again in a week and sooner if we need to. Goodbye for now."

Amid much laughter and cheerful well-wishing, the Visioneers sign off. The scene in the Visioneering Room disappears and the world leaders sit quietly reflecting on everything they have just seen and heard.

The Darker Side of Enterprise

As the Visioneers fade from the scene and the atmosphere in the Visioneering Room hangs heavy with expectancy, you're conscious of another force building up, dictating for you the next piece in the drama you are unravelling for your audience. You sense the powerful presence of Charles Dickens beside you, speaking again the words he said when you and your mentors first set the Visioneers upon their path.

He had warned of the darker side of human character. "It becomes manifest," he had said, "in individuals whose very presence seems foreordained to bring disaster and misfortune by attacking the very heart of noble enterprise."

Dickens had spoken of the archetypes of wickedness, reaching their worst in "the high priest of incarnate evil, intelligent and lithe of mind, but totally absorbed with illusions of grandeur, himself portrayed in his mind as conquering hero sweeping all obstacles aside as irritants to his deluded dream of conquest."

And George Cardinal, speaking from his heart at the bitter recollection of the evil that had destroyed his friend, Luis Valdez, had seen the fine line that divides the actions of most people between good and bad. If the force of incarnate evil is allowed to go unchecked, then it becomes a magnet to gather around it acts of lesser but accumulating ill, until the whole becomes a festering disease. On the other hand, people can take the opposite path, if inspired by lives of nobility and worth, and the scenario that then unfolds becomes a triumph and celebration of life.

The Visioneers and the watching world leaders lie in the vortex between the two alternative futures. Which way it goes will depend on the strength of the opposing forces and their ability to attract the allegiance and commitment of the great mass of struggling humanity. The full contest between good and ill is about to be joined, and your role is to present it to those most powerfully positioned to influence the outcome.

Again, you step before the world leaders to prepare them for the scene to follow.

"You have met the Visioneers," you say, "and you've heard that they intend to bring before your assembly at the United Nations the critical importance of their mission. This is the same assembly that now stands empty and adjourned while you sit here to broaden your understanding about the future. You've been detoured in time, so to speak, into this assembly here, the Visioneering Room of myself and my mentors, whom you have met. You've heard and experienced their presentations of past, present and future. Now you've met the Visioneers and seen what they're about. There's one last force to which we must expose you.

"This is the force of evil that we know only too well infects our world. You can call it by whatever name you like, and attribute its presence to whatever cause you choose. But there it is, nonetheless, and we must deal with it. Already, it has struck the Visioneers a devastating blow in the brutal assassination of one of their members. They've turned this setback to good advantage. However, the accumulated power of this evil now stands massed against them. Into this battle, for battle it certainly is, you, too, will soon be ensnared.

"Watch now as the encounter is joined."

As you withdraw, a new scene comes up in the centre space of the Visioneering Room. An ice-covered lake in the Swiss Alps appears in the foreground. Less than a kilometre wide, the lake on its far shore is dotted by a cluster of rustic cottages. Moving closer, the scene reveals a rocky outcrop on the lake's edge visible through the snow. The rocks act as a natural barrier to movement along the shore. Beyond the outcrop, the land rises gently, and standing among the trees a turreted wood mansion, painted in bright yellow with white trim and green tiled roof, presents an imposing view to someone approaching from the lake. Closer inspection reveals a high brick security fence on either side of the property running back to disappear in a cluster of trees. The building is set back about fifty metres from the lakeshore in a series of low terraces with steps running down from a broad patio to the lake. Moving in closer still, the scene now shows a high steel-mesh security fence running the full width of the property to the other fences on either side.

Through the fence, on up the steps, across the patio and into the house through square-paned folding glass doors, the scene opens out into a magnificent and opulently furnished room with a shining light oak floor and matching wood trim and high cathedral ceiling showering the room with light and space. Opening off the large room a smaller alcove is fitted with a compact set-up of computer and electronic communications equipment with several TV monitors, cameras, and switching equipment. It's not unlike what was just seen at Visioneer Headquarters in Los Angeles.

At one end of the room, an oak dining table, golden-grained and elegantly carved, is set for breakfast with four places. A maid in trim black and white uniform brings in a number of hot entrees in covered silver serving dishes. She sets them on a long buffet together with an assortment of croissants, jams, marmalade, fruit salad and silver coffee pots. Glancing quickly around the room, she ensures everything is in order, then withdraws.

From a door at the other end of the room a man enters. Tall, slightly stooped, he moves with a barely perceptible limp. He pauses briefly to glance at several sheets of paper he takes out of a facsimile machine in the communications centre as he passes. Nodding and reading as he goes, he continues on to the breakfast table. He is dark complexioned, swarthy Latin features, with a prominent aquiline nose, thick bushy eyebrows, and steel grey hair combed back severely. His age would be mid to late sixties. He is dressed casually in black, tailored slacks, and blue cotton shirt, monogrammed with a large white C on the pocket. At his throat a richly embroidered silk cravat hangs loosely. He presents an imposing figure of authority.

· He sets the pages he's been reading on the table and turns to help himself to food from the buffet.

At that moment, another person joins him. It's a woman, in her late forties, also of Latin heritage. She is attractive though slightly severe: coal black hair pulled back in a bun, wide mouth, high cheek bones, dark searching eyes under arched eyebrows. Dressed in an elegant green and gold jumpsuit with wide flowing sleeves and loose bodice, she commands immediate attention as she moves briskly across the room.

"Ah, Elvira, my darling, good morning." The man puts down his plate and goes to greet her. "I must say, you look lovely in that outfit. You bring the breath of spring to these snowy Alps."

"It's hard to be the breath of spring this early in the morning," she replies, her voice high pitched and rasping like a fine file on soft metal, "but we'll do our best. What time did you get up, Carlos? It seemed like the middle of the night when I heard you moving about the bedroom."

"And I thought I was being so quiet." His voice is thick and loud.

"Let's face it, Carlos, you're not one to be quiet at any time," she replies, going to the buffet for coffee.

"Well, I seem to remember at one part of the evening, you weren't so quiet either."

"Come on, you can't embarrass me. I just happen to enjoy love-making, even with an old carrion bird like you."

"El Condor is no carrion bird. He's the great eagle of the Andes who swoops and soars and carries his beloved away on wings of pure power."

"You really love that image, don't you. The strong and masterful, El Condor, ruler of all he surveys from the dizzying heights."

"Well, if it fits, you wear it. It's a new name for me. I like it."

"Yes, my dear, and I love to be here under your wings. Now, quiet, here comes Larry. Good morning, Larry, come and join us for breakfast."

The newcomer is a fat and balding man in his middle fifties. His face is flabby and sallow, the unhealthy complexion heightened by thick, horn-rimmed glasses, hiding tiny eyes. He wears country tweeds, rumpled and bulging about his corpulent frame.

"Yes, good morning, Elvira and Carlos." His voice wheezes and grunts its way around his words. "Something sure smells good here."

"Come, help yourself, my friend," says Carlos. "There's eggs, bacon and sausages, a good American breakfast."

"Oh sure," replies Larry, "Just like Sunday morning in New York." Behind the wheezing, a strong nasal, New York accent is clearly evident.

The three of them sit down to eat, Carlos and Larry each at one end of the table and Elvira in the middle.

"Well, I've got the reports here on the latest shipments," says Carlos. "Most of it seems to have got through. Now, you'd better see to it that those hot shot Americans pay up, Larry, when you get back there tomorrow."

"Don't worry, don't worry," replies Larry. "Everything's under control."

"Don't tell me you two are going to talk business at the breakfast table," complains Elvira. "Here we are in the middle of the beautiful Swiss Alps and I've got to listen to talk about drug shipments to New York. It's tasteless and depressing."

"It's a commodity, my dear," Carlos' voice betrays a tone of annoyance. "We've got millions of customers out there who are willing to pay any price to get what we can give them. It's the only thing that gives them any pleasure in life. They can walk away from it any time they like. But they never do. It's a blessing to them. Don't you say so, Larry? You're a good God-fearing man. You know how much comfort our product brings to souls in distress."

Larry, with a mouthful of scrambled eggs and bacon, mumbles a wheezing angry response: "Don't mock me, Carlos. You can say most anything you like about what I do, but don't mock me on the subject of religion."

"Oh, the nerves are still raw, are they?" rejoins Carlos. "But I wasn't mocking you. I'm deadly serious. As a television evangelist, you were sensational in touching people's souls. You knew what they wanted to hear. Just follow the teachings of the Lord Jesus, and God will shower all blessings on you—just as He did on the Reverend Larry Porter. Why look at me, you would say, not in so many words, but there you were right in front of them, wearing a thousand dollar suit and a diamond on each hand. How could they not look at you and see that you were successful? So, your message was clear, look at me and see the blessings of God. You were good. You were very good, Larry.

"Then when you took to blowing a little crack, you got better, and when the word leaked out you were a double sensation, and the people knew if the Reverend Larry Porter could perform like this with a little crack blowing in his brain, why it must be good for you. You were touching people in their souls and taking them away from their daily miserable lives.

"And you would've been okay if the church leaders had left you alone. But they were jealous, Larry, and first chance they got they went for the jugular."

"That's right," Larry explodes, slamming his knife and fork down on the table. "That's exactly what they did."

"Just like they did it to Jesus before you," adds Carlos, warming to the subject.

"Yes and that's what I told them, too," fumes Larry, then pauses. "Say, Carlos, are you sure you're not mocking me?"

"No! Upon my word, no. I've nothing but the greatest admiration for you. Just ask Elvira. Come, my dear, what do you say? Am I not always praising Larry for his contribution?"

"Oh, come on, you two," she replies, gesturing with both hands. "Do we have to have this performance again? I've heard it a dozen times, now. Larry's a defrocked, disgraced, whatever you want to call it, television evangelist. It happened over two years ago, when he was exposed for a bit of crack blowing and sexual horsing around. You picked him up out of the gutter and made him one of the key men in your drug-running business. Now, he's just giving millions of Americans a new way to have a high, and he's good at it. So why do we have to have this repeat performance every time you two get together?"

"Ah, my dear, Elvira," says Carlos, "you don't appreciate the hidden depths here. Larry is the quintessential man of our time. He understands the yearning of the masses for spiritual uplifting, but he understands, too, that they want their pleasures of this world. So what better combination than the gospel of salvation and a little chemical opiate to help it along. Isn't that right, Larry?"

"Yes, it is." Larry is now very excited. Small flecks of foam mix with egg at the edges of his mouth as he speaks out. "I gave that ministry of mine the whole depth of my being. I brought thousands and thousands of people to the Lord. I showed them that if they would just trust God, He would heap blessings on them manyfold and they could have everything they wanted in life. I made them good, hardworking, devout people, striving to be the best they could be, and if they took a little chemical stimulation when they needed it, why that was all right, as long as the Lord came first in their hearts.

"But the world wouldn't let me continue in that teaching. They hounded me out. Cast me adrift. Ruined me. Now I can buy all the assets of that ministry many times over—and, believe me, it was no small operation then. We had millions of dollars of real estate and broadcast facilities across the United States. Now I can buy it all back, and one day soon I will, and set up a ministry such as the world has never seen."

"Bravo, Larry! Bravo!" Carlos applauds.

"Oh, Larry, come off it," Elvira responds. "You're just a vindictive little man out to get revenge, and you happen to be doing very well at it, thanks to Carlos."

"Vindictive! You can talk!" Larry is storming. "Look at you. Elvira Ramos, widow of ex-President Enrico Ramos, ousted from his country for fraud and corruption. You've got access to millions of dollars he socked away in Swiss bank accounts, but still that isn't enough for you. No, you've got to come and screw with Carlos Palmira, the great El Condor. Sweeten the bed in his eyrie, while you plot with him to get arms shipments out of the U.S. and Germany, and France, and Britain, and anywhere else you can, so you can build up the rebel forces to overthrow the government and come back into power yourself, like some great she-hero out of antiquity."

"Say, Larry, that's pretty good." Carlos is nodding approvingly from his end of the table. "You're calling that just about right."

"Yes, I know it," retorts Larry. "And don't think I don't appreciate the other half of the strategy. If you can flood the country with drugs through the rebel forces and get enough people hooked, then they'll just welcome you all in and the government will be out overnight. And, of course, because I'm the best drug runner you've got, I can make that little plan really work out for you."

"So here we are," smiles Carlos, "One happy family having a nice breakfast together."

"I resent your tone, Larry." Elvira doesn't intend to let matters rest there. "Don't try to equate my situation with yours. I wasn't any Bible thumping evangelist, promising riches for prayers. My husband and I gave the people good law and order. We worked hard and long. We brought in foreign capital and built up industry. Anything we took off the top was a percentage for our efforts. Great people play hard for great stakes and get huge rewards for their efforts and for the risks they take. When they hounded us out, it broke my husband's heart, and he died a shattered man. Well, I'm not going to let it rest at that. All of my life went to serve my country, and those people who sit in power there now are going to pay for what they did to us. Elvira Ramos will be back. And when I am, there won't be a rat hole deep enough for them to hide to escape what's coming to them. The people will want me back. You'll see. And the ones that don't, well, they're just like dust in the wind. We'll blow them away into oblivion."

"Enough, now," Carlos interrupts authoritatively. "You've each said your piece, and that's an end to it. Both of you are here because I chose to let you participate in my empire. It's for mutual benefit, because that's the way the world works. I'm a man of my time. I understand it better than probably any one else on Earth. That's why I can play with impunity on the whole world stage. Each of you wants your own piece of that, and you can have it, as long as it works to my benefit, too."

Carlos pushes back his chair, gets up, and strides around the room as he continues to speak. His limp, barely perceptible at first, grows more pronounced as his passion rises.

"I've seen clearly that in the last half of the 20th century, the world has become an open, deadly amphitheatre where mankind is engaged in many jousts, few of them friendly, and most are skirmishes to the death with increasingly higher penalties all around. None of us knows what the ultimate outcome will be, but while the deadly games are being played, whoever understands best the conditions of the conflict can reap enormous rewards. That's the essence of my genius and that's how my power will grow.

"I know that there's no longer any moral authority in the world. Whatever works for the moment is right. I see it, and I exploit it. I sell arms to whoever wants to fight. I buy weapons from whoever wants to sell them to whoever wants to buy them. I arrange for money to move around the world, in search of the best return, no matter what the project, so long as there's a return on the investment. I run an international network of drug trafficking. I arrange for flows of public funds, because there are always corrupt officials who'll take a pay-out for giving me control. I arrange bribes of union leaders to shut down industries and ports and public services. I buy off management to achieve the same results. I sit at tables with heads of state. I meet with religious leaders of all faiths. I give generously to charities if it pleases me to do so.

"I come and go in the world as I please. I'm a power broker. I understand the raw and naked grasping for power among men and women who acknowledge no higher authority than their own ambition. My enterprise is based on human greed and it flourishes well.

"But I understand the limits and threats to what I do. While communities and nations are in conflict I can prosper. If they come together around a common purpose for the future, I can have some problems."

Carlos pauses and stands silently, staring out at the lake. Larry ventures a comment.

"Well, I don't think you've got much to worry about," he says, "There's no sign of the world coming together on anything."

Carlos whips around and storms back to the table and pounds it with his fist.

"You don't think so, hey? Have you no eyes to see what's going on? There was the beginning of a change with the break up of the communist block, and the tearing down of the Berlin Wall, and the collapse of apartheid in South Africa. But I didn't put much stock in any of that for fundamental change, because the major preoccupation of everyone everywhere was economic self-interest. Every nation and community was still at each other's throat and there was still plenty of room for me to ply my trade.

"But now in the last six months, there's a different move afoot. There's this group called Visioneers that have sprung from nowhere and they're beginning to have an effect, precisely because they're putting energy back into communities to take responsibility for one another. We've seen neighbourhoods cleaning up their drug problems and getting homeless people off the streets into housing. Self help projects are cropping up all over Africa and South America. Kids in school are beginning to think this way and are having an impact on their parents. It's the start of something significant; so, don't tell me there's nothing going on, because there is, and I don't like it."

"Well, I don't know, Carlos," Elvira interrupts. "As I recall, there was a lot of news about them when that priest was killed a few months ago, but there's really been nothing much since then."

"The word was you were behind that, too, Carlos," adds Larry.

Carlos swings on him. He erupts in anger and stabs an accusing finger into the flab of Larry's chest.

"Don't you ever presume to say anything like that in my presence. I made you what you are, and I'll break you here and now, if I choose. Do you understand that, Larry?"

The other's face turns pale under its sallow complexion.

"Yes, Carlos," he barely whispers.

"Then get out of here, now! The sight of you sickens me all of a sudden. Come back in an hour and I'll talk to you then about these drug shipments before you leave for the States."

Without a word, Larry gets up and quickly leaves the room.

"You certainly are testy," says Elvira, "Did you have to be so hard on him?"

"Don't you push my patience either, Elvira. Your rope is not much longer than his. You want to know why I'm paying so much attention to this. I'll tell you why. Last night, I monitored a video conference of these Visioneers. They're so sure of themselves, they didn't even bother to scramble it. They're reporting developments from all over the world. More important than that, though, their leader, a man named Mark Venture, is planning to meet with the heads of governments when they meet in special session at the U.N. in New York next week."

"Can he do that?"

"I don't know. He's been able to pull off some other spectacular things."

"But you needn't concern yourself too much. You've got much better contact with those people than Mark Venture can ever have. Why it wouldn't surprise me if half of them were on your payroll."

"Elvira, dear," Carlos' tone has become menacing again. "You are beginning to irritate me, too. Go on and leave me alone. I have another appointment shortly. I'll see you at lunch."

Elvira pouts a little, but says nothing, and quickly leaves the room.

Carlos turns back to the coffee pot.

"Sonya!" he calls loudly.

The maid appears.

"Sonya, clear these plates away. I'm expecting a visitor shortly. Leave that other setting there for him."

The maid is busy with her work for a few minutes, then leaves. Carlos sits again at the table, drinking his coffee and studying the reports he had set aside during his conversation with Larry and Elvira. A few minutes later, he is roused by the intercom.

"Mr. Palmira?"

"Yes?"

"Johnson, sir. We've arrived at the front entrance."

"Good, bring him in by the side door."

Carlos returns to his reading. He looks up when two men enter the room by a door at the opposite end from where the house guests had come and gone. One of the newcomers is dressed in a chauffeur's uniform. He is gently guiding the second man by the arm, for this one has a leather blindfold over his eyes. He's a young man, lightly built, dressed all in black and wearing the black and white checkered headdress of a Palestinian.

"Mr. Kamal Rashid, sir," announces the chauffeur.

"Thank you, Johnson," says Carlos, rising. "Remove the blindfold and leave us. I'll call you when I want you back."

The chauffeur does as instructed, then leaves. Kamal Rashid stands blinking in the bright light of the room. Carlos greets him, extending his hand. The other takes it.

"Ah, Mr. Rashid, welcome. I apologize for the blindfold, but I'm sure you understand the reason for the precautions. May I offer you some breakfast? It's a long drive from Geneva. You must be hungry."

"Thank you. I don't eat much," replies the young man. "Some bread and a glass of water will be fine."

"Here, have some fruit too," urges Carlos. "Won't you sit down. I'm just finishing my own breakfast."

The young man sits at the place set for him and begins to eat slowly, watching his host carefully.

"I'm sure you recall our previous meeting," says Carlos, fixing him with a steady gaze. "It was in Amman several months ago. You were interested in some assistance I might give the Palestinian cause. After that, you leapt into world prominence with the hostage taking of Esther Fisher in Jerusalem, though I don't believe your name was ever publicly linked to that business."

Carlos pauses. Kamal Rashid says nothing and continues to eat.

"Yes," continues Carlos. "It was strange how that came out. Apparently the hostages were released without incident into the hands of the leader of that group to which Esther Fisher belongs—the Visioneers, I believe they're called. An Australian named Mark Venture is the leader, I understand. You met him. Can you tell me what kind of man he is?"

"I came here to discuss arms shipments for the Palestinians." Kamal's voice is cold and hard. "I have no interest in these other questions."

"Ah, but you see, Kamal, I do. And that makes a difference, especially when you are here as my guest. I have some real interest in these Visioneers and I thought you might perhaps be prepared to satisfy my curiosity on a few points, especially if you think I can be helpful to you."

Silence settles between them.

"You see, Kamal," Carlos continues. "I have a question in my mind. Our original discussion in Amman doesn't seem to have led anywhere. That's unusual for me. I have products and services which my clients always find useful. But in your case, nothing has proceeded, and it's been several months, so I find that most unusual. And in between, there's this strange business of your capitulating to Mark Venture, and I'm wondering if there is a connection."

"I capitulate to no one," replies Kamal in the same hard, cold voice. "I released the hostages because it was to our advantage."

"Oh, and what advantage was that? Have you noticed any improvement in the Jewish position towards the Palestinians since then? Has Israel given back one square kilometre of the Arab land that it occupies? Have the Palestinians living under Israeli domination been given equivalent citizenship rights to the Jews? Are your people any better fed, clothed, educated, housed than they were six months ago when we first talked? Is there any sign anywhere of an international effort to establish a Palestinian homeland? I'm not sure what advantage you believe you've gained by capitulating, excuse me, by negotiating, with Mark Venture."

"Perhaps your intelligence isn't as complete as you think it is," replies Kamal.

"Oh, I agree, that's entirely possible," Carlos says expansively. "That's why I asked you here. I wish to be well informed. I can, however, share some information with you about Mark Venture. He plans to speak to the heads of governments at the United Nations next week. Were you aware of that? I see not. Don't you think that's a little strange, if you're so far in their confidence—the Visioneers, I mean? I understand you do maintain some regular contact with Esther Fisher. Isn't that true?"

Again, Kamal declines to answer.

"I see. Well, perhaps you can draw your own conclusions about what Mark Venture will say at the United Nations about the Palestinians. No doubt, you believe they rank high on his agenda among all of the other issues he's involved with. It's strange, though, that you know so little about his intentions. I'm sure you do know, though, about the plans for his marriage to Esther Fisher in Jerusalem in two weeks. Perhaps you're invited. Are you invited, Kamal?"

"I don't see how that's any concern of yours."

Up to now, Carlos Palmira has maintained the affable tone with which he began. Suddenly, it changes. He fixes his gaze steadily on the young man and every word is intended to cut deep.

"You see, Kamal Rashid, I want to know who I'm dealing with, here. Am I talking to a man who's willing to act for his cause? If so, the gathering of thousands of people in Jerusalem for a high profile international wedding makes an inviting target. On the other hand, if there's no interest, then I can draw my own conclusions. And there's another side to this dispute where my interests might better be served."

The two men sit staring at each other intently. Carlos speaks again.

"I have found your attitude here less accommodating than I expected. I have no further time for it now. You understand my meaning well. You will go now and in two days my agents will speak with you in Amman. Think well on it, Kamal Rashid. El Condor does not begin or abandon a project lightly."

Carlos goes to the intercom on the wall and shouts brusquely: "Johnson! Come here and take Mr. Rashid away!"

In a minute, the chauffeur, Johnson, is back in the room reaffixing the blindfold on the departing guest. There's no further exchange between Palmira and Rashid. The latter is escorted out and Palmira crosses to the communications centre. He punches a code into the system. A man's voice answers over a speaker.

"Wolfgang," says Palmira, "It's El Condor. I have a message for transcription to Amman. It's to be coded top secret. The message reads: 'Meeting with Rashid unsatisfactory. Initiate plans as discussed for the Venture-Fisher disruption. Examine Rashid further. If he remains unreliable, move to second option, and see that the Palestinians take the blame. Continue discussions with the Jewish side. Secure payment for all arms shipments now. Delivery to be in one week. Keep the pot boiling. El Condor.' That's the message. Transmit immediately and confirm to me when received and understood."

Carlos crosses the room and returns to his coffee and the papers on the table.

The Battle Lines are Drawn

For a full minute, the scene of Carlos Palmira seated alone in his luxurious Swiss retreat remains fixed in the Visioneering Room with the world leaders watching. Then everything withdraws in reverse from how it first appeared, running backward from the room to the outside of the house and grounds, down to the lakefront, back across the lake until the house is a small dot in the distance. The scene fades away, and you step forward once again to speak to the audience.

"Without moral authority or a common vision, the world is a vacuum, open to the incursions of El Condor and his like. Into this vacuum Mark Venture and the Visioneers are seeking to release a massive flood of human energy to build a decent future for the planet. The outcome is uncertain. You are among the foremost players. Watch now as the scenario unfolds."

The scene changes to show Mark Venture again seated at the communications centre at Visioneer Headquarters in Los Angeles.

"Hello! Is that Peter Hemphill?" Mark is speaking into the system.

"Yes, this is Peter Hemphill," a voice replies over the speakers.

"Just a minute, Peter. This is Mark Venture in Los Angeles. I'm using our video set-up, so I'm going to punch you up on the big screen. Is that okay with you?"

"Sure," replies Peter, "warts and all. I've got you on our video phone. You're looking well."

Peter Hemphill comes up on the big screen above the console. He's wearing his customary pin-striped, double-breasted business suit. He looks trim, fit and younger than his forty-two years.

"You're looking good, too," says Mark. "Life as Under Secretary-General of whatever you do at the U.N. must be agreeing with you. How are you making out with my request to speak with the world leaders?"

"So-so. I've spoken to the Secretary-General. He's sympathetic enough. He still remembers those speeches at the Valdez memorial, and he's been watching you ever since. The main agenda is full, but we've got you down for remarks at an informal breakfast session."

"Thanks, Peter, I appreciate what you're doing, but that's not good enough. I've got to have a presentation to the General Assembly."

"It's impossible, Mark. You'd have to be a head of government yourself to get that."

"Or receive an extraordinary invitation."

"Yes, you could receive an extraordinary invitation, and the Assembly would have to approve it."

"Fine, we'll work on that."

"Do you have something in mind?"

"No, but I have a week to come up with it."

"Okay, Mark, but I'll keep the other option open for you."

"Thanks, Peter. You're a good bureaucrat. Why don't you reserve space for a reception and celebration at that place with all the trees where we had lunch. What was it called, Woodlands?"

"Yes, Woodlands. What do you have in mind?"

"Oh, I don't know. Just reserve the whole place for a couple of hours, say at the end of Day Two of the conference, after I've spoken to them."

"On whose tab?"

"Why, yours, of course. It'll be an official function."

"And what's the purpose?"

"To celebrate the General Assembly's endorsement of the Congress of the Global Mind."

"No doubt you'll tell me beforehand what that is."

"Just plan to be in the General Assembly and you'll hear all about it."

"Okay, Mark, but I'm still keeping the second option open for you. Now, I have some other news. The word has just come in from Chile. The army captain who killed Luis Valdez has been sentenced to life imprisonment. The verdict was that he was acting alone."

"Was there any reference to El Condor?"

"Nothing."

"Do you believe that?"

"No, but he covered his tracks well, just as I thought he would."

"I understand. Well, it's not the end of it for me, Peter. Do you have that dossier ready on El Condor that I asked for?"

"Yes, I've just updated it with the highlights and verdict of the trial."

"Can you download it to me here?"

"Sure thing. I'll get it off to you right away."

"Thanks, Peter, I'll be in touch again soon. Goodbye for now."

The scene clicks off and Mark turns to face Bill Bates who came in during the last part of the conversation.

"Hello, Bill," Mark says quietly. "I guess you heard most of that. I need time to think. Tomorrow's Saturday. Can we get away somewhere over the weekend and work on all of this?"

"Why don't you come up to my country place at Ojai. It's just a couple of hours north of here in the hills—a great place for thinking."

"Sounds good to me. Let's go first thing in the morning."

The scene fades, then comes up again quickly on a bright sunny morning. Mark and Bill are sitting in a garden on red cedar lawn chairs. Around them a small patch of lawn, bordered by a variety of low shrubs, stretches back to an orchard of dark green citrus and avocado trees. Both men are dressed casually in slacks and sweaters for the mild temperature of a late winter day in Southern California.

"It's Saturday evening in Jerusalem," says Mark. "I'm going to call Esther. This is a good time to get her."

"You go ahead," replies Bill. "I've got some things to take care of inside. Let me know when you're ready to talk."

Mark calls Esther on the speaker phone and listens to it ringing in Jerusalem.

"Hello, Esther Fisher speaking." Her voice is warm and friendly.

"Hi, darling! How are you?"

"Oh Mark, I was hoping it would be you. Where are you?"

"Well, I'm out in the country at Bill's retreat at Ojai, just north of L.A. It's a beautiful spot. Not too different as far as countryside is concerned from what I've seen of Israel."

"I'm glad you can get away for a change of scenery. But Mark, I have something important to tell you. It's just happened."

"What is it?"

"Just half an hour ago a package was delivered here. I didn't see who brought it. I just got buzzed on the intercom and was told a letter was being left for me. When I went down to pick it up, I found it was a message from Kamal Rashid. You know we haven't heard from him since he called you as you were leaving Jerusalem last October. That was when he told you about El Condor. I'm sure you remember."

Mark stiffens at the second mention of El Condor in as many days.

"Yes, go on, Esther. What does he say?"

"Well, it's about El Condor again, and, oh Mark, I'm frightened. I'm not sure what it means. I'll read it to you. You should probably record it, too."

Mark hits the record button on the telephone.

"Go on, darling. I'm listening."

"It's rather rambling and a little disoriented and not addressed to anyone in particular, but it's obviously intended for both of us. The handwriting is very hard to read, too, but I'll do my best."

" 'This is a message from Kamal Rashid. You will remember me. Our ways have not crossed again, but I know your work. I wish you no harm, but others do. This is a warning to be careful. Your friend, Valdez, was killed on orders from El Condor. You are now his target. Your wedding in Jerusalem is dangerous and foolish. El Condor plans to attack. I have spoken with him in his place in Switzerland. I have no use for him. He believes in nothing but money and power. You must cancel your wedding in Jerusalem. It is too dangerous, too many people. El Condor will attack and blame the Palestinians. It will achieve nothing.

" 'El Condor told me you will speak at the United Nations. What will you say about the Palestinians? We want our land. We want justice. We can stop the killing if we get that. You must argue for that. There can be no peace until we are satisfied.

" 'But attacking the wedding is not the way. I am against that. So I warn you. Do not hold the wedding in Jerusalem. Do not tempt El Condor. He is very dangerous.

" 'I support your work in the world. But the Palestinians must come first. Work for that and we will support you. That is my message. Kamal Rashid.'

"That's it, Mark. Isn't it terrible? What are we going to do? We can't just let this kind of evil win out. But I'm so afraid."

The edge of tension in her voice cuts a vivid contrast with the beautiful Californian sunshine. Mark feels torn and distraught.

"Oh, Esther, I'm just sick at heart that you have to deal with this. A wedding is a celebration of all that's good in life. It's our celebration together with our friends and those who love us. It's our special day, and to think there are thugs out there who would want to destroy it. But we've known the security risk all along. We'll just have to increase the precautions.

"But I see some good news in this. Look at Kamal Rashid. He's come back to us, not with a gun to your head this time, but as close to being a friend as we can expect. That's a positive sign. Of course he wants his cause argued, but I think his friendship has come first, and I'll find a way to acknowledge that.

"And the other good sign is El Condor, himself. It may be perverse logic, but we've obviously got his attention. And that can only mean he sees what we're doing as a threat to his empire. I've just been reading a dossier on him that I got from the U.N. The man is an international criminal of the worst order. If he sees us as a threat, then how many more of his kind must be feeling the Visioneers breathing down their necks? The only way we can stop these people is to stand up to them, and we're starting to do that in pockets of success all over the world.

"Now El Condor—I don't know why I'm calling him that. There's no grace or majesty of the eagle about him. He's just a piece of slime that too many authorities in too many places have allowed to come to the surface. His real name is Carlos Palmira. Now he intends to make the grand play against us. But he won't be able to. We've got the right of it on our side, Esther, and during the next week we'll pick up so much momentum, that Palmira will start to see his empire crumbling around his ears."

"Oh, Mark, yes, I really believe that, too. There's just so much positive support coming in from all sides now. We can't let this threat get in the way. I'm working closely with the security people here. I'll alert them to this new piece. And I'll speak right away with Mohammed Hussein. He has excellent connections with the Palestinians and with other Arab leaders. If enough of them can come around to Kamal's way of thinking, then El Condor, or Palmira, or whoever he is, won't stand a chance, and we'll make our wedding one of the greatest events in the whole history of Jerusalem."

"Well, now you're talking. You go for it, my love. But promise to keep in touch. If you get any whisper at all of something I should know about, call me right away. You can always reach me through Bill's office. Take care, darling. You're more precious to me than life itself. I love you very much."

"Yes, Mark, I know. And soon we'll have some time together to share. Goodbye, my love."

Mark hangs up. He punches the play button on the telephone and listens again to Kamal Rashid's message.

" . . . Do not hold the wedding in Jerusalem. Do not tempt El Condor. He is very dangerous.

"I support your work in the world. But the Palestinians must come first. Work for that and we will support you. That is my message. Kamal Rashid."

Mark clicks off the recording. He's very agitated. He stands up and begins to pace around, speaking out loudly to no one in particular.

"What's wrong with this world? Black-hearted treachery everywhere you turn. And there's Esther, having to deal with this at a time when she should have nothing but joy in her life."

His pacing takes him in the direction of the orchard at the end of the garden. He moves among the trees, irresolutely picking at their leaves, as he continues to speak out the thoughts in his mind.

"And everyone has a cause. There are too many causes in the world, and not enough vision. The whole thing's become a stew of corruption, so that maggots like Palmira can breed and grow because strong people are too busy fighting for their self-interested causes. The weak ones become the victims: tossed out on the garbage heap of drug addiction, rounded up and put into armies and trained to be killers, left starving and poor while the money that could help them is laundered off into international bank accounts and poured into military budgets.

"And all the while the Earth cries out in pain. Men argue and debate and strut and parade and kill while the Earth slowly dies around them. Paradises are turned into killing fields, or garbage dumps, or cesspools. And still men argue their petty causes, while the one great cause goes unattended: the preservation of life and peace on the planet.

"And who do I think I am that I can change the course of all of that? I encourage Esther to go ahead and put her life in danger, while I continue here to play on the world stage. Is it all a pathetic delusion? Are the Visioneers just a cruel dream, with no substance, no hope, no promise for anything better? Have we been born only to see the final consummation of mankind's bitter destiny? God in heaven, if this is what you intend, then tell it to me now, and I'll walk away from all this tumult to spend whatever time there is with Esther in some quiet, protected place!"

As Mark cries out these last words he is looking defiantly up to the sky, fists clenched, his body filled with the tension of his mind. Behind him, moving quietly between two long rows of orange trees, a figure appears dressed in a simple saffron-coloured robe He comes closer. Mark turns, sensing another presence, and finds himself staring into the luminous brown eyes of Baba Satyananda.

"Baba!" Mark exclaims. "Are you really here? Or is this another of your appearances?"

"I am always as real, Mark, as you will allow me to be." His voice, pitched low, rises and falls with gentle melody. "Your heart is heavy, my good friend. Why so? You're approaching your time of greatest triumph."

"Oh? Well, I tell you, Baba, how I feel right now could be described in many ways, but triumph doesn't come to mind."

"Then you must change your mind and make room for triumph to sidle in. You're in the current and must swim with it. Your concern for Esther, while rich and loving, must not distract you from the main goal. Esther is in the flow with you, Mark, she can hold her own."

"I'm not worried about her holding her own. I'm concerned about her safety. She's more dear to me, Baba, then all the rest of this. Without her, none of it makes any sense to me."

"Then embrace it all, Mark, and give no thought to a single piece. It's all flowing together now and you're the architect of the whole. There are countless millions of people in the world depending on you to keep the vision clear. I've told you before, your work is for the living. And you said it yourself, do you remember, to all of those people who mysteriously gathered at St. Paul's church to honour Luis Valdez? You charged them to go forward from that time with the one great idea that by leading with their visionary minds, they could create the kind of world that they and all the people of the world would choose to live in, and all of their children after them? Do you remember that, Mark?

"And you weren't speaking only to that assembly there, but to the whole world, and already it's been picked up and repeated many, many times as the Visioneers have gone forward to act. So you shouldn't wonder that El Condor and those like him are afraid of what you have begun. It should be no surprise that he'll come out of his eyrie and swoop to another attack. But this time it's a whole united throng of decent caring people for which you and Esther are the symbol of hope. Against this front, El Condor's power can't prevail, if you'll only stand firm."

"Be my mentor, then, Baba, for I feel besieged on all sides, and I need guidance."

"In realizing that, Mark, you've already moved the greatest distance. You're not alone in this. The great power of God flowing through the universe is at your hand. Reach out to take it and you'll find it there to carry you through.

"You've heard my teachings on several occasions now. Let me summarize them and add another for your coming test. You must know and remember that the human race is on a journey. It's been travelling most recently along a dark passage and has emerged to find itself at the brink of chaos and despair. But you and the Visioneers, and the spirit and thinking that you represent, have appeared to lead them away from the brink toward the horizon. In caring for your brothers and sisters in all lands, you will build a new economy for the world and new institutions that will be the foundations for millennia to come.

"Now I've come to add another teaching which you must know and remember as you move on. It speaks directly to what troubles you today. It is this. The force of evil is a real force in the world, and you must be ever vigilant to restrain it. It sets the minds of men and women against the pathway to the light. It entraps them in the snares of self-interest and blocks them from the flow of love which is the dominant force of the universe.

"You and the Visioneers must be forever vigilant to see the force of evil for what it is. It can never prevail, for love is more powerful, but it can damage and destroy. You've begun your work. It's positive and bold and will bring a new renaissance to the world. But stand vigilant against the force of evil, confront it whenever it appears, and call upon the limitless power of the love of God flowing through the universe as your strength for each encounter.

"I'll leave you now, my good friend, and follow in my heart as you journey to your triumph with your band of Visioneers."

The two men embrace for a long moment in the quiet seclusion of the orange grove, then each turns to go his separate way.

Mark hurries back to the garden. Bill Bates is already looking for him.

"Say, there you are," Bill calls out. "What's up Mark? You look a bit excited."

"Yes, I got some bad news from Esther. That El Condor character—his real name's Carlos Palmira—he's out to get us. Esther's been tipped off by Kamal Rashid, you know, the terrorist who captured her last October. He says that Palmira is planning some kind of attack at our wedding in Jerusalem. The idea is to blame it on the Palestinians. I tell you if he escalates this on a big enough scale, not only will Esther and I be dead, but it could set a torch to the whole Middle East."

"Yes, I see what you mean. But you've always known there was a security risk in Jerusalem. That place is just one hotbed of violence."

"Yes, but I guess I've only just realized the extent to which we've got forces of real evil lined up against us. It leaves us with two choices. We can either back off and downplay this whole visioneering thing into local community action groups. Or we can take people like Palmira on and show the world it doesn't have to be held up to ransom."

"So what's the strategy?"

"The strategy, Bill, is to press on, but we've got to make a really big play. A highly publicized intervention at the U.N. is essential. If the General Assembly comes out with an endorsement, particularly when the government leaders are there, then there'll be no stopping the momentum, and Palmira will have to think twice before he tries something that could backfire on him."

"So what do you want me to do?"

"I want you to activiate the news networks right away. Get us some good coverage worldwide. I'll make as many appearances as I can, but everyone needs to be out there hustling. What we need to do is spend the next few hours preparing the text. Then we'll set up another video conference, say, for tomorrow morning, to finalize it, and then we're away and racing."

"Okay, buddy, you've got it. But I want you to promise me one thing in all of this."

Mark looks at him quizzically and sees a shadow of concern pass across his face.

"What is it, Bill?"

"Promise me, Mark, that if things, well, start to go wrong, your first concern is going to be for yourself and Esther."

Mark nods.

"Okay, Bill, and thanks. You're a good friend. But nothing's going to go wrong. I have it on good authority that God is on our side, and that gives us quite an advantage. Now, let's get to work."

Bill Bates looks hard at his companion, as the two men go inside.

The Choice

For a moment the garden setting holds steady in the Visioneering Room then slowly dissolves away. In its place a cavernous room appears, completely bare, with concrete floors, no windows, and high walls made of grey cinder blocks. At the back are two doorways, one on either side, closed. The light, already dim, grows weaker, until the room is bathed in an eerie glow.

A spotlight comes up, focused on the door at the back on the left side. Then a second spotlight snaps on, trained on the other door. All other light fades. The setting and the Visioneering Room are in complete darkness save for the two bright spotlights fixed on the two doors. The world leaders in the audience sit quietly, watching attentively.

The left hand door opens and the figure of Carlos Palmira, El Condor, appears and steps through into the room. The door closes behind him. He moves forward, the spotlight following. The other door remains closed. He comes to the very front, then stops, staring out at the audience. His face is severe, the prominent aquiline nose casting a slight shadow on his dark features in the glare of the spotlight. He is dressed as before in black tailored slacks and blue cotton shirt with its monogrammed C on the breast pocket. The embroidered silk cravat hangs loosely at his throat.

At the back, the other door opens, and Mark Venture steps forward into the room. He, too, is dressed as before in cream corduroy slacks, white shoes, light grey sweater with a large blue V monogrammed prominently on the left side. As he comes toward the audience, his stride is confident and easy. His handsome suntanned face betrays no emotion, but looks out squarely to the front, relaxed and attentive.

El Condor speaks.

"It's a question of staying the course," he says. "I've got the world under my feet and I can tread wherever I choose. What matters now is that we keep building, staying one step ahead. America is solid; Europe and Japan, almost in place; Asia and Africa, waiting to be plucked. Everywhere, opportunity opens up.

"The world's an open door. People are easy prey. They'll do anything to get what they think they want. They'll tear each other apart if they have to. The leaders are puppets, dancing on strings, trying to hold on to power, willing to do anything to stay on top, while their opponents scheme to topple them, stopping at nothing, turning a blind eye to everything, when it suits their purpose. Politics, industry, business, the arts, even religion, it's all open to me now. The world's an empty void and I mean to fill it with my enterprises."

Mark Venture speaks:

"We have to give the people hope. We've made a start, and it can run like wildfire. Getting the image right is the key. Once they have the vision, then the rest will follow. Without vision, there's just an empty void, and all manner of corruption can slip in.

"It all comes back to spirit, recognizing the human energy coursing through the world, tapping into it, focusing it around a vision of common purpose, where everyone can play a part. We have to touch people in their hearts, in their deep internal wisdom, getting down below the blockages of their ideology and their limited beliefs."

El Condor: "Men are basically selfish and will cut each other's throat for what they think is a slice of the main action. Women are the same. Give them a piece of privilege and they'll trample each other into the dirt to hold onto it."

Mark Venture: "People are energy systems. They'll come together and move with great power around a vision they believe in, around an enterprise of value, around a cause that gives them hope for a worthwhile future. We must tap that spirit and give it the leadership it needs."

El Condor: "Most leaders are corrupt or corruptible. All they want is power. I can play them off against one another like children in a candy store."

Mark Venture: "The supreme motivating concept of the future is synergy: men and women of all nations coming together under leaders of great vision, who see that the pursuit of a common ideal, one world, one Earth, one people, is the reason for all existence."

El Condor: "The world is flying apart. People are the instruments of their own destruction. I can reap rewards on every front. It's all open for the taking."

Mark Venture: "We're at the birth of a new renaissance. The moment of breakthrough is at hand. The Visioneers are on the move. The world lies open for fulfillment."

El Condor: "In the end, power is all that counts."

Mark Venture: "In the end, love will bring in peace."

"In the end, all of us must choose: the way of El Condor and his like, or the way of Mark Venture and the Visioneers."

The last words are spoken by yourself. You have stepped on stage in a central spotlight between the other two. They turn and without a further word exit separately by the way they had come. The lights come up and you stand alone in the stark concrete room facing your audience.

"I stand here," you continue, "in this bare place, symbol of the prison of our thoughts, unless we break free, to create a sweeter space.

"You have it all now: the bitter course of human development to today, and where that course unchecked will take us. You have caught, too, a glimpse of the alternative: empowered human beings of every land breaking free of the bondage of the past and present and travelling forward into a future of synergy and vision.

"You were brought here as leaders of the nations on this planet to see the choice. Soon you'll return to your own assembly, and there you will make your choice by what you decide or don't decide to do, and by how you act as leaders to your people.

"And now I bring this session to a close."

The walls around you disappear.

"I bring back the world, the Earth, our planet home."

The large rotating globe of land and sea and sky returns to its place of prominence in the centre of the Visioneering Room.

"And I hand you back to our mentors to bid you farewell and God speed for the next step of the journey."

PART FOUR

Going
for
Gold

CHAPTER SEVENTEEN

Through
the
Golden Arch

IT'S A TRANSFORMED WORLD THAT SPRINGS into view in the Visioneering Room. Shafts of golden light stream out from every direction, intersecting, cascading, dancing around the great suspended globe in the centre space, and sweeping out like bands of the aurora borealis to play upon the ceiling and, indeed, every space of the large, round room.

The world leaders stare in wonder at the flickering festival of light, looking around, up and down, smiling at the beauty of it, nudging one another, as they see their features transformed in the golden glow, a veritable sunbath of translucent delight.

"Hallo, there! Whoop! Hallo to all of you!"

The voice is cheery and resonant. It booms around the room.

"Welcome to the future of the Visioneers! Come with me everyone. Step right up. Cross the barrier. Take a leap forward with your minds and reach for gold."

The cheery voice belongs to Charles Dickens. He has come striding into the room, appearing from behind the golden, glowing globe, and now stands dramatically poised, in full view of every eye, striking the stance of a master magician. He has donned a billowing red velvet cape for effect along with a top hat and white gloves. In his right hand he brandishes a brass-tipped walking stick, while his left hand carves the air in magnificent flourishes.

"You have seen the landscape of the limited," he continues, "now come with me into the mindscape of the possible. This time, the images will not dance upon this centre stage, but will rather play in your mind, your own creations, as I lead you forward, your humble but enthusiastic guide to a possible future space, the world of the Visioneers.

"Close your eyes and let your minds slide down along these sunbeams of light. Down, down, you go. Come with me now, come along, sliding down, warm and glowing. Here we are arriving at the end, coming into a great wide marketplace in the sunshine filled with throngs of people streaming around among stalls with coloured canvas tops piled high with everything.

"There's fresh fruit brought in from every country. It spills out along tables, spreading everywhere. See the boxes and baskets of apples, cherries, strawberries, raspberries: all red, fresh and succulent, picked at perfection, and growing ripe and sweeter even before your eyes. And look here at the grapes, piled high in bunches: red, green, black, bursting with the sunshine that warmed and ripened them. Everywhere you look there's more of the same, and different. Now it's oranges, oh how round and glowing; and thick bunches of bananas, hanging down as if right off the tree. And pineapples lined up like squat, plump soldiers in coarse greatcoats. On and on we go through nuts, berries, jams, pickles, honey, candies, chocolates, cheeses, coffees, tea, milk, yogurt. There's no end to it. No, no end in sight. Just going on and on. And what about the bread, oh dear, I almost forgot the bread, fresh baked, filling the air with its come-buy-me-now aroma of yeast and flour, exquisite, tantalizing in long loaves, short loaves, bagettes, buns, bagels, and buy-me-now-eat-me-soon boxes of pastries, cookies, muffins and sumptuous desserts.

"And that's just the food! Intermingled with all this are the clothes and the crafts, and every product of hand, mind, eye, machine, for beauty, pleasure, necessity, comfort. It's the great, wide bustling marketplace of the world, with people flocking together, buying, selling, trading, bantering, enjoying the fun, the energy, the spirit of living.

"Outside the trading area they sit in coffee shops, and restaurants, and meeting places, all manner of people, of every nationality, every ethnic group, speaking many languages, listening intently, learning from each other: discussion and dialogue, intense, passionate and lively.

"Let's listen in. Every group has an issue or a problem—as many opinions, ideas, beliefs, attitudes as there are people. But they all speak of one thing—life, the joy of it; the give-take, up-down, you-me, all-of-us-to-gether excitement of it. And they all ask one question, on every lip, raised over and over again: How is the Earth today? What have you heard? Is our work helping to promote a good life for everyone on a healthy planet? What is our part of the project? Is our piece fitting right? Where do we need to make changes?

"And they all speak of one place, the Assembly, the World Assembly of the People. In many languages they refer to it as the Centre and the

Source, the Centre for coordination, the Source for information, advice and encouragement. And each group speaks of itself as an Assembly and a Centre and a Source. And they speak of the Network, the grand interlinkage of all the assemblies and centres and sources into a great buzzing central nervous system for the planet, working to keep the Earth safe and healthy, planning step by step to bring to all people on Earth good lives of prosperity and satisfaction.

"And after the meeting and the dialogues come celebrations. Men, women, children, all mingling together, singing, dancing, feasting, telling courage stories of hope and achievement and success. See the costumes! Hear the music! Listen to the laughter! Feel the excitement dancing and darting, bouncing and bobbing, weaving its wonderful, magical spell over people who've come together in spirit and fellowship and a sure sense of life that's full, growing and well worth the living.

"These are the people of the Earth, our future world, the world of the Visioneers, everyone a Visioneer working with each other to nurture and sustain all life, while our knowledge grows and multiplies."

He pauses and looks steadily at the assembly, then continues:

" These are the people, but where are you, the leaders, the heads of our nation states? Where are you in this future world of People's Assemblies?

"Look closely and see, there you are. Still leading the government in your parliament or congress, but working now with constituent assemblies all across your land, supporting these bands of Visioneers, giving them the encouragement they need, holding up the vision of your country as a caring contributor to world peace and prosperity for all, linking your policies to those of the World Assembly, keeping people on track in building a shared vision for the planet.

"Your huge bureaucracies are smaller now, greatly reduced in this new world of citizen participation. Your armies are smaller too, modified to peace-keeping brigades and corps of volunteers, bands of adventurers, working with their like in other countries across the world, nurturing growth and development wherever it's needed. You're honoured and respected as the leaders in a commonwealth of nations, building a global economy of cooperation and partnership.

"Look closely. Do you see yourself? Perhaps you don't. For some of you, the change will be hard, perhaps impossible. But you still have time. This is the world waiting to be invented. I show it to you now, so you can choose. Think deeply, consider your role. You still have time. Watch closely now. Look deep inside your mind. Other shadows are coming.

"See here, look now, here's one you know, Anne of Green Gables. Follow her as she adds her piece."

Anne has come on stage beside Charles Dickens. Her soft and eager voice floats over the assembly, leading them to search their hearts for where yet they might choose to go.

"Come ride with me on the sunbeams," she says, "and let's look for the children. What are they doing in this future world of the Visioneers? Oh my, there are so many of them! Look at them in every land, not only in your own country, but in every country in the world. Can you see them in their schools, open friendly places, with many adults, too, coming and going, mingling with the children, everyone a teacher, everyone a learner, everyone learning from everyone else?

"And there's so much activity. Can you see it? Look hard, look see the children working together on projects, caring for their neighbourhoods, building fun places for parties and celebrations, flocking to the libraries. Look at those libraries. My, have you ever seen so many books and magazines and television screens and computers? It makes the head swim. They're great learning centres, just like the marketplace with its products, and vendors and customers. Here we've got marketplaces for learning, with everyone involved, but especially the children.

"And look, we can see them in every city, town, village in every country. The world has become a great learning place, and the children are moving around, travelling, visiting other cities, other countries, and they're having conferences on large television screens, all around the world: children from Africa, India, China, America, Europe, Australia, all ages, many colours, and they're talking together about the Earth, how they're caring for it, how everyone is doing. Is there enough food in your village? What can we do to help? We've got a new plan here. Do you think it will work for us, too? Can you come and show us? How are things in your neighbourhood? You should see what we've done. There's fish back in the river now, and we can go swimming at the beach again.

"Can you see these children with me, the children in your own country, the children of the world, the children of hope for the future, well-fed, laughing, studying, playing, working, learning to care for each other and to care for the Earth? They're learning to be friends, to listen to one another, to understand differences. They're learning to live their lives with vision, seeing a prosperous and peaceful world where there's enough for everyone, learning to commit themselves to building that kind of future.

"Oh, please, look hard and see those children! See them in your hearts, in your minds, in your imaginations. See yourself as the leaders who will bring that kind of world to the children of the future; not starvation, or fear, or anger, or violence, or war, or killing, or hatred; but love, friendship, laughter, and a good, clean, healthy Earth to live on."

"Yes, if you all can hold that kind of vision," a new voice has taken up the theme from Anne, "you can build a world the like of which we hitherto could only dream."

John Kennedy is back on stage. His voice is strong, powerful, reassuring, filling the room with energy and excitement.

"This is the hour of vision, the time to see beyond all time past into a possible future. Look with me now and see the bounty of a new kind of leadership for the world. See yourselves coming together into the General Assembly of the United Nations and saying to a listening world, 'We, the leaders of the free and independent nations of the Earth, see that our common welfare lies not in the strength of our military might or our economic production, but rather in the spirit of cooperation that we can fashion from a forge of optimism.

" 'We see that the world is weary of the old ways of conflict, greed, and aggression. There's no more future in that. The Earth is trembling. People are afraid. Even in the richest countries they cry out in anger and frustration as things crumble around them. Hope has been snatched away. Time has come as a thief in the night and stolen away hope. Now, our task is to bring it back.

" 'We know that we must move beyond current policies and beliefs to find a new understanding. This is the age of learning. We, the leaders of all of the nations on Earth, commit ourselves to bend every effort, to grasp each opportunity, to focus all resources on building a fellowship of human awareness across the planet. Together we can continue, moving into the future as one great band of resourceful travellers, accepting with every step the responsibility of sustaining the rich and fragile heritage that God has given us on this, our planetary home.' "

As President Kennedy sends out this ringing challenge for a new kind of leadership for the world, he is joined by the oldest warrior of them all, Winston Churchill. The elder statesman moves to centre stage to stand beside Kennedy and Anne. When he speaks, his voice resonates with power, seeming to fill every mind with the prophetic portent of his words.

"You have been asked to step forward into a future age of which all of you in part will be the architects. On your shoulders now rests much of the responsibility of what shall be.

"The time has come to choose. You can either look backward to past folly or forward to future enlightenment. Where we have been as a rag-tag collection of feudal states and tribal nations, can no longer be regarded as any acceptable measure of where we must go.

"Make no mistake. There is a dark cloud hanging over the prospects for humanity, heavier now than any we have ever known. To chart the direction, to steer the course, to give heart to all who are embarked on this perilous voyage. This is your responsibility.

"In leading, your strength will be in following. In accepting power your role will be to empower. In giving direction you must learn to take it.

"There is a current now flowing through the minds of individuals in every land, which, if brought together, can become a tidal force of energy for the new age. You have been shown here the briefest glimpse of it in the enterprise of our Visioneers. Before you return to your own endeavours you will be given the opportunity to support or hinder that enterprise. You have seen the alternative. Now you must decide how you will act.

"But as you go, let me say one word more. The building force of collective human consciousness of which our Visioneers are the symbol and the portent, is irresistible. It issues from the universal source for survival. It can be fought, it can be diverted, it can be restrained, but it can never be overcome. Your individual moments of truth now upon you demand decisions on how you will act to support or retard this swelling wave of human consciousness for survival. In your own hands now lies the choice."

Churchill finishes his address in characteristic defiant surveillance of his audience, fixing them with a steely, steady gaze. Before there's a chance for any reaction, Charles Dickens appears again, stepping up beside the others and addressing the world leaders with a theatrical sweep of his flowing cape and brass-tipped walking stick.

"So now the time has come to test your learning," he exclaims. "We're sending you out to the world of the Visioneers. You came here by way of a silver bridge from your own assembly at the United Nations. Now you'll leave through a golden arch to an alternative future."

As he speaks, the huge globe that has hung suspended in space throughout the presentations now dissolves. In its place a golden arch appears, rising tall and brilliant to the ceiling. Through it a translucent glow shimmers mysteriously. The world leaders shift uncertainly in their seats, glancing at each other uneasily, wondering what next they can expect from this drama in which they've been caught up.

Charles Dickens continues:

"Go now. Go out from this assembly. Go your various ways into the world of the Visioneers. We send you out into the glow of future possibility. Step through the arch and take the learning you've tasted here with you. When the time is right you will return to your own world, but for now you have the opportunity to play on a different stage. On the other side of the arch you will find the General Assembly of the United Nations, but not as you left it. It's two days earlier and you have a decision to make. Will you entertain a presentation from Mark Venture concerning United Nations support for a Congress of the Global Mind? Go now, the world and the Visioneers are waiting."

If the world leaders have any thought of holding back from this next experience, they're not given the chance to exercise it. As one they are lifted from their seats and propelled toward the gleaming golden arch. The mentors step back, Churchill and Kennedy on one side, Dickens and Anne on the other, forming a farewell party for the departing dignitaries.

As those from the front row reach the arch, there's quite a deal of shuffling and resistance. The first to come up is a tall black leader from an African state. He looks quizzically at the arch and the mentors and screws his face into a grimace. Laughing, John Kennedy steps forward, shakes the other's hand and escorts him to the arch. The shimmering golden glow on the other side of the tall columns dances before them. Kennedy, still smiling broadly, gestures for the man to go through. He pauses, staring at the strange opaque curtain of light, then shrugs his shoulders, looks back at his companions, and laughs ruefully.

"Oh, what the heck," he exclaims. "Maybe there's a prize for coming first. It's time for Africa to show the way."

With that he steps foward and is swallowed up from sight. An instant later his head and shoulders reappear. The smile on his big round face is as broad as a sunrise.

"Say," he shouts, "they weren't kidding! This is the General Assembly room over here, and all of our seats are empty, waiting for us. Come on through. We've got some work to get done."

With one last loud chuckle he withdraws again, his face disappearing instantly, but his smile, as on the Cheshire Cat, seeming to hang there an instant longer.

General pandemonium erupts in the Visioneering Room as the world leaders push forward, now eager to get moving. Most want to shake hands with the mentors and say something pleasant as they pass. Some are disconsolate and silent and a few are hostile and rude. The last to leave is the woman president from South East Asia who had spoken to Churchill earlier in the session about the problem of moving people away from the path of least resistance. She smiles warmly at all of the mentors.

"It looks like I'm at the end of the line," she says. "This has been a most extraordinary experience. I don't know who or what is real in any of this, but even if it's all a dream, I want to say thank you. Many of us have heard deeply what all of you have said. We won't forget. Goodbye. This is most strange, most strange. I wonder what will happen next."

Still murmuring quietly to herself, the woman steps through the arch and out of the Visioneering Room. The place now stands strangely empty. The four mentors look at each other without speaking. Softly you come in to join them.

"Thank you," you say, "the next time we meet, the world will perhaps be a little nearer to where we're trying so hard to take it. Now we must leave things in the hands of Mark Venture and the Visioneers. May God grant them the strength and spirit to carry it off."

Without a further word they're gone. You look once more around the empty room. The golden arch goes, the globe returns. You close your eyes and open your mind to the future.

CHAPTER EIGHTEEN

At the United Nations

MARK VENTURE IS SITTING IN HIS OFFICE at Visioneer Headquarters in Los Angeles when the call comes in from the United Nations in New York. It's Peter Hemphill, Under Secretary-General for Political Affairs. On the videophone his usually urbane features are showing unmistakable signs of excitement.

"Well, I don't know how you did it, Mark," he says, "but you just got your invitation to speak to the General Assembly. You're on at 10 o'clock tomorrow morning."

"Hey, that's great news, Peter," replies Mark. "What's the story?"

"Well, not much. As you know, the session only got underway this morning. We've got 150 heads of state here, from almost every country on Earth, with an agenda a mile long of issues and problems to deal with, and would you know that the very first item that comes up wasn't even on the agenda."

"Which was what?" asks Mark.

"Which was you, bless my soul," retorts Peter.

"That's nice. Who introduced it?"

"Would you believe, the United States, seconded by China."

"Hey, that's impressive!"

"Impressive!" Peter Hemphill almost explodes down the telephone line. "It's just impossible! Two of the most powerful men on Earth calling for Mark Venture to come and speak to them."

"Was there any debate?" asks Mark.

"No, it passed unanimously in a matter of seconds. It was all worked out beforehand, but none of us here at the U.N. knew it was coming. I've heard in the last few minutes that some leaders were a bit uneasy about it, but the majority seem to be on side. Now the officials here are upset, because the agenda's all screwed up and no one knows whose pet projects are going to get dealt with."

"The good old bureaucratic imperative," sighs Mark. "We finally get a chance to tackle the future of the world head on, and the officials are upset because the agenda's been changed. May we be preserved against closed minds."

"Listen, Mark, you got one miracle this morning. Don't push your luck."

"Okay, Peter, I hear you," laughs Mark, "but I'm ever the optimist, you know. Which reminds me. Did you reserve Woodlands for tommorrow evening's celebration?"

"You know," replies Peter, "I actually did. Don't ask me why. I didn't think you had a chance of pulling off a presentation to the General Assembly, but something still told me to reserve for the celebration. Now, who do you want me to invite?"

"You're better at that kind of thing than me, Peter. I'd like all the delegations represented. I'll invite the world leaders personally, but you should get the word out, so they can try to put it on their schedules. And we need to include the non-governmental groups, particularly the ones that've been helpful to the Visioneers. And the press, too, of course. Say, what about the press? Do they know about this invitation for me to speak to the General Assembly?"

"The word just went out. Any second now you should get your first call."

Right on cue, Bill Bates comes hurtling into Mark's office.

"Mark, you son of a gun!" he shouts. "You did it! You're on for the U.N."

Mark roars with laughter. Bill pauses, sees Peter Hemphill on the video screen, also laughing, then joins in.

"I might've known you'd have your own pipeline on this," Bill exclaims. "We must've really got their attention! That was some news broadside we let loose last week."

"Whatever did it, Bill," says Mark, "I'm very grateful. Now you and I have got to put our heads together. Thanks for the call, Peter. I'll be in touch again when I get to New York tonight."

"Okay, Mark, goodbye for now."

As Peter Hemphill clicks off, Bill Bates lets out a wild war whoop and dances around the office.

"Yahoo! We've got 'em, Mark! We've got 'em. After this there'll be no country in the world that can't afford to pay attention to the Visioneers. Do you want me to come to New York with you?"

"You bet. Get us a couple of plane tickets for as soon as possible this afternoon. Right now, I'm going to call Esther, and then I'll patch in as many of the Visioneers as possible on the video network. It's a great day, Bill, and tomorrow it's going to be better."

On the Plaza of Nations

When Mark Venture and Bill Bates step out of their cab at the Plaza of Nations in New York City, they're greeted by a roar from the crowd pressing against the police barricades. Good-humoured shouts can be picked out against the general hubbub.

"Go for it, Mark!"

"Good on you, fella. Tell 'em where it's at!"

"Hey, where's Esther, Mark?"

"Yeah, you shoulda brought Esther!"

"Who's that other fella? Esther's a lot prettier."

"The world's depending on you, Mark!"

A battery of reporters and television crews are pressing forward. Bill Bates is almost beside himself with glee. He waves to the media people, recognizing many faces, going over to shake hands. Mark sees one familiar face. It's Pamela Barrett, who has been covering the phenomenon and growth of the Visioneers for ZNN, ever since her first meeting with Mark in Jerusalem. The last time he had seen her was on the steps of St. Paul's Church at the memorial service for Luis Valdez.

"Hello, Mark," she calls. "Have you got a word for the viewers?"

Mark finds himself staring into a galaxy of camera lenses as his spirit rises with the excitement of the crowd.

"This is a great day for the world," he says, "when people come out because they care."

Then he notices behind Pamela a group of school children, boys and girls, mixed nationalities, all in white shirts and blouses emblazoned with a big V. They're pressing forward behind a toothy, freckle-faced girl pumping a large Visioneers flag up and down on a long pole, waving it high above the heads of the group. Beyond the children and the rest of the crowd, standing out in the stiff breeze on their poles, are all the flags of the member nations with the blue and white U.N. flag most prominent of all.

"Look here!" Mark shouts. "This is what your viewers should see: these children with their Visioneers flag waving proudly with all the others."

He goes over, leaning across the barricade, reaching into the field of waving hands. Reporters and cameramen trip over themselves trying to refocus away from arriving dignitaries over to Mark among the children.

For a few minutes, elegant black limousines and world leaders are ignored as attention shifts to the children. Sensing their moment, the kids break out spontaneously into the chanting *Song of the Visioneers.*

"We are the ones, going to the fore.
Big ones, little ones—all of us are here.
Small world,big world, reaching out to all.
Up, up, and upmost—the mighty Visioneers!"

The effect on the rest of the crowd is electric. They all pick up the song and soon it reverberates across the plaza. The cameramen are now clambering over one another to get their shots. Mark laughs uproariously. He links arms with Bill Bates and they fall in behind two dignitaries who happen to arrive at the critical moment, and together the four of them march across the plaza toward the gleaming glass tower of the Secretariat building.

In the General Assembly

Inside, at the meeting of the General Assembly, the atmosphere could not have been more different. As Mark stands at the podium ready to speak, he looks out across the sea of faces, knowing that he's about to address the most powerful assembly of people ever to come together on the planet. The setting, too, seems to have been crafted for this extraordinary moment. The huge dome-shaped room exudes infinite space, dwarfing the participants in their leather chairs behind the rows of polished wood desks. The individual vertical bands of timber which enclose the space are not walls that separate this place from any other. Rather they serve to contain it, as an environment crafted by human creative intelligence for a mission, if not holy or sacred, then surely approaching such high purpose. Above, the concentric circles of lights, suspended below the radiating arms of the flattened dome, seem to serve both as a source for seeing and as the illumination needed to enhance understanding.

All of the energy and design of the assembly hall, however, ultimately has one focus. It is the huge circular symbol of the United Nations, swimming high up in the wooden panneling descending like a shaft of light from the dome above, in the full sightline of the participants. In this they know, if they choose to think about it, that the symbol of the two reeds of olive branches cradling the Earth calls for wisdom and tolerance at a level that has so far eluded all collective efforts to attain. Standing before this symbol, looking out to the leaders of the world's nations, Mark knows a profound sense of moment and significance.

The stage has been further set by the introduction he was given by a woman he hadn't met and didn't know. She had spoken, it seemed to Mark, in riddles of some experience, some great secret shared by all of them as leaders, but unknown to anyone else. A few minutes earlier she had stood at the podium, a dimunitive figure in simple, white silk sari, speaking without note or paper to her fellow world leaders. Her words had created the opening for him to move through with his address.

"Fellow members of this great General Assembly," she had said, "this morning we stand at the threshold of possibility. We have come to this moment perhaps as participants in a continuing collective dream, I'm not sure, but whatever is happening, I feel certain we're being instructed by a higher power to reach for understanding that normally escapes us. The implication, I believe, is that if we can discover some truth during this time of suspended disbelief, then perhaps we can carry it back to the deliberations we must surely make and the responsibilities we must surely assume for future life on this planet.

"We've been shown the path of history. We've been asked to consider, if we can, that path in the clear light of reason, unencumbered by ideology, religion and cultural bias. All of us are having enormous difficulty with that. When we are asked, as we have been, to go further, and set aside personal ego and self-aggrandizement, then the challenge does, indeed, seem to be beyond mortal capabilities. But if we cannot achieve those levels of understanding here in this Assembly, then how can we expect to find them among the people in our countries. We are being given the highest test of leadership, to model the behaviour required to bring about collective high performance. Will we be found wanting? I hope we won't, but I fear we shall, that is, unless we can learn more truth in this continuing time we have together of experience in a different reality.

"The man who it seems is to be our chief guide for this experience is with us this morning, Mark Venture, leader of the worldwide movement of Visioneers, which has apparently now spread into all our countries. On our return to business yesterday we found his request before us to speak to us about what needs to be done to chart a future course for the world. Of course, we know something of Mr. Venture and his Visioneers from what we have been shown. Indeed, the essential difference between this new reality and our normal life, seems to be that we now have to lead our governments in a world filled with Visioneers. None of us knows what that means. Presumably Mr. Venture is here to tell us. Judging by what I've been able to read in the world press, and by the exuberance which greeted his arrival here this morning, it appears that Mr. Venture is already a well-established force.

"It therefore gives me great pleasure to ask him to speak to this Assembly."

That had been his introduction. Now Mark begins his address.

"Your Excellencies, Ladies and Gentlemen, leaders of the world's united nations," he begins. "What an extraordinary introduction! It seems, if I heard correctly, that you consider yourselves to be temporary participants in my world. All I can say is that as far as I'm concerned, there's only one world, and here it is; there's only one United Nations and this is it; and there's only one assembly of world leaders, and that's you. Indeed, I'm greatly honoured you have given me this time out of your pressing schedule to speak to you this morning.

"What I have to say comes not from any authority within myself. I don't speak to you as a representative of a vested interest or as an elected leader of any constituent assembly. I speak to you rather as the channel of a human concern that is swelling up with great force across the planet, transcending all national boundaries and all cultural, ethnic, and religious divisions. The concern is for the quality of future human life.

"All of our history has been played out in territory. Like the animal kingdom of which we are a part, we are creatures of territory. Our passions and behaviours, and our physical brains which give rise to them, have been forged over countless millennia in the confines of particular territory on the planet. We have fought for and defended our territory. We have engaged in conquest, coalition, and compromise to expand, enhance, and consolidate our territory.

"Now, quite suddenly, in the flicker of an instant in cosmic time, all that has changed. It no longer is of any great significance to bicker or dispute over discrete geographical territory. There is only the planet, for which we must be stewards. On the planet our continents and countries remain, but no longer as separate, independent, or sovereign states. They now exist only as landscape, threads and patterns of the total integrated fabric, which is the Earth, our planetary home.

"For all of you here, leaders of territorial states, this is an issue of great significance. It's almost incomprehensible, but not quite. For somewhere deep in the mystical resources of collective human consciousness there is awareness of the change that has come about, and there are flashes of insight of what we must do, as the supreme intelligent species on the planet, to respond to the new conditions for life.

"Out of this awareness, fragile, flickering, and tentative, was born the concept of visioneering. This means the coming together of human consciousness from every corner of the planet—from every country, community and household—to engineer the future way the human race will conduct its affairs in harmony with the physical environment on which, ultimately, all life depends.

"From this hesitant beginning, in the space of a few short months, the idea of visioneering has spread like wildfire around the globe. People are coming forward as Visoneers everywhere. The understanding of what to do is anything but perfect, but everywhere now there are people striving to lift their conscious awareness to this new planetary level, breaking out of the narrow confines of old paradigms and ideologies that no longer work.

"What needs to be done varies enormously from place to place. But always the action is centred around three overarching principles.

"First there is commitment to the sanctity of human life. This is no moral or ethical pronouncement requiring simple obedience and punishment for violation. Rather, it grows out of awesome contemplation of the mystery of life itself, and a deep appreciation that every human being is linked through a creative mind to a source of infinite intelligence, which is the energy source of the universe. Our various religious beliefs lead us to describe this mystical relationship in different ways, but central to it is a profound appreciation for the magnificence and universality of our humanness. From this understanding we know that all life is sacred, that all men and women are our brothers and sisters, and that it is a violation of the order of the universe for us to take the lives of each other, whether in battle, anger, or any other form of hostility.

"Second is the law of love. This grows out of the first. If we turn our minds to the wonder of creation, we cannot help but be stirred by emotions of love, compassion, and respect. We will love the source of creation, however we might understand that concept. We will love our fellow human beings as participants and continuing co-creators of reality. We will love the Earth and the life it supports in which we see ourselves as participants and beneficiaries.

"The third principle is to know of the aberration that exists concerning the other two. This is to acknowledge the reality of evil in the universe and to be vigilant against it. Evil becomes manifest in acts that deny justice and respect for the life and well-being of others. It's as real in acts of international aggression as it is in familial and community violence. It's an abhorrent abomination to the law of life and must be recognized and resisted wherever and whenever it becomes manifest. It's a subtle and disrupting force which can infect the minds of any of us. Against it we must be personally and collectively vigilant.

"What then are the lessons in all of this that we might draw for this General Assembly of united nations? First and foremost will be an understanding that nationhood is not sovereign. Only creation and the Earth are sovereign. All human relationships and arrangements are matters of consensus which continuously need reworking in the context of a viable long-term future for humanity. While all of us are citizens of our nation states, we are first and foremost stewards of life on the planet. This is the new reality that overrides all other considerations.

"We can clearly draw the lesson from history that no tribe, nation, religion, or ideology can dominate the entire world. From our vantage point as citizens of an emerging 21st century, we see that all attempts to do that in the past were manifestations of the aberrant evil I have just described. They were perpetrated at incredible cost to the well-being of life. They were gross assaults on the principles of life and love, and to the extent that they were celebrated as victorious accomplishments of the day, this can only be interpreted now as immature understanding of the responsibility of humanness. There's no place or room for such ambitions in the future.

"The human race for all of its known history has been engaged in the waging of war. All thought, action, codes of conduct, and symbols of social approval have been grounded in that warlike imperative. In recent years we have escalated that predisposition for conflict to the point where we are in continuing danger of destroying all life on the planet—if not through military might, then through economic competition and technological barbarism.

"Hence we have been catapulted in only one or two generations to a moment of psychic time and space where the old paradigms and beliefs we had judged to be successful must now be recognized in many, though not all, respects to be terrible failures.

"The outcome of human history is that we are looking for an entirely new invention. All of the cultures of the world have to be reinvented in the context of an overarching planetary culture. In this process there will be no place for revisiting past ambitions. Nor should we rely on compromise or coalition. They are too fragile arrangements on which to bet the future of the human race. No. What we are engaged in here is the act of creation. To the extent that we understand our history we can now move into the future unencumbered by it. Indeed, there's nothing we can do about history, other than to understand it as the foundation for creating the future. We can do nothing about changing the past, but we can do everything about creating the future.

"The Visioneers for whom I speak have looked at our world today and said that they do not accept things the way they are; rather, they anticipate what they can be in the future. They don't accept that people in many nations represented in this Assembly should live in fear of attack either from neighbouring countries or from the armies and police of their own governing authorities. They don't accept the levels of grinding poverty and deprivation endured by much, if not the majority of the world's population. They don't accept the tribalism, racism, or the barbaric hatred expressed by different sectors of the human race against one another. They don't accept the levels of mental stress and family breakdown associated with economic life in even the most advanced industrial societies. They don't accept the drug and alcohol addiction that destroys the creative potential of millions of lives across the planet. None of this is acceptable as a standard of relationships among members of a species gifted with an awesome potential for creative thinking and logical reasoning.

"As bad as these relationships are, it's even more reprehensible to think that this intelligent human species would persistently poison the earth, the air, and the waters of the planet in pursuit of an economic way of life that ultimately brings with it no measurable increase in human happiness. Worse still, this destructive and internally inconsistent economic behaviour beckons as a model for all humanity to seek to attain. Surely this brings with it the crowning indictment of a civilization gone berserk through the pursuit of unmindful profligacy and greed.

"All this is unacceptable as the basis for anticipating what might be. The only anticipated outcome for a continuation of these present warring, conflictual, competitive, self-interested, aggressive behaviours will be a rapid degradation of the quality of all life everywhere on the planet within the lifetimes of generations already born, let alone those unfortunate enough to come later.

"Against all of this the Visioneers are crying out with a resounding 'No! This is not acceptable!'

"So what are they doing to change the direction? They are first and foremost engaging millions of people across the world in a process of creative learning. They are wakening the dulled imaginations of a tidal force of human potential to create a different outcome. They are stirring up the listless energy of a population at drift to identify a shared vision of what life can be like on this planet in the 21st century, instead of what it is likely to be like if conditions don't change. The visions are stirring, among children in school, senior citizens in all communities, corporate chieftains, municipal leaders, teachers, professors, farmers, industrialists, scientists, engineers, but above all among people in their households, in their communities, on the streets, in their villages, wherever they live, wherever they can be reached, however they can be brought to awareness and encouraged to join a visioneering team to make a difference.

"Which brings me now specifically to why I asked to speak to you today in this highest assembly of people of the Earth. As leaders of the nations you are in powerful positions of influence to move policy and practice in the direction that it must go. The world is clearly on the wrong course for a viable future. As Visioneers, people are showing they are prepared to accept responsibility for changing direction. But they need leadership and resources from public institutions of government and administration.

"They are crying out for the abandonment of policies that would pour sixty to a hundred times as much money into equipping a soldier as to educating a child; that would choose the commissioning of nuclear submarines and intercontinental balistic missles over the provision of health and welfare to people in need; that would spend a million dollars on a single military tank rather than on a thousand classrooms in Africa where 30,000 children could be educated for a year.

"Even more reprehensible are direct policies or convenient blind eyes that lead to the international trade in arms, as if this is good business, a good return for petro dollars, a good recovery of research and development costs. You can't expect to get a right result out of a wrong action. Clearly, the sale of arms and their use against military and civilian populations, and in the destruction of property and the environment, is as wrong-headed and morally bankrupt as anything an intelligent human mind can conceive. Yet it has been and remains still a cornerstone of the way human populations deal with each other on the planet. It has to stop and the best way to do it is right here in this Assembly where leadership for such change could come down with tremendous force.

"However, even if we put this militaristic aggressiveness to rest, the Earth will still remain imperiled. The sad and tragic truth of so-called civilized behaviour is our propensity to wage war against the living system which gave us birth so many millennia ago, and on which we continue to depend for our survival. The cry has gone out for sustainable development, but as a world system, we are so far from even beginning to approach that objective that the concept has a bitter internal contradiction to it.

"The people of the Earth need with desperate urgency to reinvent the concept of development and the economic system that supports it. So far, our only knowledge is of growth. Since leaving the societies of hunters and gatherers we have known nothing of sustainability. The industrialized world has been founded on a materialistic appetite that has become the engine of environmental destructiveness.

"As populations grow, as technology becomes more lethal in its impact, as an ever widening group of nations learn the trick of industrial development, so the potential length for any kind of quality life on the planet becomes shorter and shorter. In this arena we have turned our backs on the perennial wisdom of the ages. Every religion and philosophy known to humankind has denied the possibility of securing happiness through limitless material acquisition. Yet in every board room, in every economic conference, on every page of every economic journal, on every television set, every evening, in every industrialized country of the world, this is the gospel that is preached and accepted without question as the way of the world by vast populations content to call themselves consumers.

"People have become willing participants in an economic system based on the premise of growth without limit. This fuels and is fueled by corruption at all levels, in every corner, by officials, executives, tradespeople, merchants, politicians, heads of state, to the point that it seems almost no one is averse to pushing the system further than it can reasonably go.

"But in the end what awaits is a lingering death, for the penalty for this behaviour will not come suddenly. It will creep upon us, as it has already begun to do, in changing climatic patterns, failed crops, poisoned fish, mysterious diseases, famine, disruption, and chaos.

"Knowing this, what are we to do? Well, the Visioneers have begun— by opening their minds to creative learning—which creates the future vision, assesses current reality, and charts the path of action. Now, we're calling on you as leaders of the nations of the world to throw your prestige and power behind a worldwide thrust for creative learning. We're asking you to reconceive your role of leader as a facilitator of learning, to shift use of the Earth's resources in the direction of learning for a viable future.

"A plank in this platform was laid by Unesco in 1985, when in its conference on adult education it adopted a Declaration on the Right to Learn. It asked the question, Who will decide what humanity will become in the future? It answered it by declaring that learning is a fundamental human right, which includes not only the right to universal literacy, but also the right to imagine and create.

"Ladies and Gentlemen, leaders of the world, the time has come to go beyond that Unesco declaration, and even the United Nations Convention on the Rights of the Child, to go beyond to convene a worldwide Congress of the Global Mind.

"The Congress will not be a meeting to debate and agree on words about what should be done. It will be a great symbol for the transcendence of the world to a planetary society of creative learning. It will be an event of epic proportions. It will engage people in every community on the face of the Earth that can be reached by modern communications. It will share with them the crisis of civilization now upon us, and invite them in free and open participation to invent solutions that will work for them in their community, and which can be shared with their brothers and sisters across the Earth.

"Such a Congress is grounded in the belief that people must be given the knowledge and the freedom to learn how to do what to do. We can no longer mastermind the future of the world out of central planning and intelligence agencies, out of government think tanks, policy boards and the like. No. The way into the future is through empowerment of people to learn the lessons of history and move into the future in full creative flow in assemblies of their peers.

"The process has already begun. The visioneering projects around the world are testimony to its power. Now I'm calling upon this great Assembly of leaders to endorse it and provide to it the resources needed to make it a bold and historical declaration of the indomitable will of the human spirit to rise to the challenge of creation.

"We have prepared a full and detailed proposal on the concept, copies of which have been distributed to all of your delegations. We are proposing that the Congress be held in approximately seven months from now in late October. The scope and format will be determined by our joint planning efforts.

"In the spirit of everything I have said to you today, and in support of your own quest to bring enlightened leadership to the world at its time of greatest crisis, I call upon you at this Assembly to endorse the holding of the Congress of the Global Mind for the future well-being of humanity.

"Ladies and Gentlemen, the people of the world have put their trust in you as their leaders, to bring to them a future of decency and hope. The Earth and all life on it is in its critical hour. We are imperiled by the power of our intellects and the weakness of our bonds. Here in this world assembly, and only here, can the cool voice of reason unite with the passionate cry for love, to carve, for the preservation of the planet, the new tablets of human conduct that lie blank but ready in the fertile imaginations of all of us. Can we commit today to begin? Will we give out a message to the waiting world that we are ready for the task? May we act now with the wisdom of the ages at our backs and the unlimited possibilities of the future in our eyes! To this agenda I ask your full and unqualified commitment."

Mark stops speaking. A hush as deep as time itself settles on the Assembly. How long it lasts no one knows. Then it breaks. Moving as one, the assembled heads of governments come to their feet to applaud both the words of courage and the heart of the speaker who had delivered them. Whatever may be their individual thoughts at this moment, they rise together, to give a thunderous acknowledgement of the intent of what they have just heard.

As the applause continues Mark steps away from the podium. In his place an old friend appears to close the session. It is M'buta Mutsandu, President of Yarawi, the elder statesman of the Visioneers. His full round face is wreathed in the smiles of an exuberant moment. He waits for the applause to settle then speaks out boldly in his rich African voice, full of the music of his homeland.

"My friends, for an old man to see this day is a great privilege. It is a rare and extraordinary moment in the history of the world. You have come to this Assembly fresh from experiences of reality unknown to the people now listening and watching across the globe. I was not part of that experience with you because I belong to the world of Mark Venture and the Visioneers. But now we are all here together and you have just had your first opportunity to experience the energy of a human cause that transcends all past limitations and looks with optimism at what might be.

"We are standing now before a huge billboard in the sky, a giant screen large enough for all the world to see that asks the question, 'What if?'

"What if the peoples of the world could put aside their differences and see themselves as co-creators of a better present and more hopeful future! What if they could turn the energy they expend on conflict and competition to projects of cooperation and mutual well-being! What if we chose to redirect resources now wasted on the business of destruction to enterprises of enlightenment! What if, my friends, we really did decide to build a world based on the principles of life and love!

"These are the questions now on the world agenda. Mark Venture and his Visioneers have laid the foundation. Now they're asking us to help build the structure. That opportunity is at hand. Before we leave this Assembly tomorrow we must decide. Will we join with the Visioneers in creating the Congress of the Global Mind? Can we make it the first worldwide demonstration of the unity of humankind and commitment to creative learning for the future? I sincerely hope that we decide to act on this.

"For now, it remains only for me to thank Mark Venture for his message and the hopeful heart with which he brought it here. From this General Assembly of the United Nations, Mark, thank you."

Again, prolonged applause fills the hall. President Mutsandu waits for it to subside.

"Finally, on behalf of the Secretary-General and Mark Venture, I am pleased to extend an invitation to you all to attend a celebration of this occasion at Woodlands this evening at 7:00 p.m. I believe your permanent delegates will know the place well. May we find there the generosity and the spirit that must guide us in our work!"

At Woodlands

The event at Woodlands that evening is a festival for life. The guests are embraced by nature skillfully crafted within the most unnatural confines of a New York warehouse. The place exudes the same audaciousness of tree, shrub, flower, and fish as when Mark had seen it first at lunch with Peter Hemphill—only now it seems more so. Designed as a meandering maze of paths and gathering places in a setting of fern and forest, the space swallows up its occupants, sending them on adventures of discovery and unexpected encounters at every turn.

Everywhere dishes of fruit and vegetables, in exotic hot and cold creations, mysteriously appear within hand's reach, suspended from tree branches, balancing on rocks, hiding behind flower pots. At every turn in the many paths, pockets of conversation swell up and engulf the wanderer. The whole is a dance of becoming, a Visioneer's adventure place.

And indeed, there are many Visioneers on hand, easily distinguished by the bright blue and white V button they're all wearing. Bill Bates has been active in rounding up the American contingent of Julia McCarthy, Arthur Rhinegold, Diane Koplitz, George Walker, and Senator Wilfred Brown. Others have come in especially, wherever and whenever they had been able to leave their responsibilities at short notice. George Cardinal is prominent in his buckskin jacket standing tall among all comers. "Momma" Theresa, round, smiling and rosy, rolls along the pathways, creating spontaneous pools of laughter wherever she settles for a moment. Indira Murti graciously engages conversation. Carmen Santander sparks rhythm and dancing by a corner brook. Daniel Thomas recites ribald poetry and encourages others to follow suit.

But the toast of the evening is Esther Fisher. Miraculously she has appeared at the last moment. When Mark had last spoken to her in Jerusalem it seemed impossible that she could come. But now she's here, too late for Mark's address in the General Assembly, but this evening present as his full partner as he and the Secretary-General greet their guests.

And my, how the guests come pouring in! At least fifty heads of governments are able to make a brief appearance before going on to other engagements. All are enthusiastic about Mark's presentation and assure him of their support. Peter Hemphill has done his work well in inviting the permanent delegations. He has also included members of Congress and U.S. Senators with special international responsibilties, as well as representatives of many non-governmental organizations and foundations active in fields of human advancement. The Mayor of New York stops by, delighted with the spark that events like this give the labouring city. In all, the occasion clearly announces the emergence of the Visioneers on the international, not to mention the American, social scene.

At about 8:00 p.m. Mark and Esther make their way to the centre of the sprawling expanse of plants and people. This is like a clearing in the forest, site of the wild garden of herbs, shrubs and flowers. One gets to it by a gradual descent along the wandering pathways. Looking out from there, it is, miraculously, possible to see most of the other gathering places in the restaurant, clustered along terraces that overlook the wild garden.

A microphone has been set up. Mark goes to it and calls for attention. Conversation subsides and people gather to listen.

"Friends," he says, "thank you for coming out this evening to celebrate with us. When I spoke to the General Assembly this morning, I described a world in trouble. As I look around me here I see a world of hope. Intelligent and concerned men and women of every nation, freely exchanging ideas and fellowship. We have gathered here in a space crafted by human intelligence, but taking as the source of its imagination, the natural beauty of the world. That's what we must be about in the future: learning how to blend our creative human impulses with the natural rhythms of life on the planet. We've got a long way to go, but with your good sense and commitment we're taking the first steps. Thank you for coming."

Mark's face now lightens visibly as he continues.

"I believe most of you have noticed that I've been joined this evening by my fiancée, Esther Fisher. In fact, I know very well that most of you noticed little else when we met you as you arrived. Considering Esther is less than a week away in finalizing preparations for our wedding next Sunday in Jerusalem, I consider her presence here tonight to be one of the marvellous miracles that have come to mark my life as a Visioneer. Esther would like to speak to you."

Mark hands the microphone to Esther and steps back. Applause breaks out around the room. Esther stands quietly confident, a delicate, tiny figure, in a crisp white knit dress with a large purple amethyst at her throat.

"It's wonderful to see you all!" she says, "and to know that at any time the love and fellowhsip in this room flows just as freely in millions of places where men and women of good will gather together to enjoy the warmth of human spirit. We can have our assembiles, we can work hard on our task forces, but nowhere are we more in touch with who we are as human beings, than in gatherings like this.

"I'm so thankful now for what my life has become that I just wanted to be here and share with you this evening. I knew Mark would make a wonderful speech in the General Assembly this morning. It's already having its impact in the world, and I believe with all my heart the world is ready to listen now. Because people want so much to live in peace and to look forward to long and fruitful lifetimes in a future of expanding hope. As Visioneers we can make that happen. Not just for a lucky few, but for all people everywhere. We must work every day on making that real and not divert our energies along paths of conflict.

"It almost seems like yesterday that I was delivered from one of the most terrible forms of conflict that human beings can engage in. That's the infamy of terrorism. There's nothing more terrible than when innocent people are savagely attacked by an unknown aggressor, and their freedom is taken away, and their lives become a torment of terror and fear.

"My land and my people have been a touchstone for such actions for more years, it seems, than most of us care to remember. I've been in the heart of it. I know it from the inside. And I can say that it must not be the way of the world in the future.

"Nor will it be. My captors let me go, and I work every day on seeking to multiply the good to them of that act of compassion. That's what we must strive to make the way of the world, good multiplying good: the synergy of hope, rather than the tyranny of hate.

"I mention this to you this evening, my friends, because in a few days Mark and I are going to make our solemn vows of love to each other in a very public way in the city of Jerusalem, one of the world's great centres for sacredness and love, but ironically torn apart by hate and conflict. As we make our vows there, we want the watching world to see in that our statement of hope for the world."

Esther's voice begins to falter a little as she continues. Those standing close can see a tremble about her lips and moistness in her eyes.

"We've recently been warned that there are elements abroad, forces of the grossest evil, that will attack us on that day, and seek to put the blame on the Palestinians. Mark and I want to take this moment here tonight, surrounded by friends, to say we don't believe that such wickedness is meant to be."

Esther is now too visibly moved to continue. Her voice has faded and tears fill her eyes. Mark steps forward and takes her hand. Biting his lower lip, he continues the address, his own voice perceptibly edged by the emotion of the moment.

"Friends, this is not really the topic of a celebration, but we live as yet in an imperfect world when hard realities must be faced as they come. Esther has raised the conflict that now touches us personally. But we know that because we are public figures, it touches the world as well. Therefore, tonight with the world watching through all of you here and our good friends in the media who were also invited, we simply want to reiterate our commitment previously made to the Palestinians who captured Esther. We look only for a just and equitable outcome to the situation facing them and their Jewish neighbours, and we'll use all of our influence and resources to secure it. We stand for the future built out of understanding of the past, but not enslaved to it."

He now smiles rougishly at Esther who looks up shyly at him. He gently brushes a tear from each of her cheeks with the tip of his forefinger. Squeezing her hand more tightly, he gestures broadly to the people all around.

"We would love to invite each of you personally to our wedding. It already seems that half the world is coming anyway, and the other half will watch on television. We know we have your prayers and good wishes, as indeed all of you have ours, through your enterprises for the good of the Earth. Thank you again for coming. Please continue to enjoy your evening here. God bless you all."

"*Shalom!*" adds Esther, strongly.

"*Shalom!*" returns a chorus from the guests.

The evening closes quickly after that, with people taking their leave in lively good spirits. It's a continuous stream, some they know, others they don't, everyone wishing Mark and Esther well. They feel themselves surrounded by a cocoon of good will. Here in this space between the potential and the danger of their initiatives, they touch the hope of what can come.

The flow quietens for a minute, then Mark looks around and sees they are being approached by a tall, dark-complexioned woman. Strikingly elegant and beautiful, she moves with the gracefulness and assurance of one who knows the source and use of power. Her green sheath evening dress reveals a figure mature but well contained, and her bare shoulders curve with the lines of classical beauty. A presence moves with her that Mark finds strangely disturbing. The broad, engaging smile carries a severity, barely perceptible, but confirmed in the faint glaze of hardness in her almost coal black eyes. Mark touches Esther on the elbow to draw the approaching figure to her attention. The slight additional pressure of the touch alerts her to his guardedness for this encounter.

The woman has arrived and extends a slim, jewelled hand, first to

Mark, and then to Esther. Behind her, two Latin men in evening dress maintain a respectable distance.

"Good evening Mr. Venture and Miss Fisher." Her voice is high pitched but finely modulated. "I'm sorry we didn't meet when I arrived. I'm afraid I was a little late. My name is Elvira Ramos. You may know of my late husband, President Enrico Ramos. Some of my friends from our delegation were kind enough to include me in their party."

She motions at the men behind her, but makes no move to introduce them. They smile and nod to Mark and Esther. Elvira Ramos continues:

"I must admit I prevailed upon them somewhat. I have heard so much about the two of you and the Visioneers that I certainly didn't want to miss the opportunity to meet you."

"You're most welcome," replies Mark. "I hope you enjoyed the evening."

"Oh, most certainly. I can't begin to tell you how much I'm intrigued by what you're doing. You see, the reason we were late is that I was watching the excerpts from your speech this morning on the evening news. Truly most remarkable. I'm sure the United Nations have never heard anything like that before. You really are out to transform the world, aren't you?"

"Only people can transform the world, Mrs. Ramos. Our role is to help the process move along."

"Well, you certainly appear to be doing that. You came down very hard in your remarks on the predisposition of nations and their leaders to wage war and to resort to force to exercise their power. Are you then a peaceful man, Mr. Venture?"

"We said again this evening what we stand for," Mark replies, staring deep into her black eyes.

"Ah, yes, you stand for a future unenslaved by the past. But, you know, sometimes one must regain the past to build the future, and where there are factions who resist, conflict surely is inevitable."

"If the principles of life and love are put first among people of good will, the conflict resolves itself."

"But it's finding those people of good will that can be so elusive."

"We've had no difficulty in that," Esther intervenes. "Already there are millions throughout the world moving to bring about necessary changes."

"Do you include Jerusalem in that, my dear?" Elvira Ramos is surveying Esther closely. "I wasn't surprised to hear you say this evening that you've received threats against your wedding there. Do you think that by declaring it to the world the threats will go away?"

"The threats may not," replies Esther steadily, "but the evil behind them will be disengaged."

The other woman stiffens slightly, then visibly relaxes, her smile engaging them both. She extends her hand to leave.

"I can see the two of you are indeed of like mind. It presages well for your future. May I wish you every happiness."

With that she moves away, her two companions nodding behind fixed smiles and following.

Before Esther and Mark have a chance to speak, Peter Hemphill is at their side.

"I hope she didn't unnerve you," he says. "There's someone else here I want you to meet. She has something important to tell you about Elvira Ramos."

As Mark turns, he looks into the smiling eyes of a face he already knows. It's the woman who had introduced him this morning at the United Nations. In the press of business following his remarks, there still had been no opportunity to meet her formally. She is as small and comfortably gracious in appearance as their previous guest now leaving had been tall and severely glamorous. Mark knows instinctively that he likes her. She is dressed simply in a navy blue evening dress, high necked and full sleeved. Her short, slightly greying hair is gathered neatly to highlight a frank and open face.

"I would like to present President Miriam Suchinda," Peter Hemphill is continuing. "Mark Venture, of course, you know, Your Excellency, and Esther Fisher you have seen much of this evening."

"Indeed, yes," she smiles, extending her hand first to Esther, then to Mark. "I'm so glad to meet you both for a moment in private. First, Mr. Venture, I want you to know that your words and spirit have touched me deeply. I and my country are small players in world affairs, but we have means of influence, and I intend to use them on your behalf."

Mark nods his appreciation, but doesn't speak, sensing she has something more to add.

"I'm not sure what you know, Mr. Venture," President Suchinda continues, "about the experience which the world leaders have shared concerning the matters you raised with us this morning."

Mark shakes his head.

"I see," she says, "then perhaps you're not to know. But there's something I must share. Does the name El Condor mean anything to you?"

Mark and Peter Hemphill exchange glances as Esther gasps, just barely audibly.

"Yes," replies Mark, "we have good reason to know that name. I prefer to call him by his real name, Carlos Palmira."

"Then you should also know that the woman to whom you were just speaking, Elvira Ramos, is Palmira's, shall we say, intimate companion."

This time Esther is visibly startled. Mark turns to Hemphill.

"Peter, how come Palmira's mistress is at our reception?"

Hemphill shrugs his shoulders.

"It's a tangled web, old boy, but at least we're not caught in it. If you wanted to get a message to El Condor tonight, I would say you've done it."

"Mark," Esther asks nervously, 'what do you think she meant about Jerusalem?"

"What did she say abut Jerusalem?" President Suchinda asks before Mark can answer.

"Well, nothing direct," says Mark, "but she clearly implied that we can expect trouble there."

"Now listen carefully," the President continues. "This much I can tell you. El Condor, or Palmira, sees the Visioneers, and you in particular, Mr. Venture, as a threat to his operations. He has issued orders, I'm not sure to whom, that there is to be a strike against you at the wedding."

"You know this for a fact," asks Mark.

"Yes," she replies.

"Who else knows it?"

"All of the world leaders do—at least, we do through this experience that we've had together."

"Well, then surely someone's going to do something to stop it!"

"I'm not sure. You see, well, it's hard for us to make the connections on all of this. To be quite honest, we don't know what's real and what isn't."

"Now, that's the second time you've said that, today." Mark's irritation has begun to show. "First in the General Assembly and now here. I'm sorry. Your Excellency, I'm obviously missing a piece of the puzzle, but I can tell you, Palmira is real. Ask Peter. He gave me the U.N. dossier on the man. I've got good reason to believe he was responsible for the murder of one of my friends. If he's issued orders to strike at our wedding, then he means it."

"Very well," President Suchinda is already turning to go. "I'll act on this right away. I meant what I said before, Mr. Venture. I agree with you. We have to take care of the Earth first. God bless you both."

Peter Hemphill moves to go with her.

"No, it's all right, Mr. Hemphill," she says. "I have a driver waiting at the door. You stay here. I'm sure you have matters to discuss."

She is gone.

"Peter," says Mark, "what's going on? What's this experience she's talking about? What do the world leaders know about El Condor and me that I don't know myself?"

"Search me, Mark. You're the one who's put this whole thing together, not me. I thought you had it figured out."

"So did I," says Mark. "Now, I'm not so sure."

Esther touches Mark's sleeve.

"Look, Mark, there's Mohammed. I think he should be told about all of this right away. I'll call him over."

A few moments later Mohammed Hussein has joined them. He looks distinctly at home here in the diplomatic circles of the United Nations. For a second, Mark recalls the more heart-stopping diplomacy that the two of them had engaged in with the terrorists outside Bethlehem. He greets his friend warmly. Mohammed is obviously well pleased with himself.

"I'm glad we've got a moment to speak," he says. "I wanted to tell you, I've been talking tonight with the permanent heads of most of the Arab delegations. There's a good feeling out there towards you, Mark—and you, too, Esther. Oh yes, I know that makes you tense a little, but the point Mark's been making is starting to get through. The Earth must come first. They're looking for a symbol that can make that point clear among so many divisions and conflicts. And you know, you two may just have hit on it, by choosing to hold your wedding in Jerusalem.

"It's the ancient city of hope for three great faiths, and the focal point for so much of the hatred and conflict among them. If something can emerge from this that will let the world see a new Jerusalem, then I think it could really be the symbol for the world we're trying to create. That's the gist of the conversation I've been having with the ambassadors, and believe me, I've never heard that kind of talk before."

"Bless you, Mohammed," says Esther, "for bringing that up right now. We've just been hearing the opposite scenario: Jerusalem as the place where Mark and Esther's dreams come to an end, with who knows what consequences for the world."

They quickly fill him in on the discussions with President Suchinda and Elvira Ramos.

"Well, one thing's certain now," Mark says in summary, "and what you've just told us confirms it, Mohammed. Our original intuition was correct and we're going to push on. We can't tell how it's going to come out, but we have to believe in ourselves and keep moving ahead"

"Did I hear someone say something about moving ahead?"

They all turn to see that Pamela Barrett from ZNN has come up. Bill Bates is right behind her.

"Well, doesn't this bring back memories," Pamela says, laughing. "Mark, Esther, and Mohammed. The last time I had the three of you together—in Jerusalem, remember?—we gave the world an interview it'll never forget. Are you ready to do another one? You know, you people have got something going. I don't know what it is, but I'm sure glad to be a part of it. I can't wait to see you two getting married on Sunday in Jerusalem. That's going to be another showstopper for the globe."

Mark and Esther exchange glances.

"You know, Pamela," he laughs, "along with the timing of a real pro you've got the sensitivity of an angel. For that, I'll give you an exclusive when the word comes out tomorrow that the U.N. will support the Congress of the Global Mind."

"Oh," says Pamela, "you've got it on good authority that they're going to do that, have you?"

"On the best," says Mark.

"You bet," puts in Bill Bates. "I tell you what, Pam. Let's do the interview tomorrow on the Plaza of Nations beside the flags at noon."

"It's a date," she says brightly. "Goodnight, you guys, and thank you for what you're doing."

Suddenly to all of them there that seems to sound right.

Back on the Plaza

The next day, Wednesday, dawns sunny and cool. At 8:00 a.m. Mark takes Esther to the airport for her flight to Israel. As he drives back into the city, afterwards he muses over what lies ahead: for Esther, the final hurried preparations for the wedding; for himself, this last day in New York to move the agenda with the U.N; then an evening flight to Israel to assume his own responsibilities for the wedding. Hanging over it all, is the fear and uncertainty of what Carlos Palmira might do. In that regard, the recollection of their encounter last night with Elvira Ramos leaps to mind. No wonder he had been uneasy when he saw her coming towards them. To know that Palmira's serpent coils lay that close to the heart of their enterprise has been a rude awakening.

But today's another day.

In his hotel room at 11:00 a.m, he receives a call from Peter Hemphill.

"You did it, old boy," the diplomatic voice is edged with excitement. "The General Assembly has just voted unanimously to endorse the Congress of the Global Mind. It's the first time in history anything has ever gone through like that."

'I know," replies Mark. "There's something moving the leaders to act. President Suchinda was hinting at it last night. But it's like being in a racing river. You have to keep swimming with it or you'll drown. Can I meet with you and the Secretary-General this afternoon to discuss details?"

"I thought you'd ask that. The General Assembly adjourns at noon. How does 3:00 p.m. sound?"

"Good. I'm on a 7:00 p.m. flight to Israel. Right now I have to get to my noon interview with Pamela Barrett at the Plaza of Nations. You should drop by."

"I just might do that."

As Mark puts down the phone, Bill Bates is at the door to take him to the interview.

On the Plaza, word has gone out that the General Assembly is adjourning and that some of the world leaders will be coming out. Tourists and lunchtime crowds are gathering. When they hear that Mark Venture is also on hand, it creates a diversion toward the place where Pamela Barrett has set up for the interview. As he looks out on several hundred faces from the platform the television crew has set up, Mark whispers to Bill Bates:

"You didn't by chance have anything to do with this, did you, Bill?"

"You do your job, Mark," replies the other, "and I'll do mine. After all, there are official world leaders and unofficial ones. A little bit of joint publicity is good for everyone."

On camera Pamela Barrett is very friendly.

"Well, here we are again, Mark: from rescuing hostages in Jerusalem to convincing world leaders to support the Visioneers, in six short months. How do you feel about it all today?"

"Thankful," Mark replies, "thankful that people across the world are gathering together to take responsibility for the future, to put the Earth first, before their own self interest. That's a monumental turn in human thinking. I'm thankful to be able to help with that."

"What does today's decision by the United Nations mean for this work?"

"It's a watershed. You can't move very far or fast on a people's agenda if their governments aren't on side. Today the governments of the world have unanimously agreed to give support to an enterprise that will make it possible for people to learn how to move forward on a vision of what the world can be like, not just for them personally, or for their community or country, but for everyone everywhere."

"Isn't that going to run up against a lot of vested interests?"

"Yes. And that's part of the learning, to unlearn that kind of thinking. Otherwise within fifty years—and that's a span that'll include all of today's children and grandchildren—within fifty years most of those vested interests will be overwhelmed by major unanticipated consequences of today's self-interested behaviour."

"Are we talking then about a future Commonwealth of Nations to replace the idea of the United Nations?"

"Yes. That's probably closer to it, but still only part of the issue. I want to make it clear that today no one knows the answer to the question. We have to invent the solution, and that's a much more creative piece of work than any of the technological innovation we pride ourselves on."

"And who's going to do the invention?"

"The people are. That's the point. We rushed into the 20th century telling most people on Earth that they aren't creative. All they were good for was conforming to the innovations created by a select few. They were herded together in factories, schools, cities, economic systems, and political institutions—all designed by great innovators and put in place by the power of wealth and military and police force. People were given enough education and training to fit the pattern and try to make it work. Now it's out of hand, but still running full tilt, like a nuclear reactor gone berserk, realizing humanity's worst nightmare of a destructive force that's out of control."

Mark has warmed to the subject. His words, as well as being recorded by the television cameras, are being heard by the people nearby through speakers erected by the crew. The crowd grows larger and presses in as the interview continues.

"So, what's the first step to turn this around?" Pamela Barrett asks.

"The first step's already been taken. The Visoneers are out there demonstrating to people that they can learn how to be creative about a preferred future. But so far it's isolated activity. It's happening on every continent, but there's no sense yet of a whole Earth effort. That's what the Congress of the Global Mind is about."

"We don't have much time left in the interview, but can you tell us something about this Congress?"

"All I want to say today is that it will be a huge worldwide exposition of creative learning. Using every conceivable means of communication the people of the Earth will share their dreams and ideas with one another of how we can move forward into a sustainable future."

"Aren't there a lot of repressive regimes in the world who won't much go for that?"

"You would have thought so, but today's decision by the General Assembly was unanimous. That doesn't mean there won't be hold outs. But it's very significant."

"Are you suprised by that?"

"Yes and no. When I first asked to speak to the United Nations, I certainly put up my own personal vision and hoped they would go for it. But I couldn't be sure. Now I have the sense that the world leaders are being moved by a larger unifying force."

"Do you think they've had a vision?"

"Perhaps they have," Mark nods slowly. "Perhaps they have."

Pamela Barrett now smiles confidentially as she changes the subject.

"Before we close, Mark, you and your fiancée, Esther Fisher, have a rather important event for yourselves coming up on Sunday. Do you want to say anything about that?"

"Well, yes," he laughs. "I plan to be there. I wouldn't miss it for the world. Seriously, though, we've been touched by the good wishes from people all over the world for our marriage. Finding joy in another's happiness is a wonderful human quality. We just wish we could share it with all those who care."

"Well, you will, through the magic of television."

"That's true. I'm sure you'll give it great coverage."

"Jerusalem hasn't been a particularly happy place for you and Esther. Do you have any fears about further trouble?"

"Jerusalem is a sacred city for both our faiths. Its troubles stand as a warning to the world of divisions that destroy hope. Our marriage there is a very personal statement for us about our hope for the world. We believe there's great power for good in such forthright declarations."

"Thank you, Mark Venture. Good luck with your enterprises and your wedding. The world wishes you and Esther Fisher well."

"Thank you, Pamela, and to everyone who cares."

As the interview ends, spontaneous applause breaks out from the crowd that has stood quietly during the taping. Mark finds himself pressed on every side for autographs and from people who simply want to say, good luck. He lingers long about it, and it isn't until Bill Bates enjoins the help of several security guards that a path can be cleared for them to their waiting car. As they drive off, hundreds of hands are raised in a former symbol of hope when the world was ravaged by war, the V for victory sign. Now it takes on an added meaning, as V for visioneering. One of Pamela Barrett's cameramen is quick to catch this as perhaps the most important footage of the interview.

El Condor Again

Across the Atlantic Ocean, it's late evening in Switzerland and an interested observer is watching a news bulletin from ZNN on the concluding day of the special U.N. General Assembly for heads of governments. Carlos Palmira is seated alone in his communications centre, a thin wisp of smoke curling above his head from the slim cheroot on which he leisurely draws as he watches the newscast.

It's standard reporting on a wide range of political, economic, and social issues: agreement in principle on world trade, commitment to strategic arms limitations, reductions in polutant emission levels, war on drug trafficking—issues that have been on the agendas of less significant meetings for two decades, now shifted for discussion to the world leaders. Predicatable discussion, predictable reporting, except for one item. The commentator introduces it:

"Since the surprise appearance yesterday before the Assembly by Mark Venture, well-known throughout the world for his concept of visioneering, there has been speculation on what action, if any, the world body would take on his proposal for U.N. support for a Congress of the Global Mind. The decision was taken today: unanimous approval. What exactly this means is not yet clear. The details are to be worked out under the direction of the Secretary-General. However, if endorsement means even tacit support for what Mr. Venture presented in his speech to the Assembly yesterday, then this decision could have a dramatic impact on the shape of the world to come."

The commentator continues with a summary and clips from Mark's presentation, laying particular emphasis on the ideas of limited sovereignty for nation states and constituent assemblies of people from all countries. He then announces that Pamela Barrett conducted an interview with Mark

Venture earlier in the day and proceeds to play the tape. Carlos Palmira
hits the record button on his machine and pays riveted attention to the
interview. When it's over, he winds it back and runs it again. He then
switches the machine off, and grinds out the cheroot that had been burning
unnoticed between his fingers. He gets up and strides around the living
room, his left leg dragging a little more slowly than usual, highlighting the
barely perceptible limp in his gait.

The buzzing of the intercom breaks the silence.

"Yes, what is it?" he snaps.

"Mrs. Ramos calling from New York, sir," says a secretary's voice.

"All right, put her through."

The large screen lights up on the console panel of the communications
centre. Elvira Ramos appears curled up on the elegant sofa in her living
room. She is wearing only a designer cut green silk negligee, tied loosely,
and carefully draped to show her to advantage.

"Hello, Carlos, darling. Can you see me?" her voice is petulant and
coaxing.

"Yes," he says, "I hope you're alone."

"Carlos!" she reprimands. "You could say I look lovely. I'm keeping
myself for you. You know that."

"Yes, you do look lovely," he replies. "As to the other, I suspect you
know where your best interests lie."

"Oh, you are a grouch," Elvira complains. "It's too bad, and I don't
think my news will cheer you up, either."

"What's your news?" he asks.

"Have you seen any reports from the U.N.?"

"I just watched one from ZNN."

"Oh, you did? So did I! Isn't it marvellous how they do that! We're
thousands of kilometres apart and watching the same newscast at the same
time. Did you see the interview with Mark Venture?"

"Yes, I did."

"Isn't it interesting? He's really caused quite a sensation here. I went to
a reception he hosted last night."

"Why would you do that?"

"Because you aroused my curiosity, dear. I thought that anyone who
put the mighty El Condor on edge must be, well, exceptional."

"And?" Palmira's voice is hard as steel.

"Oh, I wasn't disappointed. He's very direct. I think people like him for
that—even the ones who spend most of their life weaving intrigues. His
fiancée, Esther Fisher, was there. For a Jewish girl, she seems to have some cut
to her. She's obviously nervous about something happening at their wedding
in Jerusalem on Sunday. You haven't started something, have you, Carlos?"

"If you have nothing further to add," retorts Palmira, "we should
terminate this call."

"Oh, I'm sorry if I upset you." Elvira sits up, a line of concern creasing her face. "I didn't mean anything by it. But they did say they had received threats."

"Did they name sources?"

"No, but they implied that by making it public they hoped to, let me see, 'disengage the evil,' I believe was the phrase."

"Elvira, it was nice of you to call," Palmira cuts in sharply. "Now, it's late here and I still have a lot to do. When are you coming back?"

"Oh, I'm not sure, in a few days, I expect."

"Good, let me know. Now, goodnight."

Without waiting for a response, Palmira breaks the connection, then immediately makes a call himself.

"Wolfgang? El Condor. I have word that the Venture-Fisher connection has received a warning. What do you know?"

"Nothing on that, sir," comes a gutteral reply.

"Check on it. It could be Rashid."

"Yes, sir."

"Get everything ready, but put it on hold. We may have to abort. What about the payments? Have they come through?"

"Not yet. I've been tracking them. I'm not sure what the problem is. There seems to be some nervousness down the line."

"Keep on it and let me know when you have something."

Palmira begins pacing the room. Again the intercom interrupts.

"Another call, sir. It's Mr. Porter. I believe he's calling from Washington."

The image of Larry Porter, crumpled and flabby appears on the screen. He looks much the same as when Palmira last saw him at their breakfast meeting in this room. Something is clearly agitating him. His horn-rimmed glasses are sitting a little more askew than usual on his sallow complexion.

"Carlos," he wheezes. "I'm switching from video. I'll transmit on 'deceptor'. Stand by."

The picture goes and thirty seconds later his voice comes back.

"Are you receiving?"

"Yes," replies Palmira.

"Carlos, this is urgent and I want it well scrambled."

"What's going on?"

"I'm not sure yet, but it could be bad. I got wind of stuff coming out of the Justice Department today that I thought we'd buried years ago, you know, charges on money laundering and pay-offs. I'm not sure what else. Worse still, it seems there's something going on in other countries, too: Britain, France, even Japan."

"Why would this start up all of a sudden?" Palmira's voice betrays no emotion.

"I dunno. It's as if, well, there's something coming from the highest levels to stir things up. One of our fellas thinks it might have something to do with the U.N. conference. You know, the Presidents get together and talk. And that Visioneer fella you spoke about, he's been here shooting his mouth off."

"I see. All right. I'll start checking. You keep your eyes and ears open."

"What are you going to do?"

"One of the best strategies," Palmira says cooly, "is to attack. Perhaps the world needs a diversion. Call me on this line if you have anything further to report."

Palmira breaks the connection, thinks for a moment, then places another call.

"Wolfgang? El Condor again. Move that item we spoke of before from hold to ready alert. And intensify the check on Rashid. I want a report tomorrow morning."

Palmira snaps another message into the intercom:

"Get calls out to the committee. I want everyone on a teleconference within the hour."

He takes out another cheroot, lights it, and sits smoking quietly in his armchair, waiting.

CHAPTER NINETEEN

Destiny
in
Jerusalem

WHEN MARK VENTURE ARRIVES at the apartment Esther has rented
for him in Jerusalem, it's already late afternoon on Thursday. With travel
time and zone changes, almost twenty-four hours have passed since he left
New York. In the compressed days between now and the wedding, this
seems like an eternity. Behind him, he left a spectacular success at the
United Nations. The follow-up meeting with the Secretary-General and
Peter Hemphill was also excellent. That relationship is poised for success.
In the days before him to the wedding the prospects should be equally
propitious. And they would, be, except for the dark unknown cloud of El
Condor's intent.

Esther was excited and radiant when she met him at the airport in Tel
Aviv. On the way to Jerusalem, she had briefed him on the preparations for
the wedding. The official guest list is almost three hundred people, but
several thousand onlookers are expected to come out to watch in the open
air amphitheatre where the ceremony is to be held outside the walls of the
Old City. Excitement and interest is mounting every day. With high profile
figures from the fields of business, government, culture, entertainment and
religion beginning to arrive, the world media are also gathering. While not
being billed as the wedding of the century—there is, indeed, some stiff
competition for that designation—it has begun to take on those dimensions.
Perhaps a more appropriate title was coined by *Woman's World* magazine
some weeks ago, and now picked up by the daily press in several countries
since Mark's and Esther's appearance in New York. THE WEDDING OF

THE FUTURE, was the headline, "Visioneers unite in love and the world comes to celebrate." Well, indeed, the world is gathering, sometimes pressing a little too close for comfort.

Mark is overwhelmed with admiration for the way in which Esther is managing the whole affair. He would like to give her more help now that he's here, but other matters are more pressing. Esther reminds him of the one overriding all the rest as he begins to unpack his bags.

"I received another call from Kamal Rashid yesterday," she says. "He's still warning us against going ahead. I gave him the phone number here. I'm sure you can expect a call from him shortly." Her voice breaks a little and Mark catches a glimpse of the anxiety pursuing her. "Oh, Mark, are we right in continuing? If anything should happen and innocent people are killed or injured, I could never live with that."

"I know, darling," he says, folding her in his arms. "There are developments every day now. All we can do is keep our faith and give others a chance to do what they can. If we have to cancel at the last minute, we will. But it'd be a savage blow for the momentum we've gathered. Worse still, it would strike at the heart of what we're about. We can't let this kind of wickedness go unchecked."

"It's so like what happened to Luis." Esther's voice is a murmur against his chest. "We can't endure that again."

"And we won't." Mark's voice is firm. He takes her face in his hands and gently kisses her on the lips. "There's a powerful force built up in the world from Luis' sacrifice. That's working for us now."

Shortly after, Esther leaves, and Mark turns his attention to settling in.

He places a call to Peter Hemphill in New York.

"Hello, Peter. I've just arrived in Jerusalem. Do you have any news for me?"

"Well, yes," replies Peter. "Some things are beginning to happen. I'm not getting everything direct, you understand, but it seems that President Suchinda has been true to her word about intervening and there's a move against Palmira. One of the businesses he operates is a financial organization that poses as a legitimate bank with branches in many countries. Banking regulations and justice people in several jurisdictions have held concerns about this for years. They suspect it's a front for money laundering and financing arms deals. You know the kind of thing. There never seemed to be enough evidence anywhere for anyone to move to shut it down. But now that looks like a possibility. If it happens, Palmira's going to be in a lot of trouble. That's all I can tell you now, but it looks promising. I've got your number there. I'll call you as soon as I hear something more."

"Thanks, Peter. I've just spoken to Esther. Apparently our contact here is still adamant that something's going to happen at the wedding."

"Mark, that's awful! What a cloud to have to work under! What are you going to do?"

"Mostly keep the faith. Your news helps. I'm going to be taking it up with the authorities right away. I'm sure they'll have their own networks to pursue. Please keep in touch."

As he puts the phone down, a profound weariness settles on Mark. A combination of travel, jet lag, and concern for the situation presses on him. He lies down to rest, but before he closes his eyes, the phone rings. It's Kamal Rashid.

"Mark Venture," he says. "Why haven't you listened to me? Why have you come back to Jerusalem? There's nothing here for you but danger."

"Look Kamal," Mark replies. "No one appreciates the gravity of the situation more than me. And I understand fully what it means for you to be giving us this warning. I don't take any of this lightly. But ever since we began this work with the Visioneers, we've faced enormous risks. There are people in every country now who are putting their lives on the line, because they believe completely in the importance of what we're doing. Our commitment to be married in Jerusalem after what happened here to Esther and her friends is an important statement from us to the world. We can't put that aside lightly."

"What statement? What is Jerusalem to you?"

"It's hard to put into words, but I believe people will feel it when they see the ceremony on Sunday."

"There may be people dead on Sunday because of this. You may be dead. Esther Fisher, too."

"Kamal, if I believe on Saturday night that there's a chance of that, then there'll be no ceremony on Sunday."

"Why wait until then? Nothing will change in two days."

"Everything may change in two days. All I can tell you is that as a result of what's been happening at the United Nations in New York this week, there's action being taken at the highest level against the man you call El Condor."

'I saw you speaking on television. You didn't mention the Palestinians."

"I didn't mention anyone in particular. I was dealing with the principles we have to follow as a human race if there's to be an Earth in the future worth living in—let alone a Palestine or Jerusalem or any other place that people cherish. That's why I'm not prepared to back off readily from what we've committed ourselves to do here."

There's a pause on the line while Kamal Rashid considers this. Mark decides to shift his approach.

"Look, Kamal," he says, "I want to put a proposition to you. You're convinced that there's going to be an attack against us. I want you to try to find out how it's to be done and who's supposed to do it."

"Ha!" the response is derisive. "There's much sand in the desert, Mark Venture."

"Oh, come on, Kamal. It's not going to be the Palestinians, you're seeing

to that. And El Condor is behind it. He can't have too many agents in a place
with the kind of security that Israel's got. Will you try?"

There's another pause.

"Very well," Kamal says finally. "I'll call again tomorrow."

"Tomorrow," repeats Mark Venture.

And the conversation is over.

The Danger Escalates

Friday, 7:00 a.m. Over steaming coffee, fresh fruit, and bagels, Mark has
breakfast with Esther and the team she has assembled to manage the
logistics of the wedding. It's an all female cast: her mother, Rivka; her two
sisters, Judith and Deborah; Jenny Lovicks, who had been her companion
when they were kidnapped by terrorists; Mina Roth, now fully recovered
from injuries suffered in the bomb blast that destroyed her apartment; and
a host of volunteers, young Visioneers, mostly students, recruited by Jenny
to assist. They're working out of temporary office space, rented by Esther
for the past two months, ever since the announcement of the engagement
and wedding date.

The conversation is lively and enthusiastic, full of the excitement of the
task. Everywhere around them there are telephones, already ringing, for
international callers have no respect for time. Fax machines and copiers are
humming amid desks piled high with papers. On one wall a plan lays out
the details of seating arrangements and traffic flow for the wedding site.
They're excited to have Mark with them, though he quickly realizes that in
this setting he's merely part of the project to be managed, and he listens
appreciatively to the stories of challenges undertaken and overcome.

The only sombre note is introduced by Esther's mother, Rivka:

"We know the rumours, Mark, of possible trouble at the wedding." She
continues to speak as she moves around among everyone, deftly pouring
coffee from a pot in one hand and orange juice from a jug in the other.
"We've had our share of such calls here. It's always upsetting, of course,
but we Israelis are used to such things. The country is a sea of rumours. But
there's news on the radio this morning, and in the papers too, that it could
be serious. We're certain to get calls. What are we to tell them?"

He looks at the faces turned towards him. They are mostly young with
a zest for the life before them. Then, there's Rivka, a beautiful woman in
her late fifties with lines of determination touching the corners of her eyes
and mouth. As he looks at these women, Mark catches a glimpse, a fleeting
instance among his thoughts, of what a world of caring would be like.
Against it the black ugliness of violence spreads a deep and sordid stain.

"I can't tell you that the rumours are true or false," he says softly.
"There's good reason to be concerned, but we're doing everything we can

to ensure the safety of the day. What you can say to everyone who asks is that their well-being is our sacred trust. We won't endanger them. What I must say to you, however, is that you need to have a way at the last moment of telling people not to come, if we decide to do that."

Rivka has come up to where Mark is standing with Esther beside him. She takes each by the hand and looks deep into their eyes.

"We'll do what you say, Mark; but I can already see around you the shield of God. You will win this struggle as you have the others."

Mark embraces her and kisses her warmly on the forehead.

"Thank you, Rivka. Your courage, and that of everyone like you, is our greatest shield."

He relaxes and smiles at everyone.

"Now, I've something very important to do myself. My parents are arriving at the airport shortly from Australia. I'm going to pick them up. You'll all have an opportunity to meet them later. Keep on with your good work."

Two hours later at the Ben Gurion Airport at Tel Aviv, the sight of his father pushing a luggage cart with his mother following a few steps behind, touches Mark with a similar wave of compassion as he had felt at breakfast among the women. These are good people, for the most part untutored in the ways of the world, but willing to set out for a strange and unknown place to be with their son for his greatest celebration. Here they would move for a moment with dignitaries. At home again, they would just be Bob and Alice, sharing their memories of an adventure in Jerusalem. It's all the Bob's and Alice's, Mark murmurs to himself, in every country, on which the world so desperately depends.

They are very tired from the flight, and though bursting with curiosity to see the sights of the Holy Land, a quick return to the apartment with Mark is as much as they want for the present. Esther has arranged adjoining separate living quarters where they can have their privacy while Mark continues with his work. For the moment, however, son and parents catch a brief time to be together.

"Weddings are funny things," says Bob, over a cup of tea on the balcony. "They suck everyone up like some bloomin' great sponge, then afterwards they get squeezed out and run away."

Mark almost laughs out loud. How long is it since he's heard anything like that? His father has never credited himself with having much in the way of "book learning" but he has a profoundly healthy way of understanding life. Physically, Bob Venture had been a big man, and still is, though a little stooped now with age. He had spent almost all of his sixty-eight years working on the land in Australia, a farmer from a long line of farmers, mostly wheat and cattle. His skin is tanned hard as leather from the sun, but his still handsome face is as open as the skies that have weathered it. Alice, too, shows her years of companionship to her husband in the hard work of farm life; for the sun and labour can take its toll on the women of the land. But this morning, sipping tea on the balcony in Jerusalem, with her son, in her crisp blue cotton dress, and her hair newly "permed" for the wedding, she's a presence of quiet, good decency in a world not always well endowed that way.

"Take this place, for instance," Bob is continuing. "I dunno all the history by a long shot, but how many times have armies poured in here over the centuries, sucked up by the sponge of history, then been squeezed out at the end of it, to run away like water on the sand that's gone without a trace. Weddings are like that too. People thrown together, hopefully not fightin' too much, but just a temporary splash, and then it's gone. The young couple are left with their memories and the struggles still to come. I s'pose that's all right, but sometimes I think we ought to put more effort into keepin' the show on the road, rather than just bangin' it up at the start. I dunno. What d' you think, Mum?"

"I just know I'm happy for Mark and Esther," Alice replies, "and glad to be here with them, even for a little while. They're doing important work in the world, and it's wonderful that they've found each other to do it together. There's many would give their eye teeth for half as much. That's why the world is paying attention. With all of the vindictiveness and fighting, people everywhere still want something beautiful to believe in. Mark and Esther are doing that for them."

At that the two of them fall silent. Mark surveys them affectionately.

"Mum and Dad," he leans forward, speaking barely above a whisper, "you can never know how much it means to have your support and good sense at this time. Thank you for being here."

The phone rings. It's Kamal Rashid. Mark takes it privately on another line, while his parents prepare to rest.

"I have news," Kamal says. "It's not good for you. Nor for me, either. I don't have much time, now. There's trouble everywhere. El Condor has put word out that I turned down his help for arms and money for the Palestinians. The ones listening to that kind of talk don't want to know about the price that comes from dealing with a man like that. I have meetings to go to now to try to convince them."

"Tell them this isn't the time for stirring up trouble. They'll play right into his hands. He's only interested in escalating the conflict on both sides. Do you have any more news on his threats against Esther and me?"

"Yes. It's as I said. He doesn't back away once he's given the order. I don't have many details. I may have more later. There's to be a bomb somewhere. I don't know where. Probably at the wedding site. It may already be planted. He has agents here doing it. They're not Arabs. I don't know who they are. Probably Europeans. I have to go. My advice is still the same. Avoid this trouble and cancel the wedding."

"That's not the solution, Kamal, and you know it! Talk to your friends.

See if you can get them to help us and then we can help them. Try, Kamal, try."

"I must go," Kamal's voice is expressionless. "I will call again when I can."

The phone goes dead in Mark's hand. For a long minute he stands staring at it.

El Condor Makes His Move

Carlos Palmira is seated at the console of his communications centre. On the screens around him, eight faces look out. They're all men: white, black, Chinese, Japanese, Indian, Latin, Semitic. Grim-faced and hard-eyed, they stare from their electronic boxes.

"So," Palmira is saying, "it seems that in the last twenty-four hours the International Trust and Credit Corporation has become the centre of a lot of interest. I've heard your reports. Now here's what I want you to do. There's to be no panic. You understand me? Nothing to suggest we've got anything to hide. That's the first point. The second is to remind some people who they're dealing with here.

"It's time to call in our markers. We haven't worked all these years getting into the pockets of officials for nothing. They need a clear message from us, all at once. If they move to prosecute now the smell will go all the way up to the highest level. Big heads will roll. Your job in the next eight hours is to make that clear. I don't care how you do it. If you need to demonstrate the consequences of crossing us, go ahead. A few examples will spread quickly around the network. Do I make myself clear? Are there any questions?"

"Yes, one here." It's the Chinese who has spoken. "We can deal with our own local operations, but this sudden interest in our affairs has an international push to it. What can be done to stop that?"

"I have a strategy," Palmira replies. "Within forty-eight hours the international community will have a situation on its hands that will make interest in us less pressing. That'll give you more time to defuse the situation locally. For today, just keep the lid on. Next week the world will be different. Now, if there are no further questions, this session is over. I'll hear your reports in eight hours."

The faces are gone.

Palmira punches the intercom.

"What's happening on that call to Larry Porter?" he snaps.

"We can't locate him, sir," a woman's voice replies. "No one seems to know where he is."

"What do you mean, no one knows where he is? He's got a pager. Why haven't you called him on that?"

"We've tried everything, sir, but we just haven't been able to reach him."

"Well, you haven't tried hard enough," Palmira is barking now. "This ·is a multi-billion dollar operation and I can't make a phone call. Put out an alert! Get people looking for him and have him phone me within half an hour."

"Yes, sir." A pause, then: "We have Mrs. Ramos waiting for you on the line."

"What does she want this time? All right, put her through. But get me Larry Porter, d'you hear?"

"Yes, sir."

Elvira comes up on the central screen. She presents a marked contrast to her last appearance. In New York, it's only 5:00 a.m. and Elvira obviously hasn't put herself together for the day. She's wearing slacks and blouse, her hair is uncombed, and what make-up has made it to her face is streaked and uneven from hasty application.

"Carlos!" It's almost a scream. "What's happening? I've been trying to get through to you for hours, but those bitches in your office said you couldn't be disturbed. I've been up all night. Ever since those men came here at midnight. Carlos, I've had some agents here asking me questions. They wanted to know about you."

"Elvira, if you have something to tell me, you know you're to call on a business line."

"Carlos, don't you understand? I'm scared. I want to know what's happening."

"Elvira, my dear, you should relax and enjoy your holiday. Do you understand me? New York is a wonderful city for a holiday, all of the theatre and art, everything you like. Don't worry about business. Everything is fine here. Why don't you have some breakfast and call me from the office later. Now I must go. Goodbye, Elvira."

"Carlos . . . !"

But he cuts her off and snarls into the intercom, "What do you mean by putting anyone through to me on an open line?"

"But . . . I thought, Mrs. Ramos . . . ," the secretary's voice is uncertain, quavering.

"Especially Mrs. Ramos!" explodes Palmira. "Now, what's happening with that call to Porter? Have you found him yet?"

"No, sir, we're still trying."

"Why is it that everyone around me is always trying, but never doing? It's not even six o'clock in the morning yet in New York. How many places can he be? If you don't get something on him in the next fifteen minutes, I'll have the hide of all of you. Do you hear me?"

Without waiting for an answer, Palmira snaps off the intercom and punches another code into the console.

"Wolfgang, is the Jerusalem project on track?"

"Yes, sir, everything's under control."

"For once someone tells me something's working well! Who's handling it?"

"Harrigan."

"Good, he knows his business. It has to be flexible, but we've got to keep it under control at all times. He knows that, doesn't he?"

"Yes, sir. He's got it worked out. We can brief you when you're ready."

"Okay, that's good. I'll let you know. I've got other things to deal with right now. But you keep on top of it, Wolfgang. I'm holding you accountable. This is a big play. It's got to be effective and we've got to make sure the blame sticks in the right place."

A Developing Situation

In Jerusalem, it's now 2:00 p.m. and Mark Venture is in the office of Colonel Aaron Greenberg, chief of security operations for Israeli Special Services. The two men have met before, when he had interrogated Mark and Esther after she was released by the terrorists six months ago. Given Mark's rise in prominence since then, Greenberg is a little more friendly this time, but only marginally so. Though clearly impressed by the world attention Mark is bringing to Jerusalem, the hard-edged colonel is irritated that it comes with a high security risk.

"So it seems we have a developing situation here, Mr. Venture," he ᵧs. "You've got several hundred important people gathering together ᴊnd the word's out that someone intends to blow you up. Not a pleasant scenario. It seems that you and Miss Fisher attract this kind of thing. Tell me, have you considered a different line of work?"

"Have you, colonel?" Mark shoots back. "Now come on, man, we're both doing things that invite risks. What we need to do here is work together to manage what you call a developing situation. Esther has kept you informed all along, so we know that the usual security checks are in place. We now have to focus on this new information about a bomb."

"And all we have to go on there is the word of Kamal Rashid," Greenberg replies. "You've never clarified for me, Mr. Venture, your relationship with this man. He's not on our list of Palestinian terrorists, you know, because of his benign behaviour in the past. From what we know of him he's perfectly capable of engineering an attack himself. This bomb rumour could be just that—a ruse to make us look in the wrong place."

"No, you're wrong about Rashid, Colonel," says Mark. "He's got a lot better understanding now of what will work best for his cause. He doesn't want the Palestinians mixed up in this. He's trying to warn us off."

"Then perhaps you should take his advice and cancel the ceremony."

"With the whole world watching? That's a strange suggestion coming from an Israeli. What conclusion would people draw from that? Since when has Israel backed down because of threats from the outside?"

"Ah, but that's because the very life of the country is at stake," Greenberg eyes Mark shrewdly.

"Well here, colonel," Mark returns the stare, eye to eye, "the life of the world is at stake. Why do you think so many people are paying attention to this? It's not because Mark Venture and Esther Fisher are some kind of celebrities getting married. There's some of that, true, but that's not the real reason. No, it's because we're giving people hope. Hope that if they stand up for a vision grounded in decency and respect for life, then that's the best way of ensuring that it will happen. Where we need your help right now is keeping the vision alive."

"You've got some strange bedfellows here." The hint of a smile plays at the edge of Greenberg's tight-set lips. "An Israeli soldier, a Palestinian terrorist, and an Australian adventurer. What sort of a vision can we offer the world?"

"The best," Mark rejoins swiftly, "the one that's buried deepest in the human psyche. It goes back a million years before cultural divisions were invented by over-active brains. It says simply that cooperation and survival are the first order of life. We now have to show what the truth of that means for a 21st century race of technologically powerful human beings."

At that moment, Greenberg's intercom buzzes.

"Yes?" he says.

"There's a call for Mr. Venture," says a secretary.

"It must be Peter Hemphill from the U.N.," says Mark. "I left this number at the hotel in case he called."

"Put it through," Greenberg tells the voice.

Mark picks up the phone on Greenberg's desk.

"Mark Venture here."

"Mark, it's Peter Hemphill. I gather you're at Israeli security?"

"That's right. Have you got some news?"

"Yes. There's been a sudden turn of developments."

"Just a minute, Peter. I want to put you on the speaker so Colonel Aaron Greenberg can hear this. He's head of security for Israeli Special Services. Is that okay?"

"Certainly, I'm sure he'll be interested in this."

Mark nods to Greenberg and pushes the speaker button.

"Okay, Peter, go ahead. We're listening."

"The F.B.I. have picked up a fellow by the name of Larry Porter. They've suspected for some time that he's been running Palmira's drug operations in the U.S. Now, he's confirmed it himself. It seems he's talking so fast no one can keep up with him."

"Larry Porter?" Mark muses aloud. "I've heard that name before."

"No doubt," says Peter, "he made a lot of news four or five years ago. He was one of those hell-fire and brimstone television evangelists. His network covered the whole North American continent. It was called 'The Kingdom Comes'. Rather clever, eh? The only problem was the Reverend Larry got himself confused with the King he was preaching about. He started to shoot a little crack on the side and entertain the ladies after hours. When he was finally nailed for it, the press gave him the usual brief publicity, and then the congregation buried him."

"And now he's surfaced again as Palmira's drug king?" asks Mark.

"Yes, seems he has a penchant to look for kingdoms to rule. Of course, I don't have any real details yet. The interrogation's going on right now. What's of more interest to the U.N. is the international machinery that Palmira's got set up to handle the cash flow from dozens of little kings like Larry Porter across the world. The operation's called the International Trust and Credit Corporation. I suspect it's high on corporation, meaning Palmira, and rather short on trust and credit—but there you have it. I'm sure Colonel Greenberg knows about them."

"Yes," Greenberg responds, "there's a branch in Tel Aviv . . . "

It seems that Greenberg is going to say more, but he stops short. Mark eyes him quizzically, then steps into the silence.

"Peter, where does that leave us with Palmira right now?" he asks. "Is anyone going to move on him, do you think?"

"I don't know. It depends what the day brings. I'll stay here at my listening post for as long as I can before I have to leave to catch my flight to Israel. I gather there's still a wedding going on there for me to attend?"

Mark looks at Greenberg as he replies.

"Yes, there certainly is. Since I last spoke to you we've had a warning about a possible bombing. I'm working with Colonel Greenberg now to contain that situation."

"All right, Mark. I'll get back to you again before I leave—sooner, if something breaks. Oh, and by the way, there's one more piece, you'll be interested to know about."

"What's that?"

"Elvira Ramos, you know, the femme fatale who turned up at your party at Woodlands, she's just skipped out of New York."

"Heading back to Switzerland?"

"No, Colombia, I believe."

"Oh? Is there anything significant to that?"

"Who knows," Peter sounds diplomatically resigned. "The F.B.I. were talking to her last night. Could be that she's smelled a rat in El Condor's eyrie and is now looking for another nest to camp in."

"Peter," Mark laughs bitterly. "Your imagery is marvellous. But if the birds and animals had a choice, I bet they wouldn't want to be associated with Palmira or his girlfriend."

"I suspect you're right, old boy." Peter ends the conversation. "I'll speak to you again soon."

Greenberg disconnects the speaker phone and sits strangely silent for several moments staring at Mark.

"So," he says finally. "It seems that you're in the middle of a rather tangled web."

"Nothing so sticky," replies Mark, " that we can't cut our way out of it, and tear the whole evil structure down as we go."

"Perhaps." The brief trace of humour that had come to Greenberg's eyes before the phone call from New York, has now gone. In its place he fixes a cold, hard stare on Mark Venture. "You need to be careful what you define as evil, Mr. Venture. You may be surprised at some of the other strange bedfellows you find along the way." Now his tone changes again and moves to military preciseness.

" All right, if there's the possibility of a bomb out there, then we'd better look for it. I'm going to seal the area off right now and keep it that way until after the ceremony. We'll search under every rock and blade of grass, but do it as quietly as possible so as not to arouse too much speculation. However, there's bound to be some fall-out. I take it that if you get any more information from your various contacts, or if you change your mind about going ahead, you'll let me know immediately?"

"Of course, colonel. And look, I want you to know how much I appreciate what you're doing here."

"I'm a soldier, Mr. Venture. I do my job. I'm not out to change the world, but I want to keep the piece I'm responsible for under control."

Mark nods and moves to leave.

"Oh, by the way," the colonel says to him at the door, "*Mazeltov* to both of you for Sunday. It means good luck."

Mark nods at him, smiles and leaves.

The Rehearsal

An hour later at 3:00 p.m. Mark and Esther gather with the rest of the wedding party at the amphitheatre outside the Old City walls where the ceremony is to be held. This will be the only opportunity for a rehearsal. It's also Mark's first chance to see the site and get a measure of the operation to be managed.

Esther has chosen well. Nestled in the Hinnon Valley skirting Mount Zion, the amphitheatre is on the site of the Old Sultan's Pool, named for Sulerman the Magnificent, who built the walls of Jerusalem in the 16th century. The whole area is about 200 metres long and 70 metres wide. At the northern end a stone stage with acoustical shell has been set up for outdoor performances. Here, against the backdrop of the walls and with the Old City of Jerusalem looking down, Mark and Esther will make their vows to each other.

At the moment, however, all is preparation. Greenberg has moved swiftly. A work team of soldiers dressed in fatigues is setting up barricades while another squad moves around, searching the area. There's nothing obtrusive about the operation, and anyone who didn't know the significance of the action would see nothing unusual.

The group on stage pays no attention to the soldiers. They've been assembled under the firm tutelage of Rabbi Ruvain Ben Sabbath. The first time Mark and Esther had seen the rabbi, the situation had been much different—when he conducted the funeral service for young Joshua Roth, tragically killed in the bomb blast last October. Now, six months later, with a new bomb threat facing him, Mark winces involuntarily at the memory.

The rabbi, however, is moving full stride with what he knows is his opportunity to orchestrate the ceremony of a lifetime. It would be challenge enough to preside over a strictly Jewish wedding with the whole world looking on, but here he's faced with an ecumenical event on an outdoor stage with several thousand people expected to come along as spectators and participants.

Not the least of the rabbi's challenges is his Christian counterpart with whom he will share the role of celebrant. The Reverend Gordon Ringthorpe has never been one to take a backseat in a performance. He and Mark had gone to school together in Brisbane in Australia where Gordon had been known as the Ring of Fire. As a teenage impresario he had produced rock concerts that were legendary among a whole generation of Brisbane youth. When he later discovered his vocation to the Anglican priesthood, the musical fire in his soul, rather than being extinguished, had been fanned with spiritual fervour. The result, twenty years later, was a musical ministry for Christ that had packed tens of thousands of hand-clapping converts into football stadiums and cricket grounds all across Australia. When thinking about who to ask to officiate for his world-stage wedding in Jerusalem, Mark hadn't taken more than a moment before picking up the phone to call his old friend, Gordon Ringthorpe.

If this were not challenge enough for the good rabbi, Mark had gone one step further and asked Mohammed Hussein to be his Best Man. Now the three faiths of Jerusalem that had many times torn the city apart over the centuries, would be presented for the world to see in the Wedding of the Future—a grand global celebration of the Visioneers.

The Reverend Gordon Ringthorpe is tall and lean. His long, hungry face, huge arm span (wide enough, according to Mark's father, Bob, to circle the fat lady's dancing daughters), and his long, loping stride give him the appearance of the world's largest stick insect, as some of his less kind associates have dubbed him. Dressed today in green corduroy slacks and sweater of many colours, he seems well content to maintain the image. This is his first visit to the Holy City and he leaps onto the stage fresh from a feast of sightseeing.

"Jerusalem the Golden!" he shouts. "My word, rabbi, the very stones sing with spirit. What a privilege! What an opportunity to present this to the world in the love of Mark and Esther! Friends, " and his long arms seem to embrace them all, "this is going to be a smash!"

That sets the mood for the rehearsal. Esther and the rabbi have been over it many times previously. Now with good-humoured prompting and questioning from the lively reverend, the planning assumes new life. The rest of the wedding party also catches the spirit. Deborah Segal and Mohammed Hussein as Matron of Honour and Best Man confidently assume their support roles to bride and groom. The two sets of parents, just getting to know one another, are light-hearted and friendly. Bob Venture and Esther's father, Tevi, while hardly understanding half of what the other says, have already struck a common bond as patriarchs of the new order. They offer their Australian and Israeli witticisms to whoever will listen, with future visions of the Bob and Tevi comedy team on international television. Two others complete the party, Natan Goldman, the full-throated cantor who will sing the Hebrew Prayers and blessings, and "Momma" Theresa, already well known to television audiences around the world as the irrepressible spirit of the Visioneers. Her role will be to engage the audience in the amphitheatre to become full participants in the event, celebrating with Mark and Esther, and with the whole watching world, the spirit and energy of what is happening here.

On the sidelines, Esther's other sister, Judith Kaplanski, is working with Bill Bates to manage the public relations and media. Already, an assembly of more than a hundred international journalists and reporters have converged on the city for the event, and many are milling around on the edge of today's rehearsal, anxious to probe for their unique angles and perspectives. Judith and Bill are holding them at bay while the others go through their paces on stage.

At 4:00 p.m. the rabbi and the reverend wrap it up.

"Friends," says Rabbi Ben Sabbath, "in a little while, the eve of the Sabbath will begin. With the lighting of the candles in homes all across the country, Jewish people secure for themselves the space to be with God in quiet reflection and prayer. For our party here it will be the most precious of Sabbath's, the quiet prelude before the greatest celebration of two precious and unique lives joining together to become a greater force for peace and love in the world. Until we meet here again on Sunday, *Shabbat Shalom*, and the peace of God go with you."

"Yes, and may we go now," adds the Reverend Ringthorpe, "with the prayer of St. Francis in our hearts. Come, let's join hands here together and say the words after me: 'Lord, make us the instruments of your peace.

Where there is hatred, let us sow love. Where there is injury, pardon. Where there is death, life. Where despair, hope. Where there is darkness, light. And where there is sadness, joy.' Until we meet here again, friends, on Sunday, the great day of Christian celebration, may God protect you and keep you safe, here in his holiest of cities, the great and glorious, Jerusalem. Amen."

With that, the small band breaks up. The family members are to meet again in two hours at the home which Esther and her parents are sharing in Jerusalem, for a Shabbat dinner. As they move away, the ring of reporters, no longer prepared to be held at bay by Bill Bates and Judith Kaplanski, close in. Cameras flash, microphones thrust forward, film crews focus. Mark and Esther move quietly, smiling through the throng. A formal press conference has been set for tomorrow evening, and the reporters don't expect to get much comment before then, but still, they push for advantage. A few of Colonel Greenberg's security people are on hand to help clear the way to the waiting cars. Questions hang in the air:

"Hey, Mark and Esther, what next for you and the world?"

"How does it feel to be this close?"

"Is Jerusalem ready for this?"

"What are the soldiers looking for?"

"Where are the Visioneers?"

"Is there a bomb threat?"

"Hey, come on guys, what can you tell us? The world wants to know."

At the car, Mark turns and says:

"Thank you all for your interest. It's wonderful to see you here. We'll answer all questions at the press conference tomorrow. We look forward to having you at our wedding. Until then, enjoy Jerusalem, it's a wonderful city."

To a further barrage of questions and camera flashes, the cars drive off, leaving Colonel Greenberg and his men to secure the area.

A World of Shadows

Back at his apartment before going on to dinner, Mark receives his next call from Kamal Rashid.

"So you're determined to continue with this?" the now familiar thrust of the Palestinian begins.

"Yes," Mark replies, "unless you have some definitive evidence why we shouldn't."

"In a world of shadows, Mark Venture, you don't get definitive evidence. You get suggestions, glimpses, illusions, lies, and half truths. Nothing definitive."

"Then I'll pick my way among the shadows as best I can, Kamal. Do you have any further news for me?"

"There's word that El Condor is in trouble. It's been impossible all day to reach any of his main offices, either here in the Middle East or around the world. But we do have evidence that he's been dealing with the Israelis. The International Trust and Credit Corporation in Tel Aviv is the centre of it. Now that my associates here see that he's not to be trusted, they're more willing to listen to me."

"Do they know he's planning to implicate the Palestinians in an attack at the wedding ceremony?"

"Yes, I've told them all. Everyone's trying to find out what they can, but there's no further news yet."

"You know that Israeli security has sealed the area off?" Mark tells him. "They're searching with a fine tooth comb for a bomb. There's no way anything's going to get past them."

"Ha! You're more foolish than I thought to put your trust in the Israelis!"

"Listen, Kamal. I'm putting my trust in a lot of people. You included. I'm assuming you won't let me down. The stakes are too high here for anything less than total effort. If we work together we can get through. I've told Greenberg what you're doing. Why don't you contact him direct and coordinate your effort."

"I'd rather go to bed with a serpent."

"Kamal, the only time I have any doubt about our ability to get through this, is when I hear stuff like that. I don't want to be the meat in the sandwich between you and Greenberg. Why can't you trust each other?"

"Some things just aren't possible, even for you, Mark Venture. Now I must go. I'll contact you again at noon tomorrow."

The Shabbat Dinner

When Mark arrives with his parents at Esther's apartment, the sun has already set and the Sabbath has begun. A hush has descended over the Jewish sections of the city as people, even those with minimal commitments to a religious life, participate in the ancient traditions of the Sabbath, to rest and refresh themselves on the seventh day.

Inside the Fisher home, the Ventures feel themselves graciously welcomed into the peace of the family circle. Esther, Tevi and Rivka, Deborah and Judith with their husbands and four young children, all gather to receive their guests, quietly murmuring *shabbat shalom*, as they shake their hands or gently embrace them.

The Sabbath candles are already lit and stand together in simple silver candlesticks, the table spread for the meal. There they'll burn, symbols of spirit, until they're fully spent at the end of the evening.

Tevi asks everyone to gather in the living room for a simple Sabbath service before the meal. Standing beside Esther, Mark feels her small hand slide gently into his. He draws her closer, beginning to feel now the strength of the bond linking their lives together.

"'*Ve yehe erev ve yehe boker yom sheshe*,'" Tevi has begun, reading from the *Siddur*, the book of Shabbat Services. "'And it was evening and it was morning on the sixth day. Thus the heavens and the earth were finished, and all their host. By the seventh day, God had completed his work which he had made, and rested on the seventh day from all his work in which he had been engaged.'" Tevi is quietly reading in Hebrew, then pausing, and translating into English. "'Then God blessed the seventh day and hallowed it, because on it he rested from all his work which he had created.'"

Tevi closes the book and continues quietly speaking to the group. "We, too, like God, have been busy this week creating the coming celebration for Esther and Mark, so now it's fitting that we rest from these labours and share this Shabbat dinner as we bring our two families together.

"In honour of this special occasion I ask Esther, to say the blessing over our Sabbath bread."

Esther embraces Tevi and kisses him gently on both cheeks as she goes to the table, and looks down on the coiled loaf of golden yellow egg bread, the challah.

"*Baruch ata Adonai*," she sings the blessing in the sweet clear voice of one who has grown up with the centuries of tradition. "Blessed art thou, O Lord our God. *Elohanu melech ha olam*. King of the Universe. *Ha motze lechem min ha aretz*. Who hath brought forth bread from the earth."

Esther breaks the bread into small pieces around the plate. Tevi is continuing:

"Now for the blessing of the wine."

Tevi goes to the table and takes the bottle of sweet red wine, the Mogen David, and holds it up for the family to see. He sings the blessing in Hebrew:

"*Baruch ata Adonai, Elohanu melech ha olam, boray pree ha goffen.*"

"Blessed art thou, O Lord our God, King of the Universe, who created the fruit of the vine," Tevi says the blessing in English. He pours the wine, a little into each glass, and together he and Esther serve the bread and wine to the others.

When all have been served, Tevi continues to speak to them:

"We have blessed and drunk the wine, and blessed and eaten the bread, and we are together now as a new family stretching across the world. We can thank the Lord, too, for granting us the life and the sustenance, the well-being, and the health to be together at this time for the most precious of occasions, the marriage of a daughter and a son. This ranks highest among our joyful events, for it speaks to the essence of all our traditions, the celebration of peace and love. Esther and Mark will go one step further on Sunday and show to the whole world how not only two lives but two faiths can be brought together in love and peace. It seems to me that for too

long the world has been fearful and suspicious of such bonds. I admit, that
I, too, have had such fears. But as I look at them tonight and search in my
heart for what I know matters most, I see only richness and blessing coming
from this union.

"So now, could we all join hands here before we eat our meal together
and sing our lovely Jewish song *Hevenu Shalom Aleichem*—Let us Bring
Peace. It's a simple message. We ask the angels of peace to bless us. The
Jewish people have always loved peace. We want it in our homes, and on
the street, and everywhere we go. We want the weak and the strong, the
small nations and the large, to live together in harmony. We look forward
with great hope to the day when there'll be peace all over the world. As
Mark and Esther through their love and work bring that day closer, let us
sing together, *Hevenu Shalom Aleichem.*"

Tevi begins slowly in a rich baritone to sing the haunting melody, then
the others join in, picking up the tempo, raising their voices to a fast paced
crescendo, then suddenly letting it drop away, as they begin slowly to step
to the words, then as the tempo rises, to break into a dance, picking it up,
until voice and feet of all the bodies in the room are joined in a great
dancing chorus as mothers and fathers, sons and daughters, husbands and
wives, sing and dance for peace among us, and with us, and upon us
forever.

At the end of it, breathless and excited, Bob Venture, looking taller and
straighter now than he has been all day, puts one arm around Tevi's
shoulders, and waves with the other to everyone in the room, saying, "If
there's one thing Mum and I have learned, by comin' all these thousands
of kilometres, it's that this great argumentative, contrary place we call the
world can be a decent happy family if we give it half a chance. So *shalom,
shalom, shalom* to all of you, and great bonza good luck, too!"

With that everyone sets to with a willingness to load their plates, buffet
style, with the meal of baked chicken, corned beef, chopped liver, cucumber
salad, hard boiled eggs and thick slices of full grained bread. On the side,
a large steaming pot of chicken soup, loaded with diced onions and carrots
and spiced up with parsley, dill, and pepper, sits bubbling, waiting for the
adventurous. At the end comes the strudel. Oh, the marvellous strudel!
Somehow Rivka had found time to lovingly roll, pull, and stretch the dough
until it was thin enough to see through. Loaded with plum preserves,
chopped nuts, bread crumbs, raisins, shredded apples, and a large table-
spoon of cinnamon mixed with half a cup of sugar, it was cut into diagonal
slices and baked into golden brown sticky magnificence that now comes
piping hot from the oven where it has been left warm, ready for serving.

At the end of the evening, as Mark and Bob and Alice pull on their coats
to leave, the memory of the shared time and laughter clings to them, along
with the strudel, like a warm cocoon of friendship that has already set fast.
As they leave under the clear, star-filled Jerusalem sky, it does seem, indeed,

that peace can be, must be, will be upon them and all people everywhere forever.

El Condor Tightens His Grip

When the phone rings back in the apartment, Mark looks at his watch and sees that it's 11:00 p.m.

Peter Hemphill is calling from New York.

"Hello, Mark," his voice is calm and steady as usual. "We're getting to the end of a long working day here. I'm about ready to pull out and head for the airport. All being well, I should be there in time to join you for the reception tomorrow night. The Israeli government is still going ahead with that, I assume?"

"Yes," Mark replies, "the Minister of Culture is hosting. It's very good of them to do it."

"They won't get anything but brownie points. You and Esther are the talk of the world. Seems I can't catch a news report here from any country without hearing about the Wedding of the Future. How's all that going for you?"

"It's still on course."

"What about the bomb threat?"

"That's still there. The security people have got the whole place sealed off now. As far as I know, they've still found no trace of a bomb. What's your news? What did the day bring for Palmira?"

"Not as much damage as I had hoped. This morning it seemed as if we might have had a shut-down order coming out against his international banking operation in several European countries at least. But by late morning here and close of business there, things seem to have changed. There's a report, too, on the London evening news about the body of a prominent British financier found floating in the Thames, and another one from Paris of a French politician blown up with a car bomb. Both can be linked to Palmira's International Trust and Credit Corporation. I don't know, but it seems to me that Palmira's network is beginning to give out some hard messages. It's going to take a lot of political guts to blow the lid on this operation. Nothing's likely to happen now until after the week-end. It looks like you're going to go into your wedding celebration with El Condor still in his eyrie watching you."

"What about Larry Porter? You said earlier he was incriminating Palmira, at least in drug trafficking."

"Yes, well I haven't heard much more on that, either. As far as I know, they've got him locked up. They'd need to, anyway, for his own protection. But I get the impression that the Justice Department here wants to slow down a bit on that, too."

"Do you think Palmira's got something on some people there?"

"Given the way he operates, it's almost certain he has."

There's a pause in the conversation. Then Peter comes on again.

"Look, Mark, I know how you're feeling. I have to leave now, but I've got people here who'll be in touch with me twenty-four hours a day. If anything new comes in, they'll let me know. We'll review the situation together when I get to Jerusalem tomorrow."

"Okay, Peter, you have a good flight. Thanks for calling."

"Goodbye, Mark, and *shalom* from everyone here at the U.N."

"Yeah, Peter, *shalom*."

With the Visioneers

Saturday morning dawns sunny and warm with the promise for the weather pattern to hold for the week-end. At 9 o'clock Mark picks Esther up at her apartment. They're on their way to the highlight of their pre-wedding events—a celebration with the Visioneers. All week their friends have been arriving, largely unnoticed by the news media, and quietly registering in private accommodation arranged by Esther in a guest house near the village of Ein Karem on the outskirts of the city.

They swing into the curving driveway and pull up before a rambling stone building cut into the hillside among a cluster of olive and cypress trees. All is quiet as they arrive. The peace of the Sabbath morning rests unbroken save for the occasional motor vehicle passing unseen along neighbouring roads.

Their arrival, however, has not gone unnoticed. Before they reach the entrance to the lobby, a bustling figure of a woman comes out to greet them. She recognizes Esther immediately.

"*Shabbot shalom*, Miss Fisher," comes the cheery greeting. "And good morning, sir. You must be Mr. Venture. I'm so pleased that I can meet you personally and wish you *mazeltov* for tomorrow. It's so exciting. Everyone's talking about it. And your friends—oh dear, what a group! They're all here, waiting for you. We're very honoured that you chose our guest house for them. Come along, please, this way, they're all waiting for you. I'm so pleased to meet you all, the Visioneers, staying here with us. It's such an honour!"

The good lady keeps bubbling along in her personal stream of associations as she leads the way through an open courtyard to the back of the building, where suddenly a twin panorama opens before them. Below, in the distance, the picturesque village with its rich collection of Christian monuments lies nestled snugly in the Ein Karem Valley. Immediately before them, an expansive paved terrace stretches away on both sides bordered by low stone walls and an abundance of evergreen shrubs. Spread around the terrace are small wicker tables with glass tops covered with baskets of fruit, cheese, bread, and rich desserts. Easy chairs of every design and comfort level are scattered around the terrace in random and rambling array among the tables.

All this Esther and Mark see at a glance, but only for a moment as backdrop to the assembly of people waiting to greet them. They're all here! The original band of Visioneers, first assembled in the Visioneering Room, seemingly so long ago, but now gathered together again, here, today, in Jerusalem, the splendid entourage for tomorrow's nuptials.

Who can say who should be mentioned first among such a group? They're a seamless pattern of personality. They come forward as a wave to greet their friends. In a moment it's a spontaneous celebration of laughter, hugs, kisses, handshakes, backslapping, and excitement. Just as Charles Dickens originally pictured them, they're here, fresh from adventure and enterprise around the world:

M'buta Mutsandu, in his white robes, from Africa; Irene Henshaw peeping over her schoolroom glasses, from Aberdeen; General Soulière and his chestful of medals, from Paris; Karl Ibsen, Norwegian skin bronzed from his sojourn in Africa; Jeremy Hiscox, rumpled in erudite tweeds, from Cambridge; Sally Hearst, fresh-faced from high school in New Zealand; Nicholai Andropov, young and sad, from Moscow; Daniel Thomas long hair longer, still carrying his Welsh spirit in Russia; Boris Gunther, big boned and rustic, back in Germany; Junichi Yakasawa, all business and steady, from Tokyo; Carmen Santander, dark Spanish eyes still dancing in India; Bill Bates, relaxed and expansive in the best American style; George Cardinal in his irremovable buckskin jacket, from Canada via South America; "Momma" Theresa Romano, the world's favourite mother, from Italy; Lin Yuen, bespectacled optimist out of Bejing, China; Mohammed Hussein, steady friend from Jordan; Indira Murti, silk-saried, with Carmen, from India. All are here, the original assembly of friends, except for Luis Valdez, still mourned and greatly loved, but here, too, in spirit and memory.

For more than an hour Mark and Esther move among their friends, hearing their stories, sharing their triumphs and set-backs. It's a whirlwind tale of seized opportunity, striving hard to put heart and hope back into people, ordinary folk achieving the exceptional. Now with the triumph of their greatest week—Mark's coup at the United Nations and tomorrow's fairy-tale wedding—all is expectancy and promise. And they're here, each one, to show their unquestioning love for one another and the great work they're doing together.

For Mark and Esther it can be only a short visit, an interlude in the crowded run-up of scenes before the main event. But for both, nothing will be more precious than this brief time with those with whom the adventure began.

Esther speaks for both of them as they prepare to leave:

"Dearest friends. What can we say, but thank you. Thank you for being who you are and for coming here to be with us. When we began, who could see where exactly we might go? Visioneers and adventurers all of us, brought together, and set loose to create a new reality, now unfolding and coming together in a parade of hope for the whole world. What we've already done can never be taken away. What we can still do together, and with the millions who have been touched by our dream, will be the wonder of the new millennium.

"Thank you again for coming. God keep and care for you as precious souls. With all our hearts, from both of us to you, *shalom!*"

Mark and Esther leave quickly without a further word and head back along the quiet streets into Jerusalem.

A New Twist of Danger

Mark drops Esther off for morning services with her family at the temple. He's back at his apartment when the phone rings at noon with the expected call from Kamal Rashid.

"You must stop now, Mark Venture," comes the warning. "It's out of control. It's too dangerous. Your safety can't be ensured. It will be a terrible tragedy. Cancel the ceremony now, while you still have time."

"Come on, Kamal," Mark rejoins, "why do you always start out this way? Why don't you tell me what you're doing to strike at the core of this business rather than giving me these doleful warnings? What new information have you got? Who are these people we're supposed to be afraid of? How are they going to strike? How can we get to them first? How do we stop them and not run away from them? Give me some facts, man, not more warnings!"

"Facts!" the voice almost shrieks back at him. "You want facts among a forest of lies. I told you before, it's all shadows and illusions, but one thing is clear: the wedding is going to be attacked."

"How?" demands Mark. "There's no bomb planted. Nothing's been found. The area's sealed. Nothing can get past security. How are we to be attacked?"

"We've been told," Kamal snaps back, "that because of the added security you've put in, the attack will now be by snipers."

"How do you know that? Where do you get this stuff from? First it's a bomb, now it's snipers! How do I know this whole thing isn't just a cruel hoax you're concocting?"

"You don't know, Mark Venture. But how much are you prepared to risk? I've called you as a friend. Now you insult me. Why do you do that?"

"All right, Kamal," Mark eases his tone. "I've been pushing for a long time to hear you call me a friend. Now, you've said it, and I believe you.

Who are these snipers? How many of them are there? Where will they be?"

"We've learned that the operation will be handled by a man named Harrigan. He's worked for El Condor before, and we know he's somewhere here in Jerusalem. If he's in charge, he'll probably use two or three others. No more than that. It's too hard to control."

"All right, now we're getting somewhere. I'm going to tell Greenberg what you've just told me. And now I want you to listen to what I say. I believe you're trying to help us. And I believe there's a real danger out there. But if we're to head it off, this cloak and dagger stuff has got to stop. Do you understand what I mean? I'm relying on you and Greenberg to protect us. I can't be the middleman any longer. I'm not going to be here to take any more of your calls, probably until after midnight. And I don't want to talk to you on a mobile phone because this fellow Harrigan is probably listening for that. The only thing that makes sense is for you to work with Greenberg. Now will you do that, Kamal? Will you call him?"

"I've told you before," Kamal's voice is trembling with passion, "I won't call any murdering Israeli!"

"Then give me your number and I'll get him to call you."

"Ha! Do you think I would give my telephone number to Israeli security? They'd be crawling all over us in minutes."

"Well, blast it, Kamal!" Mark explodes into the telephone. "There's got to be a way out of this. The safety of Esther and me and God knows how many other people depends on you and Greenberg working together."

"Your safety depends on yourself," Kamal retorts. "Call off the wedding."

"I won't do that," Mark replies. "It's no solution."

"Then may Allah decide for you!" says Kamal. And the phone line goes dead.

Mark immediately calls Greenberg. He tells him Kamal's information.

"So when we don't find a bomb, the enemy becomes snipers," Greenberg is cynical, suspicious.

"Look, colonel, I know what you're thinking," says Mark, "but I believe Kamal is desperate to avoid trouble here. He's not making this up. What do you know about this fellow Harrigan?"

"Oh, I know about him, all right. But I don't know where he is. We'll put out an alert. But I tell you, if we haven't got something more definite by the end of the day, then I think you'd better call this thing off. That'll be my recommendation to my superiors, too. Israel doesn't want a black eye here, either."

"Colonel, if the world depended on good people giving in to bullies for fear of black eyes, we'd be in a pretty sorry state."

"We are in a pretty sorry state," Greenberg replies calmly. "But as I told you before, I'm not out to save the world. I'm just interested in keeping my corner clean. Now I have to get on with it."

"You do that, colonel," says Mark. "I'll talk to you later."

Mark puts down the phone and looks up to see his father, Bob, standing in the doorway, looking at him.

"I wasn't listening, son," he says, "but I gather you've got a few crocodiles crawlin' around in the pond."

Mark nods.

"Well, if you're in there with 'em," Bob says, crinkling his eyes and rubbing his hand across his chin, "the only thing to do is keep swimmin' quietly toward the bank, and count on the laws of nature to get you out."

Mark smiles at his father.

"Thanks, Dad," he says. "As usual, you're right. Now I've got some thinking to do. I'm going down to the wedding site. Will you and Mum be all right?"

"Sure, you go ahead. We're goin' out to see Jerusalem. We'll leave the crocodiles alone."

A Powerful Encounter

As he comes down into the amphitheatre, Mark sees right away that Colonel Greenberg has posted a guard around the whole perimeter. Considerable activity is going on as workmen bring in special seating for the invited guests. A huge multi-coloured canvas pavilion has been erected to one side of the bandshell where the wedding meal will be served to guests following the ceremony. The thousands of other spectators expected to attend will be able to obtain food and refreshments from a line of stalls set up market style along the other edge of the field below the Jerusalem Brigade Road. In the centre of the open area in front of the bandshell and behind the special seating, a large square is roped off, which will be cleared for dancing following the ceremony. As he looks out over the preparations, Mark sees in his mind's eye the whole expanse filled with people and the human energy generated by the event they've come to celebrate. In twenty-four hours this will be the reality unless the tragedy that Kamal Rashid is predicting comes to intervene.

Mark's mind is dark with this last thought as he clears himself through the security check point, barely noticing the exchanges of recognition among the young soldiers and other people on hand as he moves through them. He has no intention to question or direct any of the preparations. That's all under control, in other hands. He's not even sure why he has come, but something is speaking to him, urging him to seek here for the answer to the terrible question now in his mind. Only twenty-four hours away and the shadow of El Condor's wings still hangs ominously over everything.

He leaves the construction area and walks back along the edge of the field, glancing up at the houses in Yemin Moshe. Could the man, Harrigan, even now be setting up in there to fine tune his surveillance of the site, training powerful telescopic sights on the open bandshell? Would Greenberg send his men through every one of those possible vantage points? If he did, how could he control for every possibility? And on the other side among the trees below the road, dozens of possible spots for a sniper to lurk. How could they all be cleared? And thousands of spectators on the grounds themselves. How was it possible to protect people who wanted to celebrate in openness and freedom from an evil virus that might be hiding in that mass?

With these thoughts still troubling him, Mark has moved halfway along the valley floor on the Yemin Moshe side. He clambers up a rough embankment to get a better view. Above him, he can see the soldiers patrolling. He turns to look down. Again he sees in his mind tomorrow's full festival with himself on the stage and Esther beside him, in white wedding dress and veil, the two of them under the chupa, the ancient awning of the Jewish wedding ceremony, and Esther, open to life, fragile and vulnerable. Suddenly, the thought of her in the focus of the sniper's rifle sights brings a wave of abhorrent terror flooding through his mind and body, and he trembles with the passion of raw, undiluted rage.

"Mark, Mark! Why are you so troubled?"

He looks around, startled. He had thought himself alone. He sees no one. Perhaps one of the soldiers . . . ? But, no, they don't know him. Did he just imagine it?

"Mark, this is no time for doubt. You're on the threshold of your greatest achievement."

He turns again, looking the other way, and there, standing a little above him to the left on a rough outcrop of rock, he sees the saffron-robed figure of Baba Satyananda.

"Baba! Is that you? Are you here?"

"Of course, why would I miss the most joyous celebration of our time?"

"Is it Baba? Up until this moment I would have agreed. I've been pushing on regardless, convinced that nothing could hurt us, just as I was before Luis was killed. And now here . . . Oh, Baba, I've just seen Esther up there on the stage in the rifle sights of some monster that would destroy her, and me, and everything we stand for."

"Mark! Mark! Listen to me. That can't happen, not now, not if you keep on the journey you've begun. You must keep your mind fixed on what you've said to the world in so many ways now, about love and life and the great vision for humanity of reaching to preserve the Earth and all its treasures. They're not the words or thoughts of one who would falter now, even in the face of the greatest peril."

"Oh, yes," Mark picks his words painfully out of the agony of his doubt, "I've said all that, and I know it's true in the larger perspective; but here, now, in the telescopic focus of a sniper's rifle aimed at the heart of the most precious life for me on Earth, how, Baba, how can I take that risk? What have I gained if I hold up a symbol to the world and lose a treasure that will break my heart and crack my soul? It's too much, Baba! It's just too much! This time the world is asking more than I can afford to risk."

"For leaders of true greatness, Mark, the world can never ask too much. For such men and women are not shaken by the world. Rather they shape the world with their vision. They drive unerringly to the heart of all that matters, and in the fierce intensity of their courage they gather to them a force so strong that evil can't endure in the face of it. They're locked unshakably into the rightness of what they do. Their power while on this course is unassailable. They have seen and grasped the star of truth, and while they hold it, nothing on Earth, no force of mind, machine or physical strength, nothing, can prevail against them.

"You must see now, Mark, that on such a course you're truly aimed, and it would be a crime against moral order for you to deviate one degree. You're in charge here. Your leadership strength is undisputed. It's gathering all the energy it needs for success around it. You're in the vortex of a changing paradigm to shape the future of the world, and I'm here to tell you that this is your time. This hour is yours. After you there'll be others whose time will be then. But yours is now, and you cannot, must not, will not flinch from doing what you know you must do!"

Never before in their several encounters has Baba spoken to Mark with such intensity. Throughout the exchange neither man has moved one step from his position. Between them now is a force so strong that Mark instinctively feels that he could reach out his hand and grasp it in his palm like a red hot rod of steel. Staring across into the fathomless depths of the brown eyes opposite him, he asks one last question.

"Tell me, Baba, that if I do as you say, that if I hold unshakably to the course that I believe to be true, if I do that, tell me that Esther will be safe."

Baba surveys him steadily for several moments without answering. Then, even before he hears the words, Mark knows the answer in his mind.

"In such a time as this, my good, strong friend, there are no questions, only answers. Go now, and do what what you know you must do. The rest will follow as it will."

For a moment longer Mark stands transfixed by the energy of their exchange. Then he nods, turns away, and heads back across the amphitheatre to his waiting car.

A Memorable Occasion

At 6 p.m. Mark calls for Esther to take her to the press conference. After that they'll go directly to the state reception. Esther is dressed for the latter event in a stunning evening gown with a high collar and deep V neckline curving elegantly to reveal the classic beauty of her shoulders. A simple string of pearls and matching earrings complete the captivating effect. As they leave the apartment, Mark places a shawl around her shoulders and whispers to her:

"You're so lovely, my darling. I can hardly believe my good luck in knowing tomorrow you'll be my bride."

"Why, thank you, Mark," she replies, brushing her hair gently against his cheek. "And look at you, all handsome, too, in your dinner jacket and black tie. I feel pretty lucky, myself."

In the car with Esther beside him, Mark knows that he must share with her what he senses of the next twenty-four hours ahead of them.

"Esther," his voice is calm and steady, "I wish I could tell you that we have perfect security for tomorrow, but I can't. Greenberg is doing everything he can, but the risk is still there."

"You've heard something more from Kamal?" she asks.

"Yes. He's still advising us to cancel. If Greenberg had his way, I think he would prefer that, too."

"And what about you, Mark. What do you think?"

He pauses for several moments before replying, staring into the stream of car headlights coming towards them.

"I think, my darling," he says quietly, "that the world is waiting for us. We're in a flow from which we mustn't turn away. Staying in that flow with a sure sense of what we're about is the greatest guarantee we have of safety and success."

She reaches across and takes his hand.

"I think so, too," she says, barely above a whisper. "This is the first real test of our strength and determination to continue with what we know is right. My mind is clear with the energy of everything around us. I can see us shining with success in everything we do. I know you're worried, darling. I am, too. But more than that I'm certain we're meant to carry on and show the world what our love and our lives really stand for."

As he hears her words Mark's heart swells with a tenderness and pride for this wonderful spirit that no longer merely sits beside him, but has entered, somehow, into his being. He remembers Baba's words, scorched into his mind: "Such men and women are not shaken by the world. Rather they shape the world with their vision . . . They are locked unshakably into the rightness of what they do."

To Esther he says: "Thank you, my love. I think I'm only now just beginning to know you. God grant me a lifetime to do that better." Then he adds: "I should tell, you, too, Baba is here. I saw him this afternoon."

"I'm glad you told me," Esther replies. "He's a strong force for both of us, but especially for you."

Then she changes her tone, brightening substantially:

"Now, what are we going to tell these people at the press conference?"

"I think," Mark replies, catching her mood, "that we should tell them to hold onto their hats. The world has never quite seen before what we'll show them tomorrow."

As they swing up to the entrance of the convention centre where the press conference and reception are to be held, they see that a crowd of fifty to a hundred people have gathered. The number is remarkable, considering that the event was not publicized. Several uniformed attendants descend on them, opening the doors, spiriting the car away, clearing a path through the crowd. But Esther holds back from entering the building. These people have come out to greet them and she wants to acknowledge it.

Smiling and laughing up at Mark, she takes his arm and leads him down along the line of well wishers. It's a cross-section of Jewish Jerusalem, predominantly young people out to enjoy Saturday evening, but many older faces, too, and a number of families with young children, all pressing forward to shake the hands of the smiling couple who have attracted their interest. Press photographers and film crews are on hand too, anxious to capture informal coverage of Esther and Mark among the people before moving to the formal session inside. The street scene ends when a small girl pushes her way through the crowd and self-consciously presents Esther with a tiny bouquet of flowers. Esther stoops and kisses her, then holding the flowers up and waving she leads Mark into the convention centre.

The press conference is a hubbub of activity. Neither Mark nor Esther in all of their previous interviews has ever seen the like of it. Bill Bates has orchestrated the whole thing into a performance. They enter down a central aisle into a room packed with more than a hundred people, mostly from the media. Powerful spotlights pre-positioned for angles come on as they enter and follow them down to a small central stage festooned with flowers and draped at the back with a huge blue Visioneers flag with its large white V standing out boldly. At the front to one side a string quartet brings them in lustily with a Mozart symphony while the audience stands and applauds. Waving and looking very much at ease with the attention, the smiling couple on whom all this is focused step up onto the stage and take their seats in two elegant wing chairs placed there for them. A boom microphone is lowered down just above their heads, while at a podium off to one side, Bill Bates with a flourish of his hand ends the musical introduction and proceeds to get the conference underway.

It goes on for thirty minutes with a cut and thrust of questions ranging from the banal to the profound. All manner of interests are in the room: news, fashion, religion, politics, science, economics, youth, women, minorities; all of this comes tumbling out, as these purveyors of world opinion probe for what lies at the heart of the fascination that people around the globe have found in the lives and actions of these two quintessential

Visioneers. Finally, towards the end of the time, comes the question Mark has been waiting for.

"We've noticed an unusual amount of security activity around the wedding site over the past two days. Are you expecting trouble? Does the memory of what happened to Luis Valdez haunt you, Mark?"

It's blunt and insensitive, but so much like most of the world that's listening for the answer. The room grows very quiet. Mark speaks very deliberately as he answers.

"We're taking the precautions that the world requires because we live in imperfect times. As you all well know, Luis Valdez gave his life in sacrifice for ideals that most people had believed unattainable. Esther and I honour those same ideals completely. Tomorrow we'll give public witness to our conviction that already around the world, in every land, people are moving to relationships grounded on those ideals of love and respect for life as the requirement for quality living in the 21st century. When Luis began his mission the world didn't know those truths the way it knows them now. His sacrifice generated the life force for tomorrow's future.

"I hope that answers the question. The essential point is not to focus on the externals of security precautions, but rather to declare the requirements for behaviour that would make such precautions unnecessary. We trust that you will tell the world that."

Bill Bates deflects any further questioning on safety issues for the wedding, and right on time at 7:30 p.m. he declares the session over. Taking their cue, the string quartet starts up with a lively excerpt from Vivaldi's *Four Seasons*, and Mark and Esther leave the room.

They are met at the door by Anton Salman, Israel's Minister of Culture, a short stocky man with waves of curly grey hair rolling back from a high forehead. He greets them profusely, pumping Mark's hand and blushing more than a little when Esther comes close and gently embraces him.

"Ah, it's good to see you again, Esther," he says. "Last time we met I was bringing you Israel's thanks for your contributions to art and culture in our country. Now, tonight we honour you and Mark for your contributions to the world."

"Thank you, Mr. Salman," Esther replies, "you're very kind."

"My word," the minister continues, "you two do create an atmosphere. That was an excellent press conference. I caught the last ten minutes. Just excellent. I wish we could always do as well with the press. Well, now, come along, we've got a room full of people waiting to meet you. You too, Mr. Bates. Here, Esther, you take my arm. What do you say, Mark? Your turn tomorrow, but tonight you can share her a little."

He steps off with Esther on his arm, keeping up his stream of conversation and smiling benignly to everyone he passes along the spacious passageways and exhibition halls of the convention centre. Mark winks at

Bill Bates and the two fall into step behind, leaving the minister to enjoy his prize. In a few minutes they come to a side vestibule where they pass by security guards trying to look inconspicuous, but nevertheless intent about what they do.

Inside, they enter a small exhibition hall featuring contemporary Israeli art and sprinkled with comfortable easy chairs for conversation. Twenty or thirty people are distributed around the room, looking at the art or quietly talking, women in elegant evening gowns and men in tuxedos and black tie. Another string quartet, two men and two women, is playing something by Beethoven. Behind the quartet, two sets of double doors stand open, revealing another room with more people inside.

With the appearance of the minister and Esther, an aide gives a signal to the quartet who immediately break out into a stirring performance of the Finale from Rossini's *William Tell Overture*. Even without percussion and brass this music grabs the attention of everyone within earshot. Conversations stop, heads turn, groups open out, and through the middle steps the minister, now with lively, quickened pace, moving almost at double time, with Esther on his left arm, almost running to keep up, while with his right hand the minister vigorously conducts the music, all the while smiling as expansively as waves dancing on a seashore on a sunny day. Mark and Bill Bates take their cue from the minister and fall into a brisk pace behind him and Esther. The four of them pass through the open doors into the room beyond.

Mark gasps at the magnificence of the setting. It's a grand exhibition hall with tall marble pillars reaching up to support an elegantly molded ceiling in pure white plaster featuring an intricate pattern of swirling designs like clouds in a windy sky. Around the room numerous small alcoves crafted in white marble open out, each one featuring a bright mosaic of Jewish folklore, carefully illuminated to bring out the highlights. In the far wall facing the open doors, huge glass panels reach up five metres in a set of grand arches with sparkling diamond glass-work filling the arches. Through the glass, glimpses of an elegant courtyard can be seen, beautifully illuminated with concealed lighting to show off a plantation of evergreen shrubs and a long, rectangular reflection pool.

All of this is gradually revealed to Mark as, following the minister and Esther, they sweep around the room with Rossini's music galloping along in company. But if the room is magnificent, the stunning assembly of guests is equally so. More than a hundred people are present in grand accoutrement. The shimmering splendour of the ladies brightens up the room with colour and sparkle, along with the quiet sobriety of the gentlemen in their formal dinner suits. The minister and his small entourage swing by going around the room. The centre area clears as people move back. Applause begins, the minister smiles even more broadly and continues gliding along. The music reaches its thundering conclusion, and right on cue, as if masterfully choreographed, the minister arrives dead centre at a small podium in front of the glass panels, placing himself between Esther and Mark, while the applause swells to an ovation. With a final flourish, the minister cuts his hands away, the applause ceases, and people press forward to listen and observe.

"*Chaveyrim!*" the minister greets them. "*Erev tov! Baruch Haba!* Friends from all around the world, good evening! Welcome to Jerusalem! What a wonderful occasion!

"On behalf of the government and people of Israel, I am delighted to welcome you all here to our tribute to our guests of honour who have caught the attention and admiration of the entire world. Tomorrow, there'll be a wedding under our clear blue Jerusalem skies, when the whole world will pause for a while to watch and celebrate. Tonight, as special guests representing your countries, and your noble enterprises, you have an opportunity to meet these remarkable people, the spirit of the age, giving the best hope for all that you would want to see in the world.

"We all know the challenge of the times in which we live. Under these conditions it's all too tempting to step aside and let others carry the action, often with difficulty and danger. Not so, for the guests we honour this evening: Esther Fisher, already distinguished among Israel's artistic community and well-known now throughout the world; and Mark Venture, who has swept into prominence for his contributions to world peace and enterprise. We are honoured that they have chosen Jerusalem as the place for their wedding, and tonight is our opportunity to show our appreciation.

"But it's not the time now for speeches. I want you to mix and mingle, and I'm sure you will all want to give your own good wishes to Esther and Mark. Food and drink are on hand. Enjoy the evening. We'll have a short ceremony here in about forty minutes."

That's the signal for the quartet to begin again. For those who notice, they open with Tchaikovsky's love theme from *Romeo and Juliet*. A host of waiters and waitresses in trim black and white serving dress appear in grand procession, then fan out to every corner of the room, bearing aloft trays overflowing with sumptuous hor d'oeurves and glasses of Israeli wines, brandies and liqueurs.

For the next half hour Mark and Esther are swept along on a tide of excited well-wishing. Many of the people are their friends from around the world, including, of course, the Visioneers. Their family members are all present and the minister is particularly attentive that they're well looked after while Mark and Esther greet the other guests. Most of the people there are carrying out important work in education, science, health care, cultural activities, and spiritual support. It's a universe of national and ethnic assemblies, all enthusiastic and enlivened with the expanded prospects of their work under the stimulating spirit of visioneering.

On the political side, many countries have sent official representation through their ambassadors. There's a sprinkling of royalty from various houses in Europe, coming on behalf of foundations and non-governmental, non-sectarian enterprises of good work spread all over the world.

Peter Hemphill has arrived, too, officially representing the United Nations. He smiles ruefully at Mark through the crush of activity. Mark whispers for him to wait afterwards, for they must speak. Mohammed Hussein, too, is on hand, and Mark includes him in the invitation.

Now the minister is back, this time bringing in tow one of his colleagues who has just arrived, Haim Shamir, Minister of Defence, a huge mountain of a man, tall and physically powerful, as if his appearance has been matched to his responsibilities for Israel's security. Mr. Shamir extends a huge ham of a hand to Esther who feels her own delicate fingers swallowed by it. To Mark the hand pressure is firm. He looks into deep blue eyes in a large weather-worn face.

"Perhaps we could have a word afterwards, Mr. Venture." Shamir's voice is deep, his English thick and heavily accented. "About tomorrow's arrangements, you know."

Mark then notices a familiar figure behind the minister in full dress uniform, Colonel Aaron Greenberg. The minister motions him forward. Greenberg extends his good wishes to Esther who smiles warmly at him. As the colonel shakes Mark's hand, Haim Shamir adds from the side, "Colonel Greenberg has briefed me on the situation, Mr. Venture, and there are some details I would like to confirm. We will find a quiet place to talk after the ceremony." With that, the two men move off while Esther and Mark continue to greet their guests.

One other person of particular note to come by is Cardinal Claudio Vachiano. Mark remembers vividly their first meeting at the Vatican and subsequently the Cardinal's serene presence as he presided over the memorial service for Luis Valdez. Now here he is again, in the holy city of Jerusalem, officially representing His Holiness, the Pope, but personally delighted that he can follow once more the adventures of Mark and Esther and the Visioneers. Dressed in the scarlet robes of his office, he presents a striking appearance, even in this assembly of sparkle and glitter. He is accompanied by one of his own clerics, but also by Rabbi Ruvain Ben Sabbath and the Reverend Gordon Ringthorpe, the latter two dressed less conspicuously in formal evening wear.

"We are well met again, Mark," the cardinal greets him as a friend, "this time on a much happier occasion. Esther, you are an inspiration to the world. May I offer you both the very best wishes of the Holy Father and myself. The impact you're having on the spiritual life of the world does not go unnoticed, even in the somewhat rarified atmosphere of the Vatican. And your choice of Jerusalem as the setting for your betrothal is particularly symbolic. We're delighted to be part of your celebration."

"Thank you, Your Eminence," Esther replies. "You do us great honour."

"And you're keeping excellent company with the Rabbi and the Reverend Gordon," adds Mark. "If our wedding does nothing more than create an opportunity for you three to set the world straight, it will be enough."

"Ah, wouldn't you just know," the Reverend Gordon puts in, "we've already begun drafting the Jerusalem Declaration of Fellowship on the Mount. We should have a first draft to try out on the world tomorrow."

"That is, of course," adds Rabbi Ruvain, with a twinkle in his eye, "if we think the world is ready for it."

"I have a suspicion," Cardinal Vachiano smiles wistfully, "that as the world witnesses this ecumenical Jewish-Christian wedding, that it might just decide it's ready to cross more barriers than most of us ever dreamed were possible. But look, my dear friends, we must not keep you. I see your good host has come to reclaim you. God keep both of you in His love forever."

The cardinal places Esther's hands on Mark's, then holds them both in his for a moment, the large ruby ring on his finger sparkling in the light. They bow their heads in acknowledgement of his blessing, and the cardinal withdraws, as Anton Salman, Minster of Culture, comes up.

"Well, what do you say, you two?" he fusses around them. "Can I steal you back now? It's time for a little bit of ceremony. And I'm sure you both have something you want to say."

The minister leads them back to the podium where he proceeds to get things underway. The string quartet, which has moved to the centre of the large room, breaks into a lively rendition of *Hava Nagila*, as the guests gather around, some sitting in the easy chairs sprinkled about the room, others preferring to stand. A small platform has been set up for Esther and Mark, similar to the arrangement at the press conference, and they take their seats a little self-consciously in front of such a prestigious gathering.

As the minister had promised, the ceremony is brief. The Mayor of Jerusalem is on hand to acknowledge with obvious enthusiasm the importance of the occasion, and to commit the full efforts of a city that has seen so many wonders over a four thousand year history, to this latest opportunity to be at the centre of world attention. The minister himself speaks on behalf of the Israeli government. He then invites Peter Hemphill to comment for the United Nations, to recognize the recent acceptance given by the world body to the Visioneers' proposal to create a Congress of the Global Mind.

"In the context of that achievement," Peter concludes, "I can pay my own personal tribute to the enterprise that Mark Venture has brought into world affairs. From a curiosity attracting sensational media attention, he and Esther have established the Visioneers as a spirit of hope for the future of a world that needs so much of it. I salute them, and ask you all to join me in expressing the world's good wishes on their union tomorrow."

Mark and Esther step down from the platform and come forward to the microphone, waiting for the applause to subside. Esther speaks first.

"What can I say but thank you," she says, her eyes sweeping the assembly, as she stands graciously poised before them, a petite but strong presence beside her admiring companion. "Mark and I have hardly dared to dream over the past few months that this time would really come, but now, here you all are, making it real for us, and for that our gratitude, no matter how great, can never be sufficient.

"When you set your face toward a dream, it sometimes seems a little hard to make the footsteps follow. It's then that you need the love and support of those you can truly call your friends. We feel that support very strongly here tonight. We have chosen, Mark and I, to dream a big dream, and we know that it has meaning only as it comes to be shared by others. And here, tonight, in my city of Jerusalem, I see our dream shining so brightly that I dare to hope it will light the world.

"I am an Israeli, born right here in Jerusalem, a new child in a place more ancient almost than the mind can imagine. Because I was born here, I am a child of conflict and contradiction, knowing in my home the love that runs so deep in a Jewish family, but seeing in the streets around me the ugliness which comes from people declaring themselves to be mortal enemies. My family moved away from Jerusalem, so I haven't lived here for many years, but wherever I went the scenes of that conflict, the image of the torn city, burned in my memory. Then suddenly, a few months ago, as you know I was plunged into the heart of terror. The nightmare returned, more terrible than any fear I had ever known.

"But now tonight, on the eve of my wedding to this wonderful man who has come into my life, I can say that from that ordeal of terror has come the greatest hope I have ever known. It's hope— no, more than that—it's absolute conviction, that even those who have declared themselves to be enemies to the point of death, can find a pathway to peace.

"If we can show that understanding here in Jerusalem; if we can declare here a new beginning that puts an end to violence, and shows that no pattern need be endlessly repeated; If we can do that here, in this eternal city, then we will have said to the world, it can be done.

"So those are my thoughts, as I thank all of you for being here. My greatest wish is that tomorrow, all those who watch will see the truth of what we mean to do, and choose also to embrace it in their hearts."

As she says these last words, Esther glances up at Mark and takes his hand. The audience is hushed. Holding Esther's hand, Mark adds his own remarks.

"Truth, indeed, is at the heart of it," he says. "To the world, Jerusalem stands for a particular meaning of truth. It's the individual decision, braver than all the forces arrayed against it, to risk everything to the point of death, because of what you believe the world can be. Because of what you understand about right and wrong. Because of what you declare to be the way human beings ought to live and treat each other. You realize that in acting on this truth, you have only one chance. If you choose to back away, that chance will be lost forever, and the world will be so much poorer for it. That is the truth of Jerusalem.

"We are here to declare that the world is coming home to Jerusalem. For too long have we all been guilty of accepting imperfections as inevitable, of saying that it is the way of the world, when it isn't the way of the world at all, but just the way we have chosen to look at truth.

"Can we, as in ancient tradition, imagine ourselves as travellers, standing together on the Mount of Olives, looking towards the Old City of Jerusalem before entering the gates? There we see its walls before us, as countless others must have done. But no longer do those walls enclose a deep, impenetrable secret. No longer does the city appear just as an emanation of the hills and valleys as old as time itself. Rather it glows now as a new and brightly shining light to the world."

Mark's voice has risen with the excitement of the vision. Catching his emotion, Esther steps in.

"Tomorrow as you come to celebrate with us at our wedding," she adds, "and look up to those walls, we hope with all our hearts that you and all the watching world will see that light shining there."

"To that, may we truly say, Amen," Mark concludes. "For Esther, for myself, for our families, for all of us, thank you for coming. Until tomorrow, *shalom!*"

Minister Anton Salman, tears clearly standing out in his eyes, immediately breaks into a strong baritone voice singing *Hevenu Shalom Aleichem.* Instantly, the string quartet picks it up, then all the Jewish voices in the room join in, and as it goes around and around, growing faster and faster, everyone in the room begins singing the building melody. The minister leads Esther and Mark away, and they leave the room with the song for peace ringing out behind them.

An Operational Plan

In the outer vestibule they are met by Haim Shamir, Minister of Defence, and Colonel Greenberg. The minister extends his hand to Mark, nodding his big head in long undulating sweeps. Again comes the bone-crushing grasp of his firm grip.

"Very good, Mr. Venture," his thick voice booms at them, "and you, too, Miss Fisher. 'The world is coming back to Jerusalem,' you say. I like that." He lowers his voice and continues. "Now we must have our little chat about how we keep Jerusalem safe for the world. I have a room reserved for us. Will you accompany me, please."

Esther turns to Minister Salman. "Thank you for a wonderful reception," she says. "You have made me very proud to be an Israeli."

"It's Israel who is proud of you," he replies.

Mark adds his own words of appreciation, and the minister leaves to return to the reception. At that moment Peter Hemphill and Mohammed Hussein appear. Mark turns back to the Minister of Defense.

"Mr. Shamir," he says, "you know my friends Peter Hemphill and Mohammed Hussein. I would like them to join us for our discussion."

"Of course," replies the minister. "Shall we go?"

Down the hall they enter a small meeting room furnished with oak chairs and table and a large electronic whiteboard. A pot of coffee with cups sits on the table.

"Please, make yourselves comfortable," the minister says as he serves coffee. All take a cup except Mohammed who declines. Shamir sits heavily in a chair.

"The purpose of the meeting," he continues, "is to iron out final details on security for tomorrow. I must say I find it regrettable that we must discuss this now, but given that you say you have received certain warnings from Palestinian sources, we have to take every precaution. Perhaps, colonel, if you will summarize . . . "

"Yes, sir." Greenberg stands stiffly at the head of the table by the whiteboard. "We've searched the area thoroughly and have declared it free from any explosive device. We've set up twenty entry gates equipped with scanners. We've sent a communique to all media outlets, asking them to announce that members of the public who plan to attend the ceremony should get there two hours early to ensure there are no last minute line-ups at security. Refreshment stalls are available on the grounds so that people can make a picnic of it while they wait.

"We are, therefore, satisfied that no disruptions will originate from within the site. Concerning the alleged threat of attack by snipers from outside the grounds, the situation's more difficult to control. In this regard, we can't guarantee 100 percent safety. Mr. Venture has told us that his Palestinian source says the attack will be directed by a man named Harrigan. We assume this to be Patrick Harrigan, an Irish businessman who operates an import-export agency in Jerusalem. We've had reason for some time to suspect Mr. Harrigan of dealing in arms shipments to the Palestinians. We haven't been able to confirm this, and we haven't located Mr. Harrigan. We do believe, however, that he's in the country."

"Of course," the minister interrupts, "none of these allegations have been confirmed."

"Mohammed has something to contribute on this point," Mark adds.

Mohammed speaks evenly and quietly, measuring his words: "The source of the allegation is a Palestinian, Kamal Rashid. I've spoken with him. He's genuinely making every effort to prevent an incident. He's concerned for the safety of the wedding party. He admires Mark and Esther.

Above all, he doesn't want the Palestinians implicated in any way in an act of violence here."

"Kamal Rashid is an Arab, and a terrorist with a criminal record," Haim Shamir asserts authoritatively. "You can understand why we are sceptical."

"Yes, we can understand that," says Mark, "but I want you to know that I view Kamal Rashid as a friend, even though I could find reason to see him otherwise. We can use such friends at a time when an outside element is threatening our lives. Perhaps, Peter, you can bring us up to date on that."

"I'm not sure how much all of you know," Peter says, "about the man who appears to be behind all this, Carlos Palmira." He pauses and looks at Shamir and Greenberg. They return his gaze. Silence hangs in the air.

Then Peter continues. "He has a reputation for making profits on both sides of a deal. But even a powerful man can only be successful at that game for a time. In the last few days, Palmira has seen his empire cracking. He knows that next week it may come down around his ears. I believe he sees Mark as a primary cause in turning the tide against him. If he can attack Mark tomorrow and blame it on the Palestinians, he figures he'll give himelf the space he needs to get out of the mess he's in. That's why I think we need to take this threat very seriously."

"We always take matters like this very seriously," rejoins Shamir. "If I was more confident of the source of the warning, I would move to cancel the cermony. Indeed, that's what Colonel Greenberg has recommended. However, things have gone so far now that Israel's honour is on the line. I am not inclined to back away. I understand that's your position, too, Mr. Venture."

"Yes," Mark replies, "but for a different reason. Tomorrow's event will speak to the world in a way no other means could. To cancel the ceremony would strengthen the hand of those against us."

"That's true, Mark," Peter Hemphill interrupts, "but the safety of Esther and yourself is at stake here. You've got to look at that very seriously. From what I've heard about Palmira, I'm convinced he'll stop at nothing."

Esther intervenes. "Thank you, Peter. We know where your heart and concern is. You too, Mr. Shamir and Colonel Greenberg. But you all have to understand that Mark and I both believe we are being guided in what we do. We are very grateful for your concern and protection, but we are determined to continue."

"The Israeli government sees its responsibility to support you in that," Shamir responds. "I've asked Colonel Greenberg to prepare an operational plan for tomorrow. He'll outline the details now."

All eyes turn to Greenberg standing by the electronic whiteboard. He presses a switch and a map of the wedding site and surroundings appears on the board.

"This shows where the wedding party will congregate on the stage under the acoustical shell," he points out. "The sightlines for any sniper attack are shown by the three arrows. We're 90 percent sure we can prevent anyone from operating from these vantage points. However, there's always the unexpected. So we have our own surprise."

Greenberg is stiff with efficiency and certainty as he clicks the next slide onto the whiteboard. It shows the same plan without the arrows.

"The enemy is set for one scenario," the colonel continues, "now we turn the tables on him by changing the set-up at the last minute. The stage and shell here are fixed, but we've built a second stage on a motorized flatbed. It's concealed here in a tent behind the other one. At the last minute we bring it out and drive it to the far end of the field. Then the ceremony continues as a mirror image of what the enemy had been expecting. The guests have been prepared for this with instructions in a sealed envelope distributed as they arrive. They're told not to open the envelope unless directed. My men will be stationed along all rows to see everything goes smoothly. Most people will simply have to turn around to face the other way. The invited guests will be escorted to the centre to new chairs brought out by my men as the stage is put into position. It'll all be done in ten minutes, and the enemy will have the situation completely reversed on him."

As he was speaking Greenberg had sketched on the whiteboard to show the new set-up. He continues: "Now, how do we expect the enemy to act when he see's what's happening? He'll try to move to new positions. We will have ground troops dispersed to spot any such movement. In addition, high flying reconnaissance aircraft circling out of sight, but with powerful cameras able to pick up the movement of a cat in the alley, let alone a man with a weapon. The whole operation will be monitored from command headquarters set up here in the tent behind the original stage. If there are snipers out there we'll have them within minutes of when they try to move. While all this is going on out of sight of people in the amphitheatre, the wedding ceremony will continue as if nothing has happened."

Colonel Greenberg stops speaking and looks at the group. Shamir leans forward and slaps the table.

"Well, gentlemen and Esther, what do you think?" he asks.

Mark sits staring for a long minute at the reversed image Greenberg has drawn on the whiteboard. It's a brilliant operation that no one would expect. It's designed by a tactical mind concerned, as he well remembers Greenberg saying to him, with keeping his own corner of the world clean. It has every element of effectiveness and safety built in. Why then does he feel, somewhere at the back of his mind, that it's not right?

Then he hears Baba's voice, in that same part of his mind, saying to him: "You're in charge here . . . You're in the vortex of a changing paradigm to shape the future of the world . . . " That's it! A changing paradigm!

Greenberg's plan comes from the old paradigm of strategic action to defeat an enemy. It's based on getting control of all the variables, then moving people to fit the plan. It's well designed to achieve its objectives: safety of the wedding party and capture of the enemy. But it's the old paradigm, with no provision for trusting the other party that's out there, Kamal Rashid and his Palestinians. At the end of it, the world will have witnessed a marvellous coup, the triumph of one force over another, but it will not have seen a demonstration of the truth of Jerusalem: courageous personal action, belief in fellow man, and faith in a loving, protecting God concerned with righteousness.

Mark knows the room is waiting for his reply. He looks at Esther, and senses that she can read his thoughts.

"It's brilliant strategy," he says, "but I believe we must see it as a contingency. We do this only if all other efforts to resolve the situation have failed."

"But, of course," Shamir responds. "We're not here to dazzle the world with strategy. The best outcome is to have the ceremony proceed without any disruption."

"Then I would like to ask you, Colonel Greenberg, if I have your assurance that you'll make every effort to work with Kamal Rashid between now and the start of the ceremony, to apprehend this man Harrigan and his associates."

"We're already working on that," Greenberg replies.

"Yes, but have you had any contact with Kamal Rashid and his group?"

"No, and I don't expect to. I don't know where he is, and he's not likely to call me."

"If he does, will you work with him?"

"Of course," Greenberg replies, "but if I were Rashid, I'd be reluctant to step forward."

Esther speaks again: "Perhaps if Kamal could be given some assurance of immunity, he'd feel more confident. Can you do that, Mr. Shamir? It would give Mark and me a lot more assurance if we knew everyone was working together."

The minister looks long and hard at the two of them.

"Yes," he says, "even with thousands of people present, that wedding aisle will be a very lonely place for you. You are a very brave couple. You have my word on our full cooperation."

"Thank you," Mark says quietly. He turns to Mohammed Hussein. "Mohammed, do you think you can reach Kamal and tell him what the minister has said?"

"I'm not sure," Mohammed replies, "but there's a good possibility."

"All right," says Mark. "I'll leave that to you. Now, one last point, colonel. We have to work closely together to decide if we need to switch to the contingency plan."

"That will require first-class communication lines," Greenberg asserts.

"Then wire me up," Mark responds. "That's a technical matter. You can do that. We can practically be inside each other's head from now until the wedding."

Greenberg considers for a moment, then nods. "All right, Mr. Venture. We'll use an MCD, a minaturized communication device. I'll get the equipment right now. We'll see how this works. But I'm the one who'll decide on the final course of action"

"Fine." Mark stands up and offers his hand to Shamir. "Mr. Minister, it's good to know that you and your security forces are on hand. I believe tomorrow will be a great day for all of us."

"Yes, Mr. Venture, I think so, too." He smiles at Mark and Esther. "I'm sure Miss Fisher has told you that we Jews have an ancient prayer which says, 'Next year in Jerusalem.' This discussion has changed that. Now it's 'Tomorrow in Jerusalem.' "

"And it's not just for the Jews, Mr. Minister. It's for the world. 'Tomorrow in Jerusalem!' It has a good sound to it."

Tomorrow in Jersusalem

It's 11 p.m. when Mark gets back to his apartment. He calls Esther for one last conversation before their wedding day.

"Hello, darling," he says, smiling at her image on the videophone. "Last night as a single. How do you feel about that?"

"Lonely," she replies. "Tomorrow night will be much better. And you?"

"Lucky," he says. "Of all the changes that have come into my life in the last six months, you're the best."

"We're both very lucky to have found each other."

"Yes. I just wish you could enjoy tomorrow without any fear of danger."

"I've already put all thought of that away. Mother has seen the shield of God around us. With God and Mark Venture looking after her, what more could a good Jewish girl want?"

"Just a good night's rest, I expect. I love you very much, darling. I'll see you at the wedding."

"Good night, Mark. God keep you in His care."

As her image fades, Mark reaches up to touch the tiny electronic box tucked into his ear. He's not yet used to the feel of it. He moves his hand to the pinhead in his collar. A low buzz sounds in his ear. Then he hears Greenberg's voice.

"Yes?"

"Just testing the MCD, Colonel," says Mark. "Am I loud and clear?"

"Right inside my head."

"Well, goodnight, then. Call me when you're ready."

"Good night, Mr. Venture. I'll speak to you tomorrow."

"In Jerusalem," says Mark, and touches the pinhead again to disconnect.

CHAPTER TWENTY

The
Wedding

S UNDAY MORNING DAWNS CLEAR AND BRIGHT over the city of Jerusalem. For five people it's to be a day with destiny: for the world a breath in history. To the Visioneers and your hope through them for a better future, it comes as a turning point.

First of the five is Esther, rising early, to be greeted by her mother and father already up with coffee brewing. Speaking quietly with smiles and soft words, mother and daughter begin unhurriedly the preparations to create the bride the world is waiting to see.

Second is Mark, also up early, out in the darkened streets before sunrise, running, sharply awake, rehearsing the possibilities and probabilities of the day in his mind, before he makes contact with anyone else. The cool, fresh breath of the morning invigorates, enlivening the prospects for the day with anticipation and edge.

Colonel Greenberg is third. By sunrise he's at the wedding site, wearing dress uniform, preparing to attend formally at the ceremony, if circumstances permit, but expecting more likely to be fully engaged in managing the events and the safety of the wedding party. Around him his men are moving with quiet authority to secure the checkpoints and sweep through the site and surrounding areas to maintain a strong surveillance.

Fourth, in a cramped stone building in a narrow street in the Arab Quarter of the Old City, Kamal Rashid sits alone, waiting for the full light of day to come. He waits, too, for the telephone at his elbow to ring with the news that can help to avert the disaster which he now feels to be sweeping rapidly towards them.

Thousands of miles away, the fifth of this interlocked group sits in the darkness of early morning, keeping an all-night vigil for news of the assault he has ordered against the celebrations in Jerusalem. The lurid glow of the lighted instrument panel in his communications centre falls on the hard, rock-like features of Carlos Palmira, self-styled El Condor, readying to swoop for a kill.

The Tension Unwinds

The wedding is set for 2:00 p.m. By mid-morning a steady flow of sightseers is pouring into the amphitheatre. Under the bright clear sunny sky, a carnival atmosphere prevails. A row of multi-coloured canvas refreshment stalls have been set up along one side below the Jerusalem Brigade Road. People, dressed casually for a day's outing, move easily through the checkpoints, chatting good-humouredly with the soldiers, showing no apprehension for the presence of such strong security. Blankets and cushions are spread over the green grass of the grounds as early comers select the best vantage points behind the chairs for the three hundred official guests. The soldiers have marked out with white chalk lines rows and aisles for the spectators so that everything is kept orderly.

Colonel Greenberg is watching the proceedings from just outside his command headquarters in a small tent by the acoustical shell. The stage under the shell has been lavishly decked with flowers, surrounding the traditional marriage canopy, the chupah, already set in place, with four elegantly carved wooden poles and a richly coloured floral canopy of pure silk. Running up to the stage along the aisle between twenty rows of chairs, and extending several hundred feet out into the amphitheatre, is a magnificant red carpet. Coming down along this carpet in a few hours time Esther will be seen by millions of people on every continent, the bride of the future, radiant and smiling, welcoming the world to join with her and Mark in their celebration of happiness.

To record the event, a single television crew from the ZNN network is already at hand, putting the finishing touches to their set-up. They will be using three large fixed cameras with hydraulic chairs to get varied elevation levels for best shots, plus one hand-held camera operating on stage for close-up shots of bride and groom during the ceremony. Pamela Barrett will be providing the commentary for worldwide distribution in English, while two dozen other television personalities will provide commentary in as many languages for their audiences.

All of this preparation Greenberg watches with steady approval, while at the same time receiving a flow of continuous reports from his patrols, within the grounds, along the perimeters, moving among the houses in the neighbouring artists' community in Yemin Moshe, and as far away as the ramparts of the Old City walls. Greenberg is sure the area is clear of any would-be assassins, and he intends to keep it that way. The entire space has been sealed off to all but local traffic and people arriving for the ceremony, and the soldiers are checking everyone. Backing all this up is Greenberg's contingency plan of reversing the configuration for the ceremony on the amphitheatre grounds. He is reluctant to initiate this because of the disruption, but he has already decided to do it, if he isn't satisfied that by half an hour before the start of the wedding he can guarantee 100 percent safety to the wedding party. He glances up to the sky where he knows a high flying reconnaissance aircraft is already patrolling, providing uncannily accurate surveillance of the entire area.

◆ ◆ ◆

It's 11:30 a.m. and Mark is in his apartment waiting for Mohammed Hussein, his Best Man for the wedding, to arrive. He should have been there half an hour ago. At noon they're scheduled to leave for the wedding grounds in an official car provided by Greenberg. The car is already waiting downstairs. Mark had spoken to Mohammed at 8:00 a.m. when he was still trying to make contact with Kamal Rashid. There's been an uneasy silence from that quarter for almost twenty-four hours. It's as if the Palestinian has set everyone on edge and is now going to leave them there. Mark knows that Mohammed is doing his best, but time is running out.

Communication with Greenberg is working just as planned. Mark has spoken to him several times on the MCD. It works just fine. With the instrument now tucked into the lapel of his tuxedo jacket there's no sign that he's in contstant contact with a remote party.

The telephone rings. Mark grabs for it.

"Mark, it's Mohammed here."

"Where are you? What's happening?"

"There's been a development. I've just spoken to Kamal. He's still waiting on the other line. He has a lead on where Harrigan is, you know, the man who's supposed to be Palmira's mastermind here."

"Yes, I know, go on. What about Harrigan?"

"Kamal has word that he's holed up in a building in Yemin Moshe right beside the wedding site. Greenberg's men are swarming all around there, but so far they've missed him. Kamal is somewhere in that vicinity too, but he can't get through because of the soldiers."

"Well, he's got to talk to Greenberg. Have you told him that?"

"Of course, but he still wants to do it his way."

"Well, you tell him from me that I'm putting my life and Esther's in his hands and I expect him to work with Greenberg. Surely he can see, too, that it's the best strategy for him politically. The Palestinians have everything to gain from cooperating with the Israelis at this point. You have to make him see that."

"I'll try," Mohammed replies. "I'll get back to him now. Hopefully, I'll be at your place in half an hour."

"Okay. I'll alert Greenberg. Good luck."

Mark touches the pin-head transmitter in his lapel and instantly Greenberg answers.

"Colonel, there's some news. I've just spoken to Mohammed. He's talking right now to Kamal Rashid. Kamal says he's located Harrigan somewhere in Yemin Moshe, but can't get through because of your men. Mohammed's trying to get Kamal to speak with you. Will you work with him?"

"If he knows something we don't, of course we will," Greenberg replies. "But I'm not playing cat and mouse with him on this. Do you have anything more specific on location?"

"No, nothing. You'll have to work with Kamal."

"I'm on alert for his call."

"Good. Let me know when something breaks."

Mark disconnects. He turns and catches a glimpse of himself in a full-length mirror. He smiles ruefully in spite of the situation. All dressed up in his black tuxedo for the wedding. We're off to a heck of a start, he reflects. Then he thinks of Esther, imagines her loveliness and vulnerability in her white wedding gown. His fingers involuntarily clench into balled fists.

"Come on, Mohammed!" he mutters aloud. "You've got to pull this off."

◆ ◆ ◆

Colonel Greenberg searches the rows of houses in Yemin Moshe with his binoculars. Attractively remodelled in the nineteenth-century style of the original construction, the stone buildings look inviting and peaceful. But the experienced soldier of many campaigns knows that behind the friendly facade can lie the greatest danger.

"If you're up there, Harrigan," he mutters, "we'll flush you out."

The cellular telephone on his belt buzzes. He snatches it up.

"Greenberg," he snaps.

At first there's silence on the other end, then breathing, barely audible. Finally, a voice.

"This is Kamal Rashid. You know who I am."

"Yes. Do you have information on Harrigan?"

"Yes. I could deal with this myself, but your soldiers are in the way."

"Just tell me what you know and we'll take care of it."

Silence.

Greenberg presses: "Look, Rashid, we both find this distasteful. Up to this minute I've doubted everything I've been told about what you said about bombs and snipers. Now I'll tell you this: on my word as a soldier, if you can give me information to protect the people in my charge, you'll get the credit for it."

"I don't trust you, Greenberg. But this time I have no choice. The Palestinians must not be blamed for what can happen here. I'll give you directions to where Harrigan is."

♦ ♦ ♦

Fifteen minutes later at quarter after noon, Mohammed Hussein arrives at Mark Venture's apartment.

"I'm sorry I'm late, Mark," he says. "I did the best I could. What have you heard?"

"You did well, Mohammed." Mark shakes his hand warmly. "I've heard from Greenberg. Kamal made contact. Greenberg and his men are moving in."

"Whew!" Mohammed raises his hands and looks up to the ceiling with a wry smile. "Maybe Allah and Jehovah and Jesus are really going to bless what we're about here today."

"Yes, Mohammed, maybe they are," Mark replies, "but I'll settle for some good cooperation between the people on the front line, and that seems to be happening at last. Come on, we must go. I want to get down there as soon as possible."

He goes to the door and calls into the adjoining apartment.

"Hey, Mum, Dad, Mohammed's here. We're leaving now. We'll send the car back for you."

His parents appear, Bob's rustic frame dressed for the first time in its life in a tuxedo, and Alice looking very smart and proud in pink with her hair freshly styled and just enough make-up to say: "Here I am, that's my son, and I'm proud of all of us!"

"Well, good luck, Mark," Bob says, shaking his hand. "You, too, Mohammed. Look after him, now. He's been charging the fences a bit, here, this morning. Got a few things on his mind, I expect. But you can't afford to get tangled up in the barbed wire now, you know."

"Good advice, Dad," Mark smiles. "We'll do our best to keep out of trouble. We'll see you in a little while."

In the car they ride mostly in silence, both waiting to hear some word from Greenberg. At 12:35 p.m. the next message comes through on the MCD.

"We've got the place surrounded," Mark hears Greenberg say. "We're moving slowly, not to give ourselves away. There's no sign of anything out of the ordinary yet. We're evacuating the houses on either side. I'll let you know when there's something to report."

"Okay," Mark replies. "Mohammed's with me. We're on our way to the site. Good luck."

At 12:45 p.m. the car comes down into the amphitheatre. With only a little over an hour before the start of the ceremony, the place is now a hive of activity. Several thousand sightseers have poured in and taken up positions on the grass. While no official guests have arrived yet, a phalanx of photographers and reporters is in place to greet them, with a few hundred other spectators packed in behind. The guests will be arriving by limousine and coach during the next half hour. Mark and Mohammed are the first of the wedding party to appear, and as such create quite an uproar. People press forward to shake hands. A chant of "Mark! Mark! Mark!" starts up. On the stage, several steps above and behind the wedding canopy, a group of musicians and choir members in tuxedos and formal evening dresses are still setting up. When they hear the chant from the crowd, they hastily strike up the music of the *Song of the Visioneers*. It bounces out over the people on the large speaker system to the back of the amphitheatre and up into the surrounding neighbourhoods. The crowd picks it up and Mark and Mohammed find themselves being welcomed in grand style as the words are sung over and over again:

"We are the ones, going to the fore,
Big ones, little ones—all of us are here.
Small world, big world, reaching out to all.
Up, up and upmost—the mighty Visioneers!"

The music ends, Mark steps up on the stage and waves both arms vigorously above his head in acknowledgment. A thousand camera shutters click, and a final roar goes up from the crowd. If there had been any question about the enthusiasm of the people for this event, it's now well and truly answered. Mark and Mohammed go into the tent set up for the convenience of the wedding party beside the stage, and the people, now well rehearsed, settle down to wait for the arrival of celebrities.

Five minutes later, Greenberg's voice comes in on the MCD. "We've got him, Mark!" It was the first time the colonel had ever used Mark's first name and his voice had an exuberant edge to it. "He was perched up here in a false attic. That's how we missed it the first time we went through the house. He had quite a set-up: high powered rifle, telescopic sights, and a clear view of the stage. He was watching you up there when we burst in on him. It looks like he's been here for a few days. He had a full supply of food for at least a week. One thing, though, this is not Harrigan. I don't know who he is. We're interrogating him now."

"Do you think there's any more of them?" asks Mark. "And what about Harrigan?"

"I don't know yet," replies Greenberg. "We're pressing him for answers, and my men are going through every house again. We should know something within the half hour, then we can decide what to do about the ceremony."

"What about Kamal Rashid?"

"I haven't heard from him again. I think he's somewhere in the neighbourhood. Looks like you were right about him. I'll be the first to say so. Now I want to see what we can get out of this fellow."

"Go ahead, colonel, and good luck."

◆ ◆ ◆

The next contingent to arrive are the celebrants—Rabbi Ruvain Ben Sabbath and the Reverend Gordon Ringthorpe accompanied by Cantor Natan Goldman and "Momma" Theresa from the Visioneers. Their reception by the crowd is again wildly enthusiastic, expecially when people recognize Theresa and start a chant for "Momma! Momma! Momma!". The musicians again launch into the *Song of the Visioneers* and Theresa, unable to restrain her enthusiasm, goes to the microphone and her bewitching voice rings out and down along the Hinnon Valley, until every foot and hand in the crowd of thousands is stamping and clapping to the beat. When she finally comes down from the stage the cheering and applause rise like a wave over Mount Zion and rush on and up to the Old City walls.

The mood for a festive celebration is now firmly set. As the guests begin to arrive shortly after, cheering breaks out even for people nobody knows. With each outburst, the crescendo is building for the arrival of the bride and the beginning of the main event.

Meanwhile on the slopes above the amphitheatre, a completely different drama is taking place. Kamal Rashid is moving furtively along the deserted streets of Yemin Moshe. With the alert he had given to Colonel Greenberg, the Israeli soldiers who had been patrolling the streets have now concentrated their attention on the front row of buildings overlooking the amphitheatre. For a few minutes Kamal has had the opportunity to come in from the back and move towards a building taller than most of the others, some distance away, and on a different sightline to the amphitheatre from the one he had sent Colonel Greenberg to. In here, Kamal expects to find Harrigan.

His information is not precise. It had come to him early this morning from his men who had finally beaten it out of a man who was a known associate of Harrigan. Apparently two striking positions have been set up. One in the house that Greenberg has already stormed, and the other further back. Kamal isn't sure if Harrigan, himself, is in either one. He had told

Greenberg that he thought Harrigan was in the first, but now that he sees the position of the second on the ground, it looks more like a command post, and he suspects that if Harrigan is anywhere, he's in here. Kamal had held this second piece of information back from Greenberg. He knows that he has to share the operation with the Israelis, but if he can still handle part of it himself he intends to do so.

He vaults over a low brick wall, reaches a side door to the building, tries it. It opens, and he's inside.

♦ ♦ ♦

At 1:35 p.m. Mark has still heard nothing further from Colonel Greenberg. They've been joined in the tent by Mark's parents, which now completes the wedding party on the groom's side. They'll be following the Jewish tradition of each set of parents accompanying their respective half of the bridal couple in a procession to the chupah, where they'll stand with their son and daughter under the canopy during the marriage ceremony. Esther's parents will come with her and precede her down the aisle.

Outside, most of the official guests have now arrived. The television cameras have been covering all of this, so the world is already watching. The wedding party is able to follow things on a monitor inside their tent. It's an impressive list of dignitaries from around the world: royalty, ambassadors, philanthropists, business people, scientists, nobel laureates, academics, religious leaders, heads of international agencies, celebrities from show business and sport, students from many countries, family and other personal friends of bride and groom. And finally, there are the Visioneers, coming in as a block at the end to another ringing outburst of the *Song of the Visioneers*, complete with handclapping, cheering, and some marching and dancing by children at the far end of the amphitheatre. The spectators back there are able to watch everything in detail on two huge video screens on either side of the field. In all, it has quickly shaped up as a major media event with the main part still to come.

At 1:40 p.m. Pamela Barrett, the ZNN commentator, comes into the tent looking for Mark.

"Hi!" she greets him as an old friend. "Here we are again, Mark. It's real fun this time. I'm so glad for both of you. I've only got a minute, but I just wanted to pop in and say hello. As you can see, we started the telecast with the arrival of the guests. We missed the antics with you and Theresa when you arrived, but we'll be catching you all again when the procession begins. The crowd is sure warmed up for this. It's going to be a smash! Good luck to both of you. I'll catch you again later."

With that she dashes off to continue her commentary.

At 1:45 p.m. Greenberg finally comes through. Mark steps aside to a corner of the tent to hear more clearly. Mohammed notices and comes over.

"Mark, can you hear me?" Greenberg is asking, the same exuberant edge to his voice as before.

"Go ahead, colonel," Mark replies, "you're coming in clear."

"We've nailed a second one, just a few doors down the street from the first. It's not Harrigan either, but both are confirming separately that Harrigan, himself, wasn't part of the kill. I'm inclined to think he's monitoring it from somewhere else. He knows by now that we've taken his men out, and he's probably getting out fast himself."

"You think you've got all of them, then?"

"We can't be sure, but that's my guess. The surveillance plane reported some movement further back up the hill. We're checking that now. But it's too far away to be a strike position."

Mark looks at his watch.

"We're just over ten minutes away from the scheduled start of the ceremony," he says. "What are you recommending about your contingency plan?"

"I think we've removed the need to make that change. I say go ahead with the ceremony as planned."

Mark knows this decision should sweep over him like a wave of relief, because he didn't favour Greenberg's contingency plan from the start. But there's something, somewhere at the back of his mind still troubling him.

"What about Kamal?" he asks. "Have you heard anything further of him?"

"Nothing," Greenberg replies. "Unless he calls me, I've got no way to reach him."

"Give me a moment, will you, colonel."

Mark shuts off the transmitter, closes his eyes and breathes deeply. Mohammed, watching him closely, comes up.

"What is it, Mark?" he asks. "What's happening?"

"Greenberg says they've nabbed a second sniper. He thinks they've got them all and is recommending we go ahead as planned."

"Well, that's good news, isn't it?"

"Yes, I guess so, but I don't know, there's something still not . . . Great Scott! Mohammed, do you see that?"

"See what?" asks Mohammed, turning to follow his gaze.

"There, on the television monitor. Is that Baba Satyananda? Do you see him?"

"Why, yes," replies Mohammed. "I didn't even know he was here. I'm sure he didn't arrive with the others. Now, that's strange. If I didn't know better, I'd say he was looking directly at both of us and smiling."

The television image zooms in as a close-up. The luminous brown eyes look out at them as a gentle smile plays on the lips and Baba gently nods his head up and down. Then the camera cuts away to another image.

"What is it, Mark? What does that mean?"

"I'm not sure, Mohammed," Mark says softly, "but I think Baba just came by to reassure us."

He clicks his transmitter back on.

"Colonel, can you hear me?"

"Yes, I'm listening."

"We agree with you. We'll go ahead as planned."

"Good. And oh, by the way, I've just received word your bride is at the entrance to the amphitheatre. *Mazeltov*, to both of you."

◆ ◆ ◆

Pamela Barrett and the other television commentators are perched high up to one side of the acoustical shell on a specially constructed stand, giving them a full view of the stage, the wedding guests, and the several thousand other spectators. Just below Pamela one of the cameramen is riding his camera unit like a bucking horse, as he bobs it up and down and swings from side to side to follow the action in all parts of the ground.

Pamela has just received word that the bridal limousine and its escorts are at the gate. She takes up her commentary:

"I'd like to welcome again our viewers all around the world to our live coverage of the wedding of the future. Esther Fisher and Mark Venture are getting married today in this glorious outdoor setting in the eternal, holy city of Jerusalem. Many of you I know are watching in the dark hours of your part of the world, but for us here in Jerusalem we have a beautifully clear sunny day. The temperature is mild, and everywhere I look I see people in holiday spirit, out to enjoy what all of us have been anticipating as a great celebration.

"There have been rumours of disruption, even violence, by terrorist groups, ready to focus attention on themselves and their grievances. To guard against this the Israeli security forces have been extremely vigilant and you can see evidence of it wherever you look around the grounds. However, none of that seems to have deterred the people and they've come out in their thousands today to join the the celebration.

"If you've been following along with us up to this point, you will have seen the arrival of the official guests, a colourful and distinguished assembly of three hundred people, with some form of representation from literally every country. It's extraordinary how this event has caputured the interest of the world. Esther Fisher and Mark Venture have been catapulted in six months in the imaginations of people everywhere to become the symbols of the beauty, decency, and hope that the whole world is searching for. This is their day, but it's also a day of promise and celebration for everyone else, and as we move now to the moment when the ceremony will begin, you can feel the excitement building up all around.

"I've just received word that the bridal limousine is at the entrance to the grounds. We can't see it from where we are, but there's a buzz running through the crowd, so I think a lot of people caught sight of it as it came in with its police escort. The bride will wait up there in her limousine for several minutes now while the rest of the procession gets underway. No doubt you can hear the beautiful, electronic organ that's playing processional music. I can just imagine what's going to happen when it strikes up the bridal music and six or seven thousand people come to their feet looking for the bride.

"Now look! Down there at the wedding pavilion where the groom's waiting. Something's happening! Yes, here we go. The celebrants are coming out first. Now, because this is an interfaith wedding we've got both the rabbi and the Christian minister. There's Rabbi Ruvain Ben Sabbath and the Reverend Gordon Ringthorpe. The rabbi is wearing white vestments and small white cap, yamacha, and the minister is in full white Anglican vestments edged in green with a large gold cross on the back. He's wearing a yamacha, too, in recognition of the Jewish tradition.

"Behind them there's the cantor, Natan Goldman, and there, will you look at that, with him is Theresa Romano, known everywhere throughout the world now as 'Momma' Theresa, the lovely mother figure of the Visioneers. Normally she's dressed all in white, but today, I'm sure so she won't compete with the bride, she's wearning soft blue, just flowing around her, full length—and with a garland of blue and white flowers in her hair.

"Next, looking very distinguished in formal tuxedo is the Best Man, Mohammed Hussein. He represents the third faith, Islam, that's part of this ecumenical wedding party today. He's come in here on his own so that the groom can follow the Jewish tradition of accompanying his parents in the procession. Yes, and here they are, Mr. and Mrs. Venture, Mark's father and mother from Australia, and with them, the man himself, taller than both of them, bronzed, handsome, the bridegroom, Mark Venture.

"Now, as you can see, the procession is going up and around behind the official guests seated at the front of this huge mass of people. There they are now coming across to the centre of the amphitheatre and they'll process right down that magnificent red carpet back towards us here at the front.

"Here they come now. First the rabbi and the reverend, and the crowd is starting to cheer a bit. Both men are smiling and nodding. This is certainly not going to be your formal church or synagogue wedding. These fellows have got merriment in their eyes. Now here's the cantor and Theresa, and I'm sure you can hear the crowd: Momma! Momma! Momma! Theresa's face is a wreath of smiles. Now here's Mohammed, looking a bit lonely on his own, but he's getting his share of cheers, too. But, wait for it. Here it comes, the roar of the crowd as Mark and his parents come out onto the red carpet. Mark! Mark! Mark! The chant's going up, and people are reaching out to shake hands. Mark's diving from side to side trying to oblige. Now his father's getting into the act, shaking hands all around. Everybody loves it! Mrs. Venture looks a bit bewildered by it all, but she's marching along, head up, looking really proud in her lovely pink outfit.

"What can I say? If this is the beginning, what do we still have in store in this never before wedding of the future? Here they come now, making their way up onto the stage. The rabbi and the minister are standing just behind the canopy, the chupah, with the cantor and Theresa off a little to the side. Now, here's Mark leading his parents to stand on his side of the chupah and turning to the crowd to wave. Everyone's standing up, even the formal guests at the front, applauding. I've honestly never seen anything like it!

"Mark is waving with his hands, indicating they should all sit down. It's starting to subside. People are taking their seats. We can finally hear the music again. We all know what we're waiting for now, the bridal music, and when that strikes up, I'm not willing to guess what's going to happen!"

♦ ♦ ♦

As the wedding procession begins down in the amphitheatre, up on the hillside in Yemin Moshe another scene unfolds. When he entered the house where he thought he might find the elusive Harrigan, Kamal Rashid was surprised to find the place apparently empty. It's obviously in the process of being renovated. Tools and construction materials lie around everywhere. The work is quite recent because fresh plaster sits mixed in a pail. But there's no sign of any workmen. Perhaps that explains the unlocked door. They had gone out for a while, possibly for lunch, and are not far away.

Kamal takes his time, moving stealthily from room to room, revolver in hand, satisfying himself that no one's there. He then moves carefully up the stairs to the second level. One or two stair treads creak agonizingly loud as he steps on them. At the top he pauses, watching, listening. He waits for a full three minutes, but there's no movement or sound. Cautiously, he proceeds. This floor is empty too, also being renovated. He checks every room before turning to the next set of stairs. This time it's a spiral, making one full turn on its way up to the third floor. The stairwell is dark. The door at the top must be closed. No light comes down.

Step by step Kamal moves, pausing, listening on each one. Nothing disturbs the silence of the house. Somewhere in the distance he can hear the sound of music and cheers. But inside, nothing. Then, half-way up, in the final, darkest stretch of the stairs, the briefest sound, a rustle, then something hard crashing down into his face, knocking him backward, a boot, heavy heeled, with a full driving force of a leg behind it. Off-balance and hurt, Kamal falls. Suddenly someone's on top of him. There's a brief glint of steel in the half-light at the bottom of the stairs before he feels a searing pain in his side. Enraged and hurt, he summons all his strength and flings his assailant off. He still has his revolver in his right hand. With his left he involuntarily reaches for his side to stem the searing pain. He feels blood, warm and wet, running through his fingers.

But there's no time for that. His attacker is coming back at him. At point blank range Kamal fires one shot into the hurtling body. The sound of the gun explodes like a canon in the confined space. The figure checks, then falls heavily on top of him. With a curse, Kamal pushes him off. In disgust and disbelief, he stares down at a face covered by the blue checkered mask of the Palestinian headdress. He tears the mask aside and finds himself staring into the dying eyes of a young Arab man he knows as Anwar Kutub, a hot-headed fire-brand who had been one of his most violent opponents in his refusal to buy arms from El Condor.

Nauseated, both by the pain in his side and the realization that Palestinians are now involved in this business, Kamal begins to claw his way back up the stairs to whatever lies in store on the third floor.

♦ ♦ ♦

As he comes up the hill to the house where his men have already moved into position, Colonel Greenberg listens to the cheers coming from the amphitheatre below. It's going to be quite a celebration down there, he thinks to himself. God grant there's nothing in this house that can affect it. He can't see that there will be, because the place is at the wrong angle for a good sightline to the acoustical shell, and a grove of high trees out front would make it even more difficult to see anything clearly.

The only reason for checking the place out is that the reconnaissance aircraft had spotted a man coming down to the area after the street had been cleared. He had entered the house by a side door. It was probably nothing out of the ordinary, but they needed to check it out. Greenberg had taken the calculated risk to let the ceremony go ahead, because he feels certain that in capturing the two snipers down below, he has removed any immediate danger to the wedding party. He isn't happy about not having caught Harrigan, but he hadn't really expected him to be at the operational end anyway. Greenberg's mind, too, is on Kamal Rashid, wondering where the young Arab is, and what's going to be the end of this affair for the two of them.

Outside the house he asks the officer directing the operations: "Well, what have we got here?"

"Not much, sir," the officer replies. "This place is empty. We checked it earlier in the day. It's being remodelled. The workmen are down watching the start of the wedding. My men are keeping an eye on them."

"Well, let's go through it again, then," says Greenberg. "Did you check that side door?"

"Yes, it's open. We can go in that way."

Just as he reaches the door, Greenberg hears what sounds like a muffled gun shot.

"What was that?" he exclaims.

"Sounded like a shot, sir, from inside!" the officer replies, but Greenberg is already on his way in.

◆ ◆ ◆

With a final burst of energy, Kamal Rashid heaves himself to the top of the winding stairs. He is stopped by a locked door. Feeling around in the dark, he holds his revolver close to the latch and blows it apart. The door swings open. Inside, a small attic room is lit by a single light and a small window at the front. The window immediately catches his attention. Just inside a telescope is set up, and beside it a black box with headphones attached, a transmitter of some kind. Beside that, a small television monitor glows in the half light, its volume turned down to a whisper. An empty chair stands next to the equipment.

Kamal lurches in, looking for the operator, but there's no one in the room. He feels a wave of nausea sweep over him, his eyes lose focus. He fights it off, then sees a side door half open. He stumbles over to it and looks through. Another set of stairs running straight down. He sees the blur of a figure at the bottom. His legs give out from under him. He falls through the doorway, as he grips his revolver with both hands and fires two more shots down the stairwell. Unconscious, Kamal Rashid lies sprawled half in and half out of the room across the small landing at the top of the stairs. This is how Colonel Greenberg finds him one minute later when he comes crashing into the room.

Greenberg quickly sizes up the situtation.

"Look to that man!" he barks to one of his own men, just behind him. Without waiting, the colonel bounds over to the equipment at the window. He kicks the chair aside, noting that the television monitor is tuned to the scene in the amphitheatre below. He looks through the telescope. It doesn't make sense. As he had concluded beforehand, the house doesn't have a good view of the amphitheatre. The telescope isn't even focused on the stage. Instead, it's trained on the television camera operator, immediately below the broadcast platform where the commentators are describing the scene in the amphitheatre. It doesn't make sense.

Greenberg picks up the headphones and puts them on. The microphone is open at the other end. He can hear the roar of the crowd. Then a man's voice with an Irish accent comes over the headphones.

"This is getting very exciting down here, Harrigan. It'll be almost a shame to spoil the day."

Greenberg looks at the television monitor. He sees a close-up picture of Esther in her bridal gown coming down the red carpet to where Mark is waiting for her beside the wedding canopy on the stage.

With a sudden sickening spasm in the stomach, he realizes what's going on and knows that it's out of his control to stop it.

◆　◆　◆

What Greenberg saw on the monitor was the culmination of a bridal procession to live forever in memory. When Mark and his parents had reached the stage, a hush had settled over the amphitheatre. So still was it for a few moments, it seemed the Earth had come to rest, right here in Jerusalem, with the blue sky arching above over the ancient land and the sun sending long afternoon rays down to play on the people, all waiting now for only one thing, the entry of the bride. Into this space of time and sound, there suddenly steals the bewitching opening chords of Tchaikovsky's Love Theme from *Romeo and Juliet*. The famous melody rises hauntingly at first in "tenor" tones on the organ, as if sung by Romeo, then fades almost to silence, only to well up again in higher treble as Juliet responds. The melody grows, "sung" now in duet, finally to fade in soft harp-like chords of quiet expectancy.

Another hush settles. Everyone strains ear and eye for the next moment. Then the organ erupts in thunderous acclaim of the triumphal entry of the bride. Half-way up the amphitheatre, behind the official guests, coming from the side through the other spectators, Esther appears. When she reaches the centre aisle and steps onto the red carpet, the whole assembly comes to its feet with cheering and applause. Esther has arrived. She pauses there in full and radiant view of every eye, a delicate figure in dazzling white, carrying her bouquet of spring flowers. She stands alone for a few moments looking out modestly from behind the traditional Jewish veil, down the long stretch of carpet to the man waiting for her at the wedding canopy.

As the music swells louder, and the cheers of the crowd turn to a hand-clapping chant of "Esther! Esther! Esther!", the bride is joined by her parents, and her sister, Deborah, as Matron of Honour, and the procession begins, Mr. and Mrs. Fisher leading the way.

Almost immediately, order dissolves in the excitement of the crowd. From her vantage point above the television cameras, Pamela Barrett describes the scene for the watching world.

"Oh, you won't believe this," she exclaims, "but there are literally hundreds of young girls pouring out from the rows of people, and they're all carrying baskets of flowers, and showering them all around Esther. Oh, goodness! The bride is quite cut off from the rest of the party. They're just going on ahead laughing, while Esther has slowed to almost a crawl as these little waifs in their party dresses dart all around her, spreading their flowers as she comes. The carpet has become a sea of blossoms. I've never seen anything like it.

"I've just stolen a look at Mark. He's standing up there on the stage laughing uproariously. Now he's greeting the bride's parents and Matron of Honour; they've arrived way ahead of the bride. Esther is just coming up to the back row of official guests. The children are dropping back now. Her bridal dress is absolutely covered in flowers. They're dripping off her as she comes. She's like a gorgeous flower herself, shedding blossoms as she moves.

"Now here she is, almost at the end of this incredible procession. The bridal music has come up again. This whole park full of people is just alive with the energy of the moment. There's Deborah, the Matron of Honour, coming back to straighten out the bridal dress a little, and brush off a few flowers, preparing Esther to join the groom. And he's just standing there laughing, opening out his arms as if to say 'Wow! That's quite an entry. Now come on up here, and let's get married!' "

◆ ◆ ◆

Indeed, Mark is enjoying the spectacle immensely. With the news that the snipers had been apprehended and the decision to go ahead with the ceremony as planned, he had experienced a swift flood of relief. There has been no further word from Greenberg. Whatever is still going on up in the streets of Yemin Moshe, obviously no longer holds any threat to them down here.

It's at that moment, that the MCD receiver crackles into life, and he hears Greenberg's voice in his ear, above the chords of the bridal music and the cheering and applause of the crowd.

"Mark! We've got a problem! I think there's another gunman, and he's right down there where you are. Mark, are you receiving me?"

Like the stab of a knife, Mark feels the searing pain of fear at his heart.

"Yes! Tell me! What is it?" he snaps. The smile has fled from his face, though he still stands looking down at the beautiful figure of Esther coming towards him, no more than ten metres away.

"I'm not sure," Greenberg's voice is back. "But I think it's the camerman under the commentator's stand, just off there to your right. My nearest men are a few minutes away, but I don't think we've got that much time. He knows something is up and may fire at any second."

Mark doesn't wait for another word. With a bound he leaps off the stage and a few strides carry him to Esther. Watching and describing, Pamela Barrett struggles for the meaning of this sudden change.

"Good heavens!" she gasps to the listening world. "Whatever is Mark doing? It looks like he can't wait. But no, there's something more to it. He's actually grabbing at Esther, and pulling her over into the front row of guests! He's pushed her right down! I can't see either of them now. What is this? Something must be wrong! Here's Mark again! Good Lord! He's coming this way, just sprinting towards us. What is this? What's he doing?"

In the minute that's passed since he leapt from the stage, an eternity of thought has flashed through Mark's mind. He pulled Esther to safety down among the crowd, whispering just loud enough for her to hear, "I'm sorry darling! There's trouble."

With that his next thought is for everyone else. There's no telling what a panicked gunman might do. He has to keep him distracted. He has to give him a target: himself, but not too easy! In a stride, Mark comes around in front of the first row of guests and starts weaving and dodging his way towards the cameraman. He's at least twenty metres away, a great gulf of distance, endless time, an eternity of waiting for the bullet to smash into his chest, tearing him forever away from Esther.

Up behind the camera, a cold-minded assassin struggles with his own flood of thoughts.

"What's happening? Where's Harrigan? They know something. What's he doing? I can't see them. Do they know it's me? How could they know that? The plan's foolproof. They must've got Harrigan. There he is again. He's coming this way! He knows all right. Well, okay, man, I can take you out, and a whole bunch more besides. Now, what? Who's this freak? It's that buzzard in the robe again. Who is he? Get out of the way, you freak! All right, take it then! What's wrong with this gun? Shoot! Shoot! Nothing! Gotta get out of here!"

Up above, looking down on all of this, Pamela Barrett continues to describe the spectacle, hardly knowing that she's speaking.

"I don't know what's happening. There's something wrong. Good heavens! Is there someone else? I just thought I saw . . . He's in the monitor, but he's not there really. Am I crazy? That man Baba! I've seen him before, but where is he? Now what? The cameraman is jumping out of his seat. I don't believe this. Mark's at the camera trying to pull him down. What is this? He's getting away. No! Mark's got him. He's tackled him on the ground! Here come some soldiers. They've got the cameraman. He's kicking and struggling. They're taking him away. Mark's getting up. He seems O.K. Where's Baba? Where's Baba? I don't see him anywhere. Oh, I can't tell what's going on!"

Up in the house in Yemin Moshe, Colonel Greenberg has watched the whole episode on the small monitor beside the telescope. Ironically, the cameraman with the weapon had filmed everything and his camera was the one switched on for the world to see. Except for the last few seconds when Mark had pulled the man to the ground, everything had been seen live. Even then, the telecast was disrupted for only a few moments, before the hand-held camera had been swung around to continue filming. Now, as Greenberg watches, Mark gets to his feet.

"Mark, can you hear me?" In his excitement, Greenberg is shouting. Mark winces and puts a hand to his ear. Greenberg lowers his voice. "I'm sorry," he continues, "Are you all right?"

"Yes," Mark replies, "I think so. You've got some explaining to do, colonel. Are there any more surprises at your end?"

"God knows, I hope not. Rashid is here wounded. I'm not sure about Harrigan yet. My men are after him. But, one thing, tell me. Who's that fellow in the saffron robe, and where is he now?"

"Baba?" Mark asks. "You mean Baba? Was he here?"

"What d'you mean, was he there? He was running right in front of you when you went for the camera."

Mark suddenly realizes that once again Baba Satyananda has mysteriously intervened in his life. This time he probably saved it.

"Okay, colonel," Mark says to Greenberg. "You take care of your end, I'll look to things here."

Though still unsure himself of all the pieces, Mark knows he has to move quickly to restore calm. No more than two or three minutes have elapsed since he launched himself off the stage, so people have not had much time to react. His first thought again goes to Esther.

When he gets back to her, Mohammed is there before him, helping her out from the crush of wedding guests.

"Darling, are you all right?" Mark asks.

"Yes", she murmurs, "but Mark, look at you, you're all scuffed and bruised."

"Oh," he replies, "I hadn't noticed. Are you okay to go on?"

"Yes," she says. "Is it safe, now?"

Mark nods, "I think so." Then he remembers Baba. "Yes, I'm sure it is. But we have to look to our guests. Mohammed, can we get the music back?"

Mohammed nods and signals to the organist to play. Instantly, the grounds and the surrounding hills resonate to the soaring bridal music. Deborah comes down to straighten out Esther's dress. Mark takes his bride by the arm and together they mount the steps to the stage where the rabbi stands waiting under the chupah. A tiny cheer breaks out from somewhere in the crowd. Someone picks it up and in a moment it seems that all Jerusalem is cheering for the marriage of Mark Venture and Esther Fisher.

When they stand side by side under the wedding canopy and the cheering and the music have ceased, Mark quietly asks the rabbi for the microphone to address the people. He turns, Esther with him, and together they stand side by side looking out.

"Friends," Mark says. "I wasn't scheduled to speak quite yet, but as you've noticed, a number of unexpected things happened in the last few minutes, and I think you deserve an explanation. First of all, for Esther and me, let me thank you all for being so wonderful. It's a great joy for us to know you wish us well.

"Unfortunately, as you've just seen, there are others who don't. What you saw was an attempt on our lives. I can't give you the details. I don't even know them all myself. But this much I can say, Esther and I owe our lives at this moment to a number of people. First among them is Kamal Rashid, a young Palestinian, who throughout the past week has doggedly warned us about a conspiracy, and finally during the past hour was instrumental in turning it aside. Kamal's now lying wounded, I don't know how badly, a short distance from here. May I ask you all to take a moment now with Esther and me to say a prayer in silence for the safe recovery of this brave young man."

For a full minute a canopy of silence hangs over the amphitheatre, as even the children sense with their parents that Mark, Esther, and the world owes much to this man, whoever he might be.

"Thank you," Mark resumes. "The second person to whom we owe our lives is Colonel Greenberg and his Israeli soldiers. Without their constant vigilance, we wouldn't have made it to or through this day. The colonel is listening to these words as he continues his work all around us here. Thank you, colonel."

Another wave of cheering and applause breaks out from the crowd.

"Finally," Mark resumes, "I have a word for a man who I'm sure is watching us, and who now knows that the ruthless scheme he hatched to kill us and blame it on the Palestinians is now as throroughly dead as the rest of his wretched enterprises soon will be. The full truth will come out soon. For now, Esther and I again say thank you to those who protected us. Life is wonderful! All of you are wonderful! Please join us now for our celebration."

Mark turns back to Rabbi Ben Sabbath.

"Rabbi, why don't you get this show on the road!"

Mark and Esther raise their joined hands once more to the roar of the crowd, and turn back to face the rabbi.

◆ ◆ ◆

Carlos Palmira has watched it all. Sitting alone in his telecommunications centre, he had stared in disbelief as Mark leapt from the stage and within the space of three minutes, before the eyes of a watching world, smashed the master strategy for the foolproof assassination. Now as he hears Mark do all but identify him by name as the mastermind behind the scheme, Palmira feels steel fingers of fear clutch at his heart. He knows that as his own fingers stab a code into the instrument panel in front of him, searching for an explanation on the failure in Jerusalem, elsewhere around the world, other electronic messages are already flashing his name and drawing a net tighter around his operations and his freedom. At the other end of his frantic attempts to make a Middle-East connection, an ominous, unanswered buzzing is all he hears. In a frenzy he pounds his fist into the instrument panel.

"Wolfgang! Wolfgang!" he screams at the persistent buzzing. "Where are you? What's going on?" But the continuous, unanswered signal is all he hears.

He stabs the panel again.

"Yes, sir?" a male voice answers immediately.

"Johnson, get the limousine out, and call Geneva to prepare the jet. We're leaving for Colombia. I'll be ready in fifteen minutes."

As he heaves himself to his feet, Palmira takes one last look at the television scene in Jerusalem. The camera is panning an exultant cheering crowd while Pamela Barrett stumbles with a confused commentary of speculation on what has happened. The camera returns to the wedding stage and zooms in on a radiant Esther dabbing with her handkerchief at a cut on Mark's forehead, as the two of them stand under the canopy waiting for the rabbi to begin.

Palmira angrily snaps the switch off and limps out of the room.

♦ ♦ ♦

Up in the house in Yemin Moshe, Colonel Greenberg stands looking down into the drawn, pallid face of Kamal Rashid. They've done what they can to stem the flow of blood from the knife wound in his side, and wrapped him in warm coats waiting for the arrival of the ambulance. The young Arab's pulse is barely above a flicker as he struggles to hang on to life.

"Poor fool," Greenberg says more to himself than to anyone else, "you try to go it alone, and this is what it gets you. Nevertheless, we all owe you a lot, that much I have to say. Things could've been a lot worse."

Greenberg has just said as much to an irate Defence Minister Shamir, who had exploded onto their hotline as soon as he, along with the rest of the world, had seen the events in the amphitheatre. Greenberg still doesn't know most of the answers. Who was that cameraman? How did he get through the security checks? Are there any more of them? Have you got Harrigan? Is it safe to let the ceremony go on? Are the Palestinians involved?

The last question had reminded Greenberg of the young Arab lying dead on the second floor below. Where does he fit in? There are just too many unanswered questions! Fortunately, the minister had the sense to leave the decisions to Greenberg. The biggest question is whether the wedding party is now safe from further attack. For that, Greenberg has to use his intuition that Mark knows what he's doing in calling for the rabbi to proceed. If only they could get Harrigan, then they'd have some answers.

Greenberg hears a low moan. He looks at Kamal again and sees that his eyes are open. They flicker in recognition of the Israeli colonel.

"Take it easy," Greenberg says, kneeling beside the Palestinian. "You've lost a lot of blood. There's an ambulance on the way."

Kamal's lips try to form a word. Greenberg lowers his head beside the young man's face to hear.

"W-ed-ding?" Kamal asks.

"It's all right," Greenberg replies. "They're all safe. You did well."

"H-ar-rigan?" Kamal asks again.

"We haven't got him yet," Greenberg replies, "but we will."

Kamal begins to roll his head, becoming agitated. A trace of blood is at the corner of his mouth. He tries to form words, but nothing comes. His eyes beg Greenberg to listen.

"Don't try to talk," Greenberg says. "That can wait till later."

Kamal rolls his head again. This time he manages a whisper.

"The-other-one . . . " his voice trails off.

"You mean the one downstairs?" Greenberg asks. "Did you shoot him?"

Kamal nods, barely perceptibly. His eyes are full of agitation.

"Not-one-of-us," he whispers.

Greenberg nods. He touches Kamal's arm.

"All right," he says, "I understand. We know what you've done today, son. It's a good thing. Now rest. The ambulance will be here soon."

Even as Greenberg speaks they hear the siren. When the paramedics arrive, Greenberg steps aside to let them do their job. At that moment his radio phone bursts into life.

"We've got him, colonel: the man Harrigan!"

"Where are you?" Greenberg snaps.

"Two doors away. He was hiding in a small yard. We followed a trail of blood. The Arab must've winged him."

"Is he all right?"

"Oh, yeah, good enough."

"Okay, bring him back downstairs here, I'll meet you there."

Greenberg turns back to Kamal Rashid, now on a stretcher.

"Did you hear that Kamal? We've got Harrigan. You winged him."

But the young Palestinian's eyes are closed. The paramedic shakes his head at Greenberg.

"Unconscious, sir," he says, "we're on our way to the hospital."

Greenberg nods. He suddenly finds himself caring very much that the young man lives, as he follows them down the stairs.

♦ ♦ ♦

Down at the wedding site, Pamela Barrett is still trying to unravel events for the television audience around the world.

"Well, there you are," she says. "You've heard Mark Venture say there was an attempt being made on their lives. One of our own cameramen has been apprehended. I'm absolutely amazed. I know that man. Well, I mean, I don't know him well. Come to think of it, he only recently joined the team, about a week ago, I think. His names is Michael Sullivan. But who would've thought he could be involved in something like this? I'm looking right down on the camera where he was working. There are three Israeli security people checking it out. I think they've spotted some kind of weapon built into the camera. How could that be? It's incredible. Right under our very noses.

"And how did Mark know? We can run a replay for you now. Look, he just leaps down off the stage, knocks Esther aside, so she's down among a group of guests. Now here he comes running around straight for the camera. Now look, look there. This is the most incredible thing! Suddenly, out of nowhere running beside Mark, this other figure. I'm sure it's Baba Satyananda. He's an Indian mystic and has been associated with the Visioneers. I remember him well from the memorial service for the Visioneer, Luis Valdez, held in New York State a few months ago.

"But the incredible thing is that Baba Satyananda doesn't seem to be here. I'm sure I don't understand that. Now here's the rest of the replay. That's Mark tackling the cameraman. Baba has gone. Now the security forces arrive and take the man away, and Mark goes back to Esther.

"Well, there you have it. Some of the most incredible footage ever shot live on television. The only thing to compare with it also comes fom the Visioneers, when Luis Valdez was gunned down last year while speaking live to a world audience, just as we are today. It seems that the Visioneers have a flair for creating incredible television. Perhaps this is the way they're meant to get their message through to the world. There's something quite remarkable and magical about these people. I don't know what it is, but I sense it. It's almost as if they're playing out before the eyes of the whole world the age-old struggle between good and evil, and that they're some-how involving all of us in the drama, and showing us that a better world is possible.

"And who was Mark referring to when he said some man was watching who was responsible for this attack? No doubt I'll have some word on that soon, and when I do I'll let you know.

"But now we must go back to the coverage. As you see, all this time the crowd has been cheering Mark and Esther, as they seem determined to go on. They sense the danger is past and that the ceremony should continue. I know the whole world wouldn't want it any other way.

"It looks like the rabbi is ready to begin. We'll go down to him now."

Let the Magic Begin

Like the magical moment in a symphony when a melody of unsurpassed beauty distills out of strident discord, so the wedding ceremony of Esther Fisher and Mark Venture begins. It's as if all the tumult of the preceding time was staged to now usher in this exquisite piece of soul-touching elegance. As the scene unfolds, the spectators in the amphitheatre, and the countless millions watching on television around the world, are drawn together to hear the very heart-beat of humanity. Almost as a suspension of time, the participants and the onlookers, the dancers and the dance, flow with the essence of life enriched by reaching for the loveliness of love.

It begins. The last resounding chords of triumphal music drift away down the Hinnon Valley and a hush settles over the amphitheatre. Into this space steals the golden voice of the cantor calling through all the traditions of Hebrew heritage on the name of the divine Creator: "*Baruch ata Adonai, elohanu melech ha olam, boray pree ha goffen.*"

The words and plaintive voice rise and fall in bewitching cadence, repeating and repeating, reaching out across the valley, as if calling on the ancient walls of the holy city above to sing them back in sign of blessing on this assembly.

"Blessed art thou, O Lord our God, King of the Universe, who created the fruit of the vine." Rabbi Ben Sabbath now speaks the words in English, raising his hands to embrace in gesture the couple before him and all who've come to share the celebration. Deborah, the Matron of Honour, raises the veil from Esther's face, and the rabbi continues:

"Mark and Esther, my thoughts and words today are for you, but I share them in the company of an expectant world which has gathered to listen and participate, because you have touched their hearts. You know already that the greatest satisfaction in life is to take on a big and worthwhile challenge, not to shy away in fear or apprehension, but to face it in full heart with the sure conviction that you will surprise yourself with what you can accomplish. To do that alone is a great thing, but to do it together in a partnership of love is the greatest blessing. Already, each of you has built a life of meaning. Now, from this day forward, your separate sparkling streams will flow together in a stronger river of human life committed to great purpose.

"It's a wonderful prospect, not only for both of you, but for all those who will be touched by you. I believe that God is the great guiding force behind human evolution and that here, today, in the presence of all these witnesses, He means to join your lives for the greater good of humankind.

"History has been a long and winding journey, but I believe that through the process of trial and error, the human race has the capacity to learn. It is learning the truth and wisdom of what the prophets have called upon us to establish as standards of individual and collective behaviour.

"And we're not speaking now simply of our dealings with each other in local or even national communities, but on the great global stage, such as has been assembled this day to be in celebration with you. This is the stage of intercultural and interfaith understanding, so your joining today not only of your lives, but of your two religious traditions, is also a sign to the world of the supreme importance of embracing wholeness, the single greatest principle of the universe.

"Because my tradition is Judaism, may I end these words with the categorical imperative of my faith, which can be found in the concluding paragraph of our daily prayer service: 'To improve the world under the Kingdom of God.' On that great mission I know that each of you is already firmly embarked. Now, together in love, and with God's blessing, you will from this day on be an unassailable force for the good and the peace that comes with it."

As the rabbi concludes, a choir of twenty young men and women seated on a platform at the back of the stage rise. With a lively introduction from the organist they deliver a resounding performance of *Hevenu Shalom Aleichem*, repeating it over and over to footstamping accompaniment from the crowd. When the music stops, the Reverend Gordon Ringthorpe comes forward to speak to the bride and groom.

"It is indeed good to improve the world under the Kingdom of God," he says, "but in doing so, the power comes from knowing the truth of what Jesus taught here in this Holy Land two thousand years ago: that the Kingdom of God is within. That was then, and is today, a truly amazing concept. What it means is that the universe is a flow of life, a great surging, pulsating, flood of energy, and that every human being has the potential to be in the full flow of that energy; and that when we are, our power to bring goodness and harmony is unlimited, not only in our own lives, but in the lives of all who feel the rightness of the energy flowing through us and around us.

"Millions of folk throughout the world are already sensing that energy in you, Mark and Esther. You are not only a treasure to each other, but you're a source of great riches for the world. The spirit of the Visioneers, for which you stand up so boldly, is demonstrating over and over again, in every country, among the rich and poor alike, that people acting together to enhance life can and do make a difference. What a wonderful source of hope that is in these times of great anguish for the future of the world! You're returning to people the power to take the good of the Earth into their own hands, and to enjoy its natural abundance, without seeking to impose the narrowness of human will upon it.

"We're seeing here today in this remarkable spectacle of faith and love, proceeding in the face of some wretched wickedness, of which I'm sure I don't know the details, but proceeding triumphant, because it's grounded in, built on, sustained by, the unlimited flow of universal energy.

"My friends, all of you here in the holy city of Jerusalem, and all of you out there in the boundless world of television. We're sharing in a great moment of human history. We're witnessing the triumphant ascendancy of love: the love between a man and a woman lifting them on to a pedestal of partnership, but also the universal love that flows in abundance all around us, and which we only need to reach out and embrace to bring to this Earth what the good rabbi already sees in his vision: the glorious and continuous improvement of the world.

"It's good for us to be here! It's so good for this to be happening! It's a time for which we can indeed sing *Halleluyah*, for God is showering his great blessings on the Earth. For Mark and Esther, for the peace of the world, for the future of humankind, let us all stand up, sharing our faiths, and sing *Halleluyah* until the walls of the great city up there fairly rock with the surging energy of our praise!"

With that, the powerful electronic organ again bursts into life, and with the Reverand Ringthorpe leading them, the choir sings an arrangement of *Halleluyah* which he had specially prepared. It rises and falls and dips and dives in a captivating rapid beat that goes around and around without ever seeming to repeat. In less than a minute the congregation is picking it up. The reverend dances back to where Mark and Esther are standing under the canopy. While the choir continues to sing he spins the bridal couple around to face the people, then brings the parents, the Matron of Honour, and the Best Man into formation on either side of Mark and Esther, everyone holding hands across the stage singing *Halleluyah*. "Momma" Theresa, the cantor, and the rabbi are pressed into singing service on the fringes. Then the Reverend Gordon bounds to the front of the stage in long, loping strides, singing and conducting the choir and wedding party, before he turns to the audience and brings them full scale into the performance, first the right-hand side, then the left, then both groups together. Thousands of voices pick up the melody and toss it to the hills and the sky and the Old City walls, until the very Earth seems to be singing the Halleluyah praise to God for life and love on the planet.

No one keeps track of time or the number of turns the chorus takes around the assembled multitude. It's a seamless pattern of escalating, unfettered exuberance, until finally the long arms and flying vestments of the irrepressible reverend sweep upward, hold for a moment, then cut away, and the music stops. For a mystical moment a silence as deep as the universe holds in the amphitheatre, then explodes as wave after wave of cheering and applause breaks out. Waving and acknowledging the acclamation, the reverend ushers everyone on stage into their correct positions, and hands the ceremony back to the rabbi.

At first the good man is speechless. Those near enough, along with the television camera, see the tears standing out in his eyes. He comes forward to Mark and Esther, turns them to face each other a few feet apart, and says in a breaking voice:

"Friends of Mark and Esther and co-conspirators for creating a better world, I give you our loved ones to exchange their vows."

For a long moment Mark stands looking at Esther. As the television camera closes in upon him, a huge viewing audience throughout the world sees the scuff marks on his jacket and the scratches on his face from the struggle with their antagonist. Beyond that, however, they see in his clear and steady gaze at the woman he has chosen to be his wife, a look of total and steadfast commitment. He speaks without note or hesitation, never moving his eyes from hers:

"Dearest Esther, there are many ways to speak of love, but I know of only one. It is to say with clear conviction that, I love you. I know you already know it, but here my choice is to declare it before all those who wish us well. I love you. Henceforth wherever I walk upon this Earth, for as long as breath holds in my body, never will there be a doubt of the bond that holds us together. With all my heart, I love you.

"We have begun together upon a journey to do important work. For me, were I to undertake it alone, it would be of great significance; but to be able to share it with you is a privilege beyond expression.

"Our love for each other is bound closely to our love for life, and especially to our desire to nourish the finest qualities of human spirit. To this we bring the treasured memories of our earlier lives, before we knew each other. To that we add the richness of our separate faiths, made richer now by our willingness to share and learn. In all of this I know with the certainty of the stars and all the universe that my love for you will be unwavering.

"It comes from the deepest parts of my being.
It is strong to meet the challenges ahead.
It is robust to be there for the duration.
It is tender, to respond to the soft and gentle loveliness
that I have found in you.

Take my heart and hold it.
It belongs to you.
Take my love and feel it.
It is given to you.
Take my life and share it.
It is there for you.
Take my all and every part.
Keep them close within your heart.
Given freely, given sure,
Yours to keep and hold secure."

As Mark stops speaking, a silence holds deep across the assembly in the amphitheatre. In sharp intimate focus on television screens across the watching world his gaze rests lovingly on his bride. Slowly now the cameras begin to move, shifting the focus toward Esther, whose lips tremble a little, then steady, as she searches for words that come from the core of her heart. In a voice as soft and warm as breath upon a mirror she responds:

"My dearest Mark, before God and this great multitude of people who care for us and what we believe in, I declare to you this day and forever the love that fills my soul.

"My life has been, is, and will continue to be an odyssey in search of growth, wisdom, friendship, and love. It is pulled toward a vision in which humanity in all its awesome beauty, diversity, and genius is searching to achieve some yet-undiscovered better state.

"I believe that all of us at some profound level can reach within the unfathomed depths of our minds and there, with grace, touch the very face of God. For me, I know it is my destiny, to go now on those inward and outward journeys in company with you.

"This is my great joy, to have found after long years of searching, a soaring spirit who could embrace and enlarge my vision, pulling me ever more strongly towards the golden future I could taste. God, who was watching, has brought us together. Through times of difficulty and danger we were kept safe, and now we stand before the whole world on this sacred and joyful day to declare the unlimited power of our love.

"And with love comes commitment, to each other and to our dreams for a world filled with the energy that comes from pursuing good. In symbol and substance of that bonding, I stand today before family, friends, and a worldwide community of enlightened minds, to make my commitment of marriage to you from my deepest heart.

"I bring into this marriage all that I am: my mind reaching every day to be better and more knowing; my heart striving to be fuller, deeper, and kinder; my spirit searching for courage and patience in adversity and soaring beyond mountain tops in joyous celebration of triumph. I bring the child I am in playful abandon, and the mature woman of sensuous tenderness and mystery.

"I promise this day
to be trustworthy and full-hearted in love,
and open and generous in spirit.
I promise to walk beside you
as a full partner
in spirited health;
in times of low energy,
in times of good fortune
that surely await us;

and in times when we strive together against adversity.
In sunlit and cloudy days and in starry and stormy nights,
I promise to nourish you in love all the days of my life."

Nowhere in all the watching world is there a doubt of the bond that
has now been set between these two. They continue to stand for a long
moment looking into each other's eyes, hands clasped, oblivious of everything around them.

After that, the remainder of the ceremony moves swiftly, the formal
celebration of what their vows have already said more firmly than any
ritual can proclaim. They exchange rings. The rabbi declares them married
by the laws of Moses and the State of Israel. He offers them the cup of wine
to share while the cantor sings the seven blessings, the Berachot, concluding
with the expression of the pure joy felt from the streets of Jerusalem to the
bounds of the universe for the celebration of this and all marriages sealed
in love.

The rabbi then hands to Mark a wine glass wrapped in a napkin for the
ancient ceremonial tradition of the bridegroom breaking the glass. Smiling
broadly, Mark holds the glass high above his head and turns to face the
congregation and the television cameras.

"I'm told," he says, "that no one seems to know for sure the reason for
breaking the glass. Let me offer, therefore, what Esther and I wish it to
signify today. Everywhere around us we see a world crumbling under the
weight of human conflict and destructiveness. To reverse that trend, to
make a resounding impact across the face of the entire Earth, we and our
friends have released the life-giving spirit of the Visioneers. Today, here in
this holy city, linked by television to everyone who has the heart to know
and the eyes to see, we declare now and for all time, with the breaking of
this glass, that the old ways of destruction have been shattered, and the new
ways of love are in ascendancy."

With that Mark places the wine glass on the floor of the stage, raises his
right foot high, arms extended above his head, holding for a moment, and
then with grinding force brings his heel crashing down onto the glass.
Immediately, a great cry of "Mazeltov!" goes up from the crowd. The
Reverend Ringthorpe shouts, "Halleluyah!" The organist strikes a number
of triumphal chords on the organ. Mark turns to Esther. She launches
herself gladly into his arms, and to continuing shouts of "Mazeltov!" and
"Halleluyah!" the two share for themselves and the cheering world a long
and joyful marriage kiss.

While the crowd continues to cheer, Mark takes Esther by the hand and
the two of them move to the side of the stage where they disappear from
sight inside a small curtained area. This is their time of yichud, in keeping
with the Jewish tradition of bride and groom sharing a few moments
together after the marriage ceremony.

Outside on the stage, the Reverend Ringthorpe has moved again to centre. He comes down in front of the marriage canopy and speaks to the people.

"Mark and Esther have given us the symbol of the broken glass shattering the forces of evil and destructiveness in the world," he says. "But we have the opportunity here today to go even further—to embrace and celebrate the most powerful symbol on Earth for ushering in an age of peace and prosperity.

"Mark and Esther have shown us the way. Today they've brought together not only their lives in a celebration of love and commitment, but their religious faiths of Judaism and Christianity as well. And they chose to do that in the face of grave personal danger here in this holy but unhappy city of Jerusalem.

"And all of us have witnessed the miracle of what happened. Protected by their faith in the ultimate triumph of their mission, they've given the world a spectacle and a lesson that surely now must steer our hearts and turn our minds to the good that can be done in the world."

With sweeping gestures the reverend now embraces everyone around.

"My good friends, hear me," he exclaims, "Rabbi Ruvain Ben Sabbath, Mohammed Hussein, all of the wedding party, all of you here as honoured guests, people of all faiths from every country, all of you out there in this vast crowd of well-wishers, you people of Jerusalem, and all of you watching on television, a vast family of humanity from every nation, all of you, all of us, now being swept together by the course of events set in motion by love—hear me. Can we not now find the voice to cry out together in a common language of peace, and say that here this day we will acclaim this ancient city of ages, this holy city, this Jerusalem, to be from this day forward the symbol of peace and love for the world, to be the New Jerusalem, not of the heavenly kingdom, but of an earthly renaissance, to usher in the new millennium? Can we not this day say 'Yes!' to the vision of worthwhile accomplishment that Mark, Esther and the Visioneers have laid before us? Can we not open our hearts to the wisdom of the ages, to the flow of energy in the universe, to the love of God that embraces all creation?

"Oh, my friends, if we could only this day in our hearts make that commitment to this holy city, do you not think that we would then in our minds find the way to make it work politcally and spiritually for the good of the whole human race? Can we not begin then, my friends, to let our hearts be touched by the song of ages, the song of peace, the song of love, the song of a New Jerusalem offering new hope to a new world for all time?"

During the closing words of the Reverend Ringthorpe's dramatic and unexpected plea, "Momma" Theresa Romano has come forward to stand beside him at the front of the stage. Introductory chords on the organ accompany her arrival. Then, softly at first, but building slowly to a full volume that seems surely to engulf the world, she sings the bewitching words and melody of *The Holy City*. In the inspirational beauty of the music and the clear, shining brilliance of Theresa's voice, the performance transcends for the audience all thought of differences in religious faith, catching them ultimately in the grand vision of its closing theme, the New Jerusalem, welcoming the whole of humanity, its streets and walls ringing with choirs of angels singing "Hosanna for everyone!"

Her song delivered, Theresa stands glowing with the performance, as the last resounding chords on the organ fill the amphitheatre and cascade down the valley. Before the music has died away, Mark and Esther come running from their private place, right down to the front of the stage, where they embrace Theresa and the Reverend Ringthorpe, just as someone in the audience cries, "Bravo!", and then another, until the whole amphitheatre is on its feet shouting and applauding.

What might be seemly or appropriate at a wedding has long since been forgotten by everyone witnessing and participating in this extraordinary event. There seems no end to the drama and the energy as event piles on event, each succeeding one stretching to outdo the one before. Nor is the next and closing part to be any different.

Before the acclamation following Theresa's performance has barely subsided, the first trumpet chords of the processional music ring out on the organ. The crowd breaks out into a fresh uproar. Esther on Mark's right-hand side, takes his arm, and beaming widely at everyone, each of them waves vigorously with their free arm acknowledging the reception out in the amphitheatre. Then as the music breaks into the full march, the newly-weds step boldly off the stage down the aisle along the red, flower-strewn carpet stretching out into the crowd.

Up on the television platform, Pamela Barrett is doing her best to maintain composure as she describes the scene.

"To the end," she exclaims, "to the absolute end, this ceremony defies all comparison! Have you ever seen anything like it? There they go, bride and groom down the aisle, but it's not a reception they're receiving, it's nothing short of adulation. Look, I can see, royalty, and ambassadors, and politicians, and generals down there, all with tears streaming down their faces. They're applauding, reaching out, touching Mark and Esther as they go by. And now those little girls are back out there again with fresh baskets of flowers, just strewing them in a cascading petal path in front of the wedding couple. And now the other people are coming off the stage to join the procession. It's a bit chaotic. I'm sure everyone has forgotten their proper place. But who cares? Certainly not the audience! They're just applauding everyone, but especially Theresa and the Reverend Ringthorpe. They're coming down together. I'm sure that wasn't scheduled, but after their Jerusalem performance, they're just inseparable.

"And now Mark and Esther have reached the far end of the red carpet at the back row of official guests. Oh, no! I don't believe it. Will you look at that! They're supposed to follow the carpet around to the right behind the guests and over to the pavilion for the reception. But instead of that, they're continuing on up through the crowd of people, right onto the grass. I don't know how Esther's going to manage that in her high heels. Whoops! There she goes, almost fell over. Now what? Oh, my gosh! They're putting them on chairs! Will you look at that. Mark and Esther are being hoisted up on chairs by some big strong fellows, and there they go, right up the centre aisle, right in amongst thousands of people, riding above their heads, bobbing up and down, like they're on the back of an elephant, King and Queen of the Visioneers riding among their subjects. I tell you, Antony and Cleopatra had nothing on this.

"The rest of the procession has stopped on the carpet at the back of the invited guests, waiting for Mark and Esther to come around. But they're going to be waiting for some time. It's a long way to the back of this amphitheatre. Mark and Esther are already more than 100 metres back there and still going.

"The organist is doing a super job. He's keeping the music going right along. It's just like a carnival down there. In all my years of broadcasting popular events, I've never seen anything like this."

And well might Pamela Barrett say so. For this is the culmination of a grand journey of the human spirit. Two souls launched in love and adventure upon a path in life laid out by God, but theirs to choose for the following. And follow it they have, full-hearted, through danger and triumph, now enjoying the return in spirit from those whom they've inspired with their love and life.

As we leave Mark and Esther here, riding high on their chairs above the cheering crowd, we can draw breath and wait for them to enjoy the full taste of their celebration of love. From this energy source we will now receive the stimulus to move on to the next and tumultuous act of the Visioneers, the convening of the Congress of the Global Mind and the launching of humankind into the fresh light of the new millennium.

To this and everything of spirited love, may we truly say, "Amen!"

PART FIVE

The Congress of the Global Mind

CHAPTER TWENTY-ONE

Transition

Y OU'VE GONE FOR GOLD AND FOUND IT. You began the search by daring in your mind to imagine that the world could be moved towards better future prospects. You found mentors to help you see the possibilities more clearly. You created your band of Visioneers and sent them out to act, to touch the minds of millions with the idea that they can create a better future. You took aim directly at the world's political leaders, captured them, and brought them to your Visioneering Room. You took them through the escalating tragedy of the human journey and confronted them with the stark reality of future chaos and despair.

Then you brought the two worlds together: the collapsing structure of the one you know, and the reborn possibilities of the one you can imagine. You sent the world leaders out to meet the Visioneers. You brought Mark Venture before them in the General Assembly of the United Nations, where he spoke with the authority of one who has already transcended in his mind the limiting beliefs that choke the human spirit. He presented to them the fundamental principles of life and love, and challenged them to confront directly the reality of evil, including that lodged in their own hearts. He called for their support for a brave new idea: the convening of a Congress of the Global Mind, in which all the people on Earth will come together to embrace a new mindframe, to become a world community of enlightened people guided by a positive future vision.

And the leaders accepted his challenge. They pledged their support for the Congress to be held in late October, just over a year since the Visioneers first came to world attention. Then you sent Mark out to join with Esther to raise human spirit for the coming time. They invited the world to join them in the celebration of their marriage in the holy city of Jerusalem. It was to be a symbol of celebration of life and love for the planet. But into this bright space for a final crushing assault swept the dark shadow of Carlos Palmira, the self-styled El Condor of treachery and corruption. For one breathless moment the future of your enterprise hung in the balance, as concentrated evil sought to destroy the celebration of light. But then, in a moment the danger was gone, swept aside by the irrepressible spirit of the new order now quickening around your central players, and beginning to change hatreds almost as old as humankind itself. In a final burst of joyful abandon, your lovers committed themselves each to each and the world cheered wildly for the very joy of such a union.

So now you've done it. You've exposed the vein of gold. It lies before you, glittering and beckoning. Now you must mine it to reap the reward. The world stands waiting to join the Congress of the Global Mind.

Back to Your Thinking Room

It seems so long since you were here in the comfortable space of your thinking room. The cheerful warmth of the log walls and the crackling fireplace welcome you home. Outside, the snow still lies across the valley and on the Rocky Mountain range. The sky is a cloudless blue where the sun hangs low, barely touching the peaks with shimmering brilliance, while long shadows spread across the valley floor.

The four comfortable leather chairs, so much alive with the memory of your mentors, stand empty now. It's not yet time for your friends to join you. You still have some unfinished business to attend to before the planning of the Congress can proceed. You settle down in your own chair before the fireplace and close your eyes to consider.

You left Mark and Esther in the triumph of their wedding procession in Jerusalem. Lying in hospital only a short distance away, Kamal Rashid struggles for life. In the house in Yemin Moshe, Colonel Greenberg watches the T.V. monitor on the surveillance equipment set up by Patrick Harrigan, while he waits for his men to bring in the elusive head of the assassination team. Finally, several thousand kilometres away in Switzerland, Carlos Palmira, the perpetrator of the attack on Mark and Esther, climbs into the back seat of his Mercedes limousine to begin the long drive along twisting mountain roads to Geneva, where his jet is already being prepared for his escape to Colombia. In your imagery mind you now bring resolution to these pieces.

Light over Darkness Shall Prevail

Daylight is fading rapidly as the imperturbable Johnson, Carlos Palmira's chauffeur, guides the powerful Mercedes along the last few miles of mountain highway before coming down to Lake Geneva. Gentle flurries of snow sweep around the car, enclosing it in a travelling cocoon of light reflected from its headlights. Preoccupied with driving, Johnson pays little attention to his employer sitting behind the closed glass panel separating front and back seats in the limousine.

Palmira is settled deep in the leather seat. For most of the drive he's been relentlessly scanning reports and dictating memos into the car's computer. But now with the light fading and an unaccustomed weariness settling upon him, he has closed his eyes to relax.

Suddenly he has the sense that he's not alone. His eyes snap open and he does, indeed, see a shadowy form sitting beside him. In an instant he's wide awake and alert. In response to Palmira's startled movement the other figure turns his head.

"Ah, you're awake. Good. We must speak, and you don't have much time."

Palmira is dumbfounded. The voice is lilting, almost musical, speaking perfect English with a trace of Eastern accent. Palmira edges away to his side of the car.

"Who the devil are you?" he gasps. "What's going on?"

A soft chuckle greets the outburst.

"Oh, no, Senor Palmira. I'm not the devil, though I'm sure you share his company more frequently than mine."

Palmira, starting to collect his wits, snaps on the interior light. He now sees the other quite clearly. There's something familiar, then his mouth drops open in recognition.

"You can't be," he exclaims, " . . . on the television . . . the one with Mark Venture! It's not possible!"

There's no reply.

Palmira hammers on the glass behind his chauffeur's head and slides the panel aside.

"Johnson!" he roars. "What's the meaning of this? Why did you stop and let this man in my car?"

"I beg your pardon, sir?" Johnson asks over his shoulder. "Stop? We haven't stopped, sir. Too blooming dangerous to stop on this road. Someone's likely to plough into us from behind."

"Then how did he get in?" shouts Palmira.

"Who, sir? I'm sorry, I don't understand."

"Are you telling me you can't see this man here sitting beside me?"

"Excuse me, sir, but, no. I don't see anyone."

Palmira says nothing more to his chauffeur. He slides the glass panel closed, and leaves the interior light on. He looks deep into the dark brown eyes of the man sitting beside him.

"All right," Palmira's voice is little more than a hiss through clenched teeth. "What's going on?"

"I see you recognize me," replies the other, "though we haven't met before. My name is Baba Satyananda."

"You were there, on the television screen in Jerusalem, but they said you weren't there in person. Now you're here. I can see you and hear you, but my driver can't. What the hell is this about?"

"Hell? Devil?" Baba replies serenely. "Your images reveal your mind, senor. I come in quite different guise than that."

"Then tell me. Why have you come?" Palmira's voice is steady, but around his heart he feels an icy hand of terror.

"Good," replies Baba. "You've come to the point quite quickly. Your mind is rational and paying attention. Your time is short. You'll need all your faculties to hear well before you go."

Baba pauses. Palmira sits, pale and attentive.

"Know this," Baba continues, "that today the Earth took a new course. It's one where you can't go. The direction was set in the beginning, for creation began in the light, and the light will continue forever. This is universal law. You, and others like you have set your face against the light and you'll pay the penalty for that.

"All human souls have the choice: to walk in and follow the light, or to turn aside and follow paths of darkness. You and countless millions before you have chosen the second way. And your numbers and power have grown so prodigious over time that in these days you have dimmed the light of the world. In so doing you have precipitated the crisis, which now has come to the Earth.

"This had to be. It's part of universal law. All life is evolving, but it doesn't move, as many think, in incremental steps. It changes in giant leaps triggered by moments of crisis. At such a moment the world has now arrived, and your destiny, chosen freely and designed by yourself, was to be the ultimate force of darkness that triggered a flashpoint of new light that will now blaze brightly to dispel the darkness.

"Evil fears the light. You chose as your destiny to become evil incarnate on the Earth, spreading your corruption into every field. But across your path of darkness came a new light, the light of the Visioneers, born out of the impassioned drive in minds across the globe to break free from the darkness that was spreading and threatening to engulf the planet.

"You saw that light in part for what it was, a threat to your evil enterprises. But beyond that you couldn't see: that it was indeed the light heralding the enactment of universal law, the very light of God spreading out like a sunburst to reclaim the Earth from darkness."

Baba's eyes fix Palmira with an intensity so strong that he feels himself driven backwards into the plush upholstery of his luxurious limousine.

"Know this now, Senor Palmira, that the energy of that sunburst will consume you and all your wretched enterprises. As a signal to the world that a cleansing has begun, the evil empire you constructed will come crashing down. You sought to be invincible by spreading corruption into every level of every jurisdiction in which you chose to operate. But you didn't understand the power of light: that when turned to high intensity it can sweep at the greatest speed in the universe into every corner. The Visioneers understand that power. They have directed the light of truth into the hearts and minds of people all across the planet, setting their consciousness ablaze with a new understanding.

"The Visioneers are enlightening the minds of people everywhere, to know they have the power within themselves, when they search for their inner light, when they work together to build shared visions of the future, when they embrace the laws of life and love, then they have the power to transform the planet, and they will.

"Against this force you and your like are as dust in the wind. You may obscure the vision for a time, but in the end you're swept away. For you that time has already come. For your compatriots it will follow swiftly. Know this and take it to your grave. May your soul with its burden find a path."

The car sweeps around a corner of the road, the snow flurries lift, and the lights of the city spread out below. Johnson glances in the rear vision mirror. The interior light is on, and he sees his employer crumpled strangely in the corner. Other cars speed by and he turns his attention to the road. There's a break in the traffic, and he looks again in the back seat. Palmira lies still as before. Johnson flicks the intercom switch.

"Mr. Palmira, sir, is everything all right?"

No answer and no movement. He turns up the volume and calls again. Still no response. There's a pull-off on the road just ahead. Johnson swings the car into it. He springs out and opens the back door. One look at the ashen face, wide-eyed but unseeing, tells him more than he wants to know. He fumbles for Palmira's pulse, but finds nothing except his own mounting palpitation.

Fifteen minutes later in the cold glare of the hospital emergency ward a young white-coated intern brushes aside the curtains from around the bed and emerges to face the chauffeur.

"This man was your employer?" he asks.

"Yes, doctor," replies Johnson. "That's Mr. Carlos Palmira. He's very important."

"Yes, but now he's dead. A massive heart attack, I expect. The post-mortem will tell us more. He would've had no warning. He literally blew up inside. Please come with me, and we'll begin the details."

Aftermath

Next morning news of Palmira's death sweeps the world. Mark hears it first from Mohammed Hussein. Mohammed is one of the few people who knows where the bridal couple spent the evening at a private villa outside the city. On the telephone his usually measured voice is racing with excitement.

"Mark, I wouldn't have bothered you this morning if it wasn't important," he says.

"It's all right, Mohammed," laughs Mark. "I know that. What is it?"

"Peter Hemphill's with me. He's just got word of something that will surprise you."

"Go on. I'm listening."

"There's a confirmed report out of Geneva that Carlos Palmira died there last night of a heart attack."

Mark's breath escapes as a whistle through his teeth.

"So," he says. "Providence steps in!"

"Call it what you will, but it makes the world a different place. I think you should speak to Peter. I'll put him on."

"Hello, Mark," Peter's voice is also energized. "Some news, eh, for the first day of your honeymoon?"

"Yes, it certainly is. What's your assessment, Peter? What's this mean for the action that started last week against his . . . What do you call it: International Trust and Credit Corporation?"

"Too soon to tell for sure, old boy. That's such a tangled mess, anything could happen now with Palmira gone. But there's something else to consider that's going to have an influence."

"What's that?"

"Well, you know that Greenberg nabbed Harrigan yesterday and that he was refusing to talk about who set this whole thing up. I just spoke to Greenberg. He's going to use Palmira's death as a lever to try to get Harrigan to spill the beans. If Harrigan names Palmira, I tell you, that'll blow the rest of this wide open. There'll be so many people trying to get off Palmira's band wagon that some of them are likely to get killed in the rush. I don't know whether you and Esther realize it yet, old boy, but you two are so idolized after all that happened yesterday that anyone who even breathes a word against you is going to be hung out to dry. My guess is that when Harrigan gets to thinking about it, he'll want to get out from under some of that by dumping the blame on a dead Palmira. Then I think the house of cards will come tumbling down pretty fast. And don't forget the F.B.I.'s got Larry Porter in New York ready to sing about Palmira's hand in the American drug scene."

"Isn't it incredible, Peter," Mark is musing aloud, "that one man could breed so much rottenness into the world, and I'm sure we don't know the half of it yet. It can only happen, because others go along with it. We've got to strike at that! Maybe this is meant to give us the launching pad. Maybe we've endured all this at the hands of Palmira, so that we could come to this moment in time, and strike out to move people's minds to clean the mess up."

"Well, I don't know, old boy," Peter replies, "but if anyone can do it, you and Esther can. Now I'm going to let you go back to that bride of yours. When are you two leaving for your honeymoon?"

"What's today, Monday? On Wednesday we'll be in Australia."

"Well, enjoy. And give my love to Esther."

"I'll do that. She just walked in. Goodbye for now."

Mark turns to greet Esther. He sees her as loveliness in a pink bathrobe. She slips into his arms and kisses him softly.

"Good morning, darling," she says. "I have a thought for you: God made yesterday for us and kept us safe. Today we're meant to begin something new for the world."

"What, no time off for a honeymoon?" smiles Mark.

"Oh, yes, that too," Esther replies. "It will all be part of a piece. You'll see. Now, tell me, what was that phone call about? I bet it will prove me right."

Mark tells her. She reflects for a moment.

"You know what I think of first?" she says quietly, taking his hands, and looking up at him intently. "I think of Kamal Rashid lying near death in hospital. It was Kamal who saved us yesterday. He saved us to be here this morning when Palmira's gone. It was part of God's plan. We must go to him, Mark. There's nothing more important to do today than to be with Kamal."

Two hours later, Mark and Esther are sitting at Kamal's bedside. Around them, the support systems of intensive care help the fragile body cling to life. The knife wound from his attacker has gone deep into Kamal's left side, high up into the chest cavity, just missing the heart. Massive internal bleeding and shock have left him with only the thinnest line to life. Esther reaches out to take the young Arab's hand, to hold it clasped gently in both of hers. In the clinical sterility of the place with the cold, grasping hand of death nearby, her vibrant health and energy shine like the sun. She speaks softly to the unconscious figure.

"Kamal, this is Esther. Mark is here, too. Both of us have come to thank you for saving our lives. Now you must save your own. If you can hear me, Kamal, please know that we understand what you did, and we'll make sure the world understands, too. We put our trust in God, Kamal, and He worked through you to keep us safe. There's a plan unfolding now. None of us sees it clearly, but you were meant to play this role, to save our lives and turn away the force of evil. Great good will come of that, and you'll live to see it, Kamal, if you fight as hard for your own life as you've fought in the past when you were driven by anger. The world has a great chance now to move to a new age of peace and understanding, and you've played your part well to make that happen. You can rest now, Kamal, but you can't die. You must get your strength back to be a leader for your people. You've taken the right path, and you must live to show others that way.

"I speak to you from the core of my heart to say that I know the full meaning of what you've done. I'll make sure the world knows it, too. Fight on, Kamal Rashid, fight on for your strength to bring a new message to replace the bitter hatred of the old. You have set your feet in the right direction. God will keep you safe."

On the other side of the bed, Mark also touches Kamal's hand.

"Kamal, this is Mark. Esther has spoken for both of us. We'll go on now to do what we can for the world. We look for you to join us again, soon, good friend."

Outside the intensive care unit, Colonel Greenberg is waiting to speak with them.

"He should never have tried to go it alone," the colonel says. "He could have saved himself this grief."

"He did what he thought was right, colonel," Esther replies. "He's come a long way from the angry young terrorist who took me prisoner. So have you, colonel, come a long way. I pray both of you will keep going in the same direction."

Mark hands a small flat package to Colonel Greenberg. It's the MCD he wore throughout the wedding ceremony.

"Here, colonel," he says, "I'm returning this. We took a big risk, the three of us. But we've come through. And both of us owe a lot to that young man lying in there. Esther and I are moving on, but you'll be staying. We look to you to have an influence here in the spirit of visioneering."

"I'm a soldier, Mark. I'm not out to change the world."

"Yes, you've told me that before. Well, yesterday the world changed in spite of and because of you. Now you have to think about that. When you do, you'll see what to do next." Mark extends his hand. "Goodbye, colonel. I'm sure we'll be working together again, soon."

Outside the hospital, Mark and Esther run the gauntlet of a crush of reporters. Esther turns aside a flood of questions to make a simple statement.

"We came here to say thank you to a brave young man who was instrumental in saving our lives. He's unconscious and desperately ill. As an Israeli citizen, I would like the world to know what a debt of gratitude we owe to this young Palestinian. I have prayed to God to grant him a safe recovery, so that he can continue to serve the world well."

"Now as Mark and Esther," Mark has his say, "we'd like you all to know that we're off to enjoy our honeymoon."

Glimpsing the Vision

For Mark it's to be a chance to revisit his roots in the company of his new bride. For Esther it's to venture again to the strange south land that had always for her seemed to live in mystery. For both, it turns out to be a time when they set their feet on a path destined to lead to a new vision for the world.

They come in to Australia from the north, not unheralded of course, for now these two can no longer go unnoticed in the world. Even the sleepy city of Darwin turns out a small reception at the airport for its two distinguished visitors.

From there they fly to the centre, to Alice Springs, to the heart of where it seems time began, or, if it didn't begin here, then not far off. The vast expanse of red emptiness spreading out to far horizons seems to hold its breath, waiting, waiting for something that when it comes will be a great awakening.

Mark and Esther are quickly captured by the spirit of the land. They have only two days to experience it, but into that time they pour their enthusiasm which flows into the boundless sea of energy around them, as if the whole Earth is draining down into this one place, a vast reserve of strength to be there when needed.

"Mark, do you feel it?" Esther asks as they stand close-pressed by the towering red walls of Standley Chasm, a few miles west of Alice. "There's something happening here, I don't know what, but I'm sure it's part of a great change about to come."

Later they fly south to Ayers Rock.

"Look, Esther, there it is," Mark points excitedly through the tiny window of the light plane, bobbing in the desert heat. "Have you ever seen anything like it?"

Below them jutting up out of the empty spinifex plain, the great red monolith stands beckoning. Later, on the ground, touching its searing red precipices, clambering over it 300 metres above the dusty red earth below, exploring its caves and outcrops, they feel drawn and held by this great red magnet at the centre of time and space.

"What is it, Mark? What is it about this land?" Esther asks as they stroll later hand in hand in the cool evening air. Above them the mass of Ayers Rock changes colour in the fading light, as the sun sets far away in the west, behind the primordial humps of rocks called the Olgas, cataclysms of another age and, perhaps, portents of one to come.

"I don't know, Esther. But there's more to this than the fascinating landmarks. We were meant to come here together. Both of us can feel it. I've lived my whole life in Australia, but never came here before. It's been waiting for us, both of us together. Now we have to listen and discover what it means."

Whatever the explanation for the sense of presence they both share, it's not to be revealed now. Two days later, they are in the air flying southeast to Sydney.

What a transformation! From the emptiness of the red centre they are catapulted into the cacophony of one of the world's great cities. They've tried to make this a quiet visit, but that proves useless. They gave their flight number and arrival time to no one, but several hundred people are at the airport to greet them. This is a newly discovered favourite son returning home with his beautiful bride, and no one's going to pass up a chance to celebrate. Banners, Visioneers flags, welcome signs are all ducking and bobbing in the air above the heads of the crowds outside the terminal. It's a warm autumn day in April, and when the police had realized two hours ago that they were going to have a crush on their hands, they had cleared all the spectators outside into the sunshine. When Mark and Esther come out, a great cheer goes up. "Good on yer, mate!", "Three cheers for the little missus!", "On yer Mark, get set. Go, Esther, go!" All of these and a hundred other variations of advice greet them as they walk along police barricades, shaking hands and joking with the crowd.

This is the arrival, but the royal Sydney welcome comes next day, Sunday. At noon the Lord Mayor calls for Mark and Esther at their hotel. Thirty minutes later they're out on the magnificent harbour on the deck of a twenty-metre motor launch, swinging out from Circular Quay past the soaring great "sails" of the Opera House, coming around in a wide sweeping arc to go under the huge "coathanger" of the world famous bridge.

But the greatest part of the spectacle is the boats. Oh, the boats! All day yesterday and this morning the radio stations were giving out word that Mark and Esther would be on the harbour, and everyone was invited to come and greet them. And they do: hundreds and hundreds of small craft, private yachts, motor launches, speed boats, tiny sailing skiffs. Everyone is out, forming a haphazard, multicoloured, totally disorganized flotilla, out to greet their celebrities, Sydney-style, on the harbour.

As if by magic when the Lord Mayor's launch with its official guests appears, the chaos on the water turns to order. Mark puts on an admiral's uniform with a three-cornered hat. Esther stands beside him on the deck in a shining white sun dress, her curly auburn hair billowing in the breeze. As their launch comes out into mid-harbour the flotilla opens up to create a passage, a hundred metres wide with water police patrolling on either side. The busy ferry traffic is interrupted and many of the squat green and black craft are pressed into service, bringing crowds from the shore out to join in the fun.

Down the sparkling blue passage goes the Lord Mayor's launch with Admiral Mark and Esther on the deck. The tumult of horns, whistles, hoots, and cheers that greets them ranks among the noisiest ever heard on the harbour. Halfway down the first run to the bridge, Mark takes off his admiral's hat and gives it to Esther, much to the roaring approval of every noise device on the water. Under the bridge they turn around and come back down the other side of the passage, so that everyone gets a close-up look at the world's favourite Visioneers. Every boat is flying the blue and white Visioneers flag with the bold V standing out bravely in the brisk breeze.

It's a triumphal passage! If Sydney couldn't play host to these two for the wedding, then it's certainly not going to miss the opportunity for the honeymoon. When the Lord Mayor's launch gets to the end of the passage, it comes about. The flotilla had closed in the passage as the launch came through, so that now as it turns, it faces a great wide arc of bobbing, cheering, hooting, whistling craft. Mark and Esther stand on the deck, each one now carrying a Visioneers flag and waving it vigorously above their heads, Esther still wearing the admiral's hat. The launch executes a series of short zig-zagging manoeuvres, acknowledging the flotilla; the *Song of the Visioneers* booms out across the water from loudspeakers set up by the Opera House; a dozen boats fitted with watercannon fire great volleys of spray into the air; and as a finale, a tremendous roar of "Three cheers for Mark and Esther!" rips across the harbour from shore to shore. The two Darlings of the Day stand side by side giving one last wave through the cascading water and noise of horns and whistles until their launch turns and speeds off down the harbour. Mark and Esther become private citizens again, while behind them the flotilla disperses, and Sydney goes back to enjoying its regular Sunday on the harbour.

Two days later, there's a repeat performance in Brisbane. This is Mark's home city and it's determined not to be outdone by Sydney in welcoming its own. Without the other's magnificent harbour, Brisbane puts on a ticker-tape parade through its main streets and an unforgettable fireworks display along the river. Smaller celebrations go on all week, culminating in a huge public reception at the Exhibition Grounds on Sunday, where fifty thousand people come out to share an ecumenical religious service with their famous guests.

Massed choirs of children have been pressed into quick rehearsal for the event. On the day, they stand grouped two thousand strong around a stage in the centre of the Exhibition oval and sing their hearts out. Hymns of praise and courage songs flood the area: children's voices, singing for their future! At the end all two thousand stand to sing new words to *Waltzing Matilda*, the Australian ballad known around the world. Tears spring to Mark's eyes. He grips Esther's hand tightly as she stands shining beside him.

"Once a jolly Venturer came down to Jerusalem
Seeking to show that the world could be free;
And he sang as he came and travelled

in that Holy Land
You'll come a Vis'ning, my darling, with me.

Vis'ning my darling. Vis'ning my darling.
You'll come a Vis'ning, my darling, with me.
And he sang as he came and travelled
in that Holy Land
You'll come a Vis'ning, my darling with me.

Along came a Fisher girl, who lived there in Jerusalem,
And met the young man with his plans to be free.
He told her his dreams and she slipped into
his loving arms,
Singing, You'll come a Vis'ning, my darling, with me.

Vis'ning my darling. Vis'ning my darling.
You'll come a Vis'ning, my darling, with me.
He told her his dreams and she slipped into
his loving arms,
Singing, You'll come a Vis'ning, my darling, with me.

Down came some evil men to trespass in Jerusalem,
To strike out the light that would set the world free.
But up sprang the loving hearts to act against
the evil ones,
Singing, You'll come a Vis'ning, my darling, with me.

Vis'ning my darling. Vis'ning my darling.
You'll come a Vis'ning, my darling, with me.
But up sprang the loving hearts to act against
the evil ones,
Singing, You'll come a Vis'ning, my darling, with me."

Now there's a brilliant light, shining in Jerusalem.
Blazing so bright that the whole world can see.
And we call for all nations to make the world
a Holy Land,
Singing, You'll come a Vis'ning, my darling, with me.

Vis'ning my darling. Vis'ning my darling.
You'll come a Vis'ning, my darling, with me.
And we call for all nations to make the world
a Holy Land,
Singing, You'll come a Vis'ning, my darling, with me."

Choked with emotion, Mark speaks to them.

"Yes, we will," he cries out. "We will make the world a Holy Land. It's a wonderful image! There's a spirit set free now that's sweeping the whole world. Boys and girls, men and women in every land are filled with it. It's good, it's strong, and it's true. God bless you all for coming out today! Wherever we go from here into the world Esther and I can never forget this scene here today, and your song. Keep singing, boys and girls! Keep singing loud and strong until the leaders of all the nations do indeed make this world a Holy Land!"

True to his advice, they start the song again as Mark and Esther step down from the stage into an open-top white convertible. They cruise slowly around the arena, waving to the children packed into centre oval and to the throngs of other people crowded into the stands all around. As they come to the gate to leave, the children in the choir break out into the *Song of the Visioneers*. The crowd picks it up and Mark and Esther leave the Exhibition Grounds with the now familiar words in every land ringing out into the cloudless blue Brisbane sky.

"We are the ones, going to the fore.
Big ones, little ones—all of us are here.
Small world, big world,reaching out to all.
Up up and upmost—the mighty Visioneers!"

Esther's Dream

The next day Mark and Esther make the last visit on their Australian journey. They go again to Mark's childhood home. They've been staying with his parents in Brisbane, and it's hard to leave so soon. Bob and Alice Venture are still full of their Jerusalem experience. Since returning, they've become celebrities in their own circles, telling the story of the wedding day over and over again. Now with Mark and Esther actually at hand, their lives are full to overflowing. They find it hard to let their famous son and daughter-in-law go, but all four know that this is something Mark and Esther must do alone.

Mark had brought Esther here before, in the heady days of their early courting, when the Visioneers were first spreading out around the world. He had come back then to find himself and the strength he would need for what lay ahead. He had brought Esther with him to let her feel the pulse of this spot, the place on Earth that had fashioned his boyhood spirit. Since then, he has touched the heart of her own country. Now together, man and wife, united in love and purpose, they come one more time to listen to the land.

Last time the creek had been running high, and they had left the car at the ford to walk down to the homestead. But it's been dry for many months now and the creek is down to a trickle; so they cross it in the car and drive down along the two dirt vehicle tracks, through the tall yellow grass and the sombre iron-bark trees.

Mark's brother, who now owns the property, had been in with his wife to clean the house for them. Mark and Esther plan to spend the night there. From the outside the place is much the same as when they'd come before, the collapsing fence, the sagging verandah, the unpainted weather-board walls. Inside, however, everything is fresh and clean. The windows have been thrown open to let in a cool breeze, the kitchen is well scrubbed and over-generously stocked with food. Fresh cut flowers in vases brighten the whole house.

The large double bed has been made up for them in the room that Mark remembers as his parents' bedroom. Standing there looking in with Esther he feels strange at first, recalling the little boy who had crept into the room in the early hours of Christmas morning with a brand new meccano set tucked under his arm to show his mum and dad what Santa Claus, or Father Christmas as he called him then, had brought. The memory passes, and Mark feels good to be here.

Time moves quickly. They explore the property again as they did last time: the crumbling sheds and barns, the old orchard where a good crop of grapes and blackberries are growing wild among the orange and plum trees. They eat their evening meal early in the old kitchen, then set out in the gathering darkness to go to the rocky outcrop above the creek, where last time they had sat under the stars and thought about their friends the Visioneers who were just beginning their work across the world. The same stars are still ablaze in the sky, while around them on the ground a gentle stillness spreads like an invisible cloak.

Instinctively they both recall the night they had spent camped out under the same sky at Ayers Rock almost two weeks ago. There both of them had felt a strange pull of the Earth, a surging energy field, prescient with power. Here the energy is softer, but enfolding, a sense of reaching out, linked not only to the powerful pull of the centre, but embracing everything that stretches far beyond the dark horizons of this tableland, across the oceans to the continents and their people around the globe. Filled with this presence, Mark and Esther fall silent and sit content for many minutes among the rocks, feeling the wholeness of the life force embracing them.

After a time, Mark puts his arms around Esther. She comes close to him. He kisses her gently. Hand in hand they make their way back to the house. In the bedroom, Esther slips easily out of her dress. Mark folds her in his arms. It's a moment of ultimate peacefulness. They cling to each other, feeling the warmth of their bodies spreading around them, then rising in a quickening passion of the pleasure that they know in their lovemaking. Esther tips back her head, her lips parting to call for the sensuous kiss that will then flow down her body to the full white tenderness of her breasts, where Mark's lips are now caressing her, his arms strong around her waist, lifting her to the bed, where his body settles on her, so she feels his weight and the spreading desire for him to come reaching inside her, gently at first, but then with the firm thrusting power that floods her to the tip of her being, and rushes through him until he feels himself linked to her and she to him in the rising ecstasy of the moment, rising, rising, cresting, until finally it explodes and they can again be quietly together, secure, warm and fully bonded in their love.

The quiet lush evening now embraces them, as they lie in each other's arms and slide gently into sleep. Mark knows nothing further for several hours, until suddenly he wakes and sees the first sign of dawn lighting the sky just visible through the window. Beside him, Esther is breathing gently. He reaches across to bring her closer. She sighs heavily and cuddles up to him. More awake now, he lies there holding her. She moves restlessly in his arms. He notices her breathing, more pronounced, becoming quicker. She trembles in his arms. Her head tosses from side to side. She moans softly. More restlessness. He feels her body stiffen, then arch slightly, tensing up like a spring. Her head tosses more quickly, then with a cry she snaps awake, her eyes wide open, staring at him in the pale light of the coming dawn.

"Oh Mark, Mark," she whispers. "I saw it."

"Saw what, darling?" he asks. "You were dreaming."

"Oh, yes," she replies. "Yes, but I saw it. Oh, quickly, Mark, I want to tell you, I must tell you before it goes."

She sits up.

"Come on," she says. "We have to get up. I need pencil and paper. I have to show you. Oh, it's so clear. Come on, darling, help me, please."

She's already out of bed, gathering her robe around her. Mark follows. She leads them to the kitchen. Still partially in her dream, she fumbles unsuccessfully for something to write on. Mark is smiling at her. He sits her at the table and produces a pad and pencil.

"There," he says, "now what do you want to show me?"

"Oh, Mark, it was so strange. At first it didn't mean anything, just a lot of weird stuff, I can't remember what. But then suddenly it was clear. I was up in the sky looking down, and below me was Ayers Rock, just like we saw it as we flew in. And I could feel that energy again, only much stronger, maybe because I was lighter than air, and it was pulling me down. On the top of the Rock where you and I had walked, there was a pool of brilliant white light, and I was pulled into it. From there I could see shafts of light radiating out and upwards, but going in different directions. There were five of them. I remember it quite clearly. It looked just like this."

On the pad she puts a circle in the centre of the page and draws five lines radiating out from it.

"Then I was lifted up and drawn along one of the lines. This one here running northwest. And in an instant I was looking down at the Earth again, but it wasn't Ayers Rock anymore. Do you know, it was Jerusalem. I swear to you. I saw it so clearly, I mean the whole city, in every detail from the air."

She makes another circle on the paper marking Jerusalem.

"And then, do you know," she continues. "I saw four more shafts of light radiating out from there, five counting the one I had followed from Ayers Rock."

She draws them on the paper.

"And then I followed one of them, this one, here, going northwest again. And there I was looking down on a wide green valley, with high mountain ranges on both sides. I don't know where it was. I had never seen it before, but the air was clear and sharp, like it was very high up and I felt the same strong energy there. And from a place close in to one of the ranges there were shafts of light radiating out again, only four this time. I followed one, still going northwest, and I came to another large city. I'm not sure where, but I sort of half recognized it. I've never been there, but I think it was Beijing, because I was looking down on this huge square in the middle of the city, and I think it was Tiananmen Square. From there, there were three shafts of light, and I followed one south: and do you know I was back at Ayers Rock."

All the time she's talking, Esther is drawing circles and lines on the paper.

"There's some kind of pattern here," she says. "I don't know what it is, but they're connecting up, aren't they? From Ayers Rock I followed a different shaft of light this time, going east, and when I looked down I was in the mountains again, and I recognized the place. Even though I've never been there, I knew it right away from photographs, just perched way up in the Andes. It was Machu Picchu, the Lost City of the Incas, and the energy there was very strong. Three more shafts of light radiated out, and I kept following one going east until I looked down on a great square mountain top. It must have been in Africa, I think. From there, a shaft of light went north, but I followed another one going east, and I came back to Ayers Rock.

"When I got there this time I felt really drained, as if all the energy had been drawn out of me. Probably no wonder, because I'd been around the world a couple of times. Then I woke up, and you were there holding me, and I had to tell you about it, because it was all so clear and powerful. Look, you can see here on the paper, there's a pattern of some sort. I'm sure it means something, darling . What do you think?"

Mark sits staring at the set of circles and lines that Esther has drawn. At first it looks like a jumble. Six circles, each one with five, four or three lines radiating out from it, some connected, some not going anywhere. Four of the circles are named: Ayers Rock, Jerusalem, Beijing, and Machu Picchu.

The other two appear to be in high mountains, one possibly in North America, and the other somewhere in Africa.

Mark takes the pencil from Esther and begins to draw connecting lines.

"I think, my darling, you've definitely been given a message of some kind. I'm not sure what yet, but look, if you start to join these lines just as you've drawn them, but imagine this flat sheet of paper as a round globe, so that you've got lines going around the back of the paper, so to speak, then I think what you've got is a way of dividing the world up into a number of segments, with each of these circles being a focal point."

"Yes, I see what you mean, I think, but I can't quite visualize it. And I still don't understand what it's all about."

"Neither do I," replies Mark, "but my hunch is that it's got something to do with the Congress of the Global Mind. We still haven't decided on the world centres for that and the way they're going to be linked together. I think you may have given it to us in one brilliant piece of intuition."

"But Mark, do you know what more it means? I didn't just make this up. Some of these places I've never seen. Perhaps going to Ayers Rock triggered something off. We both felt the energy there. But more important than that, what it means is that we're being guided now by some higher power to do this work.

"Do you remember what I said to you on the first morning after our wedding in Jerusalem? I said God was keeping us safe and that there is a plan. And remember those celebrations in Sydney and Brisbane, and people coming out in thousands to see us. It's all part of a great awakening. Oh, Mark, it's so exciting."

"Yes, Esther," Mark takes her hands and looks across the kitchen table at her, "and do you know, I think it really began when we were here last time. I knew then, though I hadn't asked you, that I was going to marry you. I knew there was a part missing in me, that I could never do what was being asked of me without that piece being filled in.

"You're there now, my darling. We've passed all the tests for togetherness, and some of them were pretty rough, but we're there now. We've got this wonderful partnership, and we've seen the first real sign of it this morning."

Mark gets to his feet.

"And now," he says, gesturing towards the window, "let's look for another sign. See out there. It's the sun coming up through the trees, and I just bet if we go out onto the verandah we'll get some old kookaburra to laugh. And he won't be laughing at us. As sure as the sun's rising, he'll be laughing with us, for a new day, and a new life, and a new world. What do you say we go out and give it a try?"

Arms around each other they walk out onto the verandah in the early morning sunlight. Immediately, from a tall gum tree out in the next paddock, the caw-caw, cackling laugh of a kookaburra breaks out. A few seconds later, it's picked up by another, on the other side of the house, then another, then another, until the whole of the bush is filled with their laughing. And on the verandah of the old homestead, two lovers, arms around each other, tousle-headed and sleepy-eyed, throw back their heads and join in the chorus: for the new day and their new life of meaning together.

CHAPTER TWENTY-TW0

Design

A HA!" YOU SAY TO YOURSELF. "They've already got things moving, those two two wonderful Visioneers."

"Ahem!" A not exactly apologetic cough interrupts your reverie. You open your eyes. You are sitting in your thinking room, but you're no longer alone.

The four of them are here: your mentors, returned, waiting for you to pay attention. They're standing in front of their chairs, looking just the way they did when you first met them: Winston Churchill in dark suit, bow tie, gold watch chain; Charles Dickens wearing his nineteenth-century suit with high stiff shirt collar and cravat; John Kennedy looking relaxed but ready for business in grey suit, blue shirt and tie; Anne Shirley mostly in red hair, and still dressed in her high-necked, puffy white blouse and long swishing green skirt.

It was Charles Dickens who had signalled their presence.

"Well now," he says, seeing that he has your attention. "Here we all are for the final sortie, eh! You've done well. Yes, very well, all things considered. It's coming together nicely. You kept us on the edge of our seats in Jerusalem. Now you've got us guessing again with this dream piece in Australia. But it's time to lay out a coherent plan for the rest of it. Wouldn't you say so, gentlemen and Anne?"

There are murmurs of approval from the others. You sense that your mentors are just a little annoyed with you, for excluding them for so long.

You spring to your feet, hastily seeking to reassure them of their central role in designing the outcome.

"Well yes, absolutely," you say. "I'm so glad to have you all back. It's really good to see you. I'm very honoured and very grateful for your help." You shake hands warmly with each of them. "Won't you please sit down?"

John Kennedy slaps you on the shoulder, relaxing the atmosphere.

"Aw, come on," he says. "Let's loosen up a bit here. You're doing a fine job, you and your Mark Venture, and now Esther is very strong, too. That's the way it should be. Our job was to get you going. Now you're flying. What more could a bunch of mentors like us wish for?"

"Thank you, Mr. President," you reply. "That's very kind of you to say so."

"Hrrmph!" Winston Churchill has cleared his throat. "That's all well and good," he growls, "but we have a master strategy here. And we must make sure we see it through."

This is one mentor who wants to keep his hand in the action. He continues:

"Now let's get down to business."

The others sit. Churchill moves to one side where he can address all of you. He strikes his oratorical stance, thumbs hooked into his vest pockets.

"We've got the world leaders primed with that extraordinary speech of Mark Venture's to the United Nations. Fine piece of work, that. It put the case exactly. Carlos Palmira is out of the way and his rotten empire's about to collapse. We can make a lot out of that. The Visioneers are set to pour into the vacuum. It's a good strategy, but timing's critical. We've got a little over six months before the Congress convenes. What we have to do now is build up the momentum."

Churchill now adopts his most parliamentary pose to deliver a telling speech:

"The dawn is breaking on the long day of our final triumph.
Our heroes and heroines stand ready for the test.
Across every continent the lines of communication will be erected.
Into every city, every village, every household, the word must go out,
    that this will be the world's greatest challenge,
    with riches for the taking far nobler than any spoils of war.
For we are set to create on Earth the Empires of the Mind:
Enlightened, ennobled, and empowered
    against the cowering forces of darkness,
Which conquer we must
And conquer we shall!"

"Oh bravo, Winston! Bravo! Well said!" Charles Dickens is applauding. You and the others likewise admire the old warrior's eloquence.

"Yes, and here's what we must do," Churchill continues. "A budget has to be set up for the event. The General Assembly approved it, now we have to move quickly to get the commitments in from the countries, before they start to change their minds. That's a first order of business for Mark Venture with the U.N. Secretary-General."

"How much are we talking about here?" asks John Kennedy.

"Whatever it takes," inserts Charles Dickens.

"Yes, that's right," replies Churchill. "We run it like a war campaign. Just keep spending until you get the job done."

"Okay. I go along with that," says Kennedy, "but we have to make sure the public relations are good. People will continue to pay while ever they believe in it."

"Excuse me, gentlemen," Anne has now joined the conversation. She had applauded enthusiastically Churchill's stirring speech, but during this last discussion about budget and public relations, she has become increasingly agitated. She leans forward in her chair, eyes wide open and appealing.

"I'm sure you've all had much experience in fighting wars and mounting campaigns, but I just want to say that I think this is different. In fact, we have to make it different, because if it isn't, then we'll just get the same results as before, some winning, some losing, and nothing settled. You've said it so well, Mr. Churchill. It's the world's greatest challenge. We're building the new Empires of the Mind. But it's not the old mind of conquest and control. No, it's the new mind of life and love. That's what Mark Venture said to the United Nations. That's what Luis Valdez told the world in his broadcast before he was killed. And the world has learned from that. You've seen them come out in thousands to his memorial service. You saw the reception for Mark and Esther at their wedding in Jerusalem, and the whole world was watching that. You talk about public relations, Mr. President: Mark and Esther's wedding was the greatest public relations event in history.

"I may only be a simple young girl, gentlemen, but I know when people are touched to their hearts. You heard the children singing in Brisbane: 'And we call for all nations to make the world a Holy Land.' That's what they sang for, that's what ordinary people in the whole wide world are singing for. And we've given them a chance to have it, all of us, by creating the Visioneers, who are running with nothing more than human spirit and hope and a belief in a better world that they can build with their minds.

"And we're ready to help them reach for it now, with our wonderful Congress of the Global Mind. It was your idea, Mr. Churchill. It's a marvellous idea. It's the greatest idea in the world. So let's not spoil it now by talking about budget and public relations. Let's just go on and help our Visioneers do it, by giving them the confidence to trust in the energy of their minds for changing the way the whole world thinks, and, therefore, how it acts."

"Oh, Anne, Anne, you've done it again." It's President Kennedy putting his arms around Anne, who is trembling and biting her lip, trying hard not to burst into tears. "You've put us right. Dear Anne, you're such a precious jewel. Thank you. Gentlemen," he says, turning to the other two, "Anne is saying that what we have to do from here is to let things flow. You know, Charles, you had it right when you described the world as a marketplace to the heads of government as they were leaving the Visioneering Room. Does everyone remember that? Tell it to us again, Charles, so we can all catch the vision."

Delighted with the opportunity to present, the ebullient novelist comes to his feet. All four of your mentors are now spread around the room. You sit entranced by the performance. Dickens takes up his position by the fireplace.

"Why, yes," he says. "I was leading the leaders. I wanted them to see in their imaginations the world of the future as a marketplace full of food and clothes and crafts and machines, all produced by fine creative minds striving for the best. And with that comes abundance to overflowing, all people everywhere touching and tasting and having whatever they really need, because they are working in a spirit of trust and support.

"And I saw within the marketplace the coffee-shops and the restaurants where people meet to eat and talk about how well they are caring for the Earth. And they talk about Assemblies and Sources and Networks where they are planning and coming together, not to be rich or powerful, but to be complete, to be people of integrity and compassion with a love for the Earth and all life on it.

"And Anne, yes, I remember, you added your vision of the children and how they are learning, not in schools like factories, but in great marketplaces of ideas and connections and books and projects in the community, the whole world as a community of people learning how to care for each other and the Earth.

"And, oh, Mr. President, how well I remember you laying your vision of leadership on top of that! Leadership that would give back hope to the world of a wonderful future built on trust, cooperation, and learning.

"And, Mr. Prime Minister, your final superlative summing up. Your charge to the world leaders to go out and empower their people to become a tidal force of energy to create the new age of enlightenment.

"Oh, it was a magnificent vision that we gave them, those leaders, going out through the golden arch into the world of the Visioneers. And now it's ready to come into place. Here we are poised to give it birth. The stage is set. The audience is seated. Take up the curtain, and let the final act begin!"

"Hrrrumph!" The great Churchillian expletive again resonates around the room.

"Very well," his voice is gravel grinding through gears. "I hear what all of you say. So be it. We may not be engaged here in a war, but we are, I can assure you, embarked on an enterprise of great complexity. It will test our wits to the utmost to pull it off. How much I'd give to be out there in the fray to get it done!

"But that, I know, is not my role, nor the role of any of us here. The Visioneers will do the work. We are their guides and must give them full support. To do that in their final act, the four of us here must now move to a new level of involvement with the Visioneers."

He pauses and looks around. Every eye is fixed on him.

"We must meet in session immediately with Mark and Esther in the Visioneering Room."

This is a turn you hadn't anticipated. So far, the Visioneers have been your confederates. You brought them in on the silver bridge to the Visioneering Room. You greeted them and gave them their mission. Then you began to work directly with Mark Venture as their leader. Your own mentors played a separate role advising you. You used them to conduct the session with the world leaders whom you had spirited out of the United Nations. But now, Churchill is suggesting a new development, that the mentors work directly with Mark and Esther to guide the progress of the Global Mind project. It's a new idea. What do the others think of it? You don't have long to wait to find out.

"Yeah, that's a good idea, Winston," John Kennedy responds. "I've been kind of interested in meeting those two. We've loaded them up with a lot of responsibility. They'd probably appreciate knowing more about what's behind it all. You're right, we should do it."

"Oh yes, I agree, too," says Anne. "I've wished for so long I could tell them how important their love is to the world. Let's bring them in, now."

"Well, there's always a new turn on any road," Charles Dickens now adds his comment. "I remember playing my characters many times on the stage, but this will be the first time I've actually met any. Not that Mark and Esther are purely my characters. I just gave them birth. You've breathed life into them. Yes, I think it would be an interesting next step. Capital idea, Winston, let's do it right away."

With that kind of response, what choice do you have? You move to set up the meeting.

The New Team

The Visioneering Room is the way it was when the Visioneers first arrived. A great round meeting place full of light, with tiered seating and wooden desks rising almost full circle from a centre space. Here the huge iridescent hologram of the Earth turns and glows. In brown, green, gold, blue and white of ocean, land and sky, it fills the room with the beauty of a living planet.

You have grouped a small cluster of chairs in the open space facing the rotating globe. Alone for a moment, you reflect on all that's happened here: the first meeting of the Visioneers; the early planning sessions with Mark Venture before he moved his headquarters to Los Angeles; the tumultuous entry of the world leaders; the terrifying experiences of man-made hell on Earth; and the final triumphant exit of the leaders through the golden arch into the world of the Visioneers.

"Why Mark, look where we are. Isn't it wonderful?"

It's Esther's voice. You look up and see them coming hand in hand around from behind the globe, the two honeymooners, fresh from their adventures in Australia.

"Hello," you say, going to greet them. "It's so good to see you back here in the Visioneering Room."

"Yes," Mark replies, warmly shaking hands, "and if past experience is a guide, I'm sure there's a good reason for it."

"Why yes," you reply. "You might say that. I've got some people I want you to meet."

Immediately on cue your four mentors come in from around the other side of the globe.

"Mark and Esther," you continue, "I'd like you to meet my four mentors who are working with me. Now they wish to work directly with you, to go the step beyond and build the vision of a spectacular future. Allow me to present Anne of Green Gables, Charles Dickens, John Kennedy, and Winston Churchill."

"Oh, dear!" Esther is awestruck. "I'm so honoured. I can hardly believe it. Mark, did you know about this?"

"Well, only vaguely," Mark replies. "I knew there were some guiding hands at work, but, well . . . " He gestures to all of them. "As Esther says, we're most honoured."

Churchill breaks the ice on the other side. His eyes have a merry twinkle to them.

"We're the ones who have the honour here," he says. "You two are leading a valiant fight with courage and determination. Your finest hour is approaching. We're here to lend you strength, but in the end, it will be you who will carry the day."

He comes up and shakes their hands warmly. Then greetings pass all around, each mentor echoing Churchill's words of praise. The mood relaxes. You feel the energy and know that you're in the presence of an extraordinary exchange. They sit down in the chairs, all except Churchill, who signals that he's about to lead off the discussion.

"I'll come right to the point," he says. "Time is of the essence. We have six months in which to prepare to stage the most memorable event in human history. All of us understand the concept. Now we must put flesh to the bones.

"The first issue is to design the structure. We must create a way to enfold the Earth, not as the broken pieces of a shattered vase, such as the nations and the peoples are today, but as a superlative whole fabric, such as we see before us here in this magnificent globe.

"The Visioneers have begun the process by striking out with their sorties into every land. You've done well, Mark and Esther, by blanketing the planet with symbol and image of what the human spirit can attain. The world leaders have been thoroughly chastened and challenged by what they've experienced here. We sent them out with notions of a World Assembly to revitalize the concept of united nations. Now, through the Congress of the Global Mind, we'll give substance to this new order."

"So that's it!" Mark interjects. "I thought it must have been something like that. When I spoke to them in the General Assembly, they seemed almost as if they'd come from another planet."

"Yeah, in a sense they had," John Kennedy chuckles. "We gave them a good shaking up using Charles' Scrooge experience. And your speech, Mark, followed right on cue. They're ready now for a new enfolding, as Winston puts it, but the only way they'll get there is for the people to push them. It's a new way of looking at political life on the planet."

"Why, that's what it means!" Esther has sprung to her feet. "Excuse me, Mr. Kennedy and Sir Winston," she says, "but last night, at least, I think that's when it was, I had a dream. No, it was more like a vision. I can see now it fits with what you're saying. May I share it?"

"Go ahead," replies Churchill, "that's why we wanted you here."

"Oh, if there was only some way I could draw on this globe, then I could show you."

"Go ahead," you say, "just describe what you want. It'll come up."

"Why then," Esther smiles, "it was like this. I saw a number of centres where the Earth's energy was really strong. I don't know why, but I could feel it. Four of them were places I recognized. There was Ayers Rock, in the centre of Australia; Jerusalem, my home; Beijing, more specifically Tiananmen Square; and Machu Picchu, the lost city of the Incas in Peru."

As Esther speaks, each of these places lights up on the globe. She looks amazed. The others smile.

"Why, that's marvellous," she says, looking at you. "Are you doing that?"

"You might say so," you reply.

"Well, perhaps you can help me with the other two," she says. "I'm not sure where they are. The first is a valley in high mountains somewhere in North America."

"That'll be Colorado," says President Kennedy, as quick as a flash.

"How do you know that?" asks Charles Dickens.

"I've read *Atlas Shrugged*," he replies. "You know, Ayn Rand's book about how the world's most creative and productive people gathered in this valley in Colorado to protect their genius from the despoilers. Besides, I've been there. Say, Esther, was it a long green valley between two mountain ranges, with a feeling of high energy all around?"

"Why, yes," Esther replies, "that's exactly how it was."

"Crestone, Colorado," Kennedy says. "Put it on the globe."

You do so. Esther looks nonplussed but continues. "The other place was also in the mountains, and I'm fairly sure it was in Africa: a big, square-topped mountain, as wide as all the world, and covered with snow."

"Kilimanjaro," says Churchill.

"Aha, Winston," chuckles Kennedy, "so you've read Ernest Hemmingway."

"Yes," replies Churchill. "And I also know Africa. That's Kilimanjaro to a tee. Put it on the globe."

"I'm glad you chaps read such good novelists," Charles Dickens exclaims from the sidelines. "I'm really impressed."

You add Kilimanjaro to the globe in east central Africa. Everyone sits looking silently while it makes one complete revolution. Then Esther continues.

"Now there were shafts of light radiating out from these centres like beams," she says, "and Mark was showing me that if you connect them up in a certain way you get the Earth divided up into segments."

Following Mark's thoughts, you put the lines on the globe.

"Why, that's incredible," Mark exclaims, looking at you with admiration. "That's exactly the way I saw it. Do the rest of you follow? See, we've got seven segments here, all triangular shaped, each one sharing a side of its triangle with three other segments, and at the bottom we've got a kind of a circle with Antarctica in the centre and taking in the southern portions of Australia, South America, and Africa."

"Oh, that's wonderful," Anne has jumped to her feet, clapping her hands. "It's a perfect way for people to look at the world. All the countries come together in their segments, but at the same time, they fold outwards to be part of other segments, and they're all pulled together into the six centres. Why, Esther, it's a splendid vision! You've given us the way to organize for our Congress of the Global Mind."

"Yes, Anne, I believe you're right." Churchill has gone over to the globe and is scrutinizing it more closely. "Will you stop it here just as Jerusalem comes round. Yes, that's it, right there. Can you all see how Jerusalem is at the strategic centre of the whole thing, with links out to every segment and every other centre? And it's also at the heart of the great areas of population in Asia, Europe, and Africa. Ladies and gentlemen, I believe we're looking at the site for the World Assembly. Jerusalem is destined to be the world's universal city, the centrepiece of the new millennium!"

"Why, Mark!" Esther can hardly contain her excitement, "that's exactly

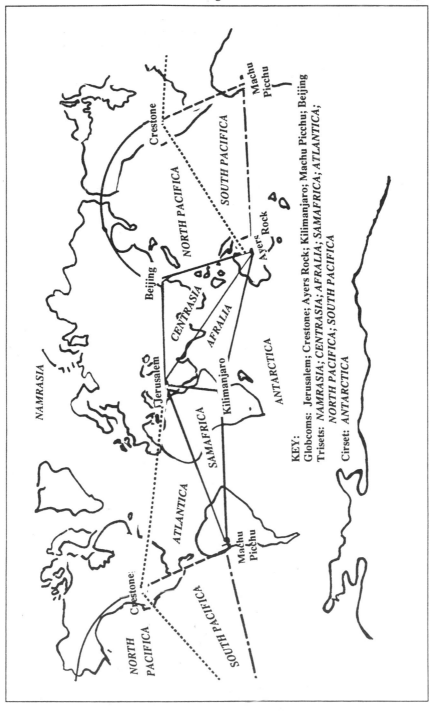

The World of the Visioneers

KEY:
Globcoms: Jerusalem; Crestone; Ayers Rock; Kilimanjaro; Machu Picchu; Beijing
Trisets: NAMRASIA; CENTRASIA; AFRALIA; SAMAFRICA; ATLANTICA;
NORTH PACIFICA; SOUTH PACIFICA
Cirset: ANTARCTICA

what the Reverend Ringthorpe said at our wedding! And who could ever forget Theresa singing about the New Jerusalem? And here it is again, right out of my vision, with all of us seeing it and focusing our thinking on it so we can understand it better. It's true! I'm sure it's true! Jerusalem will be the new centre and symbol for peace and love in the world!"

"Yes, Esther, that's right," John Kennedy is rocking back in his chair studying the globe. "And I'll tell you something else that's up there. Jerusalem will be drawing in strength from the other high energy centres that you've pin-pointed, and particularly from Colorado, because I believe it's positioned to be a stabilizing force for human spiritual development in the years to come. The axis between those two centres will be the link of the old with the new, and the world will be transformed by it."

"Well, we're certainly making progress here." Charles Dickens now enters the discussion. "I don't claim to have any prescient visions to contribute, but I can give you some descriptive terms to tidy up the picture you've presented. That's the stock and trade of the scribe, you know. First up, I see each one of the six centres as a global command post, so I suggest you call them 'globcoms'. Next, you need a name for each of the triangular shaped segments. How about 'triset', signifying a three-centred piece? The eighth one is more like a circle, so we can call it a 'cirset'. Now I have names for each of the pieces.

"Right at the top of the world, including northern Asia, Europe, and much of North America, we've got NAMRASIA. That's number one.

"Below that, including much of the Middle East and stretching across southern Asia through the Philippines and Indonesia down to northwest Australia, we'll call CENTRASIA. That's number two.

"Further south, that narrow wedge from Saudi Arabia and northeast Africa, across the Indian Ocean to northwest Australia again, can be called AFRALIA. That's number three.

"Now we'll go west to catch most of northern and Central Africa across the Atlantic Ocean to central South America. This piece I've called SAMAFRICA. That's number four.

"How do you like this? Has it got a ring to it?"

"Carry on, Charles, you're doing fine," laughs John Kennedy. "You're just renaming the world, that's all you're doing."

"Well, that's nothing new for you political chaps," rejoins Dickens. "Just ask Winston, there. He's done it a few times."

"Go on, you rogue," growls Churchill. "What are your other names?"

"All right," Dickens continues. "Next we go north to take in the north Atlantic seaboard, including the northern part of South America, the Caribbean, the eastern side of North America, and across to north Africa and Mediterranean Europe. We'll call that ATLANTICA. That's got a ring from the past, eh? Good old Atlantis and all. That's number five.

"Now we'll go to the Pacific and catch its northern rim including parts of North America, Asia, Japan, New Guinea and northeast Australia. That's called NORTH PACIFICA and it's number six.

"Of course, south from there catching the southern part of North America, some of South America and much of the eastern half of Australia, we've got SOUTH PACIFICA. That's number seven and the last triset.

"At the bottom of the world taking in Antarctica, and the southern parts of South America, Africa and Australia, as well as all of New Zealand, there we've got the cirset of ANTARCTICA. That's number eight.

"Ladies and gentlemen, I give you the New World Order, at least in name."

To much applause all around, Charles Dickens takes a mock bow. As he had named them, the new words had come up on the globe; so rotating in front of them the group can now see a world comprised of NAMRASIA, CENTRASIA, AFRALIA, SAMAFRICA, ATLANTICA, NORTH PACIFICA, SOUTH PACIFICA, and ANTARCTICA. There's silence for a time while everyone takes it in. Then Mark speaks.

"Friends," he says earnestly, "I believe we've done something quite extraordinary. We've put together the structure the Visioneers need to move the people on Earth into a new understanding, a new consciousness of life on the planet. We needed a new focus, and this is it: one that moves away from the centrality of nation states, and allows people in their natural communities to identify with a part of the Earth for which they can be responsible.

"We'll put three Visioneers in every one of the six globcoms, as Charles calls them, and from there they can connect both electronically and personally with all of the trisets that touch their centre. That way we'll have continuous and overlapping activity. Esther and I can remain free agents, moving around all globcoms and trisets.

"The main task will be to mobilize creative learning in every one of the regions, getting it down into every household, so that no one is missed. And we've got only six months to do it. It'll require the greatest concentrated learning effort the world has ever seen. What we're aiming at here is to free people's minds from the negativity and doubt, that hang like a thick blanket over the Earth.

"I'm excited now to be on with it! We've made a great start. I can see where we must go from here: building up momentum, until it breaks like a thundering wave as the Congress opens and every person on Earth is involved in creating the Global Mind."

At his last words Esther sits bolt upright.

"Oh, Mark!" she exclaims so sharply that the others turn to her. "Yes, I see that. I see exactly what you mean. It will be a creation." She comes to her feet and steps over to stare at the globe for a moment, then turns to the others, her face shining with inspiration. "Our Congress will not be a meeting, and not just an exchange of ideas. It will be an act of creation. More truly, it will be a re-creation, a rebirthing of the world, a grand evolutionary leap of human consciousness. We already have the model for it, written thousands of years ago in scripture by minds that didn't have the knowledge we have today, but inspired minds, nevertheless, inspired by the power of God moving within them. Oh, I can see it! I can see it so clearly now! The story in Genesis, the foundation of so much of the world's religious faith. It can become a metaphor for our time. It'll give us a way for every living being on Earth to experience the new creation.

"Our Congress will last for seven days. Just as the Scriptures tell of God creating the world in six days and resting in celebration on the seventh, so our Congress will re-create in six days what the world needs for its re-birth into a golden age. On the seventh day we'll rest and be thankful, and then we'll celebrate. Oh, how we'll celebrate! For we'll look everywhere, in every land, and we'll see so much that's good. Then we'll say to ourselves, all of us, all of the millions of us throughout the world who've been part of the experience, we'll say to ourselves: 'This is good. This is very, very good.' Then we'll rest from our labours and celebrate."

She pauses, eyes closed, smiling, her face a radiant glow with the vision in her mind. The others sit transfixed, waiting for her to go on, sensing that this is a moment of revelation for the work that lies ahead.

"It began in darkness," Esther now continues, eyes closed, almost in reverie. "Darkness was upon the face of the deep. And God said, 'Let there be light.' That will be our first theme. The opening day of the Congress will be a glorious festival of light, dispelling the darkness of negativity and destruction.

"On the second day God created Heaven. That will be our second theme: a day of contemplation, searching in our hearts for the meaning of a higher purpose that includes all people as one.

"Then on the third day God created the dry land out of the waters of the deep and called the dry land Earth. The third day will be our Earth Day, and everywhere people will join together and declare their plans for recreating the glory of that part of the Earth on which they live.

"On the fourth day God created the sun, the moon and the stars. This will be our Day of the Universe, a day for reaching with our minds to contemplate the infinite wonder of the stars and our place among them.

"On the fifth day, God created the creatures of the sea and the air. This will be our Day of the Oceans and the Sky, and we'll turn our thoughts to how we must care for those delicate creatures and the precious living systems that support them.

"On the sixth day, God began by creating the creatures of the Earth, of the dry land, and the last of these, with special responsibility for all the others, was man, created in God's own likeness. 'Male and female created he them,' and placed them in a glorious garden 'eastward in Eden.' So the sixth day of our Congress will be our Day of Birth. Together across the whole expanse of human habitation on the planet, we'll honour our civilization and our traditions, while we look into our hearts to see what we must do to preserve the Earth for all eternity. Then, together, as one great family on the planet, we'll commit and dedicate ourselves to that great mission.

"And on the seventh day, God ended his work, and He rested and blessed the seventh day and sanctified it. So, too on the seventh day of our Congress we'll rest from our search for wisdom and understanding and take pride in all that we've accomplished."

As she finishes speaking, Esther continues to stand facing the group with her eyes closed and her hands clasped together in front of her. Her mind lingers on in the vision of a world celebrating its rebirth. Silence hangs in the room.

Anne rises and comes to Esther. The young girl, visibly moved, puts her arms around the other and kisses her gently on both cheeks.

"Oh, thank you, Esther," she says. "Thank you for showing us how to go. Now I can see it, too." She turns to the others. "Can all of you see it? For seven whole days the world will pause from its headlong rush into the chaos that otherwise surely lies ahead. Coming together in projects of great worth, people will put aside their differences and dislikes. Around those magnificent themes of creation, they'll build the framework for unending millennia of peace and harmony on the planet. It begins here today, a dream in Esther's mind, which she shared with us, so that we, too, can catch it, and from us into the world, until it becomes the very dream of dreams that changes life on Earth forever."

Esther has opened her eyes and stands looking lovingly at Anne. She takes the young girl's hand and the two of them stand there together, tears running down their cheeks as their spirits rise, and the compelling power of their vision floods out and fills the room.

The voice of Charles Dickens, modulated and resonant, steals into the silence:

" 'Earth has not anything to show more fair:
Dull would he be of soul who could pass by
A sight so touching in its majesty.'

"If William Wordsworth could say as much about the city of London cloaked in the beauty of the morning, what might he have said of the vision these two young women have given us today? Where, indeed, is any poet, any master craftsman of word and image, who could in our hearts stir up such ecstasy of anticipation?" He has joined Esther and Anne.

The other men, too, have come to their feet. Dickens continues:

"My friends, we came together here to plan the final act of the great drama that we're giving to the world. But not in my wildest anticipation, nor in the loftiest soaring of my most eager imaginings, could I have foreseen the shining sublimity of what has just been placed before us. Yes, my dear Esther and my precious Anne, I can see your vision. So, I'm sure, can all of us here, we men so well accustomed to battling in hard reality. You've given us a glimpse of God again moving in His Earthly garden. May we now say, yes to such a dream; yes to its inscription in the minds of all on Earth; and yes to the commitment and the labour to make it so."

They cluster together, a tight circle of strong friends, earnest conspirators for a divine unfolding. You stand aside for the moment, not in isolation, but as one privileged to have experienced a great moment in human thought.

Humbled, but enlivened by the rising hope that the vision glimpsed indeed can be, you let your companions slip away, and turn your mind to making it so.

CHAPTER TWENTY-THREE

Preparation

Iт's EARLY MORNING ON THE NEXT DAY, and you're back in the Visioneering Room with Mark and Esther. If the enterprise is to move posthaste, it's necessary to get the Visioneers together, and what better place to do it than here where it all began six months ago. You hadn't by any means fully understood then where things might go. Now you find yourself being driven by a timetable set by the Visioneers to see the world through to a rebirth. And only six more months to do it in! With the grand design described by Esther and the others filling your mind, your energy is up for the action. Outside, the sun shines brightly on the snow-covered landscape. It's a pleasant spring day in the mountains. A warm Chinook wind has blown in from the Pacific, giving the exhilarating feel of shirt-sleeve weather in the thinning snow. A short way off the silver bridge stands ready to bring in the guests, and the red carpet of welcome awaits their arrival.

The Visioneers Return

Now here they come, the jolly band of Visioneers, with President Mutsandu as usual leading the way. The last time they were together was in Jerusalem for the wedding. That was just two weeks ago, it hardly seems so long. They're all still full of the excitement of that day.

As they approach the building, Mark and Esther hurry out to greet them. Immediately a shout goes up, and what order there was in the procession immediately evaporates, as they all rush forward to greet the newlyweds.

A few moments later they're coming in. You're there to meet them. How proud you are! Your own band of Visioneers, already stirring hearts and minds around the globe, but now destined to usher in a new creation. You know them all so well now, each one more ordinary than exceptional, but all of them together, an extraordinary force, because they have set themselves a high purpose, and have now become it.

You greet them each by name as they come by: President Mutsandu, General Soulière, Mohammed Hussein, Indira Murti, Boris Gunther, Theresa Romano, Daniel Thomas, Karl Ibsen, Carmen Santander, Nicholai Andropov, Sally Hearst, Bill Bates, George Cardinal, Lin Yuen, Irene Henshaw, Jeremy Hiscox, and Junichi Yakasawa. All just as you remember them from the first meeting, colourful, distinctive, enthusiastic, citizens from many lands and many cultures, but all children of the Earth, and shining with excitement to carry out their mission.

Within minutes they've all found a place and Mark is addressing them.

"Welcome friends!" he exclaims, "and were I to say it a thousand times, I couldn't mean it more. Good, dear friends, how wonderful to see you all here in this place of destiny for each of us. Esther and I can't begin to tell you how much your support has meant to us. In Jerusalem our enterprise reached a turning point in many ways. From there we all emerged triumphant to world acclaim. Now today, Esther and I are here to share with you the vision of what comes next.

"It will be magnificent! We can give you only the outline, because that's all we have. The rest of it is in your hands to create. But what we can tell you, is that our enterprise is guided. We're meant to bring forward a transformation on the planet. All that we've done to date has just been prelude to what's to come. We've been tested, pushed to the very limit of our endurance, and we've won through to grasp this moment. The forces aligned against us are enormous, but we have them on the run, and within the next six months we'll drive through them with a determination so strong that nothing will stop us.

"To give you heart, Esther and I can tell you that within the last few hours we've been made aware of powerful mentors at work for us in the background. They have already prepared the world leaders for changes that I'm sure none of us can fully comprehend. But this much we do know: the changes will constitute an overwhelming shift towards peace, goodwill, and love, and away from the violence, and division that have been the curse of the human race for thousands of years. Though we can't expect perfection, I can tell you that what we'll do together will be miraculous."

Mark pauses to look around the group. No one says a word. All are following with rapt attention. He continues:

"We're about to set up six command posts in strategic locations around the world. From these points we'll direct the preparation of people in every country to be participants in our Congress of the Global Mind. You're all familiar with the concept of the Congress as a means to engage the entire population of the planet in shared responsibility for the future. You know, too, that the United Nations has agreed in principle to support this project. Now it's up to us to get it done.

"When we first spoke of the Congress several weeks ago, the concept wasn't clear. Even when I proposed it to the United Nations, it was still only a shadow in my mind. I knew it was to be our great work, but it seemed that something yet had to happen before it could begin to take its form. Now I understand that Esther and I had first to undergo a test of our courage and commitment in Jerusalem. You all were witness to what happened there. It was as if both we and the world were being prepared for what could follow, if only we held true to our course.

"Now in the aftermath of all that happened, I can tell you something wonderful. Esther was shown a glorious vision of what the Congress is meant to be. Together with the mentors, whom I mentioned before, we've shaped it to the point where now we can tell you about it.

"This is Esther's dream and I'll ask her to share it with you."

Smiling, Esther comes to the front as Mark withdraws, giving her the space. Her eyes shine with the same brilliance as when she spoke from her heart to the mentors only a few hours ago. Her voice is soft and flowing as she weaves for her fellow Visioneers the magic of the vision she has seen. Behind her as she speaks, the globe displays the pattern of the command posts, the globcoms, and the trisets that will fold the people of the Earth together in preparation for the Congress. When she describes the unwinding of the Congress through the seven days of creation, the globe melts away, and in its place the Visioneers see a huge blue dome arching up to the ceiling of the room. Esther stands under the dome and around her a magical display of lights, like a kaleidoscope of bewitching patterns, captures the splendour of her images, until, at the end, it silently explodes into the cascading brilliance of celebration and joy.

"From this moment on," Esther is concluding, "the Earth can never again return to the old destructive pattern. A critical mass of people in every triset will have moved their minds to a planetary and universal awareness. A Planetary Peoples Forum will be created in a New Jerusalem, and its messages of peace and progress will spread around the Earth like the brilliant rays of the brightest star in Heaven."

As she finishes, above her and around her a shining white object comes spinning slowly, first as a speck of light out of a vast universe, then growing into a huge five-pointed star which bursts into such dazzling intensity that every eye in the room must be shielded from its brilliance. Then it softens. Esther has stopped speaking, and a hush hangs in the room.

Mark rejoins Esther, taking her hand. Standing with her, the white star shining above them, he speaks to the Visioneers again:

"Friends, that's the vision that will guide our mission of the next six months. We've got a lot to do to prepare ourselves. It will be hard, unending work, but the joy and certainty of our success will burn in our minds. Nothing can prevail against this. I know it as sure as I know my heart."

As he says this, Mark suddenly becomes aware of another presence in the room, a sense of higher energy and power suddenly around them. A murmur goes up from the Visioneers. They've seen him. Mark and Esther turn to look behind. There, coming towards them, as if materializing out of the blue dome, is Baba Satyananda. As usual, he wears the simple saffron robe that flows around him as he moves. He comes down between Mark and Esther and, taking each by the hand, leads them forward a few paces. His face glows with the benign warmth of a great Master. His voice caresses and comforts his listeners.

"The Earth has waited a long time for this moment," he says. "How, therefore, could I let it pass without coming to be part of it? Our beloved Esther and Mark have set the scene, not only by what they've said this morning, but also through their courage and commitment in the face of gravest danger. It would do me great honour to add my own words to support their vision."

"We're the ones who are honoured Baba," Mark replies. "From past experience, I know when you come by that something spectacular is about to happen. The floor is yours. All of us are eager to hear your message."

Mark and Esther move away, leaving Baba alone to address the Visioneers.

"My friends," Baba continues, "the stage is set for a great transition on the Earth, but the outcome is not certain. We're moving here on cosmic scale. In time, light will dispel darkness, but the hour and passage of the transformation will depend on the choices made by many millions of people on the planet. Your destiny is to be the agents of the change, but how well it moves will depend on the power you bring to the task. It begins with yourselves. Your achievements to date have been extraordinary. The world is paying attention as never before. But the change required in the transition encompasses more than normal human consciousness can conceive. Your task, therefore, is to raise consciousness to a higher level, where current perceptions will be seen as the limitations that they truly are.

"This shift to higher levels of awareness is not easily achieved. It requires mental discipline and skills unknown and unpracticed on the planet by most people for many thousands of years. The cumulative result of this limited perception is the chaos and despair that now everywhere abounds. To change that requires a massive shift from the current prevailing belief that nothing different is possible.

"People are locked into their present understanding that the only reality is what they perceive around them with their five senses. For the most part this consists at best of conflict, argument, and discrimination in a neverending struggle between those who have and those who don't, between those who win and those who lose. At worst, the reality is violence, bloodshed, hatred, persecution, corruption, and a certainty that control of the weak by the strong is the natural order of life in the world.

"These beliefs and behaviours have pulled a shroud of death and destruction over the planet. Oh, my dear beloved friends, how might we weep for the Earth and the burden she bears! The beauty and prosperity that could abound is replaced instead by fear and minds filled with cynicism and limitation. Such minds fail and fail and fail again to create a beautiful civilization of peace, love and harmony, because they have not discovered such qualities in themselves.

"And yet, my dear valiant friends, I'm here to say that such a glorious alternative reality truly exists, locked in the consciousness of the same minds who still perceive so little of it. Today's world of negativity and limitation has been created by the prevailing collective unconscious. A new world tomorrow of harmony and love will be the outcome of a new collective unconscious, born of a new learning.

"Mark has called this creative learning. You are its role models. To bring it to the world in its full power you must manifest it in your own thinking. The work that now awaits you is of the highest order in the universe. To achieve it you must control your energies by deep and frequent meditation. You must be centred and in balance, absorbing the light of the universe into your minds, becoming one with the flow of the life force. As your own power grows in this way, you will be the guides and mentors to the countless millions who must follow if the transformation to the new reality is to be achieved.

"It has been revealed to you today through Esther's vision how you are to establish command posts for aligning the Earth's energies with the higher consciousness of people everywhere on the planet. More will be revealed to you as you meditate and work together over the coming weeks to set this beautiful structure in place.

"It remains now only to begin. Today, here, now, we take the first step. I have come as your guide and mentor to show you how with your minds you will set God's great plan in motion."

Baba pauses in his address. His face is shining with the same radiance as the star above him. He turns away from the Visioneers and raises his arms in silent open embrace of the energy he has described. The globe reappears, settling into its customary place, but now with the blue dome and white shining star overhead. The globe is still lit with the flashing lights and names of the globcoms and trisets set up with the mentors. Baba, still with arms raised, turns back to the Visioneers.

"Join with me now, my friends. Come, take your place around the globe where we will quiet our minds and bring in the power of the universe to set our work in motion."

Silently the Visioneers move from their seats to gather around the globe. Baba asks them to sit on the thick blue and white carpet on the floor. There, sitting upright, eyes closed and hands resting easily in front of them, the Visioneers move in their minds as Baba leads them in guided meditation.

First he takes them into deepening relaxation of body and mind with steady, even breathing. Then softly, barely audible at first, but rising like a breeze resonating across open landscape, he begins to chant the sound of "om". Others join with him and their simple chant rolls around the room, nurturing their minds to embrace the thought energy slowly gathering to uplift them. Baba ceases his chant and leads them with his voice.

"Your mind is as still as a glassy pond resting in the quiet serenity of green field and open sky. Now, slowly with effortless motion, you ascend, the Earth dropping away in shades of green and brown and gold below, until they touch the blue of the ocean swell, reaching out to the far horizon where the setting sun spreads a crimson glow across scattered clouds. Upward you float until the horizon has become the curve of the Earth and spreading out below you in its canopy of dark space and distant stars, the planet shines as bright and blue as new creation.

"Your mind swims in awesome contemplation, then begins to stir with an energy coming from the stars. It passes through your consciousness, drawing you with it into a flowpath to the blue planet which is now no longer apart from you, but has merged into your mind. Points of energy erupt as bursts of white light and they reach in bands around the circling globe, crossing into segments, locking into place, forming the pattern described to you before by Esther.

"You are aware now of your companion Visioneers moving with you along the embracing bands of white light. All of you move off in twos and threes, moving to the centres, all around the Earth, but all of you still in contact through your minds. You feel the energy of the Earth, locking in the energy from the stars. Each of you is separate, but you act as one, holding the energy, feeling the Earth grow strong with you as your minds blossom in the ecstasy of creation.

"You hold that pattern now and look down across the Earth and see millions of people, caught in the turmoil of a great turbulence as earth and ocean heave around them and their cries ring out as stabs of pain in your mind. But still you hold the pattern, forcing your energy down and around the struggling scenes of desperation. Gradually they become less frantic, settling out, and you sense a peace enfolding everything around. As you hold the pattern, you see each other across the centres, helping the Earth to settle, finding a new rhythm to replace the turmoil of before. You know that together you have held the pattern.

"All is still now. The Earth is enfolded in a blue-violet haze. Its energy is strong and steady, and it fills your mind with the sound and song of all creation."

Baba's voice resumes its chanting, louder now than before, rising and falling, rising and falling, surrounding the Visioneers with its continuous, pulsating rhythm. Then, almost imperceptibly, it begins to draw away, like an ancient caravan moving out into the immensity of the desert until lost to sight. The chanting has stopped. The room is filled with silence. As the Visioneers open their eyes and join each other in full consciousness, they see that Baba has left them.

Their conversation is soft but intense as they come to their feet, gathering together in groups, sharing their emotions, knowing that the time has now come for them to begin. Esther and Mark have joined them. They shake hands all around, and linger a little longer in the gentle mind space that Baba has created for them. They know now what he meant by the need to teach such skills of mind to millions throughout the world. It's an awesome task, but they're ready to begin. Quietly and deliberately they return to their places to start the planning.

Back to the United Nations

Standing in Peter Hemphill's corner office in the United Nations building in New York, Mark Venture looks out across the vastness of the city. It's a sobering vista. A thousand times ten thousand minds, and it still wouldn't account for the concentrated population within a hundred kilometre radius of where he stands. And yet already far out beyond those limits, his handful of Visioneers are sprinkled around the globe taking upon their shoulders the preparation of the planet for the birth of the Global Mind. It's a wild, audacious thought, but as sure and certain in his mind as if it were already accomplished.

In New York he has come to secure the resources of the world's nations for the project. It has been a good beginning.

"Well now, there we are, the best blend of English tea, made with water properly boiled to toast your triumph." Peter Hemphill has returned to his office bearing a tea set of fine English china, consisting of cups, pot, milk jug, sugar basin, silver tongs and spoons. "Now, old boy, say when for the milk, and tell me how many lumps of sugar."

"Just serve it strong and sweet, Peter," Mark smiles at his friend, knowing that any other choice would most likely have been ignored.

"Excellent taste," responds Peter, "it matches your charming disposition."

Mark moves away from the window to drink his tea with Peter in the comfortable sitting area of the office. His companion gives him a searching look.

"I must admit you still continue to amaze me," he says. "In one afternoon with the Secretary-General you've secured more funds for your Global Mind project than all the rest of our activities combined."

"That's because people with vision know that when we've accomplished this task," replies Mark, "many of the others won't be necessary anymore."

"I don't know how many proposals I've heard like that," says Peter, waving his hand in the air, "including ones from some of the most powerful people on Earth. But you're the first one to pull off anything like this."

"Not me alone, Peter. There's a powerful team effort going on out there, including yourself, you self-effacing bureaucrat."

"Be that as it may, old boy, it's still a miracle. Now that you've got the funds, what next?"

"Why, we're going to set up the globcoms and lock in the trisets," replies Mark.

"Sounds like a visit to the chiropractor," says Peter. "Where the dickens did you get such names?"

Mark laughs out loud. "You got it right, straight off, Peter. It was Charles Dickens, himself, who invented them."

Peter looks at him, searchingly. "I'm sorry I asked," he says finally. "Go on, tell me more."

"Well, it's just as I explained to you and the Secretary-General in our meeting earlier," Mark replies. "The globcoms will be the centres for our operations. Given the short timeline for the project, we'll build temporary, pre-fabricated structures, but each one will be distinctive. The heart of each will be its communication centre. We'll need the best technology in the world in that department. Bill Bates is already talking to suppliers. I'm off tonight to begin negotiating on sites with the authorities in each country involved. The U.N. will be a great help in speeding that through."

"What about Esther?" asks Peter. "When are you truly weds going to get time to spend together?"

"Certainly not as often as we'd like," says Mark. "Esther will be focusing on publicity. We have to make sure that people understand what's happening."

"Well, after all the bad news that's coming out now about Palmira's Trust and Credit Corporation, I should think people will be looking for something a lot more wholesome. Esther's just the one to do that."

"What do you think about the I.T.C.C., Peter?" Mark has become serious. "Has the operation really been smashed?"

"Oh, yes, I believe so, but you know in a garbage heap as vast as that, there's a lot of rats slipping away into holes before the authorities can prosecute. And there's a lot of official stalling, too, in many countries, precisely because those same officials were part of the network. Still, Harrigan's implication of Palmira in the assassination attempt against you and Esther has done a lot to speed things up. You two are such darlings of the media that anyone who does anything to harm you is going to be torn apart. Of course, with Palmira himself gone, it's much easier. He had no heir apparent to follow him, so the whole thing's come apart in a lot of internal warfare."

"And with people like Larry Porter out of the way, that surely helps," adds Mark.

"Yes, poor old Larry, King of Palmira's U.S. drug scene. He's going to be out of circulation for a long time. But you know, the sad part is that the only reason these guys are successful in the first place is that there's a market out there for the stuff. Just because a supplier gets put away doesn't mean the problem disappears. Behind every Larry Porter there's a hundred others waiting to take his place to meet the demand. Until you break that chain, nothing really changes."

"Well, that's what the Visioneers are out there doing. I can tell you the world's going to see some very dramatic results in the next six months."

"I wish you well on that, Mark," Peter says earnestly. "If we could only claw back some of the wasted energy and money that goes into that, the world would take a quantum leap forward."

"We will, Peter, we will," Mark declares with the authority of one who knows what can be done. "Oh, and tell me, speaking about claws, whatever has become of Palmira's girlfriend, Elvira Ramos?"

"She's still lying low in Colombia, as far as I know. She could be very dangerous to you and Esther, Mark. It's that kind of loose end that still makes me fear for your safety."

"You're a good, friend, Peter. But just as we couldn't back away from confronting Palmira, we can't allow our work to be impeded by the likes of Elvira Ramos. This is Holy Grail stuff we're working on here. No vindictive woman is going to stop us."

"For your sake and the world's, I hope you're right," Peter Hemphill replies.

After that, their talk is of details for managing the U.N. involvement in the project. Then Mark leaves to catch his plane for Beijing.

On the Stones of Tiananmen Square

The weak sunlight filters down through the pollution haze above the capital city of China. Mark, dressed warmly against the chill in parka and mitts, stands looking around in the centre of an almost deserted Tiananmen Square. With him two other men, similarly dressed, stamp their feet and beat their hands together, to keep the circulation going. Around them, their warm breath puffs up in tiny clouds as it mixes with the frigid air locked in over the city.

One of Mark's companions on this unusually cold spring morning in Beijing is Jeremy Hiscox, the quiet, but energetic Professor of History from Cambridge University. Jeremy's first assignment with the Visioneers had been in England to bring in the interest and support of a worldwide network of foundations. He had been very successful at that, capturing the attention of British and European royalty in the enterprise. This had been instrumental in first bringing the Visioneers to world attention when Prince Rupert of Wittenstein had introduced three of them to an Extraordinary General Conference of Unesco in Paris.

One of those three, Junichi Yakasawa, is Mark Venture's second companion on Tiananmen Square this morning. Since that early Unesco appearance, Junichi has been active in his native Japan stimulating interest in the Visioneers with the assistance of Ahio Morita, a wealthy industrialist who has been throwing his wealth and influence behind Junichi. But progress has been slow in that country of vast new wealth. Economic growth and very little intercultural mixing keeps the Japanese people isolated from much that goes on in the world. However, Mark and Esther's wedding broadcast live from Jerusalem created quite a stir in Japan, and now the attention of the country to the presence of the Visioneers has been aroused.

The reason why Jeremy Hiscox and Junichi Yakasawa are in Beijing this morning with Mark, is that they have been assigned to the globcom to be erected on Tiananmen Square. They'll work with Lin Yuen, the Beijing based Visioneer, on this. Together with Mark they're now waiting for him to join them.

As they watch, they see a small group coming towards them across the vast Square from the direction of the Great Hall of the People. When the group is closer they can see that one of them is in a wheelchair, bumping along over the rough surface of the Square. Closer still, another figure breaks away and strides ahead to reach them first. It's Lin Yuen.

Dressed in the manner of the Chinese with light exterior jacket and several layers of clothing beneath, Lin smiles warmly at his friends.

"Good morning," he says, "I'm sorry if our reception is a little chilly for you, but perhaps it serves to highlight the warmth in our hearts for your coming."

"It's good to be here, Lin," Mark replies, smiling at the warm formality of the greeting. "You know this is my first on-site visit to Beijing. Is this where you'll build the dome?"

"Right where you're standing," replies Lin, "in the middle of Tiananmen Square. I would like you now to meet the gentleman who has secured permission for us to proceed with this."

The rest of the group is approaching. There are two women and one man walking, all dressed like Lin in grey jacket and pants. The fourth member is in the wheelchair being pushed by the man. Though they've never met, Mark recognizes him immediately as Zhao She Yuhan, the very old Chinese gentleman he had seen with Lin Yuen and Mohammed Hussein in the Great Hall of the People. This was in the early days of the Visioneers when Mark had been looking out from the Visioneering Room to see what his companions were doing in various parts of the world.

He remembers the scene in the Great Hall vividly. Zhao had looked out on to Tiananmen Square and recalled the bloody tragedy of the conflict between students and soldiers that had so shocked the world in 1989. He had then shared his vision of a coming celebration on the Square that would stand forever in contrast to the other scene of infamy.

When he is introduced to Mark, the old man pushes aside the blanket covering his legs, and motions to the others to assist him to stand. The two women hasten to respond. When he is standing, frail and trembling like a leaf, Zhao extends a parchment-like hand to Mark in greeting. He speaks barely above a whisper, with Lin translating for him.

"You've come out of another place to be part of our Chinese destiny." His clear and penetrating gaze searches Mark's face. "What you're doing is a great thing for the world. For China it provides the opportunity we've never had to become a full participant with the rest of the human family on the planet. There are still many here in power who do not understand why that must be our destiny. But at least they've allowed an old man his wish to make this small beginning."

"We're greatly honoured and enormously assisted by your interest," Mark replies. "China will play a leading role in creating the Global Mind. The centre we'll build here will be a powerful source in aligning the Asian trisets with the rest of the world."

Mark waits for his words to be translated, then adds to Lin: "Have you told Mr. Zhao how the globcoms and the trisets will operate?"

"Yes," replies Lin. "He's most intrigued. We've spent hours together studying it on a globe."

Lin explains to Zhao what he and Mark have just discussed. The old man speaks again.

"Those of us in China who keep ourselves inwardly aligned, know how much our great civilization has been nourished by the energy of the Earth. In recent times we've slipped into the danger of forgetting that. Your Visioneering project will help to bring us back. We'll service it here in this beating heart of our great nation with a structure that came from the mind of another great Visioneer, who did much to prepare the way for what you're doing now."

The old man waits for his words to be understood by Mark. He smiles to see recognition in Mark's eyes. He continues with Lin translating.

"Ah, I can see you know who I mean, that great friend of the Earth, Buckminster Fuller. He and I had many opportunities to discuss how in time the world must become one. He could see that it was but a breath away if men turned their minds to it. We'll be proud to build one of his great geodesic domes here in the centre of Tiananmen Square to help create the Global Mind he could already see."

As he hears these words coming from this frail figure, Mark is moved with a strong sense of certainty in the growing strength of what the Visioneers are doing. Though around them now this morning nothing appears changed, yet everything has changed. Moving in the strong mind of the man before him, the vision of one world, one planet is now about to break free and create its own reality.

"We'll be proud," Mark replies, "to see the Tiananmen Dome as one of the great anchoring structures of the Global Mind. Thank you for your vision and your confidence."

They talk a while longer, a small band of adventurers setting their minds to the enterprise. Then they disperse, all to their different responsibilities to get the task done.

Setting up the Globcoms

Beginning in Beijing, Mark's immediate intent is to ensure that each of the globcoms is cleared for construction. He has established a deadline of two months to get them in place, no later than the end of June. The ceremony for locking in the trisets is set for July 1st.

With discussions over in Beijing, he travels by plane via the polar route along an approximate triset line over Manchuria, Siberia, Alaska, western Canada to Denver, Colorado in the southwestern United States. Next day he swings his rental car up the driveway to a sprawling ranch house, just south of Crestone, in the San Luis Valley with the snow covered Sangre de Cristo Mountains stretching away north and south.

The American team has been assembled to establish the Colorado globcom. Bill Bates is on hand for the first meeting, though he doesn't intend to be part of this group. His main responsibility continues to be communications out of Visioneer Headquarters in Los Angeles. George Walker, who has taken the most active role among the Visioneers in promoting creative learning to business, will play a leading role here. Several years ago he had bought thirty acres of recreation property near Crestone. Now he's offered it as the site for the Colorado globcom.

The other members of the on-site group are Diane Koplitz and Nicholai Andropov. Diane is still marvelling over the ease she has found in moving from the high density community of Sausalito just north of San Francisco, to the 3000 metre high open spaciousness of the San Luis Valley. Along with George Walker, Diane is one of the American team of Visioneers originally recruited by Bill Bates. Over the past months she has attained worldwide prominence along with Esther in promoting partnering roles for women and men in building a culture of caring for the future. Her calm equanimity has provided a good complement to Esther's stimulating radiance. Within her new role in setting up the globcom she intends to raise the profile on her partnering message, reaching to every country in the world.

The last member of this team, Nicholai Andropov, is the sad-faced Russian teenager, who, among the Visioneers, has had the hardest time in seeing a future of hope. The upheaval and disillusionment in his own country has made it difficult for him to be optimistic. However, because of his appearances with "Momma" Theresa and Sally Hearst he has become a popular figure among teenagers around the world. Now from this globcom reaching across America and Europe he'll have a new platform on which to play his part.

They all greet Mark enthusiastically when he arrives.

"It's incredible!" says Mark, marvelling at the sheer beauty of the surroundings. "George, this is the most spectacular country. It has a rhythm to it. I swear I can hear the Earth singing!"

"You can, good buddy, you can," George replies, delighted with Mark's comment. "Except I think it's the whole universe you can hear. I call it the Celestial Chorus. I tell you I can come up here with nerves frayed to the edges from pressure and stress and within minutes I'm singing right along. Just ask Bill. Look how relaxed he is."

"You said it," Bill Bates responds cheerily. "One more day here and you'll need a team of horses to drag me away."

"What wonderful energy for the globcom!" says Mark. "Give me the picture so I can see it in my mind."

George Walker warms to the task.

"It's going to be a pyramid," he says. "When the exact locations of the other globcoms are set, we'll get the sightlines from here to Jerusalem, Beijing, Ayers Rock and Machu Picchu. That'll give us the four corners for our own base. On that we'll build the classic pyramid structure with a lot of glass and light. It'll be a jewel dancing with light to lift the energy of everyone it touches."

"Yes," Diane Koplitz intervenes, "and the pyramid structure will bring with it all the wisdom and mysteries of the ancient civilizations of which it's the symbol."

"Both ancient and modern, past and future fused together," muses Mark.

"Exactly right!" George exclaims enthusiastically.

"And Nicholai," Mark asks, turning to the young man. "What do you think about all this?"

"I think," Nicholai replies slowly, "that it's a good thing we do here for the young people of the world. Their energy is restless, and,—how do you say it?—unfocused. I think our pyramid will be an inspiration to them to quiet their minds for building a new Earth."

The young man blushes with embarrassment as the others look at him admiringly.

"God grant that our work spreads your young wisdom across the planet," Mark responds, putting his arm around Nicholai's shoulder. To everyone he says: "Friends, I salute you. The Crestone Pyramid will be our shining beacon to help light the way of the world. I can hardly wait to see it."

◆ ◆ ◆

From Colorado, Mark soars over the Pacific Ocean to Australia, arriving at Cairns in north Queensland. He has travelled the southern stretch of the North Pacifica Triset. With mind and body drugged from jet lag, he's beginning to appreciate the immensity of the task the Visioneers have undertaken. All that distance and he has travelled down only two sides of one of seven trisets, not to mention the cirset of Antarctica, circling the bottom of the globe. What a priceless jewel of a planet human beings have been entrusted with! The profound implications leap into his mind. Reinvigorated, he catches a plane for Alice Springs. Several hours later he's again at Ayers Rock, where with Esther, only two weeks earlier, he had felt the mysterious forces of this vast, empty land.

Set up in temporary camp on the flat spinifex plain a few hundred yards northwest of the Rock, the Australian contingent of Visioneers await him. It's a mixed crew: Boris Gunther, the German farmer; Daniel Thomas, the Welsh poet; and Sally Hearst, the schoolgirl from New Zealand.

Boris Gunther had been with General Soulière and Junichi Yakisawa at the sensational introduction of the Visioneers to Unesco. Since then he has worked in his native Germany where his successful Visioneering projects sit in uneasy contrast to a swelling national pride and resurging pockets of the same brutish thinking that had once shaken the world. On the positive side, however, the reunification of Germany has also signalled the possibility of unity across the globe.

Daniel Thomas has spent all of his time as a Visioneer in Russia, where he had begun with Bill Bates and continued after Bill had left to go back to the United States. Daniel had formed a deep and lasting bond with his Russian friends, and had only reluctantly assumed his new assignment. However, he has left a strong team in place there and is confident they can continue.

Sally Hearst is the ebullient inspiration to teenagers all over the world. In her native New Zealand and neighbouring Australia, she has become a household name. Through her efforts, hundreds of thousands of teenagers launched Visioneering projects that have shaken the older establishment complacency to its roots. She's delighted now to be part of what is for her a "home-based" team, deep in the heart of Australia, but reaching out through the triset network to every other globcom.

"Well, what have you got planned for the down-under anchor point on our system?" Mark asks as the four of them sit in the shade of a canvas awning on one of the trailers. "It'll need to be something strong to hold the balance."

"Aha! Just as solid as that big rock over there," replies Boris Gunther, waving at the great red monolith shimmering in the afternoon heat. "It's our inspiration," he continues. He spreads out a large sheet of blueprint paper on a camp table. It's a rough sketch of the globcom. "See, we've made it low and massive like the Rock, with five sides, but it's not a pentagon. We don't want any associations with military establishments, you know. Half of it is foursided with the angles set by the sightlines to the other globcoms around the world. That's the northern half. The southern half is a semicircle to open out on to the cirset of Antarctica. That's our special responsibility here, and we've made it a feature."

Daniel Thomas sweeps his arm in an embracing gesture to the south and breaks into verse:

"Where the sea and the sky
And the sky and the sea
Stretch out from the earth
Into destiny:
That's where we'll set to make our stand
In the rock hard centre of a great red land."

"Ah, Daniel, ever the poet," Mark smiles. "One day soon we'll harness your talent to write the song of the new creation."

"Oh, he's already working on it," Sally intervenes. "When we've got the words and the music, we'll put it out over the network. Then perhaps everyone on Earth will see that their own destiny lies in the light of the shining planet."

The silence of unspoken agreement settles on them. Mark looks warmly at his three companions. "I can't begin to tell you," he says, "how much it means to me to know that you three are here, along with all the others, building together to make a new beginning. God bless you and your efforts! Your great Australian Rock will be a good anchor for our enterprise."

◆ ◆ ◆

From Australia and the flat expanse of its vast red centre, Mark now moves along quickly to two more globcoms, each set high in mountains on two large continents. The first takes him back across the Pacific Ocean along another triset line to Machu Picchu in the Peruvian Andes in South America.

He comes in by helicopter from Cuzco on a misty morning to precede the influx of tourists who arrive each day by train. His daredevil, grinning pilot whips the helicopter around patches of cloud and towering mountain peaks to reveal below them the awesome spectacle of the ruins of a lost civilization. Despite the excitement of the ride, Mark catches a moment to reflect on the implications of what he sees below. To know that centuries ago an Inca empire flourished with great accomplishment in architecture, engineering and administration along the dorsal spine of the Andes, and to see it now in ruins, is to be humbled by the portents of what can happen to any civilization put together by human beings.

The helicopter lands in a flat area near the outer rim of the ruins toward the topmost level of the series of terraces. Three members of Peruvian officialdom appear out of the stonework along with the three Visioneers who will establish this centre. Unmistakable among the group is the towering George Cardinal, resplendent this morning in his usual buckskin jacket. He greets Mark warmly as the brother and friend of what has already been for him a long and hard campaign.

The other two members of the Visioneering team are Carmen Santander and Irene Henshaw. They make a lively contrast: the dark skinned, Latin beauty of Carmen and the subdued, pink-skinned seriousness of Irene. Since the Visioneers first began their work, Carmen has spent most of her time in India with Indira Murti and Baba Satyananda. Well aware now of how miraculous power can move among people, she is exuberant to be here in the magic of one of the Earth's most treasured places. Irene's work has been more ordered and traditional, striving from her base in Scotland to bring creative learning into school curricula around the world. For her, a sojourn in Machu Picchu is a time in a fantasy world of uplifting spirit far removed from the grind of daily work.

George is already leading Mark and the two women away from the helicopter and hovering officialdom. The big Indian moves with great strides and within minutes Mark finds himself gasping for breath in the 3000 metre high altitude of this incredible place. His mind reels with the combination of the thin air, the grand spectacle of the jagged mountains, and the mysterious aura surrounding such human craftsmanship at this inaccessible perch on top of the world.

"This is where we'll put our site," George is saying. "It won't be very large, space is tight here, and the authorities are reluctant participants anyway. However, we do have approval to go ahead. What do you think? Can't you feel the energy soaring like an eagle all around? I'm not sure what to make of it yet. To my native sense, I somehow feel that this is no place for people to trespass. This is the land of the Great Spirit. Perhaps that's what these ruins mean. It was no place for people to come to build such a city. Now it's gone. What we do here must not be a trespass. It must be a focus for a limited time to capture the energy and use it for our healing purpose. But we must never forget from where the energy comes."

"George is so right," Carmen has intervened. "What we need here is something really brilliant and crystalline to reflect and transmit the bouncing radiant waves we can feel all around. We'll make it like a diamond with four points on the base and four reflecting sides, then with another four facets on the top coming to a point. It'll sit here like a sparkling gem for as long as we need it."

Irene Henshaw adds to the description: "We'll position it so that the sightlines from the four centres to which we're linked will strike the reflecting sides, that's Colorado, Australia, Kilimanjaro, and Jerusalem. Can you see it, Mark? Our jewel in the mist holding the balance for our part of the Global Mind?"

"Yes," Mark replies. "I can see it. Your Andean Diamond will be just as precious as all of you."

The four of them stand together in a small excited group seeing in their minds the birth of a new creation. A short way off, the three official keepers of the park at Machu Picchu stand stroking their chins and wondering what foolishness these visitors are about.

Two days later, Mark comes into the second of the two high mountain globcoms. He has crossed two continents and the South Atlantic Ocean to fly in, again by helicopter, over one of the world's great spectacles. This is the rainy season in east Equatorial Africa and they have been dashing in and out of storm clouds all the way from the Nairobi airport. The last one had deluged them with sheets of driving rain while jagged lightning bolts and gigantic thunder claps exploded all around. Then suddenly they break free of the clouds. Spread out below, and stretching away, up, up, up above them, swallowing their fragile beating bird of a machine in a vast white sea of snow, sweeping out to the very ends of the Earth, lies the square solid mass of Kilimanjaro.

His team of Visioneers is waiting for him inside the boundaries of the national park. The helicopter circles looking for the place. A flare goes up from a clearing just off an access road.

"There!" shouts Mark to the pilot. "There they are! Take us in down there."

The rain has stopped, but he steps out into a sea of mud. He hadn't come prepared for this. His light shoes sink over their soles in the thick brown soup, until he struggles over to a stretch of grass. Looking up, he sees striding towards him from the treeline the Visioneering version of the Three Musketeers in khaki shirts, shorts and broad-brimmed hats; smiling President Mutsandu, distinguished General Soulière, and sun-tanned Karl Ibsen. All three are laughing uproariously at his discomfort.

"Ho! Ho! The birdman from back of Burke!" chortles Karl Ibsen.

"Non, non, it's the flying Dutchman's Australian cousin," says General Soulière.

"Why, no," insists President Mutsandu, "I believe it's our intrepid leader Mark Spiderman dropping in on his silken cord."

Mark stands with his hands on his hips glaring at them as ferociously as he can, as they come splashing through the mud towards him.

"All right, you clowns," he shouts, "where's the taxi?"

This brings another burst of laughter from the three, who by now have reached him and are pounding him on the back and shaking his hand.

"It's good to have you here, Mark," says Mutsandu, "but come along, come along, we know you don't have much time, and we have something to show you, over beyond those rocks and trees."

Mark shoots a withering look at where they want to take him, and at the slippery swamp between him and there. Then he shrugs his shoulders and says, "Oh, what the heck! One day I'll get you three out on Sydney Harbour in a full-blown gale." With that he steps out with them up to his ankles in mud heading for the other side of the clearing.

Among the trees they pick their way for a short distance along a narrow game trail, then come out to a sight that pulls Mark up breathless, and not this time from the altitude. The sun has broken through the tangled storm clouds, and before them it lights up the full cinemascope panorama of Kilimanjaro. They are standing on a rocky ridge with the land falling away gently in front of them, so that the mountain fills the whole scene with trees, rocks, cliffs, crags and its immense snow fields soaring to the top and on up into the clouds.

Mutsandu looks at Mark with great pride in his dark African eyes.

"This is where we'll build our centre," he says. "It'll be a great round tower, but not too high, for who can be foolish enough to imitate this mountain. But it will be strong and good for its purpose and at its centre will be the intersection of the sightlines from Machu Picchu, Ayers Rock, and Jerusalem. We'll hold the balance of the Global Mind here for Africa."

"A citadel with a friendly face," adds General Soulière.

"A simple human space in the midst of God's great grandeur," Karl Ibsen contributes. "We think that's appropriate. What do you think, Mark?"

"Yes, it certainly is," replies Mark, unable to take his eyes off the mountain. "I was told that Kilimanjaro means 'shining mountain'. Your Kilimanjaro Watchtower will be a shining light for what we're about to do."

They stand a while longer watching. Then the clouds roll over and close off the mountain. Together they make their way to where the tents have been set up at their campsite.

♦ ♦ ♦

In Beijing, the Tiananmen Dome; in Colorado, the Crestone Pyramid; in

Australia, the Australian Rock; in Peru, the Andean Diamond; in Africa, the Kilimanjaro Watchtower: and now in Jerusalem, at the centre of it all, the five-pointed Star of Jerusalem, universal symbol of light, with five glowing points.

This is the structure that the Visioneering team in Jerusalem has decided to build. Meeting with them on a windy hillside on the western outskirts of the city, Mark Venture is eager to hear the details. Though he has arrived bone-tired from almost two weeks of jetting, helicoptering, driving, climbing, walking, and otherwise finding his way to the globcom sights on every continent, his spirits are high now that he's back In Jerusalem.

Esther was at Tel Aviv to meet him. They had one night together and then came on to Jerusalem to meet up with the team. It's mid-morning now and they're standing on the site the team has chosen for the globcom. Stretching away before them is the panorama of the New City, with the Old City and its gleaming Dome of the Rock in the background.

The Jerusalem team is Mohammed Hussein, Indira Murti, and Theresa Romano. Esther is a member *ex officio*, but like Mark she expects to be away more often than she's there. The other three have been active in securing the site and preparing preliminary plans for the building while Mark was away visiting the other centres. They're as anxious now to hear his report as he is to hear theirs.

"What we're doing," he says, "is stretching a membrane across the Earth that's going to act as a healing force, perhaps like a cocoon. People in every land will become bonded once they raise their consciousness to the planetary level. It's already happening in isolated pockets, but when our network is up and operating, it'll release such a flood of energy that millions of people will be gathered up by it. I wish you could have been with me to feel the power of those places where we'll have our command posts. And what about your team mates! Oh, if you could only see them! Big George Cardinal, striding around Machu Picchu; General Soulière at Mount Kilimanjaro; Lin Yuen with his great confederate, Zhao She Yuhan, planning to build a geodesic dome on Tiananmen Square; young Nick Andropov working on building a pyramid in Colorado; Daniel Thomas writing poetry in the shade of Ayers Rock, and all the rest of them, all out there, putting our structure together piece by piece. All of it ties back to Jerusalem, to the centre of the vision. And now it's your turn. Tell me about it. Tell me your plans. What have we got here? What do you plan to build?"

Theresa Romano, bubbling over with excitement, can contain herself no longer.

"It's a star!" she exclaims. "It's a star! We saw it right away, when we found this land and came out here, even though it was already getting dark, and there above us were all the stars in the heaven, and below us all the lights of the city! And even then, without talking about it, all of us could feel the pull from the other five centres out across the world, and we knew in an instant we were to build a star, with five points, going out to the other places. It would be our centre, and soon become the light of the world, the Star of Jerusalem, the New Jerusalem, just as in the song I sang at your wedding, and like your vision, Esther, the New Jerusalem, shining like a star for the whole world to see!"

Before she has finished speaking, big wet tears roll down Theresa's full round cheeks. She looks adoringly at Esther and Mark, hugs each of them, then both of them together. Helpless to know what to do or say, she turns to her two companions, Mohammed and Indira, and cries: "Tell them! Tell them! That's what it will be, the beautiful Star of Jerusalem!"

Mohammed is laughing out loud.

"Oh, Theresa," he exclaims, "you're priceless. What more can we say? You've already said it all!"

"Yes, indeed," adds Indira, also smiling broadly, "and you know, Esther and Mark, I'm certain God is working one big miracle for the Earth at this time, and that you two with your love are at the centre of it."

At that Theresa again bursts into tears, all the while trying to smile with the happiness she feels. The others gather closer around her, and all of them stand together without speaking, looking out over the city that has come to mean so much to all of them. And each one ponders what it will mean to the Earth when Theresa's words are fulfilled and they have built the Star of Jerusalem.

CHAPTER TWENTY-FOUR

Communication

N OW LET ME SEE THAT I'VE GOT THIS RIGHT." Pamela Barrett is interviewing Esther in the Jerusalem studios of the worldwide ZNN network.

"There are six command centres, which you're calling globcoms, and they're located on different continents. The one here in Jerusalem will be the centre, and it'll be built in the shape of a star?"

"That's right," Esther replies. "I've got preliminary sketches of all of them here, so we can show the viewers."

"Wow!" Pamela laughs. "Get ready out there, folks. Here's another ZNN exclusive on the future of the world as designed by the Visioneers."

Esther laughs, too. She radiates happy energy, wearing a dazzling wool sweater of blues and greens and gold. Her long auburn hair has been styled for the interview so that it sits in waves on her shoulders, dancing and shimmering in the bright studio lights. She excitedly tells the story of the visioneering plan.

"This is the Star of Jerusalem, in pure white, sitting on a hillside overlooking the city. Now here's the Tiananmen Dome, a Buckminster Fuller geodesic dome right in the middle of Tiananmen Square."

"And the Chinese authorities have gone for that?" asks Pamela, incredulously.

"Absolutely," Esther replies. "The Chinese have a very important role to play in the new world awakening. Now look, here's the Crestone Pyramid, that's in the heart of Colorado in your part of the world."

"Hmm! Shades of Ayn Rand and *Atlas Shrugged*," says Pamela. "I read that book years ago, but I still remember the secret valley in Colorado where all the great minds gathered to save the world."

"Well this isn't going to be secret," Esther responds.

"Not after this morning, anyway," puts in Pamela. "Several hundred million people around the world now know about the Crestone Pyramid in Colorado. Let's see the others."

Esther continues showing the sketches of the squat red rock in Australia with its huge semicircular window looking south to Antarctica; the sparkling diamond in the misty ruins of Machu Picchu; and the solid round watchtower on the slopes of Mount Kilimanjaro.

"Now, if we look here on the globe, you'll see how all this comes together." Esther goes over to a large globe set up in the studio.

"You know, the irony of all this doesn't escape me," Pamela comments to the viewing audience. "Here's this young woman, standing beside the Earth, telling the whole world how it's going to be saved from itself. Can this be real?"

"Of course it is." Esther's face lights up with excitement. "Don't you feel the power of it, even here in this tiny, cramped studio? People all around the world have now got the means to communicate with each other and share their visions of what they want life on the planet to be like. It's the people of the Earth, the ordinary people, who are going to come together in their millions from every country and race to create the future."

"It just gives me goose bumps thinking about it," replies Pamela. "Go on, tell us what all those lines and strange names are about. What do I see there? Centrasia and North Pacifica? Is this George Orwell's *1984* revisited? I hope not!"

"No, absolutely not," Esther says earnestly. "Orwell had a very pessimistic vision that's already been proved wrong, even though the world's now in the grip of another peril. What we're doing here is giving people a framework so they can work together to build the best possible future for everyone."

"Well, Amen to that. So what's the plan?"

"It's not so much of a plan as an unfolding. See here, we have each of the globcoms I've already mentioned. Now, they're linked together in these three-sided patterns, which we call trisets, except for the one around Antarctica, which is more like a circle, so we call it a cirset."

Esther then names all the trisets.

"The brave new world!" Pamela chimes in.

"You can call it that if you like," Esther replies. "But again it's nothing like what Aldous Huxley wrote about in his book. Both he and Orwell had dark visions of what would happen to the world because nations just put new technology on top of old thinking. We're starting with the thinking and showing people that once they change that, and begin to get the vision right, then a whole new future of positive possibilities opens up. I'd like to call it a smart new world?"

"And tell me," asks Pamela, "how are the Visioneers going to create this smart new world?"

"The Visioneers aren't going to create it," replies Esther. "We're just putting the opportunity there for people to do it. You see, if people are going to find solutions to the problems that are plaguing us, they have to move from their old positions of, 'I don't trust you', and 'If you get that, I'll lose this.' While ever people are holding on to those old positions, including their ideas about territory on the Earth, then we just get further and further into trouble. What I've just shown you and your viewers around the world is a way of getting out of that."

"But how does it work? I mean, you've got these beautiful strange buildings, what do you call them, globcoms? You've got the globcoms in these wonderful places around the world, and now you've got these trisets criss-crossing and zig-zagging their way around the globe. What's it all mean? Where does simple little Pamela Barrett fit into all this?"

"First of all, Pamela Barrett isn't so simple," Esther now warms to the topic, "and neither are 90 percent of people in the world. They're very creative human beings. But they've had their most creative agenda, to build a world fit to live in, taken away from them by the political structures they've built. Even in democracies, people are feeling helpless to be able to do anything in the face of powerful politicians and huge tax-eating bureaucracies. Well, we're out to show them it doesn't have to be like that. That's just the choice they've made to date.

"And here's where Pamela Barrett comes in. Just look at you. All these months you've been following the Visioneers with your telecasts. Now here you are giving millions of people the instant opportunity to begin to think another way. We've got incredible communication possibilities in the world now. We just have to use them on a positive agenda.

"And that's what you see here on this globe. It's a huge planetary communications network. It recognizes that people and their organizations and their communities are all energy systems. And the planet is an energy system. What we're doing here is aligning the Earth's energy systems with people's energy systems, and when you do that right, human consciousness will come through with the right solutions. I don't expect you or the people out there to understand it all today, but over the next few months you'll start to feel it. Then we'll come to the Congress of the Global Mind as a great new awakening for the planet."

"Ah, the Congress of the Global Mind," Pamela interrupts. "We've heard your husband, Mark Venture, talking about that. Are you going to give us any details?"

"No, not today. We want the idea to emerge in the minds of the people as the network I've shown you gets set up. What I can say, though, is that the event will be an extraordinary act of creation and celebration, like nothing the world has ever seen before."

"Not at least since the first creation," says Pamela.

"Yes, not since the first creation," Esther smiles wisely in return.

"Well, there's something for everyone to tune in for next time," says Pamela. "Now, we have another guest here. It's Arthur Rhinegold. I'm sure everyone will remember that Arthur produced Part I of the film called *The Visioneers*. It told the story of the Visioneers up to that incredible memorial service for Luis Valdez. As we bring Arthur in, I just want to run the last few minutes of the film showing the service."

Immediately, the clip comes on, showing the enormous crowd of people who seemed to come out of nowhere to the parish church of St. Paul's in New York State last October. The moving speeches by George Cardinal, Baba Satyananda, and Mark Venture outside the church again resonate in the minds of the viewers. And then "Momma" Theresa leads the crowd in singing the new words to *Amazing Grace*, to end with the stirring *Song of the Visioneers*, which continues to flood out as the credits roll and people move off quietly away from the ceremony.

The studio cameras in Jerusalem come back to Pamela Barrett, catching her as she wipes tears from her eyes.

"Oh!" she says. "Do I ever remember that day! Arthur Rhinegold, you genius you, it's great to have you here. Now you're going to tell us about *The Visioneers Part II*, right?"

"Absolutely. It's opening in a theatre near you soon." Arthur Rhinegold has joined Esther on the set, both of them now sitting to talk to Pamela. He's the same casual, flamboyant Arthur who was brought on to the American visioneering team by Bill Bates back in the early days of the movement. He's wearing white cord slacks and a bulky, blue sweater with a huge white V for Visioneer on the front of it.

"And what's the story of the new film, Arthur?" asks Pamela.

"Why half of it's right here beside me. The beautiful, courageous Esther Fisher, now married to the dashing Mark Venture. We've got the whole of that unforgettable wedding ceremony as the finale. I think it's even more powerful than the Valdez memorial service you just showed from Part I."

"Tell me about it!" exclaims Pamela. "I was right there! My own camera operator was a hired assassin, and Mark Venture leaps off the stage and pulls him down out of his perch. I'll never forget it!"

"Yes, that and everything else about the wedding," Arthur continues. "Just a marvellous piece of cinematography. But there's a lot more in the film than that. We've got the events of the whole hundred and fifty days between the Valdez memorial and the wedding. It includes the most exciting footage of visioneering projects all over the world: organizations turning themselves around, kids leading community projects, seniors leading groups of grey power for a better world. We've got Esther and her team of women setting up partnering programs in many countries. Then there's Mark Venture at the United Nations. What a coup that was! And finally, there's all that intrigue with Carlos Palmira, the great El Condor of evil, and his phony International Trust and Credit Corporation. I tell you, this is a blockbuster. You won't want to miss it."

"And Part III, Arthur? What about Part III?" asks Pamela.

"We're already shooting it. It begins with Palmira's death and the collapse of I.T.C.C. It follows Mark and Esther to Australia with incredible scenes on Sydney Harbour and in the Brisbane Exhibition Grounds. Now we've got crews out filming the building of those globcoms Esther has just told you about. We'll follow the whole thing through to the staging of the Global Mind. By then, I tell you, this world won't know what's hit it. And we'll have the whole story on film and in the cinemas within weeks of the end of the Global Mind event. It's a film-maker's dream, but I can't tell you how personally moved I am to be part of a project like this. It's the greatest thing to ever happen in the history of the world and I'm living it as it happens. And here beside me today is this incredible lady, Esther Fisher. I just choke up thinking about it!"

Esther laughs, blinking away tears.

"Okay, Esther," says Pamela. "Last words to you. It's almost time to go. What do we look for next in this unfolding drama?"

"Well, the next major event will be the lock-in of the trisets on July 1st," Esther replies. "That's just over six weeks away. Between now and then, I'll be travelling the world telling the story wherever I can, and the other Visioneers will be out and about, doing the same thing."

"And ZNN will be close at hand reporting it," concludes Pamela. "Esther and Arthur, thank you for coming. We all look forward to creating a smart new world with you."

Fanning Out

"Come along, Pamela, just a few more steps and we're there," Esther calls back to Pamela Barrett as they climb up to the highest level of Machu Picchu where the Visioneers are building the globcom. For some unexplained reason their helicopter pilot had dropped them off at a lower level. They've been climbing for thirty minutes to get here. The camera crew is even further back, struggling with their heavy equipment. It's mid-June and a thick blanket of snow covers the ground.

"Oh, boy!" Pamela gasps. "This might be okay for you, but this girl isn't in shape for it."

Esther, up ahead, cries out, "Look, there it is! Oh my, will you look at that! It really is a dazzling bright diamond in the mountains."

As Pamela catches up, she gasps not just from the exertion, but mostly at the sight in front of her. Perched among the ruins of the ancient Inca city the Andean Diamond shines in the bright sunlight like a spacecraft from another world. It's built from prefabricated slabs of crystal-like thick plastic sheets. Thirty metres long and ten metres high, it dwarfs everything around, except for the towering mountain peaks. It is, indeed, multifaceted like a diamond, and sits securely anchored to withstand the strong winds that can sweep with a vengeance over the mountains.

George Cardinal, Carmen Santander, and Irene Henshaw are on hand to greet their visitors. This is the last stop by Esther and Pamela on a sweep around the globcoms to give on-site reports to the curious world about progress with the global project. It's just two weeks from July 1st, now called Visioneering Day, when the official launch and lock-in of the trisets will be held.

George is anxious to show them the inside of the Diamond. It has two levels. The first is administration, storage, and living quarters. The second is a surrealistic world of communications. Above and around them the clear facets of the diamond shape allow the light to pour in from outside. Everywhere is a hive of activity as technicians install computer and communications equipment. It could well be the flight deck of a star ship.

"Where's Captain Kirk and Mr. Spock?" asks Pamela, goggling at the scene before her.

George Cardinal laughs. "You'll have to settle for Chief George and Visioneers Carmen and Irene," he says, "but we're going to do wonders here on Earth as fantastic as anything the good ship *Enterprise* encountered in the galaxy."

Esther smiles to herself. The comparison with the famous heroes from *Star Trek* is a good image of what the Visioneers are about in their enterprise on Earth.

"Look, here, I want to show you this," says George.

At the centre of the Diamond is a small flat command panel fitted to a stand at waist level, like a lectern. Attached to the panel a small rectangular metal plate the size of a sheet of writing paper, shows four lines radiating out from a centre point.

"These are our sightlines to the other globcoms," George continues. "When Mark gives the word from Jerusalem on July 1st we'll transmit and receive a continuous signal along these lines from the other sites. They will work the same way. We've had quite a job getting all that lined up around the curvature of the Earth. We couldn't have done it without help from NASA. Those people have been terrific."

"That's the kind of story I want to get, George," says Pamela, "to let people know this is for real, and that prestigious agencies and organizations are coming on side to make it work."

"You and Esther have been doing a great job on that over the past few weeks," says Carmen. "Even perched up here in Machu Picchu, we've been catching all of your newscasts. The geodesic dome in Tiananmen Square, the pyramid in Crestone, the tower on Kilimanjaro, the Rock in Australia, and the great Star in Jerusalem: it's just like a magic world growing before our eyes."

"Yes, Carmen, and we've only just started," says Esther.

"Say, I want you to repeat that for the cameras, Carmen," adds Pamela. "A magic world! Yes, that's what it is in a way, but you guys are making it come real."

"We all are, Pamela," says Esther, "that's the power of it. Now let's get going on the camera work while we still have the sunshine."

"That's a bitter irony, too," Irene Henshaw speaks for the first time, a little sadly. "To think that we're now so exposed to ultra violet radiation that we can't enjoy the sunshine anymore. It's a terrible legacy for the children."

"We're changing that, Irene," says Esther. "As sure as there's life and health in each one of us now living, we're going to change that pattern for the future, and bring back hope for our children. Let's get to work on it now."

Visioneering Day

The time to lock in the trisets and officially launch the start of the Global Mind project is set for 5:00 p.m. on July 1st, Jerusalem time. This will provide a reasonable opportunity for most people to participate during waking hours, from early morning in the United States, South America and Canada, to afternoon in Europe and Africa, to late evening in eastern Asia and Australia. Mark had sent out a request to world leaders to proclaim July 1st as "Visioneering Day." He has good reason to be pleased with the response as more than a hundred countries have done so. The visioneering theme has captured the imagination of so many people now, that millions are coming out for parades, projects, competitions, and all manner of activities to promote the spirit of the day.

However, most of the interest centres around the lock-in of the trisets. All across the world people have been talking about this for weeks. Esther has done her work well in promoting it. One would have to be a recluse in a cave, or otherwise very isolated from world affairs, not to know that an unusual event is occurring today.

By now several million people throughout the world have been officially designated as Visioneers. From a start of twenty in the Visioneering Room ten months ago, this is spectacular. But it has only just begun. Most of the growth has occurred in the last two months since Mark and Esther's wedding. Now, in true network marketing style, the growth is moving exponentially. The theme of "each one reach one" has caught fire, and every

day the numbers increase by several million. At Visioneer World Headquarters in Los Angeles, Bill Bates has expanded his operation several
hundredfold since its beginning, and now with local offices in thousands
of locations throughout the world, visioneering has become a phenomenal
growth industry.

But still, it has only just begun. So far visioneering is seen mainly as an
activity, projects to do positive things, both in business and community
affairs. It has yet to reach the deeper levels of human consciousness, to be
seen as a philosophy, a way of life, a structuring of economic, social and
political arrangements to shift the relationship of human beings to their
planet. That's the purpose of the Global Mind project. And it begins today
with the lock-in of the trisets.

The ceremony will be a worldwide electronic communications event,
mixed with various levels of on-site participation at the different globcoms.
The number of people who can be involved at each centre varies enor-
mously according to conditions. It ranges from a few dozen at Machu
Picchu at mid-morning to almost two hundred thousand on Tiananmen
Square in the late evening.

At the Crestone Pyramid in Colorado the ceremony will occur in the
early morning, and a large pancake breakfast has been set up in the open
air for an expected five thousand people who've been gathering in the area
over the past twenty-four hours. At Ayers Rock in Australia, the timing will
be late evening, and even here in this remote location more than a thousand
people have come in by plane, bus and car to camp outdoors and celebrate
around blazing campfires. At Kilimanjaro it will be late afternoon as in
Jerusalem, and several hundred visitors to the national park are on hand at
the Watchtower to join the celebration.

In Jerusalem it promises to be somewhat a repeat performance of Mark
and Esther's wedding. The glistening white Star of Jerusalem was built on
an open hillside with enough space around it to accommodate several
thousand people. A carnival atmosphere of coloured tents and tantalizing
food stalls has mushroomed over the past few days. Now, as 5:00 p.m.
approaches, the crowd has gathered around the perimeter of the building,
facing five large electronic screens at each point of the Star, waiting to see
what's going to happen.

And all around the world similar scenes are occurring. In many places,
the Visioneers have decided to come together in community centres and
the like, while millions of others will stay at home with their families to
watch on television. From high-rise to ghetto, from farm house to town
house, from seashore to prairie, from mountain chalet to jungle village:
wherever the message of the Visioneers has penetrated, people are gathering to participate, more than a billion of them around the globe.

From 4:00 p.m. onwards Mark and Esther are in the Jeruslalem control
centre. As in the Andean Diamond, it's on the second level. By swivelling

their chairs they can see down each arm of the Star, knowing they're in a direct line with another globcom across the Earth. At each point of the Star banks of windows let in the light. Above the centre, a large clear bubble looks out to the sky. The whole building is constructed around a radius of twenty metres, and at its highest point is fifteen metres off the ground. Surrounding Mark and Esther in concentric circles extending out to the beginning of each arm of the Star, banks of computers and communication equipment operate under the watchful eyes of a dozen technicians. The other Visioneers, Mohammed, Indira, and Theresa, sit together going over the details. An air of quiet expectancy hangs in the room.

Mark systematically calls each of the other globcoms, making sure they're ready. One by one they come in. Everything's fine. Ten seconds to go. A transmission signal beams out via a constellation of satellites orbiting the Earth. It's a brilliant white V on a sky-blue background. Several hundred million television sets around the world pull in the signal. A fanfare of music goes up. The symbol of the Visioneers melts into the shimmering blue-white view of the Earth from space. The music softens. The image of Mark and Esther appears on the screens.

They are dressed in a new uniform of the Visioneers. A blue V-necked sweater for Mark and a blue blouse for Esther with high collar open at the throat. Prominent on the left breast of each is a pocket-sized white V, encircled by a white line signifying the Earth.

When Mark speaks, his words are in English, but people listen to him around the globe in more than thirty languages.

"Friends," he says, "friends of the Earth, everywhere, welcome to our celebration of new beginnings. We're assembled in a vast planetary envelope of communication to participate together in the birth of a new era. It's been a long time coming. The human race has been enduring the birth pains for thousands of years. But now, it's the destiny of those of us who are alive on the planet today to be present at the delivery.

"Good morning, good afternoon, and good evening to you all in our twenty-four hour world. We're privileged and deeply moved that you've joined us in your hundreds of millions around the globe.

"My name is Mark Venture and with me is my partner, Esther Fisher. Soon we'll be joined by our colleagues and friends here and around the world. We are the Visioneers, coming together with you to help create a new reality for the planet."

Esther speaks.

"From inside the cocoon of our present understanding," she says, her voice and eyes alive with light and energy, "we're moving to become the glorious butterfly of a new planetary civilization. With Mark, I welcome you all and thank you for joining us wherever you are.

"During the past months, I've developed a deep feeling of being connected, an overwhelming sense that all of us are partners in an enterprise of divine importance. Mark and I are deeply moved by the outpouring of joy and goodwill that you've shown towards us. I feel it here now, an envelope of energy surrounding the planet, holding us together and lying open to our creative minds to shape a new life together on our precious Earth.

"Together we're striving to create a new vision. It will shift us from the preoccupations of the past to the important realities of the future: to know that there are no boundaries on the Earth except for the ones we've created in our minds; to know that material wealth and beauty becomes ugly poverty when it destroys the very soil and air and water on which our human life depends; to know that we're part of a flow of continuous life and have a great responsibility to preserve the planet for future generations."

"All of that lies at the heart of anyone who becomes a Visioneer." Mark has picked up the commentary. As he continues to speak the camera sweeps to show the interior of the Jerusalem globcom. "We introduced ourselves to you several months ago and what you see around us now is the growth that has come with your support. This is the Star of Jerusalem, the heart of a global network which in a few moments we'll lock into place." The camera is now showing the exterior of the building and the people gathered around. "Outside you see all those who have assembled here, and soon, around the world, you'll see their counterparts: Visioneers all, creating the new reality, joining with millions more like you in your own communities to make the changes."

The camera has now come back to Mark and Esther. Esther picks up the commentary again.

"Yes, that's what it means to be a Visioneer," she says, "to understand that we are architects of change, spiritual people, who'll care for each other and the planet, and so fulfill ourselves. We understand that the place to begin to solve world problems is in our own consciousness. From there we move to our neighbourhood, working together, listening to each other with empathy and tolerance, and moving to create the synergy that comes from many minds and hearts striving together to build communities of peace, harmony, and understanding. This Star of Jerusalem is the new, universal symbol for that, a symbol of light and peace: one which holds for all people, whoever they are, a special meaning of oneness and unity. And from here, like the unfolding of the butterfly's wings, will come the lovely new world that will be ours and our children's forever."

"So let the celebration begin!" Mark exclaims, clearly excited now by what he knows is about to happen. They both stand and move to a large globe on another set. It's an exact replica of the globe in the Visioneering Room, showing the planet shimmering in its bright earth tones, with the six globcoms marked as glowing red lights.

"Here is the Earth and our global command centres," Mark continues. "We call them globcoms. This is the Star of Jerusalem where Esther and I are speaking from. In a moment we'll reach out from here by electronic signals to bring in the other centres. As we do so, they'll come up on your screens. We'll proceed in an orderly way around the globcoms to trace out the eight segments of the Earth. As each of these pieces, called trisets, comes in, we'll return to Jerusalem, which is at the centre. All of you living in that triset will be then welcomed to the family on Earth and you can celebrate that in any way you like."

"Go for the big cheer!" Esther puts in. "Let's give this the recognition it deserves. At the end when everyone is in, we'll really celebrate."

"Now for Trieset Number One," shouts Mark, striding back to the command centre. He faces west looking down the arm of the Star pointing towards Crestone in Colorado The camera swings in behind him. Viewers around the world see the long stretch of the arm with its banks of windows and a yellow line painted on the floor running dead centre to the point.

"Come in Crestone," calls Mark.

With a great fanfare of trumpets the scene on the television screens cuts away from Jerusalem to show a towering pyramid stretching up into a clear blue early morning Colorado sky. It is forty metres tall on a thirty-metre square base. Built of thick slabs of crystal-like clear plastic fitted together in a black alloy frame, the structure stands like a sentinel and listening post high up in the broad San Luis Valley. All around it a hive of good natured activity is underway, as people of all ages in western jeans and corduroy shirts and jackets bustle around barbecue stands, where eggs, sausages, bacon and pancakes are sizzling merrily for breakfast.

The camera sweeps inside to the command centre. Here the American team of Visioneers is on hand beaming broadly, all wearing the same blue and white Visioneers outfits as Mark and Esther. All of them are present: the three residents, George Walker, Diane Koplitz, Nicholai Andropov, supplemented for this morning's opening ceremonies by Bill Bates, Arthur Rhinegold, Julia McCarthy and Sentator Wilfred Brown.

George Walker reaches up, as if catching a high flying ball. "I've got it, Mark!" he shouts. "Hello, to the world from the Crestone Pyramid!" Every-one cheers and waves. Then, winding up for a dramatic pitch, George Walker faces north along a yellow line running to a corner of the pyramid. He tosses the imaginary ball with a powerful throw, shouting, "Take it away Beijing!" and the camera cuts to a flood-lit Tiananmen Square, where a huge geodesic dome shines against the dark night sky of northern China.

The Square is a surging mass of people, milling around, not doing anything in particular, other than packing in as tightly as possible around several dozen large television screens showing the events from the globcoms. The camera moves inside to a similar scene of smiling faces as in Crestone. Lin Yuen is there, along with Junichi Yakasawa, and Jeremy Hiscox. All wear Visioneers uniforms. In pride of place, dead centre of the dome in a high backed easy chair, looking like the commander of a star ship, also wearing a bright blue Visioneers uniform, is Zhao She Yuhan, his ancient wrinkled face, creased in an enigmatic smile.

A grinning Lin Yuen cups his hands to catch the pitch from George Walker. He politely bows his head.

"Thank you, Crestone," he says. "The Tiananmen Dome receives your message; and now back to Jerusalem!" He faces east along another yellow line running out to the edge of the dome and bowls the imaginary ball underhand back to Jerusalem.

Mark is there to receive it, smiling broadly, Esther at his side by the globe, which is tilted down so that the top of the Earth is in full view and the three centres just visited, Crestone, Tiananmen Square, and Jersualem, are all flashing red.

"So now we bring in the Triset of NAMRASIA," Mark exclaims. The triangle of the Earth defined by the three centres now floods in blue across the northern stretches of Asia, Europe and North America "All of you people living there, welcome as the first members of our new Earth family," says Mark.

"Good visioneering to all of you," adds Esther.

"And now," Mark is back at command centre, facing along the south-west arm of the Star, "come in Australia."

Instantly the screens of a billion viewers around the world are filled with the squat five-sided shape of a flood-lit building under a star-filled night sky in central Australia. The south facing wall is an arc of glass windows. A huge campfire blazes merrily, the reflection of the flames leaping and dancing in the wall of glass. Around it several hundred men, women, and children are engaged in various activities of merrymaking. When they become aware that the eyes of the world are on them, a group of wags suddenly breaks out in a feverish imitation of an aboriginal corroboree, with several partly clad dark figures leading the way.

Inside, Boris Gunther sits at the command centre like a teutonic general, while long-haired Daniel Thomas scampers around pretending to catch the long pass from Jerusalem.

Sally Hearst stands back, hands on hips, laughing at her companions. As in the other centres, all are wearing their bright blue Visioneers uniforms.

Finally, in a flying dive, Daniel catches the imaginary ball, then passes it to Boris, who calmly says, "The Australian Rock has received your message and passes it on to the Tiananmen Dome."

He does this by swiveling his chair to face north along a yellow line running out to a corner of the building. The scene on the television screens then moves back to Beijing and from there again to Mark at the globe in Jerusalem. Now a sector on the globe floods in green comprising all of southern Asia including China and India, then over to the Middle East and south to northern Australia.

"We bring in the second Triset of CENTRASIA," says Mark, "and to almost half the people on Earth, welcome to the family.

"And now, come in Kilimanjaro!"

It's daylight on a sunny afternoon outside the Watchtower with the towering snow-capped Kilimanjaro in the background. It's a leisurely scene, about a hundred people sitting around in canvas chairs, drinking and chatting as they watch the festivities on a large television screen. Inside, on the upper level of the tower, President Mutsandu, General Souliere, and Karl Ibsen sit in a circle. They look up together, like a perfectly programmed set of blue uniformed Visioneer dolls, watching for the imaginary lob shot from Mark in Jerusalem to come in through the glass dome on the top of the tower. Stony faced, they all look down together as it lands at their feet. President Mutsandu stands up. "Thank you, Mark," he says solemnly, "the Kilimanjaro Watchtower receives your message and we pass it on to our friends in Australia." With a smile from Daniel Thomas towards Africa, the message passes around again to Jerusalem and Mark.

"Welcome to Triset Number Three, AFRALIA," he says, "and all its people. Now to Machu Picchu."

The Andean Diamond comes up shining on the television screens. Snow covers the ground outside. There are no people around. All are inside. The Diamond squats bright and mysterious among the Inca ruins. In the command centre George Cardinal sits at the controls, dressed in his Visioneers uniform. Carmen Santander and Irene Henshaw stand by, smiling.

Mark's voice booms in from Jerusalem:

"George, you look great in uniform."

George Cardinal looks solemnly out along the yellow line running towards Jerusalem. "The Great Spirit moves in strange guises," he says. "Be watchful for him at all times. To my brothers in the Watchtower I now pass the signal." With that he turns to face Kilimanjaro, places his hands together, at arms length out in front, and nods.

In this way Mark now brings in the remaining trisets: SAMAFRICA, ATLANTICA, NORTH PACIFICA, SOUTH PACIFICA, and lastly, the cirset of ANTARCTICA. As each one comes in a new flood of colour pours over the globe. When it's all done, the world, more than anything else, looks like a brightly coloured beach ball in red, green, yellow, blue, black, purple, brown, and orange.

Mark and Esther stand back surveying their handiwork while the world looks on. Esther turns laughing to face the cameras, reaching for Mark's hand. They stand together in front of the globe.

"Now will you look at that," she says, "see what we've begun to do today. We've created our planet home in the image of a child's big round beach ball, made for fun and enjoyment. It's a wonderful image, but it's more, much more than that. You've all been part of a fine creative act of good fellowship. During the last sixty minutes all of us have travelled many times around the globe, sensing the powerful energy from those magnificent sites where our globcoms are built. They are there. You've seen them, strong and sure, holding the energy lines to bind us all together.

"And now we're all gathered into trisets, looking out onto our wonderful beach-ball world in a new way, understanding that the old bitter divisions and conflicts of the past don't have to bind us into a terrible future. In the words of our *Song of the Visioneers*:

'We are the ones, going to the fore
Big ones, little ones—all of us are here.
Small world, big world, reaching out to all.
Up, up, and upmost—the mighty Visioneers!'

"Today we've taken a bold new step. Over the next four months you'll have time to think about what you've participated in today. The Visioneers among you are growing in numbers every day. Each one is reaching another, then another, and another, until soon there'll be no one on Earth who hasn't had a chance to hear and be touched by the power of what's in motion to bring in the world of peace and love we all long in our hearts to see."

"Yes," Mark adds, "the cornerstones of that new world are now firmly laid. What remains is for all of us to build on them with courage, never doubting for a moment that what we're doing is part of a divine plan for the future of the world.

"I'd like now to bring in our friends who are working with us here in the Star of Jerusalem to begin to make this holy city the centre for peace and love in the world. You've met them before in other situations with the Visioneers. My good friend, Mohammed Hussein, Best Man at my wedding and staunch ally and supporter through some terrible times before and around that event. And dear Indira Murti from India, where she's been working with her people and a great spiritual leader, Baba Satyananda. You see the four of us now standing here before you, four people from four separate faiths who have grown to know that in the hearts of all true believers these faiths are one: just as our planet is one, just as we all can be one if we let our hearts and minds move to create that future."

Mohammed and Indira have come forward to stand with Mark and Esther in front of the globe.

Esther speaks again.

"But there's one more of us here," she says. "One that the whole world has grown to love as a mother whose special dream is to bring love and care to the children of the world. Come on in, Theresa. It's time for us to sing for the joy of the new world."

Theresa needs no further encouragement. Her round face wreathed in smiles, she joins the others. Like them, she wears the blue Visioneers uniform, fitting loosely over her ample frame. In her hair a bright red hibiscus flower glows with the warmth of her smile. Standing bravely before a watching world of more than a billion people, she closes her eyes, and without accompaniment sings the new words she has already taught the world to the bewitching melody of Amazing Grace.

"Amazing Grace, how sweet the sound,
That calls to us to hear.
We once were lost, but now we're found;
The time to come is near.
Amazing Grace, our hearts inspire,
Show us the way to see.
Our dreams, our hopes, our great desire:
To grow, to live, to be!"

Motioning with her hands she now invites the world to join her. A soft accompaniment comes up, as she begins to sing it through again. Outside, in the early evening the people of Jerusalem sing it with her. Across the world on the spinifex plains of central Australia the voices rise. On Kilimanjaro, on Machu Picchu, around the pyramid at Crestone, even in Tiananmen Square with the words on the big screen and where the music sounds strange to their ears: at all the globcom sites, the people are singing along with Theresa. But beyond that, far beyond that, in every city, town, village, house, bar, community centre, school, hospital, office—wherever the people have been watching—they join with Theresa and the Visioneers. Together, with full heart, caught in the magic of the moment, they sing of the amazing grace that so many are beginning now to feel enfolding them, preparing the way for the coming of the Global Mind.

CHAPTER TWENTY-FIVE

Feed-Forward

T HE WORLD IS READY, BUT NOT YET SET. Like a runner at the starting blocks, it has taken position for the race to come. Now is the moment to focus the mind, to tense every muscle for the leap to action, when the starter's pistol fires. It's the time of feed-forward, to align every element for the great performance.

The Visioneers have just four months to prepare the planet for the transformation to the Global Mind. Hope runs high across the world. Positive energy pours out from every project in every place where a band of Visioneers has gathered to make a difference. But around it all, there yet remains a web of negativity spun by minds not willing to let go, still intent to hold fast to gains of personal advantage, no matter what the cost to others and the Earth. Into this engagement the spirit of the Visioneers now pours full strength.

Kamal Rashid Returns

From his bed in a security ward in a hospital in Jerusalem, Kamal Rashid has watched the telecast locking in the trisets. As the last stirring chords of *Amazing Grace* die away, and the final scene of a smiling Mark and Esther waving to the world fades with the music, he clicks off the television set and stares long and intently at the blank screen.

It's over two months since a thrusting knife tore at his heart muscles in the house in Yemin Moshe on the day of Mark and Esther's wedding. For most of that time he has lain in a coma close to death. Dimly he recollects words in his mind that seem to have been spoken by Mark and Esther at his bedside, encouraging him to recover to lead his people. There are other memories, too, or perhaps they're dreams, he doesn't really know: faint images of Esther, coming to visit, touching him, telling him to get well.

Then two weeks ago he regained consciousness, and Esther did come to him, and sat at his bedside for an hour, telling him about the move by the Visioneers to create Jerusalem as the sacred city, planetary centre for a new world vision, and asking for his help to be leader and a spokesman for the vision among the Palestinians.

And Colonel Greenberg, chief of security operations for Israeli Special Services, had been there, formal and questioning, but somehow not the belligerent enemy of old. He told Kamal of Harrigan's capture, of his confession to the assassination plot against Mark and Esther, of his implication of Carlos Palmira, known as El Condor, head of I.T.C.C , the International Trust and Credit Corporation. Kamal knows, too, of Palmira's sudden and somewhat mysterious death, and the collapse worldwide of I.T.C.C. Now he lies in hospital, an Israeli prisoner, an alleged terrorist, regaining strength, pondering the future.

Elvira Ramos Again

Across the world in a sprawling mansion, behind a high security wall, in a deeply wooded valley in southwest Colombia, Elvira Ramos has watched the triset telecast, her breakfast untouched on a tray before her. Dressed in a green silk bathrobe, she displays the same hard-edged beauty as when she was at another breakfast, a few months earlier, with Carlos Palmira in Switzerland. Sitting with her this morning, another woman, trim, bespectacled and plain, watches a little apprehensively as she sees Elvira's mouth tighten at the end of the telecast.

"Carlotta," says Elvira, switching off the set, but still staring at the blank screen. She speaks to her companion in Spanish. "I asked you to get details of Esther Fisher's speaking engagements. Will she be in this part of the world again soon?" Her voice carries the even, high-pitched tone of superior to subordinate.

"She'll be in Los Angeles, in two weeks," replies the other, "but not in South America for almost two months."

"What's the event in Los Angeles?" asks Elvira.

Carlotta consults a notebook in her hand. "She's speaking to a women's group on 'Visioneering Partners'. It's a two day conference for business and professional women across the United States. They're expecting 2000 delegates."

Elvira considers for a moment.

"Get me complete details," she then says. "I need to travel to Los Angeles right away. Arrange a flight for tomorrow afternoon. That's all for now."

Recognizing that she has been dismissed, Carlotta leaves the room. Elvira turns to a white videophone beside her. She enters a code. A man's voice answers.

"Gilberto, this is Elvira. I want to speak with you on video."

"But, of course, my dear." A swarthy hard featured face of a man in his middle fifties appears on the phone's small video screen. Thick black eyebrows and a broad flat nose belie the geniality in his voice. "It's good to see you, Elvira," he continues. "What can I do for you?"

"Gilberto, I may need to speak with some of your people in Los Angeles about removing a problem that's been bothering me for some time. Could we meet to discuss it this afternoon?"

"Does it have anything to do with the telecast you've been watching this morning?"

"How do you know what I've been watching?"

"My dear, I know Elvira Ramos well enough that she's not normally out of bed before noon. Your passionate fixation with the exploits of two people broadcasting from Jerusalem this morning is no secret either. I just put two and two together."

"Did you watch it?" Elvira asks.

"Yes," Gilberto replies.

"What do you think?"

"I think someone should do something to stop them. But that isn't so easy anymore, since Carlos' bungled effort. Things are very tight for all of us right now."

"Can we discuss it this afternoon?" asks Elvira.

"But of course," he replies. "Shall I expect you about three?"

"Yes, that'll be fine."

Elvira breaks the connection and pushes her untouched food irritably aside.

Breakthrough in Consciousness

It's as if a light suddenly comes on in Kamal Rashid's mind. Ever since his first encounter with Esther and Mark he has sensed something mystical about them, something larger than the narrow framework in which he has battled for his own cause, the right of the Palestinians to their own land. He saw it first that morning in Bethlehem when Mark walked in unarmed to where Kamal was holding Esther hostage. Mark said he had come to make room for a miracle to happen. Now here it is, a miracle just unfolded before

Kamal's eyes and he had failed to see it, because his mind was still searching in another place. But, now, in a flash, he sees that the whole picture has been taking shape, piece by piece, over the past six months.

First, the attention of the world was grabbed by the murder of Luis Valdez and the memorial service broadcast by satellite to every continent. Then Mark spoke to the world leaders at the United Nations and they supported his call for action to promote a life of decency for everyone on the planet. Next, flying in the face of Kamal's own warnings about Palmira's murderous plans, Mark and Esther had emerged triumphant in Jerusalem while Palmira went to his death, and his evil empire crumbled around him. Now, in the space of a few more weeks, the whole world is locked into a pattern of communications no one would ever have considered possible, and Visioneers are increasing by thousands every day to set their communities on the way to prosperity and peace.

In a flash Kamal remembers Mohammed Hussein's words that morning in Bethlehem when he came in with Mark. "Standing right here among you," Mohammed had said, "is a man unarmed and unafraid, leading a group of ordinary people who are working tirelessly to bring the world to its senses, before it becomes such an abomination that no one can live on it: Arab, Jew or anyone else." Yes, Kamal realizes, now it's happening, and the way for him and his people must be to join that flow.

He reaches for a buzzer beside his bed and presses it. A nurse responds to his call.

"I want to speak to Colonel Greenberg," he says. "Will you please bring me a telephone?"

Untangling the Mess

At that moment, Colonel Greenberg is sitting with his Minister, Haim Shamir, Israeli Minister of Defence. They're in Mr. Shamir's office, where they've been watching the triset telecast.

"Well, colonel," asks Shamir, "what do you make of that? Do these people really know something that old war horses like you and me don't, or is this whole thing just a mirage?"

"I don't see the whole picture, sir", replies Greenberg, "but all the contact I've had with them tells me they're working with some extraordinary force that defies explanation."

"I never thought I'd hear anything like that from you, colonel. Do you think they were involved with Palmira's death?"

"They're not assassins or murderers, sir. Absolutely the opposite, I'm sure. But yes, I think indirectly they were involved."

"How so?" The minister is now eyeing Greenberg closely.

"You'd know better than me," the latter replies, "but I think somehow they got right to the top, and whatever support Palmira and the I.T.C.C. had just evaporated."

"And left people like you and me with a mess to clean up, eh, colonel?"

"Israel's dealings with the I.T.C.C. were rather modest, all things considered," Greenberg replies.

"Yes, but when all things *are* considered, we were involved," Shamir muses. "And that's not going to be helpful to our image on the world stage, if word gets out."

At that moment the minister's intercom buzzes.

"I'm sorry to interrupt you, sir," says a secretary's voice, "but there's a call for Colonel Greenberg from Kamal Rashid. I thought you might like to know."

Shamir raises his eyes at Greenberg.

"Put it through on the videophone," says the minister. "Both of us will talk to Mr. Rashid."

Shamir pulls the videophone over so that both of them are in front of it. Kamal's face comes in pale but excited. Shamir nods to Greenberg to speak.

"Hello, Rashid," says the colonel, "as you can see, I'm with Minister Shamir, but you can speak freely to both of us. What did you want to tell us?"

Kamal looks surprised and nervous.

"It's all right, Rashid," says the minister. "Colonel Greenberg has been keeping me fully informed on your discussions with him. If you have something more to add, we'd both like to hear it."

"Well," Kamal begins, uncertainly, "I want to say that I've changed my mind about working with you to help draft a peace accord between the Palestinian people and Israel. I think I could get something moving."

Shamir and Greenberg exchange glances.

"And what's the deal on that, Rashid?" It's Shamir who asks the question.

"There's no deal," Kamal replies. "I want to get something started. I don't know how much I can do, but I want to try."

Colonel Greenberg jumps in. "It sounds like you and I need to talk, Rashid. I'll be there as soon as I can. Thank you for calling." Greenberg breaks the connection. To Shamir he says: "I thought it best to intervene, sir. This could be a breakthrough. I didn't want to scare him off."

"Greenberg," says the minister, "if I didn't know better, I'd say you're starting to act like one of Mark Venture's Visioneers."

They look at each other carefully for a moment, then Shamir bursts out laughing.

"Go on, man, get on with it," he says. "And let me know how you make out."

Colonel Greenberg stands up, nods, and leaves the room.

Treachery in Los Angeles

In Los Angeles Elvira Ramos wastes no time in making contact. The man who appears at the door of her hotel suite is immaculately dressed in dark suit, white shirt, and red tie. In his mid-forties, he carries himself with authority. His handsome Latin features are chiseled in a hard mask of calculated efficiency.

"I'm Alberto Gonzalez," he says directly.

"Yes, please come in," Elvira replies, holding the door open for him. As he walks ahead of her into the sitting room, she notices the clean straight lines of his expensive clothes tailored to his athletic frame. He turns quickly to look at her, black eyes searching, hard.

"Please sit down," she gestures to a comfortable chair. He sits. His eyes never leave her face. She has dressed herself for the meeting in a black skirt, black and white checked jacket, and slightly ruffled white blouse with high neckline. Her dark hair is pulled back tight, framing the sharp lines of her face. They sit in silence for a moment looking at each other across the room.

"I believe Gilberto has told you something of my interests," she begins.

"Yes, but I wish to hear it directly from you," he replies.

"I haven't made a firm decision yet," she says. "This discussion is exploratory. Do you understand that?"

"What you are considering is extreme action." His reply is as hard as his presence. "I don't explore such matters lightly. If you're serious, we can talk further. If not, we end now. Anything beyond this moment bears high cost to you."

"Money is not the issue," she replies.

"When you contemplate eliminating human life, there are costs other than money. You begin to incur them the longer this conversation continues."

Elvira's carefully controlled tension snaps open for a moment.

"Look, Mr. Gonzalez," she exclaims. "I'm speaking to you about a business transaction. Neither of us will be involved in the details. Others will take care of that. At our level we have to be satisfied of each other's credibility. That's what this conversation is about."

"Exactly," he replies, "and I want to be sure you know what you're getting into with this plan."

"And I want to know that if I give the order to proceed it will be done without trace to me."

"Yes," he says, leaning forward a little in his chair, "and what I'm here to tell you is that the higher profile the target, the more difficult the execution and handling of the consequences. Esther Fisher is very high profile."

At the mention of the name Elvira's hands clench into manicured fists.

"Can you take care of it?" she asks. Her voice is brittle and sharp like broken glass.

"Yes," he replies.

"Fine." Elvira nods and sits up straight. "Now, tell me how you'll proceed and I'll decide whether we can do business."

Ripples Spreading Out

It's one day since the triset telecast. Mark calls from Jerusalem to speak to Peter Hemphill at the United Nations in New York.

"Well, Peter?" he asks. "What's the fall-out? What are you hearing from the official delegations about our triset operation?"

"It's a bit of a mixed bag at the moment," Peter replies. "Everyone's nervous, of course. No one's ever seen anything like this before. You hear the news the same as me. People in the streets everywhere seem to be very touched and are moving to form action groups, but there's a lot of confusion at the political level."

"The reports coming from our visioneering centres are really wild," says Mark. "Every place is jammed solid with enquiries. Our training programs and information packages are the hottest items around, at least, in many places, though it's not like that everywhere. Not that I expected it would be, mind you. Clearly there are repressive regimes in many countries holding things back. That's why I want to get your sense of it at the official level."

"I expect we'll know better in a week," Peter replies. "If I were you, I'd come over here right away and make your rounds through the delegations. Some of them are pretty confused."

"Good advice, Peter. I'll be there tomorrow or the next day. We've got something breaking here with Kamal Rashid and the Palestinians that I think could be pretty exciting. I'll give you details when I can."

Thirty minutes later, Mark, accompanied by Mohammed Hussein, meets Colonel Greenberg outside Kamal Rashid's hospital room.

"Well, colonel," says Mark. "This sounds promising. Anything new?"

"Not since yesterday," replies Greenberg. "I told you I met with Rashid and he asked for this meeting with the two of you and Esther. Where is Esther? Is she coming?"

"She was tied up on something else. She'll join us as soon as she can. Shall we go in?"

Kamal Rashid is sitting up in bed in crisp white pyjamas. Cleanly shaven, he looks alert, though still gaunt. An intravenous drip is attached to his right arm.

"Hello, Rashid," Mark greets him warmly. "It's good to see you looking so well. Esther will be along shortly. Colonel Greenberg tells me you have some important things to say."

"Hello, Mark Venture," Kamal replies. "I see you come dressed as a Visioneer in the uniform you wore on television."

"Yes, this is our official dress now. We've got our operational plan in place and we're on feed-forward to the Global Mind. We intend to look the part every day, so people will see the Visioneers in action. How about you? Are you ready to join us? It's thanks to you we're here at all. We'll never forget that."

"You have a big dream, Mark Venture. Maybe I'm ready now to come at least part-way with you. I'm glad, too, that my brother Mohammed is here. Please sit with me, and you, too, Colonel Greenberg."

When the three men are seated around the bed, Kamal continues.

"Do you remember, Mohammed, when you came with Mark Venture and David Roth to Bethlehem where we were holding Esther and her friend hostage?" Kamal pauses and looks at Greenberg. "I know up until now, colonel, I've never admitted involvement in that incident, and Mark was true to his word and never disclosed it. But none of that matters anymore." He speaks again to all of them. "In the last weeks I've been to death's door at the hands of one of my own countrymen, who chose to take sides with Carlos Palmira against my judgment. Now I lie here, a prisoner in an Israeli hospital. Who Kamal Rashid was before, no longer seems important to me. I've had time to think. Then, yesterday I saw your broadcast to the world. And I remembered the vision that both of you, Mark and Mohammed, spoke of that morning in Bethlehem. I couldn't see it then, but I remember the words: Arab and Jewish neighbours existing side by side as prosperous trading partners in a world growing rich with the products of cooperation. It seemed impossible then, but now, somehow, I think it can be done."

Kamal, still weak from his injuries, and struggling with the emotion of his words, falls silent.

Mark speaks softly.

"Kamal, good friend, you've learned that to speak about impossible things, you must first move your position to higher ground. From there, they no longer seem impossible. That's what the Visioneers are doing, moving people to higher ground in their minds. It's a great day for the world to hear Kamal Rashid say he's moving."

Before Kamal can reply, Esther enters the room, dressed as a Visioneer, breathless from hurrying. She touches the young Arab's hands and joins the others around the bed. Kamal now looks at all of them.

"I have a thought," he says, "not very clear as yet. But I would like to form a team of Visioneers made of up Palestinians and Israelis. We could call it PALIS. Its purpose would be to bring our people together to work on cooperative projects. I think that might be possible."

With an excited shout, Mohammed exclaims, a little louder than usual hospital decorum permits: "What did I tell you? I've been saying it for months, ever since your speech to the United Nations, Mark. There's movement to end the conflict and bloodshed. Mark and Esther, you gave us a symbol for it in the New Jerusalem. Now Kamal, you can be its spirit as a Visioneer. God is great! God is good! Now we have a place for hope to grow!"

Esther speaks to Kamal softly.

"When you were lying here deep in coma," she says, "I begged you to fight for your life to return as a leader to your people. Thank you for doing that. And I thank God from all of us for being with you." She looks around smiling and adds: "Our common God is indeed very great and very good."

Mark looks across the bed at Colonel Greenberg.

"Well, colonel," he says, "as the authority figure here, what do you say about this young prisoner?"

"I think," replies Greenberg, "I need to talk to my minister."

Within the hour Greenberg is in Haim Shamir's office.

"So," the minister is saying, "our young terrorist wants to change his stripes, and our old soldier says we should give him the chance. There's blood on his hands, colonel. We can't forget that."

"We're not sure about that, sir. But we do know about his actions to prevent a disaster at the wedding ceremonies. We'll have a lot more to gain by being lenient now, rather than trying to prove charges in a protracted court battle."

"Yes," muses Shamir, "and with the news about to break on our I.T.C.C. involvement, we could use some good publicity. I'll take it up with the Prime Minister. Thank you, colonel. Keep me informed on any new developments."

Waiting in Los Angeles

Elvira Ramos has been in Los Angeles for almost a week. Most days she spends in her hotel suite struggling with her thoughts. Alberto Gonzalez knows his business. She has no doubt about that, but he had pressed her too hard on her motives. He was offensive to the point of being insolent. The man's a professional killer. She's paying him well for his trouble. What right did he have to browbeat her about motives?

Carlos had always wanted to make the grand play, the great El Condor. And look where it had gotten him. He could have removed Mark Venture in a hundred different ways, but no, it had to be a grand spectacle, in full view of the world. And how that had backfired! Now Carlos is gone, and with him just about everything else. And where had that left her? Elvira Ramos, laughing stock of the international circle. And meanwhile the whole world's talking about a new heroine, Esther Fisher, sugar-coated little Jewish bitch from Jerusalem. What a place to be from—a stinking cesspool in the desert! Now here she's parading around the world with Mark Venture; the perfect couple, saviours of the planet. And Elvira Ramos is camped out in the jungle in Colombia. Well, not for much longer.

She doesn't need to know about how it's to be done. That's Gonzalez's business. And he doesn't need to know about her motives. That's her business. Blast him for being an arrogant Latin stud! Sitting there undressing her with his eyes while all the time he insulted her with his words. But she has it under control now. Gonzales knows his place. He will take care of it, when she gives the signal.

Fed up with her thoughts, Elvira seeks distraction in the television set in her room. Mid-afternoon inanity of American television does little to help. But it's a diversion. She passes rapidly through the channels. She pauses at the ZNN news network. She recognizes Pamela Barrett, the commentator who had described the wedding from Jerusalem, and Carlos' ridiculous fiasco. Pamela Barrett is reporting something new out of Jerusalem.

"The Israeli Government has just announced that it's dropping all charges of terrorism against Kamal Rashid. Rashid is the young Palestinian who was seriously injured from a knife wound several weeks ago while seeking to intervene in a death threat against Mark Venture and Esther Fisher, the well-known Visioneers, at their wedding in Jerusalem, last April.

"Rashid has just been released from hospital and in an interview with ZNN he made a rather startling announcement. In association with Mohammed Hussein, one of Mark Venture's principal Visioneers, Rashid is putting together a group to be known as PALIS. That stands for Palestinians and Israelis. The purpose is to begin work at a grass roots level to build cooperation and trust among their people. That's a far cry from the terrorist activities Rashid has previously been accused of. It's also in keeping with the approach of the Visioneers, to begin projects among people that will eventually lead to better solutions at a political level.

"Of course, we can't be sure where this initiative is going to go. There hardly seems to be a tougher place to look for successful cooperation, but the Visioneers have been working magic all around the world over the past six months, and this may well prove to be another example. ZNN will have a full report on this development, including interviews with Kamal Rashid, Mark Venture, and Esther Fisher at a later time.

"Closer to home for our American viewers, the visioneering news is that Esther Fisher will be in Los Angeles next week to speak to a national conference called 'Visioneering Partners'. On the way from New York, where she has a number of other speaking engagements a few days earlier, she'll make a stop at the Crestone Pyramid in Colorado. This is the American so-called globcom, established by the Visioneers as part of their triset operation for the planet. Ever since the telecast last week of the opening of the globcoms in various parts of the world, thousands of visitors have been pouring into the little town of Crestone to see what this is all about. We have some footage here to show you. Any visitor who goes to Crestone next Friday will have the added attraction of seeing Esther Fisher."

As Pamela Barrett continues to talk, scenes of crowds of people pouring into and around the Crestone Pyramid are shown against the magnificent backdrop of the Sangre de Cristo Mountains. Elvira Ramos sits transfixed, watching. Then suddenly she switches off the television set and reaches for the phone.

"Operator?" she says. "I want information on how to get to Crestone, Colorado. Could you please have someone call me back about that right away."

Experience at Crestone

It's mid-afternoon when Elvira Ramos catches sight of the glistening, crystalline pyramid reaching up into the sky. Just a smudge in the distance at first, it slowly takes form as she comes closer. She is driving north from Alamosa where she had flown in from Los Angeles via Denver that morning. It's Friday afternoon, the day that Esther Fisher is visiting the pyramid.

Elvira is still not sure why she's doing this. All week she had struggled against the impulse to come, but finally it proved overwhelming, and here she is. Tomorrow Esther will be in Los Angeles where the lives of the two women may well intersect tragically. Today, well who knows, but something has drawn Elvira to come. She has taken the precaution of travelling under an assumed name, Corina Montego. In Los Angeles, she had registered at her hotel as Francesca Costilia. There must be nothing to connect the presence of Elvira Ramos with events surrounding Esther Fisher. That's why coming here to Crestone when Esther is visiting seems so foolhardy. Elvira almost turns the car around to go back to Alamosa. But an irresistible curiosity to see Esther in this setting, to know what's attracting the world to this woman, compels her to carry on. She'll keep her distance. She'll be careful. Just a quick look and she'll leave.

A paved road leads directly to the pyramid, but as she comes within a kilometre of the towering structure, Elvira turns off along a side road. She's not yet ready to face the pyramid. The road winds up onto higher ground tucked under the Sangre de Cristo Mountain Range, which at this point rises precipitously straight up for several hundred metres above the valley floor. With the pyramid dropping away behind her, Elvira passes scattered mountain chalets tucked in among stunted pinion pine and aspen trees in new leaf. The whole valley spreads out below as a sea of mottled green.

What is this place? Why is that pyramid here? The questions crowd into Elvira's mind. She passes a number of other strange buildings, not North American design, but Eastern, rather like temples or monasteries. She catches glimpses of figures in coloured robes walking among the trees. She remembers having read somewhere that this was a popular place for various spiritual communities. Why are they here in the mountains of Colorado? Suddenly she feels decidedly uncomfortable. This is no place for Elvira Ramos.

The car comes to a dead end at the base of a towering mountain. The only way out is by means of a tight turnaround among large rocks and thick brush. The feeling of unease grips Elvira more tightly. She spins the car around. Stops. Backs it up. Tries again. Too fast. In a shower of flying gravel the car lurches sideways and slides into a ditch. Engine racing, one rear wheel helplessly spinning, it settles down in soft earth. Stuck.

Elvira gets out, angry to the point of tears. She has no mechanical mind, absolutely no idea of what to do. She looks around. Nothing. No one. Only rocks and trees. And a beautiful shining, black car that has no possibility of going anywhere. Elvira's reserve breaks. She kicks the front wheel with her dainty pointed sandals, buries her head in her arms on the hood of the car, and begins to sob convulsively.

"Pain and solutions both begin and end in the mind. That is truth."

The voice is just loud enough for Elvira to hear above her sobbing. She looks up, trying to stifle the tears. She sees no one, then turns, and there, standing close by is a tall male figure, wearing a long saffron-coloured robe that falls simply from his shoulders to his feet. His brown luminous eyes survey her closely, while a faint, enigmatic smile plays around the lips in the light brown face.

"Oh!" Elvira gasps. "I need help. My car is stuck."

"Yes, I see that," the man replies.

Sensing a solution at hand, Elvira quickly regains control of herself.

"If a few of you from the temple, or whatever you call it, get together, you can push it out," she says.

The man doesn't reply. He just stands there, continuing to survey her in the same measured way.

Irritable now, Elvira becomes demanding.

"Well, are you going to help?" she asks. "I have a very tight schedule to keep."

"Yes, I know about your schedule," he replies. "It's one that you would best reconsider."

"What do you mean?" Elvira is hostile now, but still uncomfortable. "Who are you to say that to me? All you need to do is gather up some of your friends to help. I don't appreciate comments about what I do."

"When what you do disregards the sanctity of human life, you can expect to pay the consequences deeply."

He still hasn't moved. His eyes unwaveringly stare into hers. Elvira feels fingers of fear grabbing at her. She still tries to force her way out.

"How dare you speak to me like that! Who do you think you are?"

"My name is Baba Satyananda. You will do well to remember that you met me on the road above the Crestone Pyramid when Esther Fisher was visiting. She is my special charge. She is protected. The aura around her is her shield."

Elvira gasps and steps away. She bumps into the car and feels her way nervously towards the door. Remembering that there's no escape there, she stops. Her voice has lost its edge. Fear closes around her throat.

"Baba Satyan . . . ," the word trails off. "Yes," she continues, barely above a whisper, "I've heard of you. At the wedding. They say you intervened. But here, in those robes . . . I thought you belonged to a temple."

"My community is wherever people do good. For the other, there is strong justice. You will do well to remember that, Elvira Ramos. Remember, too, the aura that protects Esther Fisher. You can go now. If you drive your car gently it will take you down to the pyramid."

He nods his head towards the door of the car. Trembling, her chest tight with pain, Elvira mechanically feels her way to get behind the steering wheel and start the engine. Effortlessly the car glides forward. When she turns her head to look back to where Baba had been standing, there's nothing but the empty road.

With no sense of time or conscious awareness, Elvira automatically guides the car along the mountain roads and down to the soaring pyramid. Growing taller as she approaches, it fills her mind, far beyond its actual size, with an overpowering presence of shining white energy, held to the Earth by the strong black bands of the frame.

A large crowd is gathered around the entrance just beyond the parking lot. Still barely conscious of what she's doing, Elvira parks her car. As she walks up to the rear of the crowd she sees a raised speakers' platform. A buzz of excitement goes through the crowd. Applause breaks out. Onto the platform steps Esther Fisher, wearing the blue and white uniform of the Visioneers, with her shining auburn hair hanging loose on her shoulders. She raises her arms in acknowledgement of the applause and prepares to speak. Elvira hears no words. Her attention is entirely consumed by the golden aura she sees shining around Esther's figure. Does anyone else see it? Elvira has no idea. Baba's words burn in her mind: "She is my special charge. She is protected. The aura around her is her shield." Transfixed, Elvira stares at the phenomenon for several minutes. Esther is speaking, but the words have no meaning for Elvira. She turns away and hurries back to her car.

Aftermath in Los Angeles

When Esther arrives at her hotel that evening in Los Angeles, a message is waiting for her. It is handwritten on hotel stationery, sealed in a hotel envelope.

"Miss Fisher:
It's imperative that I speak with you this evening. Please contact me in Room 1202, no matter when you arrive. It is urgent and personal. Elvira Ramos."

The name immediately leaps into Esther's memory: the tall, elegant woman in a green sheath evening dress at Woodland's restaurant in New York, associate, confidante, mistress of Carlos Palmira. Esther's immediate impulse is to seek assistance. Bill Bates and other members of her travelling party are at hand. But something tells her she should do this alone. It's after midnight when she calls Room 1202. A woman's voice answers immediately.

"Yes?"

"This is Esther Fisher. I received a message to call."

"Yes, thank you. I'm Elvira Ramos. You may remember me."

"Yes I do."

"May we speak?"

"Now? It's very late."

"Yes, I know. I'm sorry, but it's important. I only have this evening."

"Very well, I'll meet you in the hotel lobby in ten minutes."

When Esther arrives in the lobby, Elvira is already there. Esther recognizes the other woman immediately. The same classical beauty exudes but something nervous and distraught detracts. Her expensive clothing is carelessly worn, her makeup slightly smeared.

Elvira stands. She doesn't reply to Esther's greeting, but stares hard at her uncomfortably long. Finally, Esther asks:

"Is anything wrong?"

"It's still there," Elvira's voice is distracted.

"I'm sorry," replies Esther. "I don't understand."

"Did you know you are protected by an aura?"

Esther is embarrassed, uncomfortable. Something is definitely not right with this woman. She's about to reply when Elvira raises her hand.

"No, please. Let me tell you what I want to say and then I'll leave. I came to Los Angeles because—no, it doesn't matter why I came. That's changed now. It's all cancelled. You see, I went to Crestone to hear you speak, but instead I met your protector, Baba Sata . . . , I don't know, it's an Indian name. He said that you're protected. He's put an aura around you. I can see it now."

It's Esther's turn to stare.

"What are you saying?" she asks. "You met Baba Satyananda up at Crestone? But he's not there. At least, I didn't know that he was."

"It's no matter. I expect he's always around you. I didn't imagine it. He was definitely there. You're very fortunate to have such protection."

"Why are you telling me this?"

"I don't know. Perhaps I wanted to meet you again. Now I must go. Thank you for seeing me."

Elvira turns to go.

"Mrs. Ramos," Esther calls after her. "Is there something I can do for you?"

But the other woman doesn't turn. She has her bags with her at the hotel desk. She signals a sleepy night clerk to bring them to a cab outside, and she disappears into the night.

Back in her room, Esther puts through a call to Mark Venture in New York. A sleepy voice answers.

"Mark, darling, it's Esther. I know it's still early morning there, and I'm sorry to wake you. But I just had a strange meeting with Elvira Ramos. Do you remember her?"

Mark is immediately alert.

"What was that about?" he asks. "I thought she was in Colombia. She's bad news, Esther. What did she want?"

"I don't know. But she told me she was up at Crestone and met Baba who said he was protecting me. It's really bizarre."

Mark is silent for a moment while he considers.

"Listen, Esther, darling, please. I don't know what that's about. But if Baba's intervening it means there's danger around. I want you to get hold of Bill Bates right away. Don't worry that it's early in the morning, and tighten up the security around there. It may be nothing, but I don't want you taking any chances."

"All right, darling, I will. But what do you think it means, that she saw Baba like that?"

"It means that you're being protected to do your work. Both of us are. All of the Visioneers are. The likes of Elvira Ramos can't do anything to stop the process, no more than Carlos Palmira with all his wealth and power could either. We're getting set now for the Global Mind. Once it comes, the world will never be the same again! Stay well, my darling, take every care. I'll be with you again soon."

CHAPTER TWENTY-SIX

Culmination

ESTHER'S WORK IN LOS ANGELES PASSES without further incident. Nothing more is heard from Elvira Ramos. At least, not immediately. A week later in New York, Mark receives a call from Peter Hemphill in his apartment.

"Mark, I just got wind of something. I think you'll find it interesting. It's about Elvira Ramos. She's dead."

"What? How did it happen?"

"That's not clear. She was found at her house outside Cali in Colombia this morning by her maid. According to the report there were no signs of foul play. The police are saying suicide at the moment, but I'm not so sure."

'What do you mean?"

"Well, ever since you told me about that incident between Esther and Elvira in Los Angeles about a week ago, I've been keeping my nose to the ground. My theory is that if she was in Los Angeles to set something up to harm Esther, and then changed her mind because of her experience at Crestone, she may well have put some things in motion that finally caught up with her."

"How so?"

"Well, what I mean is, if you mess around with professional killers, and then don't follow through, they get pretty nervous about how much you know, and might well conclude that you're better off dead with your mouth closed permanently. Now, it's only a theory, but it's plausible."

"There's some wretched stuff out there, Peter." Mark's voice betrays his disappointment.

"It all comes from wretched people, old boy," rejoins Peter, "and you and your crew are certainly doing a lot to make that better. Now I've got another good-news bad-news story for you."

"Oh, yes?"

"The bad news is that the Israeli government has had to 'fess up' to having some arms trading deals with Carlos Palmira in the past through the I.T.C.C. It's really nothing worse than what a lot of other governments have been up to, but it's a bit embarrassing for them."

"What's the good news?"

"Well, as you know, ever since Israel released Kamal Rashid, he and Mohammed Hussein have been making some headway with their PALIS idea. Now, the good news. What I'm hearing through some of the Arab delegations around here, as well as the Israelis, is that the pressure is starting to build up on both sides from a lot of people who are getting involved. They want a political solution so that Israelis and Palestinians can get on with living decent lives together."

"You know, Peter, a breakthrough there would do so much to lift the morale of the world."

"Well, keep working at it, old boy. You've already pulled off a few miracles."

"Yes, Peter, they're coming in every day now. We're in the final three months of the run-up to the Global Mind. These next few weeks will be critical. Thanks for all your news. I'll keep in touch."

Countdown

As Mark has said, the next few weeks are critical. Everywhere the Visioneers redouble their efforts to get momentum. They sow the idea of build-up, a countdown to something extraordinary on the planet.

Carefully staged publicity releases come out from Visioneer Headquarters through Bill Bates. Esther continues her tireless schedule of visits around the globe. Mark patiently explains and re-explains the concept to the delegations at the United Nations. Prestigious international planning committees are at work designing each globcom's participation in the coming Congress. The news outlets are picking it up. Newspapers, magazines, television, radio: all forms of media feature stories every day on exploits of Visioneers around the world. Excitement is building. Everyone is getting set for the event to come.

The primary thrust is to get people working together through their trisets. A new significance is given to the adage of, "Think globally, act locally." Act locally to build relationships. Act locally to put aside negativity and conflict. Act locally to tap the creativity of people to find solutions to situations that for generations have seemed unsolvable. Act locally, but think globally through the trisets, and tell the success stories every day.

Thousands of reports come to light by the minute—good news stories from every quarter. A Global Visioneering Network is set up by Bill Bates in partnership with ZNN. By the beginning of August the Network is bringing reports twenty-four hours a day of the major events in every triset.

No artificial border can stop the flow of activity. People in China send aid and encouragement to communities in India. Americans and Canadians reach out across the Atlantic and Pacific Oceans. Europeans work with Africans while Australians partner up with South Americans and Asians. Cities, towns, villages, wherever they might be, look beyond national borders and continents, seeing themselves as part of this triset, linking to that triset, working with the globcoms. All of it is coming together in a worldwide flow of positive activity to celebrate the beauty and abundance of the planet.

Of course, not all of this runs smoothly. The world is too turbulent a place for that. The old agendas of conflict, violence, industrial unrest, poverty, and suffering are still there. But a light of reasonableness has begun to shine through the gloom. Everywhere there's a sense that people, millions of them on every continent, are beginning to change their minds and discover the untapped potential of human consciousness to create harmony and order: to begin, indeed, to think as part of a Global Mind.

Prelude

It's mid-October and one week before the start of the Congress. In the Star of Jerusalem, Mark and Esther make last minute preparations for another telecast to the entire world. This is the prelude to the Congress, the culmination of the months of work now behind them. All of the other globcoms are standing by. As before, the broadcast begins at 5:00 p.m. Jerusalem time, to catch the world from early morning in North America to late evening in eastern Asia and Australia.

The numbers on the studio's digital clock flash to 17:00; the Visioneers theme music comes up; the familiar white V on the sky blue background appears on the world's television screens; the blue-white view of the planet ripples through the symbol of the Visioneers; a bright pinpoint of light spins in from black space, swells to a star, and bursts in brilliance on the Earth at the site of Jerusalem. Out of the cascading shower of light Mark and Esther look out to the world.

"Welcome from Jerusalem." Esther smiles her salutation.

"To our Visioneers and friends from dawn to darkness across the Earth, greetings and good spirit," Mark adds.

"This is our moment to anticipate the future," Esther continues. "Across the planet for the past four months we have seen an awakening to life. Today, swept along on the crest of that rising wave, we look up and see before us the golden sands of a new, enlightened world. Seven days from now our wave will carry us up onto the beach and we'll begin together the glorious celebration of the Global Mind."

"That's the future," Mark continues, "our minds leap toward it with excitement. But today and tonight we honour what we have already done. From the Star of Jerusalem, centrepiece of this global network, we take you now on a sweep of our planetary home, across the trisets and through the globcoms, showing you what we already have, displaying how the spirit of the Visioneers has touched and enlivened the planet."

With that, the television screens of more than a billion viewers explode in a starburst of cascading light. The top of the globe appears, showing the landmasses of Asia, Europe, and North America grouped around the North Pole. A searing red laser light streaks across the picture, tracing out the triset of NAMRASIA, flashing up the globcoms in Jerusalem, Beijing and Crestone. The Tiananmen Dome comes into view where Lin Yuen, Jeremy Hiscox and Junichi Yakasawa take up the commentary. Like Mark and Esther, they are dressed in the now familiar blue and white uniform of the Visioneers. They run scene after scene of visioneering activity across northern China and Mongolia, into the republics of northern Asia, right up to the frozen tracts of Siberia, across Russia to Ukraine.

Then the Star of Jerusalem comes back again, where Mohammed Hussein, Indira Murti, and Theresa Romano pick up the story, taking the viewers through Syria and Turkey into eastern Europe, across Poland and Germany into Scandinavia.

The countries are mentioned by name only in passing. What's important is the activity in the streets and the countryside, where people of all ages, countless cultures, innumerable occupations are shown working together, unconscious of borders or differences, working together on projects to make life better. Everywhere the cameras go they pick up the familiar blue and white uniforms of the Visioneers, moving among the people. They tell stories of pride and accomplishment, cooperation and enterprise: scarred landscape restored, bankrupt factories brought into production, farming revitalized, bureaucracies energized, communities working together. Nowhere are there scenes of violence or bloodshed: no weapons, no military vehicles, no soldiers in uniform, only the Visioneers in blue and white; enlivening debate; challenging assumptions; pushing people to think, to dream, to believe in themselves, and to dare to act to make a positive difference.

Now the Crestone Pyramid comes up, with George Walker, Diane Koplitz, and Nicholai Andropov. They bring in other people of western

Europe, across the British Isles, over the North Pole to Iceland, Greenland, Canada, and the northeastern United States. All of this together, lights up the top of the world as the triset of NAMRASIA, held together with the balancing energies of its globcoms and the enthusiastic spirit of the Visioneers.

But that's only one-eighth of the story. From there the other trisets come in, bringing with them almost another five billion people, across oceans, mountain ranges, deserts, industrial concentrations, lush farmland, jungles, and ice fields. Across all degrees of latitude and longitude, through every climatic zone, the trisets of the visioneering world are swept together. Holding the balance, pushing the communications, engaging the spirit, the remaining globcoms show their work: the Machu Picchu Diamond, the Australian Rock, the Kilimanjaro Watchtower, and all of their people.

It's a glorious kaleidoscope of human energy linking with the energy of the Earth, flowing together in an unfathomable ocean of opportunity, achievement, and enterprise. As it sweeps to a finale, the *Song of the Visioneers* comes up, and marching across their screens viewers everywhere in the world see their children, countless millions of them, of every race and colour, their voices raised, their eyes shining, singing:

"We are the ones going to the fore.
Big ones, little ones—all of us are here.
Small world, big world, reaching out to all.
Up, up, and upmost—the mighty Visioneers!"

As the last chords of the children's singing fade away, the image of the blue and white living planet Earth comes up again. It holds for a moment, then slowly dissolves into a sea of liquid golden light. Music of a gentler rhythm rises slowly, harmony of creation, the melodic tonal beauty of the Baroque distilling into the evocative, mysterious strains of Eastern meditative chant.

The light scatters. It breaks away revealing the lush green of a garden setting. On a white bench before a flowering hibiscus tree, a man wearing a saffron-coloured robe sits with his eyes closed, gently rocking back and forth. Some of the viewers recognize him from brief appearances at the memorial service for Luis Valdez, and at Mark and Esther's wedding in Jerusalem. For most, however, he's a new actor on the stage of the Visioneers. He raises his head and looks out to the world through luminous brown eyes.

"I am Baba Satyananda," he says quietly, "and I bid you welcome from my Place of Peace and Serenity here in the ashram at Ventagiri in India. For many months I have followed the adventures of the Visioneers and my heart leaps with joy as I watch with you this evening and see all that they have done. They are poised now to bring to the world a new beginning. I speak to you a few words so that you may know of where this change comes and why this is the time for it.

"You must know that these are days of great urgency. A turning point has come. The countdown is upon you, the people of the Earth, to make massive shifts in your relationships to each other and to the planet. The Earth is part of a perfect universe of love, forever in creation, flowing with an energy that is the source of all life. Your role as the highest form of all creation on the planet is to discover and embrace that universal energy and order all activity on the planet in the harmony of its perfect way.

"Through the technology of your science you have released powerful activity on the planet. It could be directed to do great good, but mostly its impact is destructive, because you have not aligned your consciousness with the flow of the universal life force. You work at cross purposes to your own ultimate benefit, and an aura of dense and destructive negativity envelops the planet.

"The mission of the Visioneers is to break down that negativity by leading you to find a new wisdom in your minds. It begins with a few and spreads to the many. When people embrace it, a new peace and energy moves throughout their communities. They become places of care and nurturing where children can be raised in an environment of love and truth. And the truth they learn is not a truth that seeks for pleasure through acquisition, but a truth that finds happiness through loving and sharing. Ah, you may say, that is not the way of the world. And you would be right. It has not been the way of the world. But it is the way of the universe, and you are being challenged now to bring the two together, into alignment.

"You begin with yourself, to find peace in your heart, and the power of God which is within you. Then you build relationships of trusting cooperation with others. From this you find universal prosperity, because you know that when consciousness is aligned with the life force, the world becomes a place of abundance. It only manifests as a place of conflict and scarcity when you perceive it that way in your minds. For whatever you think in your minds and hold in your hearts, becomes manifest in the world around you.

"To the leaders of the world who are watching, hear these words, and lead your people along the path of peace. To the leaders of business and government and communities, the same universal principles apply. Turn now to the energy of love and sharing and away from the energy of conflict and bitter competition. The Earth cannot bear the force of mounting negative forces. It will groan and creak and crumble under the pressure, and you and your children will have lost forever your heritage to live in peace and tranquility on our wonderful planetary home.

"In the days to come the Visioneers will show you the joy of following another path than the one you have been pursuing. You will experience the power of becoming one great river of human consciousness flowing together in the Global Mind. Then it will be up to you to choose: to choose the path of trust and love and sharing, or the path of anger, hostility and conflict. Choose well, my dear ones, for the future of the planet and your children are in your hands."

Baba's message is finished. He smiles gently to the world. The same evocative music of rich melodic tones comes up again. Baba's image fades into the picture of the fragile blue planet hanging in black space. Then this, too, fades into the blue and white symbol of the Visioneers suspended in the centre of the Star of Jerusalem. Mark and Esther re-enter to stand before their symbol and close the telecast.

"Choose well, Baba has advised, "Mark exclaims. "We must learn to see the future for what it is destined to bring, and not the illusion of what is around."

"If we can see a glorious and prosperous future for everyone on the Earth," Esther continues, "then we will work to create it. If we can't first imagine it, we can't ever do it."

"Thank you for joining us, from wherever in the world you've been watching," Mark concludes. "In a few days' time we'll come together again in the celebration of the Global Mind. Details of where and how you can participate, if you don't already know, are available in your community or through any Visioneer.

"Esther and I bid you goodbye for now, with a wish that the peace for which we all search in our hearts becomes manifest around you and brings you joy."

The Visioneers theme music comes up, the lights fade. The telecast is over.

Reaction

Mark has barely been off the air for an hour, when a call comes through on his videophone at the Star of Jerusalem from Peter Hemphill at the United Nations in New York. The usually unflappable Peter has a decidedly strained look on his face.

"I'm sorry to have to tell you this, Mark," he says, "but there's been a blow-up after your broadcast—which, by the way, I thought was absolutely brilliant."

"Thank you, but what's wrong?" asks Mark.

"Some of the heavies have hit the panic button. They see too much of this visioneering stuff starting to erode their power base in their own countries. Frankly, I'm surprised it didn't explode before this. They're demanding an emergency meeting of the General Assembly for next week before the opening of the Congress. The Secretary-General asked me to get hold of you. The two of you need to talk. I'll connect you in a moment. First I wanted to tell you about this myself."

"Thanks Peter. I've been expecting it. I think I might just go them one better than an emergency debate at the U.N."

"What do you mean?"

"I'm sorry, I can't explain right now. I have some checking to do first. Let me speak to the Secretary-General."

Showdown in the Visioneering Room

Mark's conversation with the Secretary-General changed the course of everything. Instead of accepting a meeting in the General Assembly, Mark declares that the meeting will be in the Visioneering Room.

So, once again, you, the creator of this whole adventure, are brought back into the action. If you had any sense before that the characters were beginning to take over the control of your creative journey, your suspicions are now confirmed. When you first began thinking your way through this exercise to create a viable future for the planet, you had seen yourself at the centre of events, carefully determining what each next step would be. However, at your last meeting with your mentors, that began to change. They were impatient with you for not consulting them more frequently. Then they had upstaged you by demanding that they meet with Mark and Esther. Now Mark has gone one step further. Faced with an ultimatum from some of the world leaders to reopen debate on the Global Mind project in the General Assembly, he has instructed you to pre-empt their initiative by rounding up everyone, bringing them to the Visioneering Room, and setting up a no-holds-barred exchange with himself, Esther, yourself, and all of the mentors.

So here you are, the leaders once again in the rows of seating, reluctant and noisy, while Mark and Esther stand up front calling for silence. The four mentors, Churchill, Dickens, Kennedy, and Anne are seated behind Mark and Esther, facing the Assembly. You, at the side, wonder what's going to happen. You don't have long to wait.

Mark has had some success in achieving order, but one by one the leaders are coming to their feet, attacking the idea of visioneering as unworkable, complaining that they were hoodwinked into supporting it, and demanding that everything be scaled back. Not all are antagonistic, however. On the other side of the debate powerful and passionate arguments are made for what the Visioneers have accomplished and the hope all this has engendered in people otherwise destined for lives of misery. But still the chorus of dissent swells loud. It's too much, they say. Too radical. Unworkable. Certain to bring chaos. Unrealistic. The tide of negativity comes in. Minds begin to close. Those that struggle to withstand the flood begin to weaken. The carcinogen of doubt begins to work its poison, and faith in the miracle of visioneering starts to fade from the majority in the room.

Into this thickening gloom steps a mighty spirit.

"Have you so soon forgotten?" he roars. Crashing his chair aside, Winston Churchill has leapt to his feet. He propels himself forward to stand squarely before this assembly of power. His nostrils flare. Blood red, his dogged face thrusts forward and his eyes fix the audience with rivets of steel.

"Here in this very room," he thunders, "you saw and felt and heard the dire consequences of continuing past thinking into future time. The masterful Mr. Dickens played them out for you. They burned in your minds again when you heard Mark Venture speak to you in the United Nations, and you enthusiastically endorsed the Congress of the Global Mind. Now, a few months later, when the inconvenience and threat of changing direction touches your administration, you begin to vacillate, change your minds, say what you thought perhaps will not be so.

"Well, let me tell you again. Nothing is more certain than the slide of this planet into abject despair and desolation, far worse than anything we can believe or imagine, if men and women of new high mind do not emerge to steer it on another course.

"We shall play the scenes for you again, but this time place them in contrast with what you have just seen presented by the Visioneers after only a few months of their work.

"Then you may choose: you may choose to walk through the doorway to the future where current thinking takes us, or you may choose to pass through to where the Visioneers are proposing the world should go.

"You have been brought here to decide. This is a place of unremitting and binding choice, as fixed and sure as when you pass across the boundary between life and death. Mr. Dickens and Mr. Venture, with your assistance the process will begin."

There then follows a spectacle as extraordinary as any previously presented in this room. The space in front of the assembled leaders divides in two with a beam of white laser light separating them. Charles Dickens moves to stand in a spotlight at the lower left facing the audience, while Mark Venture takes a similar position, lower right. The space behind Mark remains in darkness. On Charles Dickens' side, activity springs into light.

The leaders are quick to recall the replay of the dreadful scenes they had seen before, when they were shown the future by the mastery of Dickens. Nothing is omitted: the horror of one hundred million children exterminated by a wall of water in the blood red canyon; scenes of violent, high-technology combat reeking with the stench and carnage of mutilated bodies; ugly vistas of ruined landscapes; cities thick with smog; factories and machinery lying idle; hordes of unemployed people in long unending food lines; dying and stunted vegetation. The final set of scenes presents massive assemblies of violent people, railing against their politicians, burning buildings, bombing churches, storming the legislatures. The faces of the political leaders jostled and pushed aside by these angry crowds are the faces of the leaders looking on in the audience.

That side of the room darkens, and behind Mark a different panorama unfolds. It's a replay of what was seen on television a few days before when the watching world was taken on the journey through the trisets. The leaders in the Visioneering Room see again countless millions of people of every nation, culture, colour and religious creed engaged in positive projects of cooperation. Among them the blue and white uniforms of the Visioneers stand out as working symbols of a worldwide creative force for good.

The lights now come up on both sides of the laser barrier and Churchill again steps forward to address the assembly.

"You have seen," he says. "Now comes the moment to choose."

The final scenes played out on both sides come up again and are frozen in full view of the audience. Churchill continues.

"Those of you who will choose to join your mirror images among the rioting masses may now get up and do so. Remember only this: if you choose that path, it will be your certain future. It is coming as it is shown. If you choose it, then it is yours. Those who want it, proceed now to claim your future."

No one moves. Churchill waits while time hangs heavy in the room. He then turns a belligerent , provocative gaze on those who had argued strongest before against the Visioneers. His voice growls with the passion and the anger of a lion enraged.

"What? None of you wish to journey now where moments before your empty heads and wagging tongues would take you? No travellers now on the highway of bravado? No one who any longer would choose to plow ahead to collective and personal oblivion?

"Well then, may we conclude that if you are not for the one, then at least you will not obstinately oppose the other? Silence? I accept it as agreement.

"Perhaps my colleagues have something further they wish to add. I thank you for indulging the passion of one who has already used a lifetime in bitter struggle against the consequences of human wickedness. Like you, I would not willingly again choose such a path."

President Kennedy comes forward.

"Friends," he says. "None of you can know the exact details of the future, but you all can search your minds for higher purpose to guide your choices. The Visioneers would have us do that. You owe them the opportunity to show you their crowning piece."

Anne adds a word: "For the sake of all the unborn children, choose well for life and love."

Charles Dickens gestures to the scene behind him and exclaims, "No greater purpose can we hold than to safeguard the world from a future such as that."

Mark and Esther come forward. Esther speaks.

"It's a privilege to share the space with noble and powerful minds. I bid you God speed in all you do to guide the future of the world."

Mark concludes: "Leaders of the world, we go forward now to embrace the Global Mind. Your leadership and vision have greatly assisted us in reaching this point. Thank you for that, and for your presence here. Go in peace. When next we meet may it be in triumph."

Standing alone, but deeply a part of all the action, you look for one long moment at the assembled people in the room. With Mark and Esther you wish to them all God speed, high principles, and good judgment. With that you send them out to play their roles in the now opening drama of the Global Mind.

CHAPTER TWENTY-SEVEN

The Global Mind

IT BEGINS ON SATURDAY EVENING, LOCAL TIME, in Beijing on Tiananmen Square. This is the moment the world has been waiting for. So high is the interest that everywhere on the planet, no matter what the hour, people are watching, to be there at the beginning. A profound expectancy has settled across the Earth. Never before in the history of the planet has such a concentration of human energy been brought to bear on a single event.

Awakening: The Festival of Light

The ceremony is equal to the occasion. This is Day One of the Congress of the Gobal Mind, the glorious Festival of Light. It represents the birth of the universe, the beginning of all creation, long held in human minds as the ascendancy of light over darkness, the separation of form out of the emptiness of the void.

When the television cameras capturing the event for the world begin to run, there's nothing but darkness. The whole of Tiananmen Square and the surrounding area for many blocks lies plunged in complete blackness. Against this dark, empty space, the ceremony begins with the voice of Jeremy Hiscox, speaking from inside the Dome on the Square, announcing the opening passage from the Book of Genesis:

" 'In the beginning God created the heaven and the earth. And the earth

was without form, and void; and darkness was upon the face of the deep
. . . And God said, Let there be light: and there was light.' "

As the last words proclaim the age-old wish of all humanity, the centre
of Tiananmen Square explodes in a blaze of white light as electricity surges
through a hundred thousand bulbs and the magnificent geodesic dome
bursts into life before the watching world. And with the light comes the
sound: the sound of a great fanfare of trumpets, championing in their
resounding clarion call the exuberant triumph of the light over the darkness.

Then, out in the still empty blackness of the vast Square all around the
Dome, another spectacle of light begins. Ten thousand tiny batteries
illuminate as many candles, each one held in the hand of a child, and the
Square is suddenly a glitter of walking light. The fanfare of trumpets has
ceased. Replacing it, rising with equal energy, the clear, bright voices of
the children ring out, each one amplified for the listening world with a
personal microphone. The song they sing, over and over, as they step out,
invisible bearers of their beacons of waving light, marching around the
Square, the song is the one the world now expects to hear, the *Song of the
Visioneers*. They sing it first in English for the world, then in Chinese for
themselves, then alternatvely in both languages over and over, as they
march around the Square:

"We are the ones going to the fore.
Big ones, little ones - all of us are here.
Small world, big world, reaching out to all.
Up, up, and upmost - the mighty Visioneers!"

Now the children, still singing, break from their marching formation
and begin to weave their lights into intricate symbolic patterns displayed
for the television cameras high above the Square. The candles dance and
wave in many colours as the symbols come and go: the white crest of the
Visioneers, changing to the blue and white planet Earth, changing to a
multicoloured pattern of the trisets cutting across the globe. In the final
image the children create a magnificent butterfly in red, blue and gold,
which spreads its gigantic wings across the great expanse of the Square,
grand symbol of an awakening world. As it hovers there in all its splendour
for the whole world to see, the *Song of the Visioneers* comes to an end, the
fanfare of trumpets sounds again, and floodlights blaze out on every side
of the space. The worldwide audience now sees what until then was
hidden: more than a hundred thousand spectators standing around the
perimeter of the Square, all of them carrying small blue and white
Visioneers flags that now leap into life as a waving forest of motion. The
children in the centre, each dressed in a blue and white Visioneers uniform,
suddenly break rank and surge around in a churning, shouting charge of

human energy. The Tiananmen Festival of Light has opened: the Congress of the Global Mind has begun.

But this is only the very tip of the beginning. All around the world communitiies have planned their own festivals of light, ranging from the grandest extravazaganza on Broadway's Great White Way in New York City, to the simplest torch-lighting ceremonies in thousands of African villages. Throughout the evening and into the next day the festivities continue, each place working out its own schedule according to the local time zone.

Back on Tiananmen Square on Sunday afternoon, marking the end of the first day, a vision is fulfilled. The ancient Zhao She Yuhan looks out from the Great Hall of the People and sees what had only been a dream when he first described it to Lin Yuen twelve months earlier. Two hundred thousand people have come together to share food, fun, and fellowship. They are out to celebrate. And oh, what a grand celebration it is! But more, much more than that! What a moment for China and her people, showing the spirit of participation with the rest of the world in the next millennium! And presiding over it all stands the structure Zhao had not at first envisioned but conceived of later, the shining geodesic dome, symbol now to the whole world of the spirit of the Chinese Visioneers. With quiet satisfaction the old man celebrates his people's entry into the emerging Global Mind.

Day of Meditation

Day Two begins on Sunday Evening in Machu Picchu. By now most of Europe, Africa, and Asia would normally be asleep or, further east, be waking to Monday morning. But so enthralled has the world become with what is happening in this global congress, that when Day Two opens, more than a billion people are joining in from every continent.

This is the Day of Meditation. George Cardinal will lead it. Seated in the company of his fellow Visioneers, Carmen Santander and Irene Henshaw, in the Machu Picchu Diamond, he appears to the world as the proud chieftain. Wearing his full headdress in equal pride with his Visioneer's uniform, he looks out boldly to the world. Across the continents people see the same determined courage as when he spoke in memory of his fallen brother, Luis Valdez. Tonight his message resounds with no less force.

"We take as our theme for this great world Congress the story of creation from the Book of Genesis." He pauses a moment for reflection before continuing. "We do this not as the text from any one religion, or as the special truth of an event we can never comprehend, but rather as a statement of how much we people of the Earth need to reach for a spiritual home. I, myself, am born of the forests and the plains, and the hard, cold, icy tracts of northern winters. All of you joining me this day have your own special origins. But together we are no less than the children of one common God, whose perfect order flows around us in the universe.

"Our inspired text describes Day Two of creation as the time when God made the firmament and called it Heaven. So let it be. We can seek forever to find the words to describe the greatness and the splendour of creation. It goes far beyond our human comprehension. Our task today is not to dwell on the words we cannot find, but on the inner wisdom that if we stretch our minds to seek, will lead us to touch the mind of God.

"I am too simple a man to know the mystery of these things. But what I see is the perfection of the leaf that breathes for the tree, and the drop of water that enlivens the soil. And I see in these every day, the miracle of a continuing creation.

"Knowing this, my heart weeps at how we human beings, priding ourselves with our great intellect, and seeing ourselves as masters of industry and commerce, how we in all our arrogance separate ourselves from our earthly home. Further still, we separate ourselves from ourselves, forgetting that all of us are born of the same source and depend for our survival on its continuing care and nourishment.

"On this Day of Meditation we are asking you to set aside as many hours as you can, to reflect on the miracle of your life and of your responsibility to share it to enrich the lives of all you touch. Let us, today, as one great family on the Earth, reach out in our minds to embrace the unity of all things. Let us listen to the wind, to the waves on the beach, to the snowflake falling, to the jungle steaming. Let us feel the pain of each other's suffering and of the wounds we inflict on our mother Earth, and let us resolve in our hearts and minds to learn how to live together in the oneness of creation."

With these words George Cardinal has set the theme for the day. Across the planet, Visioneers now convene in assemblies from unversity halls to mud huts. Here, they seek first in meditation to still their minds from the clamour of the world, and second to listen together, one to one, and one to many, to draw closer to the truth of what binds the Earth together in a Global Mind.

Manifestation

Days Three, Four, and Five of the Congress are the days for celebrating the divine order of relationships on the planet. On the third day, the Book of Genesis tells that God created the dry land which He called the earth. This is Earth Day at the Congress. On the fourth day, God created the sun, the moon, and the stars. This is the Day of the Universe. On the fifth day, God created the creatures of the sea and the air. At the Congress this is the Day of the Oceans and the Sky.

Over the seventy-two hours spanned by these three days, people everywhere on Earth are engaged and challenged, on a scale never before attempted, to understand that their planet is a delicate living system, as miraculous in its smallest part as it is awesome in its totality. It is presented and seen as a gift of a divine mind, part of a perfect order, filled with the energy of continuous creation, that links it forever to the unfathomable, unknowable immensity of the universe.

Earth Day is led by the Visioneers in the Crestone Pyramid. As the hours pass, the shimmering brilliance of this grand structure, captures the hearts and minds of people everywhere. Thousands flock in from all across North America to be part of what's happening. In outdoor settings among the trees, with the tall mountains looking down, they come together, strangers at first, but soon accepting one another as fellow travellers, on a journey of understanding. They see the Earth as their common home where they can be nurtured and grow on their passage through time and space. Their responsibility in return is to care for their planet, and to engage their minds fully in understanding how this is to be done.

Inside the Pyramid, George Walker and his team of Diane Koplitz and Nicholai Andropov, beam messages out to the participating world that speak to this same awareness. The messages are received by millions of Visioneers across the globe, who, at some point during the twenty-four hours of Earth Day, gather with a group of people in their community, to consider what they must do to preserve and nourish their part of the planet.

The day closes in Crestone with the unforgettable spectacle of the setting sun shining on the Pyramid and five thousand people grouped in front of it singing softly of their affection for their planet home.

Day Four, the Day of the Universe, is conducted from the Watchtower on Mount Kilimanjaro. It begins in the evening under a perfectly clear, star-filled sky. President Mutsandu introduces the theme for the Day as he stands at the ramparts on top of the Tower looking out to the immensity that surrounds. He speaks in the soft rhythm of his African home as the cameras track across the night sky. He speaks of his boyhood in his native village, when from time to time he would snatch precious moments to stand alone like this and feel himself drawn up to float among the stars, to search there for the master-hand that made them. As a man now, and leader of his country, he never has a stronger sense of power than when he can step aside from all the insubstantial trappings of office, and walk alone on the savannah under the wide vault of the African sky. The camera rests for a moment on the huge black mass of Kilimanjaro humping up into the stars, then settles quietly on the genial face of the President.

"My friends out there in the world," he continues, "all of you, wherever you are, watching me right now, let me say to you one or two words that might speak to your heart. I am not a learned astronomer or cosmologist, not even an amateur one. Such scientists are standing by and will speak to you soon from the great universities of the world. They will describe the leaps in knowledge that take us far beyond in understanding anything our ancestors could know about our place in the universe. All of that is wonderful and important; but for me, and I hope for you, its greatest truth is that our world is a precious jewel, exquisite and rare. And it is ours to care for, lest its lustre diminish.

"On this fragile planet we have grown rapidly in the last few years of this single century into a very large family. Many of us are undernourished and starving. That is no way for a family to look after its members. We must build a future that allows all of us to live well together. My charge to you, as you now take time to consider the place and meaning of our world in the immensity of the universe—my charge, and my most heartfelt plea, is that you consider and craft from your shared visions a new image and wisdom for human beings. It is the wisdom that we need now to play our role as full, magnificent participants in the divine inspiration that lies behind and around all creation.

"Go to your deliberations in peace and good spirit, my dear friends, and build together the power of a Global Mind."

With these words President Mutsandu ends the transmission from the Watchtower. All around the world, and continuing for the next twenty-four hours, telecasts are shared among millions of viewers of the best that science can offer in understanding the mystery of the universe. It is powerful and enlightening, but nowhere is its message stronger than in the heartfelt plea from this African leader, whose mind seeks only to discover and nourish the nobility of people as divine, spiritual beings with a responsibility to nourish the only world they have. When the day closes, millions remember, more than the science and the stories, more than the spectacle of sunbursts and supernovas, what they remember, is the graciousness of this leader and the wisdom of his words from the Watchtower at Kilimanjaro.

On Day Five the attention of the world is turned to the oceans and the sky. It is led from the heart of the Earth's smallest continent, where oceans surround while the sky envelops, and the land lies pressed like a dry red leaf in pages of unending blue. This is Australia, the great south land, Earth's largest island, sitting alone between two great oceans and opening to the south to the vast and little visited waters of the Antarctic.

From here, in the squat five-sided globcom at the centre of the country, Sally Hearst and Boris Gunther begin the telecast on Wednesday evening local time. It's a short introduction designed to set the stage for the highlight to come tomorrow noon. They present the context for scientists around the world, oceanographers and marine biologists, to bring the message that the oceans are the Earth's great reservoirs of life, not only for the food they provide, but more for their stabilizing force among vast planetary interactions. As the currents sweep through the oceans in rotating whorls of surface motion, they run like veins and arteries of a living being, maintaining the life-supporting temperatures unique to our planet in the solar system. Together with the air in constant interaction they bathe the land with the moisture that is the very essence of all physical life. It's a page from any child's geography lesson, but presented now to human eyes opening to a new awareness: to know that how we choose to act in life can change, has changed, the balance of these great external forces. We are now not only actors on the stage of life, but also have become the producers and participants for ensuring its continuation.

This is the theme picked up and driven with the piercing accuracy of a marksman's arrow by the presentation from Ayers Rock on Thursday noon. A circling helicopter banks slightly in the shimmering blue heat of the unending sky, and the cameraman on board brings in the full view of the great blood-red monolith. The signal bounces off a satellite a thousand kilometres above the Earth, and more than a billion people watching around the planet see the huge rock swirling and rushing towards them as the helicopter sweeps down in a careening dive. The focus for this precipitous rush is at first a black dot on the top of the mountain of rock, but then it leaps rapidly to size as the camera zooms in. Bare-headed, stripped to the waist, his long black hair blowing in the dry hot breeze that cuts across the surface of the Rock, Daniel Thomas stands defiantly staring out across the empty spinifex plain stretching away to the horizon. As the helicopter roars overhead and speeds off, the scene switches to Daniel up close, shot by cameras covering him on the Rock itself.

Bronzed like a sculpture from too much sunshine during his six months' sojourn in the heat, Daniel Thomas looks directly into the camera and speaks:

"Look and see around me here and store it in your mind for understanding. This is the very heart of the hot red centre of everything that can happen when the moisture is sucked from the land. Look up and see above me here the great blue vault of eternity, the very hurtling place of rockets to the stars, pressing down, pressing me, pressing this great red rock into the earth. Look and know that this is life without life, the grand spectacle for feasting the eyes, for uplifting the soul; but know, surely know, if this was all there was, there would be nothing.

"Look around you where you are. Where are you? Bustling city? Mountain top? Heaving ocean? Pleasant countryside? Tropical jungle? Working? Playing? Full of life? Close to death? Rich and comfortable? Poor and starving? How are you? Where are you? Who are you?

"Listen. It's the motion all around, the pulse of life, the grass growing, the warm-cold-wet-dry-wind of everything.

"Listen and look and know that you're a part of it all, and that it is a part of you. And who are you? What do you have? Who is your neighbour? What does he have? What does she have? And what do all of us have? Only this. Only this air, only these oceans, only this life, only this planet.

"Look. Listen. See. And learn what you must know. It's all around, hidden but knowable, in books, libraries, broadcasts, magazines, newspapers. The wisdom of the ages. The news of the day. All of it there for your knowing, if you will open your mind to it and listen. Listen. Listen for the voice of God speaking to you. Through your neighbour. Who is your neighbour? Listen. Listen, and you will find the answers."

The camera sweeps away from Daniel Thomas, traverses the stunted green growth on the red plain, then comes to the squat globcom, where it zooms in, and cuts to Sally Hearst, young Visioneer, handing the baton to her fellows across the Earth.

"We leave you now," she says, "to your own reflections on what you've seen and heard. Be Visioneers, all of you. Learn and know. And out of your new knowing, please build together what we all need: a Global Mind, that can find, and know, and continue to learn what we all must know for life together, on the planet, forever."

Day Six

It's late afternoon on Thursday in Jerusalem. Mark Venture is making final preparations to open the telecast for Day Six from the Star of Jerusalem. He places a call by videophone to Bill Bates in Los Angeles. Though it's only 5 o'clock in the morning in California, Mark expects Bill to be hard at work. He's not disappointed. Bill comes on looking fresh-faced and alert.

"Well, Bill," Mark asks, "how are we doing?"

"It's a smash, Mark! It's an absolute smash! I'm so excited I've given up sleeping. Not that there's time for it anyway. These round-the-clock, round-the-world days are something else.

"We've been monitoring the situation every day and, as I told you yesterday, we seemed to be picking up momentum as the week wore on. Of course, you know last Saturday's opening in Tiananmen Square was a show-stopper. There were more than a billion people watching that. We expected things to slow down a bit during the week as people went back to work. And they did at first. But then each time one of those telecasts came on from a globcom we had close to a billion viewers every time. But that's not all. The ZNN network is replaying it continuously. It's almost as if there's no other news in the world. And there isn't: no wars, uprisings, demonstrations, stock-market crashes, major accidents, floods, earthquakes, or negative whatevers. It's as if the whole world has gone sane for a week. Those Visioneers out there are doing a great job. They've got groups organized around the major telecasts, either live or taped, depending on what time it is when they're broadcast. Julia McCarthy told me from New York that it was 10 o'clock last night when Daniel Thomas came on, and then after that, discussion groups went on until 3 o'clock in the morning. Now, they're all up again, getting ready to listen to you."

"No doubt about you, Bill," Mark laughs. "You're a great inspiration."

"Well, it's true," Bill replies, "I've got the statistics here. The whole world's paying attention like it's never done before."

"What about the hold-out countries?"

"Well, yes, we've still got them, but, you know, even there, people are finding ways to tune in. I mean, you can't hold this thing back, and sooner or later those repressive regimes are gonna realize that."

"Well, it's all good news, Bill. I'm glad to hear it."

"Yeah. Now you and Esther go and give 'em heck, Mark. What day are we up to? Six? This is when you bring men and women into the scheme of things. That should be a challenge."

"Well, with your good news, Bill, we're certainly up for it. Thanks again for the encouragement. I'll speak to you after the telecast."

Birth Day

The telecast for Day Six, the Birth Day for humanity, begins with Esther sitting with Mark on Thursday evening at the command centre of the Star of Jerusalem, reading from the Book of Genesis:

" 'So God created man in his own image, in the image of God created he him; male and female created he them. And God blessed them, and God said unto them, Be fruitful and multiply and replenish the earth, and subdue it: and have dominion over the fish of the sea, and over the fowl of the air, and over every living thing that moveth upon the earth.' "

"When those words were written two thousand years ago," Mark takes up the commentary, "they represented the best efforts of the time to explain the greatest mystery of all, the mystery of creation, the birth of human consciousness, and what it meant for the maintenance of life on the planet. Today we see with new eyes, and with minds enlarged by knowledge that expands our understanding of how we're meant to live and be.

"On this sixth day of our Congress, we invite you all to join with us to determine how our consciousness is to take us into the future. On every continent, in every community, linked together in a global web of communications, we must turn our minds now to understanding what we have to do to create our common future."

"And the place to begin is with our minds." Esther takes over from Mark. She stands and moves to the large model of the globe that hangs permanently at the centre of the Star of Jerusalem. It shines in the full beauty of its earthly tones, without any subdivision of human boundaries.

"Can we understand as we look here at our planet home," she continues, "that the thought energy of our minds is part of the same energy that keeps the Earth alive? We're a part of that, and it's a part of us. We know now that everything is energy, and that we human beings have a unique role to play. The energy of the universe courses through our minds every moment with the same creative force as from the beginning. This means that if we bring our minds together, we will have available to us all the creative power of the universe to build a future of harmony rather than division. This is what the Visioneers are doing. We're bringing together the collective energy of human consciousness to create a powerful Global Mind, where no thought will persist of the issues that previously divided us."

"This is the exciting story of evolution," Mark comes in again, joining Esther at the globe. "If we turn our minds to look beyond the seeming chaos and disruption of so much that surrounds us, we can see the unfolding of a divine plan. From its elementary beginnings human consciousness is on a journey towards enlightenment. For most of the way the path seems to have been dark and dangerous. But from time to time great souls have come by to give direction. Their lives and wisdom are part of our collective heritage. The enormous wealth of scientific knowledge is also available to us. Armed with all this, we're now on the threshold of making a great leap forwards in the evolution of consciousness. Ironically, at the same time we're struggling for survival. We're at the fork in the road. Everything's on grand scale. Down one route lies the horror of massive destruction. Down the other, we can expect a tough time of it, but we'll have the certainty of winning through in the end.

"The Visioneers are out there with you in the world to make sure that together as a human family we take the right fork in the road. This Congress is the moment of awakening. As Esther says, we're pushing for the birth of a Global Mind, the breakthrough to planetary consciousness, the complete and overwhelming awareness that the only way forward is through human relationships flowing with love."

"That's the energy of visioneering!" Esther's eyes are shining with excitement as she speaks. "We know the power of human consciousness. We believe this is the moment of breakthrough. Everything's coming together. We've set up the globcoms to focus the energy. They've been working with you in your trisets, drawing all of us into one human family, where everyone is filled with the consciousness of love and caring for the planet and for all life on it. For what do we have if we don't have life? It's the most precious gift in the universe, and we have it here on Earth in abundance, but only if we nourish and sustain it."

"So this is our Birth Day," Mark continues, "our day for declaring commitment, millions of us around the planet, declaring commitment for life, putting aside the violence and destruction of past history, and looking ahead with the full power of our creative imaginations to vision a planetary future full of life, love, and prosperity for all.

"For the first time in history we're assembled as a planetary family. Esther and I speak to you here from Jerusalem at the centre of many networks, but all around the world the lines of communication are open. We have the chance today to create the Global Mind, a life force of energy for the planet.

"So, let the day begin! Globcoms, are you ready? Crestone? Tiananmen Square? Machu Picchu? Ayers Rock? Kilimanjaro? Come in all of you!"

As Mark calls them by name, each of the five globcoms comes up in split image on the television screens of people watching around the world. The Star of Jerusalem appears in the centre, with each of the other five at the end of a point. Mark's voice continues over the picture.

"This is our network. Wherever your meeting place is in the world, keep tuned to this signal, and know that you're part of this great global network. The Visioneers with you will lead the meditations and discussion. During the day you'll be asked to decide: Do you wish to be part of the Global Mind? Thousands of centres have been set up in every triset to hear your report. Visioneers are on hand to listen and feed the information in to us. In twenty-four hours we'll be back to give you the result. Go with good heart and God speed to bring in the Global Mind."

Yes

Exactly twenty-four hours later, as the daylight fades toward sunset in Jerusalem, and the Sabbath is soon to begin, Esther and Mark sit again at the command centre of the Star of Jerusalem. Grouped around them, the other Visioneers can hardly contain their excitement. All day Mohammed Hussein, Indira Murti, and Theresa Romano, have been working with hundreds of volunteers, compiling reports coming in from thousands of centres around the globe. Now the moment has arrived to share the news with the world. The signal to begin is given. Mark speaks to an audience of almost two billion people.

"Welcome to the Global Mind!" he exclaims. "Millions of you have spoken, and our communication lines are still jammed solid with reports coming in. The message is clear. Yes, you say, to peace on the planet! Yes, to the end of arms shipments to make war! Yes, to a Planetary Peoples Forum to promote the development of equity and justice! Yes, to the universal spread of creative learning! Yes, to the spirit of the Visioneers, active in every quarter, to put up the vision for peace and prosperity, and to focus every mind on the planet to see that it comes in!

"And you're saying no to governments that would jostle for power and spend outrageous sums of money on weapons of destruction! No, to business and activity that can further harm the planet! No, to beliefs and values that generate waste and the irresponsible squandering of precious resources!

"But above all, it's a yes for life! And a yes for the learning that will lead to life, away from violence, destruction, drugs, crime, and mindless consumption. It's yes to knowing that the only way forward is for all of us to change our minds about the meaning of life. And it's yes to bending every effort to learn together what the new meaning must be so that all of us can benefit."

"What a wonderful message this is!" Esther is speaking now. "To know that more than a billion people in every country on Earth are saying the same thing, and are willing to turn the creative energy of their minds to make it happen! And if it's a billion people today, then it can be three billion tomorrow, and everyone on the planet the day after that. We know, and you know, that we can't change the way things are immediately. But we also know that nothing can change at all until we begin to change our minds. And then beyond that we know the greatest truth of all, that what we decide in our minds to do releases all the power in the universe to make it happen.

"Knowing that, my friends and Visioneers, then know, too, that you have today created the Global Mind. You have enlivened the Earth with a strong channel of universal consciousness to be a sure and steady guide into a future of hope and prosperity for all."

"Hallelujah!" shouts Theresa, unable to restrain herself any longer. She rolls to her feet and tugs Mark and Esther out of their chairs, embracing them, and waving to Mohammed and Indira to join in.

"Oh, Hallelujah! Hallelujah! Hallelujah!" Theresa shouts over and over again. Music comes up, the same *Hallelujah* theme that she sang at Mark and Esther's wedding. She leads it now for the world. The other Visioneers join in. The television screens of the watching people on every continent cut to split image and all of the Visioneers come in from all of the globcoms, singing *Hallelujah* with Theresa. Then in every Visioneering Centre around the globe, and in every place where people are watching—more than two billion of them around the planet—they come to their feet, singing *Hallelujah*, for the Global Mind and for the future it promises to bring.

The music rises and falls, rises and falls, going around and around, with the one word, "Hallelujah," shouting its emotion of joy and praise, meaningful in every language, crying its universal message of hope for the planet forever.

Then the singing ends and the television camera closes on Esther standing alone behind a table where two Shabbat candles stand unlit in simple silver candle sticks. She takes a lighted taper and sings the ancient Jewish benediction for the lighting of the Sabbath candles:

"*Baruch ata Adonai*. Blessed art thou O Lord our God. *Elohanu melech ha olam*. King of the Universe. *Asher kidishanu Bemitzvotav*. Who sanctified us with your commandments. *Vetzivanu le hadleek nair shel shabbat*. And commands us to light the candles of the Sabbath."

"We've come to the end of the sixth day of creation," Esther continues. " 'And on the seventh day God ended his work which he had made; and he rested on the seventh day from all his work which he had made. And God blessed the seventh day, and sanctified it: because that in it he had rested from all his work which God created and made.'

"The Sabbath has begun here in Jerusalem and we invite you now to share its peace and rest around the world. To all of you who have joined us in this Congress we say, 'Peace and love.' For what we have all done today in creating the Global Mind we say, 'Hallelujah!' From the globcoms of the Visioneers around the world, to everyone on Earth, we say, 'Go and rest. Share the joy in your hearts. You've done a wonderful work. We'll be with you again soon. God bless you all.' "

Mark moves in beside Esther. The other three Visioneers gather around. The Hallelujah theme comes up again. They wave to the watching world. The picture fades. The Congress of the Global Mind has ended.

Why Not?

The week of the Congress was a masterpiece of precision. The work that follows is a triumph of achievement. The world is no longer as it was. Everywhere people are empowered to act. It's as if a great wave of relief has swept across the planet. Suddenly, it's all right again to be optimistic. No one knows for sure what the new thinking will mean. For everyone it will bring some hardship along with benefits, for old ways don't give place to new without some pain of passage. But in this first week the enthusiasm is unquenchable.

The Star of Jerusalem is at the heart of it. Recognized now as the centre of a new global network, it receives an unending flood of messages from around the world. Most significant among them are the ones from world leaders to Mark. It takes a few days, but then they start to come. Pressured by constituencies and badgered by the media, the leaders have no choice but to respond. The mood is overwhelmingly positive. "Congratulations," they say, "You have done a great service for humanity. My government looks forward to working with you to design the structures to preserve world peace and to create new avenues for economic prosperity for people everywhere."

The media is schizophrenic. It wants to praise, but finds it hard to believe. The old paradigms are strong. But the voice coming from the people is stronger. They believe in the Visioneers. They have been stirred in their hearts. The young are the most outspoken. They demand to be heard. Everywhere they ask the question: "Why not?" And by the end of the week it's a very brave editor or journalist who will choose to answer by saying: "It can't be done." The hearts and minds of the people on the planet have been stirred to act, and "impossible" is not a word they choose to hear.

The high point of the week comes for Mark and Esther on Wednesday morning. They receive a phone call from Kamal Rashid. The young Palestinian wants to meet. Mark invites him out to the Star of Jerusalem. When he arrives, Kamal comes not by himself, but with a delegation of young men and women, Palestinians and Israelis. All of them are wearing the uniform of the Visioneers.

"This is my PALIS group," Kamal tells Mark and Esther. "We've worked together for many weeks, but especially during the seven days of the Global Mind. There are ten of us here, but each of us is at the tip of a network of a thousand others. We want you to tell the world that we've decided there will be peace between the Palestinians and the Israelis, and we'll see that it happens. We thought that would be a good message for you to announce to the world."

Mark looks at the young man and is speechless. Esther catches her breath and whispers, "Oh, Kamal, if only that could be so."

"It can and it will," he replies. "Because of what you have taught us in your life and work, we can see now that in the past we've put wasted energy into destroying each other's dream. We've changed that. Now we'll build a new dream together. You may tell the world. We've decided."

Mark and Esther do indeed tell the world, and suddenly there seems to be an overwhelming response of: "Why not?" Touched by the energy of the Global Mind, people hear the announcement in a new way. If the only future for the planet is along a path of peace, then how can we step aside here from such a course. There are differences and difficulties. There are hatreds that go back for thousands of years. But this is a new time now. The end is clear. We must have peace. The thought is in our minds. There will be dangers, and difficulties, and setbacks; but the end is clear. And we will find our way to it. Why not?

By the end of the week, this was the question in everyone's mind. Why not? Why not peace in the Middle East? Why not an end to aggression and hostility? Why not shut down corruption in high places? Why not override the drift to drugs by giving people a new sense of the power in their minds? Why not set aside the benefits of greed by showing the rewards that come from pursuing lives of meaning and worth? Why not expect the best of people and help them to achieve it? Why not replace tough negotiation with synergy and deep listening? Why not live together in love and fellowship? Why not take charge of the future of the planet and learn to live in the flow of a universal life force? Why not create a Global Mind and learn to see our lives fulfilled through our contribution to this higher force? Why not learn to be the magnificent beings we were meant to be? Why not?

And at the heart of it all lie three images now shining in the minds of everyone who has been touched by the work of the Visioneers. First, hanging alone in space, the beautiful blue planet, Earth, sings with the music of the spheres and calls softly but urgently: "Be with me." Second, emblazoned on its sky-blue crest, the bold V of the Visioneers calls to those who pause to listen: "Work with me." Third, standing astride its place in destiny, the City of Jerusalem opens its arms to the world and cries: "Come with me."

Together at the crossroads of history, the Earth, the Visioneers, and a New Jerusalem stand waiting for their calls to be answered.

Why not?

CHAPTER TWENTY-EIGHT

The End
and
The Beginning

Y OU'VE DONE IT NOW. FROM THE TURBULENT, uncertain beginning, when you struggled with waves of crushing power that seemed impossible to master, you've triumphed and created in your mind a future vision of the Earth reborn. Along the way you were joined in your imagination by a remarkable group of friends and mentors. They've grown close to your heart. They came into your mind, born out of your searing passion and need to see a way forward for the Earth, which you love with all your being. You're a child of the universe. Your consciousness is filled with the life force that moves among the stars, and you will not, cannot let it go. As you turned its energy full up to look for a future to which the Earth can move, you created your Visioneers to take you there, and together, all of you working in harmony, you formed the Global Mind.

It exists now in your imagination as an embryo for a new birth. You've done your best, you and your mentors and your Visioneers. It's time now for you to step back, to let it go, to allow the force you've created to do its work. It's been a grand adventure. Sadly, you know that it's now come to an end. It's time to say goodbye, and open the doorway to the new beginning.

Friends Gather

Looking out from your thinking room, you've never seen the mountains more spectacular. They are dressed in the same fall colours as when you first came here, just a year ago. Golden shards of aspen blaze among the green spruce and pine climbing the mountains, right up to where the glaciers hang in shimmering crystalline white and blue, feeding their melting waters into the aquamarine lake on the valley floor below.

As you stand looking out, you feel your mentors gathering around. The warm energy of their presence builds for several moments before you turn to greet them.

"Hello," you say. "I was expecting you." You wave your hand at the vista through the window. "It's a wonderful scene, isn't it? The Earth feels right today. Thank you for helping me to get here."

No one speaks for a moment. The four of them stand silently surveying you. They look just the same as when you first met. Winston Churchill is in the centre with Anne beside him, the elder statesman in suit and vest, a marked constrast to the youthful glow of the young girl, whose shining red hair and long green skirt radiate all around her the energy of enthusiasm and hope. On the one side next to Churchill, President Kennedy stands easily in dark blue business suit, while at the other end of the group beside Anne, Charles Dickens exudes the theatrical presence of creative author in his nineteenth-century black suit and high, stiff-collared shirt and blue cravat. You look at them standing there together, and a wave of affection runs through you for these stalwart souls. They've grown as dear to you as life in your struggle on the journey.

The men are strangely silent, and it's Anne who steps forward to embrace you and speak for all of them.

"How wonderful it's been to be a part of your dream!" she says. "Dreams are the places where everything begins. And here in your thinking room the five of us have conjured up such a dream as the world will surely catch to make its own. We've done it with full heart, holding nothing back, and that's where the magic lies. When you give your mind completely to creating something noble and worthwhile, it sets everything around you alive and dancing. That's what we've done. Oh my, how they've danced! Those wonderful Visioneers, all with their own dreams for what might be. We've done it here together in one great glorious dream for the future of the planet. Now I just know the people will pick it up and make it real."

"Yes, Anne, you're right." John Kennedy speaks out. "And we're not quite done with it yet. We've got one last piece to do to push it over the top.

He turns to you. "It's time to bring the world leaders back. We sent them out to have a taste of living on a planet filled with Visioneers. Now it's time for them to return to their own places and show the leadership to bring in the new world vision. What do you say, Winston and Charles? Are we ready for the last hurrah?"

"Yes, indeed we are," Churchill's gravel voice fills the room. All eyes turn to him. "There are moments," he continues, "in the course of things, which, if you pick them right, can make all the difference to what will follow. There've been many such moments in our story to date, but none is greater than this one to come. Let's go to it, now."

"Oh, well scripted, gentlemen and Anne!" Charles Dickens exclaims enthusiastically. "I sense we're heading for a dramatic finale. So," he turns his darting eyes to you, "let the Act begin."

Let's Bring in the Visioneers

You need no further encouragement. This is to be your triumph, too, and you're eager to embrace it. In a trice you shift the scene to the Visioneering Room where the five of you stand looking out towards the silver bridge. The view is back the way it was a year ago when the Visioneers first came in. The end of the bridge touches the grassy hillside between two tall shining pillars.

"If we're to have a grand finale," you say, "then we must get all the characters on stage. Let's bring in the Visioneers!"

And so they come, jostling along the bridge just as they did the first time, but no longer strangers, for now they're friends of a long campaign. Onto the grassy slope they come, linking arms to march up to the Visioneering Room on a broad front, Mark and Esther in the middle. It's the original nineteen Visioneers, first created in the mind of Charles Dickens, but now so real they seem a force in their own right, marching up the hill in triumph. Only Luis Valdez is absent, the one tragic figure in the story, but his courageous initiative at the beginning is so much a part of their success that his spirit seems always present.

You and your mentors go out to greet them. A shout goes up as they see you there. Then they break out into the *Song of the Visioneers*. Even before the now familiar words and melody ring out across the mountain slopes, you sensed that it was coming. Born of this place, created in the spirit now so strong around, how could the song not be sung in the closing act of the drama?

But not this group alone, for look, coming across the silver bridge, there's another band of Visioneers, their voices rising with the others. The front rank turns to look and then sings louder, stronger as they recognize friends and compatriots of the campaign coming together. The new arrivals are the first wave of Visioneers who took the time to listen and act in the beginning when everything was getting underway.

At the head comes Mutsandu's African contingent full of the colour and energy that have set their continent alive with hope. With the Africans come the Europeans, Lord Nigel and Lady Pamela Feversham, who first heard the story from Jeremy Hiscox and Irene Henshaw at the Grampian Arms in Scotland; Prince Rupert of Wittenstein, who put the message before the Unesco conference in Paris; and the rollicking Russian crew of

Vladimir Rostov, Anna Borodino, and Boris Dubrovsky who met with Bill Bates and Daniel Thomas in clandestine fashion on the beach at Lake Radovichy.

From China the ancient Zhao She Yuhan is there in his wheelchair, assisted by Diane Koplitz from the United States, and close behind her the other members of the American team: George Walker, Julia McCarthy, Senator Wilfred Brown, and Arthur Rhinegold. After them come a dozen teenagers, marching along merrily as representatives of the 25,000 who were at the Vancouver rock concert on the night that Theresa Romano stole the show. Bringing up the rear, several other familiar faces who played a central role in nurturing the dream march together: Peter Hemphill, Cardinal Claudio Vachiano, Rabbi Ruvain Ben Sabbath, the Reverend Gordon Ringthorpe, and Pamela Barrett.

Last of all, striding along, side by side, heads up, shoulder to shoulder, come the two whose presence here tells the story perhaps best of all: Colonel Aaron Greenberg of Israeli Special Services and Kamal Rashid, former Palestinian terrorist and now head of the PALIS group for peace in the Middle East.

This is the second wave of Visioneers and they spill off the silver bridge between the shining pillars, spreading out across the hillside, with arms linked, to form a second phalanx pushing up behind the first.

And all the while as you and your mentors watch the procession coming up the hill, the singing continues, growing louder and stronger the closer they come. Just as the song has engulfed the world with its passion and its energy, bouncing from satellites in orbit to the largest cities and remotest outposts, so now it reverberates across the mountains where it all began, sung now in chorus by those who gave it birth, the original Visioneers, singing with you and your mentors, full voice, full heart, full hope for the future:

> "We are the ones going to the fore.
> Big ones, little ones—all of us are here.
> Small world, big world, reaching out to all.
> Up, up, and upmost—the mighty Visioneers!"

The Leaders Return

Inside with backslapping and handshaking all around people merrily bustle about looking for positions. You are the centre of it all. These are your Visioneers, all together for the first time in the Visioneering Room. What an occasion! What a moment of triumph! But the best is still to come.

It's a tight squeeze, yet everyone finds a place. At the front of the room the huge golden arch through which the leaders had passed when they went out into the world of the Visioneers, is now again in place, waiting for their return. You position your mentors with the original Visioneers on the floor of the room in a semicircle facing the arch. The other group has gathered at the back, leaving the rows of benches for the leaders when they come in.

Standing proudly in front of them all, you wave your hands for silence, ready to announce the entrance of the heads of governments from around the world:

"Friends, co-conspirators for a new world coming, Visioneers all of you, welcome! You can't imagine the excitement I feel seeing you all here today, knowing that we've already accomplished so much, and sensing now how what we've done will take root and grow. In a moment I'll bring in the world leaders. A few months ago I stole them out of their debate at the United Nations and brought them here to see in their hearts the future possibilities for the world. Then I sent them out to experience your world, to interact with you in the building of the Global Mind. And now it's done! Against all the arguments for saying it can't be done, it has been done. In your world, it has been done. Now the task is to move it from imagination to reality. And to begin that mighty work we'll bring the leaders back here one last time, one last taste of the spirit of visioneering, before they go, back to their debate, back to the task of assisting the world to take a new path of hope into the next millennium. Are you ready with me to greet them?"

A chorus of, "Bring in the leaders!" fills the room. From somewhere the stirring beat of triumphal music comes up. All eyes turn to the golden arch. You move back among your mentors and Visioneers. The first world leader steps into the room to the sound of enthusiastic applause.

It's the same black African president who had led them out. He comes boldly through the shimmering golden light behind the arch, then pauses and blinks momentarily at the warmth of the reception greeting him. A broad smile lights up his face, and he raises his hands in acknowledgement and pleasure, and steps forward in quick beat to the music.

After that the other leaders come through in a steady stream. In ones and twos and threes they enter, moving easily, smiling and relaxed, pleased with the reception and evidently pleased with themselves. You watch them closely, looking for signs that might give you hope, a sense that their experience has shaped their thinking towards a visioneering future. You can't be sure, but mostly the indications seem good. There's a different energy about them this time. Of course, it's not 100 percent. That would be too much ever to expect from this group. But as they pass by, smiling, some pausing to shake hands with you and the mentors and Mark and Esther, you have a sense that, yes, there surely is momentum here to help carry the world to where your dream would have it go.

When everyone is seated you stand in front to address them. The golden arch disappears and in its place the familiar globe of planet Earth returns. Your voice is confident and strong as you speak out:

"Leaders of the world and Visioneers every one, welcome back to the Visioneering Room. We're well met here in this place of new beginnings. My heart leaps up to see you all, to know that from what seemed at first a small idea we have stretched so far. Of course the greatest test is still to come. Can what we have created in imagination endure to transform the real? With all my heart I believe it can, and believing that, I'll continue to focus every effort to make it so. But this part is done. For my mentors and myself I can say that we've completed what we set out to do. We sought to put up a vision for the world that promised hope because it called upon the very best that men and women have to offer through their spirit. We called the spirit visioneering, and here in this room we have the noblest of the noble, who took the energy of their minds and applied it to the task until the job was done, and all the world was linked in one great Global Mind.

"To you leaders of the world we said, 'Come and look. Lend us your support, and see what visioneering can do.' We asked you to put aside the bitterness of divisive struggle and let the magic of people seeking to set themselves aright perform its miracles. And that you saw. In a few short months of concentrated effort people learned to come together in ways that previously seemed impossible. Now we ask you to take the wisdom of what you saw and apply it to the world to which you'll soon return.

"This is the greatest test of leadership, to draw from others the full power of what they have to offer, and hold them fast with courage and integrity to a fine enobling vision. That's what it means to be a Leader-Visioneer. We're asking you to take back that model to the world, and with it build the new millennium of peace and prosperity for the planet."

The room has listened in silence to your words. You pause and look around. No one moves or speaks. You step to one side and turn to face the slowly spinning globe. This is your final word to those whose actions can so affect the outcome for the world:

"Please look to the planet. Each of us with all our grand ambitions is but a speck of dust. Our brief and struggling lives depend for every breath on the mighty heart that beats forever there."

Every eye in the room is fixed on the globe. It continues its slow rhythmical turning for a moment longer, then slowly dissolves. In its place standing side by side, unmoving, two new figures look out to the audience. A gasp goes up from the watching Visioneers. One is immediately recognizable to everyone in the room: the saffron-robed Baba Satyananda. The other wears a plain white cassock of the Catholic church. His face, as he looks out serenely to the audience, is as relaxed as when he spoke to millions of television viewers from the Mission of Santa Maria in the Andes Mountains of northern Chile, moments before his life was taken from him by a vicious act of terror from the world he wished to change. Father Luis Valdez has returned to be among his friends as the final scene in the Visioneering Room draws to a close.

Baba Satyananda speaks first:

"I have come to say goodbye. The world has been a hard and divided place. For one brief span of time we have held it together as Visioneers. The divine bright light which guided us on that course continues to shine forever to direct your way. Seek for it in your heart and you will surely find it.

"With me, as you see, I have brought my brother Luis. His great spirit from the first proclaimed the truth of the Visioneers to the world. As you go, you can do no better than to take such wisdom in your hearts. He would speak to you again, this one last time."

Luis' voice has the same rich cadence as when in life he addressed the world.

"My beloved friends," he says softly. "It wasn't meant for me to journey with you to your final destination. I simply said as best I could the truth of what I saw: the dawning of a new age where people will hold to a vision that allows them to be all that they can be in God's pure love. In these last few days you have reached for the Global Mind and touched that vision. You have seen its transforming power for the world. In your achievements, my life has surely been fulfilled. God bless and guide you in the work to come."

The figures of Baba and Luis fade away. The globe returns to its customary place. Every person in the room, Visioneer and head of government alike, is transfixed by what has just been seen and heard. You come to the centre and stand before the globe, looking out to the sea of faces, waiting, waiting for a sign to tell the way to go.

Within moments it comes, and oh, how your heart leaps again with the excitement of what it means! The world leaders are getting to their feet. One after the other they stand and speak. Countries large and powerful, others small and poor, it makes no difference. One by one they declare themselves for the spirit of the Visioneers. America leads off, then China, Bangladesh, Saudi Arabia, Britain, France, Russia, Brazil, Zimbabwe, Japan, Australia, Germany, Canada, then many others following in rapid succession. From every continent they stand and speak, praising the Visioneers for what they've done, declaring their commitment as leaders to ensure the dream's not lost. They promise action to give their people courage and freedom to build their future and to stretch their thoughts across the Earth; to see the planet alive and whole and glowing with the Global Mind of human consciousness reaching for its highest level

With every declaration a new wave of applause and cheering breaks out, led by the Visioneers, but then picked up by the whole assembly, until the room, and indeed the very mountainside itself, seem to tremble with the energy of what has been unleashed. In the centre of it all you stand humble but exalted, hardly daring to believe that what's afoot can indeed be real. Words completely fail you. Your mind leaps away, transported to the highest, wildest flights of possible imagination. All the dangers and afflictions, the atrocities and the tragedies, all the despair of clashing conflict and debilitating destruction, all, suddenly, in the magic of this moment, all of it, gone, swept away by the rushing, rising wave of irrepressible hope and enthusiasm for the future!

Suddenly you realize the room is quiet. Every face is turned to you, waiting for you to act, but you've lost all sense of what to do. It seems too much, all this, so much more than you had hoped for. What to do? How to bring it to a close? How to end a dream you would wish to last forever?

Mark Venture and Esther Fisher come to your rescue. Standing with you now on either side they raise your arms in salute to the assembly, and Mark cries out, "To one who dares to dream, the prize is given! To the boldest Visioneer amongst us, the one who dared to imagine that this could be and made it so!"

Hugging you with joy, Esther shouts for all to hear: "Bravo for your courage! Bravo for your dream! Bravo for your inspiration to all who now can stand up and declare themselves as Visioneers!"

With that the whole assembly comes to its feet in spontaneous applause. Celebration is in the air. You have no idea what to do, but it happens anyway. Vaguely you remember your mentors gathering around, even Churchill's face is wreathed in smiles as he grasps your hand while the others openly embrace you with great affection. Then the Visioneers come crowding in: Theresa Romano, Bill Bates, Mahommed Hussein, and all the others, pressing around in the warmth of their strong friendship. President Mutsando's rich, deep voice is laughing and booming above everything else. Theresa shouts "Hallelujah!" Others laugh and shout it back. It's all movement and energy, light, laughter, and life. Moving, moving, moving onward to a new beginning. Everyone is moving.

The world leaders are going out the doors, down the grassy hillside in the sunshine where the silver bridge lies waiting. You forgot to put out the red carpet, but nobody cares. The women in high heeled shoes kick them off and walk happily on the grass. The Visioneers are crowding out, too, forming a guard of honour for the leaders as they pass through and onto the bridge. Somehow you're there at the head of the bridge, shaking hands, waving goodbye, enjoying the magnificent energy of human hearts and minds on a quest for adventure and achievement.

The last of the leaders is travelling across the bridge. And now it's time for the Visioneers to go. There's no thought of further delay. It's all in flow. The work's been done. The journey's over. Everyone's saying goodbye and moving onto the bridge. Everyone but Mark and Esther and the mentors. You keep them with you for a little while longer. But the others are going, and as they leave Theresa leads them all, one last time, in the *Song of the Visioneers*. And they go off singing it, louder and livelier than ever, stretching out across the bridge, disappearing from view into the soft haze where the bridge arches up into the sweeping blue dome of a perfect sky. And long after they've gone it seems you can hear their voices, singing clear with the force and energy that can transform the world:

"We are the ones going to the fore.
Big ones, little ones—all of us are here.
Small world, big world, reaching out to all.
Up, up, and upmost—the mighty Visioneers!"

Let's Not Say Goodbye

Suddenly it's quiet again. Turning to your six remaining companions, you say: "Please, come with me. I would like a few more minutes together."

You take them to your thinking room. It's a short walk across the hillside, past the Visioneering complex. Mark and Esther haven't been here before. You bring all of them in through the heavy slab wooden door with its rustic brass latch and solid black hinges. As ever, the fire crackles in the field-stone fireplace. The five chairs are clustered together in their usual places in the middle of the room. You find two more and bring them up for Mark and Esther. Everyone sits.

"This is my thinking room," you say to Mark and Esther. "I began here on my own, but then my friends joined me." You smile at the other four. "I guess I needed them, and somehow they found me. This is a special place. It's reserved for meetings with my mentors. I've brought you here because I'd like the two of you also to be my mentors. At least, that's part of the reason, though probably the truth is, I don't want to say, goodbye."

"Then don't," says Mark.

"No," adds Esther. "Let's not say goodbye. We can remain as close as your nearest thought. After all," she smiles wistfully, "this isn't the end of anything; it's only the beginning of everything still to come."

You look around at all of the faces.

"What do you think?" you ask. "Have we really done something that can make a difference?"

"Oh, yes!" President Kennedy says enthusiastically. "All that anyone can ever do to shift the ground a little is to get out there and lead with the mind. The world gets into trouble when people sit back and leave the visioning to someone else. You've shown them that there isn't anyone else, only all of us together. So you invented the idea of visioneering, and we helped you run with it, and between all of us we thought up a storm and turned it loose. Now the world can never let it go, because it's thought energy, and that never goes away, just whizzes around forever. We've given people something to think about, and think they will, and that's when they'll begin to make a difference."

"Better than that," Churchill adds his piece, "they'll grab the bone and gnaw on it like a hungry dog until they get the juice out of it. We've shown them that there's only one bone with no way for anyone to steal it for themselves, so they've all got to learn to gnaw on it together."

"Oh dear, I'm sure that's true, Mr. Churchill," Anne comes into the conversation, "though I do prefer another image. All that gnawing is a little, well, primitive, I would say. I'd like to think we've shown the world how to come out of its cocoon and turn into a butterfly. Do you remember those children on Tiananmen Square? All of them with their coloured lights formed that magnificent butterfly that filled the darkness of the empty space. That's what the Visioneers will do, all of them learning how to be brilliant butterflies themselves, and coming together to build the very grandest butterfly in all the universe, and that will be our Earth."

"Well, I think we could say that we're in agreement, then," Charles Dickens smiles roguishly at everyone. "We've got waves of thought energy keeping the dogs alert while they gnaw on their gigantic bone and watch the butterflies darting all around." He turns to you. "It's a good thing there's no more of us, else the picture might become a little cluttered. For me, I just want to say I think we've put some good spirit out there; you know, like the kind old Scrooge finally found in Christmas; so that, in the end, it could be said he knew how to keep Christmas well. If we've helped people to see how to keep a Christmas spirit alive in the world, across all the dark days and the light, then I think we might say we've done our bit, and that even Tiny Tim might be heard again to remark, 'God bless us, every one!' "

"Well, God bless you, every one," you say, now standing and inviting them all to join you in a close circle of friendship. It's a tender moment as the true warmth of their embrace touches not only body, but heart and mind as well. You feel the tears standing out in your eyes as you look at them all and know that it's time to go.

"Let's not say goodbye," you smile at them. "For Visioneers and travellers of the heart there's no such word. For all that's passed between us and for whatever lies ahead, let us simply say, Amen."

You close your eyes, and when you open them again, your friends and mentors have gone.

Outside, the sun still shines brightly across the gentle space. Where the silver bridge and Visioneering Room had stood for so long as part of your dream, only the open hillside now remains, running down to the forests of spruce and fir below.

The structures of your dreamscape have done their work. Far out beyond the bounds of this quiet space where you have built your sanctuary, a larger vision now unfolds. It moves in your thoughts, and surely if it there can find a passage, then likewise must it grow and spread across the mindways of the planet. Its whispers touch the ears of those who listen deeply. Its vistas spread before the eyes of those who look awakened. Its promise reaches out to touch the heart of those who know the purpose for their being.

Open and exposed, the Earth now waits expectantly for human thought to stir, to grow, to reach, to touch, and at last to know what it must do. You have set your thoughts to seek and find that path. Your call is out to all who would choose to also walk that way. The Visioneers are gathering. For success to their enterprises big and small, might we truly say, Amen.

Readers of the heart, continue here . . .

Afterword

Dear Fellow Readers:

If you are like me, you are full of awe at what you have just read. The Visioneers, their authenticity and truth, have entered deeply into your heart and mind. In most reading experiences you are left to wonder, "What can I do about this?"

But *The Visioneers* **is a tract for action,** for next steps, for "what ifs." These are meant to be applied in your own life. The action steps are outlined below.

Become a Visioneer

Action Steps

1. **Make your first printing limited edition of The Visioneers a special personal treasure.**
   Set it up, at desk or bedside or armchair. Pick it up to read parts again, or to choose truths that apply to you. Write these as little notes for yourself. Put them on desks, mirrors, refrigerator doors, or your favourite spot, wherever you can see them regularly.

2. **Use The Visioneers in your daily life.**

   Think about it:
   as you drive to work, it will empower your day; as you fall asleep, it will seed your dreams; as you walk in the woods or along the beach, or through the streets, it will allow your own possibilities to take form.

   Speak to your heart partner about it:
   at the dinner table, it will add meaning to your relationship; as you walk together, it will enhance your romance.

   The Visioneers is a philosophy for your whole life. Embrace it. You will become a Visioneer.

3. **Give The Visioneers book or tapes to those you care about as a gift of life:** at Christmas and other religious festivals; for birthdays, anniversaries, and special occasions; or just to honour your friendships.

4. **Become a Visioneer.**

   Join *Visioneers International*, centred in Vancouver at the home office of the Publisher of this book. This will enable you to receive regular information on the work of Visioneers and the spread of visioneering groups as they are formed around the world. Owners of a first printing limited edition may become charter members of the first group forming in Vancouver, Canada.

Visioneers International is temporarily sponsored by the Publisher, Creative Learning International Press. It will become a centre for reporting and celebrating visioneering projects. When it is able to stand on its own, it will be established as a not-for-profit organization.

5. **Choose your first visioneering project.** Any act of positive service, worth, or value to one or several or many human beings on the planet on which we live, can qualify, as long as it embraces the principles of Visioneering:

Answers yes to the questions:

(a) Is it friendly to the Earth, its citizens, and its living systems? (Yes)

(b) Will it improve the quality of life for the person, persons
     or community to whom it is directed?   (Yes)

(c) Will it empower your own life?   (Yes)

Answers no to the questions:

(a) Is it harmful to anyone?   (No)

(b) Is it harmful to the Earth or its living systems?   (No)

My first visioneering project is:

_____

_____

_____

6. **Log your project** by phone or fax to *Visioneers International* in Vancouver:
   Phone: (604) 734-2544
   Fax: (604) 734-9723
   Note: All visioneering projects are eligible for awards.

7. **Consider the possibility of forming a visioneering group** in your enterprise, organization, school, community or network. Two Visioneers are sufficient to begin. Ideas on how to start are available by ordering the *Visioneering Groups Starter Kit Pack*.

Building Momentum

If each reader of this book begins the process with the action steps outlined above, within a very short time, there will be millions of Visioneers worldwide. *That is the plan.*

The words of Margaret Mead, the late world-renowned anthropologist, provide good advice to Visioneers: "Do not wonder how one small human being can change the world. That is the only way it has ever been done." Every dream, no matter how extraordinary, started in the mind of a single human being.

We encourage you, as the reader, to transform your own life by making a contribution of service and meaning to a person and/or our planet. *Become a Visioneer.*

In our times,
when a powerful person engages another
to catch the whole dream,
the two have enormous power.

And when these two
engage the mind of only a few others,
they can and will together
create the future.

—*Geraldine Schwartz*

How To Order

The following products are now available:

The Book: *The Visioneers*, a novel by Desmond E. Berghofer: a transformative reading and learning experience.

The Tapes: *The Visioneers*, a set of 10 audio tapes, based on the novel by Desmond E. Berghofer. The tapes are a dramatized reading in 20 exciting half-hour segments by Desmond Berghofer and Geraldine Schwartz. This is a transformative listening and learning experience.

Visioneering Kit: Ideas and guidelines on starting a visioneering group in your own community.

Book Plates: Gift stickers which are to be affixed to the inside cover of the book or the lid of the tape container. The message reads as follows:

> Dear _____:
> I/we give you The Visioneers as a gift of life to celebrate _____
> May it empower you and touch your life as it has mine.

This is followed by a blank space for a personal note, the date, and your signature. A gift sticker will be included on request without cost, or it can be affixed to your gift with your message. (See **Gift Service** on page 525).

Membership in Visioneers International: Join the network of Visioneers.

New products to follow:

Following the release of the book and tapes in October, 1992, a variety of products to support the growing communities of visioneers will be available. These will include T-shirts, bumper stickers, posters with quotes, Post-It notes, banners, flags, hats, and any manner of support products our creative minds can conceive. Please send for your copy of the catalogue.

Prices (1992-93)*:

The Book	Set of Tapes	The Visioneering Kit**
$19.95 CDN	$39.95 CDN	$5.95 CDN

Plus shipping and applicable taxes

Membership in Visioneers International: $12.00 CDN per year

*For information on all matters after 1993 contact Creative Learning International, Vancouver, Canada.

**These are handling costs only.

The Gift Service:

Books, tape packages, or any visioneering products can be mailed directly to any place in the world. These may include book plates already affixed to the book or set of tapes which contain the personalized statement of the giver forwarded to us by phone, fax or letter. (See Book Plates on page 524 for format).

ORDER FORM

To: Creative Learning International
     503-1505 West 2nd Avenue
     Vancouver, B.C.
     Canada V6H 3Y4

Please send: Price   Number   Total

_____   copies of The Book   _____ x _____ = _____

_____   sets of Tapes   _____ x _____ = _____

_____   copies of Vis. Kit   _____ x _____ = _____

_____   Membership   _____ x _____ = _____

_____   Book Plates   _____ X _____ = _____

                                            Subtotal   _____

Taxes (Canada)   GST 7% Book/Tapes   _____

                     PST 6% Tapes (Only BC residents)   _____

Shipping   Canada add $5.00 CDN   _____

                        US & Foreign add $6.00 CDN   _____

                                  TOTAL   _____

Make cheques, money orders, or purchase orders payable to
Creative Learning International

     Or charge to: VISA ☐   MASTERCARD ☐

     Expiry Date   _____

     Number   _____

     Signature   _____

For information write to the above address.
Order by phone or fax using your credit card
Phone (604) 734-2544   **Fax (604) 734-9723**
To order by mail or fax please photocopy or handcopy this order form.
To order by phone please have relevant information available.

Ideas from the Book

About the world . . .

" . . . swelling up across the whole vast richness of the human minds on this planet is a revulsion at our failure as the most noble creature on God's Earth to live up to our nobility." (page 152)

" . . . it's time now for us to take back into our own hands the responsibility for building a vision of the future that's full of the joy of human cooperation and caring." (page 153)

"And the time has come for the idea that we can, by leading with our visionary minds, create the kind of world that we would choose to live in for ourselves, and for our children, and for their children after them." (page 203)

"I have this sense, that somehow the world is listening in a way that it's never listened before, and that if someone, today, speaks the right words they'll be heard, and the world will have turned a corner." (page 196)

About leadership . . .

"For leaders of true greatness, . . . the world can never ask too much. For such men and women are not shaken by the world. Rather they shape the world with their vision. They drive unerringly to the heart of all that matters, and in the fierce intensity of their courage they gather to them a force so strong that evil can't endure in the face of it." (page 352)

About the future . . .

"The supreme motivating concept of the future is synergy: men and women of all nations coming together under leaders of great vision, who see that the pursuit of a common ideal, one world, one Earth, one people, is the reason for all existence." (page 289)

"Today's world of negativity and limitation has been created by the prevailing collective unconscious. A new world tomorrow will be the outcome of a new collective unconscious, born of a new learning." (page 437)

About business . . .

"We look for productivity gains through smart new systems, but the way you really get leaps in productivity is in the hearts and minds of people. The new paradigm that's out there for business is to understand that human consciousness is the most important resource we've got." (page 114)